Susan Lewis

SUMMER MADNESS

DANCE WHILE YOU CAN

arrow books

This edition published by Arrow Books in 2004

Arrow Books
The Random House Group Limited
20 Vauxhall Bridge Road, London SW1V 2SA

Random House Australia (Pty) Limited
20 Alfred Street, Milsons Point, Sydney,
New South Wales 2061, Australia

Random House New Zealand Limited
18 Poland Road, Glenfield
Auckland 10, New Zealand

Random House (Pty) Limited
Endulini, 5a Jubilee Road, Parktown 2193, South Africa

The Random House Group Limited Reg. No. 954009

www.randomhouse.co.uk

A CIP catalogue record for this book
is available from the British Library

Papers used by Random House are natural, recyclable products made from wood grown in sustainable forests. The manufacturing processes conform to the environmental regulations of the country of origin

ISBN 0 09 190289 4

Printed and bound in Great Britain by
Cox & Wyman Ltd, Reading, Berkshire

SUMMER MADNESS

Susan Lewis

arrow books

Acknowledgements

I would like to thank Jo Birch for giving me the invaluable benefit of his yachting expertise and for introducing me to the magnificent vessel, now moored in San Diego and known in this book as the *Valhalla*. My love and thanks also go to Richard and Tricia Strauss for rescuing me from Mexico and making my stay in San Diego such a happy and memorable experience.

To all my friends on the Côte d'Azur with whom I have shared so many wonderful summer madnesses.

Also I would like to thank everyone at Heinemann for their loyalty and support. And a very special thank you to my agent, Toby Eady, whose advice and friendship I wouldn't be without.

For Carl and Brenda

They'd followed it all on the television news – the accident, the murder, the arrest and then the release. It was sensational stuff, with enough speculation and scandal to keep the American, Mexican and Argentinian press in headlines for weeks. There was more money in the two families concerned, the Santinis in Buenos Aires and the Mallorys in San Diego, than the two Mexican peasants, Sanchez and Ortega, could ever hope for in ten lifetimes. But there was plenty, plenty, plenty for them in this lifetime if they kept their mouths shut.

The battle between San Diego and Buenos Aires rumbled on long after the press lost interest. Still Sanchez and Ortega said nothing. They collected their dollars, drove their flashy American cars, lived it up in grand Mexican style, while they guarded their secret and waited.

Delacroix, the boss, took care of everything. He alone knew the price they'd eventually be paid for their secret. But for now he played the game, kept Sanchez and Ortega happy while he moved between the underworlds of Buenos Aires and Mexico City letting it be known that his was the gun at the Santini and Mallory families' heads. He had been feared and respected before, now he was becoming a legend. Oscar Delacroix, one of the three people in the world who knew what had really happened that fateful day off the coast of Puerto Vallarta. Oscar Delacroix, the man of many faces, the man of a hundred photofits, the human chameleon whose gun was for hire and whose soul was committed to the highest bidder that day.

Delacroix, Sanchez and Ortega, the guardians of a secret that was rumbling steadily, inexorably, terrifyingly, away from

the Mexican shores . . . A secret that was seeping into the ocean and washing itself up on the shores of Europe . . . A secret that was soon to explode with horror and devastation in the wrong people's lives . . .

1

'I can't believe it's over, can you?'

'Not really, no.'

'It's the end of an era.'

'The gravy train stops here.'

'Speak for yourself. Some of us have got work to go to.'

'And some of us don't ram it down other's throats.'

'Now, now girls.'

'Any more boxes going? I'm full up over here.'

'Fred's bringing some more.'

'Put some music on someone.'

A few seconds later the chaotic, open plan offices where a slightly bemused and future-wary production team were throwing and catching, shouting and banging around as they packed up their belongings, began to throb with the catchy beat of the series' theme tune. Instantly everyone stopped. They weren't sure whether this was what they wanted to hear right now, but somehow it was appropriate. One of the secretaries began to cry. *Private Essays*, the series they'd all devoted their lives to for the past three years, was at an end.

A door at the far end swung open and Louisa Kramer, the series' creator and Sarah Lovell, the series' producer, teetered into the mayhem.

'Looks like someone's had a good lunch,' one of the PAs remarked.

'Not a drop has passed our lips,' Sarah hiccoughed.

'Not a drop,' Louisa echoed, trying to keep a straight face.

Everyone was grinning.

Sarah looked around at the packing cases, the open filing cabinets, the empty noticeboards, the general debris of three years' hard labour. 'Oh God, I suddenly feel depressed,' she groaned.

Laughing, Louisa took hold of her and danced her through the cane partitions and cluttered desks in the hilarious swing and bob routine some wag had choreographed to go along with the theme tune.

'Champagne's on its way,' Sarah cried, waving out as she disappeared into her office to begin her own packing.

Louisa's secretary came beetling over with a stack of unedited cassettes. 'What shall I do with these?' she asked.

'Sling them!' Louisa cried dramatically, and with a jaunty backward kick of her heel she threw open her own door and shimmied into her office.

It was chiefly due to Louisa and Sarah that the *Private Essays* ship had been such a happy one these past three years, for Sarah's dry and often risqué wit coupled with the infectious ring of Louisa's laughter and remarkable talent for writing scripts that were not only brilliant but shootable had bonded everyone into a formidable team. The series was only ending now because Louisa felt it had run its course, that it was better to go out on a high – in other words around number two or three in the ratings – than drag it on the way so many other producers did with their successes. She was ready to start something fresh and the fact that the TV station which broadcast *Private Essays* had lost its franchise had given her the perfect opportunity to call it a day. As soon as they'd heard that *Private Essays*, the nation's leading one-hour drama series, was about to be pulled other broadcasters had bombarded Louisa with offers to continue with them, but she'd remained firm. Not that the decision had been easy for it was *Private Essays* that had made her, Sarah and Danielle Spencer, the star, household names. Were it not for the fact that Louisa and Sarah were so young the press probably wouldn't have paid them much attention, but to be heading up a multi-million pound production at the age of twenty-seven in Louisa's case and twenty-nine in Sarah's was obviously, at the time, deemed newsworthy. And that the three of them had become such close friends during the course of the production, partying the nights away in all the trendy night spots of London, mixing with the rich and the famous, causing wonderfully juicy scandals and still managing to churn out a hit show had made them great fodder for the gossip columnists. Danny most of all, for hers was the beautiful, unbelievably sensuous face the public saw on their screens every Friday and her stormy, sensational and riotous love life made spectacular reading.

The break-up of Sarah's marriage just after the series started had brought the press flocking again. Was someone else involved? Was it true she was seeing Phillip Standeven, one of the TV station's more flamboyant controllers? Was he going to leave his wife? So many questions about something that had made Sarah's head spin with the sheer incredibility of it all. I mean, had they *seen* Phillip Standeven!

It had been much the same with Louisa when just over a year ago her relationship with Bill Kovak, a freelance director, had ended. During the time they were together the speculation about wedding bells, the outrageous suggestions of miscarriage and stolen pictures of blissful togetherness just went to show how wrong the press could be.

Still, she reflected, tipping the contents of her top drawer into a shoe-box, at least it was over now, mainly thanks to Danny who had rescued her from the trap of her own misguided attraction to the wrong men. Violence had been a part of her life from such an early age that until Simon, the gentle, crazy and adorable man she lived with now, had come along she'd been terrified that maybe in some appalling, masochistic or unthinkably deranged way, she was responsible for it. That maybe she was incapable of having a relationship with a man without the constant threat of both physical and mental abuse. However, knowing Simon had put her mind at rest on that score and it was only the packing away of old newspaper cuttings that had made her think of Bill now.

'Oh shit, what a mess,' she grumbled aloud as she pulled open a deep bottom drawer and gazed despairingly down at the chaos. She looked hopefully around the room searching for something marginally less daunting to tackle, then started to laugh. Next door Sarah was complaining so loudly about her own slovenly state of affairs that Louisa decided to go and sympathize.

'It's so fucking depressing,' Sarah complained as Louisa strolled into her office to find her sitting in the midst of a pile of old scripts and story outlines staring down at a photograph of the three of them, she, Louisa and Danny, taken for the launch of the series. 'Talk about a trip down memory lane, I feel like slitting my wrists all of a sudden.'

Louisa's luminous brown eyes were dancing with laughter. 'Why don't you have some more champagne?' she suggested.

'Good God no, if I do I'll start seeing double and its bad enough as it is. How are you doing?'

'Not much better. I knew we should have gone to Spain with Danny.'

'Don't remind me.' Sarah's round, cheerful face and normally bright, laughing blue eyes were filled with despondency.

'Oh come on,' Louisa laughed. 'Only an hour ago you were telling me how much you were looking forward to making a new start.'

'That was before I was sitting here facing all this. For some nasty little reason it's reminding me how long it is since I last had sex and I swear to you I didn't set out to break any records.'

'Hey everyone!' Camilla, the redheaded associate producer called out. 'Frank's just rung from wardrobe, they're selling off the costumes if you're interested.'

'Have the sets gone into the crusher yet?' Sarah asked, tucking her sleek, short blonde bob behind one ear as she looked up at Louisa.

'I imagine so,' Louisa grinned, her lovely eyes sparkling with mischief. She was tall, extremely slim and her soft, tawny brown hair framed her elfin face in a sixties, Quant sort of way. Her full, wide mouth had a gentle hypnotic quality and her smile could make people blink with its radiance.

'Why do I feel that my whole life is going through a

shredder?' Sarah grumbled. 'It's all right for you, you know what you're doing next . . .'

'Sssh,' Louisa said, putting a finger to her lips as she glanced over her shoulder.

'It's OK,' Sarah grinned, 'your secret's safe with me. How are you feeling about it now?'

'As nervous as hell.'

'Yeah, I imagine I would be too,' Sarah commented. 'And I'd be ecstatic. Aren't you?'

'Of course. I'm going to get some coffee. Want some?'

A few minutes later Louisa was back in her office, sipping her coffee as she gazed thoughtfully out the window. What a day this was! Talk about immaculate timing. To have discovered she was pregnant on the very day *Private Essays* was coming to its final conclusion seemed quite stupendously fateful. She'd only told Sarah so far, she would tell Simon tonight when, for once, they had managed to make their busy calendars coincide to give themselves an evening at home in their still relatively new apartment in Bedford Park. They'd really pushed the boat out when they'd bought it, sinking every penny they both had into it and virtually crippling themselves with mortgage repayments. But neither of them had ever had money before, they'd come from ordinary, working-class backgrounds where to have an extra couple of quid in your pocket at the end of the week was almost unheard of. Well certainly in Louisa's gran's case it was, probably it wasn't quite so drastic for Simon's parents. Nevertheless, the thrill of earning such inordinate sums of money had intoxicated them both and they'd spent and squandered and lived it up this past year as if they were Bonnie and Clyde at the height of their luck. Well, Louisa had, Simon was more sensible when it came to money, only ever buying things that virtually guaranteed a return on his investment. He was the smart thinker, the steady influence and the man who had given Louisa more confidence in herself. She could hardly wait to see his face when she told him about the baby, he'd be over the moon, she just knew it.

Turning back to the onerous task of clearing out her desk

Louisa set down her coffee and began sorting through the clutter. It was such a drag doing this sort of thing, especially when she just couldn't make up her mind what to keep and what to junk. Sighing wearily and putting her feet up on the desk she flicked idly through a batch of photographs, wondering if maybe it wasn't an idea to junk it all. She had a video cassette of every episode, Simon had had a copy of each script bound in leather and embossed in gold for her thirtieth birthday and she couldn't think of anything else she really needed. Except the odd bric-a-brac she kept on her desk – the silver paperweight, the leather blotter from Aspreys, the Tiffany pen and pencil set. And of course the framed photograph of her gran with the entire cast of *Private Essays.*

Louisa smiled mistily to herself as she picked the photograph up. She could almost hear her gran's voice, filled with awe and pride the day Louisa had won her first award for writing. She'd been fourteen at the time and her play, her very own play, had been put on at the Royal Court in London! She and her gran had never been to London before, so when they'd got there everything had been an adventure. The big shops, the thundering Underground, the dazzling theatre lights and the overwhelmingly swish hotel in Chelsea. They'd been too shy to go down to the posh restaurant for dinner with its formal waiters and glittering chandeliers, and not even knowing that such a thing as room service existed they'd popped out to see if they could find some fish and chips.

Louisa laughed to herself. She knew now of course that Chelsea wasn't big on fish and chips, but what fun they'd had during that first trip to the Big City. Her gran had treated herself to a new suit in the C&A and had almost burst with pleasure when an assistant told her she looked pretty snazzy. Louisa had bought a new dress in Top Shop which had cost her nearly twenty pounds, and the play's producers had sent a taxi to take them to the theatre on opening night. There were even pictures of them in the paper the next day, mainly because Louisa was so very young. Whenever Louisa looked at those pictures now she wanted to laugh and cry at how lamentably under-dressed and awkward they had looked among so many glitzy, sophisticated.people.

Over the years that followed they'd become more used to the limelight as Louisa's talent for writing had blossomed. When she was eighteen she was offered a job on a script-editing team for BBC radio and it had almost broken her heart to leave her gran and the little council bungalow they'd shared since Louisa was two. Her gran had put on a brave face, telling her she had to get out there and make something of herself and not worry about an old woman who had more friends than she knew what to do with.

When *Private Essays* finally went on air the press who had come to know Florrie Kramer over the years made almost as much fuss of her as they did of Louisa, Sarah and Danny. Florrie had become one of the nation's favourite grans and to her chuckling delight she even received fan mail. That her success had brought such happiness to her gran was more than Louisa could have hoped for. Life hadn't been easy for Florrie, not that she ever complained, but taking on a two year old at the age of sixty-one had been quite a challenge when all she had was her old age pension and a paltry child allowance to live on. But she'd always managed to keep a pound back to go to the bingo on Saturdays. She'd won fifty pounds once and had put it into a post office account for Louisa. There had been so many gestures like that over the years, like giving Louisa an extra lamb chop because she was a growing girl and going without herself, or making sure that Louisa's shoes were as smart and tidy as the other children's when her own had holes in them, or saving up to take Louisa on the bus to the zoo with enough left over to buy nuts for the monkeys and ice-creams for themselves. The list was endless and too painful to think about now. But at least she had managed to give her gran something back when she'd started to earn herself. Florrie loved hats and Louisa never failed to turn up with a new one each time she visited. And she'd taken her gran on holiday to Butlins because that was where Florrie had wanted to go, and she'd bought her a spanking new colour TV to replace the second-hand black and white one a neighbour had generously given her.

Florrie had been dead for two months now and Louisa still wasn't sure she'd accepted it. There had been such a turn-out at the funeral that it had overwhelmed Louisa to discover just how loved her gran was. Most of the cast of *Private Essays* had been there, all of the journalists who had interviewed her came to pay their last respects and one old man had travelled all the way from Newcastle, saying he'd fallen in love with Florrie from afar. The local bingo hall opened its doors for the mourners and Florrie's pals did all the catering. It was one of the most moving experiences many of them had had. The only person who hadn't come to the funeral was Florrie's only son, Louisa's father.

Louisa was glad he hadn't come for she knew that Florrie wouldn't have wanted him there any more than she did. Neither of them had seen him since he'd emigrated to Canada when Louisa was twelve, but neither Florrie nor Louisa had ever forgotten his visits throughout Louisa's childhood when he used to beat them, take all Florrie's money, and frighten them half to death. Florrie had never said that it was her son who had driven Louisa's mother to suicide, but Louisa suspected that was the case – she'd never questioned Florrie too closely though, for she had sensed what pain it caused her. He was the only living relative Louisa had now and she hoped never to see him again.

'Hey, what's all this?' Sarah asked, seeing the tears on Louisa's cheeks.

Louisa looked up, then smiling she tilted the photograph of Florrie and the cast for Sarah to see.

'Oh,' Sarah said, her face instantly softening. 'Life just isn't quite the same without the old girl, is it?'

'No,' Louisa said sadly, 'but it has to go on.' Then swinging her legs back to the floor she said, 'How are you getting on in there?'

'I can't tell you how many things I've found that I've accused other people of stealing,' Sarah answered with a grin. Her big floppy shirt and leggings were covered in dust and there was some kind of smudge over one of her dimples. 'Anyway, I thought you might like this,' she said, handing Louisa a skipping rope she'd borrowed and lost during one rash week of exercising about two years ago.

Laughing as she recalled the way Sarah had skipped her way round the production concourse, back and forth to the loo and even down to the studio, Louisa took it, saying, 'I've found some publicity photographs here that you took. If you haven't got copies yourself you can have them, otherwise I'll hang on to them.'

Sarah gave them a critical look-over. 'Not bad,' she said. 'I can do better now. I'll *have* to do better now if I'm going to make it my new career.'

'Are you really serious about that?' Louisa said.

'Of course I am!' Sarah cried. 'I've had enough of all this telly lark and thanks to the Waltzing Matilda I can take a bit of a breather now with no worries about paying the bills.' Waltzing Matilda was Sarah's great-aunt who, just like Sarah, had been the youngest of four children and who, as Sarah put it, had left all her dosh to a worthy cause – in other words, Sarah.

'So, do you think you'll be coming to the final bash tonight?' Sarah said.

Grinning, Louisa shook her head. 'I wouldn't have thought so,' she answered. 'Tonight is going to be pretty special for Simon and me and I can't imagine him wanting to share it.'

'No, me neither,' Sarah said, pulling a face. 'I don't know, with you not there, Danny not there and me without a brawny body to hang onto I'm not really sure I'm looking forward to it.'

'Sarah, everyone will be devastated if you don't go,' Louisa told her.

'Mmm,' Sarah replied distractedly as she gazed around the steel shelves and bookcases while Louisa answered the phone.

'Don't tell me,' Sarah said when she'd finished, 'it was Daddy.'

'Sssh!' Louisa laughed. 'Yes, it was. Just checking that

nothing was going to hold me up tonight. Do you know this will be the first night in together we've had in three weeks?'

'Well, you'd better start getting used to them because there are plenty coming up. Oh God, I'm so envious. All I want is a husband and children. Is that so much to ask? Oh, but for God's sake not a husband like the last one, I couldn't stand it a second time around. I blame him, you know, for turning me into a raving sex maniac. Frustration does that to a person. You don't get it, you start fantasizing about it and once that old brain gets hold of the libido . . . Hey! Wait! Diane, what are you doing with my mummy?' she cried as a set designer sailed by with an Egyptian mummy tucked under her arm.

'Putting it in the prop store,' Diane answered, uncertainly.

'But I've grown so attached to her,' Sarah declared. 'Can't I take her home with me?'

Diane looked from Sarah to Louisa and back again. 'Are you kidding me?' she said.

'Absolutely not! I want her. Leave her in my office . . . Can she sit down?'

'Uh, no, I don't think so,' Diane answered.

'What a spectacle we're going to make at rush hour,' Sarah grinned.

'She'll never fit into your Midget,' Louisa laughed.

'She will if I put the roof down.'

'But it's raining.'

'So it is. Well, I'll work something out. That was one of my favourite episodes so I'm not letting her go off to be all lonesome in some spooky old prop store. Anyway, what were we saying? Oh God, we were talking about my ex, weren't we? Well, we'll get straight off that subject.' Then, lowering her voice to a whisper she said, 'I know I've got tons of nieces and nephews but I don't have any godchildren. Just thought you'd like to know.'

Laughing, Louisa threw a note pad at her which missed as Sarah ducked around the door and sailed back to her own office.

At six o'clock, having finally sorted out what she did and

didn't want to keep, Louisa followed one of the porters out to her car which he loaded with her belongings then, along with a few million others, she set off into the dreary London night heading for home. She would never have dreamt it was possible to feel so happy so soon after her gran's death, but she did. She only wished that her gran was still there to share in the joy. But she felt sure that wherever her gran was she knew and she whispered a little prayer for Florrie to look after Simon and make sure he got home safely on this rainy night. It wasn't so unusual for her to do that, she'd done it most nights since her gran had died because Simon and now their baby mattered more to her than anything else in the world.

Louisa was slavishly following a Delia Smith recipe, running a floury finger down the page, weighing out all the ingredients and desperately wishing she understood what she was doing. This was one of Simon's favourite dishes and all too often her valiant efforts in the kitchen ended in misery. But not tonight! she told herself. Tonight she and Delia Smith were going to work culinary magic because she simply couldn't imagine that anyone, least of all Delia Smith who looked such a nice lady, would want anything to spoil this momentous occasion.

'Hi,' she said, licking her fingers as she took the phone from the wall. 'Oh, Elaine, no, he isn't home yet. I'm expecting him any minute . . . Is it urgent? Shall I get him to call? OK. The minute he gets . . . Oh hang on, that must be him now. I'll tell you what, let him take his coat off will you? I'll pour him a drink then he'll call you back.'

Whether Simon's secretary was agreeable to that Louisa didn't wait to find out. He was always getting called back to the office for something or other, because advertising campaigns were much like TV programmes in their erratic hours. But not tonight, she told herself as she called out, 'Hi, sweetheart. I'm in the kitchen.'

'Mmm, something smells good,' he remarked coming to stand in the doorway. 'And you've lit the fire I see.'

With flour on the tip of her nose and pastry all over her

hands Louisa turned to greet him. 'Oh Simon,' she cried, 'you're soaked. Didn't you take the car today?'

'No. I was late this morning so it was quicker to jump on the tube,' he answered, running a hand through his dishevelled blond hair. His pale blue eyes were watching her curiously and when she tilted her mouth up to his for a kiss he laughed. 'I was half afraid I'd find you in tears,' he said, kissing her briefly. 'How did it go today?'

'OK. I'll probably miss it like crazy over the next few weeks, but to be honest I could hardly wait to get out of there tonight. By the way,' she added as he turned towards the bedroom, 'Elaine just called and wants you to ring her back.'

'OK, I'll do it before I take a shower just in case I have to go back in.'

As he disappeared into the study Louisa crossed her fingers and prayed furiously that he wouldn't have to. Fortunately he didn't and half an hour later they were sitting down at one end of the big oval table in their spacious, yet cosy, sitting room with a fire crackling lazily in the hearth and the sleepy sound of a jazz piano drifting soothingly from the CD player. Outside a feisty March wind was tearing through the trees and the rain thrummed a steady beat on the windows, making the room seem even more secluded and restful. In fact everything was just perfect, even the meal now she'd pretended there was no starter. Most of that was still on the bottom of a saucepan, actually it *was* the bottom of the saucepan, but Simon didn't need to know that.

'So, how was your day?' she said, gazing at him in the candlelight and trying not to wince as she burnt her lip on the steaming hot food.

'Not bad,' he said. 'Things are moving a bit now they say the recession's over. We clinched the cat food, by the way. That's what Elaine was ringing about.'

'Congratulations!' Louisa cried, raising her glass. 'Here's to Whiskas!'

He smiled. 'Actually, it's called Purrfect Puss and before you come out with any smart ass remarks I've heard them all already.'

'I'll bet you have,' Louisa laughed. 'But you and I both know Sarah will be able to top them all.'

'I don't know whether I'd dare put her to the test,' he laughed. 'And this,' he added, pointing with his fork to his meal, 'is pretty damned perfect too.'

There were several Sarah-type comments Louisa could have made to that, but she refrained and listened as he talked some more about what was going on at the agency he part-owned.

It had nothing to do with the fact that she wasn't interested that her mind started to wander, it was simply that she was so excited about her news that she wasn't able to concentrate on anything very well. And for some reason Danny was in her mind right now, over there in Spain doing heaven only knows what because Danny had a flair for the reckless. Louisa wondered how Danny would take the news that she was pregnant. Actually, she was quite glad Danny didn't know yet because Danny had a way of taking over Louisa's life that Louisa wasn't always totally comfortable with. Not that Louisa couldn't stand up to Danny, it was usually just easier to let Danny have her way than to get into unnecessary arguments. In fact Louisa only had to take the situation with Bill, the director who had given her such a terrible time with all his ridicule and jealousy and violent tempers, to know that had it not been for Danny she might actually still be there suffering it all. It was when Bill had put her in hospital with two cracked ribs and severe bruising to her face and neck that Danny had finally acted. She hadn't allowed Bill into the hospital to see Louisa, threatening to expose what he'd done to the press if he tried, and when Louisa was ready to leave Danny had taken her to her own large, terraced house in Fulhan where to Louisa's surprise she had discovered all her possessions already installed. She had a lot to thank Danny for . . .

'Louisa? Louisa, are you listening to me?'

'Sorry,' she smiled, 'I was miles away. What were you saying?'

Simon looked at her steadily and for once, surprisingly, she couldn't tell what he was thinking. He'd finished eating, she noticed, had pushed his plate aside and was holding his glass between both hands.

'What were you saying?' she repeated.

'It doesn't matter.'

'No. It does. Come on.'

He shook his head. 'It wasn't important.'

They sat quietly, a little awkwardly, for a moment then both spoke at once.

'You first,' he said.

'No. You first.'

He sighed, pushed his fingers through his hair and rested his head on the heel of his hand.

'Simon? What is it?' she said, her brown eyes clouding with concern. He had been saying something important, she realized, and was hurt that she hadn't been paying attention. Did that happen often, she wondered. But no, she was sure it didn't.

He lifted his head and looked long into her eyes. She looked back, waiting for him to speak, but all he did was force a smile and look away.

'Come on,' she encouraged. 'What is it?'

Again he sighed, dabbed his mouth with his napkin, then pressed it onto the table. 'We have to talk,' he said. 'There's something I have to tell you . . .'

She smiled. 'I have something to tell you too,' she said. 'So why don't we take our wine over to the fire.'

He turned to look at the cosy depths of the sofa. 'No,' he said, shaking his head. 'Let's talk here.'

'OK,' she said frowning. 'Would you like some dessert or . . .'

'No. I've had enough.' He picked up the wine and refilled his glass. When he held the bottle out to Louisa she shook her head and watched him put it down with the same odd deliberation with which he had put down his napkin.

Turning his gaze back to the fire he stared so long and so hard at it that Louisa turned to look at it too. She was aware of the unease stealing over her, of the inexplicable alienness she was suddenly feeling towards her surroundings and as a quick panic tightened her heart she turned back to Simon, half-expecting, half-hoping he'd be watching her and smiling reassuringly. But he was still staring at the fire, seemingly intent on the sluggish yellow flames.

And then it hit her. The offer of a job in New York must have come up again and he was trying to find a way of breaking it to her. But it wasn't a problem any more. There was nothing to keep her here in England now, she wanted to go.

At last he looked at her and her heart lifted as the smile of reassurance came and reaching across the table he covered her hand with his own.

'I love you,' she whispered.

Lifting his hand he curled her hair behind her ear, gazing searchingly into the heartbreaking loveliness of her face. Then his eyes dropped from hers, following his hand back to the table.

'Louisa, there's no easy way of saying this,' he began softly.

'Of saying what?' she asked, hardly able to hear her own voice above the strange buzzing that had started in her ears. 'If it's about New . . .'

'Of saying I'm going to leave you,' he interrupted.

Louisa stared at him, unmoving, but feeling everything inside her starting slowly to withdraw. 'But . . . But you can't,' she said.

He looked up to find her eyes wide with shock, her full lips parted as though to say more, but nothing came.

'I'm sorry,' he whispered. 'Truly, I'm sorry, but I just can't go on living this lie.'

'Lie?' she echoed huskily.

'The lie of pretending to love you when . . .' his voice trailed off as he realized how painful his next words were going to be.

'When you don't any more?' she finished for him, looking stupefied and confused as she wondered how through this debilitating numbness she was able to say anything at all.

His lips narrowed in an uneasy smile of admission.

She looked away. Her eyes were big and haunted, seeming to search the room for something to hold on to.

'Oh God, Louisa,' he groaned, squeezing her hands. 'I don't want to hurt you. You're the last person in the world I want to hurt . . .'

'But?'

He was silent for a while, then taking a deep breath he said, 'I might as well come clean about the whole thing. There's someone else and has been for some time. She's someone I want to be with, someone I love . . .' Again he stopped, knowing he was making a real mess of this.

'More than you love me?' she said.

'In a different way from the way I love you,' he said lamely.

Without really knowing what she was doing Louisa reached out for the wine and refilled her glass. Beneath this strange, almost eerie calmness she was feeling there was something else, something she didn't want to escape, and it was growing, expanding within her and frightening her.

'Why are you telling me now?' she heard herself say. 'What made you choose tonight?'

He shrugged. 'I don't know.'

She was still holding the pain at a distance, but knew that it was there, reaching for her, waiting to claim her. 'How long have you been seeing her?' she said.

'I don't know. Six months.'

She looked down at her wine. So everything had been a sham. His concern when her gran had died, his proposal of marriage, even his lovemaking, had all been done out of pity. 'Who is she?' she said flatly. 'Do I know her?'

He nodded. 'It's Elaine.'

'Elaine your secretary? Elaine who rang earlier?'

Again he nodded.

'I see.' She knew he was waiting for her to say more, but what more was there to say except that she loved him and wanted to be his wife and that she was carrying his baby? She looked at him, almost told him, then looked away. What good would it do, he loved someone else.

'I'm sorry,' he said, and the tears in his voice made her flinch and pull her hands away.

'I've tried to tell you so many times,' he said, 'I hated cheating on you, you deserve better, you deserve someone . . .'

'Simon stop it,' she said, a sudden edge to her voice. 'Patronizing me by denigrating yourself isn't going to make this any easier.'

'No, you're right,' he whispered. 'It's just that I feel such a bastard. I mean I know the timing is lousy, what with you losing your job and your gran being dead only a couple of months, but I just can't go on like this.'

The mention of her gran was almost her undoing.

' . . . and I thought,' he went on, 'I was thinking that . . . Well, Elaine and I talked it over and we thought that perhaps it was better for you to deal with this now, I mean, rather than me being there to help you get your life back together then pull the rug from under you when it was, by going. This way, we thought, you could make a whole fresh start.'

Each use of the word 'we' was like a knife jabbing into her heart. She was staring absently at the bangles on her slender wrists, feeling oddly repelled by the dress she was wearing, the dress she had chosen for seduction and celebration. 'And when exactly have you and Elaine decided that I should make my fresh start?' she asked, her dark eyes flashing in the candlelight.

'What do you mean?'

'I mean, when are you going? Or do I have to move out to make room for Elaine?'

'Don't be ridiculous. I'd never ask you to do that. This is your home.'

'And yours,' she reminded him.

'I'll go to Elaine's,' he said dully.

'When?'

'I'm not sure. I hadn't really . . .'

'Tonight?' she cut in. 'Maybe you should go tonight.'

'Louisa, for heaven's sake!'

'For heaven's sake what?'

He shook his head. 'I don't want to leave you like this.'

'Like what?'

'I don't know, just like this. We've meant a lot to each other, we still do and I suppose, well, I suppose I know how hard this is for you.'

'No you don't. You have no idea what this means to me.'

'Then tell me. Let's talk about it.'

'What for? You've made up your mind so I think you should go. Now.'

'I can't. Not yet.'

'Why? Isn't Elaine ready for you?'

'Yes, she's ready, but you're not.'

'I've already asked you not to patronize me,' she snapped.

'I'm trying to be your friend.'

'I have friends.'

He wiped a hand over his mouth. 'You're making this so difficult,' he said.

'I thought I was making it easy. I said I wanted you to go, that's what you want, isn't it?'

'But not tonight.' The awful truth was that right at that moment what he wanted was to make love to her. Those huge, liquid brown eyes, the delicate nose, perfect, sensuous mouth and finely carved bones of her cheeks were working their magic on him in a way they hadn't for some time. And he felt so protective towards her, wanted to wrap her in his arms and hold her close. How could this be happening now when he was about to break it all off?

'What difference does it make when you go?' she said. 'What's the point of drawing it out?'

'There is no point, except I care for you and I want to make sure you're all right.'

'I'm all right,' she said breezily, but she knew she wasn't, knew that this was hurting beyond anything she'd ever imagined, beyond even what Bill had done to her. But she wasn't going to fall apart, she had too much pride for that, too much horror of repeating the mistakes of the past. What a joke, she thought bitterly to herself, for if he was smashing his fists in her face, yelling at her and shoving her about the room, she'd very likely be on her hands and knees pleading with him to stay. But as it was, she was telling him to walk out the door, to leave her for another woman and never come back. How could she be doing that when she knew that the moment he went her whole life would fall apart? Did she really want to invite such pain into her life when she knew she couldn't face it? But pain didn't come invited, it came of its own accord. She must remember that, must keep telling herself that. She wasn't responsible for what men did to her, she didn't make it happen, not any more. She'd come through all that, it was behind her now and she wasn't going to fall at anyone's feet and let him walk over her and abuse her and cheat on her the way she had once. She had her career now, her success and her reputation. She'd come a long way since those terrible days and she didn't need someone who had been deceiving her for six months, who didn't love her or want her any more. She could live without Simon, she could live without them all. So no, she wasn't going to fight this, she wasn't going to resist it at all, she was just going to let it happen.

She watched him as he got up from his chair and went to get another bottle of wine. 'If you drink any more,' she said, 'you won't be able to drive.'

'For Christ's sake!' he shouted, suddenly rounding on her. 'This might not mean anything to you, but it damned well does to me. It's tearing me apart doing this to you, can't you see that?'

'So what am I supposed to do?' she cried. 'You're the one who's met someone else! You're the one who wants to go. Or are you waiting for me to beg? Is that it? Do you want me on my knees? Do you want to humiliate me the way all the others humiliated me? You want your turn now, is that it?'

His face was twisted with rage and she knew he was going to hit her. It would be the first time he'd ever laid a hand on her in violence, but she wanted it. She wanted his abuse if only to prove to herself that she could take it and walk away from it.

But he didn't hit her. He merely put down the wine and came to take her in his arms. She pushed him roughly away.

'I don't want your guilt or your pity,' she seethed. 'Take it to Elaine and let her deal with it, you're nothing to do with me now.'

'Louisa!' he cried. 'This isn't you talking. This is someone I don't know. You're not cold, you never have been, so why now? What's got into you?'

'Maybe I've changed. Maybe I've been changing all the time you've known me and you just haven't bothered to notice. Maybe, Simon, I'm a woman who can stand on her own two feet, who doesn't need a lying, cheating bastard like you in her life to fuck her around. So please, just get out of here. I've got a lot of things to think about and I'm sorry, but dealing with your conscience isn't one of them.'

He looked at her, stunned. 'What is happening to you,' he said incredulously. 'Don't you care? Don't you have any feelings at all?'

'Yes, I have feelings, but they're not going to change your mind, are they?'

'I don't know. Maybe they would if I knew what they were.'

'You know what they are,' she said.

He looked at her helplessly, not knowing what to say or what to do. 'I love you,' he said quietly.

'But in a different way,' she reminded him.

His eyes fell from hers.

'Simon,' she said after a while, her voice much gentler now, 'I think we've reached an impasse and if you don't mind I'm tired.'

He looked up. His impotency was as clear in his almost childlike blue eyes as his dilemma. 'Do you really want me to go?' he said.

She smiled. 'What I want is for this conversation never to have happened, but it has and now . . . Well, I guess we have to deal with it the best way we can.'

He was watching her closely, something like awe in his eyes now, but it was so clouded by sadness she couldn't really tell.

'Why do I get the feeling I'm about to make one of the biggest mistakes of my life?' he said.

'I hope not,' she answered, feeling herself start to falter. He was right, this wasn't her speaking but the words just kept on coming and her emotions seemed to be ebbing away to some unreachable part of herself. But they would come back and when they did she wanted to be alone. She wanted to think about the baby growing inside her and make the decisions about her life without Simon's guilt and integrity forcing him into a marriage she knew he didn't want. Of course he would persuade himself he did, he'd probably even end up persuading her, but she wasn't going to let that happen.

'Go to Elaine's,' she said. 'She'll want to know that you've told me and I think it's better that you're with her tonight, not me. No,' she said as he made to interrupt, 'if you stay it'll only confuse things further. You can come back whenever you like for your things and we'll leave discussing selling the flat for another time.'

'Oh Christ,' he groaned, pushing his hands into his hair. 'I want you to keep it. This is your home, I know how much it means to you.'

He was right, it did mean a lot to her, but she'd always thought it meant a lot to him too. 'We'll sell it,' she said harshly. 'Either that or I'll try to raise the money to buy you out.'

He was shaking his head in dismay and bewilderment. 'Louisa, let me hold you,' he pleaded.

'You have Elaine to hold now,' she responded.

'But I want to hold you.'

'Simon, just go.'

He stood up, started to turn away then at the last minute he turned back and pulled her into his arms.

Neither of them said anything as they stood together, holding each other close and wanting more than anything never to have to let go.

In the end he was the first to break away. For one panicked moment she almost clung to him, but then she turned quickly to the table, starting to clear away. A few minutes later she heard the front door close behind him.

2

'Well, this is a nice surprise!' Sarah declared, opening the door of her Richmond flat to find her eldest sister Yvonne standing there. 'What brings you to London?'

'I've got a check-up this afternoon in Harley Street,' Yvonne answered. 'And don't start fussing, I'm completely cured, it's just routine.'

'OK, OK,' Sarah laughed, holding up her hands at Yvonne's fierce expression. 'You can come and sit for me,' she said. 'I need a model and failing anyone else you'll do.'

Yvonne slanted her a meaningful look and followed her into the sitting room. 'We're all beginning to wish you'd go back to producing,' she grumbled, 'you didn't have time to be rude then.'

'Not to you, maybe,' Sarah said, clearing a space for Yvonne to sit down, 'but you should speak to some of my team. I was a tyrant.'

'I have no problem believing it,' Yvonne remarked dryly, as Sarah went off to the kitchen to make some tea. She knew full well what a popular producer her sister had been. She also knew that behind her sunny and brazen facade Sarah was quite shy and, Yvonne suspected, not a little inhibited, a legacy from that dreadful ex-husband of hers.

Yvonne had never taken to Colin, he was much too starchy for her liking and his antipathy towards children hadn't scored him any brownie points either. You could tell a lot about a man by the way he behaved with children, Yvonne thought, and Colin's manner towards her own little brood had been as uptight as his morals. How Sarah had ever managed to fall in love with him was a mystery to the entire family, particularly when Sarah so adored her nieces and nephews and wanted nothing so much as to add to the ever mounting number of their father's grandchildren. Still, Colin hadn't actually shown his true colours until after they were married, by which time Sarah was head-over-heels in love and totally convinced that she could persuade him to have a family when the time came. She hadn't been able to talk him round, but surprisingly that wasn't the reason they were now in the process of divorce. That had something to do with Sarah having a quick fling with another man, though as close as they were Yvonne still didn't know all the details. What she did know however was that Colin had been totally unforgiving, had succeeded in making her sister feel like some kind of sexual deviant, and that for all Sarah's bravado she had been left pretty scarred by it. But her inherent courage and indomitable sense of humour had helped her get over it, as had the loving support of her family and her friends Louisa and Danny.

As Sarah came back into the room and set down a tray among the expensive camera equipment she had recently purchased in a bid to start a new career, Yvonne pondered the friendship that had evolved through the drama series Sarah had produced. At first Yvonne had considered Sarah to be the odd one out. Danny was so breathtakingly glamorous and Louisa had a quiet sophistication and elegance which totally belied her roots, that Sarah, with her exploding seams and jovial ineloquence, had seemed almost gauche by comparison. Not that Sarah was either unintellingent or unattractive, she was quite simply a contrast – and quite a refreshing one Yvonne thought – to the other two. And now that Yvonne knew Louisa and Danny better she felt that perhaps Danny was more of the odd one out.

'I'm having lunch with Louisa in an hour or so,' Sarah said, flopping down on a chair and carelessly resting her feet on a steel camera case. 'Why don't you come along?'

'I can't. I'm meeting my dear mother-in-law,' Yvonne answered, obviously regretting it. 'Maybe another time.'

'Sure, whenever you like.'

Yvonne sipped her tea. 'How is Louisa?' she said. 'How did Simon take to the idea of becoming a dad?'

Sarah's cup stopped in mid-air as she looked at her sister. 'He doesn't know, Louisa didn't tell him,' she answered. 'He left her that night for another woman.'

'Oh my God,' Yvonne murmured. 'Poor Louisa. But what about the baby? She'll have to tell him some time.'

Sarah was shaking her head. 'There is no baby, not any more,' she said sadly. 'She had an abortion the day before yesterday.'

'Oh, good heavens! Why on earth did she do that? I thought she wanted the baby.'

Sarah shrugged. 'So did she, until Simon walked out. Then, so she says, she got to thinking and realized that she didn't really love Simon, that she'd only gone along with the relationship because she'd wanted to prove to herself that she could make a relationship work. But now she realizes there's no point doing that with someone who in her heart she knows isn't right for her. Therefore having his baby wouldn't be the right thing either.'

'Oh dear, what a mess,' Yvonne sighed. 'Fancy him just going off like that. How was she the last time you spoke to her?'

Sarah pulled a face. 'Distant,' she said. 'It's like she's gone right inside herself. All the barriers are up and she won't let me in.'

'Guilt,' Yvonne said decisively. 'She can't face the guilt and is afraid someone else might make her.'

'You may be right, but in truth she's usually like that when she's working. She's got a new project on the go, so she tells me. She's concentrating on that now. Simon and the baby are in the past, she says.'

'What did Danny have to say about it?'

'Nothing. I got the feeling I interrupted something when I called her last night, but I expect she'll call me later. I'll have spoken to Louisa again by then so I'll probably have a better idea of whether she's just covering up the way she's feeling or if she really does think she's done the right thing.'

'I'm still amazed she didn't discuss it with anyone before she went through with it,' Yvonne remarked.

'She said she knew we'd try to talk her out of it and since her mind was made up she didn't want to end up arguing with anyone.'

'Would you have tried to talk her out of it?'

Sarah thought about that for a moment. 'Probably,' she said. 'At least I would have tried to make her wait a while longer before going ahead. And I would have tried to get her to tell Simon.'

'As the father he had a right to know.'

'Yes, but she was afraid he'd give up this other woman and go back to her for the sake of the baby and, so she claims, she just didn't want that. Actually I can see her point. Holding onto a man that way isn't wise and Simon's a pretty honourable sort of chap on the whole. He'd have given his secretary the elbow, stayed with Louisa and probably ended up making them all miserable.'

'Poor Louisa,' Yvonne said shaking her head. 'It hasn't been a particularly easy time for her lately, has it? What with her grandmother dying, the series folding and now all this. I can't help thinking she's done the wrong thing about the baby though, but I guess it's her business and it's not my place to judge. I've always found her a bit of a mystery really. I mean she doesn't look the introverted type at all, does she?'

'That's because she's not introverted,' Sarah laughed. 'Quite the reverse, in fact.'

'Isn't she? Well it just goes to show how wrong you can be about a person. But being a writer is such a solitary profession and she looks like she should be out there striding the catwalks. Come to think of it, that's who you should get to sit for you, Louisa, not me. Let her put up with your insufferable rudeness. And Danny. She'd be a good subject for you too. I expect you wouldn't have too much trouble getting her to take her clothes off.'

'Now that's just where you're wrong again,' Sarah laughed. 'Danny might be an exhibitionist and she might get up to all sorts of things in private, but posing nude for a camera, still or moving, is where she draws the line. Don't ask me why, but she does.'

'Tell me, has she ever had a steady boyfriend?' Yvonne wondered. 'I never seem to see her with the same man twice.'

'That's the way Danny likes it.' Sarah shrugged, leaning across to the fruit bowl and taking an apple.

Yvonne watched her for a moment, taking in her round, turquoise blue eyes, her pink cheeks and smiling lips. It was hard to be objective about your sister, but Yvonne really did think that Sarah was quite special. She might not be as beautiful and sensuous as Danny, or as striking as Louisa, but she had a certain something all of her own, something quite indefinable and totally unique, that Yvonne was amazed men didn't find irresistible.

As Sarah started to grin Yvonne realized that as usual her mind had been read, so instead of asking the question on the tip of her tongue, she waited for Sarah to answer it.

'My turn will come,' Sarah told her, crunching into the apple.

'I know it will,' Yvonne said spiritedly. 'I have no doubt about that. But I was thinking, maybe you're just not going to the right places.'

'Got anywhere in mind?'

'How would I know? I'm too long married and too long off the scene. What about Danny, she's never short of a man, where does she find them?'

'Where Danny's concerned they just materialize,' Sarah said, sticking a finger in her mouth to dislodge a piece of apple. 'She uses 'em, abuses 'em and then waits for them to come back for more, which generally they do. Do you know, she has the most varied and fascinating sex life of anyone I know. She said I could watch one time if I was around, don't you think that's mightily obliging of her?'

Yvonne sighed, shaking her head in quiet exasperation.

'Sarah, this is me you're talking to,' she scolded, 'so don't let's get into this trying to pretend you're a pervert act.'

'Who's pretending?'

'You, so stop it. It might amuse your friends, but it doesn't amuse me.'

'That's because you've got the sense of humour of a cod.'

'Can't we talk sensibly about this?'

'No, because there is nothing sensible about three years of celibacy.'

'Exactly. So isn't it about time . . .?'

'Yvie, don't preach. I know you mean well, but it's been a long time since you were single and you never were at my age.'

'Sorry. It's just that I'm concerned.'

Yvonne put down her cup and reached for her bag. 'Where are you meeting Louisa?' she said. 'Can I drop you anywhere?'

'No, it's OK. She's coming to pick me up, then I expect we'll hit McDonalds or Burger King or Belly Busters or somewhere even more decadent.'

'Well, say hello to her for me and tell her . . . Well, I don't suppose I can give a message of condolence because I don't imagine I'm supposed to know anything. So tell her she's welcome any time. It's always lovely to see her.'

'And Danny?' Sarah grinned mischievously.

Yvonne's blue eyes narrowed slightly as she looked into Sarah's. 'Of course and Danny,' she said. 'Why do you say it like that?'

Sarah's mouth tilted at one corner. 'Maybe because you never seem too comfortable around Danny,' she answered.

'Don't I?' Yvonne shrugged.

'No, you don't.'

'Well, maybe that's because I'm never too sure where the actress stops and the person begins.'

Sarah laughed. 'I don't think even Danny knows that,' she said. 'And that's what makes her so utterly wonderful and so completely exhilarating to be around.'

Danielle Spencer's entrance did not go unnoticed, but then

Danny's entrances rarely did. And Quaglino's in St James's, the in-spot of the moment, was the perfect place for making a glorious, Hollywood entrance. For, with its wide, sweeping staircase leading down to the hub of glitzy, deliciously rich and exclusive clientele, its glittering mirrors, gleaming brass rails and shiny marble floors, it was straight out of a Busby Berkeley extravaganza.

Danny's lazy, cat eyes were scanning the tables as she sauntered down the stairs in a black lace dress that clung lovingly to her breasts, not quite revealing them, but offering tantalizing glimpses of the smooth, succulent flesh beneath. Her full, sensuous lips were curved in a satisfied smile, her night-black hair cascaded in rich glossy curls around her bewitchingly beautiful face and down the exquisite length of her back. Spotting Sarah and Louisa she waved, tossed back her hair and allowed a waiter to lead her to them, stopping en route to greet those she knew.

'You look stunning,' Louisa said, as Danny sat down, putting her purse on the table and stealing a quick glance at herself in the mirror behind Sarah.

'Do I?' Danny smiled. 'Thank you. As a matter of fact, so do you. Abortion obviously suits you.'

Sarah choked on her wine as the smile drained from Louisa's face. 'Then I must remember to get one every year,' she said waspishly.

Danny looked at her long and hard. Louisa stared back, her angry, brown eyes challenging Danny to say more.

'Why did you do it?' Danny demanded. 'Why didn't you wait at least until you'd spoken to one of us? And why the hell didn't you tell Simon?'

'I've been through all that with Sarah, I'm sure she's already told you, so I'm not making any more excuses for myself to you,' Louisa retorted. Her eyes were shining with resentment, but both Sarah and Danny could see how hurt she was.

Danny's face softened. 'I'm sorry,' she said. 'I didn't mean to upset you, but I want to be sure that you really know what you've done.'

'Of course I know what I've done,' Louisa snapped. 'Do you take me for an idiot or something?'

'Not an idiot, no,' Danny answered smoothly. 'But I have to confess that I'm surprised at how philosophical Sarah tells me you're being about it all. Personally, I thought you'd have gone to pieces.'

'Then excuse me for disappointing you,' Louisa said through her teeth.

'Oh, I'm not disappointed,' Danny corrected. 'Quite the reverse, because as it so happens I think you did the right thing. I just want to be sure that you do too.'

'Well I do, so shall we change the subject?'

'Not yet. Have you spoken to Simon?'

'Not about the baby, no.'

'Do you want him back?'

'No.'

'Is that truth or pride talking?'

'Both.'

'So what are you going to do with yourself?'

'The same as I always do with myself. I'm going to work.'

'Work as opposed to hide?'

'For God's sake Danny!' Sarah cried. 'Give her a break will you? She's upset enough without you adding to it.'

'I'm not adding to it,' Danny responded, 'I'm just getting things clear in my mind before I tell you what I propose we all do.'

'And exactly what would that be?' Sarah remarked sourly.

Danny's eyes started to sparkle and, getting up from her chair, she went to put her arms around Louisa. 'I'm sorry,' she said with feeling. 'Really I am. I'm sorry about Simon, about the baby and about the way I just spoke to you. I know I'm a bitch, but I was hurt that you didn't discuss it with me first. I really care about you and I can't bear to think of you being unhappy or taking such big decisions all on your own.'

'I'm not a child,' Louisa said, returning the embrace.

'But you're so vulnerable at the moment and I'm worried about you.'

'There's no need. I'm fine. I'm upset about what happened, I'm not proud of what I did, but it's done now. There's no going back and even if I could I'm not sure I'd want to.'

Danny looked at Sarah and Sarah shrugged as if to say, 'I told you'.

'Well,' Danny said, sitting down again, 'just so long as you really are all right. Can you look me in the eyes and tell me honestly and truthfully that you are?' she challenged.

Sarah thought if it were her Danny was asking she'd poke her in the eye, but Louisa's tolerance of Danny's outrageous condescension always had been a mystery to Sarah.

'I'm all right,' Louisa smiled, holding Danny's eyes. 'I swear it. Simon isn't the man for me, I know that now. I think I've known it for a long time, but I was either too busy or too afraid to face it. So what's happened is for the best. I miss him, of course, but I'll get over it.'

'Of course you will,' Danny confirmed, squeezing her hand. 'And the right man is out there somewhere, just you wait and see.'

'I think I'm going to be sick,' Sarah commented.

Louisa burst out laughing and Danny turned her incredible violet eyes on Sarah and said, 'There's one out there for you too, you know.'

'Why do I have this overwhelming urge to slap you?' Sarah smiled sweetly.

Danny laughed. Sarah took the wine from the silver bucket and topped up their glasses. By the time she'd finished they were all laughing.

'You are the most condescending, conceited, self-centred, interfering, pompous bitch I know,' Sarah stated.

'But?' Danny prompted.

'No buts. That's it. You're appalling and you know it.'

Danny laughed again, picked up her glass and proposed a toast. 'To us,' she said, watching her reflection.

Sarah and Louisa waited for her eyes to come back to them. 'To us,' they chorused.

A waiter arrived to take their order. They weren't ready, so with an apologetic hand on his arm Danny asked him if he would mind coming back in a few minutes. Transfixed by her eyes, he said that he would but remained right where he was. Danny smiled then turned away, and seeming to break free of his trance the waiter left.

'How do you do that?' Sarah grumbled. 'The last time a man looked at me like that he was about to take my teeth out.'

'Oh, it's quite easy when you know how,' Danny said breezily.

Sarah eyed her nastily, her top lip curling, making Danny laugh.

'So,' Danny said, 'let's decide what we're going to eat and then I'll tell you what I've arranged for us all.'

They didn't take long to make up their minds, they'd been there plenty of times before and knew the menu. The smitten waiter returned, looked mildly crushed when Louisa gave the order, then went away again.

'So come on then, out with it,' Sarah demanded. 'What have you got up your sleeve now?'

'We,' Danny said, her eyes moving between them, 'are going to spend the entire summer in the south of France!'

Sarah and Louisa looked at each other incredulously. 'We are?' Sarah said.

'We are,' Danny confirmed. 'My aunt Rebecca has a villa down there that we can use for as long as we like. It'll be a great place for you to recover, Louisa, and to write. The light down there is just perfect for your photography, Sarah, and I reckon we could all do with a holiday.'

Again Sarah and Louisa looked at each other.

'Sounds like a good idea to me,' Sarah said encouragingly.

Louisa turned back to Danny, shaking her head as she started to laugh. 'You're unbelievable, do you know that?' she said.

'Does that mean you like the idea?'

'I love the idea! I can't think of anything I'd rather do than spend three months with you two just lazing around in the sun, and if it weren't for the fact that I have to use all my available funds to buy Simon out of the flat I'd be there like a shot.'

'But it's not going to cost you a bean,' Danny protested. 'Rebecca doesn't want rent from us.' Rebecca didn't, but she had suggested that they might like to pay the maid and gardener who came in on a daily basis, though Louisa didn't need to know that.

'We'll still need to live,' Louisa said, 'and with no money coming in . . .'

'OK. How about I lend you the money?' Danny offered.

'I can't let you do that,' Louisa said, laughing.

'Why ever not? She can afford it,' Sarah declared.

'I know and don't think I'm not touched by the offer because I am. It's just that it wouldn't feel right. But why don't you two go anyway? You'll have a wonderful time and maybe I could join you for a couple of weeks or something.'

Danny looked at Sarah and both shook their heads. The real purpose of going, and they both knew it, was to give Louisa a treat.

'It won't be the same without you,' Sarah said.

'Of course it will,' Louisa smiled. 'You'll be so busy having a good time you won't even notice I'm not there.'

'Look, we want you to come,' Danny said, 'and we're prepared to do whatever it takes to get you there, so stop being churlish and say thank you very much for arranging it Danny, I'd love to come and I'll worry about the money later.'

'Thank you very much for arranging it, Danny,' Louisa echoed, 'I'd love to come and I'll worry about the money when I'm there.'

'Brilliant!' Sarah cried. 'The whole summer?' she added, frowning. 'The entire three or whatever months?'

Louisa shrugged. 'If I can find someone to rent my flat while I'm away, then why not? Yes, the whole summer.'

'My, you're a hard one to persuade,' Danny commented.

Louisa laughed. 'But I'm not taking any money from you,' she said. 'From either of you. I'll find a way of managing, even if it means cleaning up after you both and doing all the cooking.'

'Oh, God spare us,' Sarah groaned. 'I've tried your cooking

and I'd happily pay you not to inflict it on us. And anyway, money can't be so tight that you have to take up charring.'

'I'm afraid it is,' Louisa grimaced. 'Simon and I never put aside a penny between us. We blew the whole lot on fast cars and fast living, so I won't only have to borrow to keep the flat on, I'll have to borrow to eat. Which is why I was offering to do the housework. You buy, I'll cook and clean.'

'Like Cinderella?' Sarah said.

Danny's eyes widened. 'I resent that,' she retorted. 'It casts me in the role of an ugly sister.'

'You'll be stupendous,' Sarah assured her.

'We're going to share everything,' Danny said, tearing her narrowed eyes from Sarah. 'And there's a maid who comes in every day, so you don't have to humble yourself for your food,' she told Louisa. 'You'll have enough for that, I'm sure. You would if you were in London, so what's the difference?'

'None, I suppose,' Louisa shrugged.

'So that's settled then,' Danny said, raising her glass. 'Let's drink to three months of pure decadence on the Côte d'Azur.'

'Decadence?' Sarah said rapturously, clasping a hand to her breasts. 'You didn't mention anything about decadence. Oh the sublime vision of it. When shall we go? My libido is telling me soon, very soon.'

'To Sarah's libido,' Danny laughed.

Louisa clinked her glass against the others'. It was a wonderful idea and she knew they were doing it for her more than themselves, but . . . But what? Why should she have any doubts when neither Sarah nor Danny did, except of course it was going to be difficult affording it. Sarah and Danny would inevitably want to hit all the high spots and she just didn't have the resources for it. But what the hell? She wanted to go, wanted more than anything to get away from London for a while and where better than the south of France to try to sort out the mess her life, or more particularly her emotions, seemed to be in? She was missing Simon terribly, had been tempted so many times to pick up the phone and call him, to plead with him to come back, but it wouldn't serve any purpose, if anything it would only make matters worse. Besides, Simon was no magician, he couldn't make the guilt go away any more than she could. Only time could do that. And maybe, getting away and living another life, at least for a while, might help her to come to terms with everything.

She started to laugh at the excitement stirring inside her and at the way Danny was bantering with Sarah. It was strange the way she sometimes felt when watching them like this, as though she was somehow on the outside looking in. She knew of course that was the last thing they'd want her to feel, but she couldn't help it. She was very different from both Danny and Sarah, whose love of noisy, outrageous, unexpurgated and unwholesome fun was an integral and wonderful part of their extrovert natures. Not that Louisa didn't join in, for most of the time she loved the parties and the glitz and crazy, impulsive and outlandish things they did. But there were also times when she felt totally at odds with who and what she was, as though, despite the way she looked and what she did, she didn't quite belong in the glittering hype and glamour of showbiz. She was, by nature, much quieter than Sarah or Danny, less confident and not always comfortable around a lot of people. And as much as she adored Danny for her incredible generosity, there were perhaps too many occasions when Danny's sophistication and autocratic manner made her feel hopelessly naive. But right at that moment she just wanted to hug Danny for the way she had stepped in and organized everything in a way that was so wonderfully typical.

'Oh shut up,' Sarah was laughing as Danny teased her.

'Seriously, I promise you,' Danny went on, 'as soon as this poor, unsuspecting, devastatingly handsome Frenchman, whoever he is, finds out you're in the vicinity he's going to be fighting his way through the forests of the Riviera brandishing the key to that old chastity belt of yours.'

'Then let's just hope it hasn't gone rusty,' Sarah commented dryly, making them all laugh. 'Or horror of all horrors, he doesn't throw it away once he claps eyes on you.'

'That of course is a possibility,' Danny admitted, a mischievous twinkle in her eyes. 'And of course there's always the gorgeous Louisa to contend with. I can see . . .'

'Oh no, no,' Louisa laughed, holding up her hands. 'I might be prepared to break the bank for this trip, but I'm definitely not putting my heart in any more jeopardy. All I want now is plenty of sun, beaucoup de vin and lashings of inspiration to get something new off the ground. The romance is all yours.'

Danny winked at Sarah. 'So when do we go?' she said. 'I thought the beginning of June. It'll give us all time to do what we have to do here before we clear our desks and our diaries for the heavenly pursuits of paradise.'

Louisa nodded.

'Sounds good to me,' Sarah said. 'Do you think we're going to get on all right together, all of us under one roof for three months?' she grinned.

Right at that moment the very idea that they might not seemed so preposterous that they all laughed. But if any of them, as they sat there at the end of March in the lavish and familiar surroundings of Quaglino's, had had even the slightest inkling of what they were about to let themselves in for, they would probably never have gone. But how could they have known when what was waiting for them in France would defy even Louisa's extravagant imagination, and would put paid entirely to Danny's taste for the bizarre, the dangerous and the reckless.

3

The time passed quickly and almost before they knew it, Louisa, Danny and Sarah, their cars as filled to the brim with luggage as they were with heady anticipation, were driving in convoy down through France. They stopped overnight in Burgundy, staying in an old farmhouse with friends of Sarah's and breakfasting outside in glorious sunshine. They arrived on the Côte d'Azur during the late afternoon, turned off the autoroute heading inland and got lost trying to find the villa. It didn't matter, they were back on the right road soon enough having stopped for a while to gaze dreamily out at the distant, dazzling views of the Mediterranean. They finally arrived at the magnificent, Provençal villa just as it was getting dark and not even bothering to unpack the cars or designate rooms they cracked open bottle after bottle of champagne until they were almost hysterical with laughter as they teased each other with the outlandish ways they were intending to fill the weeks ahead.

It took little more than twenty-four hours for their initial euphoria to fade. And by the time two weeks had passed Danny was so fed up she could hardly be bothered to speak.

Wandering listlessly out of the kitchen, hugging her cardigan around her she padded across the red-tiled hall into the sitting room. Her face was set in an expression of outright resentment. Sarah and Louisa were huddled together on one of the vast creamy leather sofas engrossed in the *Times* crossword and didn't even glance up as Danny slumped down on the sofa opposite and sighed angrily.

Two weeks they'd been here now and it hadn't stopped bloody raining, not even for a minute. In England there was a heat wave, on the Côte d'Azur there were floods! That she might just have been able to stand, but the horror of finding themselves in a place that, for all its splendour and beauty, could, thanks to its population, only be described as the furthest flung suburb of London was a fucking nightmare! Almost the moment they'd arrived they'd been pounced on by the jolly hockey-sticks brigade who lived here and invited to every cocktail party, under-cover barbecue and pretentious dinner going. Meaning that, every damned person they'd met so far was *English*! No wonder her aunt rarely came here, it was purgatory.

Maybe they should have taken somewhere nearer the coast, but how were they to know that the historic and picturesque village of Valanjou, twenty or so kilometres inland from Cannes, was going to be like this? There was no doubt that the village itself was exquisite with its steep and narrow cobbled streets, time-ravaged sixteenth-century houses and quaint arcaded square, but it was hard to work up an enthusiasm for anything when it never stopped bloody raining. And when practically every voice you heard was either English, or English mutilating French.

Actually they'd met one French person, Jean-Claude who lived in the villa opposite with his twenty-year-old lover, Didier. Louisa had struck up quite a friendship with Jean-Claude, but Danny wasn't particularly interested in gays so hadn't made much of an effort.

Thanks to Sky Gold and its repeats of *Private Essays* almost everyone around recognized Danny and though when in England she generally welcomed attention, when in another country she didn't. She was feeling trapped behind the mask of her public facade and was hating every minute of it.

Deciding it must be time for a *pastis* and ready to tell the others to go to hell if they pointed out that it wasn't yet four o'clock, Danny got up and wandered back to the kitchen for some ice.

'This is turning into a disaster before we've even started,' Louisa remarked quietly to Sarah.

'I know,' Sarah sighed, gazing dismally out of the french windows at the rain. Right at that moment it was hard to think of this house as the dazzling white villa with its red bougainvillea-covered walls and beautifully balustraded terraces they had seen in the photographs Danny had shown them. Even harder was imagining themselves swimming in the immaculate, turquoise-blue swimming pool that, when viewed from the villa, seemed to fall off the edge of the garden. Around the pool were vibrant, green potted palms, flowering shrubs, giant cacti and the occasional stone sculpture of nymph-like creatures. The garden that sloped gently into the woods all around was filled with ancient olive trees, soaring pines and succulent orange, lemon and quince trees. There was no doubt it was a beautiful place, but how the hell could they enjoy it in this sort of weather?

'Just imagine if we'd come here for a fortnight,' Louisa said, getting up and wandering over to the window. 'Our time would be up now and this would have been it.'

'God forbid,' Sarah shuddered. 'Still, it's all the more reason to stay, I suppose. I mean, just look at that pool. We can't possibly leave without taking advantage of it and the sun's surely got to come out sooner or later. After all, this is the south of France!'

'It is? I was beginning to think we were in Bournemouth.'

Sarah sighed, and closing her eyes leaned her head back against the sofa while Louisa watched the rain bounce off the wide, pale stone terrace outside where sprightly red geraniums tumbled from terracotta pots and lobelia the colour of lapis lazuli twisted itself lovingly around the balustrades. As her thoughts drifted through the winding, forest roads down to the breathtaking splendour of the coastline, so far only viewed from the car, she could feel herself almost bursting with frustration. The huge, sprawling palms, creamy white, subtropical beaches hugged by the aquamarine sea and the subtle, though unmistakable air of intrigue and wealth was like a magnet to her. And then there was the little hilltop village just the other side of Valanjou, that had fascinated her with its air of mystery and weird, sullen silence. When they'd stopped to ask the only person in sight if there was a café or restaurant in the village they were told that the nearest place was in Nice, some thirty kilometres away. An extraordinary response since Valanjou with all its restaurants and cafés was a mere three kilometres down the road. This had got Louisa's creative juices flowing as freely as the rain for she could easily envisage something sinister going on in that village that the world so far knew nothing about. And the stupendous, gleaming yachts in the harbours where the very rich were about to descend for the summer were just crying out for someone to rock their polished decks with intrigue and romance. If only she could get out there and explore it all!

'I'll bet she's gone to get a drink,' Sarah said. 'In fact, I think I'll have one too, God knows we need something to cheer us up. Whose turn is it to cook tonight, by the way?'

'Oh God, the mundanities,' Louisa groaned.

'That must mean it's your turn,' Sarah grinned.

'It is. And I haven't been to the shops to get anything yet.'

'I'll have one of those,' Sarah said, as Danny came back with the ice, set it on the bar and took a bottle of *pastis* from a mirrored shelf.

Danny looked at her in surprise. 'You will?' she said.

'Yes, why not? What about you, Louisa?'

Louisa shook her head. 'I'll have wine,' she said, flopping into one of the armchairs that was almost the size of a sofa.

Danny blinked. 'You do realize it's not six o'clock yet, don't you?' she said.

'We're on holiday, aren't we?' Louisa yawned.

'And she wants to get drunk so she can't drive the car to go and get us something for dinner,' Sarah explained.

'Oh great, so we're in for yet another riveting evening of take-away pizzas and Trivial Pursuit?' Danny grimaced, wondering how the hell this was happening to her.

'Looks very much like it,' Sarah answered. 'God, listen to that wind, will you?' she added as it howled around the house.

'It's called the mistral,' Louisa said.

'Giving it a bloody name doesn't make it any more acceptable,' Danny snapped. 'It's driving me crazy.'

'They say it does,' Louisa informed her mildly. 'Now are you going to pour or shall I?'

'Oh my God! Quick! Hide!' Danny ducked back from the bar where the steamy, rain-spattered window was reflected in the mirrors and pressed herself against the wall.

'What is it?' Louisa said.

'It's Mrs Name-Drop, who do you think?' Danny hissed. 'She's coming up the drive. Now hide.'

Immediately Sarah and Louisa dived behind the nearest sofa.

'It's no good,' Louisa whispered, peeking round one arm, 'she'll know we're here, all the cars are there.'

'Get back! She might think we've gone for a walk,' Danny whispered.

'It's pissing down with rain,' Sarah pointed out. 'She's bound to know we're here.'

'Are you saying you want to let her in?' Danny hissed, glaring at her.

'God forbid,' Sarah cried under her breath, flinching as Mrs Name-Drop's meaty fist rammed the front door so hard it might just crash its way through the three-hundred-year-old solid oak.

'Hello! Hello in there. Is anyone at home?' Marcia Barringer's plummy voice boomed.

Danny sank to her knees, edging around the bar while Louisa gripped her stomach trying to suppress her laughter.

'Yoo hoo! It's Marcia! Is anyone there?' She knocked again, so loudly the windows rattled in their frames.

'She won't go away,' Sarah warned, hardly able to speak she was laughing so hard.

'Are all the doors locked?' Danny asked, a quick panic stealing the smile from her face.

'If they are she'll only come in through a window,' Louisa choked.

'Helloooo! Danny!' Marcia called.

'Why me?' Danny groaned, making the others laugh all the more. 'What's the matter with you two? Why does it have to be me?'

'The price of fame,' Sarah laughed.

'Oh fuck!' Danny suddenly spluttered as Marcia's beaming face appeared in a tiny square of the hall window. 'Don't say she saw me. Please God, don't say she saw me!'

It didn't seem that Marcia had, for a few seconds later they heard her footsteps crunching on the wet gravel outside heading back down the drive. At least, that's what they thought, until Danny, still not totally convinced they'd managed to get rid of her so easily, crawled to the french windows and peeped out.

'Jesus Christ!' she almost screamed, clutching her chest as she came face to face with Rudy, Mrs Name-Drop's pit bull terrier.

Rudy went berserk.

'Rudy! Rudy! Do be quiet, there's a dear,' Marcia admonished, her voice barely muted by either the pounding rain or the french window. 'You'll frighten poor Danny.'

Danny lifted her head miserably, making a slow journey up over Marcia's stocky frame until she came eye to eye with the curious expression peering down at her from the jaunty oval of its jolly headscarf. Danny gave a weak smile and Marcia stooped to make sure it really was Danny she was seeing crouched down there on the floor.

Sarah couldn't hold on any longer. Her laughter came in a great whoop of unbridled mirth, while Louisa rolled around helplessly.

The fact that all three of them were picking themselves up from the floor, that Sarah and Louisa looked remarkably as if they'd been crying, seemed to pass Marcia by as she bounded excitedly into the room, closely followed by Rudy.

Rudy sniffed his way across the tiled floor, got one whiff of Sarah and pounced.

'Get this wretched animal off me!' Sarah screamed, slumping back against the wall as Rudy tried to nuzzle his way through the defence of her arms to get a good, wholesome lick of her face.

'Rudy, you little rascal,' Marcia laughed. 'Leave poor Sarah alone, will you? I don't know what it is about her,' she said to Louisa and Danny, 'but he seems to have developed quite a passion for her.'

'For God's sake, get him off, will you?' Sarah cried.

Hooting with laughter Marcia grabbed Rudy's collar, dragging him away from the object of his affections. 'He's just playing,' she assured Sarah. 'There's nothing vicious about you, is there my precious?'

'Well he gives a damned good impression of it,' Sarah remarked sourly, brushing herself down and throwing Louisa a nasty look as Louisa, almost beside herself, helped her to her feet.

'So!' Marcia declared, plumping herself down on a sofa and coming straight to the point. 'Have you seen,' here she stopped and cupped a hand around the side of her mouth conspiratorially, 'TK?'

Louisa, Sarah and Danny all looked at each other. Who was going to be the stooge this time?

'Wasn't he in the café earlier?' Louisa answered, folding her legs under her as she too sat down. Unlike the others she was more entertained by Mrs Name-Drop than she was irritated. 'I was in a bit of a hurry, but . . .'

Marcia's head whirled in Louisa's direction. 'He was in the café?' she cried, clearly miffed. 'The café in Valanjou?' she demanded.

Louisa shrugged. 'He goes there quite often, or so he tells me, I'm surprised you've never seen him,' she said, not having the faintest idea who they were talking about.

'You mean you *know* him?' Marcia said, her startling eyebrows bristling with resentment.

'Oh yes,' Louisa answered. 'We've met him hundreds of times, haven't we?'

'Oh, hundreds,' Sarah confirmed.

'I see.' Marcia's voice was so clipped the words barely made it through her lips. 'Have you ever been to his home?'

Louisa and Sarah looked at each other. 'No, no, I can't say we have,' Sarah answered. 'At least not so's I can recall.'

'Andrew and I have been invited over for cocktails tomorrow evening,' Marcia announced, certain that this would top anything Louisa or Sarah might be able to tell her about the mysterious TK.

'No! How wonderful!' Sarah gushed. 'Lucky you.'

'He lives in Opio, you know,' Marcia said, apparently pleased with Sarah's response. 'Just for the summer of course. We met him last year. Such a nice man. Of course he wasn't the king then.'

Louisa almost choked.

'The king?' Sarah said. 'Oh, is that what you call him? We call him Elvis.'

Danny gave a splutter of laughter as Marcia's mobile face was arrested by confusion. 'I don't think he's the king yet is he?' Danny said, surprising them all.

Marcia's busily darting eyes softened as they alighted on Danny. 'You're quite right, my dear, he isn't. But as we know, he soon will be. My word, his life is going to change then. It'll be like when Andrew and I first went to the Middle East. So many functions to attend, so many dreary dinners and cocktail parties. I could feel quite sorry for the poor man. I mean when it comes right down to it, when you actually sit down and think about it, who would really want to be a king? Such a ghastly job if you ask me. All those frightful people one has to be polite to . . . I was just saying to Andrew . . . Oh by the way, Danny dear, I just saw you on the TV. You did know they were re-running that wonderful series you were in on Sky Gold, didn't you?'

'Yes, I think you mentioned it once or twice,' Danny muttered.

Marcia beamed. 'I've written to tell all my friends that you're living at the end of our lane. You're our local celebrity now, you know? Do you think you might like to be interviewed on Riviera Radio? It's an English station – I'm sure I can arrange it. We've got our own magazine down here as well, *The Riviera Reporter*. I'm sure they'd love to do a piece on you.'

'Well actually, I was . . .'

'I'll never forget,' Marcia boomed in over Danny, 'the first time Andrew did an interview on the radio here. We were just inundated with invitations afterwards. It was how we got to know so many people. Of course, we don't really like to mix with the English community too often, after all, what's the point of living in France if you don't take a tipple with the natives? We were just saying at dinner the other night, while we were with the mayor of Nice. He's such a charming man. I'll always remember . . .'

Behind Marcia's back Sarah rolled her eyes and stifled a yawn. There'd be no stopping Marcia now with her, 'I'll never forget's' and 'I'll always remember's'. That would be backed up by further fawning over Danny and there were bound to be more names to be dropped and more one-upmanship before she could happily be on her way. God the woman was insufferable and wasn't it just like her to compare herself and her husband with the soon to be crowned king and queen of Belgium, whom Sarah had belatedly identified as TK, the king.

An hour and a half later, having downed the best part of a cheap bottle of rosé, Marcia launched herself back down the drive, dragging a reluctant Rudy on his lead. 'Don't forget!' she cried, turning back to Danny, 'Colour-Me-Beautiful on Wednesday and tomorrow night is B-B-Q time! I've told everyone you'll be there, so don't let me down.'

'That's it!' Danny declared, closing the door behind her. 'She's never coming in here again.'

Sarah and Louisa were rolling around the sofa laughing.

'And if she thinks I'm going to her bloody B-B-Q . . . B-B-Q! Why can't the fucking woman speak properly? Well I'm telling you, if she comes near this house again she's going to exit PDQ because I can't stand any more of it. And stop laughing you two,' she said, breaking into a reluctant smile herself. 'It's not funny.'

'You should see it from where we're sitting,' Sarah gasped. 'I thought you were going to throw up at one point. I know I nearly did. How the hell does her husband put up with her?'

'You mean you haven't had that pleasure!' Danny cried.

'He's as bad. No, I take that back, he's worse. They're a double act.'

'Oh my God! Look!' Louisa cried.

Instantly Danny plastered herself to the wall. 'She's back?'

'No, it's the sun!' Louisa laughed. 'Look!'

'Quick, get your bikinis before it goes,' Sarah cried excitedly. 'Ah, too late, it's gone.'

'But it has stopped raining,' Louisa pointed out, springing up from the sofa. 'I'm going to get some food. Set the table on the terrace, I don't care if we're up to our knees in puddles, tonight we're eating outside.'

By the time Louisa finally extricated herself from the nightmare of Carrefour, just outside Antibes, where the Godzillas of French womanhood convened for their weekly pillage and rampage, almost two hours had passed and the rain had started again. Not as heavily, but the drizzle was perhaps even more depressing than the downpour. As she hauled the heavy bags up onto the terrace and let herself in through the kitchen door she noticed that no attempt had been made to set the table outside. Well, there would have been little point, they couldn't dine in the rain.

Dumping the shopping on the kitchen table, she removed her shoes and wandered into the hall.

'Danny! Sarah!' she called. 'I'm back.' Her voice echoed through the arches that opened into the sitting and dining rooms, reverberating upwards to the solid oak beams above.

There was no response, so assuming they had gone to their separate bathrooms to shower before dinner, Louisa went back to the kitchen to start preparing their meal.

Half an hour later a succulent seafood paella, prepared by the *poissonnerie* at the supermarket, was warming nicely in the oven, delicious *crottins* of goat's cheese were ready to sizzle in the pan and the green salad was dressed and tossed. Louisa was just wondering if she had time to go and grab a quick shower herself when Sarah and Danny came into the kitchen.

'Hi,' Louisa said. 'I was beginning to think . . .' She stopped, suddenly confused by the way they were dressed. 'Are you going somewhere?' she asked.

'Yes, we're going out,' Danny answered shortly.

'Out? But I've just prepared . . .'

'We're sick to death of hanging around this bloody house,' Danny interrupted, 'so we're going out.'

Louisa stared at her. 'Don't you think you could have told me before I went to all this trouble,' she said, looking at Sarah.

'We didn't even know you were back,' Danny responded curtly. 'You were gone so bloody long we thought . . .'

'You know how long that damned supermarket takes,' Louisa cried, dimly wondering what had happened in the time she'd been away. 'And you can't go out now, the food's almost ready. Besides, I saw Jean-Claude in the lane and invited him and Didier to join us.'

'Well that sounds a wonderful evening, doesn't it?' Danny retorted. 'Us three and two gay men. Well, the pleasure can be all yours.'

'Just a minute,' Louisa protested, putting a hand to her head. 'What's going on here? Why are you being like this? What did I do?'

Sarah and Danny looked at each other. 'Are you going to tell her, or shall I?' Danny said.

Sarah looked away.

Danny turned back to Louisa. 'Quite frankly, Louisa,' she said, 'Sarah and I have just about had it with holding back on the things we want to do because you can't afford it. We've offered to pay for you, but since you so stubbornly refuse to let us we don't see why we should deprive ourselves too. So we're going out for dinner and then on to Parady'z in Monaco.'

'We appreciate the fact that you have to stick to your budget,' Sarah said awkwardly, 'and of course you can come with us if you like, but the idea of hanging around here for another evening . . .' Her voice trailed off.

'I see,' Louisa said, hoping she didn't look as hurt as she felt. 'Well, far be it from me to stop you enjoying yourselves. I hope you have a nice time.'

'Thank you,' Danny said. 'We hope you do too.'

'Why don't you come?' Sarah said.

'No, thank you.'

'You see, it's always the same,' Danny said crossly. 'We've been cooped up here for two fucking weeks doing next to nothing and that's still all she wants to do.'

'I don't believe you're saying that!' Louisa cried. 'We've been out! We went . . .'

'To all those horrendous B-B-Q's, yes I know. While they might be your idea of fun, they're certainly not mine.'

'Come on, Danny, ease up,' Sarah said. 'It's not Louisa's fault things aren't turning out the way we expected. And she has been going around gathering up all the information about what's going on here to find us something to do.'

'And it was you, Danny, who didn't want to do it,' Louisa reminded her heatedly.

'We're not talking about visiting fucking perfume factories in Grasse,' Danny retorted, 'or touring the Rainier's Palace in Monaco. God, you're so parochial sometimes!' she seethed, stamping her foot. 'We're talking about meeting people, Louisa! Going to cafés, wine bars, restaurants, places where *people* hang out.'

'Have I ever said I didn't want to do that?'

'You've never said you do,' Danny responded. 'You've always seemed to prefer sitting around here playing Trivial Pursuit or plundering the ex-pat morons for material for your precious drama or disappearing off to your computer when the mood takes you.'

Louisa looked at her, for the moment too angry and too hurt to answer. Then she turned away, not wanting them to see the tears that were suddenly burning her eyes. OK, she had never suggested that they go to places as expensive as Parady'z, but nine times out of ten it was she who suggested that they at least go to one of the numerous cheaper and cosy restaurants in the village. Danny never wanted to though, because she couldn't stand the English who frequented them. Danny preferred to stay at home where she wouldn't be recognized and

Sarah had never seemed to mind what she did. At least, that was what Louisa had thought, but obviously she had misjudged the situation.

'Well, we'll be off then,' Danny said. 'I don't know what time we'll be back, but lock up if you like, we'll take another set of keys.'

'Won't you at least stay and have a drink with Jean-Claude and Didier?' Louisa said.

Sarah turned to Danny. 'We could,' she said.

Danny looked at her watch. 'We haven't got time,' she said, 'we've booked the restaurant for eight, we'll only just make it now.'

When they'd gone Louisa picked up a spoon and stirred the paella. Then pouring herself a large glass of wine she slumped down at the table, seething with anger. Of course she was embarrassed, she knew that, not having enough money to be here was even more intolerable to her than it was to the others, but to have had it thrust in her face that way was unforgivable.

She started as the telephone rang then got up to answer it, taking another sip of wine. It was Danny's parents calling to find out how they were all getting on. Louisa assured them they were having a wonderful time, laughed and complained about the weather and told them she'd pass on their love to Danny.

When she rang off she stalked back into the kitchen, checked on the cheeses then set about laying the table. To hell with feeling sorry for herself. It would all work itself out in the morning, or at least when the damned sun came out it would, and on reflection some kind of flare-up had been on the cards for days. It was better to clear the air, let Danny get her resentment off her chest and it wasn't so unusual for her to pick on Louisa like that. Louisa didn't blame Sarah for going along with her, it was boring staying at home all the time, especially when they'd come here with such high expections of exotic weather and wild, extemporized parties. But if Danny thought she was going to get away with many more outbursts like that then Danny could just damned well think again! It had been different when she was the star of the series, there hadn't been much choice then but to put up with her tantrums and try to placate her, but they were all on an equal footing now and the sooner Danny realized it the better. She'd never put up much of a fight with Danny before, but they'd never yet been in a situation where it particularly mattered . . .

For some reason Didier hadn't come over for dinner, probably Jean-Claude had said why, but Louisa couldn't remember now. All she knew was that she had probably drunk too much and was basking like some over-fed cat in the sonorous, seductive tones of Jean-Claude's beautifully accented English while watching the lines around his humorous blue eyes deepen as he smiled.

'And you 'ave to realize,' he was saying, 'that Marcia, 'ow you call 'er, Name-Drop? as insufferable as she is, is lonely. She never 'ad any children so she tries now to make us all 'er children.'

'Heaven forbid,' Louisa shuddered, making him laugh. 'How many children do you have?'

'I 'ave two. My son, 'e is twenty-nine and my daughter, Lili, she is twenty-seven and will be a mother next month. They both live in Paris, not far from their mother.'

'Is it because of Didier that your wife is divorcing you?' Louisa asked.

'Yes. And also why my daughter will no longer see me. My son, 'e 'as to see me because I must be in touch with what 'appens at the *bureau*, but 'e is not 'appy with my love for a boy who is younger than 'im.' He laughed. 'It is not a question of age, of course, it is because Didier is male. And you, beautiful Louisa, does it give you a problem?'

Louisa laughed softly and reached out for his hand. The way she felt about Jean-Claude was the way she'd always imagined feeling about a father or an older brother. 'Not at all,' she assured him. 'Maybe it should, but it doesn't.'

'Why should it?' he asked, confused.

'Because, well, I suppose I'd be lying if I said I didn't find you attractive.'

Linking her fingers through his Jean-Claude said, 'Didier thought you might, that is why 'e would not come this evening. 'e saw your friends leaving and told me 'e would not come to spoil things for me. I told him 'e was silly, but 'e would not come. 'e thinks that still I want to make love with a woman, but as beautiful as you are, Louisa, that is no longer so. Do I offend you?'

'No,' Louisa smiled. 'Not at all.'

With their fingers still entwined they sat quietly, companionably, for a while, each with their own thoughts, until Louisa laughed.

'Why do you laugh?' he asked curiously.

'Oh, I don't know,' she answered. 'Maybe because I feel happy. Happier than I have in a long time. Now how have you managed to do that to me when I hardly even know you?'

'I think the wine, 'e 'elp a little,' he teased. 'But what about your boyfriend, did 'e not make you 'appy?'

'Sometimes, yes.'

'Did you love 'im very much?'

'I think so, at first. But looking back I think we'd grown apart long before we broke up. What about you, did you love your wife?'

'Yes. I still do, but she doesn't understand that I can love 'er when I can love Didier. But of course I love 'er in a different way now. She is a remarkable woman, I 'ope she meets someone who can make 'er more 'appy. And you?' he said. 'Will you meet someone who will make you more 'appy?'

'I don't know,' Louisa sighed. 'I've never really been able to get it right with men.'

'Mmm, it is 'ard, this business of love,' he sighed, but his eyes were dancing. 'Even when it comes we can never be sure 'ow long it will stay. Sometimes it just checks in for the night, sometimes it arrives with all its baggage for a 'oliday and sometimes it brings no baggage and stays for always. It is a crazy thing, so unpredictable, sometimes so painful, but would any of us be without it?'

'I don't know,' Louisa answered solemnly. 'Sometimes I think I would.' She smiled and squeezed his hand. 'But don't let's talk about that. Tell me some more about you. Tell me what you do with yourself down here. Where do you go, who do you see?'

He chuckled. 'Would I be boasting if I told you I 'ave so many friends that I 'ide from them? They all want to visit from Paris, from Genève, from London, from America, from all over. I say yes only to the special ones or I should never 'ave any peace. Didier 'e is very 'appy when there are lot of people in the 'ouse, but I am not so young any more. I like to be quiet sometimes and think and read and do things old men like doing.'

'How old are you exactly?' Louisa laughed.

'Fifty-eight. Old huh?'

'Very,' she answered gravely and he gave a shout of laughter.

Seated as they were in the warm glow of candlelight at one end of the long dining table, with the high beamed ceiling lost in shadow overhead and the spacious sitting room enclosed in darkness beyond, there seemed such a sleepy intimacy about the small space they occupied that only the occasional echo of their laughter reminded them of the rambling openness of the house.

'I am sorry that your friends were unkind to you tonight,' he said.

'Oh, it doesn't matter,' Louisa shrugged, embarrassed now that she'd told him. 'We'll make it up, it was just the weather getting us all down.'

'Ah, yes, that I can understand. It is not normally like this. Maybe it rains for a few days, but . . .'

They both looked round and blinked as suddenly the front door opened and the hall was flooded with light.

'Oh my God,' Sarah gasped, seeing the candlelight, half empty wine glasses and joined hands. 'I'm so sorry, I didn't realize . . .' She bumped forward as Danny came in behind her, telling her to get a move on.

'Oh shit!' Danny muttered, her eyes widening with astonishment as she saw Louisa and Jean-Claude holding hands. 'Oh, God, what timing. Look, we're sorry. We'll go out and come back again,' and grabbing Sarah by the arm she made to drag her outside.

'It's all right,' Louisa laughed. 'You don't have to go. Danny! Come back!'

Danny and Sarah stopped, looking uncertainly over their shoulders.

'We'll just go straight to bed,' Sarah declared. 'We won't interrupt you a moment longer. Oh the light! Sorry,' and hurriedly she flicked off the overhead light.

'It is all right, I think maybe we need the light to see our way into the kitchen,' Jean-Claude laughed, dabbing the corners of his mouth with his napkin and getting to his feet.

'Oh, you don't need to do that,' Louisa told him. 'I'll clear away.'

'No, no!' Danny cried. 'Why don't you two go and make yourselves more comfortable somewhere and *we'll* clear away.'

Louisa and Sarah gaped at her, dumbfounded.

'We will?' Sarah said stupidly, then, as Danny nudged her, 'We will! Of course we will.'

Louisa caught Jean-Claude's eye and both of them burst out laughing.

'I think it is time I was leaving,' he said, taking Louisa by the shoulders. 'Thank you for a wonderful dinner, I look forward to returning the favour, soon.'

'Well, what was all that about?' Danny laughed incredulously as Louisa closed the door behind Jean-Claude. 'I thought he was gay.'

'He is. We were just holding hands, nothing else.'

'Mmm, looked pretty intimate to me,' Sarah commented.

'Well it wasn't. So what are you two doing back so soon, I wasn't expecting you until the early hours.'

'We're back,' Danny answered, 'because neither of us could

finish our meal we felt so mean about the way we'd treated you.'

'So we came back to say we're sorry,' Sarah added.

'It was all my fault,' Danny went on. 'I'm a spoiled, selfish, egotistical, nasty, spiteful bitch, who took it out on you because it was raining.'

'And I'm just as bad for listening to her,' Sarah declared.

'But we're taking you wherever you want to go tomorrow night for a slap-up meal to try to make up for it,' Danny continued. 'And we're not having any arguments.'

'No, no arguments,' Sarah insisted. 'And you're also relieved from cooking duties for the next week, Danny and I will share them.'

Louisa's eyebrows were raised, her eyes were dancing with mischief. 'It'll do for starters,' she said. 'You do remember where the dishwasher is, don't you, Cinders has a headache so she's off to bed.'

'The hell you are!' Danny cried. 'You're not going anywhere until you've told us all there is to tell about Maurice Chavalier. Is he gay or isn't he?'

'You know he is. And apparently it's how he managed to shake Mrs Name-Drop, by telling her that he and Didier were lovers. As you can no doubt imagine, she didn't want them anywhere near her B-B-Qs after that.'

Danny turned to Sarah.

'Don't look at me,' Sarah cried backing away. 'I'm not pretending to be gay just to get Mrs Name-Drop off your back.'

'Why not? It would get the dog off yours,' Danny responded.

'Yeah, well, I might just prefer him,' Sarah said, turning up her nose as she looked Danny over. 'Anyway, let's get on with what we really came back for.'

'You mean it wasn't to apologize to me?' Louisa challenged.

'Of course it was, but we also decided that it was about time we did something about this godawful situation down here. We might not be able to change the weather, but our social lives we can. At least we think we can. Between us, you, Danny and I are going to do what we should have done before we left

London and that's call up everyone we know who has a house down here or might know someone who has a house here who could be worth getting to know. Because, what we reckon is that the in-people are a pretty exclusive bunch and we need some introductions. OK?'

'OK,' Louisa said. 'I'll have to rack my brains a bit, but I expect I'll come up with someone. My guess is Jean-Claude could come up with even more.'

Sarah nodded. 'Mmm, just so long as they're not all gay. Anyway, Danny's going first because she knows the most people. Got your black book, kiddo? Then get dialling.'

Danny was on the point of picking up the phone when suddenly it rang.

'Hello?' she said. 'Oh hi, Jean-Claude, yes she's right here.'

Louisa turned back from the kitchen as Danny put her hand over the receiver and mouthed, 'are you *sure* he's gay?'

Rolling her eyes Louisa took the receiver. 'Hi, Jean-Claude,' she said.

'I 'ope I am not calling too late,' he said, 'but I want you to go outside and look at the sky.'

'The sky?' Louisa said, looking curiously at Danny and Sarah.

'Can you take the phone to the terrace?' he asked.

'Yes, it's a radio phone,' Louisa answered, walking around the dining table to the french windows. 'OK,' she said, stepping out onto the terrace, 'I'm looking at the sky.'

'And what do you see?'

'I see stars, lots of stars and a moon, is it a blue moon?'

He laughed. 'Yes, it is a blue moon, but do you not find something unusual about the stars?'

Louisa was working very hard to try to remember the constellations, but wasn't having much success. 'Unusual in what way?' she asked.

'You can see them,' Jean-Claude chuckled. 'That is what is unusual. It is the first time we 'ave seen them for over two weeks. Do you understand what this means?'

Louisa had already broken into a smile. 'It means there are no clouds.'

'That's right. Tomorrow I think will be a fine day.'

'Yes,' Louisa said, turning back to Danny and Sarah, 'I think it will.'

'So maybe now your life down 'ere begins at last.'

4

Jake Mallory was used to people stopping and staring whenever he brought the magnificent, twin-masted *Valhalla* into port. She was a beautiful, one-hundred-and-twenty-foot handcrafted vessel, built in Scotland, and was one of the two great loves of his life. She was flying two flags as she inched her way into the busy harbour at St Tropez – Jake's native American and the French tricolor. Following the instructions Jake gave mainly with hand signals, the six-man crew were busy paying out the anchor, hauling and winching lines, flaking the sails and moving swiftly and efficiently about the deck.

Jake's dark, expressionless eyes moved between the rudder indicator and Bob, the first mate, who was at the bow controlling the anchor. St Tropez was not an easy port to negotiate, particularly at this time of year when its oddly horseshoe-shaped harbour walls were so crammed with vast and luxurious motor cruisers.

Eight feet from the dock with the engine and anchor chain balanced, the yacht glided gently into the mooring. The aft crew leapt onto the dock with the stern lines. Jake looked back over his shoulder. For a fleeting moment his eyes rested on a woman lying on the deck of the cruiser they were moving in alongside. She was watching Jake and raised her eyebrows slightly as he looked her way, but wasn't quick enough to wave before he'd turned away. It wasn't that he was averse to semi-naked women giving him the come on, it was just that he had other things on his mind right now.

Getting up from the steering station he moved down the deck, gazing up at the russet, pink and yellow houses with their wide open shutters and red-tiled roofs that clustered around the old bohemian fishing port. After the recent heavy rains everything looked twice as bright and sparkled brilliantly in the sunlight. For a moment he allowed himself to think of happier times he had spent there and almost smiled as he dropped his eyes to the bustling cafés, gift shops, street art and the parading peacocks of French fashion. It made a pleasant change from the great, sprawling marinas of the West Coast.

Maybe it was the claustrophobia of St Tropez that he enjoyed the most, with its narrow, shady streets where laundry hung from upstairs windows and friendly, noisy bistros spilled onto the cobbles. After the infinite, silent expanse of the sea, the isolation, the eerie calm and the howling winds that made his heart throb with fear and exhilaration, the cluttered pandemonium of St Tropez made a striking and welcome contrast. This time they'd sailed only from Corsica, but for a while the wind had registered seven on the Beaufort. His black hair was still damp from the sea-spray, and his thin, white cotton shirt and tattered jeans were stained with salt and sweat.

Time now for some relaxation, at least for his crew. They'd been on board for over three weeks, making brief calls into French and Italian ports, but never for more than an hour or two.

As he moved on along the deck towards the stern the humour in his watchful eyes was affecting the men. He was popular with his crew and was almost sorry he wouldn't be around much over the next day or so. But at least he knew where they'd be, which was more than they could say about him. He was an intensely private man and those who knew anything about him at all knew it mainly from hearsay – with the exception of Bob, the first mate. But Bob was as closed about Jake's personal life as Jake himself and had never entered into the speculation as to how Jake had come by the vicious, disfiguring scar around the socket of his left eye. It wasn't unusual for Jake to cover the scar with a patch, as he was doing at that moment, for glaring sunlight caused the eye problems.

Bob knew why they had come into St Tropez now, knew too that it would have been more convenient for Jake to have anchored off Cannes or in the marina at Golfe Juan. But Jake didn't want the crew too close to hand over the next few days, so he'd chosen a port where he knew they would have a good time even though it surely to God must give him more pain than pleasure to be there himself.

Scratching the thirty-six hour stubble on his chin, Bob came alongside Jake at the stern where a couple of crew were connecting up the *passerelle*. At five foot ten Bob was by no means as tall as Jake, nor was he so muscular, but he did have a certain something that appealed to the ladies. Possibly it was the shyness that he concealed with a gruff disinterest, or maybe it was just that they used him to get to know Jake. What the hell did he know? What the hell did he care even? He was as confirmed a bachelor now at forty-six as he has been at twenty-six, for when it came to women and the sea there was no contest. He occasionally wondered if Jake could say the same.

'Any sign of her?' he said.

'She'll be here,' Jake responded tonelessly. Then his mouth relaxed in a smile as he registered Bob's anxiety. 'Nothing's going to happen this time,' he said.

'No,' Bob grunted, not for the first time wishing that he and Jake were preparing for the Transpac or the Sydney–Hobart or just sitting on one of the quays in San Diego chewing over victories and near misses, new techniques and how many millions Jake and his old man were about to sink into the building of yet another marina. In fact Bob wished they were anywhere right now rather than the south of France, even though he knew they had no choice in the matter.

'You taking them up to the Café des Arts?' Jake asked

Bob nodded.

'I might join you later,' Jake said, swinging himself up on to the *passerelle* as a familiar black Mercedes sports car inched its way through the crowds.

'Just keep in touch,' Bob called after him. 'And for Christ's sake don't do anything rash.'

As the car came to a halt Jake turned back, grinning. Then opening the door for the driver to get out, he slid behind the wheel himself, waited for the blonde to get in the other side then drove away.

'OK, you lot,' Bob shouted to the crew, 'finish up here, then let's go have ourselves some fun.'

Consuela de Santiago Santini was strolling through the gardens of her palatial estate on the Cap d'Antibes. Her thick blonde hair was clasped at the nape of her neck by an intricate tortoise-shell slide, her flimsy silk sarong parted in the breeze to reveal long, exquisite legs that could easily belong to a woman half her age. Dark glasses shielded her gentle, green eyes from the sun, a subtle pink gloss protected her wide, generous lips. With her was Rosalind Carmichael, a woman who whilst not quite so beautiful as Consuela was nonetheless striking. She was younger than Consuela by almost ten years, but then Consuela could have passed easily for being in her early to mid-forties.

Consuela gave a cry of surprised laughter as Rosalind finished telling her about an incident on Capri a few weeks before, when mutual friends had become embroiled in an unfortunate confrontation with the locals.

'Ah, Capri,' Consuela sighed, stopping beside a fountain and sitting on the edge. 'It is so long since I have been there.'

'Then why don't you go, darling?' Rosalind said, gently.

Consuela shook her head. 'I don't think so,' she smiled. 'But I like to hear about it. About all the places you visit.'

Rosalind reached out for her hand. 'You know how I hate nagging,' she said, 'but you have turned yourself into a virtual prisoner here.'

'A prisoner?' Consuela laughed, covering Rosalind's hand. 'Is that how you see me?' She looked back at the sprawling white stucco villa that housed eight luxurious bedrooms, six of which overlooked the sea, three sitting rooms, two dining rooms and a collection of the most tasteful antiques and paintings on the entire coast. Seeing Frederico, one of her six young gardeners, poised ready to dive into the pool, she smiled fondly. Unlike the others Frederico rarely used the private beach, he didn't like to swim in the sea.

'They have all been working so hard these past two days,' Consuela murmured, almost to herself. 'There has been so much clearing up to do after the storms. You are lucky you missed them, *chérie*, it has been quite dismal here. But the sun is shining now and the sky is so beautiful, don't you think?'

'You're changing the subject, Consuela,' Rosalind chided. 'How do you see yourself, if not as a prisoner? You so rarely go out, you stay here all the time, shut up behind these walls . . .'

'Ssh, ssh,' Consuela soothed. 'You know I don't like to discuss this. I am happy here, Rosalind, very happy. I have my boys to take care of me, I have my music, my lovely garden, and all my wonderful friends who come to visit. What more could I ask for? Now come, I want you to see the new olive press the boys have made. It is quite an accomplishment, I think.'

Smiling and shaking her head in fond exasperation Rosalind followed Consuela along an oleander-lined walkway towards the vast stable block that Consuela had had converted into a Greco-Roman bathhouse on the ground floor and living quarters for her staff on the upper floor. Whether Consuela ever indulged in the sensuous delights of the bathhouse herself Rosalind didn't know, though her friends were certainly always welcome to avail themselves of its pleasures.

It was almost heartbreaking to see the way Consuela lived now when compared to the jet-set life she'd led before. Of course, no one could wish for a more perfect setting in which to lock oneself away from the world, but it was so terrible to see the sadness that seemed to flow through her every movement and the despair that stole the joy from her lovely smile. She had been known to leave the house once or twice since it had all happened, but she never ventured further than the Côte d'Azur, hadn't left France at all in almost three years.

'I am thinking of having a few friends for dinner at the weekend,' Consuela said, as they walked around the bathhouse to the hidden work area behind. 'Will you still be here, *chérie*? I'd like you to come.'

'I'll still be here. We aren't leaving until the end of next week. Shall I invite Peter?'

Consuela's eyes held a mischievous sparkle as she turned to her friend. 'Do you want to invite Peter?' she asked.

Rosalind laughed. 'Maybe not.' she said. 'Who else are you inviting?'

'I thought perhaps Mathilde, Caro, Serena, Olivia . . .'

'Olivia is here?' Rosalind interrupted. 'I didn't know. When did she arrive?'

'Just yesterday. She called me this morning. She and Gino are sailing to Morocco next week. Now, here, see my new olive press, aren't they magicians, my boys?'

Never having seen an olive press in her life Rosalind made what she hoped were the right noises. She knew how proud Consuela was of her boys, how she treated each one as though he were a cherished son – the son perhaps that she'd never had.

When Consuela had first left Argentina and moved permanently into this house where she had spent so many summers with her husband, Rosalind, just like everyone else, had been curious about the absence of any females on her staff, but Rosalind had been the one insensitive enough to ask. The grief that had clouded Consuela's eyes had been answer enough, and Rosalind had wanted to bite out her tongue. But seeing Rosalind's distress Consuela had comforted her with another answer, an answer that was also true, but certainly not the sole reason for surrounding herself with handsome young men.

'You know how I enjoy the company of young people,' Consuela had smiled. 'It keeps me young too, but girls they always come with so many problems, their lives are so complicated in comparison to the boys. And they do so like to gossip. So that is why I don't employ them. I have plenty of female company in my friends, it is enough.'

There had been a great deal of gossip concerning Consuela and her household, but Rosalind doubted that even half of it was true. She had never seen a sign of anything even remotely sexual between Consuela and the boys, had never detected as much as a glimpse of anything that would suggest that Consuela had a sex life at all.

The olive press admired, Consuela and Rosalind started back towards the house.

'Are you sure I can't offer you some lunch?' Consuela said. 'I like the boys to take a break at midday, but I can easily prepare something myself.'

'No, really, I'm not hungry,' Rosalind insisted. 'But I could use a drink and perhaps a swim. Do you think Frederico would mind if I joined him?'

'I'm sure he'd be delighted,' Consuela answered with a laugh. 'And while I go to the kitchen perhaps you can think of someone else I should invite on Saturday. It has been some time since we ladies got together. What will you have to drink? Maybe a fruit punch?'

'Sounds heavenly,' Rosalind said, stopping at one of the sunbeds and kicking off her shoes. She turned to where Frederico was doing steady, strenuous laps of the pool. 'Do you think he'll mind if I go in topless?' she whispered to Consuela. 'I only have my bikini bottom.'

'My darling, I'm sure you won't be showing him anything he hasn't seen before,' Consuela laughed. 'Now go ahead, I'll bring you a towel.'

Consuela was on the point of walking up the steps to the house when the telephone rang. Turning back she picked up the phone beside the pool.

'Yes, this is Consuela Santini,' she said, admiring Rosalind's perfect but as yet untanned body as she stepped out of her dress.

'Consuela, it's Ricard.'

'Darling, how are you?' Consuela cried. 'It has been so long since we've spoken. Where are you?'

'On tour with the band. We're in London at the moment, off to Amsterdam tomorrow.'

'Are you coming down this way? It is the jazz festival here next month, are you taking part?'

'Sadly no, but I'll try to get down when the tour is over.

Anyway, how are you? Still spoiling yourself rotten with all those wicked young boys?'

'You rascal,' Consuela laughed. 'You know you are the only one I love.'

'If I thought for even a moment that were true I'd give up everything and come to you now.'

'You wouldn't, but it's nice to hear. How is Lucinda?'

'Terrific. About to give birth again actually.'

'*Oh là là.* How many does that make?'

'Just three. Will you be godmother?'

'If you mean it then of course I will.'

'So you'll come to London for the christening?'

'Ah-ha, you are trying to trick me.'

'And failing. But I'll get you out of there one of these days. You've got to start living again, sweetheart, the world misses you.'

Consuela laughed.

'OK, look,' Ricard said, 'I've just popped out of rehearsals so I'll have to come right to the point. There's this actress friend of mine, Danny Spencer, who's staying somewhere near Cannes for the summer and I wondered if you could, well you know, sort of introduce her around a bit. I know you don't go out, but since everyone who's anyone comes to you . . . She's a great girl, you'll like her a lot. She's got a couple of friends with her, I don't know much about them except that if they're with Danny they'll be OK. Don't feel obliged, but if you could help out I know they'll be for ever grateful.'

'How old are they?' Consuela asked.

'Thirtyish.'

'Then I don't see there'll be any problem at all. Do you have a number where I can call them?'

'Sure. I was going to tell them to call you, but if you're happy to do the phoning . . .' He read out the number, blew kisses down the receiver and rang off.

'Danny Spencer,' Consuela said thoughtfully, wandering over to Rosalind who after two lengths was now lying on the edge of the pool making a start on her tan.

'Danny who?' Rosalind said, holding up a hand to shield her eyes from the sun.

'Spencer. That was Ricard on the phone asking me to take Danny Spencer and her two friends under my wing for a while. Do you think Danny could be Suzannah's and David's daughter? Isn't her name Danielle?'

'Yeah, it is. She's an actress, quite well known in England.'

Consuela looked up as Frederico's shadow fell over them. She hadn't noticed until then that he was no longer in the pool.

'Towel and suntan cream for Mrs Carmichael,' he said, holding them out.

'Oh Frederico, thank you,' Rosalind said taking them. 'He thinks of everything, doesn't he?' she whispered to Consuela as he dived back into the pool.

'More or less,' Consuela laughed. 'So what about Danny Spencer and her friends? Do you think we should invite them on Saturday evening?'

Rosalind shrugged. 'I don't see why not. It could be fun to have some fresh faces on the scene. And from what I know of Danny she's mature enough. We'll just have to hope the others are too. If not, well, what's one night?'

'Nothing. Nothing at all. I'll call this afternoon to see if they're free. I wonder if I should mention that I know her mother?'

Rosalind looked at her curiously.

'I was just thinking that if I did then it will automatically create a generation gap. On the other hand, Suzannah might already have told Danny she knows me.'

'If she had then surely Danny would have been in touch with you through Suzy, not Ricard.'

'True. So I won't cast myself in the role of her mother's geriatric friend,' Consuela smiled.

'Hardly geriatric,' Rosalind said arching an eyebrow.

'That's how the young see us, *chérie*.'

'Speak for yourself,' Rosalind quipped, sitting up as she heard a car coming up the drive.

Consuela turned and immediately Rosalind felt her stiffen. She reached out for Consuela's suddenly unsteady hand and squeezed it as they watched the black, open-topped Mercedes approach. The sun was dazzling the windscreen so they couldn't see who was driving, but then neither of them needed to see, they already knew who it was.

'Were you expecting him?' Rosalind said, holding the towel to her.

Consuela shook her head.

'How did he get in through the gates?'

'He knows the security code.'

They waited, watching the magnificent car as it glided to a halt at the side of the house. Rosalind's pulses were racing. It had been a while since she'd last seen Jake Mallory and she was wondering if he would have the same effect on her now as he'd had before.

Consuela's grip had tightened on her hand. Rosalind returned the pressure, knowing that Jake Mallory was the source of all Consuela's suffering, that it was this man's actions that had driven her friend to live this hermit-like existence.

Jake stepped from the car. He was wearing a pair of filthy, torn jeans, a faded black T-shirt and a red bandanna was tied around his untidy black hair. Rosalind almost moaned aloud. His sexuality was every bit as lethal as she remembered and the look in his piercing, grey eyes sent shivers of lust through her body.

She watched in slightly awed admiration at the way Consuela was going towards him with her hands held out to receive him. How could she do it? Rosalind was asking herself. After all he had done and for all Rosalind knew was still doing.

'Jake,' Consuela said, kissing him on either cheek. 'What a pleasant surprise.'

Jake's answering smile was more of a smirk. 'It is?' he said. 'I thought you might be expecting me.'

'But you're always welcome, *chéri*, you know that,' Consuela said turning away. 'You've met Rosalind Carmichael?'

Letting the towel drop Rosalind got to her feet. 'Hello, Jake,' she said. 'We met a couple of years ago, in Los Angeles I think it was.'

Jake clearly didn't remember but said. 'It's good to meet you again, Rosalind.' His eyes stayed on her face, but there was something about the way he was looking at her that was making her almost feel her palms, her face, her breasts pressed up against a wall while he did things to her from behind that turned her knees weak just to think of them.

'If you'll excuse us, Rosalind,' he said turning to Consuela.

Consuela smiled, and as she and Jake turned towards the house Rosalind was again impressed by Consuela's remarkable composure when she surely must hate and fear that man beyond anything else in her life.

5

'Hold it! Hold it, Jean-Claude.' Sarah cried, putting up her hands to stop him. 'Did I just hear you say that Erik Svensson, *Erik Svensson*, the internationally renowned photographer, the drop dead gorgeous, be-still-my-galloping-heart, Erik Svensson, is a friend of yours?'

''e is a very good friend, *oui*,' Jean-Claude grinned. 'We 'ave known each other since maybe ten or fifteen years.'

Sarah turned to Louisa. 'Did you hear that?' she said. 'He actually *knows* Erik Svensson.'

'He knows everyone,' Louisa said, laughing at Sarah's incredulous delight and thanking Didier as he passed the bottle of Aligoté across the table for her to help herself.

They were sitting on the terrace over at Jean-Claude's where the view of the red-roofed village way down at the bottom of the hill and the swelling peaks of the Alps in the far distance was so beautiful it was hard to believe it was real. Didier was barbecuing lamb chops and sausages while Jean-Claude laughingly impressed them with all the famous people he knew. Occasionally he winked at Louisa, letting her know when he was spinning a yarn, but it seemed that in this instance he really did know Erik Svensson.

'In fact,' Didier said, forking more sausages onto a plate. ''e is coming here this summer, is 'e not, Jean-Claude?'

Sarah looked at Jean-Claude as though she might devour him she was so dying for him to confirm it.

'Yes, 'e will be 'ere,' Jean-Claude told her solemnly. 'But maybe 'e bring 'is wife, I don't know.'

'Who cares about his wife?' Sarah cried. 'It's his talent I'm after. Do you think he'll give me some pointers?'

'Some advice,' Louisa provided when Jean-Claude frowned.

'Oh, I am sure 'e will. 'e is very 'elpful to those who are beginning. Didier, I think we have enough sausage now. Why don't you sit down and 'ave something to eat yourself?'

'So when's he arriving?' Sarah asked as Didier slid onto the bench beside her.

'Who Erik? Soon I think. 'e 'as an apartment in Monaco, but 'e will stop 'ere for a day or two 'e says. Don't worry, I will be sure to introduce you.'

'Perhaps we can invite you all over to our place for aperitifs, or dinner,' Louisa suggested. 'Sarah can cook.'

Throwing her a meaningful look Sarah turned to Didier who was quite a keen photographer himself and as they became involved in a somewhat stilted conversation given their appalling grasp of each other's language, Jean-Claude turned to Louisa.

'Have you done much writing these past few days?' he asked.

'A little,' she answered, helping herself to another lamb chop and some potato salad.

'How much is a little?'

'None actually. We've been sunbathing.'

'That I can see,' he laughed, looking at Sarah's pink shoulders. 'Will she go brown? She is very fair.'

'Yes, she'll go brown, a kind of honey colour, or so she tells me. Danny looks absolutely gorgeous, but then she already had a tan from when she was in Spain.'

'Where is she tonight?'

'She said she was going into Cannes, but Danny's plans often change at the last minute, so we'll see. I hope you're not upset that she didn't come.'

'Not at all. She is looking for adventure and she knows she won't find it 'ere, not with Didier and me.'

Louisa sighed and leaned back against the window sill behind her. 'It's so lovely here,' she said, 'so rustic and natural. It's almost as if we were in another part of France altogether it's so different from our garden.'

'That is what is so special about here,' Jean-Claude answered, 'very little is as you expect it to be.' He paused a moment to let that sink in, then continued. 'Didier does the garden,' he said, 'but only when 'e feels like it, which is why we are so overgrown. 'e claims it is because 'e wants us to be private and I pretend to believe 'im.'

Louisa chuckled and reached out for her wine. 'Did I tell you we've been considering setting up a production company down here?' she said.

'Sarah mentioned it to Didier this afternoon. I don't wish you to think me pessimistic, but it is very 'ard and very complicated to start a business in France. Not to mention expensive. Do you 'ave any contacts to 'elp you get started?'

'Not one,' Louisa answered cheerfully.

'Maybe I will 'ave some, I will think about it. 'ow did you get on by the way with ringing up your friends in London? Did they know any people down 'ere who you can meet?'

'Only more English people. Except Danny's jazz musician friend, Ricard, he's put us in touch with a woman who lives on the Cap d'Antibes. Consuela something-or-another. She called us yesterday afternoon to invite us to dinner tomorrow night. We're going, but only because Danny couldn't think of an excuse not to.'

'Why does Danny not wish to go?'

'To quote Danny, "more fucking women".'

'I see. What with gay men and fucking women, Danny is not 'aving a 'appy time, is she?'

'Not really, no,' Louisa laughed.

'But maybe there will be men at this dinner?' Jean-Claude suggested.

'I don't think there will be, actually,' Louisa said frowning. 'I can't remember now exactly what Danny said, but she made it sound like it was an all female thing. Did you get that impression, Sarah? That tomorrow night was all women?'

Sarah nodded. 'Sounds a barrel of laughs, wouldn't you say? Us three hanging out with the lace handkerchief, humming hearing-aid set.'

Didier, Louisa suddenly noticed, was looking at Jean-Claude. She turned to see why and saw that Jean-Claude was frowning.

'Is something the matter?' she said.

'No, nothing is the matter,' he answered.

'Do you know this Consuela woman or something?' Sarah asked, curiously.

'No, I don't know 'er, but if she is the woman I am thinking of then I 'ave 'eard about 'er. Didier, 'e knows some of the people who work for 'er.'

'Who work for her? Why, what does she do?'

'I think nothing. She is very rich. She lives alone in 'er 'ouse on the Cap and doesn't go out very often. But she 'as a lot of people who go to visit 'er. We 'ave 'eard stories of what 'appens there, but we don't know if they are true.'

'Really?' Sarah said, her eyes glittering with intrigue. 'What kind of stories?'

Jean-Claude's grin was mischievous. 'I think maybe I should not tell you,' he said. 'I think that maybe you should come back and tell me if they are true.' He translated this for Didier and Didier laughed.

'Yes, you tell us,' Didier said, his boyish face flushing 'We want all detail, yes, Jean-Claude.'

'Oh come on! This isn't fair,' Sarah cried. 'Just give us a hint of what to expect.'

'What we 'ave 'eard is only rumour,' Jean-Claude said. 'Some of it is good, some of it is bad. Maybe she is not a woman you should become involved with, but only, I think, because of the people she knows.'

'What kind of people?'

'Very dubious people. That is if the rumours are true. But maybe they aren't.'

'Just wait 'til we tell Danny this,' Louisa laughed, 'wild horses won't keep her away now.'

Didier said something to Jean-Claude in French and, laughing, Jean-Claude turned back to Louisa. 'You say it is an all female evening?' he said.

'I think so,' she nodded, looking at Sarah as Jean-Claude's teasing eyes moved between them.

'This is driving me nuts,' Sarah declared. 'Come on, Jean-Claude, you obviously know something we don't.'

'I think,' he said, 'that you will find plenty of men there.'

'Everyone who work for Consuela is man,' Didier added.

For the second time that evening Sarah looked extremely impressed. 'You mean she lives on her own with her own private supply of men to pander to her whims. Wow! What a set-up! This woman I've got to meet.'

'You are honoured,' Jean-Claude told them. 'I don't think many people get to see the inside of Consuela Santini's home. So,' he grinned, 'I shall look forward to 'earing all about it later in the 'ope that at least some of the rumours I 'ave 'eard are true.'

'My God, will you just look at this place?' Louisa murmured as Danny gently accelerated her open-topped BMW into the drive. 'Are you sure we don't have to pay to get in?'

Danny and Sarah laughed.

'It's like something out of a Scott Fitzgerald novel,' Sarah remarked, looking about her at the exquisite topiary, the gazebos, fountains, oriental pines, tropical palms and flowers that were so perfect and so vivid they hardly seemed real.

'Did Jean-Claude say how she'd made her money?' Danny asked.

'No,' Louisa answered, transfixed.

'Wow, will you just look at that house,' Sarah gasped as it came into view. 'It makes our place seem like a hut. It's a palace, it's got to be, I'm telling you this is a palace.'

'If it is then it's a small one,' Danny responded, feeling the sheer romance of the smooth white walls, the towering, arched french windows and the grand, immaculately carved columns wash over her.

'What's that building there, through the trees?' Louisa said, pointing to the far side of the garden.

'Looks like another house of some sort,' Sarah answered. 'Maybe it's where the staff live.'

'I'm glad we brought your car, Danny,' Louisa said, 'look at all these others. What's that one there, the powder blue one?'

'It's a Ferrari,' Danny answered, cruising slowly past it.

'Where are you going to park?' Sarah wondered aloud.

'Is she serious?' Danny said to Louisa. 'I mean how much space do you want, Sarah? This forecourt's got to be as big as a polo field. Anyway, if I'm not greatly mistaken I think someone else is about to take care of that. Hello,' she said to the young man who was opening her door.

'Hi,' he said with a devastating smile. 'I'm Carlos. Madame Santini is expecting you. If you would like to leave the keys in the car I will see that they reach you later.'

'Thank you,' Danny said, sounding every inch the lady as she stepped out of the car. 'Maybe you'd like to return them to my friend here,' she added indicating Louisa. 'She'll be driving us home.'

Louisa smiled up at him, feeling faintly ridiculous just sitting there, but assuming she should wait for him to open the door for her too. He did.

'Hi, I'm Sarah,' Sarah said smiling up at him as he held out his hand to help her from the back of the car. 'Oh God!' she gasped as her foot caught in the seat belt and she fell against him. 'Sorry. Gosh, I'm so sorry.'

Carlos smiled, set her back on her feet and gave a slight bow as he directed them towards the house.

'You did that on purpose,' Danny hissed as they walked towards the house.

'I did not!' Sarah hissed back.

'You're going to show us up, I know you are,' Danny seethed.

'Don't treat me like an idiot!'

'Then don't behave like one.'

'Shut up arguing you two,' Louisa said through her teeth, 'and swear to me again that this dress isn't too short.'

'It's only three inches above the knee!' Danny cried. 'And you look fantastic, how many times do we have to tell you?'

Which she did, particularly now that her olivey skin had turned even darker in the sun and the simple pale lemon linen dress, flat gold sandals and gold bangles on her wrists set it off to perfection.

Sarah too looked lovely. Her skin, as she had predicted, was turning honey, her bobbed hair was even blonder after a week in the sun and though a lot of people her size wouldn't have dared to wear such a revealing dress, on Sarah it simply contrived to look sexy. Besides, she had good legs and provided she remembered to keep breathing in her figure – with a little imagination – was quite stunningly hour-glass.

Danny was breathtaking in a silver, sheath dress that showed every curve of her tall, voluptuous figure. Her glorious curly black hair spilled down her back covering the bare skin, but tantalizingly revealing the very low cut of the dress as she moved. She wore black spiked heel sandals making her beautiful, bronzed legs seem even longer and even more perfect than they already were. But even she, usually so confident in her looks, felt faintly diminished by the quiet elegance and sophistication of the woman in the plain, knee-length black dress with a black velvet bow holding back her lovely blonde hair, who was coming to greet them.

'Hello,' Consuela smiled, moving gracefully down the steps. 'I'm so glad you could come. Now let me guess, which one of you is Danny?'

'It's me,' Danny said, holding out her hand. 'And this is Louisa, and this is Sarah.'

'Hello,' Consuela said, taking each of their hands in turn. 'As I'm sure you've already guessed, I'm Consuela. Now, won't you come through to the terrace and take a little aperitif before dinner? My other guests have already arrived. We're eight altogether. I hope we won't seem too formal, but this house does rather impose it on one.'

'It's a beautiful house,' Louisa said, as they followed Consuela up the steps and through the double front door into the entrance hall.

'Have you lived here long?' Sarah asked.

'It's been in my family for quite some time,' Consuela answered. 'But I've lived here permanently for about three years.'

My God, it's like an art gallery, Louisa was thinking to herself, as they walked through the capacious hall with its ornate sweeping staircase and innumerable framed portraits towards the sun-bleached doorway at the other end.

'Maybe you'd like to take a look around later,' Consuela offered, briefly turning back as she descended a set of steps midway across the hall.

'Oh, we'd love tooooo–,' Sarah cried, grabbing Louisa as her right foot skidded from under her on the polished marble. Louisa tried to catch her, but it was too late and as Sarah hit the floor Louisa was almost dragged down with her.

Hearing the thump Consuela and Danny turned back, looking down at Sarah in astonishment.

'Before you say one word, Danielle Spencer,' Sarah said savagely, 'I did not do it on purpose.'

Danny's eyes flickered to Consuela's as she struggled to suppress her laughter. 'I'm sure you didn't,' she said, almost losing it as she noticed how Louisa's shoulders were shaking.

Consuela looked at Danny uncertainly, then at Louisa, then down at Sarah. Quickly she put a hand to her mouth, but not before Danny had seen the smile. Then, unable to stop herself, Consuela started to laugh. 'I'm sorry,' she said to Sarah, offering a hand to help her up. 'I'm so sorry. I do hope you haven't hurt yourself.'

'Only my pride,' Sarah grinned wryly, taking her hand.

'Sarah, there's not enough room in this dress to laugh,' Danny protested.

'No one's forcing you to,' Sarah answered loftily.

Consuela was biting her lips. 'Are you sure you're all right?' she said. 'These floors are so dangerous.'

'I'm fine, thank you,' Sarah replied, summoning her dignity as she straightened her dress. 'And please, feel free to laugh, it'll make me feel better.'

'Come along,' Consuela said, putting an arm around Sarah's shoulder, 'let's get you a drink.'

Half an hour later, third cocktail in hand, Sarah managed to work her way across the wide, sweeping terrace that tripped in long, gently curved steps down to the pool, through the other guests, all of whom were as glamorous and probably as disgustingly rich as Consuela, to Louisa. 'Consuela seems pretty taken with you,' she said, stirring her drink and moving into the shade of a palm tree. 'What were you talking about?'

'I was just telling her what we all did in London and what we've been thinking about doing down here. In fact, she thinks she knows someone who might be able to help us.'

'Really? Did she say who?'

'I can't remember his name. She said she'd give him a call for us. He's in Nice, apparently.'

Sarah smiled as one of the gorgeous, dinner-suited boys took her near-empty glass and handed her another.

'No thanks,' Louisa told him. 'I still haven't finished this one. How many have you had?' she whispered to Sarah as the boy moved on.

'Who's counting?' Sarah replied airily, lifting her face towards the sky, drinking in the wonderful balmy air and gentle hum of conversation on the terrace. 'I could live this life,' she said. 'I wouldn't have any problem getting used to it.'

'I wonder what Consuela's story is,' Louisa said.

'Why don't you get your notebook out and go and ask her?' Sarah suggested.

'Very funny. But aren't you intrigued? I mean, to begin with, where's her husband?'

'Ah, now that I can answer,' Sarah said. 'The woman over there, Serena I think her name is, the one in the striped dress, she told me. Apparently Mr Santini died about three years ago.'

'Oh. Who was he, did she say?'

'He was Argentinian I think, the same as Consuela.'

'What did he do before he died?'

'She didn't say.'

'What did he die of?'

'I don't know, I didn't ask.'

'Doesn't she have any other family?'

'Louisa! How the heck am I supposed to know? You're the writer, you're the one with all the questions, you go and ask.'

'All right, keep your hair on. Anyway, I think we'd better go and mingle again, don't you?'

'Mmm. Listen, before you go, have you managed to get out of Danny yet where she was last night?'

'No. Have you?'

Sarah shook her head.

'Well, you know Danny, she likes to have her little secrets,' Louisa said, looking over to where Danny was laughing at something one of the women was saying to her.

'When do you think we're going to eat?' Sarah muttered. 'I'm starving.'

'Then you're in luck.' Consuela laughed, coming up behind them. 'I was just about to say shall we go inside?'

Dinner, or a little light supper, as Consuela referred to it, was served in the main dining room just off the entrance hall. All four of the tall french windows were opened onto the terrace, offering a splendid view of the pool, gardens and setting sun. Anti-mosquito spirals and candles flickered and smoked and vast chandeliers glowed softly overhead. Consuela was at the head of the beige lacquered table with Danny to her right and Olivia Woodrow to her left. Louisa was at the other end opposite Consuela with Serena Udell, the wife of a Belgian banker, one side and Caro Reuben of the Reuben cosmetic group the other. Sarah was in the middle between Serena Udell and a woman whose name she embarrassingly couldn't remember.

The atmosphere was easy and relaxed, the women obviously knew each other well and Louisa found it quite fascinating to watch them. She'd never been in the company of such wealthy and celebrated people before, and their air of exclusivity and elitism was as spellbinding as their conversation. She almost laughed as she thought of what raptures Marcia Name-Drop would of be in were she here. Surprisingly, Louisa hadn't detected even the slightest degree of snobbery amongst the women and their fondness for Consuela seemed quite touchingly real. It was as though, Louisa reflected curiously, they each harboured some kind of sadness for her, some kind of mutual compassion that Consuela neither accepted nor rejected. It was simply something that was there. What was it she was trying to say to herself about Consuela? she wondered. There was something about her that seemed as closed as an oyster and when she laughed it was as though the joy came from her lips, not her heart. When they'd spoken earlier Louisa had caught a sharpness in Consuela's eyes, an edge that suggested some inner pain or maybe it was anger, or maybe she, Louisa, had too vivid an imagination.

'She is very beautiful, no?' Caro whispered in her throaty Spanish accent.

Louisa turned to her in surprise, then smiled as she realized Caro had noticed her watching Consuela. 'Yes, very beautiful. Have you known her long?'

'*Si*, many years. I knew her husband too, he was kind, kind man. He love her very much.'

'How did he die?' Louisa asked.

'He had heart attack. Consuela, she was very sad after, she love him very much. Her life has never been same since. So much terrible things happen to her.'

'What kind of things?' Louisa couldn't help asking.

'Sssh,' Caro said, putting a finger to her lips. 'We no talk about them. Consuela, she no like it. She like to forget.'

'Does she have any family?'

'No, no family now. They all gone. She is alone. But she make her family here with the young ones. She love the young people. They love her too. They make her happy.'

Louisa looked back across the table to see Consuela laughing at something one of the boys, Frederico, was whispering in her ear. It wasn't the first time this evening that Louisa had noticed the easy, informal relationship Consuela seemed to enjoy with her staff – there had been not even the remotest suggestion of anything like the salacious, Messalina-type mistress with her humble and lust-weary slaves scenario she, Danny and Sarah had conjured on their way here. She watched as Consuela turned her attention to Danny and shared Frederico's joke and as the two of them laughed they unthinkingly joined hands.

Caro turned to talk to Rosalind who was sitting the other side of her and as Serena was listening intently to her neighbour Louisa picked up her lacy gold goblet and gazed thoughtfully out of the window. She could see a car coming up the drive and absent-mindedly tracked its progress until it came to a stop on the forecourt. The man who got out tossed his keys to Carlos who was waiting, then disappeared around the side of the house. He had been too far away for Louisa to get a good look at him, but his proprietorial air and the expensive car made her idly wonder who he might be.

She looked across the table to Sarah who was cheerfully encouraging one of the boys to refill her glass. Heaven only knew how much Sarah had had by now, but she certainly appeared to be keeping the women either side of her entertained.

Seeing that Caro was no longer talking to anyone, Louisa was on the point of turning back to her when she saw the man from the Mercedes standing in the hall talking to Frederico. She could see him only in profile, but it seemed clear that he was giving orders, making her wonder again who he might be. He moved slightly, bringing himself further into the light and Louisa felt a strange stillness suddenly wrap itself around her. Despite some kind of scar around his left eye he was quite staggeringly good looking, and the incredible strength that seemed to emanate from the hard muscles beneath his thin cotton shirt and the tightness of his jeans was having an extraordinary effect on her. She swallowed hard as though to push back the peculiar emotions that were rising in her, as light as air, more potent than the wine. He looked up, as though sensing he was being watched. Louisa started to look away, but found to her surprise that she didn't. She couldn't remember this ever happening to her before; she was responding to him in a way that was almost dizzying. As he looked back at her his dark eyes were questioning, as though wondering if he knew her, but more than that, as though he too was feeling something indefinable passing between them. He smiled and frowned, causing a sudden heat to sweep through her, leaving her almost breathless in its wake. When his eyes moved on around the table she continued to watch him, wondering how he was still managing to have such a disturbing effect on her. Then with a horrible sinking feeling she saw that he was looking at Danny and that Danny, her wine glass barely concealing her smile, was looking at him with sultry, provocative eyes. He raised an eyebrow with a drollness that made Louisa's heart trip and Danny ran her tongue over her beautiful lips.

Suddenly realizing that all her guests had fallen silent Consuela turned to look over her shoulder. 'Ah, Jake,' she said. Then turning back again, 'Ladies, I believe some of you have already met Jake Mallory.'

No one answered, but Louisa saw the way Rosalind and Caro exchanged glances. Jake looked briefly at Louisa and she almost gasped. He seemed almost angry, but the glance was so fleeting it was difficult to tell.

As he disappeared, taking the stairs two at a time, Louisa watched as Frederico appeared at Consuela's side and laid a hand on her shoulder. Smiling, Consuela reached up to cover it with her own. 'Please, everyone, if you will excuse me,' she said, getting to her feet. 'The evening is young and I am sure you would all like to take a stroll in the garden, perhaps relax in the bathhouse. As always, Frederico and the boys will be happy to entertain you.'

As she left the room both Danny and Sarah looked across to Louisa. Louisa shook her head, obviously as baffled as they were by the sudden chill that seemed to have permeated the room. Then Rosalind was pushing back her chair and standing up. The others followed suit and quite suddenly it was as though the last few minutes hadn't happened as everyone returned to their light-hearted chatter, following Frederico out into the garden.

'What on earth was all that about?' Sarah whispered to Louisa as they walked onto the terrace.

'God knows,' Louisa answered.

'Don't ask me,' Danny responded as Sarah turned to her. 'But I can tell you something . . .'

'Can I bring you anything, ladies?' Frederico offered. 'The others are taking champagne in the bathhouse, but if you prefer perhaps to take a swim in the pool, or maybe a drink on the terrace . . .'

'I think,' Danny said, raising her eyebrows challengingly at Sarah and Louisa, 'we'll take the champagne.'

As they strolled across the garden behind Frederico Louisa whispered. 'What exactly is this bathhouse? I heard someone talking about it earlier.'

'Apparently,' Sarah answered, 'so Mathilde, the woman who was sitting next to me, tells me, it's something of a ritual on these girls' nights of theirs to go and relax in the bathhouse after dinner.'

'Yes, but what is it?'

'That's what we're about to find out,' Danny said, as Frederico opened the door to the building they had spotted through the trees on their way in.

'Please relax and make yourselves at home, ladies,' Frederico said, standing aside for them to pass. 'If you need anything then you have only to ask.'

Louisa was the first to step inside and instantly stopped. Danny squeezed herself past, then she too stood still on the threshold.

'My word,' Sarah murmured, coming in behind them.

A gentle steam was rising from each of the circular and oval sunken baths, drifting lazily through the vivid green fronds of exotic palms and ferns, circling the white, delicately carved screens that partitioned the baths. Beside each bath was a white chaise-longue, and on several of these were the carefully folded clothes of the women who were already in the baths. With the exception of Frederico the boys who had waited table were all here, joined now by three or four others. None of them wore anything more than a leather pouch that hugged his genitals, and they all had a physique that belonged totally to this extraordinary Greco-Roman setting. Though the harps and lutes were purely ornamental, these were the instruments that were providing the soft music that seemed to blend with the subtle fragrances of the steam.

It was the most beautiful, most inviting film set Danny had ever seen and as though she had rehearsed it many times before she moved forward, leaving first one shoe, then the other, behind her. Dmitri, one of the boys who had waited table, seemed to appear from nowhere and waved an arm towards an unoccupied bath. Danny lifted her hair, turned her back to Dmitri and smiled dreamily as he lowered the zip. Peeling the dress from her body she stepped out of it, lowered her panties and handed them to Dmitri. Obediently he took them, laid them carefully on the chaise-longue, then took Danny's hand as she stepped into the bath.

Like a camera following the action, Louisa's eyes moved with the boy who passed them going to the bath where Olivia was resting her elbows on the side and gently kicking her legs. The boy handed her a glass of champagne, then lay down beside the bath, resting his head on one hand, ready to take the glass from her with the other.

Hearing laughter, Louisa looked to the next bath and saw Stephan sink beneath the water with Rosalind. When the two of them came up he was holding Rosalind about the waist and Rosalind let her head fall back, her hair and arms fanning out across the water as he kissed her breasts.

The whole thing was so hypnotic, so unbelievably sensual that when someone took her by the hand Louisa barely registered what was happening. She moved as Danny had moved, as though in a dream. Her inhibitions seemed to disperse in the steam as her dress fell to the floor, her panties brushed lightly over her legs and gentle hands took her, guiding her to the bath. As the warm, perfumed water enveloped her she rolled over and over, her movements as fluid as the gentle currents beneath her. Johann was sitting beside the bath, watching her, resting his weight on one arm. After a moment he got up, then returned with champagne. Louisa sipped it then handed it back. The aroma of bath oils was as intoxicating as the wine.

She swam some more and Johann increased the pressure of the jets. She pressed herself to them, closing her eyes as they gently pummelled and caressed her, turning languidly and luxuriously in the scented water, feeling the tension flow from her limbs and coherent thought unravel itself from her mind. Eventually she came to rest against the side of the bath where Johann put his hands on her shoulders and began gently to massage. She let her head fall forward, felt herself melting beneath the expert touch of his fingers.

Lifting Danny in his arms Dmitri carried her from the bath and laid her down at the edge. Danny's eyes were closed, but her hand was stroking his thigh, the leather pouch was gone. He stood over her, gazing down at her as he reached for more champagne.

On the chaise-longue the other side of the screen, Olivia was sitting beside Antonio, her hair streaming down her back, his hands stroking her waist as his lips moved indolently over her neck and shoulders.

Rosalind, covered by a bathrobe, was leaving with Stephan through a door at the back of the room. Caro was stretched out on the floor, arms above her head moaning softly as her massage became ever more intimate. Serena was still in the bath, her elbows resting on the edge, her nipples tingling under the purposeful gaze of Michel's sultry eyes.

Gradually, one by one, each of the couples got up and left through the door Rosalind had used. Some were in bathrobes, most were still naked. Louisa watched them, hardly aware of what she was seeing as Johann stroked her face, her shoulders and her breasts. She thought she saw Sarah go through the door, but couldn't be sure because at that moment Johann pulled her head back and kissed her softly on the mouth. 'Come,' he said, taking her by the hand.

Louisa turned in the water and walked up the steps to the

edge of the bath. Then she too disappeared through the door at the back of the room . . .

'You waiting for someone?'

Not having heard anyone come up behind her Louisa started and turned round. She wasn't surprised to see Jake Mallory standing at the top of the steps, the black Mercedes was still there on the forecourt and in some curious way it was as though she'd been expecting him.

As she got up from where she was sitting on a balustrade she was vaguely aware of the way her heart was pounding. The scent of the oils still lingered on her skin, but the memory of Johann's hands now seemed as elusive as a dream. 'I'm driving my friends home,' she answered.

He was looking at her in that same questioning way he had earlier and Louisa could almost feel herself floating in the intensity of his dark eyes. Standing close to him like this was overwhelming her, he was so tall, so powerful in his body and the mesmerizing aura that surrounded him seemed almost to be drawing her in.

He looked at his watch and Louisa's eyes were instantly drawn to the hard muscles and dark, leathery skin of his forearm. 'You could be in for a long wait,' he said. His American voice added such a potency to his masculinity that Louisa was almost dizzied by it.

'It doesn't matter,' she said. 'It's a lovely night and I'm quite happy to sit here and look at the garden.'

He nodded, then cupping a hand around his jaw he said, 'How about you leave the keys here for someone else to drive your friends and I'll take you home?' he said.

Louisa's heart skipped a beat. 'Oh, but you don't have to do that,' she protested.

'I know I don't have to,' he said, a latent irony filling his eyes as he looked at her.

He was holding his hand out for the keys and still looking at him Louisa dropped them into his palm. Then she smiled. He had such a warmth about him, such a softness in his dark eyes that she could feel it stealing into her senses like the heady perfume of the night.

'Where are you staying?' he said.

'Valanjou. Are you sure it isn't out of your way?'

His eyebrows flickered. 'It's not out of my way,' he said and she knew he was lying.

She watched him go back into the house then turned to walk to his car. She was aware of the turmoil going on inside her, but it felt distant, muted, like her sense of reality. How could she be feeling this way about someone she didn't even know? Why did she get the feeling that when he looked at her he knew all she was thinking, all she was feeling because he was thinking and feeling it too? She wanted to laugh. It was crazy, irrational, wonderful and terrifying. She wanted him to come back, to smile at her like that again and tell her what was happening between them. She wanted to hear him say the words that she didn't have the courage for. She wanted the reality of his touch, his voice, his presence, his incredible strength.

Hearing the front door close she turned back to see him coming towards her and almost blushed at her thoughts.

'Good guess,' he said, seeing her standing beside his car.

'I saw you arrive,' she told him, getting in as he opened the door for her.

'Do you want that I put the roof up?' he said, getting in the other side. 'It'll be colder once we start heading inland.'

'No, it's fine. I like it this way.'

Neither of them spoke then until he had turned the car around and they were gliding smoothly along the Cap towards Antibes.

'So, you going to tell me your name?' he said, glancing at her.

Louisa gave a cry of surprised laughter. 'Of course. Louisa Kramer,' she said. 'And you're Jake Mallory.'

It was his turn to look surprised.

'Consuela introduced you earlier.' she reminded him.

He nodded. 'Sure,' he said and reached out to turn on the

CD. As a sleepy, soulful voice came from the speakers Louisa turned to look out at the passing cafés and glowing neon signs.

'Have you been on the Riviera long?' he asked.

'Just over three weeks. We're here for the entire summer though.' She started to question why she'd told him that, then stopped. She'd only tie herself in knots if she went that route.

'Are you vacationing or working?' he said, lighting a cigarette.

'A bit of both. What about you?'

'I guess you could say I'm working,' he answered, inhaling deeply, holding the smoke, then exhaling.

'What do you do?' she asked.

'We build marinas. We're thinking about starting up a project somewhere in the Med, that's why I'm here.'

'We?'

'My father's the boss. He's back in the States right now.'

'Where are you from in the States?'

'California. Near San Diego. Do you know it?'

She shook her head. 'I've never been to America.'

'You from England?'

'Somerset originally, I live in London now. Do you know London?'

'Sure. I know it well.' He cast a quick glance back over his shoulder then manoeuvred the car across a complicated junction, heading out of Antibes towards Grasse. Smoke from his cigarette wafted towards her and she knew from the pungent, sweet smell that it was marijuana.

She leaned back against the headrest and stretched out her legs. The temperature was starting to drop now, as he'd said it would, but she was enjoying the rush of wind through her hair and the humorous lilt of his voice as he went on to tell her more about his plans for a marina. After a while he fell silent, and as the music changed Louisa said, 'Can I ask you a question?'

'Sure.'

'Do I remind you of someone you know?'

He shot her a quick look, his head still resting on one hand while the other rested lightly on the steering wheel. 'I don't think so,' he answered. 'Why do you ask?'

Louisa shrugged, feeling foolish for a moment and wishing she hadn't got into this. 'It was just that when you first saw me and again just now when we were in front of the house, well, I got the impression that you thought you knew me.'

She turned to look at him and saw that he was smiling.

'What?' she laughed.

He shook his head. 'No, I don't know you, Louisa Kramer,' he said.

'Oh.' She was blushing and got the feeling from the way he looked over at her that he knew it.

'So how did you come by Consuela?' he asked, changing the subject as smoothly as the car changed gear.

Louisa explained about Danny's jazz musician friend.

'I see,' he nodded. 'And Consuela's hospitality? Was it to your liking?'

He was laughing and, pursing her lips, Louisa turned to look out at the passing, night-blackened forests. 'Do I have to answer that?' she said.

'Not if you don't want to.'

'I don't,' she said and turned to look at him, her luminous brown eyes brimming with laughter. 'How do you know Consuela?' she asked.

His face seemed to darken as he said, 'Now that's a long story. One we'll save for another time.'

Louisa's heart gave such a skip of joy at the 'another time' that she almost laughed. How could she be so hopelessly infatuated after such a ridiculously short time and what had got into her that she could be so cheerfully abandoning her promises not to get involved again? But he was different. She just knew it, she could sense it in every word he said, every gesture he made. There was a chemistry between them that was stronger and much more potent than she'd ever believed possible, and even if she were able she knew she wasn't going to try to resist it.

'You going to start directing me now?' he said as they turned onto the road to Valanjou.

'It's just before you get to the village,' she said. 'I'll tell you where to turn when we're there. Where are you staying?' A sudden gulf of embarrassment opened up inside her. Dear God, that sounded like a proposition!

'St Tropez,' he answered, his eyes on the road ahead.

So he really had come out of his way to bring her home, she was thinking as they sped past the turning to the villa.

'Sorry,' she said as he turned the car around.

'No matter,' he said. 'Where now?'

As she directed him up the hill and in through the open gates she was acutely aware of the bewildering change in his mood. He seemed to be withdrawing from her, wanting only to be rid of her now.

'Thank you,' she said as he came to a stop in the full beam of the security lights.

'You're welcome,' he said, turning to look at her.

'Would you like to come in for coffee?' she offered.

He turned to look at the house then shook his head. 'No,' he said.

The pang of disappointment was so crushing that she felt sure he must hear it in her voice as she said, 'OK, well thank you again for the lift.'

He waited until she closed the door behind her then backed the car up to turn around.

'Do you like to sail?' he said, as she moved towards the house.

She turned back. 'I don't know, I've never tried.'

'Would you like to try?'

She nodded. 'Why not?'

'I'll call you.'

It wasn't until the tail lights disappeared at the end of the drive that she realized she hadn't given him her number. But no matter, she told herself as she opened the front door, he could always get it from Consuela.

6

It was around eleven the following morning when Sarah, hidden behind dark glasses and wearing a short, cotton T-shirt finally managed to stagger her way down the stairs and out into the blinding sunlight. She was stiff all over and every move was making her head throb and spin. The pool looked desperately inviting, but she was afraid to brave it in case she drowned. Louisa was just climbing out, looking unspeakably gorgeous in her black one-piece and disgustingly bright eyed.

'Sit yourself down,' Louisa laughed, picking up a towel and dabbing her face. 'I'll get the coffee and aspirin.'

Sarah flopped gratefully into a garden chair, stuck out her feet, let her hands drop to her sides and groaned loudly. 'Where's Danny?' she said.

'She hasn't surfaced yet,' Louisa grinned as she went past into the kitchen. 'What time did you two get home?' she called out.

'God knows, but I do seem to recall a sunrise blazing its way into my eyeballs. How did you get home?'

When Louisa didn't answer Sarah put her head back in the vain hope that the throbbing would subside. The sun was burning her legs, but she didn't have the energy to move. Somewhere, not too far away, a family of cicadas were screaming their heads off, grating every suffering cell of her brain.

'Here, this should make you feel human again,' Louisa said, putting down a tray of coffee, orange juice and Panadol.

'Decapitation is the only thing that's going to make me feel better.' Sarah grimaced, leaning towards the table and almost toppling into a pot of geraniums. 'Who the fuck put that there?' she grumbled, pulling her hand out of the damp earth.

'It's always there,' Louisa laughed, throwing her one of the pool towels.

'You're getting on my nerves,' Sarah said, eyeing Louisa irritably. 'How come you're not suffering like the rest of us? Oh, for God's sake, shoot those fucking cicadas someone, please!'

As Louisa's grin widened Sarah's lips gave a reluctant twitch of humour, then downing two Panadol with the orange juice she picked up the coffee and poured.

Louisa was sitting the other side of the table, her long, tanned legs hooked over the arm of the chair, her dark hair, shining and wet, finger combed back from her face. As she dropped her head back to gaze up at the sky she looked so natural and so lovely that even through the stupor of her hangover Sarah wished she had a camera to hand.

'Can you believe last night?' she murmured after a while. 'I mean, did it really happen or was I just dreaming it?'

'It happened,' Louisa assured her cheerfully.

Sarah dropped her head in her hands. 'You mean I've broken my three years of celibacy with an adolescent Rambo?' she groaned.

'I don't know, did you?'

Sarah nodded and lifted her head. Her memory was treacherously lucid considering how hard she'd tried to drown it. 'The games rich women play,' she commented, not at all sure she was glad she'd taken part. 'It's quite a set-up she's got there, isn't it?'

Louisa nodded and Sarah waited, expecting her to say more.

'Well,' she prompted. 'What did you do? And how the hell did you get home?'

Smiling, Louisa turned to look at her. 'Jake Mallory brought me,' she said.

Sarah's eyebrows shot up in a way she wished they hadn't. 'Jake Mallory!' she said. 'But how on earth did that come about? Don't tell me he was in the bathhouse too.'

Louisa laughed. 'He found me on the front doorstep waiting for you and offered me a lift.'

'Well, I never,' Sarah remarked, trying to work her way

through the cobwebs to find out what she really thought. 'Did he come in?' she said.

'No.' Putting her feet back on the floor Louisa folded her arms on the table and looked at Sarah. 'If I tell you something do you promise not to laugh?' she said.

'Right now I'm incapable.'

'This is going to sound crazy,' Louisa said, slanting her eyes towards the garden, 'but I think I've fallen for him.' Her eyes came back to Sarah. 'I mean really fallen for him.'

Sarah was nonplussed. There were lots of things she wanted to say, but she couldn't seem to form a coherent sentence right now. 'What happened?' she asked, taking a fortifying sip of coffee.

'Nothing really.' Louisa leaned back in the chair. 'I mean, I can't explain . . . We talked, but nothing physical happened, at least not in the conventional sense of the word. But, well, it's hard to say it without sounding mawkish and corny.'

'It's OK, my stomach's settling down a bit now,' Sarah said helpfully.

Louisa's tawny eyes were dancing in a self-mocking, self-conscious way. 'Has this ever happened to you?' she said, 'Where you meet a man and somehow, right from the start, you just know he's right? That he's the one who's meant for you?'

Sarah pursed her lips as she thought about that. 'No,' she said in the end, 'at least not as quickly as that. But that doesn't mean I don't believe it can happen. The French call it a *coup de foudre*, so if there's an expression for it then I guess it exists.' Her head was still so fragile that she was afraid she wasn't saying the right thing, but Louisa's expression told her she probably was. 'Do you think he felt the same way?' she ventured.

'I'm not sure,' Louisa answered. 'I mean, I might just be kidding myself, but it all felt so incredibly . . . Now you are going to laugh so I'm not going to say it. But the answer's yes, I think he might have felt it too.'

'Are you seeing him again?'

'He's taking me sailing.'

'When?'

'He said he'd call. He'll have to get the number from Consuela though because I forgot to give it to him.'

'Did he say how he knew Consuela?'

'Just that it was a long story.'

'Mmm.' Sarah wished she could get to grips with what she was really feeling about this because for some reason she didn't think it was good. She stared at Louisa thoughtfully then said. 'Look, I don't want to be the one to burst your bubble, but it hasn't been long since Simon and everything and well, you don't really know anything about this Jake . . . Well, what I'm really trying to say is, are you sure this isn't some kind of rebound reaction?'

'Positive,' Louisa smiled, obviously not in the least put out by Sarah's caution. 'This is different, Sarah. Totally different. I only wish I knew how to explain it better, but it's a feeling I have and I'm excited and terrified and completely and utterly . . .' she laughed. 'I feel head over heels in love. Or at least as near to it as you can get without actually being in it.'

Sarah laughed. 'I wish he could see you now,' she said, 'there'd be no question about whether or not he had fallen for you when you look so lovely. And if that's what he's doing to you, well, who am I to question it? Oh, look out, here comes Sleeping Beauty. God, Danny, you look worse than I feel.'

'Anyone seen my sunglasses?' Danny croaked.

'They're in the kitchen, I'll fetch them,' Louisa said, getting up.

'What time is it?' Danny asked, flopping down in her bikini next to Sarah.

'Time you and I gave up drinking.'

'How did we get home?'

'Frederico drove us in your car.'

'Oh yes. Did we really open another bottle when we got back?'

Sarah looked at her horrified. 'We didn't?' she said.

'You did,' Louisa confirmed, handing Danny her sunglasses, 'but you didn't drink much of it.'

'I wish I could say the same for the champagne,' Danny groaned. 'It always gives me such a splitting headache. Louisa, I love you,' she added, as Louisa put an orange juice in front of her. 'That's better,' she sighed when she'd finished it. 'So, what a night, eh? What happened to you?' she said, looking at Louisa. 'What time did . . . Oh God,' she groaned as a blinding pain shot through her head. 'Two nights in a row is too much. I must be getting old.'

'Ah, yes, you still haven't told us where you were on Friday night,' Sarah reminded her.

Danny turned to Louisa. It was several seconds before she answered and with her eyes shielded by her sunglasses it was impossible to tell what she was thinking. Then, to both Louisa and Sarah's surprise, she said, 'Did you see the way that man, Jake Mallory, looked at you last night?'

Louisa started to smile. 'Yes,' she said. 'I saw it.'

'You'd have had to be blind not to,' Danny commented, her dark eyebrows teasingly arched.

Sarah was about to speak when Danny said, 'That's where I was on Friday night. With him.'

Despite her tan Sarah saw Louisa's face pale. 'You were with Jake Mallory?' Louisa said, pushing her voice through the horrible chaos unfolding inside her.

Danny nodded. 'His yacht is moored at St Tropez, that's where I spent the night – at least most of it.'

'How did you meet him?' Louisa asked quietly, understanding now the look that had passed between Danny and Jake the night before.

'I met up with his crew at the Café des Arts, they invited me back to the boat and when I got there I met Jake Mallory.'

'Did you sleep with him?' Sarah said, not knowing why in the world she'd asked such a stupid question, especially when she almost felt Louisa flinch.

Danny smiled. 'Yes, I slept with him,' she said, then leaning towards Louisa she took her hand and squeezed it. 'I'm only telling you in case you thought . . . Well, I don't know what you thought when he looked at you that way, but it's better that you know now what he's like, that he turns that look on for all the women and from what I can tell . . .' She shrugged. 'Look, maybe I'm making too much of this, for all I know it didn't mean anything to you.'

Louisa looked at Sarah, then gently easing her hand out of Danny's she said, 'No it didn't. I thought he was good looking, yes, but no more than that.'

Sarah and Danny watched her walk into the kitchen, then picking up her coffee Danny said, 'Oh shit, why do I feel so awful, he only looked at her for God's sake.' Her eyes came up to Sarah's. 'Or is there something you're not telling me?'

Sarah's lips tightened angrily. 'You know there's more, Danny,' she said, 'otherwise you'd never have brought it up.'

'He drove her home, didn't he?' Danny said. 'I saw Consuela just before we left and she told me.'

'Then why did you pretend not to know?'

Danny shrugged. 'I thought . . . Oh, hell. I don't know what I thought, but what I do know is that he's not the man for Louisa. He's a bastard, Sarah, you can see that just by looking at him.'

'As a matter of fact all I saw was an exceptionally good-looking man,' Sarah retorted. 'What did Consuela say about him?'

'Only that he'd taken Louisa home.'

Sarah eyed her steadily. 'It must have been quite a surprise for you, seeing him there last night,' she remarked.

'Yes, it was a bit,' Danny admitted. 'But if you're thinking I know any more about that sudden frost when he walked into the room then you're wrong. And what is this, why do I suddenly feel like the villain of this piece when all I was trying to do was warn her what he's like?'

'But how do you know what he's like when you only knew him for a night?'

'Instinct. And tell me honestly, Sarah, do you get good vibes about him?'

'I don't know that I get any vibes at all,' Sarah lied. She wasn't sure whether they were good or bad, but considering the abrupt change in atmosphere when he'd walked into the room last night she thought they were probably bad. However, Sarah wasn't prepared to pass judgement on someone she didn't know. 'Are you seeing him again?' she said.

Danny shrugged. 'Not if it's going to cause bad feeling between Louisa and me. Is she seeing him again?'

'I don't know,' Sarah answered, wondering how long it was going to be before Jake Mallory picked up the phone and called Louisa. Or maybe, when the call came, it would be for Danny. Or with any luck the call might not come at all.

'Oh, come on,' Danny said, irritably, 'let's go and see if we can swim off these hangovers, I'm tired of talking about him.'

'You go on ahead, I need some more coffee,' Sarah said. She had the uncomfortable feeling the situation wasn't just going to go away. It was odd that Jake Mallory had had such an extreme effect on Louisa the very night after he'd slept with Danny. And odder still was the way Danny had tried to warn Louisa off. In some totally perverse way it made Sarah think more kindly towards Jake for she knew how devious Danny could be, pretending nonchalance when really she felt totally the reverse. Except Danny cared for Louisa probably more than anyone else in the world did, so perhaps she was just being over-protective. But what about Jake? Had he felt the same as Louisa? If he had then Danny's interference was only going to be a bad thing. But what about the coincidence of him sleeping with Danny the night before he met Louisa? For some reason Sarah believed that it was just coincidence, but that still didn't mean that Louisa's instincts about the man were right. But on the other hand it didn't make Danny's right either.

Getting up from her chair Sarah stripped off her T-shirt and strode naked down to the pool. She couldn't think about this now, the circles were making her as nauseous as her hangover.

Hearing the door open behind her Consuela looked up from her desk and smiled as Frederico came into the room.

'Ah,' she sighed gratefully, taking the glass of fruit punch from his tray, 'just what I need.' She took a long, refreshing sip, set the glass down on the desk and removed her half-spectacles. Despite the soaring temperatures outside the thick walls of the house kept the room pleasantly cool and Consuela, in a pale blue silk dress and cream accessories looked as elegant and unruffled as always.

'The others have taken their lunch?' she asked.

'Yes. They are down at the beach,' Frederico answered.

'And you? Will you take a swim?'

'In a while. I would like to talk to you first.'

Consuela looked up at him and seeing the slight frown between his eyes said, 'But of course. Nothing is the matter, I hope.'

'Dmitri is saying he would like to leave,' Frederico answered.

Consuela turned to gaze out of the open window. 'Is he not happy here?' she asked.

'He would like to go home to Greece. He misses his family.'

'I see. Then of course we must arrange for him to go.' She was thoughtful for a moment, flicking the arms of her spectacles with her thumb. 'Tell me, how much does he know of what Mr Mallory does here?'

'I think he knows a little,' Frederico said. 'He says Mr Mallory told him.'

Consuela's face hardened. 'Then perhaps Mr Mallory would like to see him safely back to Greece,' she said, a sarcastic edge to her voice.

Frederico remained silent, it wasn't his place to comment on what went on between Jake Mallory and his employer.

'I shall be sorry to lose Dmitri,' Consuela sighed, walking to the french windows and looking absently out at the shimmering pool. 'He is such a pleasant boy.' She turned. 'Saturday was just his third time in the bathhouse, was it not?'

Frederico nodded.

'Who was he with?'

'I believe it was Danielle Spencer, the British actress.'

'Oh my!' Consuela laughed. 'I'd have thought he'd want to stay for ever after spending the night with such a beautiful woman. But if he is missing his family . . .' She left the sentence unfinished as she attempted to puzzle out Jake's surprising choice of Dmitri to confide in. Had it been any of the others she might have understood it better, but to choose the boy who had spent the night with Danny Spencer simply didn't make sense. Unless Jake was planning something she didn't know about.

She smiled and turned back to Frederico. 'Ask Dmitri to come and see me when he returns from the beach,' she said. 'I will talk to him and find out if he is truly homesick or if it is something Mr Mallory has said that is driving him away.'

Frederico moved his tray from one hand to the other, clearly still not ready to leave.

'Is there something else?' Consuela asked gently.

'I'm afraid so.'

'Goodness, Frederico, you do look glum. Come on, tell me, what is it?'

'I have heard,' Frederico answered, 'that Danielle Spencer spent the night with Mr Mallory on board his yacht.'

Consuela's eyes flew open. 'What!' she gasped. 'When?'

'The night before she was here.'

'*Mon Dieu!* He is the last man in the world her parents would want her associating with. How did they meet?'

'I don't know, madame.'

Consuela began pacing, tapping her spectacles against her chin as she thought carefully. 'Have they seen each other since?' she asked.

'I'm not sure. I don't think so.'

'Then they mustn't. We must stop her seeing him at all costs. She is very precious to her parents and it is my duty as her mother's friend to see that she comes to no harm. I must speak with her. Yes, that's what I must do. I must make her see sense.'

She looked at Frederico, and though his eyes were sympathetic she could tell that he didn't think this was wise.

'No, no, you're right,' Consuela muttered as if he had spoken. 'She has a mind of her own, she will do as she pleases and maybe talking to her will only make the situation more attractive to her. What do you think I should do, Frederico?'

'I think that depends on how long Mr Mallory plans to stay,' he answered.

Consuela's laugh had no humour. 'Mr Mallory is a law unto himself, as we both know. His plans are never shared, least of all with me. Do you know where he is now?'

'I believe he has returned to St Tropez.'

Consuela nodded pensively. 'OK, I will contact him there. But first, tell me, what of the girl he took home, Louisa?'

'He was at the *Valhalla* an hour and a half after leaving her.'

'Good, that doesn't leave time for anything more than the journey to Valanjou so we have no need to concern ourselves with her. I suggested while they were here that they might like to meet Señor Morandi, but neither of them has called me back about it.'

Frederico could offer no explanation for that so he remained silent. He wished he knew what his employer was really thinking, what was really causing the anguish in her wide, green eyes. Although she confided in him much more than the others he knew there was still a great deal he didn't know about her, things from the past that continued to persecute her, to invade her moments of calm so that she was never truly at ease.

'I will speak to Señor Morandi,' she said. 'Maybe he can find something for Danny and her friends to do. If she is busy she will forget about Jake.'

Frederico nodded. Behind his impassive eyes was an adoration for this woman that he would never confess to her – it wasn't what she wanted to hear. What she wanted was his unspoken loyalty, his unswerving support and discretion and that she had.

'You asked me to remind you, madame, to call Mrs Carmichael this afternoon,' he said.

Consuela's eyes seemed to glaze for a moment as she withdrew into the secluded depths of her mind. 'Yes,' she said, distractedly. 'Thank you. I'll call her. Now off you go for your swim; send Dmitri in after I have taken my siesta.'

'Well, you 'ave satisfied Didier's curiosity as to what 'appens in the bathhouse,' Jean-Claude commented, watching Didier disappear into the darkened interior of the bustling café before turning back to Louisa. 'So maybe now you will satisfy my curiosity and tell me what is on your mind?'

Louisa raised her eyes from the untouched *salade Niçoise*, looked at him for a moment, then putting down her fork she fell back in her chair and sighed. 'Actually it's nothing really,' she said, smoothing her hair back from her forehead. 'I'm just trying to work through something I'm writing about.'

'Oh, I see,' Jean-Claude replied.

He watched as Louisa's troubled eyes moved absently about the sun-drenched square, following the progress of aimless tourists as they roamed the shady arcades. Catching sight of someone he knew leaning from an upstairs window of the Auberge, he waved out then turned back to Louisa. They were sitting in the shelter of the café's white parasols, but Louisa's slender legs were resting on the seat of a chair, exposed to the sun. There was obviously more on her mind than a creative problem, and guessing what it was Jean-Claude decided to broach the subject.

'Tell me,' he said, 'do you still wish to know something about Jake Mallory?'

The way Louisa's eyes suddenly fell to the table told him he was right. She hadn't wanted to bring it up herself, but it was clearly what was bothering her.

'Why, have you found something out?' she asked.

Jean-Claude picked up the bottle of rosé wine and refreshed their glasses. 'Didier, 'e ask around 'is friends,' he said. 'They say that Jake Mallory trafficks in drugs. 'e 'as a boat, many boats I think, and 'e sails around the Mediterranean selling the drugs.'

Louisa was thinking of the marijuana Jake had so openly smoked in front of her. 'Is that all?' she said.

'Isn't that enough?'

'I mean, do you know anything else about him?'

Jean-Claude shook his head.

'Jean-Claude,' Louisa smiled, drawing out his name, 'I can tell there's more, so come on, out with it. What's his connection with Consuela?'

Jean-Claude shrugged. 'Maybe 'e supply 'er with the drugs?'

'There were none in evidence the other night.'

'Maybe she doesn't know you well enough to know if she can trust you.'

'Maybe.' Louisa looked away and stared up at the crumbling, flat-fronted facade of the apartments above the café. As much as she wanted to talk about Jake she was finding it difficult. Danny's revelation had shaken her more than she cared to admit and she knew she was still in danger of trying to convince herself that she was different, that she had meant something to him, just as he had to her. And desperately wanting to overlook the fact that he'd slept with Danny as well as not wanting to believe he was dealing in drugs was also unsettling her. She was only too aware of how easily she misjudged men, of how she tried to justify their behaviour with convoluted logic, or simply blinded herself to it altogether. But it wasn't easy convincing herself that her instincts had been at fault the other night, not when she cast her mind back and pictured him, listened to him and felt the same trip in her heart now as she'd felt then.

She looked up as Didier came back, watched him sit down then turned back to Jean-Claude. 'Danny told me that she spent the night with Jake last Friday,' she said flatly. 'And now you tell me he's into drugs. So it seems I've made a bit of a fool of myself, doesn't it?'

Didier was silent, watching Jean-Claude and waiting for him to answer.

'I think,' Jean-Claude said, 'that since nothing physical

passed between you that it will be easier to recover from what 'e 'as done to your 'eart.'

Louisa gave a wry smile. 'You're probably right,' she said. 'But if he carries on seeing Danny then I know I'm going to find it very hard to watch them together, especially if I do carry on feeling this way.'

'Does it not help you to know he is a criminal?'

'It should,' she answered, her voice lilting in irony.

Jean-Claude laughed. 'But it doesn't?'

'Not really. And besides, what you've heard is only rumour, it might not be true.'

Jean-Claude arched an eyebrow and rolling her eyes at her own pathetic desire to cling to straws Louisa gave a sardonic grin. 'Well, whatever,' she said, 'I won't be seeing him again, I'm just not prepared to take the risk of getting in any deeper.'

Jean-Claude's obvious scepticism made her laugh as she flicked his arm.

'Truly, I'm not,' she said.

'Until he calls.'

'It's been five days now and he hasn't, so my guess is he's not going to. So, let's change the subject, shall we?'

'In a moment. But first tell me, did he tell you why 'e was in 'ere in France?'

'Yes. He has plans to build a marina down here,' Louisa answered, frowning curiously.

Jean-Claude nodded. 'That was all he told you?'

'Why, is there more? What aren't you telling me, Jean-Claude?'

'Nothing. I am just curious myself to know why 'e is 'ere.'

'Doesn't the marina answer the question?'

'Yes. It answers the question.'

Louisa started to speak then stopped herself. It was so plainly obvious that Jean-Claude knew more about Jake Mallory than he was letting on that for a fleeting moment she felt irritated enough to snap at him, even shout at him. But before she could, to her surprise, Jean-Claude leaned forward and took her hand.

'I will be as truthful with you as I can,' he said, gruffly. 'When you asked me about Jake Mallory the other day it was not the first time I 'ad 'eard of 'im. I did not tell you then that I knew of 'im because I did not want to tell you things I did not know for sure were true. That is why I ask Didier to ask 'is friends what they know. They 'ave told 'im nothing I 'ad not already 'eard. But there is more, I am certain of it. There is something going on between 'im and Consuela Santini and though I do not know what it is I do not think it is good. And what is important 'ere is that you do not become involved in something from which you cannot withdraw. It is true that I 'ave 'eard as many good things about Jake Mallory as I 'ave 'eard bad and I believe it will be very easy for you to fall in love with 'im. But I do not think it will be easy for you to discover that it is the bad things that are true when it is already too late.'

'And if the good things are true?' Louisa countered.

Jean-Claude's eyes darted between hers. His generous mouth was uncharacteristically hard and unrelenting.

When he didn't respond to the question Louisa pulled her hand away, her eyes still fixed on his. 'I wouldn't tell Danny any of this if I were you,' she said, 'if you do you'll be presenting her with a challenge she'll find impossible to resist.'

'And what about you?' Jean-Claude said. 'Can you resist it?'

'Yes, I think so,' Louisa answered, feeling her heart plummet with the loss of what might have been if only things hadn't suddenly got so complicated and mysterious. Then quite suddenly, quite unexpectedly, her heart tripped again and as she felt Jake's presence as though he were sitting right there beside her she could hardly believe what she was saying. Was she really so fainthearted that she wouldn't accept the challenge herself? Was she really sitting here like an injured bird, too afraid to try her wings again in case they carried her too close to the sun? Why should she listen to everything everyone told her without giving Jake a chance? And why should she deny what she'd felt during that brief time they were together just because of some unfounded rumours and one night of passion that had happened before they'd even met? No, it wasn't Danny who was going to rise to this challenge, it was her. She trusted her instincts, she knew that he was worth taking the risk for and if he called she'd see him. She'd go with him wherever he wanted to take her and if it was meant to be that she fell in love with him then that's just what she'd do. But she wasn't going to tell Jean-Claude that, she wasn't going to tell anyone at all, for what happened between her and Jake was their business and had nothing, nothing whatsoever, to do with anyone else. She just wished he'd call soon because she was so longing to see him that she couldn't think about anything else.

7

Golfe Juan was not a port Sarah would have thought of coming to. In fact, until Jean-Claude had mentioned it she'd never even heard of it. It was in the small bay between the Cap d'Antibes and the Cap de la Croisette in Cannes and was so new that in the shimmering light of the sun the paint on the smart, colourful shop fronts and cafés barely looked dry.

The jetties were laid out in neat rows between the quayside and the harbour wall that curved out around the port like a giant, protective arm. The bigger, more luxurious cruisers were furthest away, unable to manoeuvre in the crowded moorings deeper into the port.

There weren't many people around so Sarah clicked away happily, switching frequently between the three cameras strung around her neck, capturing the gleaming pinpoints of light reflecting from masts, cabin windows and the glorious blue sea beyond the harbour wall. They weren't particularly interesting shots, it wasn't a particularly photographic port, but it was, as Jean-Claude had told her, a good place to get some practice in where she wouldn't be constantly fighting her way through tourists.

As she worked her way along the port she rubbed a high-factor sun cream into her delicate, rosy skin and pulled her blue peaked cap further down over her eyes. Her shorts were nipping her about the waist and the straps of her swimsuit dug into her plump shoulders, but she was too busy concentrating on the angles from which she could shoot this port to make it look more vibrant, less polished.

After a while she was out by the incredible yachts that she would have more happily described as ships, and since the owners weren't in evidence she snapped away cheekily, trying to imagine what it must be like to have so much loot and simply dying to go on board to take a look around. It was another world on board these floating palaces, she thought dismally, and one that was totally closed to the likes of her. It was only nosiness really, for she didn't covet such wealth for herself, neither was she particularly turned on by the yachties she, Danny and Louisa had come across in the bars at Antibes. But she'd sorely like to go on board, just to satisfy her curiosity and to say she'd been. Still, there was no one around to ask, so turning her lenses around, she began shooting back across the harbour towards the rose-pink apartment blocks with crescent shaped, balustraded balconies and well-tended roof gardens and the wooded hills behind, crowded with villas.

She came upon what was clearly a private mooring where bougainvillea climbed the harbour wall and fussy little gardens edged the quayside, and passed breezily through it onto a narrow pathway with huge boulders either side and the sea beyond. She had been perched on a rock at the end of the harbour wall next to the cheery, little green-topped lighthouse for over an hour before she realized her skin was prickling painfully in the fierce rays of the sun, so reluctantly she gathered up her cameras to find relief in the shade.

As she strolled back she was mulling several things over in her mind: the exposure that would best portray the vividness of the sky; whether there was anything here worth experimenting on with the infrared film; how serious they all were about getting into some sort of business down here; was it worth even discussing it when she was pretty fed up with telly; was she ever going to get the hang of this water-skiing lark Danny and Louisa were into; the intriguing gesture of Consuela's inviting them all to lunch at the Grand Hotel on Cap Ferrat when they'd been told she rarely left the villa . . . All kinds of things were flitting through her mind when she happened to glance back over her shoulder to see a magnificent yacht gliding smoothly, no, majestically, through the waves towards the harbour. To her delight the sails were still up and the sun was in a perfect position over the Esterel, slightly hazed by the heat, to get some wonderfully dramatic shots, especially if she used the infrared film.

Two reels and several convoluted angles later, the sails were down, the yacht was anchored just outside the bay and a motorized dinghy with three people on board was heading towards the inner sanctum. Sarah stared at it, shaking her head in a fatalistic sort of way. Over a week had gone by and Jake Mallory hadn't yet picked up the phone to call either Danny or Louisa, nor had his name been mentioned again since that morning on the terrace, but Sarah had known he would come back into their lives at some point and here he was speeding across the water towards *her*.

Quickly capping up her lenses, she stashed her cameras in their bags and started off for the jetty the dinghy seemed to be aiming for. Fortunately it was the one closest to her so she arrived at the water's edge just before Jake Mallory and the others disembarked.

'Hi!' she called out, her cameras clattering together as she waved. Who the hell wanted to see the plastic palaces out by the harbour walls when there was a vessel like the one they'd just left to explore?

Jake looked at her blankly then glanced back at Bob and Jason, assuming she was greeting one of them. They shrugged, equally at a loss.

'Hi,' Jake said, swinging himself effortlessly up onto the jetty. 'How're you doing?'

Realizing that he didn't recognize her Sarah said, 'I'm fine. We sort of met at Consuela's a week or so ago. You probably remember my friends Danny and Louisa better than me, but I was there. I'm Sarah, by the way.'

'Good to meet you, Sarah,' Jake smiled, shaking her hand. 'That looks like quite some gear you've got there,' he added, nodding towards her cameras.

'Oh I'm just practising,' she said. 'I hope you don't mind but I took some shots of your boat. She's pretty splendid. I hope you don't think it an invasion of privacy,' she added looking worried.

Jake laughed and Sarah could see instantly why Louisa had fallen so hard. He was absolutely gorgeous and the twinkle in his dark eyes, coupled with the athleticism of his hard body was starting to play up her hormones. 'If it is,' he said, 'then you're welcome. You say you're practising?'

She nodded. 'I'm hoping to change careers and I've always been a bit of an amateur snapper. Hey, I don't suppose you'd let me go on board and take a look around would you?' she said, turning to gaze out at the *Valhalla*.

'Sure,' he said without hesitation, taking a patch out of his pocket and putting it over his left eye. 'I'm kind of busy myself right now, but Bob here'd be happy to take you.' He turned to look at his first mate who was eyeing Sarah with his usual suspicion – women were always throwing themselves at Jake and this one might think she was being subtle in her approach but Bob was having no problem seeing right through it.

'Hi, Bob,' Sarah said, sticking her hand out to shake his. 'I promise not to be a nuisance. Maybe you'd let me take some shots of you, you've got just the kind of face I've been looking for.'

Jake turned away to hide his laughter. It wasn't often he got to see Bob blush.

'I don't suppose,' Sarah went on as Jake handed her down into the dinghy, 'you could put a patch over your eye too, Bob, could you? And if you've got a skull and crossbones to wave around on the top of one of those big stick things it would make some pretty entertaining shots. No? OK, just a thought,' and turning aside she winked up at Jake.

Bob was looking at her with such blatant hostility now that Jake laughed outright. 'Well, partner,' he grinned, 'looks like you're in for quite an evening. You ready Jason?'

'Right there,' Jason answered, jumping up onto the jetty.

'Do you think you could show me how the sails go up when we get there, Bob?' Sarah asked, dropping her bags on the floor and making herself comfortable.

'I thought you said you weren't going to be a nuisance,' Bob grunted.

'Oh, I won't be,' she assured him. 'If you say no sails, then no sails it is.'

Still laughing Jake turned and walked off down the quay, pretty certain he'd come back to find the *Valhalla* flying every one of her kites and Bob posing on the bowsprit, complete with eye patch and G-string and flexing his brawn like he was straight off Muscle Beach.

Quite unperturbed by Bob's disgruntlement Sarah began reloading her cameras as Bob jerked the cord and started up the engine. It was a shame Jake wasn't coming along too, she was thinking to herself, she'd have enjoyed getting to know him. Not that she had any designs on him, he was far too good looking for her taste and she couldn't imagine she'd be his type either, but she was curious to find out a little more about him. Maybe Bob would be forthcoming on that front and if he wasn't what the hell, she reckoned she was going to enjoy getting under old Bob's skin for an hour or two and she could hardly wait to tell Louisa and Danny where she'd been.

A brief frown crossed her face. On second thoughts maybe she'd keep it to herself. Louisa hadn't mentioned Jake again since that morning on the terrace, neither had Danny, but Sarah knew that Danny had spent another night in St Tropez during the week, though whether Louisa knew she couldn't say. She'd probably guessed though, but at least on the surface it didn't seem to have caused any bad feeling between them.

She started and almost lost her balance as Bob's chest suddenly rang. Reaching inside his shirt pocket he pulled out a compact mobile phone and unfolded it.

'Yeah,' he barked. He waited a moment then made a noise in the back of his throat as he thrust the phone at Sarah.

'For me?' Sarah said, amazed and feeling very international.

He nodded curtly and she took the phone.

'Hi,' the deep, American voice said. 'It's Jake Mallory.'

'Well seeing as you're the only other person who knows

where I am, I believe you,' Sarah responded, looking back towards the port to see if she could catch sight of him.

He laughed. 'Could you do me a favour?' he said.

'I'll try.'

'Tell your friend I haven't forgotten. She'll know what I mean.'

'You haven't forgotten,' Sarah repeated. 'Yes, I think I can manage that. Anything else?'

'Just one thing, Bob's all growl and no bite, but I reckon you figured that out already.'

'Yeah, I reckon I did,' Sarah said, affecting his American drawl as she looked over at Bob.

'OK. Well you have yourself a good time,' Jake said and the line went dead. It was only as she handed the phone back to Bob that it occurred to Sarah that she didn't know which friend he'd been referring to. She'd assumed it was Louisa, but what if it wasn't? She didn't want to get Louisa's hopes up again, especially not if the message was meant for Danny.

'Uh, do you think I could call him back?' she asked Bob as he cut the engines and they nudged gently against the hull of the *Valhalla*.

Glaring at her Bob took out the phone and dialled. 'He's gone out of communication,' he said after four rings.

'Oh. Well, if you could give me his number I'll try again later.'

'I can't do that without Jake's say so,' Bob retorted, ''specially not the number of his private line.'

Sarah smiled so winningly that Bob's jaw visibly tightened as he fought to keep hold of his animosity.

'Then how about you let me have your number?' Sarah said. 'After all, I have the distinct feeling that you and I are going to be great friends by the end of the evening, don't you?'

Bob shook his head. 'Uh-huh,' he said. 'You don't get to him that way either. Jake wants you to call him he'll give you his number himself.'

'And what if I want to call you?'

Bob looked at her, his watery blue eyes not thawing in the

least, but he was the first to turn away. 'You want to see this baby, or don't you,' he said getting to his feet.

'What I want, Bob,' she answered smoothly, 'is to convince you that it's not your skipper's body I'm after.'

Bob started, almost lost his footing and Sarah reached out to catch him as he stumbled against her.

'Later, Bob,' she said. 'After all, we've only just met,' and at long last she managed to pull a smile from the obstinate press of his lips.

The twin-enginnned speedboat was skimming rapidly over the inky black water, breaking apart the rippling reflections of moonlight, riding high on the waves, heading towards the Ile Sainte Marguerite, just off the coast at Cannes. Jake was driving, standing at the wheel, steering with one hand while with the other he pointed to the small wooden jetty they were approaching.

Dmitri peered through the darkness. His golden hair was tangled by the wind, his green eyes were constantly darting towards Jake. He knew there was marijuana on board, Jake had been smoking it when he'd arrived at the quay, but whether there was more than what Jake kept for his personal use Dmitri had no idea and he wasn't going to ask. If they were stopped by the coastguard he'd plead ignorance, though much good that would do him.

A few minutes later Jake eased the lever back, slowing the engines and steered the boat quietly, effortlessly alongside the jetty.

Dmitri watched as two men emerged from the shadows wearing dark clothes and soft-soled shoes.

Jake turned to Dmitri. '*Vas-y*,' he said.

Dmitri climbed obediently from the boat to join the two men, listening as Jake told them that the *Valhalla* was in Golfe Juan and would sail for Corsica the day after tomorrow, stopping en route at the Ile Sainte Marguerite to take Dmitri on board.

'You OK?' Jake said, looking up at Dmitri.

Dumbly Dmitri nodded.

Jake laughed. 'Give him a stiff drink, Alain,' he said in French, 'then get him to tell you about the girl waiting for him in Athens, that should loosen him up a bit.'

Alain's humour was gruff as he slapped Dmitri on the back, while Jake started to turn the boat around.

Dmitri was still on the jetty, gazing back at the distant lights of Cannes as the boat gathered speed, ploughing into the waves, making its return journey to the mainland.

'*Viens*,' Alain said.

Dmitri turned, could see just a few lights glowing through the dense trees of the island in front of him. Why, he was wondering, did he have to leave France this way? Why couldn't he have taken a plane from Nice Airport, or even a train from the Gare de St Augustin?

Consuela, when she'd driven him to Cannes, had told him that Jake would explain, but Jake hadn't even attempted to and Dmitri had been too afraid to ask. Maybe he would have the answers when they sailed to Corsica, if they sailed to Corsica.

With each step he took, moving deeper into the night-blackened island, his foreboding grew. Why did he have the feeling that he was never going to see Athens again? Why had Consuela seemed so upset when he'd left, so angry with Jake, yet so unnerved by him too? She'd said little, but he'd sensed it in her and once again he felt chilled by the way Jake had looked at her, as though he wanted to kill her. He'd wanted to assure them that their secrets were safe with him, that he'd never tell what he knew, but his tongue had been too weighted with fear to speak. Merciful God, why had Jake sought him out in those moments before he'd made love to the English actress? Why did Jake have to tell him what was about to happen? He'd carried out Jake's instructions, but even so he hadn't needed to know. It would have been far better never knowing. But it was too late now and the burden of his knowledge was as heavy and as doom-laden as this night was still and so intimidatingly black.

8

The immense ocean-going cruiser, *Misty Nights*, was moored at the furthest point of the Albert Edouard Jetée in the *vieux port* of Cannes. Every light on the vessel was flooding the crowded decks, champagne was flowing, music blared from the speakers and excited laughter, shouts and screams rang joyously around the harbour.

Sarah and Danny were among the wild dancers on one of the spacious aft decks, jiving recklessly with one another, bumping the other dancers, tripping, catching each other and spinning into the arms of anyone who cared to catch them. Louisa was elbowing her way through the heaving mass of glittering, sun-bronzed bodies, champagne fizzing over her fingers from the three glasses she was carrying. Seeing her, Sarah and Danny grabbed their champagne, threw it back in one go and drew Louisa into the heart of the mayhem, shouting down her laughing protests as she careened into a semi-naked woman, slopping half her champagne over the woman's shoulders.

'Sorry!' Louisa yelled.

'Don't worry!' The woman cried, throwing out her hair, gyrating her hips and letting the champagne trickle over her breasts. She wasn't the only topless guest, there were plenty of others in various states of undress, most having come straight from the beach, others simply having discarded excess clothing in an effort to cool down as much as to enter into the spirit.

Pierre, who had been teaching them to water-ski off the pier at the Majestic that afternoon, had pointed out the yacht as it sailed in, telling them where they could find it later and just to ask for Guy when they got there. They'd returned to the villa to freshen up and change first, so the party was already in full swing by the time they arrived. Now, two hours later all three of them had lost track of how much champagne they'd drunk, how many dances they'd had and how many gorgeous men were on board. There didn't appear to be anyone above the age of thirty, making this a very different kind of party from the rather more decorous cocktail affairs Louisa imagined these decks were more used to hosting.

She was in a great mood, had laughed, danced and flirted her way through the evening as outrageously as either Danny or Sarah, and was feeling happier and more carefree than she had since arriving in France. What did it matter that she had seen Jake Mallory the day before at a café in Mougins, a stunning blonde sitting opposite him, gazing rapturously into his eyes? It was true, her heart seemed to jar at any thought of him, but she wasn't going to let that stop her having a good time. Guy, the chief steward, had taken quite a liking to her and he was simply irresistible. Sarah and Danny had teased her all evening about her conquest, though they were doing their fair share of flirting, especially with the two Italian brothers, Marco and Saberio, who also worked on board.

'Don't tell me you've had enough!' Guy laughed as Louisa flopped against the side of the boat.

'Never!' she cried, breathlessly. 'Well, maybe for now. This is an amazing party. What would the owners say if they found out about it?'

Guy's handsome face was simmering with laughter as he looked at her, admiring the impish light in her eyes and the fullness of her smile. 'Why, you going to tell?' he teased.

'I wouldn't know who to tell,' she laughed.

Leaning an elbow on the rail beside her he gazed seductively into her eyes. 'I'll let you into a secret,' he said, his lips touching her ear as he spoke. 'The owner knows. Who else do you think is paying for all this champagne?'

Louisa shrugged then shivered as he pressed his lips to her neck. 'I hadn't really thought about it,' she said. 'So where is he? Don't tell me . . .' The music suddenly crescendoed.

'What? You'll have to speak up,' Guy shouted.

'Never mind,' Louisa shouted back. 'I was just asking where the owner was.'

'The owner? He's in the States.'

'Sarah! What are you doing?' Louisa laughed as Sarah grabbed her arm and pulled her to one side.

'You'll never guess whose boat this is,' Sarah shouted in her ear.

'Whose?' Louisa grinned, knowing from the excitement in Sarah's eyes it was going to be someone famous.

'Jake Mallory's. Well, his father's. Pierre just told me.'

The warmth drained from Louisa's smile. 'Jake Mallory,' she repeated, feeling the words drop like lead weights on her spirits. Dear God, the man was omnipresent and as the effects of the alcohol began rushing through her head she suddenly wanted very much to leave.

Sarah nodded.

'Then where is he?' Louisa demanded querulously.

Sarah shrugged. 'Don't ask me. But I thought you'd like to know who our host was. Small world, eh?'

'Isn't it just,' Louisa commented, unable to keep the edge from her voice, angry because this had put a damper on what until now had been a terrific evening.

'Hey come on, you two,' Guy laughed, 'no more secrets. Let's dance,' and pulling Louisa back into the crowd he twirled her under his arm while somehow grabbing two brimming glasses from a passing tray.

Jake was sitting in the Caviar Club bar at the Carlton Hotel, sipping a beer while reading through the stack of papers in front of him. Since he was wearing an old, torn pair of jeans and a faded denim shirt with a black bandanna knotted around his neck he was attracting more attention than he realized. There were no actual rules stipulating dress but the other men in the small, baroque-style bar all wore gold-buttoned blazers, white shirts, yacht club ties and smart, flannel slacks. Jake had little time or regard for such sartorial proprieties, he was there to keep a rendezvous, not to impress, though had he been anyone else he might well have been politely asked to leave. As it was, the waiter, knowing exactly who Jake Mallory was, had served him his beer and left him alone.

It was amongst the few Americans in the bar that Jake was exciting the most attention, for one or two felt sure they recognized him. Only vaguely aware of their curiosity Jake concentrated on his documents until, looking up to see his guest walk in, he put the papers down and stood up to greet the woman who had delivered his car to St Tropez when he'd arrived. As she walked into his embrace Jake almost laughed at the way every eye in the room had come out on stalks. She was breathtaking and with her fine, ash-blonde hair piled with immaculate carelessness on the top of her head, her deep, royal blue silk dress that barely contained her generous breasts in its sequinned bodice, he guessed he couldn't blame everyone for looking.

He kissed her lightly on both cheeks, whispered something in her ear that made her laugh, then pulled her down beside him on the banquette.

The waiter was already there, took Jake's order and went. Jake scanned the bar, grinning as everyone looked quickly away before catching his eye. Beside him the woman crossed one exquisite leg over the other, revealing even more of her firm, brown thighs, while Jake leaned back, resting an arm along the back of the seat and lifted one foot onto the corner of the table. She was talking in a low voice, but Jake could hear her perfectly.

'I'm not sure of the details yet,' she was saying, 'but Fernando will call here in the next fifteen minutes or so.'

'Are they still in Mexico City?' Jake asked.

'He says not.'

'Then where?' Jake's face was hard now, all traces of humour had vanished.

'That's why Fernando is calling,' she answered. 'I've spoken to San Diego, they're expecting to hear from you in the next twenty-four hours.'

Jake nodded, his expression grimmer than ever. His hand,

as he picked up his beer, was perfectly steady, but the tension in his fingers was noticeable.

Some ten minutes later he was called to the phone. He was gone for some time and when he returned it was to find that his guest had ordered another Bellini.

'Drink that,' he said, 'then get onto Bob and tell him to take the *Valhalla* over to Corsica tonight.'

'Where are you going?' she asked as he pocketed his car keys and gathered together his papers.

'I'll be in touch,' he said, throwing a two-hundred-franc note on the table. Then downing the rest of his beer he left.

Ignoring her drink, the woman picked up her bag and ran out into the street after him.

Louisa was leaning against the side of the boat, her head resting on a pillar, a warm glass of champagne cupped in her hands. Looking down at it she grimaced, tossed it over her shoulder into the sea, then closed her eyes for a moment. She'd had far more to drink than she could handle, though she put the way she was swaying down to the gentle motion of the yacht. The party was still in full volume, even more people had arrived now and Guy, like Danny and Sarah, seemed to have disappeared.

She opened her eyes as a young man fell into her, and assuring him that she was all right she looked across the deck to see Danny dancing with one of the Italian brothers. His hands were very low on Danny's back, almost resting on her buttocks. Danny's arms were around his neck, the hem of her short, clinging white dress riding high.

Louisa sighed, hiccoughed and put a hand to her mouth. Since finding out that this was, to all intents and purposes, Jake's boat all the sparkle had gone from her evening. She no longer felt right about being there, wished she could go home, but hadn't so far managed to tear herself away.

'Hi, are you OK?' Danny cried, using her hair to fan her back as she leaned against the side next to Louisa.

'I'm great,' Louisa smiled. 'Where's Sarah?'

'God knows. She was with Pierre the last time I saw her. Why aren't you dancing?'

'I will in a minute. What's happened to Romeo?'

'He's gone to get more of that,' Danny answered, pointing at Louisa's empty glass. 'How many have you had?' she laughed as Louisa pulled a face.

'Don't ask. Too many to drive.'

'You'll have to get a cab home then, 'cos I don't think I'll be coming back tonight,' Danny grinned. 'And you can bet your bottom dollar Sarah's had a skinful. Ah, Saberio,' she said affecting an Italian accent as she took a bottle in one hand and a glass of champagne in the other.

She giggled as Saberio swung her round so that he was leaning against the side and she was leaning against him. As he buried his face in her neck Danny's eyes fluttered closed. 'Mmm,' she murmured, letting her head fall back. She looked at Louisa and grinned. 'God, I feel horny tonight,' she whispered.

'I'd never have guessed,' Louisa commented wryly.

'I have bet with my brother,' Saberio intoned in Danny's ear, sliding his hand over her bottom. 'We make bet that you wear nothing under this dress. Am I right?'

Danny winked at Louisa. 'Well, that's for you to find out,' Danny laughed as Louisa rolled her eyes.

Saberio's hands were now at the hem of her dress, brushing lightly over her thighs.

There was a sudden uproar on the other side of the deck as several people leapt spontaneously into the sea. Everyone rushed to the edge to watch the swimmers, shouting to them, some tearing off their clothes and throwing themselves in too. As Danny looked back over her shoulder Saberio slid a thumb under her hem, stroking it gently across the crease of her bottom.

Danny's eyes were smouldering as she turned back. 'Mmm,' she purred. 'I think you've just found out. So do you win the bet?'

'I win,' he grinned, 'but how I prove to my brother?'

'I don't know, you tell me,' Danny smile l, following Saberio's eyes back across the deck to Marco, who was idling against a pillar watching them.

'Maybe like this?' Saberio suggested, starting to roll her dress up over her buttocks, while pushing his tongue deep into her mouth.

Beside them Louisa moved restlessly, wondering if it was the heat that seemed to make everyone so sexually liberated. Then, to her amazement, naked from the waist down Danny turned around, leaned against Saberio and poured more champagne into her glass while keeping her eyes on Marco.

'Danny!' Louisa muttered.

Laughing, Danny passed her the champagne bottle and glass and rolled her dress back down as Saberio whispered something in her ear. Danny's eyes darkened and from the corner of her eye Louisa saw Saberio's hand travel up inside the front of Danny's dress.

Feeling horribly like a voyeur Louisa started to move away when Saberio let Danny go and strolled over to his brother, passing Sarah on the way.

'Where have you been?' Danny laughed seeing Sarah's bleary eyes and smudged lips.

'Disgracing myself over the side of the boat,' Sarah groaned, jerking her head back as Danny's champagne glass came dangerously close.

'What happened to Pierre?' Louisa grinned.

'God knows,' Sarah answered, closing her eyes and starting to sway. 'Oh God, just take me home someone, please.'

'Sit there,' Danny said, pointing at the empty chair next to Louisa, 'you'll feel better in a minute.'

Sarah slumped into it as Louisa turned, resting her arms on the side of the boat, to gaze out at the moonlit sea. She didn't see Saberio beckoning to Danny to go and join him and his brother, but as Danny moved away Louisa guessed they'd probably seen the last of her for tonight.

A few minutes later she was on the point of turning back to Sarah when her heart gave a painful twist and she swore under her breath. Quickly she turned her back as Jake and the beautiful blonde she'd seen him with in Mougins the day before came on board.

Guy and two other crew spotted them instantly and hurried over with champagne. Louisa couldn't hear what was being said, but she could see Jake laughing and waving the drink away. He turned to the blonde, shouted something in her ear then they disappeared into one of the cabins.

Louisa looked down at Sarah who appeared half asleep. 'Guess who's just arrived?' she said.

'Mmm?' Sarah grunted.

'Nothing. Come on, let's go home. Now.'

Sarah nodded and taking her by the arm Louisa helped her to her feet, laughing as Sarah gave a plaintive groan.

'Just throw me over and let me drown.' Sarah mumbled.

'Come on,' Louisa encouraged, 'lean against me.'

'Need a hand there?'

Louisa looked up, knowing from the voice whose face she was going to find herself looking into. As her eyes met Jake's, to her dismay Sarah staggered against the side of the boat, taking Louisa with her.

'No, no, we're fine, thank you,' Louisa assured him, trying to get Sarah upright again. 'She'll be OK once she's on dry land.'

'Sure,' he said, still smiling. 'Did she remember to give you my message?'

Louisa looked at him. So the message Sarah had blurted out in another inebriated moment had been for her. 'Yes, she did, thank you.'

'Hey, come on, let me give you a hand,' he insisted as Sarah teetered towards him, and catching her he grabbed her about the waist and steered her over to the *passerelle*.

Louisa followed, realizing that she wasn't any too steady herself. Fortunately she made it, but lost her balance momentarily as she stepped onto the harbour.

'I'm sorry,' she said, using Jake's arm to steady herself. 'I must have got used to the sway of the boat.'

'It happens to most when they've been drinking on board,' he told her. 'You'll be fine in a couple of minutes. Where's your car?'

'We haven't got one,' Louisa answered, linking Sarah's free arm.

Jake's dark eyes flashed with humour. 'Seems like I'm destined to become your chauffeur,' he remarked.

'Oh no, I didn't mean that,' Louisa said hastily. 'We can take a taxi. There's sure to be one outside the Palais.'

'My car's nearer,' he told her.

Louisa was about to protest again, but there was something about the laughter in his eyes that stopped her.

Between them they got Sarah to the Mercedes, though now she was on *terra firma* she was gratifyingly more stable on her feet. At last she was curled up on the back seat and Louisa was sitting beside Jake as he reversed the car back and headed out towards the Croisette.

'I called you earlier,' he said, glancing over at Louisa.

'Did you?' Louisa said, feeling her heart do all sorts of things she wished it wouldn't.

He smiled. 'Seems I didn't have to look any further than my own front door, as it turned out.'

'I didn't know the boat was yours,' Louisa told him, knowing she sounded ridiculously defensive.

He looked at her quizzically, then indicating to change lanes he turned the corner at the Martinez heading towards the autoroute. 'That sounds like you wouldn't have gone if you'd known,' he remarked.

Louisa's face was averted. 'I wouldn't have,' she said.

Again he threw her a questioning look. 'Did I do something?' he said.

'No, I don't think so,' Louisa answered.

'Then why do I get the impression you're ticked about something?'

'Me?' Louisa said, feigning surprise. 'I'm not ticked, as you put it. I'm fine.'

'So why wouldn't you have gone to the party if you'd known the boat was mine?'

She was becoming uncomfortably hot and sorely wished she hadn't got into this. 'What I meant,' she said lamely, 'is that I wouldn't have gone without an invitation.'

'Why do you think I was calling you?' he said.

Louisa was momentarily nonplussed, but then remembering that he'd arrived much later than everyone else and with the blonde in tow, she said, 'I really don't know why you were calling me, unless . . .' she stopped, damned if she was going to let her jealousy show by saying something as crass as perhaps she was second choice.

'Unless what?' he prompted.

'Nothing. Shall we change the subject? How's your marina project coming along?'

'Slowly,' he answered, coming to a halt at the red lights at the foot of the Carnot. 'Why else do you think I was calling you?' he persisted.

'I'm sorry,' she said. 'I've got a bit of a headache and it's making me snappy.'

He was still looking at her and his evident confusion was seriously weakening her resolve. But what she was feeling inside, the swirling emotions that were drawing her to him again, were, she had to keep reminding herself, exactly what all his other women probably experienced when they were under the scrutiny of those ruthlessly hypnotic eyes.

He pressed down on the accelerator and as the car slid into the heavy traffic of the Carnot neither of them said any more.

Sarah was the first to break the silence as they sped through the winding country roads between Mougins and Valanjou.

'Louisa,' she croaked, trying to pull herself up.

Louisa turned round.

'Louisa, we have to stop.'

Jake was already pulling over to the side of the road and burning with embarrassment Louisa jumped out, pulled her seat forward and rushed Sarah over to the bushes.

'I don't believe you,' Louisa muttered in her ear while

holding Sarah's hair from her face. 'Couldn't you have held on?'

'I'm sorry,' Sarah gasped weakly, then retching loudly she started to throw up again.

Louisa turned as she heard Jake get out of the car and watched him walk towards her.

'Is she OK?' he said, seeming as concerned as he did amused.

'Let's put it this way,' Louisa answered, 'she's a whole lot better now than she's going to be when I get her home.'

Jake laughed and at last Louisa's face softened into a smile. 'I'm sorry,' she said.

'Me too,' he said. 'I don't know what I did, but I'm sorry.'

Louisa was still smiling. 'You didn't do anything,' she told him, 'at least nothing you don't have a perfect right to do.'

'You going to explain that?' he said, lifting a hand to smooth his thumb along her jaw.

His touch was so gentle, yet so potent, that Louisa felt herself tremble. 'Do I have to?' she whispered.

He shook his head, his eyes looking deeply into hers. Then, cupping her chin in his hand, he kissed her softly on the mouth.

Louisa's eyes were still closed as he lifted his head to look at her again. He waited for them to flutter open then kissed her again, just as softly, but this time more lingeringly, running his hand around her neck and pushing his fingers into her hair.

As gentle as the kiss was Louisa could feel a slow fire starting to burn inside her. The touch of his mouth was so sensual, so tender, yet so powerfully compelling it was as though he was touching every part of her. The lazy caress of his fingers seemed to draw her even further into the allure of his embrace, an embrace that had more potency in its gentleness than she could ever have dreamed possible.

Still his lips were on hers, tasting them, parting them, moulding them to his own. His eyes were closed, his hand held her, his magnetism flowed through her. Time was standing still, they were locked in a beautiful, sensuous world of their own.

'Louisa, can I come up now?' Sarah wailed.

Jake's laughter was expelled into Louisa's throat as she too burst out laughing. They looked at each other for a brief moment then, letting go of Sarah's hair, Louisa took hold of her and guided her back to the car.

'I'm sorry,' Sarah said as Jake walked round to the driver's side. 'I know you want to kill me, but I was getting cramp down there.'

'It's all right,' Louisa laughed, aware that she was still slightly dizzy from the effects of the kiss. 'Now, you're sure you're not going to throw up again?'

'I don't think so.'

Within ten minutes they were home and Sarah had taken herself discreetly, as well as necessarily, straight off to bed.

'Are you sure this is all you want?' Louisa said to Jake, carrying a beer onto the terrace for him.

He turned and sat on the balustrade, watching her put the beer on the table. 'That'll do just fine,' he answered, inhaling deeply on his cigarette. 'What about you? Aren't you having anything?'

'Just coffee,' she said, praying that he couldn't see how nervous she was.

The air was perfectly still, with just the metallic chirping of night insects chafing the silence. The garden offered its own delicate perfume, the soft lights of the terrace captured them in a muted glow of sensual awareness. She watched him reach for his beer, following the movements of his hands, so strong and so masculine she could almost feel herself melting at the thought of what they could do to her. His long, powerfully muscled legs were stretched out in front of him and through a rip in his jeans she could see the dark hair on his thigh. Desire was pulsing so hard through her body it held her rooted to her chair. She raised her eyes back to his face to find him watching her.

'You've got exceptionally beautiful eyes, do you know that?' he said.

A voice somewhere deep inside her was crying out for her not to listen, not to be taken in by such easy charm and flattery, but of course it was too late. Just that one kiss had been enough to tell her that she was his for the taking.

'Thank you,' she said, then felt a bubble of laughter rise in her throat.

The next moment, to her amazement, she heard herself say, 'I hope your girlfriend won't mind you bringing us home.'

Jake's eyebrows lifted and raising his cigarette he took another long draw.

'She's very beautiful,' Louisa said, wishing she could stop herself. 'What's her name?'

'Marianne,' he answered and Louisa's heart seemed to split in two.

'Oh,' she smiled. Then when he said nothing, 'I saw you with her in Mougins yesterday.'

He nodded, then flicking his cigarette into the garden he tilted his head back to drink his beer. 'Time I was going,' he said, putting the half-empty bottle back on the table.

Louisa had already drawn breath to protest before she mercifully managed to stop herself. She walked with him round to the front of the house, thanking him again for bringing them home and hoping he couldn't hear the misery and shameful anger in her voice. When they reached the car he stopped, turned to face her and crooking his fingers under her chin, he said, 'Look, we both know something special is happening here, but don't let's rush it, huh?'

Louisa gazed up at him with wide, uncertain eyes.

He smiled. 'Marianne's not my girlfriend,' he said. 'No one is, and you, Louisa, have just got to be patient. Can you do that?'

'I don't think so,' she answered, making him laugh.

'Yeah, well, there are a lot of things going on right now,' he said, 'things I can't explain, leastways not yet. But I will, when the time is right.'

'Can't you at least tell me something?'

He shook his head. 'No. It's not good for you to know. And I want you to keep what we have between us to yourself. Will you do that?'

'And what exactly is it that we have between us?' she pressed.

'You know as well as I do,' he murmured, 'so stop trying to make me say things I'm not in any position to say right now. Just keep it to yourself, OK?'

She nodded.

'And don't listen to all you might hear about me, 'cos only half of it's true. You'll find out which half when, if, I'm ever able to make the commitment you want.'

'Am I so easy to read?' she smiled.

'It's not a case of reading,' he answered, 'it's a case of feeling and I feel you mighty powerfully, Louisa Kramer.' He grimaced. 'Too powerfully,' he added with a smile.

'Then why do you have to go?' she whispered.

'I just do. We're not either of us ready for this yet,' he said, brushing his fingers over the cool softness of her cheek.

'I feel ready,' she said.

'Don't make this any harder than it already is,' he said, looking ruefully into her eyes.

'Then just tell me when the time will be right,' she persisted, wanting so desperately for him to hold her, to feel his strength beneath her hands, against her body.

'I don't know,' he said. 'Soon, maybe. But . . .' He stopped and looked past her into the black of the night.

'But what?' she said.

'But no promises,' he said, lowering his eyes back to hers.

Louisa felt a coldness stealing over the unsteady joy in her heart and as if sensing it he said, 'Don't expect too much, Louisa, 'cos it may be that in the end I can't give it.'

'I wish I understood what was going on,' she said.

'I wish I understood it too,' he answered, seeming suddenly very far away.

'Will you kiss me again?' she whispered.

He shook his head. 'If I do that I'll never be able to leave here tonight.' He laughed at the mischievous look that shot into her eyes. 'I can't stay,' he told her. 'Believe me, I want to, but I can't.'

'Will I see you again?'

The corner of his mouth curved in a wry smile. 'My guess is we'll see each other again,' he said, his voice laden with irony. 'Just don't ask when, don't listen to all you hear, trust me and keep what we have for us.'

He touched his lips so lightly to hers that were it not for the sudden flame it ignited in her he might not have touched her at all.

'OK?' he whispered.

'OK,' she nodded.

As she watched his car disappear at the end of the drive she was wondering why it had only occurred to her now to ask him about Danny, when it was too late. But what difference did it make? She knew now that he felt the same way she did and though he hadn't told her anything about himself or what he was really involved in she was going to do as he asked and trust him.

9

The turn of the century Grand Hotel on the very tip of the millionaires' promontory Cap Ferrat, was one of the most exclusive and expensive on the entire coast. The rich, the famous and even the infamous could stay there in complete seclusion and anonymity if that was their wish, which was why, as a woman who valued her privacy above all else, Consuela had arranged to meet Rosalind on the hotel's sweeping half-moon terrace, shaded by umbrella pines and sufficiently distant from the other guests not to be overheard.

At that moment Rosalind was staring in horror at Consuela, wondering if she were looking at a friend or an enemy. Neither of them spoke for a moment as two uniformed waiters positioned themselves at their elbows, paused, then with a subtle flourish, lifted the silver lids from their plates to reveal the *homard aux girolles*.

'I'm sorry, Rosalind,' Consuela murmured as the waiters departed. 'Truly, I'm sorry.'

'But if he's with Peter now,' Rosalind said, 'why didn't you call me before I left? Maybe I could have stopped him.'

'I called,' Consuela said, 'but you were already on your way.'

'Oh my God!' Rosalind muttered, her face as pale as the alabaster sculptures in the gardens. 'This is going to kill Peter,' she said, gazing sightlessly at the other tables where fine wines accompanied the exquisite food and easy laughter rippled from the lips of the chic guests. 'It'll kill everything. Don't you understand that? Peter trusts me. More than that, he truly believes that the sex life we have is enough. And it is! It's just that sometimes the pressure of living with someone who's dying is too much. I have to find a release, to forget it, if only for a few hours.'

'I understand,' Consuela said, covering her hand. 'Believe me, I know what you're going through.'

'So why are you allowing Jake to do this?' Rosalind implored.

'It's not a question of allowing, you know that,' Consuela answered.

'But you must have known what he was doing.'

'Not until it was already done,' Consuela said, swallowing hard on her food.

Rosalind looked at her dully. 'How much money is he going to ask for?' she said.

Consuela shook her head. 'I don't know. It'll be a lot.'

'But didn't you tell him Peter was dying?' Rosalind pleaded. 'Doesn't he have any pity for a man whose only wish now is for a peaceful end to his life?'

'Of course I told him,' Consuela assured her. 'I did everything I could to stop him. I even offered him the money myself.'

'But he wouldn't take it,' Rosalind stated helplessly. 'I'd have paid him,' she said. 'I have money. Not as much as Peter, it's true, but . . . Oh no, Consuela,' she cried as Consuela lifted her napkin to her mouth to stifle a sob.

'Rosalind, I'm sorry,' she choked. 'Would that it had been anyone but you. But no, I wouldn't wish this on anyone and to think that this is the price people have to pay for being my friend. It's my fault, I'm as much to blame as he is, but tell me, what can I do? They wouldn't send him for trial. His family are more powerful than . . .'

'Sssh, ssh,' Rosalind soothed, aware that they were attracting several interested glances. 'It's not your fault. Please, Consuela. You mustn't blame yourself. I know what he's put you through . . .'

'He doesn't want me to have any friends,' Consuela said, her voice so choked with tears it was barely audible. 'The rumours he's spread about me . . . I know what he says, but that I can live with. It's what he does to the people I care for that I can't live with.'

Rosalind turned and stared at the glittering Mediterranean where expert skiers skimmed smoothly across the waves, windsurfers glided with the breeze and a hundred different yachts rocked and swayed in the current. 'So he's done this before,' she said, hearing the words echo in her head.

Consuela nodded. 'I wish I could tell you otherwise, but he's had those videos put together in the past and . . .' Her voice was too strangled for a moment to continue, 'and . . . he's rich, Rosalind, richer than you or I put together. He doesn't need the money. He does it for kicks. Diana and William Fitzbligh? You remember them. They're divorced now, we never see her any more. It was Jake who split them up, who destroyed her life. He put a camera in the bathhouse and had everything she did edited together with a real pornographic film. He sent copies to William's colleagues, to his clients, even to his children. Diana didn't do half the things she looks like she's doing, they're most of them editing tricks, but it looks so real and the damage . . . Rosalind, he's going to make as big a fool out of Peter as he can and Peter will . . .' she stopped, unable to go on.

'Will die thinking that that was how much I valued him and what we are to each other,' Rosalind finished, still staring blindly out to sea. 'Oh God, Consuela! What am I going to do? How am I going to face him?'

'You can only tell him the truth,' Consuela answered. 'You must tell him why you come to the bathhouse then explain the editing tricks Jake uses to make it look like it's you doing those disgusting things.'

'How disgusting are they?' Rosalind said, her eyes dilating with fear.

'They're horrible. Depraved.'

Rosalind took a gulp of wine. It was still her first glass, but already she was lightheaded with the fear of what this was going to do to the husband she loved so deeply. A man as gentle and kind as Peter should never have to be submitted to the kind of humiliation and heartbreak Jake Mallory was going to bring into his life. He had so little time left in this world, so why couldn't Jake just let him die with dignity and love in his heart, instead of the shame of seeing his wife behave like a whore or worse. She thought of how long it had taken to win over her stepchildren; what were they going to think now? Would Jake really show them?

She looked at Consuela. 'We have to go to the police,' she said.

The clatter of cutlery, strains of soft music and drifting hum of conversation filled the silence. At last Consuela shook her head, 'It wouldn't do any good,' she said. 'Remember, he has already been arrested once and on a much more serious charge than extortion. They let him go then and they'll do it again. His father's influence doesn't stop at the shores of the United States any more than the power of the United States stops there.'

Rosalind put a shaking hand to her mouth. 'Dear God, where does all this end?' she sobbed.

'I wish I had an answer for you,' Consuela said, gazing down at her empty plate. 'But you must think of yourself now. Make Peter's last days as happy as you can, the way I know you want to. Tell him to call me if you think it will help. I'll stand by you, I'll do all I can to ease this for you – for you both . . . And he won't change his will, I know he won't. He loves you too much to do that. Yes, I know right now that's not your consideration. You don't need the money, but neither do you need it being said that it was your indiscretions on a video that made him change his will. It happened to me, remember? My husband changed his will and now the disgrace is such that I cannot return to my homeland. Yes, he gave me the house, he gave me enough to run it, but everything else he took from me, including my beloved Argentina.'

Rosalind looked at Consuela's beautiful, grief-stricken face and realized that she could hardly begin to know the depths of her suffering. Rosalind knew so much more than most, but even she didn't know the full story of what had happened at the time of Carmelo Santini's death. Consuela couldn't bring herself to speak of it the pain was so great. And the question that had trembled accusingly on Rosalind's lips earlier was already answered. Consuela had the bathhouse because Jake made her.

'What are you going to do about those girls?' Rosalind asked, looking at her watch. 'They'll be here soon, have you thought about what you're going to say?'

Consuela shook her head then shivered as though a storm-cloud had suddenly passed over the blazing sun. 'I don't know what to do,' she said. 'I keep telling myself they're young, they don't have so much to lose, they can survive it, but one of them, Danny, is already involved with him. I don't know how seriously, but you know how the young are, if you forbid it they will want it all the more. You know Danny's mother, Suzannah Spencer?'

'Yes, yes, I know her.'

'It would break her heart if anything happened to that girl.'

'I know,' Rosalind mumbled. It wasn't that she was feeling unsympathetic, it was simply that she was facing a crisis herself right now and just couldn't take on board any one else's.

Consuela smiled weakly. 'But let's not dwell on what might happen,' she said, 'when the unthinkable is already happening to you.'

Rosalind's heart gave a sickening lurch as she thought of what her beloved husband must be going through even as they spoke. 'Consuela,' she said softly, 'would you mind terribly . . .'

'No, of course I don't mind,' Consuela said, reading what Rosalind was about to say. 'He'll need you now. Call me when you can.'

Rosalind started to get up then stopped as she realized she was leaving Consuela in such distress. Her loyalties were badly torn, but Peter was dying. 'I'll always be there for you, Consuela,' she said. 'You know that, don't you?'

'I don't deserve it,' Consuela smiled sadly, 'but yes, I know.'

Within minutes the atmosphere around the table had changed so dramatically that Consuela could barely catch her breath. Louisa was so overwhelmed by the hotel's splendour that Consuela found herself laughing along with her at such guileless enthusiasm. In fact both Louisa and Danny appeared in such high spirits that it was impossible not to be drawn in. And in their own individual ways they looked so lovely that heads were constantly turning in their direction. It was undoubtedly Danny who was attracting the most attention, for she was the more beautiful of the two and she looked so radiant today that Consuela decided that to broach the subject of Jake as she'd intended would be a mistake.

'Hey!' Danny said suddenly as she handed the menu back to the waiter. 'We just saw Rosalind Carmichael driving off. She looked terrible. In fact she almost drove into us she was going so fast.'

Consuela chuckled. 'That is Rosalind's usual way of driving, I'm afraid,' she said. 'Always in a hurry. So, where's Sarah? I thought she was coming along too.'

'Sarah is in her new darkroom,' Louisa answered. 'She's shot about a hundred reels of film since we've been here so we're not expecting to see her for at least a week.'

Consuela appeared interested. 'What is she photographing?' she asked.

'Anything that moves,' Danny replied, her eyes moving about the terrace, 'especially us. Every time we turn round she's right there with her camera.'

'Not that you're complaining,' Louisa retorted, laughingly.

Danny threw her a look which brought a fond smile to Consuela's lips.

'And what have you two been doing with yourselves?' she wondered.

'What haven't we been doing?' Louisa laughed. And as she recounted their hilarious attempts at water-skiing, para-sailing and even a little scuba-diving plus the parties they'd been to and the whole general chaos that was taking over their lives, Danny interjected with teasing comments and obviously feigned boredom. Though Consuela was smiling she could have wept for the loss of her own youth and such enthusiasm for life. And Louisa, she noticed, was a good deal more beautiful than she'd at first thought. Her hair had lightened in the sun and it was now a soft caramel colour, her skin had darkened and her smile was quite dazzling. She was, Consuela realized, fascinating to watch, for there was an elegance, a grace to her movements that brought out her femininity in a way Consuela had seen in few other women.

As Louisa sipped her wine she knew she was being quietly assessed and was intrigued to know what Consuela was thinking. Not that she was going to ask, any more than she was going to bring up the subject of Jake. True, Consuela was probably the one person who could tell her what she longed to know, but he had asked her to trust him and that was what she was going to do.

'Just look at her, will you?' Danny said, making Louisa blink. 'Oh, hello, you are still with us,' Danny grinned. 'You'll have to excuse her,' she added to Consuela, 'she's a writer, drifts off with the muse, you know what I mean?'

'What are you writing?' Consuela smiled.

'I'm in the planning stages of what I hope will be a ten-part series,' Louisa answered, feeling on quite a high because of all the work she'd managed to get done in the past couple of days – since she'd seen Jake.

'Did you contact Señor Morandi, by the way?' Consuela asked, covering her wine glass as a waiter tried to refill it.

'Not yet,' Louisa answered. 'But we're going to. What sort of things is he looking for, do you know?'

'I'm not really sure,' Consuela confessed. 'I've only met him once, but I think he's had quite a few successes in feature films and television.'

'Does he speak English?' Louisa asked – it was easy to forget that not everyone did when they seemed so surrounded by English-speakers.

'Mmm,' Consuela answered, taking a mouthful of the delicious *Saint Jacques aux cèpes*. 'His English is very good if I remember correctly.'

'I don't know if we'll be able to get Sarah interested,' Danny commented. 'She's dead set on changing careers right now, but you and I could always go to see him, Louisa.' She picked up a napkin to fan herself. 'God, it's hot,' she sighed.

'It'll get much hotter than this by August,' Consuela warned. 'But you'll be more used to it by then. Besides, we have some rain forecast over the next few days, that should help cool you down a . . .' She stopped and followed the direction of Danny's eyes to see a stunning blonde woman, in the very briefest of bikinis, stroll across the terrace down into the garden below. Just about everyone in the restaurant had paused to watch her, for as one of the world's leading models she was as easily recognized as she was admired.

Louisa wasn't in the least surprised when a few minutes later Danny disappeared into the ladies' room. By the time she returned she would be wearing the white one-piece swimsuit she'd brought with her and her flawless, tanned skin would be coated in oil. Today was obviously one of the days when she wanted the limelight and as gorgeous as Gretchen Gunter was even she would find it hard to compete with Danny's exotically dark and voluptuous beauty. Louisa smiled to herself. Danny was so like a child at times, so easy to read and desperate to be noticed, and with a stab of unpalatable jealousy she couldn't help wondering what Jake really thought of her.

'I am glad to have this chance to speak to you alone,' Consuela said. 'Johann tells me that you left the bathhouse earlier than the others, that the entertainment wasn't quite to your . . . How shall we put it? Taste?'

'Oh, please don't think . . .'

'It's all right,' Consuela smiled, putting up her hand. 'I'm not offended, I was just hoping that you weren't.'

'No, not at all,' Louisa assured her, feeling herself start to colour. 'It was just, well, it was simply that . . .' What could she say when the truth was that she'd left early because of Jake? It seemed so absurd when at that point they'd never even spoken to each other.

'You don't have to explain,' Consuela laughed. 'I understand.

You may have noticed that I didn't join in myself – you see it's not really to my taste either.'

Louisa looked at her, not wanting to pry, but hoping she would say more.

'Why do I have the bathhouse, is that what you're asking yourself?' Consuela said. She gazed out to sea for a moment, smiling distantly to herself as she absently stroked Louisa's hand. 'It is there for the enjoyment of my friends,' she said softly. 'It gives them great pleasure, helps them to relax from the stresses of their lives and their marriages, in an atmosphere of soothing calm and of course discretion. This sort of thing has been available to men for as far back as any of us can remember, so why should it not be available to women?'

Louisa shrugged, as if to say, why not indeed?

'But that doesn't really answer your question, does it?' Consuela went on. 'The reason that I do not indulge myself in its pleasures is really very complex and one that I have no wish to burden you with. I trust Jake saw you home safely,' she added casually, taking a sip of water.

'Yes, thank you,' Louisa answered. She paused, then no longer able to curb her curiosity she said, 'Is he – is he a relative of yours?'

Consuela laughed. 'Jake's family and mine go back over many years,' she answered. 'We know each other well.' Her eyes were dancing with humour. 'Do I detect an interest?' she said.

'No, no, not at all,' Louisa assured her.

'And what about Danny? They've seen each other once or twice, I hear. Is she smitten with him yet?'

'I don't know,' Louisa answered, inwardly reacting to the 'once or twice'. She hadn't known for sure whether or not Danny had seen Jake again after the first time, but it seemed that she had – and that Jake had mentioned it to Consuela.

'Maybe it is he who is smitten with her,' Consuela laughed, giving Louisa a conspiratorial wink. 'That'll be hard for Jake to take if it's true, he's not used to having things that way round. But maybe you should warn Danny to take care. He has something of a reputation for breaking hearts and I should hate to see her unhappy.'

'If you knew Danny better,' Louisa said, forcing herself to smile, 'I'm sure you'd agree she can take care of herself.'

'I'm sure she can,' Consuela said, picking up her wine. 'But if I were you I'd give Señor Morandi a call, because it won't hurt to have Danny's mind a little more occupied than it is.'

Later that night Louisa and Sarah were sitting quietly on the terrace, sipping rosé wine and watching the tiny crackles of light from the fire-flies.

'So what do you think?' Louisa said, having just recounted her conversation with Consuela.

'I'm not sure,' Sarah answered. 'There's obviously something going on, I mean after what Jean-Claude said to you about Jake and now with Consuela trying to get you to warn Danny off him.'

She turned to look at Louisa, studying her gentle profile in the subdued light of the terrace.

'Did Danny say where she was going tonight?' Louisa asked, still watching the fire-flies.

'Yes.'

Louisa allowed a few seconds to tick by before saying. 'Well, I guess that answers my question. Did he call her, do you know?'

'I didn't hear the phone so I don't know what their arrangements were.' She paused for a moment, sensing how badly Louisa was feeling. 'You haven't told me what happened between the two of you the other night,' she prompted.

Louisa's lips pursed at the corners as she looked down at her wine. 'Nothing happened,' she said. 'We kissed on the side of the road, as you know, and that was it.'

Sarah looked perplexed, clearly not sure whether or not to push a little harder.

Louisa lifted her glass and drank. She desperately wanted to confide in Sarah, and since Danny was with Jake again tonight she didn't see any reason why she shouldn't. Except what was there to say that wasn't going to make her look the prize fool that she was?

'I take it you do still feel the same way about him?' Sarah probed gently.

Louisa shrugged. 'I told you, Consuela thinks he's probably besotted with Danny and since they're obviously together again tonight, I guess that just about wraps it up for me, wouldn't you say?'

There wasn't much Sarah could say about that so changing the subject slightly she said, 'I think we should go and see this Morandi guy.'

Louisa turned to her in surprise. 'I didn't think you were interested in getting back into TV.'

Sarah shrugged. 'I'm not particularly, but swanning around here with nothing much to occupy our minds isn't really working, is it? And who knows, he might come up with something that will make me change my mind.'

Jake was stretched out along the saloon deck box, his feet resting on a dorade as he idly smoked a cigarette and gazed up at the night sky. The crew had gone ashore and he was relishing these rare moments of solitude. Somewhere inside the port a party was in full swing, but the noise was no more intrusive than the gentle slap of the waves against the hull. His mind was so distant from these shores that it had suspended the reality of his surroundings, just as the events in his life had suspended the joy of untroubled thought.

Taking a last draw on his cigarette, he cast it into the sea and swung himself up into a sitting position. His expression was hard, almost angry, his fists were clenched. He looked out across the sea and seeing the lights of the Carmichael's yacht disappearing into the horizon a grim smile twisted his mouth.

Hearing the gentle chug of an engine he glanced back towards the port. Bob was on his way back, though earlier than expected. There was someone in the dinghy with him and when Jake realized who it was he started to laugh.

He stayed where he was waiting for them to come aboard,

then with no more than a cursory glance in Danny's direction he looked at Bob.

Bob muttered in Danny's ear while her sultry eyes slaked Jake's body, her lips curving in a slow, promising smile. When Bob had finished she turned, sauntered across the deck and with a lingering glance back over her shoulder she descended the gleaming, varnished steps into the luxurious cabins of the *Valhalla*.

'Well?' Jake said when she'd gone.

Bob reached inside his shirt and drew out a thick wad of bank notes. Jake took it, flicked it, then tucked it inside his own shirt. 'Anything else?' he said.

Bob looked at him for a moment before answering. 'She was in Guadalajara three days ago,' he said.

Jake's eyes became suddenly hard and the shock that passed through him was visible. 'Where's Fernando now?' he asked.

'On his way to Guadalajara.'

'Is he sure it was her?'

'Yeah, he reckons so.'

Jake stared at him, but his thoughts were once again a great distance from the decks of the *Valhalla*. Then turning abruptly he said, 'I'm going ashore. Get onto Marianne. Tell her I want to see her, tonight. She knows where I'll be.'

Bob's eyes shifted downwards, reminding Jake he had a guest.

'Tonight,' Jake repeated then swung himself down into the dinghy.

Bob stood in the darkness with his hands resting on the lifeline, watching the small boat speed across the water. A few minutes later he took a phone from his pocket and called Marianne. That done, he turned towards the coach house. Time now to go deal with Danny Spencer.

10

Mario Morandi was sitting in the chaos of his office on the third floor of a nineteenth-century building just off the Avenue Jean Médecin in Nice. As his mournful brown eyes darted about the stacks of film cans, haphazard piles of video cassettes and endless reams of typed paper, his expression became increasingly anxious. The din of the traffic outside was bothering him, and each time a lorry roared past or someone hooted angrily on a car horn he winced. The heat was getting to him too, as he repeatedly picked up his handkerchief to mop the sweat from his troubled face.

There was a stack of messages in front of him, most of which needed to be dealt with yesterday and on top of them was a huge plan of a schedule which, unless he could master the art of being in four places at once, he was never going to make work.

He called himself a producer, which from time to time he was, but on the whole he was a high-faluting Mr Fixit, who couldn't say no to anyone, no matter how impossible or outlandish the request – which was how he'd come to land himself in the kind of mess that etched his naturally worried expression deeper into his face and had, he was sure, given him an ulcer.

He was about to get up from his desk when the door opened and Aphrodite, his Greek assistant, put her head in. 'Your visitors have arrived,' she told him, then laughed at the blank expression that came over his handsome face.

'The friends of Consuela Santini,' she reminded him, coming into the room and closing the door behind her.

'Yes, oh yes,' he said sounding very depressed.

Aphrodite grinned, pushed her long, frizzy brown hair back

over her shoulder and walked to his desk to dab his face with his handkerchief. 'Don't look so worried,' she told him, dropping a kiss on his receding hairline. 'It'll be fine.'

'Will it?' he asked despondently. 'I have a feeling I'm going to make a real hash of it.'

'You won't,' she assured him. 'Now, shall I run out for some lemonade?'

'Mmm,' he responded, clearly deep in thought. 'You'd better ask them if they'd like some too. Did you get any joy from Rome, by the way?'

'The lights are on their way. I've found some editing facilities for Frank Bull's production too. Ours are all booked up. Now,' she tilted his face up to hers, kissed him lingeringly on the mouth and said, 'I'd better remind you that you're taking me to dinner tonight. You promised and I'm holding you to it.'

'I'm looking forward to it,' he said and as he smiled the soft light in his hazel eyes added a quality to his sombre expression that more accurately portrayed the man behind it. 'What would I do without you?' he said.

'I really don't know,' she replied, kissing him again. 'Incidentally,' she added, nodding towards the outer office, 'only two of them have turned up.'

Morandi was suddenly depressed again, watching Aphrodite wander back to the door. 'You'd better contact Jake Mallory and tell him that,' he said.

Aphrodite turned back, looked as though she was about to say something, then merely shrugged and pulled open the door.

Morandi was already on his feet when Sarah and Louisa walked in and the first thing they noticed about him was his incredible height. It was rare to find an Italian over six feet and Morandi had passed the mark by several inches. The second thing they noticed was his deeply troubled frown. Sarah glanced at Louisa, then moved forward holding out her hand.

'I'm Sarah Lovell,' she told him, surprised by his firm, cool grip when his brow was sweating so profusely. 'And this is Louisa Kramer.'

'It is a great pleasure to meet you both,' Morandi said,

leaning further across his desk to shake Louisa's hand. 'Please, won't you sit down.'

Sarah and Louisa looked around at the cluttered chairs and Sarah felt a moment's nostalgia for the bedlam of her old office.

'Oh, I'm sorry,' Morandi said, hastening around his desk to clear some space. He sent books and cassettes crashing to the floor then held the backs of the chairs as first Louisa, then Sarah, sat down. He seemed so absurdly polite that Louisa wanted to laugh.

'So,' he said, returning to his own chair. 'How can I help you, ladies?'

Ah, there was an accent, Sarah registered, it was the first note of it, for so far his English had been incredibly Oxford. She was on the point of answering when she noticed how suddenly pained he looked. 'Are you all right, Mr Morandi?' she said solicitously.

His eyes opened wide. 'Oh, yes. Yes, I'm very well thank you,' he answered. 'How are you?'

Sarah's lips twitched. 'I'm fine, thank you, it's just that you looked a little, uh, bothered, about something.'

'*Si*?' he said surprised.

'*Si*,' she nodded when he didn't continue.

'Ah, no. I was trying to remember. I was thinking that when Señora Santini called me she said there were three of you. But now,' he spread his hands so flamboyantly it was as though he were ending a conjuring trick, 'you are two!' he declared.

Sarah could sense that Louisa was having an even harder time keeping a straight face than she was. 'Yes, I'm afraid that Danny wasn't able to come today,' she explained, 'so as you say, we are two.'

'Three including me,' he said delightedly.

Sarah looked frankly and humorously into his eyes. To her surprise he returned the look and then to her even greater surprise he started to blush.

'So, you are interested in making films,' he said and the

suddenness of his despondency caused Sarah and Louisa to look at one another in bewilderment.

'Well, uh,' Sarah began.

'We don't actually have any projects ready to go into production at this time,' Louisa said. 'We just thought it would be a good idea to meet. The market in England is slow at the moment and well . . .' She shrugged. 'It's always interesting to see what other people are doing.'

'*Si, si*, of course,' he said. 'But you don't have any projects yourselves?'

'Not at the moment,' Sarah said apologetically.

'It is of no matter,' he said, the astonishing brightness of his smile lighting up his face. 'I have many projects and not enough people to make them. I am a very busy man, I need more staff, more people willing to work, it is not easy, I must find the right people.'

'Of course,' Sarah agreed. 'Uh, what kind of projects do you have?'

'All kinds. One kind,' he corrected. 'All variations on the same theme. You don't want to make these films,' he added.

Sarah turned to Louisa, unsure whether that was a question or a statement.

'Actually,' Louisa said carefully, 'we're a little more interested in finding out how we might go about raising finance for films ourselves. Well, TV actually.'

He appeared to be quite taken with this idea and clasping his large hands together in front of him he said, 'I think yes, that maybe I can help you with that.' Again his smile was so transforming that Sarah almost felt she was meeting two totally different people. 'I have many contacts here in France and in Italy and Germany, I will be happy to introduce you,' he told them cheerfully.

'Thank you,' Sarah said.

This time when he looked at her she could feel her own cheeks starting to reflect the colour rising in his. 'Um,' she said, tearing her eyes away and turning to Louisa.

'Uh, exactly what is the theme of your films?' Louisa said,

feeling that polite interest was the best way of filling the awkward pause.

At that moment Aphrodite returned with the lemonade.

'So,' Morandi said as the door closed behind her. 'You want to make my films. I shall be glad to hand them over.'

Sarah blinked, wondering if maybe she'd passed out for a moment and missed a vital link in the conversation. When did they say they wanted to make his films?

'You have no problem with morals, I hope,' Morandi muttered, looking uncomfortably at the window. 'It is not good to have a problem with morals, it does not help.'

Sarah's loss for a response took her eyes back to Louisa.

Louisa grinned. 'Would I be right in thinking, Mr Morandi,' she said, 'that you make adult movies?'

Morandi's colour sank to the roots of his thinning brown hair.

'And you would like us to make them for you?' Louisa added helpfully.

Sarah looked at her in amazement. That had almost sounded like an offer. Then her head spun back to Morandi as he said, 'If you prefer you can act in them. You are actresses, no?'

'No,' Louisa said, hardly able to contain her laughter. 'Danny, our friend, is an actress, but I think we're talking at cross-purposes here. You see, as I said earlier, Sarah and I are exploring the possible avenues of finance in France for our own projects. Not,' she added hastily, 'that we have any objection to the films you make, it's simply that they're not for us.'

'I understand,' he said. '*Si*, *si*, I understand. My poor mother, she would turn in her grave if she knew that I make these films. It is terrible, disgusting, I am glad you no want to do it. Very glad.'

Sarah, totally bemused by now, decided to let Louisa continue. Besides, she was happy just to watch this man for she had never come across anyone who appeared so at odds with himself.

'But if you don't approve of what you do, Mr Morandi,'

Louisa said, 'then if you don't mind me asking, why do you do it?'

'Why do any of us do anything?' he sighed. 'We do for money. I start my company. It was good company. A little editing here, a little shooting there and then a request come in to do scenes for a TV programme, very late night TV programme for Holland. I take it, I help out, like I help everyone and then in comes another and another. After that it is not just the TV, it is private videos too. Now I have to make them or the boys . . .' He slid a finger across his throat.

'Boys?' Sarah echoed.

'The boys from Naples,' he explained. 'They are here in Nice. They own Nice, they own me. I do as they say, I live. But you, you no want to be involved. You are good women, I can see. You stay that way, you don't become involved.'

'No, well, no of course not,' Louisa said, wondering if her imagination was going too far or if he really was talking about the Mafia.

'You like to come to a party on Friday night?' Morandi asked.

Louisa's mouth opened and stayed that way. She turned to Sarah – time for her to take over.

'You mean Friday night as in tomorrow night?' Sarah said.

Morandi hastily consulted his diary. '*Si*, as in tomorrow night,' he answered. 'I will introduce you to people who might be able to help you. It is party at the Colombe d'Or hotel in St Paul. They are very nice people, very respectable.'

'Well, that's very kind of you,' Sarah said, smiling and frowning.

'You call me, yes?' he said.

'Yes, we'll do that,' Sarah said as she and Louisa picked up their bags.

'And please,' he added as he showed them out through the reception, where Aphrodite was frantically dealing with the phones, 'if there is anything else I can do for you, anything at all, you call me.'

A few minutes later Louisa and Sarah fell out onto the busy, noisy street, clutching their sides with laughter.

'You didn't really fancy him?' Louisa cried.

'Maybe fancy's too strong a word,' Sarah laughed, 'but isn't he a scream? Have you ever seen so many emotions cross one face in such a short space of time?'

'Never. But what's intriguing me is the way the conversation suddenly turned when his secretary came back into the office.'

'Yes, didn't it? I thought I'd fallen asleep or something. Do you think there's something going on between them?'

'Looked pretty much like it. Anyway, what do you think about this party tomorrow night?'

'I'd like to go,' Sarah said. 'I mean, if it's at the Colombe d'Or then nothing unseemly's going to happen there, is it?'

'I wouldn't have thought so.'

'Will you come?' Sarah asked. 'Like he said, we could make some useful contacts.'

'We?' Louisa said playfully. 'I thought you only came today for moral support.'

'I did. And I'll do it again tomorrow. If you're interested, that is.'

'Your altruism touches me deeply,' Louisa grinned. 'And yes, I'll go to the party.'

They paused to look in the window of a *parfumerie*. 'Do you think he's really Italian?' Sarah remarked casually as they walked on.

'If he is,' Louisa responded, 'then I'm Jamaican.'

'Do you know what I think?' Sarah went on. 'I think he's English. His accent's all over the place I know, but there's something about him that looks English.'

'I'd say you're probably right,' Louisa answered. 'But what I'm wondering . . .'

'Is why Consuela Santini sent us to a blue movie producer?' Sarah provided.

'Exactly. Except she did say she'd only met him the once, so maybe she doesn't know. Anyway, tell me, what did you make of that comment about the "boys" in Nice?'

'Mafia?' Sarah said.

'Mmm, that's what I thought and there are plenty of them around here, so they say.' She turned to look at Sarah. 'It didn't ring true to me though, did it to you?'

'No, not really,' Sarah sighed, feeling herself starting to wilt in the heat. 'If you ask me the guy's a bit of a crackpot, but we'll go to the party anyway and see if he really can put you in touch with anyone useful.'

They stopped again, rifling through a circular clothes rail outside a shop. 'Was it my imagination,' Sarah said, holding up a pair of shorts, 'or did I hear Jake Mallory's name mentioned just before we went in?'

Louisa's eyes came up. 'I thought I did, but I wasn't sure,' she said.

'It seems to me,' Sarah said, putting the shorts down as they turned to walk on, 'that something pretty peculiar is going on around here.'

Louisa could feel her insides starting to swirl. On the way over in the car she'd told Sarah the things Jake had said to her on Sunday night. She'd done it out of pique really, because for the second night running Danny hadn't come home. 'Do you think Danny knows what kind of producer Morandi is?' she asked.

Sarah shrugged. 'I wouldn't have thought so. If she did I'm sure she'd have mentioned it.'

They stopped to cross the road and said no more until they were descending the steps into the underground car park. 'I was just thinking about Rosalind Carmichael,' Louisa said. 'I think I told you, didn't I, that Danny and I saw her leaving the Grand Hotel? Consuela said that she always drove like a loony, but I saw her face and I'm telling you, she looked really upset.'

'Mmm,' Sarah said thoughtfully. 'It's all mighty odd, isn't it, and to tell you the truth I wouldn't mind trying to get to the bottom of it.'

Louisa didn't answer straight away. Despite all the evidence telling her that Danny was involved with Jake there was still a very strong part of her that desperately wanted to do as he'd asked and trust him. But on the other hand maybe she'd be doing herself a favour if she found out what she could about him now before she went in any deeper than she already was.

'How do you propose we go about it?' she said unlocking the car door.

Sarah shrugged. 'Go to all the things they invite us to, I suppose. Keep our eyes and ears open and maybe ask around a bit. And we could always try a spot of undercover work.'

'Don't let's get too carried away,' Louisa said, then laughed as she realized what Sarah was getting at. 'No, I am most definitely not going to bounce around in front of Morandi's cameras,' she declared.

'Oh,' Sarah said. 'I thought that might have been right up your street. What about behind the cameras? I can see you as a purveyor of porn.'

'Thank you,' Louisa smiled sweetly getting into the car.

'Does he strike you as the leather type?' Sarah laughed, absently watching the sunburned tourists rambling their way to and from the pebbled beach.

'I don't know, but he does strike me as your type,' Louisa teased.

'Honestly?' Sarah said turning to look at her.

'Why not?' Louisa shrugged, unsure whether Sarah was really as interested as she was making out or if this was just another of her wind-ups.

'Because the guy's a few frames short of a reel,' Sarah responded, 'which now I come to think of it probably does make him my type. And no matter what's really going on between him and Jake and Consuela and God knows who else, I got quite good vibes about him? Did you?'

'I didn't fancy him if that's what you mean,' Louisa answered. 'But you know, thinking about it, I sort of got the impression he was trying to warn us off.'

'Did you?' Sarah said. 'I didn't pick that up, but if you're right it just makes me all the more determined to find out what's going on.'

Half an hour later they arrived home to find Danny lying by the pool in a shimmering black G-string and a pair of sunglasses.

'Hi,' she called out as Sarah and Louisa got out of the car. 'I got your note. How did it go?'

'You missed a treat,' Louisa told her, laughing to hide the unsavoury feelings she was experiencing as Danny got to her feet and sauntered towards them, her magnificent body fresh from Jake's bed. 'We got ourselves a job offer and an invite to a party. Oh, and Sarah fell in love.'

'I did not!' Sarah cried.

Danny was watching her, smiling affectionately. 'You're blushing,' she teased.

'Oh, honestly,' Sarah said, rolling her eyes. 'He makes porn films for the Mafia, or so he says. Come to think of it, Louisa, if he really is working for the Mafia he'd never have told us. Not just like that when he didn't really have a clue who we were.'

'True,' Louisa agreed, sinking into a chair as they reached the terrace. 'Tell me, Danny,' she said, 'did you have any idea that Morandi was a blue movie producer?'

Danny shook her head. 'If I'd known I'd have told you and saved you the trip,' she answered. 'Unless you've decided you want to go in with him,' she added teasingly.

'Sarah might,' Louisa grinned, ducking as Sarah tried to slap her. 'And I expect the offer's still open if you're interested, Danny. How do you fancy becoming a porn star?'

Danny's eyebrows were raised. 'I don't think so somehow,' she said, the same edge to her voice as Louisa's. Then, looking Louisa full in the face she gave her such a dazzling smile that Louisa's fingers itched to slap her. If she had spent the night with Jake again, she didn't have to gloat over it.

'What time did you get home?' Sarah asked, kicking off her shoes.

'An hour or so ago,' Danny answered, picking up the suntan oil and massaging it into her heavy breasts. She knew the gardener was watching her, that he'd hardly taken his eyes off her since he arrived. He'd been her camera and she'd enjoyed the performance, carrying a drink to him on a tray, watching him try not to look at her breasts and failing. No, she had no desire to perform these little scenarios publicly, it was far better having the cameras roll inside her head and trying to manipulate others into playing out a script that was totally unknown to them. Mahmud was shy, a little too respectful, but she'd planned her scenario around it and had Louisa and Sarah not returned when they did, she'd probably be wearing nothing at all by now and asking him to rub oil on her back. Still, there'd be other occasions, just like there would with Jake Mallory. Which reminded her:

'I didn't know you'd been on board the *Valhalla*, Sarah,' she said, sitting on the ground and stretching out her legs.

'Didn't you?' Sarah said, nonplussed.

Danny shrugged. 'You never mentioned it to me. I only know because I sneaked a look in your darkroom. Those photographs are terrific, you know. Have you seen them?' she asked Louisa.

Louisa nodded. 'I told her they were,' she answered. 'The best she's taken yet.'

'Are you planning to show Jake?' Danny wondered casually.

'I hadn't really thought about it,' Sarah replied, sensing the hostility in the air and wishing they could get off the subject.

'Well I think you should. And you'll never guess who agrees with me?' Danny's violet eyes were flashing with intrigue and laughter. 'Erik Svensson!' she declared.

Sarah stared at her. 'Erik Svensson has seen them?' she said, confused.

Danny nodded. 'Jean-Claude brought him over to say hello about half an hour ago so I hope you don't mind, but I thought they were so good that I invited him and Jean-Claude in to take a look.'

'No, no, of course I don't mind,' Sarah said starting to smile. 'Did he really like them?' she said.

'He really liked them,' Danny laughed. 'If you don't believe me then you can ask him yourself, we've been invited over for aperitifs at seven. And I'd better warn you, if you're after falling in love with anyone then Erik Svensson is going to blow your mind he's so damned gorgeous. *And*,' she went on, 'there is no wife in tow, they've split up.'

'She doesn't trust the good-looking ones,' Louisa teased.

'Then she's probably the wisest of us all,' Danny laughed. 'Anyway, tell me more about this Morandi.'

'You can meet him for yourself,' Sarah said. 'He's invited us to a party at the Colombe d'Or tomorrow night.'

'What kind of party?'

Leaving Sarah to convince Danny that this was a party she really should go to, Louisa went inside to fix them all a drink. By the time she came back Danny was holding her sides laughing.

'All right, all right,' she cried, holding up a hand to stop Sarah's hilarious account of Morandi's quicksilver emotions. 'I'll come, but in the meantime why don't we invite Jake over for an evening to see these photographs?'

Louisa felt her insides churning. The last thing she wanted was to spend an evening with Jake while Danny was there. But on the other hand it was perhaps one way of finding out where she really stood with him.

'Well you can call him,' Sarah declared. 'For me, modesty prevails.'

'I would if I had his number,' Danny frowned, causing a wave of spiteful pleasure to coast through Louisa. 'He always calls me,' Danny went on, immediately dampening Louisa's triumph. 'But Consuela's sure to know how to contact him. Why don't we call her and ask her a bit more about Morandi at the same time. You can do that, Sarah, then I'll speak to her about Jake.'

'I'm not asking her about Morandi!' Sarah cried. 'She might think I'm interested. You do it, Louisa.'

'All right,' Louisa said, rolling her eyes. 'Where's the phone?'

Danny went inside to get it and dialling the number for Louisa she passed her the receiver.

'Ah, Louisa, *chérie*,' Consuela said when Louisa told her who was calling. 'How are you?'

'Very well, thank you,' Louisa answered. 'Are you?'

'I am very hot,' Consuela laughed. 'But tell me, did you and Danny meet with Señor Morandi today?'

'No, Sarah and I did.'

'Danny didn't go with you?' Consuela said.

'No, she couldn't make it,' Louisa answered, looking at Sarah as she wondered why Consuela was making it sound important that Danny should have gone.

'Ah, *Mon Dieu*!' Consuela gasped when Louisa had finished telling her about the meeting. 'I am so sorry, I had no idea. He seemed such a nice man when I met him, not that kind of person at all. Oh, *chérie*, what can I say? I would never have mentioned it had I known.'

'It's OK. No harm done,' Louisa assured her, then started to smile as she heard Consuela's gentle laughter.

'Does he really make those kind of films?' she said.

'So he claims. He even offered us parts in them.'

'*Mama mia*!' Consuela exclaimed. 'I do hope you turned him down.'

'We did,' Louisa laughed.

'Well, I must think again,' Consuela said. 'I am sure I can come up with someone else who can help you. Someone a little less, how shall we put it, unconventional.' She tutted and sighed. 'My, my,' she said. 'I really would never have thought it. He seemed such a shy man and so, well, ordinary and inoffensive. It just goes to show, doesn't it, how deceiving appearances can be? Now, I must try to remember how I came to be introduced to him, because I wouldn't want to make the same mistake again. But I can't think who on earth I know who would know a man in his field. Except . . .' She paused. 'Yes, I remember now who introduced us,' her tone was suddenly a shade darker. 'If only I'd remembered before I would never have suggested you meet him. *Oh là là*, the memory isn't what it used to be when you reach my age, and when someone appears as sweet and polite and charming as Señor

Morandi one is apt to forget who his friends are. Again, *chérie*, I am sorry. But as I say, I shall try to think of someone else. Meanwhile, how are your friends?'

'Oh, they're fine,' Louisa answered. 'They're sitting right here, roasting in the sun. In fact Danny would like a . . .' She stopped as Consuela covered the mouthpiece and spoke to someone the other end.

'I am sorry,' she said coming back on the line. 'What were we saying?'

'Uh, actually,' Louisa said, lifting her eyes back to Danny. 'We were wanting to ask you if you knew how we could contact Jake?'

Consuela chuckled. 'My dear, you are in luck for he has just walked in the door. I'll pass you over.'

Louisa's heart somersaulted and without thinking she handed the phone to Danny. 'He's there,' she whispered.

Danny blanched slightly, but took the receiver and nestled it on her shoulder.

'Hi,' Jake's voice came over the line.

'Hi,' Danny drawled. 'How are you?'

'I'm good. And you?'

'The same,' Danny smiled, winking at Louisa. 'We were just wondering if you'd like to come over and see the photographs Sarah's taken of the *Valhalla*. They're pretty good.'

There was silence for a moment before he said, 'Sure, why not? When are you thinking?'

'Whenever's convenient for you.'

'How about tomorrow?'

Danny's eyes narrowed and as the intimacy in her voice deepened to a sensuous purr, she began stroking her fingers lightly over her breasts. 'That'll be fine,' she said. 'Around eight.'

'When's he coming?' Sarah wanted to know as Danny clicked off the phone.

'Tomorrow night,' Danny answered.

'But we're going to the Colombe d'Or tomorrow night!'

'Oh gosh,' Danny said, clasping a hand to her mouth. 'I

forgot. But it doesn't matter, you can still go, I'll stay behind and show him the photos.'

Sarah glanced at Louisa. Was she also wondering if Danny had really forgotten? It was impossible to tell for Louisa's expression was giving nothing away. 'I'd rather show him myself,' Sarah said.

'I'm sure Danny'll do a wonderful job for you,' Louisa said, struggling to keep the fury from her voice. 'And I quite want to go to that party, so let's keep the arrangement as it stands, shall we?'

11

'I'm going to put a stop to this with Danielle Spencer,' Consuela hissed, her green eyes flashing with rage.

Jake's upper lip curled viciously as he looked across the bed, the patch over his left eye lending a baleful menace to his fury. The scruffy bandanna knotted carelessly inside his open collar and ripped, oily jeans made him incongruous and even more threatening in the thick bands of sunlight streaming through the open windows onto the peach and cream satins of Consuela's bedroom.

'And just how are you gonna do that, Consuela?' he sneered.

Consuela's anger sat like a mask on her normally gentle face, contorting it horribly. 'Get out of here,' she spat. 'Get out and leave me alone.'

'Are you sure that's what you want?' he challenged, his eyebrows raised mockingly.

Consuela's hands flew to her head. 'Stop tormenting me this way,' she cried. 'Just stop! I can't stand any more.'

'Consuela, this is me you're talking to,' he seethed. 'So quit the acting, you know what I want, now just tell me what I have to do to get it.'

'There's nothing you can do. There's nothing I want from you, not any more.'

'Is that so? Well I want plenty from you, Consuela, and I'm not out of your life until I get it. So where is she, Consuela? Where are you hiding her?'

'She's dead, Jake! Do you hear me? She's *dead*!'

'No,' he said shaking his head. 'She's alive.'

Consuela's mouth was trembling. 'For God's sake!' she

implored. 'You've seen the grave! How much more proof do you need?'

'That grave is as empty as your soul, Consuela,' he said savagely.

'Oh God, please don't do this to me,' she sobbed, pushing a fist to her mouth. 'She's in the grave, Jake.'

'Then how do you account for the fact she's been seen?'

'It's not possible,' she choked, squeezing her eyes tightly shut.

Jake glared at her so maliciously that it seemed to stain the air between them. 'I'm gonna find her,' he said. 'I'm gonna find her and when I do may God help you, Consuela.'

Consuela started as the door slammed behind him, then stumbled against the bed as Marianne came out of the bathroom.

Marianne crossed the room quickly and took Consuela in her arms.

'You heard?' Consuela said hoarsely.

Marianne nodded.

'It is always the same,' Consuela said, dabbing her eyes. 'He just won't believe me.'

'But why, if he has seen the grave?'

'Because someone has told him that she is still alive and he is afraid it is true . . . But it isn't true. She is dead. My baby is dead . . .' She broke off sobbing, turning her face into Marianne's shoulder.

Marianne held her, rocking her gently, until finally the tears subsided and Consuela lifted her head.

'Just thank God he didn't find you here,' she smiled into Marianne's eyes, smoothing the silky blonde hair from her face.

For a while Marianne gazed back, then very slowly, very gently she leaned forward, her eyes fluttering closed as she kissed Consuela's mouth.

A few minutes later Consuela got up from the bed and went to the window in time to see Jake's car disappearing at the end of the drive. It was a shame, she was thinking to herself, that she hadn't managed to get Danny together with Mario Morandi today for Danny was the one person, she felt sure, who could have found out for her whether or not Morandi was working for Jake. But there'd be other times and other ways, she told herself as she turned back to Marianne. And if she could pull off what was forming in her mind then Danny Spencer, great actress that she was, was going to be Jake Mallory's downfall.

'Oh, Jesus Christ,' Erik Svensson groaned, closing his eyes and pressing himself up on his arms to penetrate deeper. His narrow hips were moving vigorously back and forth, his breathing was rapid, the blood was pulsing through him – he was going to come soon, much sooner than he intended.

Beneath him Danny pounded herself violently into him, clutching the headboard and feeling her breasts bounce deliciously over her ribs. She raised her mouth as his lips came down to meet hers. Their tongues entwined, she lowered her hands, scratched her nails over his back and buttocks, and lifted her legs even higher.

The light was dim, but not so dim that she couldn't see the tightening of his exquisite face as his semen started to spurt. He looked down into her smouldering blue eyes and groaned loudly as the seed continued to leap from his body, pulsing into hers as savagely as he was pounding her.

He didn't know how this had happened, couldn't even recall the moment they'd left Jean-Claude's terrace and come over here. All he knew was that one minute they were sitting there talking and the next she was lying here on this bed and he was plunging into her with an urgency he couldn't control.

From the moment he'd laid eyes on her he'd known he had to have her. Known too that no matter how long it took, how hard he might have to work at it, it would be worth it. She was the most beautiful, most sensuous creature he'd ever seen and in his profession he thought he'd seen them all. But just those few minutes this afternoon had been enough for him to fall under the crazy, bewitching spell of those unbelievable eyes and this body that could fuck like no other woman he'd ever known.

He'd talked about nothing else since he and Jean-Claude had left the garden, had been more nervous waiting for her to arrive than he'd ever been as a teenager. Jean-Claude had teased him, reminding him that this was how he'd felt with all three of his wives when he'd first met them, and though Jean-Claude might be right, Erik was certain that this time it was different.

At last he fell over her, panting, still throbbing at every pulse and pulled her tight against him. He had only just regained his breath when she pulled herself up, lifting one magnificent breast to his lips. He drew the fat, tender nipple deep into his mouth, taking the other between his fingers, rolling it gently. She began to moan and he raised his eyes, watching her head move from side to side, saw the muscles of her face tense and realized she was nearing orgasm. He sucked harder, lowered his hand to the join of her legs and inserted his fingers as far as they would go.

'Yes, oh, yes,' she murmured, twisting his thick blond hair in her fingers.

He pressed his thumb against her, heard her gasp and began to rotate it. She started to shudder, clutched him to her, scratching him, lifting one leg over him and pushing his hand hard into her. He pumped his fingers fast, bit down on her nipples and she screamed.

'Yes, yes,' she cried as her orgasm broke. 'Oh my God! *Yes*,' and rolling him onto his back she knelt over him. He was hard again now, powerfully hard. He drew her onto him, penetrating the hot, saturated, pulsating depths of her and began to thrust.

Within minutes he was shooting into her again, hardly able to believe the incredible force of his climax, or the insatiable hunger of her passion.

It was after midnight when Erik finally emerged from the bedroom, padding barefoot to the kitchen, desperate for a drink. Fortunately he'd put on his undershorts, for Louisa and Sarah were on the terrace enjoying a nightcap.

'Hi,' he said, grinning at them sheepishly. His white blond hair was hopelessly dishevelled, his deep blue eyes were shining and his mouth looked as red and sore as it was.

'Hi,' Louisa said, unable to stop herself admiring the perfection of his physique.

'I was just getting a drink,' he explained.

'Help yourself,' Louisa said, her eyes twinkling merrily up at him.

'Danny still in one piece is she?' Sarah enquired, wincing as Louisa kicked her under the table.

Erik's eyes moved from one to the other of them. He looked so uncertain that a little devil in Sarah decided to compound matters by saying, 'Did you ever learn to shake hands first?'

'Ignore her,' Louisa told him, wanting desperately to laugh. 'I take it Danny's asleep.'

'Yes,' he said. 'Uh, can I get a drink for either of you?'

'Make yourself at home, why don't you?' Sarah muttered.

'Yes, I'd love a top-up,' Louisa said quickly, handing him her brandy glass. 'You'll find it just inside the kitchen. What on earth's got into you?' she hissed to Sarah when he'd gone.

'I don't know,' Sarah grumbled. 'Well no, actually, I do. We were supposed to be meeting him to talk about my photography and he never once took his eyes off Danny. What's more, I'm seriously pissed off at her for offering to show him *my* darkroom when it was just a ruse to get him over here to screw her ass off.'

'I see. Jealous,' Louisa stated, resting her chin on her hand.

'No. Pissed off.'

'Oh, so it's got nothing to do with the fact that you fancy him?'

'I don't fancy him. I was much more interested in my fledgling career, much good it did me. Anyway, what the hell's the matter with the woman? Has she got to screw *every* man she meets or is it just the ones we . . .'

'Sssh, he's coming,' Louisa warned. 'And if you're pissed off with Danny take it out on her, not Erik. Thanks,' she said as he handed her a brandy she didn't actually want.

'Do you mind if I sit with you?' he asked politely.

'No, please do,' Louisa said waving him towards a chair.

'I can't imagine what you must think of me,' he grinned,

but still managing to look as though he actually did care what they thought.

Louisa very nearly burst out laughing for that surely should have been Danny's line. 'Danny is a very beautiful woman,' she said helpfully.

He nodded and his deep blue eyes sparkled with such captivating humour that Louisa found herself smiling along with him. 'She is very special,' he said. 'I knew that the moment I met her. I think, I hope, she feels the same way.'

Such frankness and surprising insecurity in a man whose reputation for his conquests almost surpassed that of his profession was, Louisa thought, quite touchingly disarming.

'Oh, I'm sure she does,' Louisa said confidently, happier with Danny tonight than she had been in a while.

'You are?' Sarah said, looking at her loftily.

Louisa gave her a daggered look and turned back to Erik. 'So how long are you staying with Jean-Claude?' she asked.

'Until the weekend. Then I shall go on to my apartment in Monaco.'

'Oh, I see.'

There was an awkward pause then that Erik suddenly filled with, 'Please don't think badly of Danny for the way we behaved tonight. You see, we just couldn't help ourselves. When something like that happens between two people there is no point in resisting it, I'm sure you'll agree?'

'Oh totally,' Louisa assured him, covering her smile with her glass while Sarah gaped at him in disbelief. This poor, misguided fool was actually defending Danny's honour! Hadn't it occurred to him yet that she was the hottest thing to trot this side of the intergalactic highways?

'I should like,' he said to Sarah, 'if you would permit, to see the shots you have taken of Danny. She tells me there are quite a number. And we can, if you like, perhaps photograph her together.'

'Oh, I'd love that,' Sarah replied, her voice dripping with sarcasm. 'It sounds so cosy, doesn't it?' she added to Louisa.

Louisa was chewing her bottom lip to stop herself laughing so said nothing.

The sarcasm seemed to have completely bypassed Erik for he said, 'There are, as I'm sure you already know, Sarah, certain techniques in photographing nudes and I . . .'

'Nudes!' Sarah interrupted. 'Who said anything about nudes?'

'But I thought . . . Aren't the shots you already have . . .?'

'I don't have a single nude shot of Danny,' Sarah cut in. 'Neither do I particularly want one.'

'I'm so sorry,' he said, obviously shocked by her response though trying not to show it. 'I must have misunderstood. She has such a beautiful body. I just assumed . . . I'm sorry if I've offended you. Please, forgive me.'

The corner of Sarah's mouth tightened and Louisa could see that she was beginning to thaw. Sensing that there was a way in at last Erik took it, encouraging Sarah to talk about her preferences in subjects and as Sarah became at first grudgingly then increasingly responsive, Louisa allowed her mind to drift. Danny's sudden passion for Erik when only a couple of hours before she'd been warning Sarah that she'd probably fall for him was curious to say the least. But then so was almost everything that had happened today and she could only wish that Jake was there so she could ask him what it all meant. She wondered where he was now, what he might be doing. Would he be disappointed not to find her here when he came to see the photographs tomorrow night?

She looked up as Danny strolled onto the terrace, sleep-flushed and tousled. Going to Erik she curled herself into his lap, winding her arms around his neck and nuzzling her head onto his shoulder.

For a while Erik's good manners prevailed and he continued talking to Sarah, but it was clear to anyone listening that he was rapidly losing his thread.

In the end Danny pulled his face round to hers and smiled almost coyly into his eyes.

'Remember me?' she whispered.

Louisa didn't hear Erik's murmured response, but Sarah's everyone heard. It was no more than an elongated sigh, but there was no mistaking the smouldering resentment it contained.

Danny and Erik, however, appeared oblivious as they continued to gaze into each other's eyes.

'Oh yuk!' Sarah muttered as Erik walked his fingers up Danny's arm then snared her nose.

'Where's your spirit of romance?' Danny laughed, still gazing into Erik's eyes.

Sarah turned to Louisa, who was almost beside herself trying not to laugh. 'Is she talking to me?' Sarah demanded.

'I think so,' Louisa choked, wiping the tears from her eyes.

'Oh dear,' Danny said to Erik, 'I do believe Sarah is cross with me for stealing your attention.'

'No, no, I just love it when someone sticks their tongue down someone else's throat when I'm in the middle of talking to them,' Sarah protested.

Beside her Louisa spluttered, twisted in her chair and hid her face.

'Maybe you'd better leave, darling,' Danny said, stroking her fingers through Erik's hair. 'We don't want to make Sarah angry, do we?'

Erik looked across at Sarah, clearly hoping she'd persuade him otherwise, but Sarah simply glared mutinously back.

'I have things I must do during the day tomorrow,' Erik said to Danny, 'but can I see you in the evening?'

Louisa's eyes opened a little wider as she looked at Danny. Tomorrow was when Jake was coming round, but surely Danny wasn't going to turn Erik down, not when they seemed so besotted with each other.

But Danny did and the words she used sent an icy shiver through Louisa's heart.

'Oh darling,' she said, 'we both know we have something special here, so don't let's rush it, mm?'

Louisa missed Sarah's acid response, for Jake's voice, speaking virtually those same words, was ringing in her ears. But what she didn't miss was how upset Erik looked, and neither, it seemed, did Sarah.

'Louisa and I are going to a party tomorrow night, Erik,' Sarah said. 'Why don't you come with us?'

'Yes, why don't you go with them?' Danny said, 'and I'll stay here thinking about you and making myself beautiful for Saturday night.'

Louisa stood up and started to clear the table as Danny and Erik went back to Danny's room to get his clothes.

It was another hour or more before Erik finally left, by which time both Louisa and Sarah were in bed, so neither of them saw him get into his car instead of going into Jean-Claude's, and neither did they see him make a brief return just before dawn.

12

It was evident from the moment they began winding their way up through the lush, steeply sloping gardens of the Hotel Colombe d'Or in St Paul-de-Vence that they were heading towards an infinitely more elegant and salubrious affair than any of the barbecues or wild bashes Louisa and Sarah had attended so far. The soirée was being held in the grand, stone-columned pergola which was covered in a verdantly juicy vine with huge, succulent grapes dangling like lanterns over a sea of politely smiling faces that moved with swan-like grace between the decorously cascading fountains and vivid flowers. The low rumble of male voices occasionally pierced by the falsetto ring of female laughter spiralled languidly with the expensive perfumes and cigar smoke towards the crumbling ramparts of the town above and the magnificent blue sky beyond.

There were, Sarah estimated, around fifty people present, most of whom appeared middle-aged or older. Along with the flowers the women's bright sequinned dresses created lively splashes of colour in a forest of sombre black dinner jackets, making Sarah pleased with her choice of a royal blue silk dress that matched her eyes perfectly. It had a tight-fitting skirt that flared in neat, shiny pleats around her knees and wide shoulder straps that were plaited down the length of her back. She'd bought the dress specially for tonight, having dragged Louisa along the rue d'Antibes all morning until she'd found exactly what she was looking for. Her sleek, ash-blonde hair framed her sunny face in a loose, swinging bob and shone like silver.

Beside her Louisa looked either exotically boyish or impossibly feminine – Sarah couldn't make up her mind which – in a thigh-length cerise silk jacket, tight black mini skirt and a perky black bow tie. And Erik was just scrumptious, as she'd told him when they'd wandered over to Jean-Claude's to find him in his exquisitely tailored tuxedo.

'Did you remember to wash behind your ears?' Sarah murmured to Louisa as they hovered on the edge of the crowd, waiting for Morandi to spot them.

Louisa gave a splutter of laughter as her luminous eyes scanned the gathering with interest. 'Did you remember your breath freshener?' she answered from the corner of her mouth.

'Oh my God!' Sarah gasped, covering her mouth. 'Don't tell me I need it, please, I'll die.'

'No,' Louisa laughed shaking her head and watching Erik who was blithely helping himself to three glasses of carefully chilled Sancerre from a waiter's tray. 'Here's Morandi,' she added, nodding her head towards where he was striding purposefully through the crowd.

'Wow!' Sarah muttered, her eyes widening. Apart from looking quite disarmingly rakish in his DJ, he seemed somehow taller, more composed and confident than he had in his sweltering and cluttered office.

He was on the point of greeting them, his lean face alight with pleasure, when he hesitated, obviously bemused by Erik who was passing them drinks. Sarah moved forward to make the introductions, but of course Morandi knew who Erik was. It came as something of a surprise though to discover that Erik knew Morandi too.

'We have several mutual friends,' Erik explained, laughing at their confusion. 'You must know by now that the world of show business is a very small one.'

Sarah refrained from asking how someone in Erik's position might have come to meet someone in Morandi's for she didn't want to offend Morandi, so instead she turned a beaming smile on Morandi which to her delight made him blush.

He'd called Sarah early that morning to check that she would be coming, which was what had prompted the shopping spree, and seeing the bashful coquetry steal into Sarah's clear blue eyes as Morandi smiled foolishly down at her, Louisa took Erik's arm and they melted discreetly into the crowd.

Erik was able to introduce her to several people and Louisa felt a pleasant kick of adrenalin wash through her to hear so much talk of pre- and post-production and who was doing what on the international scene. Equally cheering was to discover how many people had heard of her and her series, though since it had sold all over the world it shouldn't have been quite such a surprise. Nevertheless it was and for the first time Louisa started to realize how very parochial she was in her thinking and her understanding of matters beyond the shores of the UK. It was embarrassing to hear so many foreign tongues with such an eloquent grasp of English when she could barely muster more than a dozen words of French and none whatsoever in any other language. It wasn't that anyone seemed to mind, but the ease with which they switched from one language to another and clearly moved so freely about Europe made Louisa acutely aware of her island mentality.

'I know what you mean,' Sarah grimaced during a snatched moment together. 'But it's making me feel frightfully international, isn't it you?'

Louisa laughed. 'Yes, it is a bit and I quite like it. Did you meet the woman from Star TV in Hong Kong? She's been the head of more TV stations in Asia and Australia than Rupert Murdoch.'

'Hi, how are you two doing for wine?' Erik interrupted.

'I think we could do with a top-up,' Sarah answered, lifting her glass to check it. 'I was just talking to some Dutch guy whose name I can't pronounce,' she went on as Erik turned to find a waiter, 'who tells me that his company have just bought *Private Essays*.'

Both Louisa and Sarah grinned, then licked and flicked a forefinger.

'How are you getting on with Morandi?' Louisa asked, turning to gaze down over the sweeping view of the valley below.

'Oh, I think he could be the father of my children,' Sarah

replied breezily, making Louisa laugh. 'Actually, I haven't seen him for a while, have you?'

Louisa shook her head, looking around the terrace. 'Oh, there he is.' She pointed through the crowd to where Morandi was standing with one foot resting on the edge of the fountain talking to two people Louisa had met but whose names she had forgotten.

Spotting Louisa and Sarah looking in his direction, Morandi politely excused himself and came to join them just as Erik returned.

'Ah, can I get you a drink too?' Erik offered.

'Uh-huh,' Morandi answered, 'I'm OK for now. Are you having a good time?'

'Fascinating,' Sarah assured him. 'You know so many people.'

Morandi seemed to enjoy the compliment almost as much as he did looking at Sarah. 'I confess I am showing off a little,' he told her. 'But I did not want you to think that my life was only what you saw at my office. And I hope that maybe you have met some people who might be of some help to you in the future. Which reminds me, Louisa,' he added, stepping towards her to allow someone to pass behind him, 'I would like to introduce you to the famous Gaston Olivier.' He turned to survey the crowd. 'Ah, there he is over there, I will go and speak to him.'

'Gaston Olivier?' Louisa repeated to Sarah with not much hope of enlightenment.

'Gaston Olivier,' Erik laughed, 'is a Parisian banker, very well known in film and television circles for backing outsiders and romping home with a fortune.'

'Which one is he?' Sarah asked, craning her neck to look past the group standing next to them.

'The one standing at the top of the steps,' Erik told her. 'There, Morandi is shaking his hand.'

A few minutes later Gaston Olivier, a man in his late fifties with flamboyant eyebrows and a wide, juicy bottom lip that rose to tuck in his top lip before drooping towards the splendid wart on his chin, had been plucked from the centre of his cronies and was at Louisa's side while Sarah and Erik were being swept into another elite little gathering by Morandi.

This was turning into quite an exhilarating evening, giving Louisa the feeling that she was at last emerging from a shell of small-minded Britishness that she hadn't even known she was trapped in. Not only that, being among so many stimulating people whose interests ran along the same tracks as hers and whose enthusiasm and energy for what they did was managing to rub itself off on her had left her mercifully free of all thoughts of Jake. Well, perhaps not totally free, for the image of Danny soaking in a perfumed bath awaiting Jake's arrival along with some exotic dish simmering in the oven and a set of outrageously daring underwear laid out on the bed kept sneaking its way into her mind. But there was more to life than an obsession with a man she barely knew and it was high time she shook herself out of it.

Gaston Olivier had all the inherent charm of a Frenchman and Louisa fell instantly under its spell, blushing modestly when he told her how delighted he was to meet the creator of *Private Essays* and showing real eagerness to hear about Louisa's plans for future productions. From the corner of her eye Louisa saw Sarah and Morandi taking a private moment together, talking softly, smiling, laughing and seeming very much to want to be elsewhere. After a while Morandi moved reluctantly away as someone called to him and Erik took Sarah by the arm, evidently in need of being rescued from a stout, over-zealous female with a veritable bush of fiery red hair and such a busy rash of freckles they looked almost contagious.

Louisa was still talking to Olivier some twenty minutes later when Erik wandered over to join them. It was immediately evident how fond of Erik Olivier was, as was almost everyone who knew Erik, Louisa had noticed. And the little group they made up seemed to become something of a Mecca for the other guests as they made their way over to speak to Olivier and Erik and, to Louisa's delight, to her too.

Standing alone for a moment Sarah took a sip of her wine as her eyes travelled around the terrace in search of Morandi.

He was a strange, paradoxical man, vacillating as curiously and touchingly between shyness and confidence as he did between English and Italian. She longed to ask him who he really was, how he had come to be here on the Côte d'Azur and why he was hiding behind a persona she had the distinct impression he wanted her to see through. But so far the opportunity hadn't arisen, there had been too many people around, too many interruptions and besides, she wanted to give him the chance to tell her himself without any prying encouragement from her.

Seeing him turn sharply away from Aphrodite over in a shady corner, Sarah smiled uneasily and would have gone to join Erik and Louisa had Morandi not turned towards her, the anger melting in his eyes as he saw her.

With so many invitations being thrown out for dinner Louisa was laughing and looking at Erik for help, but with a playful wink he allowed her to make the decision. She accepted Olivier's, assuming that Erik would too. However it seemed that Erik had other plans as he drew Louisa aside saying, 'You are quite safe with Gaston and I think Morandi and Sarah will probably join your party too, so I shall leave you shortly to go back to see Danny.'

Louisa's eyes widened with alarm. 'Uh, well, actually,' she said, hunting around for Sarah, 'I'd really like you to come.'

Erik grinned.

'No, really, I would,' she insisted.

'But Danny is all alone and you are having such a good time, you don't need me,' he told her.

Oh God, Louisa was thinking, what could she say to keep him there? And where the heck was Sarah?

Erik looked at his watch.

'Just have one more drink before you go,' Louisa said encouragingly.

Erik shook his head. 'No, I have had enough,' he answered, 'and I really would like to leave now. Please, forgive me.'

'But you're taking us home,' Louisa protested.

'Gaston will be happy to take you home. Or Morandi,' Erik responded, his brilliant blue eyes dancing with laughter.

'Look, Erik, really, I don't think you should go,' Louisa said awkwardly, realizing that she was doing this more for him than she was for Danny. 'I mean, women don't really like it when men turn up unannounced. She might have a face pack on or . . .'

'I would adore her even in a face pack,' Erik laughed.

'But Danny wouldn't like it and honestly, she really did want to have an early night.'

'Then I shall join her,' he said decisively.

Dear God, there was no easy way of telling him this, but it was better, Louisa told herself firmly, that he found out from her rather than have to go through the awfulness of walking in on Jake and Danny. 'Erik,' she began, 'I'm really sorry to be the one to tell you this, but . . . Well, you see, Danny isn't exactly alone this evening, she's uh, entertaining someone, a friend!'

Laughing, Erik shook his head and looking at his watch again he said, 'Jake is by now on his way to Mexico City. He will have boarded the plane in Paris a few hours ago.'

Louisa's luminous eyes rounded. 'You know Jake?' she said, feeling faintly dizzy.

'Yeah, I know Jake,' Erik grinned.

Louisa shook her head as though to clear it. 'And you knew that Danny was expecting him tonight?'

Erik nodded, clearly enjoying himself immensely.

'So you let her get stood up?'

'Sort of,' Erik confessed. 'A few things came up late yesterday and this morning that meant Jake had to fly out in a hurry. He told me he was coming to see the photographs at your villa this evening, so he left me to make his apologies.'

'Hang on, hang on, I've got to think about this,' Louisa said, her thoughts moving so fast she couldn't trap them. 'What you're saying is that Jake has gone to Mexico so you knew Danny was going to be on her own, but you didn't say anything?'

'That's right.' His eyes were twinkling so merrily that Louisa couldn't help but laugh.

'But I thought you were crazy about Danny,' she said.

'I am. But it won't do her any harm to have that beautiful nose of hers put out of joint once in a while, I'm sure.'

'Oh God,' Louisa laughed, 'I'm glad she can't hear you because Danny's not particularly used to people getting one over on her.'

Erik shrugged.

'Did Jake know that Sarah and I weren't going to be there?' Louisa asked after a pause.

'No. He thought you would be. I didn't tell him anything different, he had a lot on his mind at the time.'

Louisa wondered about that for a moment then said, 'So why has he gone to Mexico?'

Erik's eyes narrowed as he looked into hers. 'He has some business to attend to there,' he answered with a caution that wasn't at all lost on Louisa.

'Is he coming back?'

'Probably.'

Louisa smiled ruefully. 'I can see that I'm not going to get much out of you,' she said. 'But I get the feeling that you know what's going on. And something is, isn't it?'

'Yes. But it's up to Jake to tell you and to be frank I don't think he will.'

Louisa's heart folded around the disappointment. 'Doesn't it bother you that Danny's sleeping with Jake?' she said.

Erik laughed. 'She's not. At least tonight she's not and since I only met her yesterday I'm in no position to judge her for things she did before I knew her, now am I?'

'No, I don't suppose you are,' Louisa responded. As she lowered her eyes she looked so unhappy that Erik lifted her face back up to his.

'For what it's worth,' he said, 'I'm pretty certain Jake will be back. When, is hard to say, but this is one hell of a time for you to come into his life. He's not too pleased about it and if you knew why you wouldn't be too pleased either.'

'It's got something to do with Consuela Santini, hasn't it?' Louisa asked, probing.

'It's got everything to do with Consuela Santini,' Erik replied soberly.

'And Mario Morandi?'

Erik glanced across the terrace to where Morandi was talking to Aphrodite. 'Indirectly, yes,' he answered. Then bringing his eyes back to Louisa he said, 'You've got yourselves into a real hornet's nest here and if I were you I'd . . .'

'Hi, you two,' Sarah butted in, 'what are you looking so secretive about? I'll tell Danny,' she warned wagging her finger at Erik.

Erik laughed. 'Speaking of whom,' he said, 'I feel the telegraph wires of love a-humming so I'm off.'

'What!' Sarah gasped, looking frantically at Louisa. 'But you can't do that. You've . . .'

'He can,' Louisa interrupted. 'I'll explain later.'

'Ah, Morandi, just the fellow,' Erik said as Morandi joined them. 'I'm sure I can rely on you to see these two ladies home safely, can't I?'

'But of course,' Morandi agreed, smiling at Sarah who was gazing up at him through a rosy flush of alcohol. 'Just a quick word before you go, Erik,' Morandi said, taking Erik to one side.

'What's going on?' Sarah whispered to Louisa.

'That I can't answer, but what I can tell you is that Erik is a friend of Jake's. A very good friend, from what I can make out.'

'Really?' Sarah said, sounding interested. 'So he knows Jake is with Danny tonight? Oh God, don't tell me they're sharing her, some women get all the luck.'

Louisa pursed her lips. 'Apparently,' she said, glancing towards the upper terrace as a group of diners exploded into laughter, 'Jake is on his way to Mexico,' and she went on to fill Sarah in on the conversation she'd just had with Erik.

'Mmm, the plot thickens,' Sarah remarked when Louisa had finished.

'And thickens,' Louisa added spotting Aphrodite surging towards them through the crowd.

'What?' Sarah said, turning to see who Louisa was looking at. 'Ah, Aphro . . .' She gasped as a glass of red wine hit her full in the face.

'Bitch!' Aphrodite hissed glaring at Sarah with wild, malevolent black eyes, and turning on her heel she stalked majestically back across the terrace in a flurry of red lace.

'The cow!' Sarah seethed, taking the napkins Louisa had scooped from a nearby table. 'What did she do that for?'

'You have to ask?' Louisa muttered.

'I'm sorry, I'm so sorry,' Morandi fussed, taking the napkins and dabbing the inky red liquid from Sarah's face. 'Your beautiful dress, she is ruined. But I will buy you another.'

Everyone was looking in their direction so Sarah turned her back in disgust and fury. 'How the hell am I going to walk out of here looking like this?' she raged. 'What's the matter with the woman? Is she crazy or something?'

'She has a very passionate nature,' Morandi said apologetically.

'I'll get the car and bring it to the front,' Erik chipped in helpfully.

Sarah looked down at her lovely new dress and wanted to weep. 'Well, I won't be going anywhere for dinner now,' she said tightly.

'Please, let me drive you home,' Morandi implored.

'No, thank you, I don't fancy the idea of a bomb being flung through the letter-box,' Sarah retorted angrily.

Morandi looked crushed.

'Maybe you could go and keep an eye out for Erik and let us know when he arrives,' Louisa suggested, dipping a napkin into her white wine and using it to try and absorb the red wine in Sarah's hair.

'Where did she go?' Sarah seethed. 'I want to kill her.'

'I think she left,' Louisa answered. 'Shit, she's made a right mess of you. Your hair's turning purple.'

'Why the hell did he invite me if he was bringing her

too?' Sarah demanded. 'Does he get off on her jealousy or something?'

'He looked pretty upset about it actually,' Louisa placated.

'So he damned well should. Where's Erik? I feel a right idiot standing here like this.'

Louisa bit her lips. 'Actually, you look a bit of one,' she remarked.

'Thanks!' Sarah snapped, but the glint in her eyes told Louisa that her indomitable humour was on the return.

'Erik's here,' Morandi said, coming up behind them. 'Please, take my jacket,' he said quickly stripping it off and draping it over Sarah's shoulders.

Since Erik had taken his car to the front of the hotel they had no choice but to leave through the terrace restaurant. As they reached it Louisa took hold of Sarah saying, 'OK, just put your head down, cover your face with your hands and leave the rest to me.'

'What?' Sarah said, gulping as Louisa shoved her head down.

'Emergency!' Louisa shouted, ushering Sarah forward. 'Make way! Make way! We have an emergency!'

The astonished diners looked up from their tables, staring with bloodthirsty interest as Louisa and Sarah dashed past the Léger mural towards Cesar's giant sculpture of a thumb beside the door and hurled themselves into the back of a waiting Jaguar.

It wasn't until they were speeding through the winding back roads towards Valanjou that Sarah realized that neither of them had said goodbye to Morandi and that she was still wearing his jacket.

'Never mind, it gives you a good excuse to call him,' Louisa pointed out.

'Yes, yes it does, doesn't it?' Sarah said, obviously cheered by the thought.

'So you're not angry with him any more?'

'Depends what he does to make amends,' Sarah said with relish.

Erik laughed, then swerved dangerously around a giant

pothole in the road. Since his driving was worthy of any Frenchman or even Italian come to that, they were home within twenty minutes.

'Aren't you coming in?' Sarah said when he stopped at the bottom of the drive, confused because she'd assumed he was driving like a maniac to get to Danny sooner.

'Actually I'm rather hungry,' he answered, 'so I'm going to see if Jean-Claude has eaten yet and if not we shall go to the village for dinner. Would you care to join us?'

Louisa and Sarah looked at each other. 'Yes, I think we would,' Louisa answered, smiling.

'Just give me a few minutes to clean up and change,' Sarah said, 'and we'll be right with you.'

They were already out of the car and starting up the drive when Louisa turned back and said, 'Uh, what about Danny?'

'In case you hadn't noticed,' Erik answered mildly, 'her car isn't there.'

Louisa and Sarah turned to look.

'Ah,' Sarah said awkwardly.

'I think we can all guess where's she's gone,' Erik smiled. 'Leave her a note if you like asking her if she would care to join us when she returns. We'll go to La Table Gourmand. I'll be at Jean-Claude's when you're ready.'

'Looks like Danny might have met her match,' Sarah muttered with a grin as she and Louisa started back up the drive.

'Doesn't it?' Louisa responded.

'Are you going to tell her that Erik is a friend of Jake's?'

'No, I don't think so.'

'Very wise,' Sarah smirked. 'You know, I think I'm going to rather like Erik Svensson.'

'Mmm, me too,' Louisa smiled.

Danny was crying. Silently, unmovingly, unblinkingly. The small, yellow light in the master cabin cast the spidery shadows of her eyelashes over her delicate face. The tears flowed freely from her tormented eyes, spilling onto the pillows as she gazed blindly at the black circle of the porthole. Outside the waves splashed indolently against the hull of the *Valhalla*, above the giant masts clanked and the wooden deck creaked as someone moved stealthily across it.

It was the final shot of the scene. The camera was tracking slowly back from her face revealing the man in the bed beside her, sleeping peacefully, one arm thrown across his chest the other squashed beneath his head. A single tousled white sheet covered them both, but a perfect female leg lay exposed on the bed, just as the raw emotion lay exposed in her eyes.

This was the most delicious living out of her fantasies she'd had in ages. She was captive on board, unable to escape, only able to do her master's bidding, to satisfy his needs, to suffer the humiliation and feel a part of herself die each time he abused her. He had no idea of the love that flourished so deeply in her heart, of the desire he aroused in her, of the pain his indifference and cruelty caused her. He saw only her terror, did all he could to incite it, passed her amongst his crew for their pleasure, never witnessing the violations but hearing of them later and watching her with baleful, mocking eyes that slaked her body with contempt. How could her heart be so treacherous as to make her love a man who treated her so?

The scene faded to black and Danny turned on her side. The aura of memory tingled over her and she pushed a hand between her thighs. Sleeping with Jake's crew was no hardship but to sleep with Jake was what she really wanted. She'd known that first time, when he'd finished with her then laughed and told her she didn't look like a whore, what he'd wanted of her, what role he was casting her in and she was more than happy to play it – at least as long as it suited her she was. And right now it was suiting her just fine, the only question was, how to get him away from Louisa? Still, with Louisa's unerring talent for choosing the wrong man it shouldn't prove too difficult to convince her she'd done it again. Which, as far as Danny was concerned, Louisa had for there was no doubt in Danny's mind that Jake was as skilled a deceiver as he was a lover. It might be easier to persuade Louisa though if Danny could tell Louisa just what it was that Jake was hiding, for he was hiding something, that Danny knew for a certainty. So far she hadn't even been able to guess at what it might be and neither could she get as much as a murmur from Bob who was lying beside her now, snoring softly, with whatever Jake's secret was locked securely, unattainably in the deepest recesses of his mind. But she would find out what was going on, she would find someone to tell her and maybe, she thought, not for the first time, that someone was Consuela.

As for Erik, there was nothing she could do to stop him falling in love with her. She knew he would because he was like all the others, though she had to confess she liked him a bit more than she'd liked the others. But Jake was different. Instinct told her that his complicated, insidious and ambiguous soul was a reflection of her own. With her he had no need to disguise his cruelty, or his treachery, he could vent it as freely as he wished for whatever he was feeling, whatever he desired, whether it be violence, tenderness, hatred or love she could always summon the exact same emotion to embrace it. In other words she could handle a man like Jake, Louisa couldn't.

Feeling Bob's hand on her shoulder Danny rolled onto her back and turned to look into his bleary, bloodshot eyes. The stirring savagery of lust was starting to curl his mouth and throwing back the sheet he pointed at his groin and ordered her astride him. As she drew herself up Danny could feel herself beginning to slide into the character of her fantasy. A frightened, pleading look rose in her eyes as she knelt over him, preparing to impale herself on his solid, angry erection. Her last, conscious thought as the captive slave girl eclipsed her, was to wonder again what it was that had taken Jake Mallory so suddenly to Mexico.

13

Dropping a crumpled ten thousand peso note on the counter Jake carried his Dos Equis through the dingy, deserted bar with its scratched tables, broken chairs and ubiquitous TV blaring violence from its perch high in the corner. He selected the furthest, darkest corner of the bar where he sat facing the door, unseen but able to see.

The bartender, smearing glasses with a greasy cloth, watched him with small, aggressive eyes, sucking the corner of his moustache into hard, thin, scarred lips. *Gringos* didn't come to this bar, they had no business here unless it was bad business and this man, with a patch over one eye and a mean glint in the other was all bad. José knew, he'd seen enough men like this one to know.

Jake ignored him, kept his gaze focused on the dazzling block of light streaming in from the dusty street where ragged children scuffed a football in the dirt and flea-ridden dogs scavenged the festering piles of week-old garbage. He glanced at his watch, knowing he could be in for a long wait. Mexicans rarely kept to time and the Mexican he was waiting for might just not show at all.

He'd left France four days ago, flying first to Mexico City, then to Cancun then north to Chihuahua. Yesterday he'd detoured across the country to Puerto Vallarta, a town too full of memories – he hadn't been sorry to leave. His patience was wearing thin, already he'd spent too much time chasing around this godforsaken land, had handed out thousands of dollars to slit-eyed men with solid chunks of gold flashing on their necks, their wrists and their fingers, gaudy shirts and designer jeans straining over the muscles of their taut little bodies, and still he had nothing. He trusted few of them, knew there was little or no chance that he would find what he had come for, but the fear that he might was what drove him.

He tensed as a shadow darkened the doorway. He couldn't see the face, but knew from the shapely outline that it was a woman, from the sway of the hips that she was a hooker. She went to perch on a tall stool, leaning her elbows on the bar, flicking her black, curly hair over her shoulders.

Jake could feel her eyes on him, guessed that the kids outside, the ones he had paid to keep the wheels on his jeep, had told her that a rich *Americano* was in the bar. It wasn't long before she came over, asked him in broken English if he would like some company and sat down. Jake called out to the bartender to get the lady a drink and keep her out of his way. Feigning hurt the hooker pouted her fleshy lips, and leaning towards him to expose the deep crevice between her breasts told him she'd make him a good price. Casually lifting one foot and resting it on the chair beside his own, Jake reached into his shirt pocket and pulled out a 9mm Luger.

Her druggy eyes widened, then dropped to the table as Jake slammed down a hundred thousand pesos. She eyed it greedily, looked uncertainly back to his face, then watched as using the barrel of the gun he pushed the money towards her.

'Now beat it,' he said, sliding the gun back into his pocket.

Quickly she scooped up the money, cursed him in Spanish and returned to the bar.

Jake picked up his beer. It was as well to let the bartender know that the *gringo* carried a gun, that way he wouldn't try pulling any stunts like inviting his friends around for a little sport.

He took out a Marlboro, lit it, drained his beer and called for another. The whore brought it, set it down and sauntered back to her stool. She reminded him of Danny Spencer, the British actress who behaved like a whore. She didn't have Danny's class, but the two dark-haired beauties sure as hell shared a soul. His upper lip curled as he thought of Danny, of the games she played with herself and tried to drag him into.

Just where was she coming from, he wondered, what was she trying to prove? She had to be crazy if she thought she could control him, she was well out of her league, was flirting with the kind of danger that would destroy her if she didn't leave it alone.

His hand tightened around the bottle as he then thought of Louisa. Louisa Kramer, the writer who had stirred emotions in him he wanted left alone. But Jake was a master at controlling his thoughts and right now they belonged here in this sordid Mexican bar.

An hour passed. The hooker had long gone, the movie had changed and now it was time for him to go. His fury was such that he wanted to smash a fist through the grimy, stained-glass window, to see the blood flow from his veins to remind himself he was human, that he couldn't take much more of this. There was a whole network of people working for him all over this fucking country and still they'd found nothing. Still the rendezvous weren't kept, still there was no evidence to tell him that she was alive – or dead.

He walked to the bar, handed over some money and waited impatiently for the change.

'Señor Mallory?'

Jake swung round to find a skinny old man with drooping eyelids and a cruelly pock-marked face looking up at him.

Jake eyed him, waiting for him to speak again.

'Fernando send me,' the man said. 'I am Pedro.'

Jake glanced back over his shoulder at the barman.

'He no speak English,' Pedro informed him, then nodded to the barman to make himself scarce.

'So?' Jake demanded.

Pedro shrugged, lowered his eyes to the floor and kicked around the dust.

Jake's jaw was like rock as he slid a hundred thousand pesos from his pocket and passed it over. Pedro took it, held it up to the light, then pocketed it. His shifty eyes came back to Jake's, then turning he walked out of the bar.

Jake followed, blinking at the harsh glare of the sudden

sunlight, feeling his injured eye sting beneath the patch. The dusty street was empty, just two scrawny kids idly kicking a ball beside his car, seemingly oblivious to the biting heat of the sun. The old man stopped, asked why they weren't in school then hurled a stream of abuse in response to their smartass remarks.

As the boys ran off Jake grabbed Pedro's arm and hauled him round. 'What have you got?' he growled, his hand itching for the gun.

The old man revealed his chipped, tobacco-stained teeth in a savage grin. 'She has been seen,' he said.

Jake's eyes blazed into his. The old man had no way of knowing what those few words had done to the man accosting him, neither was he going to know. 'Where?' Jake spat.

'Twenty kilometres from here.'

'When?'

Pedro shrugged. 'Two weeks, maybe three weeks ago.'

'How do you know it was her?'

'I know.'

Keeping hold of the old man Jake threw open the door to the jeep and shoved him inside. 'Drive,' he said.

After an hour or more of bumping over rock-littered dirt roads, swerving round potholes and crashing through the gears as they headed into the foothills of the Sierra Madre the old man skidded the jeep to a halt in an ancient, crumbling village where the only sign of life was a weary, dejected mule tethered to a wall beside the faded red paint of a Coca-Cola sign.

'Over there,' he said, pointing towards a dirty white building where the word hotel, painted in blue, was barely visible above the dilapidated shutters of the upper floor.

Jake looked at it. His face was inscrutable.

'She was there. Maybe they know where she goes after,' Pedro said.

'Maybe you know,' Jake replied, turning slowly to the old man.

'No.' Pedro was shaking his head. 'I not know. But maybe they tell you.'

Jake got out of the jeep, trod the sandy road with deliberate, reluctant steps, feeling a hundred hidden eyes following his progress. She'd never have come to a place like this, not the woman he knew. The woman he knew was dead. So why was he here? Why was he chasing around Mexico, shelling out a fortune to hunt down a woman who didn't exist? Because he had to be sure, that was why.

The hotel door creaked open, the lobby was dark and empty. The smell of stale tequila curdled the air, mingling with the pungent spices of simmering chilli. Somewhere, out of sight and barely audible, a tinny radio piped music, the taste of poverty and neglect salted his lips.

He hit the bell on the counter and waited. After a few moments a worn-out old woman in a sauce-smudged apron and shabby dress emerged from a door beneath the stairs. She looked at Jake, blinked and gruffly asked him what he wanted.

Jake was on the point of answering when he heard the jeep start up outside. In a split second he was at the door, wrenching it open and racing into the street. It was too late, the jeep was already speeding back down the road they'd come in on.

Cursing himself viciously for his own stupidity Jake watched it until it disappeared from sight.

'So they'd never heard of her?' Fernando said, hours later as he paced Jake's hotel room while Jake stood at the window staring down at the grim, grey lines of the freeway and the stark oblongs of abandoned construction that stretched to the filthy brown line of the horizon.

At last Jake tore himself from the window. Exhaustion and rage was etched in every line of his face. 'No, they'd never heard of her,' he said tightly. His eyes came to rest on Fernando's, boring into him. 'I want you to find the old man again,' he said.

Fernando cocked an eyebrow in surprise. His deceptively youthful face was calm, his cultured voice was as smooth and American as the expensive clothes he wore. 'That should be possible,' he said, 'but why? If he knows nothing . . .'

'He knows who's paying him to fuck me around,' Jake snarled. 'We get to them, maybe we get to . . .'

Fernando wasn't surprised when Jake stopped, he rarely, if ever, mentioned her name.

'Find him,' Jake growled through his teeth. 'Find him and crunch his balls until he sings.'

Fernando nodded, then watched as Jake rolled himself a cigarette, sprinkling it liberally with hashish. When it was ready Fernando drew a lighter from his pocket, but he wasn't fast enough. Jake lit the joint himself, inhaled deeply then returned to the window and its depressing view of a city he loathed.

'Do you think she's still alive?' he said after a while.

Fernando sighed, flopped down on the sofa and buried his face in his hands. 'I don't know,' he answered. 'Sometimes I do, sometimes I don't. What about you? What does your gut tell you?'

'Nothing. It doesn't tell me one goddamned fucking thing.'

Fernando hesitated, then said, 'The local cops were here earlier.'

'What did they want?'

'To welcome you to Mexico,' Fernando grinned.

'They're getting better,' Jake remarked. 'It's only taken them four days to find me this time.'

'What are you going to do?' Fernando asked.

'Head back to Europe. The trail's run cold here and I have things to do in France.'

Fernando's smile was sculpted in sarcasm. 'How *is* Consuela?' he said.

Jake turned to look at him. 'Get that old man,' he said. 'Do whatever it takes to find out who's paying him. You know how to get hold of me. I should be back in France by the day after tomorrow.'

Fernando got up and walked to the door. When he reached it he turned back. 'Jake,' he said, 'have you considered what you're going to do if she is still alive?'

Jake drew deeply on his cigarette, held the smoke then exhaled slowly. 'Yes, I've considered it,' he said and the tone of his voice was enough to tell Fernando he would be wise not to press it any further.

'I look like a ruddy cabbage-patch doll,' Sarah wailed, holding up her compact and eyeing the puffy swellings on her face with unbounded misery.

Louisa and Danny glanced at each other then burst out laughing. 'You look fine,' Danny told her, pushing her feet into the ground to rock herself and Louisa back and forth in the swinging hammock chair.

'Don't lie to me,' Sarah retorted. 'I look like I'm about to erupt.'

'Stop scratching,' Louisa laughed, 'you'll only make them worse.'

'But they're driving me crazy. Oh, just look at this eyelid, will you? How the hell can I go out like this?'

'Call him and cancel,' Danny said.

'I would if he weren't already on his way.'

'Where are you going?' Louisa asked, hooking the straps of her swimsuit back up over her shoulders and curling her legs under her.

'He didn't say. Somewhere dark, I hope,' Sarah answered, picking up Danny's wine glass and taking a mouthful. 'Is this from the *caves* down the road?' she said. 'Not bad is it?'

'At less than a pound a bottle, it's pretty good,' Danny remarked. 'And don't drink it all because I can't be bothered to go and get some more.'

'Here he is,' Louisa said, as a black and yellow Renault 5 chugged and spluttered up the drive.

Sarah stared at it, following its unsteady progress with unblinking fascination. 'Awesome,' she muttered, as it groaned to a halt.

'You go and show him your mosquito bites,' Louisa laughed, 'and I'll go and get some more glasses.'

'Are you kidding?' Sarah cried, tearing her eyes from the Renault. 'I'm not inviting him over here when she's sitting there looking like that.'

Danny was wide-eyed. 'What's the matter with the way I look?' she demanded.

'Nothing, that's the trouble.'

'She'll cover up,' Louisa laughed.

'No she won't, she never does.'

'It's nothing he can't see any day of the week on the beach,' Danny pointed out, hooking the elastic of her G-string a little higher on her hips. 'Or in his profession, come to that.'

'But it's better than mine, so I don't want him to see it,' Sarah retorted.

'It's not better, it's just different,' Danny said, looking down at her golden tan, large, firm breasts and erect rosy brown nipples. 'But if you're worried then pass me the towel.'

'No, we'll go straight out.' Sarah turned to look across the garden to where Morandi was now standing awkwardly beside his car, obviously not sure whether to venture a nonchalant stroll across the lawn or wait to be invited. 'Will you just look at him,' Sarah sighed, her head to one side. 'He might not be what dreams are made of, but he kind of gets to me. What's he doing now?' she said as Morandi took something out of the car and started to waggle it in the air. Then all three of them burst out laughing as they realized he was waving a white flag.

'Isn't he just something else,' Sarah grinned.

'Haven't you told him yet that you forgive him for the Aphrodite incident?' Louisa cried.

'No, but I'll get round to it. Anyway, I'd best be off, enjoy your evening you two, don't wait up,' and carrying her sandals in one hand and her purse in the other she padded across the cool, springy lawn grinning as stupidly at Morandi as he was at her. When she reached him he put his hands on her shoulders, gazed down at the angry little rash of mosquito bites, told her she looked ravishing and kissed her on both cheeks.

'Where are we going?' she said as he cranked the door open for her to get in.

'It's a surprise,' he smiled, making sure she was settled and even going so far as to buckle up her seat belt for her. 'I'm sorry about the car,' he went on, looking so absurdly contrite that Sarah wanted to hug him, 'but mine's in the garage and this was all I could borrow at short notice.'

'I love it.' Sarah said truthfully, folding her hands in her lap as she watched him walk around the car and get in the other side.

'I don't think you would if you knew whose it was,' he said earnestly.

'Ah, I see. Well, just so long as it doesn't squirt oil at me.'

'Oh no, it won't do that,' he assured her.

Sarah shot him a look from the corner of her eye and belatedly realizing he'd missed the joke Morandi blushed.

'Does she know why you've borrowed her car?' Sarah asked, as he crunched it into reverse.

'Uh, not exactly,' he confessed, turning it around then sending it hurtling towards the gates. He was far too tall for such a little car and looked so woefully embarrassed by it all that Sarah's heart flowed over with affection. She wanted to put her hand on his, but feeling suddenly shy, she turned to look out of the window and waved to Danny and Louisa.

'Mmm, isn't this wonderful?' Danny sighed, stretching then laughing as they heard the Renault backfire in the distance.

'Sheer bliss,' Louisa agreed, sipping her wine and gazing up at the sloping red roofs of the villa where the leaves of the olive trees glistened silver in the sunlight and the blue sky was starting to turn pink. 'Aren't you seeing Erik tonight?'

'He said he'd call later,' Danny yawned, sinking back in the downy cushions and closing her eyes. 'What about you? Are you going to do any more writing?'

'Not tonight. I had a pretty good run at it today, but I need to think about the next scenes before I carry on.'

Danny's eyes were closed and as she appeared to drift off into her own thoughts Louisa flicked over a page of the magazine on her lap. The tension that had been building between her and Danny over the past couple of weeks seemed to have diminished now and the atmosphere in the villa was once again easy and friendly. Louisa wasn't ignorant of the fact that it was

Jake's departure that had diffused the situation, at least for her. Danny hadn't even mentioned it, had seemed too wrapped up in Erik this past week to care about anything else and that in itself was helping Louisa to relax, for if Danny was as keen on Erik as she appeared to be then hopefully there would be no return of the unspoken rivalry between them when Jake came back. If he came back.

Not wishing to dwell on how she might feel either way Louisa forced herself to concentrate on an article about the French television channel TF1. Since she didn't understand too much of it her mind soon started to wander, and letting the magazine slide to the floor she rested her chin on her hand and started to churn around the plot of the new series she was devising.

'Do you ever think about Simon now?' Danny said a while later.

Surprised, Louisa turned to look at her. 'Yes,' she answered. 'Quite a lot, actually. Why do you ask?'

'I just wondered. Do you ever wish you'd fought a bit harder to keep him?'

'Do you mean do I wish I'd told him about the baby?'

Danny raised one eyelid. 'Do you?' she said.

'Sometimes. He had a right to know.'

Danny smiled. 'You miss him, don't you?' she said.

'As a friend, yes.'

'You mean Sarah and I aren't enough for you?' Danny teased, batting a fly away from her face.

'Of course you are, but Simon was . . . I don't know, what was he? He was a bit like a brother, I suppose. I always used to wish I had a brother.'

'Mmm, me too. Preferably an older brother. Sarah's lucky having such a big family, don't you think? I feel quite envious the way they call her as often as they do to check up on her. It must be lovely having so many people care about you.'

'But your parents call regularly too,' Louisa reminded her.

'I know,' Danny sighed. 'I quite miss them actually, but I shouldn't be saying that to you, should I? Not when you don't have anyone at all calling you. Shit, I could have put that a bit more tactfully, couldn't I?'

Louisa smiled. 'Yes, you could, but it doesn't matter. I've got my family right here in you and Sarah.'

'That's a lovely thing to say, I know Sarah would be touched by it too.' She reached out for Louisa's hand and squeezed it. 'But we've got our families and obviously they come first for us. Not that we ever want to shut you out, we wouldn't dream of it, but it must be so hard for you knowing that the people who matter most to you have other people they care about first.'

'I don't think I've ever looked at it quite that way,' Louisa said feeling suddenly depressed.

'That's good,' Danny smiled, letting go of her hand. 'It doesn't do any good to dwell on loneliness, it only makes a person do things they might not otherwise do.'

'What do you mean?' Louisa said, turning to look at her. 'What might I not otherwise do?'

'Nothing,' Danny laughed. 'I was just trying to let you know that I understand how lonely you must feel at times, how much you must miss your grandmother – and Simon. He was quite special in his way, I think. He was so good to you and after all you'd been through with that ghastly Bill Simon was just what you needed. I wasn't too sure about it in the beginning, it's true, I was afraid you might be rushing into something on the rebound, something you'd end up regretting. Well, you probably did go into it on the rebound, but fortunately it all worked out. At least for a while it did and he certainly put you back on the road after all that fuss with Bill. You know, when I look at you,' she went on, her head to one side as she gazed into Louisa's face, 'I just can't imagine anyone ever wanting to hurt you. You're so lovely, so gentle and kind, I know if I were a man I'd just want to love you and protect you. I think that's what Simon wanted and I sometimes wonder if it wasn't you who pushed him away. It's like you can't believe that someone really cares for you, that they don't want to hurt you, so you go out of your way to make them hurt you without even really knowing you're doing it. Or you hurt yourself, like you did with the baby.'

Louisa sipped her wine and gazed thoughtfully down at the still, clear water of the pool. 'I thought what I did about the baby was for the best,' she said softly. 'I never looked at it as trying to hurt myself.'

'No, I didn't think you did,' Danny smiled. 'But Simon hurt you by telling you he was in love with someone else and then there you were, back on the cycle of pain, feeling like you deserved it and then punishing yourself for the crime of not being loved by terminating your own baby. It didn't seem to occur to you to put up a fight for Simon, you just accepted that he didn't love you because you don't feel worthy of anyone's love, not even your own. You care so much for Sarah and me, but you never seem to care about yourself. You escape into your writing, taking yourself off into a fantasy world where everything is just the way you want it to be and you don't have to face up to reality or what you're doing to yourself.'

Louisa was still staring at the pool, allowing Danny's words to sink into her mind. 'Is that what you think?' she said hoarsely. 'That I'm running away?'

Danny nodded.

'It doesn't feel like that's what I'm doing. I think about Simon a lot, it's true. I know I could have fought to keep him and that if I had I would probably have won, but in my heart I had to admit that it wasn't really what I wanted.'

'Then maybe you should ask yourself why you didn't want it? Was it because you were afraid of his love? Afraid that it would turn to violence in the end like it has in your past? Maybe you're just fooling yourself into believing you don't want him as a way of trying to protect yourself.'

'I don't think so,' Louisa said. 'I mean, I really don't believe we are right for each other. Not now. We were for a while, but it had run its course. And the truth is, had he not met someone else I'd have stayed with him just because he made me feel safe and that's not really a basis for a relationship. He deserves more, he should be loved because he has so much love to give.'

'And it's the same for you,' Danny said. 'You have so much love to give, but you can't accept it in return, so you go out looking for someone who will hurt you, it's what you expect so you make it happen.'

Louisa looked down at her glass. Danny hadn't mentioned Jake's name but Louisa was sure he was in both their minds and as much as she disliked it, she had to admit that there might be some truth in what Danny was saying. She sensed that Jake had it in him to hurt her, to hurt her badly if he chose because her feelings for him were already deeper and more acute than anything she'd ever felt for Simon. It was why she was afraid of Jake, why she was now fighting against trusting him the way he'd asked her to. She knew so little about him, but the tenderness in the one kiss they'd shared haunted her. The truth of his words when he'd told her that something special was happening between them echoed insistently in her mind. Why had he said it if he hadn't felt it too?

'I was thinking,' Danny said, 'why don't you give Simon a call and just find out how he is?'

Louisa shook her head. 'No, there's no point. And I still feel too guilty about the baby to be able to speak to him.'

Danny smiled and leaned forward to pick up her wine. 'Jake agrees, you know, that Simon had a right to know about the baby, but I'm not so sure.'

Louisa turned slowly to look at her, hardly able to believe she'd heard her correctly. 'Are you saying you've talked to Jake about Simon and me?' she said carefully.

Danny nodded. 'Oh come on, don't look like that . . .'

'But you had no right to discuss it with Jake! No right to discuss it with anyone.'

'But Jake asked. He wanted to know about you, if there was anyone in your life, so I told him what had happened.'

'I don't believe it,' Louisa cried, putting a hand to her head and getting to her feet. 'Why did you tell him about the baby? He didn't need to know that . . . Oh God, Danny, I just don't know what gets into you sometimes.'

'I'm sorry,' Danny said, looking genuinely bemused. 'I'm

really sorry. I had no idea it would upset you so much. You never really said anything about it so I just assumed it wasn't that important any more. But I can see how stupid that was now . . .'

'Not just stupid, Danny, it was insensitive. Do you really think I want the whole world to know what I did? It would have been bad enough if I'd told Simon about it, but not telling him . . . Surely you've got to understand how awful I feel about that. And of all the people to tell you have to choose Jake Mallory. Oh Danny, why? He's the last person I'd want to know.'

Danny's eyes were staring up at her and for a moment she seemed almost childishly bewildered. 'Louisa, I'm really, really, sorry,' she said. 'I just didn't think. I mean, I wasn't sure whether you'd told him yourself and I honestly didn't think it would do any harm to tell him. Oh God, I can see how stupid, no, you're right, insensitive, that was now. Shit, why did I do it? I'm sorry, really, I'm sorry. But at least I told him that if it had been his baby then you'd never have done it.'

'You said what!' Louisa cried incredulously. 'Danny, for Christ's sake, what's the matter with you?'

'But you wouldn't have got rid of it if it had been his,' Danny argued. 'I know you wouldn't. You'd have kept it if it had been Jake's.'

'But it wasn't Jake's! I hardly even know Jake. I've never even slept with him, so what the hell made you go and say something like that?'

'I didn't want him to think badly of you,' Danny said lamely.

'Then why tell him about the baby in the first place? Simon yes, but not the baby.'

'OK, OK, I can see why you're angry, and I apologize, but it's done now and well, it's better that you know I've told him just in case you were thinking about lying to him.'

'I wasn't thinking about saying anything at all, not at this stage,' Louisa raged. 'Shit, what a mess, Danny. What am I supposed to say to him if I see him again now?'

'Well I don't think he was particularly bothered about it,'

Danny said. 'He said that Simon had a right to know, but if it were him, he said, he wouldn't want to know and even if he did then he wouldn't see it as being his problem.'

Louisa watched her, shaking her head in disbelief. 'When did you have this conversation?' she asked.

'Last night.'

Louisa suddenly felt like she'd been struck. 'You saw Jake last night,' she whispered.

Danny nodded. 'On the *Valhalla*.'

'But I thought he was in Mexico.'

'He was. He got back two days ago. He called me just after he got in.'

'But you were with Erik last night in Monte Carlo.'

'No. That's where I told you I was going because I was afraid you might be upset if you thought Jake had called me and not you. But I don't like lying to you like this, Louisa, that's why I've told you now. It's better that you know the truth and what kind of man he is. I don't know what he's been telling you, but he's not for you, Louisa, not a man like that. He's a real bastard. He's leading you on . . .'

'But what about you and Erik? I thought you were mad about Erik.'

'We're not talking about me, we're talking about you because it's you who's going to get hurt here, not me. I can sleep with them both, play them at their own games, but you can't. You don't have it in you to do that, you never have.'

'But Erik's crazy about you, you said you were about him. So why are you sleeping with Jake?'

'It's hard to explain, but put in it's simplest terms Jake and I can't get enough of each other, that's why he called me as soon as he got back.'

'But what about Erik?' Louisa insisted, almost shouting as though the noise could numb the horrible jealousy churning inside her.

'What about Erik? He's just another man.'

'He's got feelings, Danny.'

'So have I. I care for him, but not the way he wants me to.

He knows I'm sleeping with Jake, he was there on board last night while I was with Jake. I spent the rest of the night with him after I'd made love with Jake. He accepts that I need other men, that he can't give me everything . . .'

'And what about Jake? Does he accept that too?'

'Not as easily, but he knows that's the way it has to be.'

'But why does it have to be that way? Why can't you commit yourself to one man?'

'I could if Jake would let me, but he won't. Not yet, anyway. There are things he has to get sorted then maybe we can give it a try. Look, I don't want to be petty about this Louisa, but I met him first, I slept with him first and it's me he calls. That's not to say I don't think he'll call you, because I'm sure he will. But when he does I think you should remember that it'll probably only be because I'm with Erik. Speaking of whom,' she added, as Erik's Jaguar turned into the drive.

With her mind still reeling from all that had been said Louisa watched dumbly as Danny sauntered, virtually naked, across the lawn then stood on the edge of the terrace and waited for Erik to come to her. As he folded her in his arms, a huge bunch of flowers in one hand and a neat little box from an exclusive jeweller's in the other, Louisa turned away stiff with the jealousy that was almost choking her. She didn't begrudge Danny her relationship with Erik, nor the expensive gifts he brought her, but she did begrudge whatever Danny had with Jake. Just to think of the two of them together made her feel sick inside. The vision of their entwined limbs, the frenzy of their passion, inflamed her anger to the point of violence. It stabbed her with a pain she had no right to feel for he wasn't hers, she had no claims on him, had shared no more than one kiss with him, but the pain was there nevertheless. He'd told her she meant something to him and like a fool she'd believed him. Worse, she still believed him because she didn't want to face the fact that he had lied to her. She wanted to hold onto the man she thought he was, the man who had made her feel so wonderful and special, the man whose feelings for her had been as immediate and as compelling as hers had for him. She moved restlessly, as though to extricate herself from the sudden power of his imagined presence. She so badly wanted to see him in that moment, to feel him touching her and watch his grey eyes darken as he looked at her and told her that nothing Danny had said was true. Then the echo of Danny's words suddenly rang in her mind, 'you go off into a fantasy world where everything is just the way you want it to be . . .'

The truth of that was suddenly razor sharp in her mind and as she sank back into the chair she felt a terrible, debilitating contempt for herself.

She looked up to see Erik wandering across the garden to join her. As she watched him she couldn't stop herself smiling. He had such a roguish look in his eyes and seemed so ridiculously pleased to see her that it simply wasn't possible not to respond.

'Hi,' he said, stooping to kiss her. 'How are you?'

'Fine.'

'You look kind of glum to me,' he grinned, slanting her a glance from the corner of his eye as he poured more wine into Danny's glass.

'It's just the heat,' Louisa said, stretching. 'How's life with you? No, don't tell me, just perfect now you're here.'

He laughed. 'You've got it.'

He turned to look at her and seeing the way his eyes were dancing she started to laugh.

'How do you fancy going into Cannes tonight?' he said.

'Oh no. You don't want me tagging along and I'm pretty tired.'

'Go and get dressed,' he said.

'No, honestly, I'm not in the mood for going out.'

'You will be once you're ready. Now, no arguments, go and get dressed or I'll pick you up and put you in the car the way you are.'

'Erik, I don't want to play gooseberry . . .'

'Louisa, do as you're told.'

Realizing she was in danger of just sitting there feeling sorry for herself if she didn't go Louisa took herself off to get changed, almost laughing as she wondered what Danny would say when she discovered Erik had invited her along. But what the hell, she felt angry enough with Danny right now to want to spoil her evening.

Just under an hour later she was on the point of leaving her room when there was a knock on the door and Erik came in.

'Danny and I are leaving now,' he said, grinning all over his face.

Louisa stared at him in amazement.

'You look lovely,' he told her.

'Erik! Erik!' she cried as he started to leave. 'I thought I was coming with you.'

Laughing, he turned back. 'I guess I'd better come clean,' he said. 'I remembered what you said about a woman not liking a man to turn up unannounced and Jake's on his way over.'

Everything inside Louisa suddenly turned weak. 'But . . . I don't . . .'

'I thought you'd want to be looking your best,' Erik laughed. 'Have a good time,' and he was gone.

A few minutes later Louisa heard his car pulling out of the drive and, as her stomach churned horribly, she went to pour herself more wine. She had no idea what was going on, or why Jake hadn't just called to say he was coming, all she could think of was what Danny had told her, to remember that if she did see Jake it was probably only because she, Danny, was with Erik.

Heading back to the hammock chair at the other end of the pool she started to rehearse in her mind all that she wanted to say. She needed the answers to so many questions she hardly knew where to begin. She thought of Sarah and wondered if she would get anywhere with all the questions she had for Morandi tonight. Then quite suddenly none of it seemed important. If there was something underhand going on, if Jake, Morandi and Erik were involving them in something they might live to regret it didn't matter. All that mattered was that he was here. That he was getting out of his car and ambling across the garden towards her, his hands stuffed into the pockets of his faded jeans, his wonderfully hypnotic eyes holding hers as he drew closer and started to smile.

Louisa's heart was in her throat. Somewhere deep down inside she knew she should be angry with him, but she just couldn't get it past the sheer emotion she felt at seeing him. For one dizzying moment she was overwhelmed by the enormity of her feelings, could hardly make herself believe that this man who had the looks, the power and the wealth to attract any woman was here to see her.

He stopped in front of her, looked down at her, then taking his hands from his pockets he stooped towards her, putting his mouth over hers. After a moment he took her by the elbows and, still kissing her, pulled her to her feet and drew her into his arms.

'Hi,' he drawled, his voice as dark and intimate as his eyes as he gazed down at her.

'Hi,' she said.

He kissed her again, touching her lips gently with his own, holding her loosely about the waist while everything inside her was fighting hard not to respond.

He raised his head again and started to smile. 'What are you afraid of?' he whispered.

'You,' she answered.

'Don't be,' he said, folding her against him and resting her head on his shoulder. 'I missed you.'

As he held her Louisa could feel herself melting into him, was aware of the way his faint, musky odour mingled with that of the sea was seeping into her senses, dizzying her yet calming her and very gently arousing her. His latent power seemed to embrace her with a touch as tangible as the hard muscles of his thighs and the strength of his arms. 'When did you get back?' she said.

'Two days ago.'

Immediately Louisa stiffened and pulled away.

'Hey,' he said, putting his fingers under her chin and tilting her face up to his. 'I tried to call you, half a dozen times, but there's no getting past Danny. Why do you think Erik came to get her the way he did tonight? I wanted to see you.'

'She said you called her, that she was with you on the *Valhalla* last night.'

'She was. So was Erik. I tried to call you then, but you weren't at home.'

It was true, she hadn't been. 'She said you made love to her.'

He grinned and shook his head. 'Not me,' he said.

'But you have made love to her.'

'Sure I did, the night before I met you.'

'Not since?'

'Uh-huh,' he smiled. 'You're looking at the only guy around here she's not making it with.'

'Then why does she say she is?'

'I guess,' he laughed, 'to make you jealous, and it's working.'

Louisa rolled her eyes, trying not to laugh, knowing she shouldn't believe him, but wanting to desperately. 'You're so sure of yourself,' she remarked.

'Not really. I was kind of scared you might be hiding behind Danny, not wanting to see me again after what I told you the last time I was here.' He smiled deep into her eyes. 'So, do I get a drink or do I get to kiss you again?'

'How about both?' she said recklessly.

'I think we'd better take the drink first,' he said, the irony in his voice seeming to lift her heart.

When she returned from the kitchen with a fresh bottle of wine and two glasses he was rocking back and forth in the hammock chair, his eyes closed. It wasn't until she passed him a drink and he opened them that she noticed how very tired he suddenly looked. Tired and strained as though there were something tormenting his mind that wouldn't leave him alone.

Taking the drink in one hand he used the other to pull her down beside him and resting his elbow along the back of the chair he began gently, almost absently, to stroke her face and neck. She leaned against him, sinking into the aura of him then turned her face to his and laughed when he bit her nose.

'How was Mexico?' she asked.

He took a sip of his drink then gazed past her at the rockery that spilled in a blaze of colour down to the gates.

It was so long before he spoke again that the glow of happiness burning inside her began to fuel itself with unease.

Then turning back to her and running his fingers into her hair he said, 'Tell me about you. What have you been doing while I was away?'

'Writing,' she said. 'Exploring the countryside with Sarah – thinking about you.'

He gave her a quick hug then pushing her gently away he took a fat, self-rolled cigarette from his shirt pocket and lit it.

As the sweet, unmistakable scent of marijuana drifted into the balmy evening air Louisa turned to look at him. He looked back, watching her with eyes that seemed to question her, with an intensity that seemed to move into her and hold her. Then slowly he started to shake his head. 'What the hell am I doing?' he said. 'I've got no right to be here, no right to do this to you.'

Louisa said nothing, she just watched him as he took a long draw on the cigarette then leaned forward to let it rest in the ashtray. When he sat back he lifted a hand to her face and ran his thumb over her lips. 'It's true,' he said as though speaking to himself. 'Something is happening here and it's happened so goddamned fast . . .' He gave a dry, almost bitter laugh. 'We've got to talk,' he said.

'OK,' she smiled, catching his thumb between her lips.

His eyes were on her mouth, then taking his hand away he pulled her back against his shoulder.

'It's kind of hard to know how to say this,' he said finally. 'But we've got to deal with reality here. We've got to look at what's happening between us and work out the best way to handle it. Maybe we should just take from it what we can, what's not going to hurt either of us, most of all you.'

'What do you mean?' she said.

'I mean that you're here for the summer. That after that,

when you go back to London, it'll be over for us. We can't take it any further than that.'

'But why? I don't understand.'

He sighed heavily and pressed his fingers to his eyes. 'There's so much you don't know about me,' he said, his voice suddenly tired to the point of exhaustion, 'and if I'm being honest I don't want you to know.'

'Is it so terrible?'

'Yeah, it's pretty goddamned terrible.' Then lowering his hand he tilted her face to his and kissed her softly on the mouth. 'Right now you're the only good thing in my life,' he said, 'and if I tell you what's really going on it's going to tarnish what we have. In some way it's going to make you a part of it and I don't want that to happen. I want just that we're together, that we give each other whatever we can, and when it comes time for you to go, you go with good memories. Can you live with that?'

'I don't know,' she whispered, looking away.

Leaning forward he put his glass on the table then pulled her deeper into his arms. 'I'm not proud of what I'm doing here,' he said. 'I'm asking you to take the decision to stop this when I can't do it myself. But I'm not going to lie to you, Louisa, there can't be anything at the end of it. You've got to know that so you can decide whether it's better for you to break away now. It's gonna be easier if you do, on both of us, but I'm a pretty selfish sort of guy and what I want right now is to go on holding you this way just as long as I can.'

'Is it really so impossible for us?' she said, looking up at him.

As he looked back at her she could almost feel how desperately he wanted to say no, but in the end his answer was unequivocal. 'Yeah, it's impossible,' he said.

Louisa looked down at their entwined fingers, his so long and masculine, hers seeming so frail by comparison. 'This is cruel,' she said. 'Why did we have to meet at all if this is the way it has to be? I mean, whichever way you look at it, it's going to hurt. Now or later.' She shrugged. 'But maybe it's better to do it later, at least that way we'll have had something.'

He laughed, abruptly, but there was no humour in it. 'Now how come I can suddenly do for you what I can't do for myself?' he said. 'I'm gonna call it quits now, Louisa. I'm gonna do it for you because I can't let you go through this, I can't drag you through it. You don't need any more pain in your life.'

Louisa's eyes moved to the garden as the carefully targeted sprinklers began to arc and spin. 'So Danny did tell you,' she said flatly.

'About the baby? Yeah, she told me,' he said, stroking her hair.

'And did you mean it when you said if it had been yours you wouldn't have seen it as your problem?'

Closing his eyes he let his head fall against hers. 'Shit, there's so much you don't know,' he groaned. 'It's got to be easier for you to know, but I can't do it. And the answer's yes, I did say that, but I had my reasons. Reasons that don't matter if we're going to stop seeing each other.'

'But I don't want us to stop, Jake. I want this time with you even if it's all we're going to get.'

'No, I can't let you do it.'

'Jake, I've got my pride, so please don't make me beg. I want to go on seeing you. I want you to go on holding me this way, for ever if it were possible, but if it's not then for as long as you can.'

'That's how you feel now, but in two weeks, a month from now you're going to see it a whole lot differently and by then it'll be too late to turn back.'

'I'm prepared to take that chance.'

'It's not going to be easy.'

'Nothing worth having ever is,' she said.

He smiled and tightened his arms around her. 'I know I'm gonna live to regret this,' he said, 'but how about you hold me too?'

As she turned to put her arms around his neck she saw how

suddenly vicious the wound around his eye had become, as though it too were suffering whatever pain he was hiding.

'What happened to your eye?' she said after he'd kissed her.

'It's a long story, not one for now,' he answered, leaning across her to pick up his wine. 'For now you're gonna tell me that you're prepared to stick by the rules I'm about to lay down if we're going to continue seeing each other.'

'Rules? You mean like love, honour and obey?' For a moment she was shocked by what she'd said, but when she saw he was laughing she laughed too.

'Definitely the last,' he said. 'And quit doing that,' he said, pulling her up as she started to kiss his neck. 'It's driving me crazy.'

'I know, I can feel it,' she grinned.

His eyes were simmering with laughter, but as he looked at her the humour started slowly to retreat. 'Jesus Christ,' he murmured. 'I so badly want to make love to you.'

As Louisa's heart turned over, the breath caught in her throat. And then he was kissing her, crushing her to him, pushing his tongue deep into her mouth. She clung to him, curling her fingers through his hair as he laid her back in his arms, fanning his fingers over her neck, pressing his thumb along her jaw. Then his hand was on her leg, moving along her thigh. She raised it, opening herself to him, groaning into his open mouth as he touched her.

There was no denying that she was as ready for him as he was for her, but quite suddenly he stopped. 'We can't do this,' he said gruffly.

'Why?'

He looked down at her for some time before his eyes started to dance. 'Are you taking contraception?' he said.

Reluctantly she shook her head.

'Then that's the first reason,' he said. 'And the second,' he added, pulling her up, 'is that we've got to talk some more. I'm not having you make any decisions about going on seeing me without knowing what it's going to entail. OK?'

'OK? Then can we make love?'

'We can make love,' he laughed, 'when we get ourselves some contraception.'

They both turned round as the automatic lights around the house and pool suddenly came on, not realizing how quickly dusk had come on them. Jake took a lighter from his pocket and lit the green spiral on the table to keep the mosquitos at bay while Louisa, still trembling slightly from the incredible force of her desire, took a soothing sip of wine.

He turned back and taking her arms from around her knees he pulled her onto his lap.

For a while they sat quietly, listening to the frogs and the crickets. He looked down at her, a certain irony in his eyes, but she could sense his inner struggle. 'Shit, I still can't believe I'm doing this,' he said, pursing the corner of his lips and looking at her as though blaming her for getting to him the way she did. Then his eyes moved past her, out towards the potted palms around the pool. 'The reason I told Danny that I wouldn't see it as my problem if you were pregnant,' he began, 'is so that Danny wouldn't know the way I feel about you. I don't want her to know, I don't want anyone to know. That's rule number one. It's not only safer for you that way, it's safer for me too.'

'But . . .'

'No, these are unconditional rules, Louisa. You have to stick by them or you're gonna find yourself in a whole lot of trouble I might not be able to get you out of. So don't ask any questions, because I've told you already that I don't want to talk about what's going on. All I want is that what you and I have stays between us and goes no further.'

'I was only going to say, what about Erik? He set it up for you to come here tonight.'

'Erik's not a problem. Erik is one of the few you can trust. The others are my crew. That's it! No one else.'

'What about Sarah?'

'*No one else.*'

'OK. But what about when we want to see each other? You know already how often Danny answers the phone.'

'There are ways around that as we proved tonight. But for God's sake don't trust her. I don't know what kind of game she's playing, but she's not doing herself or anyone else any favours by lying about sleeping with me. That's why Erik's taken her in hand.'

'You mean he's not as crazy about her as he seems? It's all a front?'

'The man is besotted with her as it happens, more fool him, but yes, it's partly a front.'

'What about Mario Morandi?'

'Who?'

'You mean you don't know him?'

Jake looked at her askance. 'Should I?' he said carefully.

'Oh, Jake, please don't lie to me. Do you know him or don't you?'

'Why does it matter?'

'That means you do know him. And it matters because Sarah's out with him tonight. Who is he, Jake? He's not an Italian, is he?'

'He's a producer who makes low-budget movies,' Jake answered.

'Consuela put us in touch with him,' Louisa said, hoping it might provoke some sort of response.

He showed no surprise, just chewed thoughtfully on his bottom lip. 'And you say they're out together tonight?'

'That's right.'

To her surprise he started to laugh. 'Then maybe, my darling, you can tell Sarah about me. But only Sarah.'

'This is starting to feel like we're ganging up against Danny. I know she has her faults, but she doesn't mean any harm, Jake. I promise you, she doesn't.'

'And providing she knows nothing she won't cause any. So just you leave her to Erik, because besotted as he might be, he knows exactly how to handle her.' Again he laughed when he saw the sceptical look she gave him. 'Erik's been around the world,' he reminded her, 'he's come across plenty of Danny Spencers in his time and as far as I can make out he's gone off at the deep end for every one of them. He's even married a couple of them, married to one right now, I believe, unless he's forgotten to tell me the divorce has gone through. If it has then don't be surprised if he ups and pops the question to Danny, myself I'm expecting it, though it won't be anything to do with me. I'd never ask him to go that far, that's his own choice. All I'm asking is he keeps her off my back because a woman like Danny can cause the kind of problems I don't even want to think about. It was just luck that Erik was staying with Jean-Claude when he was and got to meet her, the falling in love bit he did all on his own, the rest he's doing for me, to protect me and to protect her.'

'You know I'm going out of my mind with curiosity here,' Louisa groaned. 'How does Jean-Claude fit into it all?'

'He doesn't. I don't even know the man. He's a friend of Erik's from way back, nothing to do with me. Now rule number two. No more questions. You don't need to know what's going on, like I said, it's better you don't. You just do as I say and you'll be OK.'

'Does that mean I have something, or someone, to be afraid of?'

'You might. I don't know for sure, but I don't want to take any chances. Christ, what am I saying here? If I thought you were in any real danger I'd stop this thing right here and now no matter how strongly I felt. But the minute I think there might be any danger then you're out of here, do you hear me? You're on the next plane back to London and you're taking Sarah and Danny with you.'

'Wouldn't it be better if I knew what I was up against?' she protested.

'If I knew for sure there wouldn't be any danger,' he said. 'All I know is that I've got to be out of my mind to go on seeing you, but I can't give you up, not yet anyway. It's been a long time since I had anything good in my life and you, Louisa Kramer, feel better than good. In fact a whole lot better than good. I just wish to God I knew why life had thrown you at me right now, because the way things are I've got nothing to offer you and I've got no right to do this to you, none at all. I just hope you're not going to end up hating me, but I don't guess I'd blame you if you did.'

'That's hard to imagine at this moment.'

'I know. And that's why we've got to have rule number three. I don't want you to go fooling yourself that this is all going to turn out all right because it won't. You've got to believe what I'm telling you now, that two months at the maximum is all we've got and then I'm out of here and out of your life. I won't be coming back and I sure as hell can't take you with me. I've got other commitments, other priorities that will take over. There's no getting away from them and if things turn out the way I hope, I won't want to get away from them. And just so's you understand how serious this is, there are people involved in this who just might not come out alive. That's not the way I want it, but it's the way it's got to be.'

'Is one of those people likely to be you?' Louisa asked, feeling strangely as though she was drifting away from reality.

'I don't know.'

'Can I ask one last question?'

'You can ask, I'm not promising to answer.'

'Is this all to do with drugs?'

'No. It's got nothing to do with drugs. I just wish it were that simple.'

Louisa looked at him for a moment, then laying her head on his shoulder she gazed absently down towards the woods where night was spreading its darkness as inexorably as the knowledge she was going to lose him was already spreading its dread in her heart. It felt so right being here in his arms, it was where she belonged, where he belonged too. There was no way of rationalizing those feelings, they were just there and deep down inside she knew they were right. And at that moment it didn't matter that there was so much she didn't know about him, she couldn't imagine anything that would change the way she felt. Yes, there were a thousand more questions she wanted to ask, but she knew it wouldn't do any good to try. If he wanted her to know he'd tell her, he'd be as frank and honest with her as he'd been about the impossibility of a future together. She just felt thankful that he'd agreed to let her speak to Sarah. She had the feeling she was going to need to do that quite a lot over the next few weeks. And who could say, maybe during that time he would feel that he could trust her enough to tell her what was really going on and then she could give him the support she longed to give as well as the release he so obviously craved. But for now all that mattered was that they were together, that they could sit here like this and hold each other, knowing that whatever the future held for either of them, that for this short time they had everything they wanted.

'You OK?' he whispered.

She nodded. 'Just trying to take it all in. I wish I understood it better, but for now I'm willing to go along with the way it is.'

'And the minute that changes, the minute you want out, you just tell me and we'll call it quits,' he said. 'Now, what are the chances of a man getting something to eat around here?'

'Every chance,' she smiled, reluctantly unwinding herself from their embrace and getting up. 'Shall we take a picnic out here, or shall we take it to bed?'

'Uh-huh,' he grinned. 'No contraception, no nookie. We'll take the picnic out here.'

'There's a late night *pharmacie*,' she said, her brown eyes twinkling the challenge.

'Still no. I've got to leave in an hour. Hey,' he said, taking her hands when he saw how disappointed she looked. 'There'll be other times.'

'Are you sure?'

He stood up and cupped his hands behind her neck.

'I'm not sure whether I should be saying this,' she said, looking sideways into the pool, 'but I want you very much. Very, very much. But then I guess that must be pretty obvious by now.'

'Yeah, it is,' he smiled. 'And I want you too. But I'd be a liar if I didn't say that I'm worried about how much harder it might make it for us to say goodbye.'

'It worries me too, but I guess I'm just not as sensible as you, nor as strong-willed.'

Knowing how close he was to giving in he turned her away from him and made light of it by saying. 'But I'll bet you're as hungry, so come on, let's get this picnic together, then perhaps I could take a look at these shots Sarah's taken of the *Valhalla*. Erik tells me they're a knockout.'

14

Late the following morning Louisa and Sarah were strolling through the covered market in the old town of Antibes laden down with fruit, salads and flowers. Their progress was slow through the dense crowds of sunburned, straw-hatted tourists and frenetic French housewives and the walk back to the car promised to be a long, unbearably hot one as it was parked way up on the ramparts.

'I honestly don't think you've got anything to worry about,' Sarah was saying, dodging her way round a splendid bouquet of leeks that was bobbing past her. 'I mean, I know I'd believe him if I were you. And the fact that he's holding back on making love to you just confirms to me that you really do mean something to him. Otherwise he'd just screw you and leave.'

'That's what I keep telling myself,' Louisa said, shaking her head politely while smiling at the jolly round Frenchman who was offering her several bunches of freesias. 'And when I was with him it seemed to make sense, but now, in the cold light of day I just don't know what to think.'

'You just don't have enough confidence in yourself, that's your trouble,' Sarah said, stopping at a stall to pick up a fan-shaped object that unfolded into a hat and jamming it on her head. 'What do you think?' she said, tottering sideways as a busy French housewife jostled past her.

Louisa burst out laughing. 'Not really you,' she said.

'He called you this morning, didn't he?' Sarah said as they walked on. 'Why would he bother to do that if he wasn't crazy about you?'

'I don't know, but tell me, do you think I'm mad going ahead with this?'

'Probably,' Sarah responded cheerfully. They parted for a moment to let a wheelbarrow of oranges through. 'So he's sending this Marianne woman to pick you up whenever he wants to see you?' she continued as they came back together.

'That's what he said,' Louisa answered.

'Mmm.' Sarah pondered for a moment. 'Who is she exactly?'

'She works for him as some kind of runaround as far as I can make out. Funny isn't it,' she went on, 'that Morandi denied knowing Jake when Jake admitted that they did know each other.'

'My guess is that he needs permission from Jake before he says anything,' Sarah answered, taking an apple from the bag and biting into it. 'Did Jake tell you anything else about him?'

'Just that he produces low-budget films. He didn't say anything about how they were linked to each other.' She cast Sarah a sideways glance. 'You really like him, don't you?'

'He's OK,' Sarah answered breezily, but Louisa wasn't fooled. 'He's not Italian,' Sarah added.

'Well we know that,' Louisa laughed.

'No, I mean he admitted he's not. He's from Buckinghamshire. His real name's Trevor.'

The laughter bubbled from Louisa's lips before she could stop it.

'I told him I prefer Morandi,' Sarah grinned. 'So we're sticking with it.'

'So did he tell you why he's masquerading as an Italian?'

'Nope,' Sarah said, squinting as they stepped out into the sunlight and lifting her sunglasses from their chain. 'I did ask, but he's such a terrible liar I know I still haven't got the truth yet.' She sighed wearily. 'As amateur sleuths we're not doing too well, are we? I mean we haven't found out anything of any consequence. Did you ask Jake about Consuela at all last night?'

'No, I didn't. Did you ask Morandi?'

'Yep, but he was as closed about that as he was about Jake. I'm curious about Aphrodite though. He says they've been having an affair for the past few months and that he's been trying to break it off for a while, but she won't let him.

I told him to fire her, but he says he can't do it. Well, he's such a sensitive soul I don't suppose that really surprises me, but I got the impression that when he said "can't" he really meant can't. Do you think we could stop here and have a drink?' she said, flopping down at an empty table outside a café.

'So how do you feel about continuing to see him if he's still involved with her?' Louisa said, sitting down too and putting the shopping on the chair next to her.

Sarah shrugged. 'Just so long as she doesn't spray me with any more wine then I'm game,' she said. 'Do you think we stand any chance of getting anything out of Erik?'

'No. And if we tried he'd probably tell Jake and I don't much relish the thought of what Jake might say if he thought I was going behind his back trying to find things out. What are you going to have to drink?'

'A large orange juice and soda, it might help my hangover.'

'How much did you have to drink last night?'

'Not as much as Morandi, but enough. It was quite pathetic actually. There we both were knocking it back like there was no tomorrow just to give ourselves Dutch courage for when we got home and when we got there all he did was shake my hand and get back in the car. I've never felt quite so resistible.'

'Didn't you invite him in?'

'Yes, but he said he didn't want to appear presumptuous on our first date. He has too much respect for me to have anyone thinking that he might be taking advantage of me.'

'Would you have gone for it if he had come in?' Louisa laughed.

'I'm not sure. I mean I was all bravado on the doorstep, but I reckon once we were inside I'd have come over all frigid or something. However, alcohol loosened my tongue enough to tell him that I had a few problems in that area to which he replied that he didn't in any way want to rush me and that we would, when I felt ready, try to work through the problems together. Isn't that sweet?'

'Delightful. You seem to have found yourself a real old-fashioned gentleman in Trev.'

'Oh God, don't call him that,' Sarah laughed and groaned. 'Isn't it just the most dreadful name?'

'It doesn't have quite the same ring as Morandi, no,' Louisa grinned, turning to the waiter to give him their order.

'Now, tell me again what Jake said about my shots of the *Valhalla*,' Sarah said excitedly. 'Did he really want to buy them?'

'That's what he said.'

'I'd happily give them to him, you know.'

'That's between you and him. He does want you to get them blown up and framed for him though. He's happy for you to choose the frames, but they should be chrome because that will fit in with decor of the yacht club he intends to hang them in at one of his marinas over in San Diego. And then, with any luck, other yacht owners will like them and you'll have commissions coming out of your ears. It was a brilliant idea of yours to use that infrared film, he was completely bowled over by the effect.'

'Mmm, it was pretty ingenious, wasn't it?' Sarah remarked. 'You know, I'm coming to the conclusion that I enjoy shooting sea and landscapes more than I do people. I think I'll talk it over with Erik, since he's the real genius around here. When's he bringing Danny back, did she say when she called earlier?'

'No. She just said to expect her when we see her, but not to try contacting her at Erik's because she won't be there.'

'And did you give her the satisfaction of asking exactly where she would be?'

'Absolutely not.'

'Good for you,' Sarah grinned.

Feeling a shadow fall across her Consuela opened her eyes and removed her sunglasses. 'Ah, Jake,' she said, smiling up at him from where she was lying on a sunbed. 'I thought you were in Paris.'

'Your spies are letting you down, Consuela,' he remarked, sitting on the end of the bed, 'I got back last night.'

'Was it a good trip?'

'It was useful,' he said.

'And Mexico?'

'Mexico yielded up what I expected.'

'So you're no longer angry with me?'

'Angry with you?' he said. 'Now why would I be angry with you?'

'You have no reason to be, but I always feel that you are. And at our last meeting you were, as I recall, extremely upset.'

Jake's eyes were hard as he looked down at her, then picking up the suncream from the table beside her, he pooled some into his hands and started to massage it into her legs. 'You're still in pretty good shape for a woman your age, you know that?' he said.

Consuela laughed. 'Thank you for the reminder,' she said. 'Will you be staying long in France?'

'Why, do you want me to?' he countered.

She chuckled. 'It's all the same to me,' she answered. 'But it might not be to a certain young lady.'

The corner of his mouth drew down in a smile. He hadn't missed the fractional movement of a curtain in an upstairs window when he'd arrived, neither had he failed to recognize Danielle Spencer. 'You mean you haven't succeeded in warning her off me yet?' he said.

Consuela looked up from his hands. 'It would appear you've made quite an impact,' she answered, her soft brown eyes gently mocking him.

'It wasn't my intention, I can assure you,' he smiled.

'It rarely is,' she laughed. Then she was serious. 'That girl is very special to her parents, Jake,' she said quietly.

Jake was very still. 'Most children are,' he said. His eyes were suddenly burning with fury, but Consuela didn't look away.

'If you're thinking of using her to get back at me, then you'll be hurting the wrong people,' she warned.

'And you would know all about that, wouldn't you, Consuela?' he said bitingly.

Consuela looked away. 'I have nothing to tell you,' she said.

'You are chasing rainbows, Jake, and I'm not going to help you.'

'Because you're afraid of what I might find at the end?'

'It's you who are afraid. I have nothing to fear. My conscience is clear.'

He laughed, bitterly. 'And mine isn't, is that what you're saying?'

'How can it be after what you've done?'

'You know,' he said, his eyebrows arched incredulously. 'I think you're actually beginning to believe your own lies.'

She reached for a towel and draped it across her hips as she sat up. 'Jake, look at me,' she said, a tremor of passion shaking her voice. 'I am not lying. She is dead. She died that day on the yacht and we both know how she died. Now why don't you let her rest in peace? Ghosts can't talk so you have nothing to fear.'

'She's alive, Consuela,' he said. 'She's alive and I'm going to find her.'

'Why? So you can kill her again?'

His hand moved so swiftly that Consuela didn't even know it was coming until her head jerked back under the force of the blow. She gasped, covered her cheek with her hand and glared at him. 'That makes you even less of a man than you already are,' she spat as he stood up.

Behind him he was aware of the young boys grouping, ready to come to her defence. For some reason it amused him and he started to laugh. 'What do you want, Consuela?' he said. 'To see me in jail? Is that it? Is that still your burning ambition, to see me behind bars?'

'It's where you belong and you know it,' she hissed.

He nodded thoughtfully, his humour still not abated. 'If I go, Consuela,' he said, 'it'll be with your blood on my hands.'

'Mine and how many others?'

'Just yours.'

'Hah!' she scoffed. 'It's already too late for that and we both know it.'

'She's still alive, Consuela.' He smiled the reminder, but

there was a dangerous glint in his eyes now. 'When you're ready to talk you know where to find me,' he said and dropping the suncream in her lap he started to walk away.

'Jake!' she called after him.

He stopped.

'What happened to Dmitri?'

'Dmitri?' he said turning back.

'The Greek boy who used to work here. What happened to him?'

'I don't know, Consuela,' he drawled, 'you tell me.'

'Jake, I care about these boys, they're my family now.'

Jake looked up and seeing that they had moved into earshot he grinned. 'Then you should take better care of them,' he said, and tossing his keys in the air he caught them and strolled off towards his car.

Mario Morandi's apartment with its uninterrupted view of the glittering blue Mediterranean and small pebbled balcony high above the harbour at the Baie des Anges was at the peak of one of the triangular blocks which sat like four giant flared skirts on the borders of Nice. It was a small apartment, but the rooms were bright and airy with only the bare essentials when it came to furniture and though nothing quite matched it was, Sarah considered, quite touchingly him. Especially, she smiled to herself, because he was a little too big for the place. The only clutter was on the walls where paintings of all shapes and sizes jostled for space, most of which, he confessed shyly, he had done himself. Sarah looked them over with a critical eye, tilted her head from side to side, almost turned herself upside down but no matter which angle she viewed them at there was no getting away from the fact that they were some of the worst she had ever seen.

As she turned to look up at him she could barely stop herself laughing for his efforts to appear modest were hopelessly dazzled by the childlike pride shining in his eyes.

'Would you like one?' he offered, his eagerness tinged with an adorable uncertainty.

'I'd love one,' Sarah smiled. 'Which one would you like me to have?'

'I'd like you to take my favourite,' he said, his cheeks reddening slightly as they gazed at each other.

'And which one would that be?' she asked, reluctantly tearing her eyes from his.

'This one here,' he said, reaching up to lift it from its hook.

'Oh yes,' she enthused, taking it from him. 'I can see why it's your favourite. It's got so much . . . so much depth to it. Oh yes, yes. It's really quite . . .'

'Transanimatic?' he supplied, helpfully.

She turned to him in astonishment. 'You took the word right out of my mouth,' she said, looking up at him as though overawed that their minds should move so eloquently along the same tracks. 'What's it called?' she added, hoping that it might give her some clue as to what it was actually meant to depict.

'I'm afraid it doesn't have a title,' he apologized, scratching his head and making his hair stand up. 'Why don't you give it one?'

'Ah, uh, well now, let me see . . .' She was thinking fast, wishing she knew what the hell transanimatic meant. 'I know,' she said, still stalling. 'Yes, that's it. I know just what it should be called.'

He waited, eagerly, excitedly.

'Yes, that's definitely it,' she said decisively. 'Yes, it can't be anything else. It's perfect.'

His excitement was growing.

'I'm going to call it . . . Soul in Flight!'

She turned to look at him and blinked at the look of such incredulous admiration he was giving her.

'That's amazing,' he murmured, almost reverently. 'Truly amazing.'

Sarah beamed. 'I'm glad you like it,' she said happily, rather pleased with it herself. 'Soul in Flight.'

'Amazing,' he repeated, shaking his head in disbelief. 'Absolutely, truly amazing. Especially for someone who doesn't know what transanimatic means.'

Sarah's blue eyes came steadily up to his face. He looked perfectly serious, was still gazing at his *chef d'oeuvre* as though not quite able to believe its brilliance. Then she saw the corner of his mouth twitch and felt the laughter spring to her own lips. 'You're winding me up,' she cried.

'Yes,' he nodded, his lean face breaking into a grin. 'But nevertheless it's true. It's a great title for someone who doesn't know the meaning of transanimatic.'

'OK, so what does it mean?'

'It means the transference of a soul from one body into another.'

'It does?' she said, stupendously pleased with the choice now. She looked at the painting again and as dreadful as it was she suddenly adored it. 'I'm going to cherish it always and it's going to get pride of place when I hang it,' she declared rashly.

He shrugged self-consciously, but was obviously bursting with pleasure that she liked it so much. 'Would you like something to drink?' he offered, taking the painting from her and leaning it against the wall. 'I've got tea and coffee.'

'Gosh, both!' she said, shocked.

He laughed. 'Something a little stronger?'

Sarah looked at her watch. It was eleven o'clock in the morning. 'How about a *pastis*?' she suggested, devilishly.

'*Pastis* it is,' he grinned, and went off to the kitchen, leaving Sarah to boggle over the rest of his bewilderingly myopic masterpieces.

She was actually on her way to Monaco to meet up with Erik who had agreed to spend the afternoon with her and her cameras in the wooded mountains behind Vence. But she wasn't due to meet him until one, so had called Morandi to ask, on the off-chance, if he was free since she was passing through Nice. As it was Saturday Morandi was at home and had sounded as keen to see her as she was to see him. And, she had to confess, she'd been more than a little curious to take a look at where he lived.

'How long have you been here?' she asked following him out onto the balcony with the drinks.

'Just over a year,' he answered, removing a guitar from a chair to make room for her to sit down. 'My sisters came down to furnish it for me, brought me all their cast-offs and I've never been too sure whether they left my nephew behind on purpose or not.'

'Nephew?' Sarah said, looking around.

'Oh, they came back for him,' Morandi assured her, tilting the flowery green parasol so the sun wasn't in her eyes. 'He was hiding under the bed, wanted to stay, didn't want to go home.'

'How old is he?' Sarah laughed as he sat down.

'Twenty-five.' His face was so perfectly straight that Sarah couldn't tell whether he was joking or not. Then she spotted the glimmer of humour in his eyes and laughed again.

'Seriously,' she said.

'He's five,' Morandi grinned, and Sarah's heartstrings stirred at how very appealing he was when he smiled.

'How many sisters do you have?' she asked.

'Two and one brother.'

'Now there's a coincidence,' she remarked, 'so have I. Where do you fit in?'

'I'm the eldest. And you?'

'The youngest.'

'Do you have any children yourself?' he asked. 'From your marriage?'

Sarah frowned. 'How did you know I was married?' she said.

'You told me the other night.'

'Did I? Oh. Well the answer's no, I don't have any. What about you? Do you have any? No, don't tell me, none that you'll admit to.'

'Oh, of course I admit to them,' he said, clearly shocked that she should think otherwise.

Sarah pulled her lips between her teeth and looked down at the mustardy yellow liquid in her glass. They were having some embarrassingly entertaining moments on the sense of humour front here and she was only glad that Louisa and Danny weren't around to witness them.

'All seven of them,' he added, bringing Sarah's head up sharply.

She gave a shout of laughter that was a little too overdone, but she wanted him to know that she appreciated his jokes. 'Honestly! I almost believed you for a moment,' she said, taking a sip of her drink.

'It's true,' he said, earnestly. 'I have seven children.'

'And don't tell me, your wife's name is Snow White,' she chuckled.

'No, Tina. Christina actually, but she likes to be called Tina.'

Sarah's smile was starting to wane. But no, he was having her on, he had to be. 'So where is she now?' she asked, watching him through narrowed eyes.

'We're separated. She's in England.'

'With the seven children?'

'No, with three. The other four are with my first wife, Dolly.'

'Just how many wives have you had?' Sarah asked.

'Only two,' he assured her.

Sarah rested her elbow on the balcony railing and looked at him. 'Are you winding me up again?' she demanded.

'No, no, not at all. Why, don't you believe me?'

'I don't think so.'

'Would you believe me if I told you you look lovely when you're confused?' he said, and promptly blushed to the roots of his hair.

'I don't believe any of it,' she laughed, thinking there was no way a man who was so easily embarrassed by a simple compliment could have managed to work himself up to fathering seven children.

'It's all true,' he said, 'every word of it. It's how I got into making the kind of films I do, it pays well and until my paintings start selling I have to meet the alimony payments somehow.'

Well that made sense even if nothing else did. 'Yes, I was

wondering how someone like you came to be making those kind of films,' she said. 'I mean you don't really strike me as the type.'

'Then how do I strike you?' he said, smiling at her shyly.

'You know, I'm not really sure I know the answer to that,' she replied. She was tempted to mention something about Jake, but feeling sure it would distress him and bring that eternally worried look back to his face she decided not to.

'I told you some pretty personal things about myself the other night, didn't I?' she said. 'I'm not sure I remember all of them, but I hope I didn't shock you or make you think I was some kind of freak or anything.'

'All you did was make me think what a very wonderful and special woman you are,' he answered with such heartfelt sincerity that she started to glow. 'And I thought how very lucky I was to be with you.'

'Do you mean that?' Sarah cried, her sunny face shining with delight.

'How can you even doubt it?' he said, still bashful, but seeming to gain confidence by the minute. 'I knew from the moment I saw you that you weren't like other women.'

Sarah pondered that for a moment. 'Then exactly what was I like?' she asked.

'You were sweet and shy and your eyes were laughing. Your hair shone like silver, just like it's shining now and your skin glowed just like it's glowing now and you made me think of all the love ballads I've ever known.'

'Really?' she said, fascinated.

'Really,' he confirmed. 'And what's more you wear mosquito bites more beautifully than anyone I've ever met.'

Sarah burst into laughter. 'I think I like you, Mr Morandi,' she said.

'Trev, please,' he said generously.

'No, I told you before, I can't call you that. You don't even look like a Trev. Thank God.'

'But you look like a princess, which is what your name means.'

Sarah's grin was so wide it was almost swallowing her dimples. 'I'm awfully glad my friends aren't here to hear you say that,' she said.

'But I'm very glad you're here. Can I get you another drink?'

'You mean you're ready for some more confessions?' she teased handing him her glass.

'I'm ready to kiss you if you will permit it,' he answered and this time it was Sarah who blushed.

She looked up as he stood over her, feeling ridiculously young and nervous. And, as he touched his lips gently to hers, she felt her own start to tremble. His mouth was warm and soft, commanding yet vaguely hesitant. As he straightened up she gazed into his eyes, then smiling awkwardly she looked down at her hands.

'I think,' she said hoarsely, 'that maybe I'd better not have any more to drink. It'll only make me brazen.'

Hearing him laugh she looked up, then reaching out for his hand she said, 'I don't want to lead you on and I just don't know how far I can go.'

'I told you before,' he said, his eyes smiling down at her, 'that I'm not going to rush you. We have all the time in the world.'

'Have we?' she said, thinking of Jake and Louisa. 'You mean you're not going to disappear when the summer is over?'

'It's you who's going to disappear,' he reminded her, 'back to London.'

'But what about when Jake goes? Won't you be going with him?'

His eyes suddenly clouded and she felt his hand tighten on hers.

'He told Louisa that you and he know each other,' she said, 'so you don't have to deny it any more.'

He looked searchingly into her eyes as though unsure whether to believe her. In the end he obviously decided that he did. 'Did he tell Louisa how we know each other?' he asked.

Sarah shook her head.

To her surprise he let go of her hand, saying, 'I'll get you that drink.'

Sarah turned and resting her chin on her hands gazed out at the lustrous blue sea, the brilliant shards of sunlight that sparked from the yachts and the clear, velvety sky. It seemed somehow incongruous to be on the brink of discussing something whose darker side she was becoming more convinced of by the day when they were in surroundings that appeared so beautifully pure and benign. It was so easy, she was thinking, to lose a sense of reality here, and maybe in their own ways that was what they were all doing, she, Louisa and Danny. Without the constraints of normal, everyday life upon them it was as though they were drifting aimlessly through a fantasy world, untroubled by direction, unanchored by responsibility or consequence. They had found themselves a mystery and were going blindly into it as though it were as innocuous as a child's game, as though they had cast themselves in a movie over which they neither had nor wanted any control because there would never be a price to pay since all movies had happy endings and even if they didn't none of them was real.

'So,' she said still staring out at the horizon as Morandi put their drinks on the table and sat down, 'are you going to tell me how you and Jake know each other?'

He followed the direction of her eyes, watching the shimmering surface of the sea, feeling the heat pounding down on him. 'I want to,' he answered, 'but I just don't know how much of it is safe for you to know.'

Sarah felt a knot tighten in her stomach, but whether it was of excitement or apprehension she couldn't tell. 'Then why don't you tell me just some of it?' she suggested.

He took a long time thinking it over before he said, 'Jake fixed me up with my company down here. He did it because I owed him a favour, a very big favour and he needed someone he could trust to run . . . to organize certain ventures for him.'

'So you're not just soft porn?' she said, turning to look at him.

'No, but that's as much as I can tell you. The rest is up to Jake.'

She nodded, thinking that he hadn't really told her anything. 'OK,' she said. 'But what about Aphrodite? Can't you tell me where she fits into it all?'

'She's my assistant. Jake employed her, but she answers to me.'

'But you can't get rid of her because Jake won't let you?'

'If she wanted to go I don't think Jake would stand in her way, but she doesn't want to. I'm not sure how much she knows about what's going on, we've never discussed it for the simple reason that we're both afraid of revealing things the other might not know. But the truth is, I think she knows more than I do.'

Sarah was quiet for a moment, mulling over in her mind the little he had told her and deciding that she still wasn't really any the wiser. 'Jake told Louisa that it has nothing to do with drugs,' she said. 'Is that true?'

'As far as I know it's true, but Jake doesn't tell me everything.'

'What about the Mafia?'

He lowered his eyes and tilted his drink towards him. 'That I don't know,' he answered soberly. 'Consuela has a lot of contacts, knows a lot of people, so does Jake. But please, don't ask me any more. I've sworn never to betray Jake's confidence and I don't want to lie to you.'

'Can't you just give me the basic ingredient?' Sarah protested. 'I mean, if it isn't drugs and it isn't the peddling of porn, then what is it?'

'Probably just about everything else you can think of,' he answered. 'And that's all I'm going to say. Can I sing you a song?'

Sarah blinked. 'Are you serious?' she said.

He was, for picking up the guitar he strummed a few chords then started to sing: '*My eyes adored you, though I never laid a hand on you, my eyes adored you; Like a million miles away from me you couldn't see how I adored you, so close, so close and yet so far . . .'*

'I don't believe you,' Sarah laughed incredulously when he'd finished. 'That was wonderful and I just can't work you out at all. One minute you seem so shy and the next you're, I don't know, you're so . . .'

'Brazen?' he suggested.

'Not brazen, no,' she laughed, 'more self-assured, at ease with yourself.'

'I feel relaxed with you,' he said, 'but I'm trying to make a good impression too. Does that explain the schizophrenia?'

'I suppose so.' She picked up her drink and swirled it around the glass, clinking the ice-cubes. 'I like it here,' she said. 'I like your apartment, I like your paintings and I like you.'

'I'm glad,' he smiled.

'Tell me about your children. How old are they? What are their names? How often do you see them?'

'I guess I'd better come clean here,' he said, grinning awkwardly. 'I do have seven children, but they're not exactly all mine.'

'How exactly aren't they all yours?' Sarah said, with a little wave of her hand.

'Well, four of them are stepchildren. They came with my wives, but I've tried never to show any favouritism.'

'So in actual fact you have three children?'

'Two by my first wife, one by my second. I can show you photographs if you can bear to put up with a proud father,' he said.

'I think I can bear it.'

An hour later, having gone through no less than six family albums and listened to countless tales of childhood pranks, achievements, illnesses and brilliances, Sarah had finished her third drink and was sitting beside him, her arm resting against his, their legs brushing lightly beneath the table.

'She's very like you,' she said, looking down at the picture of Morandi's eldest daughter who was going to be fourteen the next day. 'Will you call her tomorrow?'

'Of course. She's hoping I'm going to tell her she can come down for a while, but it's not a good idea right now. The trouble is I'm not very good at saying no where my children are concerned. I'm afraid most of the discipline has fallen to their mothers.'

'I think they're very lucky to have a father like you. They must miss you.'

'Probably not as much as I miss them.'

'You know,' she said, feeling a lump inexplicably rising in her throat, 'I could quite envy you having such a big family. It's what I've always wanted. Not that I ever had as many as seven in mind,' she laughed. 'But my husband, he didn't want any. He just didn't like children. Strange that we should ever have got together really, considering we wanted such different things from life.'

'But you're still young,' he said softly. 'There's still plenty of time for a family, even a big one.'

'Yes, you're right,' she smiled, as his hand closed over hers. For a while she looked down at their hands then feeling him turning her towards him she looked up and watched him as he lowered his mouth to hers. Her eyes fluttered closed as he kissed her so tenderly that it sent delicious swirls of warmth eddying through her heart. He pulled her closer and ran his fingers over the plump, soft flesh of her shoulders, smoothing a hand into her shiny hair, caressing her gently, assertively yet undemandingly.

When finally he let her go he took both her hands in his and gazed down at her, his velvety brown eyes smiling yet concerned.

'I'm sorry,' she whispered, aware of how very aroused he was, of how aroused she was too. 'I want to, but I'm afraid.'

'It's OK,' he told her.

'I wish I knew what I was afraid of,' she said. 'Maybe I think you'll despise me after, I don't know.'

'Have you made love at all since your husband left?' he asked.

'Just once. In Consuela's bathhouse. I take it you know about the bathhouse?'

He nodded.

'But somehow that was different,' she said. 'It was anonymous. I didn't know anything about him, nor him about me so I didn't have to worry about what he thought of me. But I didn't like myself too much after. Oh I don't know!' she said, suddenly impatient with herself. 'I laugh and joke about sex all the time, I pretend to be a mad, bad, wild woman, but it's all a front because when it comes right down to it I know I'm frigid.'

'A woman who kisses the way you do isn't frigid,' he assured her, smiling. 'You're merely bruised and it's not sex that will heal the bruises, it's love.'

She laughed wryly. 'You make it sound so simple.'

'It will be when you come to trust me.'

'That's just it, I think I do trust you.'

'Then let's wait until you're sure.'

She smiled fondly up into his eyes. 'You're a wonderful man, Trevor What-ever-your-name-is.'

'Trubshaw,' he said.

'Oh God,' she laughed, 'how can someone as wonderful as you have such an awful name?'

He laughed too. 'Actually it's Deighton,' he said, 'but we can stay with Morandi if you like. And now, as loath as I am to let you go, didn't you say you were meeting Erik at one?'

'Oh heaven's, yes,' she cried, looking at her watch. 'Oh my God, it's twenty to already. Would you call him for me and tell him I'm on my way?'

'Of course,' he said standing up with her. 'I'll ring you, OK? And good luck this afternoon, I'll look forward to seeing the results.'

'Call me soon?' she said turning back from the door.

'Very soon,' he promised.

A few minutes later Sarah was on the point of getting into her car which was parked on the edge of the harbour when Aphrodite suddenly appeared from out of the strolling crowds.

Oh God, Sarah groaned inwardly, as a mental picture of herself flying into the oily water passed through her mind.

'I know where you've been,' Aphrodite hissed, her jet black eyes burning with fury, 'but you keep away from him, do you hear me?'

'Now hang on a minute,' Sarah said, making an attempt to be reasonable.

'Keep away from him! I don't know what he's told you, but I'm telling you he's a liar, a cheat and a blackmailer and if you don't back off right now I'm warning you both, I'll expose him for what he is,' and spinning on her heel she stormed off in the direction of Morandi's apartment block.

Because of the traffic it took Sarah over half an hour to reach Monaco. She drove straight to the Parking des Pecheurs, which Erik had told her to head for, then clutching her map and camera case got into the lift and glided sedately up through the rock to the outer ramparts of the exclusive, sunbaked town.

As she wound her way through the meandering tourists along the twisting pathways fringed by magnolias, eucalyptus and oleanders she was still thinking about what Aphrodite had said. It had shaken her, there was no doubt about that, but the drive had calmed her a little and she was able to approach it more rationally now. She had, she knew, to put her personal feelings to one side as she considered Aphrodite's accusations against Morandi. But it was hard, very hard when she had truly believed in those two hours they had spent together that he was everything he appeared to be, father, brother, friend and soon-to-be-lover. But had she seen only what she wanted to see? It was true she'd asked him about Jake, but she knew she hadn't pushed it any harder because she hadn't wanted anything to spoil the beauty of what was developing between them.

'*He's a liar, a cheat and a blackmailer.*' Aphrodite's words resounded horribly, repeatedly through her ears and as much as she hated to admit it she knew she had to face the fact that if he really was the father of seven children then maybe it was blackmail that was helping not only to support them, but to provide him with the means to take her to the kind of restaurant he'd taken her to the other night and to parties like the one at the Colombe d'Or. But who was he blackmailing?

By now she had passed the Musée Océanographique and was in the midst of the fairytale town with its narrow, polished brick roads and flat-fronted pink and lemon buildings. Gifts and postcards, T-shirts and memorabilia spilled out of tiny shop fronts, back-packing students with slender, tanned legs and greasy hair studied their maps, squinted up at the sun and flopped exhaustedly into the cafés. Prim old ladies with tightly curled hair and chic, young sundresses tottered by, poodles tucked protectively under their arms and jewels sparkling lavishly under their chins. She'd taken a wrong turn, she knew that, but imagined if she pressed on ahead she would find another way round to Erik's apartment that overlooked the Port de Fontvieille.

She wasn't too sure now that she was looking forward to the afternoon. Maybe it would be better if she and Louisa gave up on this crazy idea of solving whatever mystery they'd stumbled upon. They were out of their depth, she could sense that as fiercely as she could sense the biting heat of the sun. But deep down inside she knew she was resisting letting go. She didn't want this all to be an illusion, to find herself the victim of lies and chicanery and feel a fool for believing in someone who, on the surface at least, seemed like the answer to her prayers.

She stopped a moment to admire the palace, sitting like a huge, creamy cake beneath the jutting, barren mountain top that scaled the flawless blue heavens behind it. Then glancing at her map again she walked quickly across the Place du Palais, down the steps to the Promenade Sainte Barbe and onto the walkway that skirted the clifftops above the Port de Fontvieille.

When she reached the pale orange apartment block with its black wrought iron balconies and sienna and white striped awnings she looked up at it warily. She wondered if Danny was inside – they hadn't seen her for almost a week and though she'd called frequently she'd never said where she was. But even if Danny was there Sarah still wasn't sure she wanted to go in. Then someone came out, the door slammed behind him and Sarah pushed Erik's bell.

She rang and rang, but when, five minutes later there was still no reply, she could only conclude that he'd got fed up waiting. She could always ring Morandi to see if he'd called, maybe Erik had left a message for her there, but she wasn't sure she wanted to speak to Morandi right now.

Wandering back onto the path she put her heavy camera case between her legs and leaned her elbows on the wall, gazing thoughtfully down at the turquoise-blue waters of the harbour where white-sailed yachts and gleaming cruisers were gliding smoothly past each other on their way out to or back from the sea.

For the moment no one else was around and as the peace stole over her she closed her eyes and prayed for guidance. Or maybe it was for the courage to admit that she was so desperate to find someone to love, someone to make her feel normal and desirable again, that she was prepared to ignore what was staring her in the face and go blindly, blithely into something that was only going to end up making her even more insecure and screwed up than she already was.

Suddenly she started to smile, for somewhere in the distance, almost as though in answer to her confusion, she could hear a church organ. She turned to look along the path, then checking her map she saw that she was only fifty yards or so from the cathedral.

Picking up her case she began walking towards it and the closer she got it seemed the more fervent and demanding the organ became. Its strident, chords surged out of the silver-grey structure, filling the humid air with sound. Sarah watched in fascination as though the frenzied notes might suddenly explode through the walls and the whole cathedral collapse, slowly, melodically, before her very eyes.

When the music stopped leaving only a sluggish resonance petering into the silence, she continued to stand there, staring. A gaily painted wooden train passed in front of her and she heard the English tour guide inform his passengers that inside this neo-Romanesque cathedral, built in the late nineteen hundreds, was to be found the tomb of Her Royal Highness the Princess Grace.

Sarah watched as the sweltering tour party disembarked and moved languidly towards the cool darkened interior of the now silent cathedral. She toyed with the idea of joining them, took a step to follow, then without really knowing why, turned abruptly away and started back to the car.

15

As the car came to a stop at the end of the lane Danny picked up her holdall, turned her scarlet lips to kiss Jake on the mouth and got out. She didn't wait to watch him pull away, but continued on up the lane towards the villa, humming tunelessly to herself and smiling like the cat that just got the cream and knows there's more to come. She was at the point of turning in through the gates when she heard a car coming up behind her, radio blaring through the wide open windows.

'Hi!' Louisa cried, the genuine pleasure in her greeting telling Danny that she clearly hadn't seen Jake.

'Hi yourself,' Danny grinned back. 'Where have you been?'

'More to the point where have you been?' Louisa laughed, turning the radio down.

'All over,' Danny answered, swinging the passenger door open and getting in for the short ride up the drive.

'Oh come on,' Louisa protested. 'Stop being so mysterious. Where did he whisk you off to?'

'Who, Erik? Nowhere. As a matter of fact, I've hardly seen him since last Sunday when he came here to pick me up.'

The warmth started to seep from Louisa's smile. 'Then where have you been all this time?' she asked.

'Actually, I went back to London to see my parents for a couple of days and the rest of the time I was staying at Consuela's. She and my mother are old friends it would seem.'

'Really?' Louisa said, brightening again. 'Did your mother tell you anything juicy about her?'

'Not particularly. Where's Sarah?'

'As far as I knew she was spending the afternoon with Erik learning the tricks of the trade. In fact she thought you were going to be there too, but something must have gone wrong because you're here, her car's back and there's no sign of Erik. How did you get here, by the way?'

'Louisa! Louisa! You've just got to come and see these,' Sarah cried, throwing open the front door. 'Danny!' she squealed as she saw Danny getting out of the car and ran over to hug her. 'Where did you find her?' she said to Louisa.

'Down at the gates,' Louisa answered, closing the car door and trying not to think how tarty Danny looked in her short vermilion dress and black high-heeled sandals.

'Where have you been?' Sarah demanded.

'I'll tell you later,' Danny laughed. 'Now what was it you wanted Louisa to see?'

'Oh, just you wait!' Sarah gushed. 'They're simply out of this world even if I do say so myself. Come on, come and see for yourself.'

As Sarah bounded excitedly into the house Louisa and Danny looked at each other, intrigued.

'Da-daah,' Sarah cried throwing out her arms as they came in the door behind her. 'Aren't they fantastic!'

'Wow! They're stunning,' Danny declared, obviously genuinely impressed by the huge silver-framed photographs of the *Valhalla* that Sarah had propped up against the wall.

'Aren't they?' Sarah beamed. 'I just popped in on the off-chance to see if they were ready and *voilà*! I can hardly wait for Jake to see them.'

Louisa's eyes immediately darted to Danny, but Danny was lifting one of the photographs to take a closer look.

'I thought you were spending the afternoon with Erik,' Louisa said.

'He wasn't there,' Sarah answered still watching Danny and clearly eager for more praise.

'Aren't they wonderful?' Danny said to Louisa. 'She's obviously even more talented than we realized. In fact,' she added, as Sarah swelled with pride, 'I'd like to buy one to hang in my house in London.'

'Oh, don't be silly,' Sarah laughed. 'I'll give you one. These are all for Jake, but I can easily get more blown up and you can choose your own frame.'

'You mean Jake's already seen them?' Danny said, surprised.

'Not like this no,' Sarah answered, still radiating excitement. 'He saw the ten by eights and asked Louisa to ask me to get them blown up for him.'

As Louisa's eyes closed in dismay Danny turned to look at her. It was only then, as Sarah saw the expressions on both their faces, that she realized what she'd done. Danny wasn't supposed to know that Louisa had seen Jake again.

'Oh God,' she groaned. 'I'm . . .'

'You fool!' Danny cut across her. 'You bloody fool, Louisa. Don't you ever learn?'

Louisa started to turn away, but thrusting the photograph at Sarah Danny grabbed her by the arm and jerked her back. 'What's the matter with you?' she snapped. 'Don't you ever listen to anything anyone tells you? How much longer are you going to go on deluding yourself over that man?'

'To be frank, Danny,' Louisa responded icily, 'I don't see that it's any of your business.'

'Look, come on, you two,' Sarah said as Danny's eyes blazed into Louisa's, 'we haven't seen each other for over a week, so let's just . . .'

'You're sick, do you know that?' Danny spat. 'You've got something seriously wrong with you the way you throw yourself at a man who's just laughing at you behind your back. I tried to warn you, I told you he was no good, but you always think you know best, don't you?'

Louisa's face was pale with rage as she glared back. 'I think it's you who's sick, Danny,' she said scathingly. 'I don't know what you're hoping to prove by trying to come between Jake and me, but it isn't going to work. He's told me all the lies you've made up . . .'

'Lies!' Danny shouted. 'What lies? Come on, tell me, what am I supposed to have said that you can't allow yourself to believe?'

'He's only ever slept with you once,' Louisa yelled, 'and that was the night before he met me. He told me that himself. He told me that he was the only one you *weren't* screwing.'

'And you believed him! Jesus Christ Almighty, when the hell are you ever going to wise up? Where do you think I was last night? Who do you think just brought me home? If you'd arrived two minutes earlier you'd have seen him with your own eyes.'

As Louisa's heart twisted she glanced at Sarah as though Sarah could somehow refute it.

'Well, for your information I'm *not* seeing him,' Louisa said, turning back to Danny. 'He came here the night after you'd left with Erik and I haven't seen him since.' It was a lie, she'd seen him several times this past week. OK, only for snatched half hours here and there, but they had been precious, idyllic moments, filled with laughter and blessedly untouched by the strains of his life. She'd seen another Jake during those times, a Jake who appeared as carefree and loving as she could wish, a Jake who held her hand as they strolled in the forests, who fed her ice-cream in out of the way cafés, who constantly pulled her into his arms to kiss her and gaze deeply, wonderingly into her eyes.

'You know what your trouble is?' Danny said, fury and resentment making her face tremble. 'You always want what you can't have. No! I take that back. You always want what *I* have. You've always been the same, I can't do anything without you copying me or trying to take it away from me. And I've let you, because I felt sorry for you. You don't have any friends except Sarah and me, you don't have any family, and because of your background you're totally fucked up where men are concerned. I've tried to understand all that, I've made God only knows how many allowances . . . Jesus Christ, if you knew the lengths I've been to to try and stop you from hurting yourself and still you won't listen to me! Still you want what's mine just because it's mine. Well this time you're not getting it. This time I'm not backing down and letting you waltz off with Jake Mallory.'

Louisa's eyes were big with confusion at the unexpected

brutality of Danny's attack. 'Didn't you hear me?' she said tightly. 'I said, I'm not seeing him any more. But maybe you'd like to ask yourself why it was he got Erik to get you out of the way the other night so he could come here and see me? And while we're at it, perhaps you'd like to explain why you won't ever let him speak to me on the phone.'

'Because he never fucking asks to speak to you,' Danny cried, throwing her hands up in frustration. 'He's only seeing you to try and make me jealous! He can't stand the fact that I'm sleeping with Erik so he's using you to get back at me. It's a game we're playing, both of us, and I don't want you involved, because one of these days he's going to make the commitment to me that I want and when he does he's going to leave you high and dry.'

'Why can't he make the commitment now?' Sarah wanted to know.

'Why?' Danny said, rounding on her. 'You want to know why? OK, I'll tell you. He's already married, that's why!'

'You're a liar!' Louisa yelled.

'Am I?' Danny yelled back. 'Then ask Consuela, she'll tell you. Ask my mother . . . Better still, ask him and see what he says. He's married all right and shall I tell you about his wife? Do you want to know about her, about how he treats her? You'll like this, Louisa, you'll really get off on this! He beats her, he keeps her locked up and won't let her out for days on end. He screws around with other women, takes them home, flaunts them in front of her. He keeps her short of money, never takes her out . . . He can't, because she's always covered in bruises . . .'

'If that's true,' Sarah said, 'then why the hell are you bothering with him?'

'Because we're two of a kind. We recognized it in each other the moment we met. I can handle him and he knows it. He hates me for it, but he can't resist me either. Now tell me, is that the sort of man you want *her* eating her heart out over?'

Sarah looked uneasily at Louisa. Louisa's face was pale with shock, but nevertheless there was a flicker of doubt in her eyes.

'So where's his wife now?' she said, still sounding angry, but obviously shaken.

'How the hell do I know? Ask him!'

'Why haven't you asked him?'

'Because I don't care where she is. I don't get myself all screwed up over things that don't matter the way you do.'

'I'm sorry,' Sarah interrupted, 'but none of this is making any sense. To begin with why would Jake be bothering with Louisa if, as you say, he's already got a wife and on top of that he's got you too?'

'Is he sleeping with her?' Danny demanded, her livid eyes blazing the challenge. 'Tell me, is he screwing her?'

Both Louisa and Sarah were silent.

'You see!' Danny cried triumphantly. 'And why would he when he's getting all he wants from me?'

'But if he's the kind of man you say he is I don't understand why you . . .'

'That's just it! Neither of you understands what kind of man he is. But I do. And that's why I'm telling you to back off, Louisa. Just leave him alone.'

'But it's him who won't leave her alone!' Sarah cried.

'Jesus Christ!' Danny seethed. 'How many times do I have to tell you? He's playing us off against each other. He's using her to make me jealous.'

'I'm sorry, but it still doesn't make any sense,' Sarah said. 'Why use Louisa when he's got a wife he can make you jealous with? And why should he want to make you jealous, anyway?'

'I told you, because of Erik!' Danny seethed as though speaking to an idiot.

Sarah still looked baffled.

'You're lying, Danny,' Louisa said quietly. 'Why don't you just come clean and admit that Jake doesn't want you and that's what you can't stand – not that he wants me, but that he doesn't want you.'

For one fleeting moment Danny looked as if she might lash out with her fists. 'If that were true, then why is he sleeping with me and not with you?' she spat.

'Is he sleeping with you?' Louisa said, her eyes boring into Danny's. 'He says it only happened that once.'

'And you believe him because that's what you want to believe. Because in that sick, fucked-up brain of yours you know he's a bastard and that's what you want, isn't it? Someone to hurt you, someone to punish you for something you haven't even done. Well, if it were anyone else I'd tell you to get on with it, I'd tell you to go right ahead and get yourself abused, because I'm sick to death of bailing you out, of having to lay myself on the line for you just to save you from yourself. But no more, Louisa! No more. This time I'm not going to just stand by and watch you walk off with Jake the way I let you walk off with Simon.'

'What!' Louisa hissed. 'What the hell has Simon got to do with this?'

'You know damned well that I was sleeping with Simon before you came along.'

Louisa looked at Sarah, and to her horror saw that Sarah couldn't meet her eyes.

'I never knew you were sleeping with Simon,' Louisa said hoarsely.

'Of course you knew,' Danny sneered. 'Everyone knew, but you needed a shoulder to cry on, needed someone who could treat you halfway decently after that moron you'd got yourself mixed up with, so I bowed out and let you have Simon. It was all the same to me, he never really meant anything to me, so why not let you have him? But it's not going to happen this time, Louisa. Believe you me, you're not going to have Jake.'

'I don't want Jake,' Louisa said through clenched teeth. 'You can have him and his wife and whatever else he's hiding. And shall I tel' you why? Because I don't want anything that's been touched by you.'

'Now come on, let's calm things down here before they really get out of hand,' Sarah interceded. 'I think I've got the measure of what's going on now and Danny, you're out of order. Well out of order.'

'Me!' Danny screamed. 'How can you say that when you

know yourself what she's like. You've seen the way she always tries to steal the limelight from me. She struts around like Miss High and Mighty the successful writer when we both know she'd still be nobody if it weren't for me. It was my name that took that series to the top and it was me who got her where she is now.'

Louisa gasped.

'Danny, it was the series that made your name,' Sarah said in a low, angry voice.

'Christ, will you listen to yourself, Sarah!' Danny yelled. 'She's got you believing it now. She's come between us so many times in the past and she's doing it again. She puts on that Little Orphan Annie look and everyone feels sorry for her and rushes to her defence. I thought you were brighter than that, Sarah, I thought you of all people could see straight through it.'

'Danny, this kind of jealousy just isn't healthy,' Sarah warned.

'Jealousy! You're accusing *me* of jealousy, when it's her who's so damned eaten up with it . . .'

'Danny stop it!' Sarah snapped. 'Stop right now because I've had about as much as I can take. Louisa's told you that she's not seeing Jake any more, so he's yours to do with as you please. But I'm telling you, here and now, if I find out you're lying about any of this then it'll be me you have to answer to and, I promise you, it won't be pleasant.'

'Sarah! For God's sake, why are you letting her do this? Why are you letting her come between us the way she's trying to with me and Jake? Can't you see what she's doing? She's trying to take you away from me too.'

'You're wrong, Danny,' Louisa cried, her voice shaking with fury. 'I don't want anything that's yours, do you hear me? Nothing at all. It's you who wants what's mine.'

'Oh, and you think Jake's yours, do you? You really believe that it's you he wants. Well then maybe you should invite yourself onto the *Valhalla* one of these nights and hear the way he laughs about you. The way he pokes fun at you and tells us all how pathetic you are the way you look at him with those puppy dog eyes while falling for all his lies. You're a laughing stock, Louisa . . .'

'Danny, five minutes ago you didn't even know Jake had been seeing Louisa,' Sarah pointed out.

'Maybe not, but I should have realized it when I heard them all laughing about her. I assumed he was talking about the couple of times he brought her home, but I should have realized there was more to it than that. And maybe I would have if I'd remembered how damned stupid she is when it comes to men.'

'Just give me one good reason why he should turn her into a laughing stock,' Sarah challenged. 'Because I'm afraid it simply doesn't ring true to me. Not with a man like Jake Mallory.'

'And what would you know about a man like Jake Mallory?' Danny threw back. 'A man like him has never crossed your path before so how would you know what makes a man like him tick?'

'OK, then tell me.'

'Tell you why he ridicules her? OK, I will. He does it because he knows she fell for him the minute she set eyes on him and it amuses him to encourage her. That's the kind of man he is. I've tried to protect her from it, I tried to tell her what he's like, but she wouldn't listen. He's not the man for her, no matter how much she might like to fool herself he is. He's just screwing around with her head and she doesn't have what it takes to handle someone like that. All *she* can do is *write* about it!'

'How dare you belittle her talent like that when it's what made you who you are?' Sarah cried.

'I'm not taking the responsibility for turning her into a fucking monster,' Louisa shouted. 'And if Jake's screwing up anyone's head around here it seems to me it's yours, Danny! And why do you have to have him when you've got Erik? When you've got any other man you lay eyes on? Why does it have to be the man who wants me?'

'There she goes again!' Danny screamed in frustration.

'Can't you get it into your thick head that he doesn't want you?'

'Then what are you so afraid of?' Sarah demanded.

Danny stared at her breathlessly, her exquisite face taut with rage. 'I can see there's no getting through to you two,' she said bitterly. 'She's got you on her side and you're just not prepared to listen to what I'm telling you.'

'If it made any sense we would,' Louisa said, biting out the words.

'OK,' Danny said, forcing herself to calm down. 'OK, let's try it again. I'll concede that he might find you attractive, that one of these days when he's got you to the point of begging for it, he'll probably screw you and you, just like I did the first time, will think it's the screw of the century. But after that it changes, believe you me, it changes and that's what I've been trying to protect you from. I can stand the violence, but you can't. I've got Erik to put me back together, but you haven't. And even if, in his own sick way, he did fall for you, Louisa, he's still married. He's got a wife, do you hear me? So it's no good going on thinking that one of these days he's going to sweep you off your feet and run with you to the nearest church, because it isn't going to happen.'

'I know that,' Louisa said, her voice still clipped. 'He's told me himself that there can't be any future between us.'

'But you don't believe him, do you?'

'Yes, I believe him.'

Danny was shaking her head. 'No, I don't think you do.'

'I don't give a damn what you think,' Louisa bristled.

'I know you don't, you've more than proved that.'

'Look, come on, let's try to be grown up and rational about this,' Sarah said. 'It seems perfectly obvious to me that he's lying to you both . . .'

'To her! Not to me!' Danny interrupted. 'Everyone's lying to her and why shouldn't they when she lies to herself the way she does?'

'She doesn't,' Sarah countered. 'She's as aware as you are that there's more to Jake Mallory than meets the eye. She knows how likely she is to be hurt, she's the one who's faced that and . . .'

'Let's just drop it!' Louisa said, cutting Sarah short.

'Yes, let's just push it under the carpet, pretend it's not happening, shall we?' Danny said sarcastically. 'Let's not face the truth because the truth doesn't fit into your story, does it? You want us all to play by your rules, you want to write our lives and have us all behave the way you want us to. Well, this is real life, Louisa. We're none of us a part of your fantasy world, not me, not Sarah, not Jake. We're real. We . . .'

'I told you the last time we talked, there's not even a role for you in what I'm writing now,' Louisa snapped. 'So it's you who's in a fantasy world, not me. In fact, I can see quite plainly what's going on here, even if you can't.'

'Then tell me!' Danny demanded savagely. 'Tell me what's going on, because I'd really like to know.'

'OK, I'll tell you,' Louisa said, her dark eyes once again glittering with rage. 'You're accusing me of everything you're guilty of yourself. You're the one who's making things up. You're the one who's lying to herself. And you're the one who's lying to me to try to keep me away from the one man in the world who doesn't want you. Your ego is so damned big, Danielle Spencer, that quite frankly I'm surprised there's enough room for you all in the bed.'

'For Christ's sake, let's just stop this!' Sarah shouted. 'You don't mean what you're saying, either of you, so shut up before I knock your damned heads together.'

'Then tell her to sort herself out and keep her fucking hands off what's mine,' Danny spat.

'How can he be yours if he's married?' Louisa shot back.

'Is he married?' Sarah demanded, glaring at Danny.

'*Yes.* I told you, ask Consuela, ask my mother. Ask Erik, they'll all tell you, Jake is married. His wife's name is Martina. OK? Do you believe me now?'

Sarah looked at Louisa.

'Yes, I believe her,' Louisa said grudgingly but still angry. 'It makes sense of some of the things he's told me.'

'And do you believe that I'm sleeping with him? That I slept with him last night? That he brought me back here this afternoon?'

'I can't think of any reason why you would lie, except to try and come between us. But if he's married then you don't really have to bother, do you?'

'At last I seem to be getting through to you,' Danny sighed in exasperation.

'I think we all need a drink,' Sarah declared, turning towards the kitchen.

Louisa and Danny eyed each other, hostility still crackling the air between them. Danny was the first to back down and as the rancour melted in her eyes and her face started to soften she stepped forward to put her arms around Louisa. 'I'm sorry,' she whispered. 'I shouldn't have said all those awful things. I didn't mean them, honestly I didn't. I don't know what comes over me sometimes, it's like it's not me talking. You're the best friend I've ever had and we shouldn't let a man come between us like this. He's just not worth it.'

'No,' Louisa said, standing woodenly in the embrace. It was going to take more than an apology to heal the hurt of the past twenty minutes though, she knew that, but for now she would go along with the charade of forgiveness. If she didn't, it would mean going back to London and despising herself for it as she did, she just couldn't go without seeing Jake again. She had to find out the truth for herself. She had to confront him with his marriage, with the cruelty of his ridicule, with his continuing relationship with Danny.

'So what's happening with you and Erik?' she asked stiltedly as she and Danny followed Sarah into the kitchen.

'I don't know,' Danny answered. 'I haven't seen him since Tuesday. Maybe I should give him a call.'

'If you do, then tell him from me I don't much appreciate being stood up,' Sarah retorted. Then smiling as she handed them a glass of wine, she said, 'Are we all friends again now?'

'Yes, I think so,' Danny said, looking at Louisa for confirmation.

'Yes,' Louisa nodded, tears of angry betrayal burning the backs of her eyes as she thought of the wonderful moments she and Jake had shared this past week that had now been tainted beyond standing by Danny's outburst. They had laughed so easily together, he had seemed to treasure every minute of what little time they could spend together and even now she could almost hear the way his voice seemed to deepen when he called her to tell her he was missing her. He couldn't be lying, he just couldn't be, but so much of what Danny had said rang true. Like how he would get her to the point of begging him to sleep with her, like how he wouldn't make a commitment to Danny the way he wouldn't with her, and like both Danny's mother and Consuela telling Danny he was married. She just couldn't understand why he wouldn't have told her that himself, but there again, if he really was treating his wife the way Danny said he was he wouldn't have considered her even worth mentioning. But this wasn't the man she was getting to know, this was a stranger, a monster, a pathological liar and in her heart she just couldn't believe that Jake was any of those things.

'So what were you doing over at Consuela's?' Sarah said as they strolled out onto the terrace with their drinks. 'Availing yourself of the pleasures of the bathhouse, no doubt.' As casual as she sounded, she was extremely interested to hear the answer after what had happened earlier in the day when Aphrodite had hissed her accusations of blackmail. That all seemed such a long time ago now after the drama of the past half hour, but she was going to wait until she and Louisa were alone before tackling that.

'Actually, no,' Danny laughed. 'I was just relaxing by the pool most of the time, being waited on hand, foot and finger and trying to eavesdrop on the rows she was having with Jake.'

Sarah's eyebrows rose in surprise as Louisa flinched at the mention of Jake's name. 'Did you hear anything?' Sarah asked, tearing her eyes from Louisa.

'Not much. Except I did hear her trying to warn him away from me once. She's not at all keen on my getting involved with him, neither is my mother. Well, considering the way he treats his wife I don't suppose you can blame them. The trouble is, the more they try to turn us against each other the more determined they're making us to be together. Which is what I meant earlier, about he and I being two of a kind. But still, we don't want to get into that again, do we?' she said, closing her eyes and letting her head fall back against the chair as Louisa's lips tightened. 'Anyway, I think the main gist of what Consuela and Jake were rowing about has something to do with Mexico, but I couldn't quite catch what. I would imagine though, it was why Jake went there recently, but he won't tell me anything about it. I don't suppose he's told you, has he Louisa?'

'Why would he tell me when he's so much closer to you?' Louisa answered tartly. Then catching Sarah's admonishing look she said, 'No, he hasn't said anything to me and quite frankly I don't think I want to know what it's about anyway. How did you get on with Morandi this morning, Sarah?'

Sarah had just taken breath to answer when Danny said, 'Oh yes, Morandi. That reminds me. I know I've only ever seen him the once, but I'd swear it was him I saw driving into Consuela's as Jake and I were leaving this afternoon. He wasn't driving that beaten up old Renault then though. Oh, no, he was driving a dirty great big Mercedes saloon. You'll have to talk to him about that, Sarah, tell him you'd rather go out in style if it's all the same to him.'

Louisa turned to Sarah whose cheery face had turned stony, but with a quick flash of her eyes Sarah told Louisa to say nothing.

'I'll do that,' Sarah said, topping up their glasses. Then after a pause. 'Tell me, Danny, it must have occurred to you, what with these rows between Jake and Consuela and everything you've heard about him, that there's something not quite right going on in that house.'

'In what kind of way are you thinking?' Danny asked, her eyes still closed.

'In a kind of blackmail way,' Sarah answered, feeling the

curiosity burning from Louisa's eyes. She lifted a hand as though to say, I'll tell you later, and continued to wait for Danny's response.

'Well,' Danny said thoughtfully, 'it's funny that you mention it, because it has crossed my mind that something like that might be going on. Which was why,' she went on, sitting forward and picking up her wine, 'I took it upon myself to take a look around that bathhouse when no one was about. There's no sign of any cameras or anything like that though, no sign at all.'

'But what made you think that something like that might be going on?' Sarah pressed.

'Actually, it was something I overheard Erik saying to Jake,' she answered, screwing up her face as she tried to remember what. 'He said, "there's more money coming out of that bathhouse than ever goes into it," or something like that. And Jake said, "it can't go on much longer, we're going to get found out." Or he might have said, "she's going to get found out." I can't be sure. But anyway, when you come to weigh it up that sounds pretty much like some kind of blackmail to me, doesn't it to you?'

Sarah was nodding. 'Did you mention what you'd overheard to Consuela?'

'Yes I did as a matter of fact.'

'Well what did she say?' Louisa urged when Danny didn't continue.

'She said that yes, there was something going on which was why she didn't want me getting involved with Jake. And that was when she told me she knew my mother and felt sure that my mother would expect her to do all she could to keep me away from him. I couldn't get any more out of her than that, except that he was married, so when I went back to England I asked my mother what she knew about him. All she said was that she didn't want me getting involved with married men, and that she was glad to think that Consuela was keeping an eye on me.'

'Did your mother know anything about the bathhouse?' Sarah asked.

'No. And now, given that there was no sign of cameras or anything, I'm wondering, this is assuming someone is blackmailing someone, if it's got anything to do with the bathhouse at all. My guess is it's just between Jake and Consuela, 'cos she gets pretty upset every time he goes there and neither of them ever goes anywhere near the bathhouse. Or not that I saw. But they did disappear into her bedroom once or twice and I saw him stroking her legs once out by the pool, just like they were lovers. It turned into a row pretty quickly and he actually belted her one, but before that, well, like I said, to see them you'd have thought they were lovers.'

Louisa's head was pounding. Her emotions were too embroiled in this for her to be able to see anything clearly or rationally. She so desperately wanted to believe Jake, but things were becoming so confused now and so horribly unpalatable with this talk of blackmail, wife-beating and some kind of bizarre relationship with Consuela and with Danny that she could feel herself recoiling from the blind trust she had placed in him.

'Did your mother tell you anything, well anything untoward, about Consuela?' Sarah asked, seeing the anguish on Louisa's face and wanting somehow, if she could, to ease it by casting the shadow of suspicion in another direction. But she wasn't only doing it for Louisa, she was doing it for herself too, for whatever Jake was implicated in here, so too was Morandi.

'She didn't tell me anything we don't know already,' Danny answered. 'That Consuela's husband died a couple of years ago leaving her squillions and she's been a virtual recluse ever since. She really seems to like Consuela though, said most people do. She was one of the great hostesses of her day apparently. Had time for everyone, did all kinds of wonderful things for charities and the like. She's still quite a legend in Argentina, by all accounts.'

'Argentina?'

'That's where she's from.'

'Not Mexico?'

'Why Mexico?'

'Just a thought, since that's where Jake was.'

Danny shrugged. 'My mother seemed pretty certain she was Argentinian. So apparently was her husband.'

'Weird, isn't it?' Sarah remarked later to Louisa, when Danny had gone off to take a shower. 'Nothing seems to add up at all. There are no nice neat little coincidences that are taking us any further down the line, if anything I'm more confused than ever.'

'You and me both,' Louisa sighed. 'But then, how do we know we can believe anything Danny says?'

'I suppose we don't, and I have to confess the way she went for you just now has made me extremely suspicious about this so-called relationship she's supposed to be having with Jake. It all happened so fast that it's only now, when I really think about it, that I can see how many questions she managed to avoid. She turned it all around to say what she wanted, but even then she was contradicting herself. Like suddenly deciding to concede that he might find you attractive, when up to that moment she'd been telling you he was turning you into a laughing stock. And why is she so afraid that you're going to waltz off with him if, as she claims, he's only using you to make her jealous? It doesn't make sense.' She stopped for a moment and looked into Louisa's bewildered eyes, wondering whether she should continue. In the end she decided to. 'You're not going to want to hear this,' she said, making what she knew was a futile attempt to soften it, 'but all that doesn't mean that I don't believe she's sleeping with him, because unfortunately I do. It could just be that she's like Everest, he's mounting her because she's there. But even though there are obviously bigger things at issue here, for what it's worth, I reckon Jake really has fallen for you. Not only because of Danny's behaviour this afternoon, but because if he hasn't then he's not only got you fooled he's got me fooled too. OK, I know I only saw you together for a few minutes the other day, but I'd have had to be blind not to have noticed the way he was looking at you and, take it from me, if that wasn't genuine then my name's Trev Trubshaw.'

Louisa giggled. 'Trev Trubshaw, father of many?'

'Seven including the steps,' Sarah smiled wryly, then sighed and shook her head. 'I know I saw the pictures, but quite honestly they could as easily have been his nieces and nephews. Though why he'd lie about having so many kids beats the hell out of me. But why do you suppose he changed his name when he came here? I know Trev is a handle any of us would be glad to shed, but there's nothing wrong with Deighton. And there's nothing wrong with being British either, is there? Or am I missing the point somewhere?'

'Search me,' Louisa responded. 'It's all so way beyond me that I'm almost inclined to give up on it and never see any of them again.'

'Common sense tells me that's exactly what we should do,' Sarah said, contemplatively. 'There's no question that Danny's in it right up to her eyes even if she doesn't know it herself, but she'll just breeze through and come out the other end completely unscathed, the way she always does. It's a bit different for you and me though. We're the monogamous types who like the same thing from our men. We don't thrive on mistrust and intrigue the way Danny does, we're just plain and simple women who like to know what we've got and make the most of it.'

'God, don't make us sound too exciting, will you?' Louisa commented, making Sarah laugh.

'The thing is,' Sarah went on, 'this all started out as a bit of a lark, really. I mean, I don't know if you did, but I didn't take it all that seriously to begin with, you know the amateur sleuth bit. And let's face it, we're not exactly Holmes and Watson are we, 'cos we're just getting more and more confused as time goes on. The trouble is though that I don't think I could bear to give up now, if for no other reason than once it's all over, or solved, or whatever it's going to be, I just couldn't stand to look back on it and still not know what the hell it was all about. On the other hand, we're not only woefully inexperienced when it comes to playing detective, we're both of us too emotionally involved with the main players to be able to take an objective look at it all.'

'You feel that strongly about Morandi?' Louisa said.

'Yes, I think I do. I mean, I could wish that he wasn't mixed up in anything sordid and criminal, but there seems little doubt now that he is, that they both are, wouldn't you agree? The strange thing is that it doesn't seem to be putting me off him at all. And don't tell me it's making you change your mind about Jake, because I know for a fact it isn't.'

'You're right, it's not. I wish it were, but if anything it's making me want him all the more. And do you know why? Because in my mind I've cast him as the hero in all this. That somehow, in some corny, sixpenny novel way, he's going to turn out to be the dashingly handsome victor of all that's being levelled against him and that's got to make me about as blind and as stupid and as far from reality as Danny accused me of.'

'Oh, don't take any notice of her. Why shouldn't you have your fantasies? Everyone else does, including her. Especially her! And besides, I don't think you believe that at all. I think, if the truth be told, you're just as appalled as I am to think that there's every chance we've both managed to fall for, to put it as mildly as possible, a pair of confidence tricksters.'

It seemed such an incongruous label to hang on someone like Jake that Louisa just couldn't take it in and they were both quiet for a while as they contemplated the extraordinariness of the situation. It was a situation that neither one of them would ever have dreamt of finding themselves in when coming to what they had assumed was a little pocket of paradise, except, as Sarah remarked curiously, 'Nothing seems quite right down here, does it? I don't know if it's something in the air, or because we don't speak the language and therefore can't help feeling as though we're not part of real life, or if there's just something odd about the whole place. I mean, I honestly don't know if we'd be taking the same view of all this if we were in London, though somehow I don't think we would. Because, to my mind, the entire Côte d'Azur is like one great big film set and I sometimes get the feeling that one of these days someone is going to shout "cut" and a thousand technicians will rush in and fold up the sky, uproot the trees, carry off the mountains and pull the plug on the sea.'

'I wouldn't mind the sound recordist turning off the cicadas,' Louisa remarked. 'But anyway, as intangible and weird as it all seems, it is real and we are going to have to decide where we go from here.'

'Well, if we're going to try and get to the bottom of it then we're going to have to reassess our tactics. It's my guess that we're asking the wrong questions, or maybe we're asking the wrong people, probably both. The trouble is though, who else is there to ask? Danny's not interested enough in anything or anyone beyond herself to want to get to the bottom of it and everyone else, it seems to me, is a part of the cover-up.'

'She can't be that wrapped up in herself not to be just a little bit curious,' Louisa said. 'And she did go snooping around the bathhouse.'

'So what are you saying, Detective Kramer, that we should include her in the investigation?'

Louisa laughed. 'I don't know. Right at this moment I'm still too furious with her to want to include her in anything.'

'I don't blame you. And since we're back on that subject I'm going to tell you what I really think. I think it's you who's the challenge here, not Jake. It's you she wants to beat, not him. Don't ask me why I think that, I just do. You're probably right when you say that she can't stand it because he wants you and not her, but I reckon it's the fact that it's *you* that's really bugging her. She's always seen herself as your great protector, you know, picking up the poor little matchgirl and making the world all bright and wonderful for her. She saved you from Bill and gave you Simon . . .'

'Yes, what was that about Simon? I never knew she was involved with him.'

'Yes, she was. Only superficially, well you know Danny, nothing ever goes much deeper than the surface. But yes, she was sleeping with him.'

'Then why didn't he ever tell me?'

'Probably because it was no big deal to him either. Or because he assumed you knew and never thought it was important enough to bring up.'

'And now she's convinced herself that she got me to the top by agreeing to do *Private Essays* when you and I both know that the budgets were already in place and the time slots had been allocated long before she was cast, *and* she was second choice.'

'Third,' Sarah corrected. 'But for God's sake don't ever tell her that. And besides, it's all water under the bridge now, because she did a fantastic job as we both well know. But I reckon this is where all the resentment comes from, in that she sees herself as your Svengali and you're showing your appreciation by snatching, as she so eloquently puts it, the screw of the century, right from under her nose.'

'Well at least she's slept with him, because even he admits to that. And how, I ask myself, does she know I haven't if he didn't tell her himself?'

'Lucky guess?'

'Or he really is making sport of me and going back to the *Valhalla* to entertain his crew with tales of my puppy dog eyes and pathetic determination to get him into bed.'

'Does he strike you as that type?' Sarah said sceptically. 'Because he certainly doesn't me. Even if he does turn out to be married, a blackmailer, a charlatan, a liar, a God only knows what else, I still don't see him as someone who'd entertain his crew like that.'

'Then why would Danny say it?'

'Why does Danny say anything?' Sarah responded unhelpfully, taking a mouthful of wine. 'Anyway, if I were in your shoes I'd be inclined to give Jake the benefit of the doubt. You can always reassess the situation later if we find out he really is lying, but in the meantime there's no logical reason in this world why he would be wasting his time trying to mess up your head and get you panting for his body just to entertain his bloody crew, for God's sake!'

'What do you think of what Danny said about his relationship with Consuela?'

'Mmm, that's a tricky one. There's obviously a lot more to Consuela than meets the eye. In fact, she's so whiter than white with all this charity stuff and grieving widow bit that it wouldn't surprise me at all to discover that she's the villain of the piece here and that Jake and Morandi and, for all we know, Erik, are the ones being blackmailed rather than doing the blackmailing.'

Louisa gave a wry grin.

'Yes, I thought you'd like that scenario,' Sarah laughed. 'So you see, you're not the only one with sixpenny novel fantasies.'

'But even if it is they who are being blackmailed it still means they have something to hide,' Louisa pointed out.

'Mmm, yes well, sadly I didn't major in sleuthing so that's the best I can come up with.'

'Which, if I'm reading you correctly, is giving us the green light to get ourselves involved with two men who are highly likely heading straight for jail and for all we know could end up taking us with them.'

'I'm glad you can see the positive side of this,' Sarah remarked cheerfully. 'For a minute there it was looking all gloom and doom.'

'Anyway,' Louisa laughed, 'let's not forget that Aphrodite actually accused Morandi of being a *blackmailer*.'

'Oh yes, I'd forgotten about her,' Sarah said, suddenly depressed again. 'And I have to confess that the thought of Morandi's fluctuating personality is making me dizzier than his God-awful paintings. Did I tell you about them?'

'No.'

'They're absolutely, categorically, without any exaggeration whatsoever, terrible. So, where do we go from here? You make the decision, because since I've never yet managed to win a game of Cluedo . . . What's the matter? Who are you looking at?' she said, craning her neck to look in the same direction as Louisa.

'What I'm looking at,' Louisa said, 'is an extremely expensive, wonderfully chic, silver Jaguar pulling into Jean-Claude's drive.'

'Erik?'

'Who else? And what was that you were saying just now about having no one else to ask?'

'Of course,' Sarah cried. 'Jean-Claude.'

'And where are we going for dinner tonight?'

'Jean-Claude's. Brilliant. Except, we can't ask him anything while Erik's there, can we?'

'No, but you could always ask Erik where he was this afternoon when he was supposed to be meeting you.'

'I stand about as much chance of getting a straight answer to that as Morandi does of selling his paintings,' Sarah responded.

'But you can always try.'

As it turned out Erik had already left by the time Sarah and Louisa had showered and changed and got themselves across the road for dinner in Jean-Claude's wonderful garden overlooking the staggered, red roof tops of Valanjou – or Happy Valley, as Sarah had now taken to calling it. Danny had gone with Erik, having once again apologized to Louisa for all she'd said that afternoon. She'd promised to make it up to her by taking her out later in the week for a slap-up meal somewhere. Since Louisa couldn't afford the really expensive restaurants, she'd said, it would be nice for her to have a treat. That had annoyed Louisa every bit as much as what Jean-Claude was telling them now was making her uncomfortable.

'. . . and so I told Erik,' he said, his gentle brown eyes as grave and as meaningful as the throaty timbre of his voice, 'that I don't want to become involved with what 'e is doing. 'e came 'ere tonight to ask me to keep money for 'im, and I said I would not unless 'e told me what it was for or where it was from. 'e wouldn't do that, so I told 'im to take it away again and go to a bank.'

'How much money was it?' Sarah asked, her eyes flicking towards Didier and back again.

'I don't know, but it was a lot. I saw it. It wasn't francs, but in any currency the caseful 'e 'ad was a lot of money.'

'You didn't see what the currency was though?'

'No. And I also told 'im that I thought 'e should not be involving either of you in whatever is going on with 'im and Jake Mallory.'

'What did he say?' Louisa asked, the succulent *gambas* before her for the moment forgotten.

'That Jake was a rule for himself and that 'e couldn't tell Jake what to do. 'e also said, by the way, that 'e was going to ask Danny to marry 'im.'

'Who? Erik or Jake?' Louisa breathed, her face starting to drain.

'Erik is going to ask 'er. 'e says 'e loves 'er, but Erik 'e is a fool for a pretty face. Always 'e 'as been that way.'

To Louisa and Sarah's frustration Jean-Claude very skilfully managed to steer the conversation in another direction after that, and before they could get around to their dessert they had to move inside, for the storm that had been threatening to break all day suddenly boomed its arrival with a great, deafening crash of thunder and a downpour that was so fierce and so dense it wasn't possible to see even as far as the end of the garden.

It was just as they were leaving that the topic was touched upon again as Jean-Claude hugged Louisa warmly and told her that if ever she or Sarah needed a friend in this country that wasn't their own, then he would be there for them and would try to help them in any way he could. And when Louisa tried to take the edge from his unsettling concern by laughing and asking why on earth he should think they would need help, he told her that he knew she was seeing Jake, that he'd seen the Mercedes several times during the past week.

'I know I've had too much to drink,' Louisa said, taking a towel from Sarah to dry herself off after their quick sprint through the rain, 'because right now all I want to do is call the number Jake gave me and talk to him.'

'Then do it.'

'No.'

'Why?'

'Because he told me not to unless it was an emergency. And besides, what am I going to say? Jake, I think Danny's got some weird obsession with me and that's why she's telling people she's sleeping with you. Oh yes, and by the way, my neighbour is making me paranoid by telling me that he'll be there to help me in any way he can because he knows I'm seeing you.'

'You could always try asking him why Erik turned up at Jean-Claude's with a case full of dosh this afternoon,' Sarah suggested helpfully.

'Very funny.'

'OK, why not try asking him how, what did Danny say her name was? Martina? How Martina is these days? Or maybe more to the point, where Martina is.'

Louisa jumped as a sudden bolt of thunder crashed overhead. 'I wonder what all that money was for, or where it was from?' she said, pensively. 'He won't have got it from a bank, will he, not on a Saturday. Although some are open Saturday mornings, aren't they?'

'Then surely that would have been the safest place to leave it,' Sarah responded. 'And do you know what I'm thinking now? I'm thinking about Morandi driving into Consuela's this afternoon as Danny was leaving.'

Louisa's eyes opened wide. 'You mean you think he was going to pick it up?'

'It makes sense to me, doesn't it to you?'

Louisa nodded.

'When are you seeing Jake again?'

'I don't know. He said he'd call today, but he hasn't.'

'Mmm, well I reckon it's time we went into action and stopped shilly-shallying around trying to guess at what's going on and letting them off the hook every time we ask a question they don't want to answer. So, the very next time we see either of them I think we should confront them with what we've heard and see what they have to say about it. And if we don't get any straight answers, if they start messing us around with stuff like it's not safe for us to know and all that garbage, then we've got to tell them that in that case we don't think it's safe for us to carry on seeing them.'

'Yes, you're right,' Louisa said. 'You're definitely right, because I don't know what the statistics are for blackmail leading to murder, but my guess is they're pretty high. And I just can't forget what Jake said about some people being likely to lose their lives before all this was over.'

Both of them suddenly swung round as another deafening crash of thunder blasted overhead at the same time as flashing forks of lightning daggered over the pool.

Sarah turned to Louisa who was staring blindly out of the window and looking as shaken by the storm as Sarah felt. But what Louisa couldn't hear that Sarah could, was the echo of a crazed and portentous organ booming its baleful din from the portals of a neo-Romanesque cathedral in Monaco.

As Louisa's eyes came slowly round to Sarah's they both started to laugh, each knowing what the other was thinking, that this really was like a film set, a film set with everything, right down to the immaculate timing of the special effects.

16

Over the next few days, following the storm, the temperature dropped to a more bearable eighty-five degrees, before shooting back into the mid-nineties and seeming hotter and more stifling than ever. During the relatively cooler spell, though the atmosphere between Louisa and Danny was still at times fractious, the animosity was on the whole kept to a minimum. But now that the mercury was rising towards an all-time high it was not only shortening tempers, it was making the smugness of Danny's pleasure in Erik's recent proposal seem all the more galling. There was such a de-energizing sluggishness to the humidity that Danny's excitement was as exhausting to watch as it was to contend with. She hadn't given Erik an answer yet, and secretly she was intrigued to know what Jake's reaction was going to be, but she didn't mention that to either Sarah or Louisa. She simply swanned around the house and garden, naked but for her G-string, admiring herself in passing mirrors or lovingly massaging herself with suntan oil while flicking through magazines, filing her nails or talking to Erik on the phone.

Occasionally Danny took herself off on long, solitary drives never saying where she was going or when she would be back and, as difficult as the situation was between them, seeing her go off alone touched Louisa's heart with sadness and regret that the rift between them was widening and there was nothing, it seemed, that either of them could do about it. Were it not for the capricious delight Danny appeared to take in never saying where she was going Louisa might have tried a bit harder to repair things, but as it was Jake stood between them like an immovable mountain and any sympathy Louisa might have felt for Danny's isolation was swallowed by the sickening suspicion that it was him Danny was going to see when she disappeared for hours on end. It clearly wasn't Erik, because he often rang when she was out, and the fact that Jake had neither called nor sent Marianne to pick her up as he had on a few occasions the previous week only served to convince Louisa further that now Danny was back his attention was elsewhere.

Sarah hadn't heard from Morandi either, though she'd tried several times to call him both at the office and at home, but all she got was the answer phone. The frustration they were both feeling very nearly erupted in an argument between them when, one afternoon while Danny was out, Sarah angrily referred to Jake as the bastard who was fucking up all their lives. Louisa, without thinking, leapt to his defence, but then realizing that there really was nothing she could say to dispute that she reluctantly backed down. Sarah apologized and went off to her darkroom while Louisa settled down beside the pool to try for the umpteenth time to tie a subplot to the main plot without its seeming too contrived.

The trouble was, she realized irritably as the sun beat relentlessly down on her and she let her pen and pad slide on to the pale stone tiles, so much of her own life seemed so implausible that she was losing her grasp on reality.

A few minutes later she heard the sound of a car pull into the drive and felt herself tense. Quickly she turned her face towards the woods at the end of the garden deciding to feign sleep rather than have to put up with Danny's exultant strut towards her and half-apologetic, half-triumphant manner as she tried to goad Louisa into asking where she'd been. Louisa had only fallen for it once and wasn't going to make the same mistake again because she'd come very close to slapping Danny's face when, having given Danny the satisfaction of asking, Danny had merely drawled, 'Really, you wouldn't want to know.'

'Louisa?'

Louisa's head spun round, her heart lurching at the sound of Marianne's Australian accent.

'Jake would like to see you,' Marianne said.

Louisa would have dearly loved to be able to say no, wanted desperately to tell Marianne to tell him she was sorry, but she really didn't have the time, but as she sat up, removing her sunglasses and covering her breasts with a towel she heard herself say, 'Where is he?'

'Not far from here,' Marianne answered, showing her perfect white teeth in a smile that seemed even more dazzling than the sun.

Louisa stood up. She could wish that Jake had chosen someone a little less glamorous as his runaround since beside Marianne's oozing voluptuousness she felt gawky and skinny. 'I'd better get some clothes,' she said.

Ten minutes later she was beside Marianne in Marianne's white convertible Golf, speeding through the winding forest roads towards Opio where the occasional glimpses of the alps shimmering in the heat haze were quite breathtakingly lovely. As usual Marianne was asking about Louisa's new series, telling her how much she'd loved *Private Essays* when it went out in Australia and generally enthusing about a talent she longed to have herself.

Despite feeling ordinary and rather overshadowed by Marianne's shining blonde beauty, Louisa liked her, and generally enjoyed the brief conversations they had when on their way to meet Jake. Today, however, Louisa was in such a turmoil of nerves she was barely listening to what Marianne was saying.

It wasn't until they took a sharp turn from the main road and started to climb the hairpin bends to the top of a hill that Louisa realized where they were heading. A ripple of unease coasted over her heart, for this road led to only one place, the village that, despite its quaintness and hilltop splendour, she and Sarah had found so strange and so stolidly unwelcoming when they'd first arrived on the Côte d'Azur. Why, of all places, she wondered, had Jake chosen to meet her here, in what surely must be the only village in the whole of France that had no café, no restaurant, no amenity or attraction to entice the outsider?

There was no point, she knew, in asking Marianne anything. Marianne never spoke about Jake, except to say that he wanted to see Louisa, and besides the sinister feeling she'd got from the village before probably had a lot to do with the rain, which had undoubtedly also been responsible for driving everyone indoors and keeping tourists away.

However, as they drove slowly in through the huge stone walls that surrounded the village, Louisa saw straight away that the sun-baked square with its neat rows of empty cars and firmly, somehow forbiddingly, shuttered windows was, just as it had been before, totally deserted.

'Here we are,' Marianne said, coming to a stop outside the Mairie. 'Jake will be here in a few minutes.'

Louisa pushed the car door open and got out. 'Don't you find this place a bit . . .?'

'Bye,' Marianne smiled, cutting across her. 'I have to rush, but you two have a good time,' and before Louisa could draw breath to say more the Golf was disappearing back the way they'd come.

Louisa looked around at the outwardly innocuous facades of the tall, narrow houses, the salmon-pink walls and bright blue shutters of the Mairie; the drab and silent École Communale, the eery stillness of the *lavage*, the somehow incongruous circle of bright flowers on the roundabout, the stark oblong of the church tower jutting from the labyrinth of sloping, red-tiled roofs.

It was odd, she thought, that despite everything she had heard about Jake, the violence, the blackmail, the deceit, it had never once occured to her to be afraid of him. Not that she felt afraid now, at least not of him, but this peculiar ghost town with its hidden inhabitants and omnipresent air of menace wasn't somewhere she'd have chosen for a lover's tryst.

She wandered over to a short, stone pillar in the shade and sat down. After a while it seemed as if the silence were descending over her with all the intensity of the suffocating heat and it was only as the minutes ticked monotonously by and she found herself listening to the silence that she began to realize the strangeness of it. There were no birds. And now she came to think about it, it wasn't only here that no birds sang, for she couldn't recall hearing one for several weeks. Maybe they migrated to more temperate climes during the height of the summer, but their absence was adding to the sense of menace in this square.

A while later she turned to look back at the road and seeing an old woman, who had appeared from nowhere, her heart froze. She was standing not ten feet away, staring at Louisa with hostile eyes. Her thick arms were folded across her chest, her stout frame was bulging with animosity. Louisa attempted a smile. To her surprise the woman smiled back, but instead of reassuring her it only served to unnerve her further. The woman turned, walked away across the square, then sat heavily down on a cast-iron bench, and once again fixed Louisa with her intimidating eyes.

Suddenly Louisa was angry. She'd been waiting over fifteen minutes now and still there was no sign of Jake. If he didn't come it was a long and arduous walk back, but that wasn't really the point. The point was, that he had kept her waiting in this godforsaken time-warp of a place, where she couldn't even get a drink if she wanted one and couldn't even use the phone to call him because she hadn't brought the number with her.

Hearing footsteps approaching from the bottom of the square she turned, half-expecting to see someone else, but it was him. Immediately her heart turned over and seeing the way he was looking at her her anger started to fade, leaving in its place the misery and reluctance of having to deal with what had happened since the last time she'd seen him. She stood up, watching the easy movement of his body, feeling her own responding and knew that, despite herself, she was smiling. He looked so pleased and eager to see her that she longed with a passion bordering on desperation to just ignore all that Danny had said and go to him as freely and as naturally as she had only a few days ago.

'Hi,' he said, coming to a stop in front of her and after looking long into her eyes he cupped his hand around her throat and kissed her lingeringly on the mouth. There was nothing she could do to stop herself responding, the power he had over her was too great.

'Sorry I'm late,' he murmured, letting his gaze roam over the smoothness of her face, the liquid softness of her anxious brown eyes.

'Where were you?' she asked.

'I had some business to attend to,' he answered. 'It took a bit longer than I expected.'

'Where's your car?'

'Up at the top. I've missed you.'

She lifted her eyes from his lips and seeing the familiar expression of gentle mockery and surprise at the pleasure he seemed to take just in looking at her she felt herself aching with love for him. 'Have you?' she said.

He seemed vaguely bewildered by the question, then frowned as he remembered that of course he hadn't called for a few days. 'Yeah, I missed you,' he said firmly, but gently.

'Then why didn't you call?'

'A lot's been happening, but I sent Marianne as soon as I could.'

Louisa looked away. 'So it's got nothing to do with Danny being back that you didn't call?' she said.

'Why should it?' he asked, turning her back and looking genuinely bemused. Then his frown disappeared as realization dawned. 'Oh, I get it,' he said, 'she told you I brought her home on Saturday?'

'Amongst other things.'

'Well, I don't know what else she told you, but the reason I brought her home Saturday was because I went to pick her up from the airport. I picked her up, drove her to Consuela's where she collected her belongings then I drove her to Valanjou. And the reason it was me who did all that was because Erik was doing something else at the time, something for me.'

'Like picking up a lot of money?' Louisa said, unable to keep the accusation from her voice.

'Yes, as a matter of fact, he was,' he responded, his face darkening. 'Now come on, what is all this? I thought we agreed, no questions . . .'

'That was before Danny told me that you're still sleeping with her. That you're making a laughing stock out of me with your crew, that . . .'

'For Christ's sake, why are you listening to her? Why are you even discussing me with her? I thought I told you, she is the last person . . .'

'You want to know about us,' Louisa finished heatedly. 'Yes, you did tell me that, but what I want to know is why, Jake? Why are you flaunting your relationship with her when you're hiding it with me?'

'I'm not flaunting any relationship with Danny,' he said angrily. 'How can I be, when there's no relationship to flaunt? She's lying to you, Louisa. I don't know why she's doing that, I don't even care much. All I care about is that you stop listening to her.'

'And go on listening to you? Go on making a fool of myself over someone who didn't even bother to tell me he was married?'

His eyes were suddenly hard and as he glared down at her she could see the struggle he was having to keep his temper. 'Who told you?' he said tightly.

'Consuela told Danny.' Louisa waited, almost crippled by the need to hear him deny it, but it was obvious he wasn't going to when his question alone had confirmed it, and if that were true, then dear God, the likelihood was that so too was everything else. 'So are you?' she said dully.

'If Consuela says so, then I guess I must be,' he answered, his voice still strained with anger.

'What kind of answer is that?' she cried. 'Either you are or you aren't!'

'Right now it's the only answer I can give,' he said, 'so don't push me.'

'It's not good enough,' she said turning to walk away. 'I'm sorry, but I can't go on like this. I thought I could, but . . .'

'Louisa,' he said, grabbing her arm. 'Louisa, don't walk away.'

As she looked up at the fine bones of his lean, handsome face and saw the way it was racked with torment, the way the disfiguring scar around his left eye was suddenly so pronounced, she was almost engulfed by the longing to put her arms around him, to hold him and tell him that none of it mattered. That whatever it was, whoever it was, driving this wedge between them would be of no importance at all if he would just trust her enough to tell her what was happening.

'I want to tell you,' he said gruffly, as though he had read her thoughts, 'more than anything else I want to tell you, but I just can't right now.'

'Why? What difference is it going to make when you tell me?'

'There isn't the time to tell you now,' he answered.

'Excuses. Always excuses, but never answers,' she said.

'I'm catching a plane this afternoon,' he said, putting his hands on her shoulders, 'but if I weren't I swear, Louisa, I'd tell you now.'

'I want to believe you,' she whispered, her voice strangled with emotion as she lowered her eyes, 'but I don't know if I dare. I don't want to believe what I've been hearing, but until you tell me what this is all about, why Erik was asking Jean-Claude to look after so much money, why Danny should want to lie about sleeping with you, what your relationship is with Consuela . . .'

'Darling, look at me,' he said, his voice almost as choked with feeling as hers. 'Look at me and listen to what I'm telling you. I am not sleeping with Danny. I don't want to sleep with Danny, I never did want to sleep with Danny. She was just there, she threw herself at me and I took it. It was no more than that. A one-night stand and I never expected to see her again.'

'And the money?'

'Is money I'm taking with me to Mexico. The people I'm doing business with there want paying in cash. What Erik had was a quarter of a million dollars worth of pesos.'

'What kind of business is it?'

He looked at her for a long time before slowly shaking his head. 'Not now,' he said. 'I will tell you, but not now. I need to be with you afterwards and today I just can't stay.'

'Then what about Consuela?'

'It's all a part of the same thing,' he answered and once again it was as though his pain was being pushed to the surface. 'Louisa, please don't make me hate myself any more than I already do. I never intended anything to happen between us, it would have been better if it hadn't – for both of us. But we're here now, we've got what we have . . .'

'It's blackmail, isn't it?' Louisa said flatly. 'You're involved in some kind of blackmail.'

His eyes closed and sighing he dropped his forehead against hers. 'Were it only that simple,' he murmured.

'Aphrodite told Sarah that Morandi was a blackmailer,' she persisted. 'Morandi told Sarah he works for you.'

'He does, in a way. When did Aphrodite tell Sarah that?'

'On Saturday. The same day that Danny told us she thought the same thing.'

'Has Sarah spoken to Morandi since?'

'No, his answer phone's on all the time.'

Jake was silent, then pulling her into his arms he said, 'I told you none of this was going to be easy. I tried to warn you, but it's my fault, I was crazy ever to have started it. I should let you go now, but, God help me, I can't. If you only knew how it feels to hold you, what you do to me when you look at me. I want you, Louisa, I want you here with me to remind me that there is still some good in this world. But I know I can't keep doing this to you, hiding things and expecting you to accept it. Jesus Christ,' he groaned as he buried his face in the soft scent of her hair, 'I want you so bad it's hard to make myself think about anything else.'

As Louisa's arms went around him she just knew, deep in her heart, that no matter what anyone said this wasn't a man who beat his wife. And neither was he a man who was lying to her now. She could feel his love as though it were moving into her, drawing her closer, binding her to him. The gentleness, the concern and deep emotion that reflected themselves in his eyes, in his voice, in his touch were more real to her than anything else could ever be.

'Hold me,' she whispered as his arms tightened around her. 'Hold me close Jake and tell me that I'm not wrong about you.'

He lifted his head, looked deep into her eyes and said, 'You're not wrong,' and then his lips were on hers, his arms were crushing her and his whole body was pressed against hers telling her the extent of his desire, his passion, his unspoken love.

'Oh God,' he laughed harshly. 'Why does it have to be like this? Why can't I just . . .?' His eyes closed as though he regretted saying even that much, but then he was kissing her again, kissing her and holding her as though he might never let her go.

Then suddenly, like a great, ugly fist, Danny's words hit her. 'He'll get you to the point of begging . . .' she'd said. 'He won't make a commitment to me, not yet . . .'

Louisa pulled herself abruptly from the embrace, shaking as much with anger at herself for being so easily taken in as with hatred of Danny for spoiling what little she had. But it wasn't Danny, was it? It was him. He had said those things . . .

'For God's sake!' he cried angrily as she threw the accusation at him. 'What do you want me to say? That I'm committing myself to you?'

Yes, that was what she wanted, but at the same time she didn't want to hear him refuse.

He rolled his eyes towards the heavens as he gave an exasperated smile. 'Why are you letting her do this?' he said gently.

Louisa looked at him, the battle raging within her to resist him.

'Would you believe Erik if I got him to tell you how I feel about you?' he said.

'Why don't you tell me yourself?' she challenged.

'Because I don't have the right to tell you myself. But I will tell you this, Louisa, I want you just as much as you want me. Sure, you're telling yourself you don't right now, but we both know that what's happening between us is too big for either of us to deny. And what Danny told you, what she claims she's repeated from my lips, was either what she overheard me saying to Erik, or what Erik's told her himself. It's more likely that she overheard it, because I don't believe Erik would break my trust. And what I told him was that I can't make the commitment to *you* that I want to make. They were idle words, because he knows that already and he knows why. And as for getting you to beg me, you've got to know that I'd never let you do that, it would never get that far, because God knows I can't hold out much longer myself. The only reason I've held back until now is because I can't make love to you knowing you feel the way you do, without telling you first what you're really up against. Erik knows we haven't made love because I told him. I told him that it was going to drive us both crazy, but that I wasn't going to do it until you knew the truth. Danny must have heard that and then put it into her own words.'

'But why would she do that? And why, after I asked you that night in the garden not to make me beg, should she have used that very same word?'

'An unhappy coincidence, I don't know. But that word sure as hell never crossed my lips when I was talking to Erik.'

'That still doesn't explain why Danny would lie to me.'

'No, because I don't have an answer for that,' he said, 'I don't know Danny like you do, maybe you're better placed to come up with the answer.'

Louisa thought she probably was. But what was it all about, she wondered. What was going on in Danny's head to make her want to hurt her the way she was, to take the credit for her success, to throw her background in her face then tell her it was because of it that she excused Louisa for a selfishness Louisa was unaware of? There was something going on with Danny, something that undoubtedly had its roots in a horrible and competitive jealousy that Jake had fallen for Louisa and not for Danny. But it wasn't something Louisa wanted to think about now, not when Jake was standing there, watching her with that lazy irony in his eyes that was tinged with concern while waiting for her to tell him . . . To tell him what? How sorry she was that she had doubted him? But no, she couldn't do that, and she was sure, under the circumstances, that he wouldn't expect her to.

'Why don't we just forget about Danny and concentrate on us?' she said softly.

'You got it,' he smiled. Then pulling her into the circle of his arm he started to walk towards the narrow road running alongside the school.

'Do you find anything odd about this place?' Louisa said, taking the hand that was draped around her shoulder and lacing her fingers through his.

'Yeah, as a matter of fact, I do,' he answered. 'To be honest it gives me the creeps.'

'Mmm, me too.' She paused for a moment then said, 'I'm sorry we argued.'

'I'm sorry too,' he said, giving her a quick squeeze. 'So tell me, what have you been doing with yourself?'

'Not much actually. It's been too hot to go anywhere, so we've been lazing around the pool mainly. Oh, by the way, Sarah's got the enlargements of the *Valhalla*. I think you're going to like them.'

'Good, I'll have to try and get round to see them. And, now I come to think of it, I'm going to have to get you on board one of these days because you haven't seen her yet, have you?'

'No, but I'd love to. More than anything I'd like to see where you live.'

He laughed. 'I don't live on the *Valhalla*,' he said. 'I've got a house over in the Var where I live when I'm here.'

'A house?' she said, surprised. 'You've never mentioned it before.'

'No, I just hope I'm doing right by mentioning it now.'

'Why shouldn't you be?'

'Come on,' he said, pulling open the door to the Mercedes, 'get in and I'll drive you back.'

'So soon?'

'I told you, I've got a plane to catch.'

'Where are you going?'

'Back to Mexico,' and closing the passenger door behind her he walked round to get in the other side. The roof was up and all the windows were closed, but as Louisa made to push the button to open hers he stopped her.

'The air-conditioner's on,' he told her, starting up the engine.

As he reversed back over the gravel he was punching out a number on the phone. He let it ring on the speaker for a moment, then picking up the receiver he spoke in what at his end was a series of non sequiturs, 'Bob?' he said. 'Yeah. No, it was no good. Get onto Erik if you can and have him meet me at the *Valhalla* in half an hour. He can take me to the airport. *What!*' he hissed. 'When did it happen? Where's Morandi now? OK, find him, tell him I want to see him. Sure, I'll be right there,' and he rang off.

'I want you to do something for me,' he said, glancing over at Louisa as they drove back through the village.

'What's that?'

'I want you to promise me you'll stay away from Consuela. And, if you can, I want you to keep Danny away from her too.'

Louisa's heart gave a twist of unease. 'Am I allowed to ask why?' she said.

He didn't answer straight away so she turned to look at him. 'Do you know the story of Pandora?' he said.

'I think so,' she answered, curiously.

'Well I'll tell you just in case,' he said glancing at his watch. 'She was sent by Zeus as a punishment to Epimetheus. She came with all the gifts of the divinities and with all the beauty of the goddesses. But in her mouth were lies and in her heart was perfidy. That is Consuela.'

Louisa turned to look straight ahead, not knowing what to say.

They continued in silence as they rejoined the main road and the refreshing breeze from the air-conditioner cooled them. She looked over at him and though she couldn't see his eyes behind the sunglasses she could tell from the tightness of his mouth and the hard set of his jaw that whatever was going through his mind now was causing him a great deal of anguish, if not anger. She desperately wanted to lighten the atmosphere for these last few minutes, but couldn't think what to say.

'When are you coming back from Mexico?' she ventured and immediately wished she hadn't when she saw the strain in his face increase.

'I don't know,' he answered abruptly.

She shrugged awkwardly. 'Whereabouts are you going in Mexico?' she asked trying to sound chatty.

'Look, Louisa, I don't need this right now, OK?' he snapped. 'Just get off my back with the questions. I told you I'll tell you everything just as soon as I can, so quit hassling me.'

'Don't speak to me like that!' she retorted angrily. 'I was merely trying to make conversation.'

'Then don't.'

For a moment she was lost for words then, quite suddenly, without her even knowing how it had happened, they were in the middle of a blazing row.

'I did what I could to put your mind at rest,' he was raging, 'but right now I'm not doing any more. And if you've got a problem with that then maybe you'd better get out of my life now!'

'Of course I've got a problem with it,' she shouted back. 'I can't stand all this deceit, all this . . .'

'Make the decision, Louisa, because it's all the same to me.'

She gasped. 'Well if that's how you feel,' she seethed, 'then I'll say goodbye now.'

'That suits me just fine.'

For a second or two as alarm threatened to get the better of her anger she smouldered in silence. 'So you are a liar!' she suddenly cried. 'One minute you say you can't let me go, then the next it suits you just fine.'

'OK, I'm a liar!' he yelled furiously. 'It's what you've been trying to get from me ever since I turned up today, so you got it. I'm a liar. Does that make you happy? Is that what you want to hear?'

'If it's the truth, then yes, it's what I want to hear.'

'Then you've got it!'

Louisa turned to glare out of the window while he swore under his breath as he took a bend too fast and had to swerve to avoid an oncoming car.

'Why don't you slow down?' she snapped. 'You're going to get us both killed at this rate and I don't see why I should die just because you can't control your temper.'

His face was still stony, the knuckles of his left hand white as he gripped the wheel, but he did ease off the accelerator at the same time as he punched the CD and drowned the car with music.

Louisa immediately sat forward and punched it off again.

He let it go, glancing in his rear-view mirror as he made a right turn into Valanjou. A few minutes later he pulled up at the end of the lane leading to the villa.

When Louisa merely sat there he looked pointedly and impatiently at his watch.

'Is this how we're going to leave it?' she said curtly.

'I don't have time for this,' he responded, sounding only fractionally less angry. 'I'll call you when I get back, OK?'

'Suit yourself,' she said through clenched teeth and throwing open the door she got out and slammed it behind her.

It was just after midnight. Jake was furiously pacing the deck of the *Valhalla* while Erik stood leaning against a stanchion calmly smoking a cigarette.

'How much goddamned longer are we gonna have to wait?'

Jake growled. 'And who the hell called the police, is what I want to know?'

'Aphrodite?' Erik suggested, tilting his head so that it was in the glow of the lamp on the foremast.

Jake glowered at him, then resumed pacing.

'Look, if it had been a straightforward burglary the police needn't have been involved,' Erik pointed out. 'But there's no way he can cover up the fire.'

'How much longer are they going to hold him?' Jake demanded.

'They're not holding him, they're just carrying out their investigation.'

'At this time of night?'

'No one could find him before,' Erik reminded him. 'Now, for God's sake roll yourself a joint and calm down, will you?'

'Did you get me on a flight out tomorrow?'

'Yes. And Fernando's been contacted, he knows you're not coming in on schedule.'

Jake turned and hammered his fist against the coach house. 'This is all we fucking need right now,' he hissed.

'Hey up, here they come,' Erik said, spotting Morandi and Bob getting into the dinghy over at the harbour.

Jake stood at the edge of the deck watching them come and barely waited until Morandi was on board before laying into him with: 'Who the hell called the police?'

Morandi's face was pale, his hair and clothes were in disarray, his eyes were tired and filled with foreboding. 'Apparently it was a neighbour,' he answered. 'She saw that the office had been burgled so she called the police and by the time they came the place was going up in smoke.'

'Did they manage to salvage anything?'

'I think so. They acted pretty quickly, but I haven't had a chance to go and look the place over yet. You needn't worry about all the records though, they weren't there.'

Though it was minimal, Jake appeared mollified by this answer. 'Where's Aphrodite?' he said.

'I don't know. I haven't seen her since this morning.'

'Where were you when the police contacted you?'

'On location, where I've been most of the time since Monday.'

'And Aphrodite?'

'She was with me until this morning.'

Jake glanced at Erik who shrugged and lit another cigarette.

'OK,' Jake said, 'fill me in on what happened just prior to the burglary. Yeah, yeah, I know you were on location, but what about Consuela? Did you have any contact with her over the past couple of days?'

'Yes,' Morandi answered, wiping a hand over his mouth as the troubled look in his eyes deepened. 'I had a video she wanted, but I refused to hand it over.'

'What video?' Jake demanded.

Morandi looked at him, glanced at Erik then back again. There was something akin to real fear in his eyes now.

'What video?' Jake said through clenched teeth.

'The one of Danny Spencer's mother,' Morandi sighed defeatedly.

Jake gave a bark of laughter. 'Of course!' he said. 'What a fool. I should have known. Did she say what she wanted it for?'

Morandi seemed to shrink as his eyes once again moved between Jake and Erik. 'She said she was afraid you'd use it to try and get money out of Danny,' he answered, already wincing at the explosion he knew was about to come.

But it didn't. Instead, for several seconds, the only sound was the gentle wash of the waves against the hull.

Morandi waited, watching Jake closely, deeply unnerved by this lack of reaction. In the end it was Erik who spoke.

'The question now,' he said, 'is did she get the video out before she had the place burned?'

'We have to assume she did,' Jake answered, 'otherwise she'd never have burned it.' He turned to Morandi. 'Tell me you didn't mention anything about her to the police.'

'Not a word,' Morandi assured him.

'OK. You'd better try and find Aphrodite, make sure she doesn't start singing either.'

'Oh, she won't,' Morandi said confidently.

'Just make sure of it. Now I'm for bed, because if Consuela's already got that video then there's nothing any of us can do about it now. Where's Danny?' he added to Erik.

'At the villa.'

Jake nodded. 'Do what you can to see that she stays there. I know she's as slippery as a barrel of eels, but try,' and leaving them to it he swung himself in through the hatch, his mind now totally focused on Mexico.

17

Since there was still no sign of Aphrodite Sarah agreed to help Morandi clear up his office. He'd called her early that morning – the morning after it happened – sounding so exhausted and so utterly dejected that Sarah hadn't even bothered to question why he hadn't called her before. In light of what had happened it seemed both irrelevant and petty to be thinking of her own injured pride.

Now, as they stood among the charred debris, overturned furniture and smoke-blackened walls still dripping with water, trying to make some order of the chaos, Sarah was watching him, wishing she knew how to comfort him. He looked so downbeaten and weary she couldn't help wondering how close he was to breaking.

Looking up and catching her watching him he forced a smile, but it didn't make it to his eyes for they were too steeped in worry and helplessness to brook any other emotion.

'Have you been in touch with the insurers yet?' she asked.

'Yes, I did it just before you arrived,' he answered. 'Someone's coming over later.' Then, to her dismay, he sat down heavily on a chair and dropped his head in his hands.

'This is all such a mess,' he muttered. 'Such a fucking mess I don't know which way to turn.'

Sarah went to him, put a hand on the back of his neck and started gently to massage it. Knowing that the fire had been arson, she wondered if she dared voice what was in her mind. In the end she decided to chance it. 'You don't suppose,' she began tentatively, 'that Aphrodite was behind this, do you?'

He shook his head without looking up. 'No, I don't think so,' he answered.

'Then where is she?'

'I wish to God I knew.'

Sarah went to kneel in front of him, took his hands from his face and looking at him with her clear, sensible blue eyes said, 'I think it's time you told me what's really going on here, don't you?'

He nodded, and kept on nodding for some time, before saying, in a voice that rasped with fatigue, 'Yes, I think you're right.'

She waited, holding his hands in hers and watching the way he seemed to be searching his mind for where to begin.

'You must have guessed by now that it's blackmail,' he said forlornly.

Sarah nodded.

He laughed dryly, as though despising himself, then in a tone that was brutal and self-punishing, he said, 'I take the cameras to Consuela's whenever she asks me. I set them up in hidden niches of the guest rooms in the bathhouse – she always tells me which rooms to go into – and then we video her rich friends and all they get up to with the boys. Then, needless to say, the videos are used to extort money from the women with threats to show their husbands, or fathers, or God knows who, if they don't pay up.'

'But that's terrible,' Sarah murmured, disappointed with the inadequacy of the word, but unable to think of another.

'Oh, it's worse than that,' he said, injecting his voice with a biting revulsion. 'Some women have paid up and the videos have been put into the wrong hands anyway, just for the hell of it. Just to see the women suffer and in some cases lose everything.'

'Dear God,' Sarah muttered, thinking of the women she had met at the bathhouse the one time she had been there and wondering if any of them had yet been made to pay such a dreadful price for what they'd assumed to be after-dinner relaxation. 'But why are you doing it?' she said. 'You don't seem like a man without morals, but . . .'

'I do have morals,' he interrupted. 'It's just not wise to show them too often when you're dealing with people like Consuela Santini and Jake Mallory.'

'So Jake is behind it,' Sarah murmured, her heart going out to Louisa for how horribly she'd been duped.

Morandi shook his head. 'Depends who you're talking to,' he answered. 'Consuela claims it's all his idea. He says it's hers.'

'So how did you come to be involved?'

Morandi sighed heavily. 'Now that's a long story,' he said. 'It started about two years ago when Peter, my youngest brother, came down to the Riviera to get a job. He didn't have anything particular in mind, you know what kids are like, he just wanted to bum around for a while and have a good time. Which is what he did. Then he called me one day after he'd been here a couple of weeks and told me he'd landed himself a real cushy number with some rich lady. He said the pay was out of this world and the perks were even better. It didn't take much imagination to work out what the perks were, Peter's a good-looking boy, keeps himself in good shape and has always had a certain way with the ladies. I didn't see any harm in him being a bit of a gigolo for a while, I'd have probably done the same thing at his age given half the chance, so I didn't think too much about it. That was until he stopped calling. Two months or more went by with no letter, no postcard, no phone call. He'd never told me this rich woman's name, nor given me her number and knowing that the Riviera is virtually littered with them I didn't know where to start. My sisters were frantic with worry, so I got myself on a plane and came down here to see if I could find him. Needless to say I got nowhere. I didn't even know which town the woman lived in, never mind the street. I contacted the police, but there wasn't much they could do – students are passing through all the time, taking on temporary jobs before moving on somewhere else and forgetting to tell their families where. In the end I went back to England none the wiser and feeling twice my age with worry. It wasn't like him not to be in touch for so long, so I knew something had to have happened.

'Then suddenly one day there was a knock on my door and there he was. I could hardly believe it. I'd never said anything to the rest of the family, but I'd almost given up hope of ever seeing him again. There were two men with him, one was Jake, I forget the other one's name now, but it isn't important. They'd brought Peter back, that was all that was important to me.

'Anyway, it seemed that Peter had told Jake something about me – I'd made a few low-budget movies by then, mainly for the European market, much like I've been doing down here. There's money in it and, like I told you, I have two ex-wives and an army of kids to support. It didn't take Jake long to get around to offering to set me up in business down here, he's not a man to hang around as I've since found out. He was prepared to set me up, he said, in return for a few small favours. Well, since he'd just brought Peter back I felt it was I who owed him a favour and I was right, I did, because it wasn't until Jake had gone that Peter told me where he had been and what had been happening during the past three months. Apparently, it took him several weeks to catch on to what was going on at Consuela's, but as soon as he did he told her he wanted out. She didn't seem to mind, he said, in fact quite the reverse, she seemed to want to help him find another job, or pay for his flight back to England, or whatever he wanted. Obviously she swore him to secrecy about what was going on, and it was only later that he realized what a mug he was to have believed that she was going to let him out of there with only his word as his bond when he knew all that he did.

'That was where Jake came in. As Peter tells the story Jake arranged for someone to take a dinghy into Consuela's private beach late at night, pick Peter up and take him to the Ile Sainte Marguerite where he stayed for two or three days before the *Valhalla* came to take him over to Corsica. Jake wasn't on board, but he was in Corsica when Peter got there. That was when he told Peter what was going to happen to him.'

'And what was that?' Sarah asked clearing her throat.

'He had a choice,' Morandi smiled grimly. 'He could either

be shot right there and then and buried where no one would ever find the grave, or he could opt for being kept prisoner for the rest of his life in some place so remote he'd never even know which country he was in.'

'I don't believe it,' Sarah murmured 'That's monstrous.'

'No, that's blackmail,' he corrected. 'Or what happens to those who get mixed up in it, because innocent or guilty, someone almost always ends up paying with their life.'

Echoes of Louisa's same observation passed chillingly through Sarah's mind. 'So how did Peter get around it?' she said.

'Jake got him around it. The choice wasn't being offered by Jake, you understand, it was being offered by Consuela. Or that's what Jake told Peter and Peter believed him. And who can blame Peter for believing him, as far as Peter's concerned Jake saved his life. As far as I was concerned at the time, I believed it too, so of course I was prepared to do Jake a favour. He was perfectly straight with me, he told me it wouldn't be legal, that there was every chance one or other of us, if not all of us, might end up in jail. But he said he'd do everything he could to get me off should it ever come to that and in the meantime I wouldn't even have to think about how I was going to meet my alimony payments because he'd take care of everything. Which he has.

'So, I gave up my flat in Barnet and moved down here. By then I'd met Jake a few more times, I liked him, trusted him and believed the story he gave me. He said that when Consuela's husband died he'd left her penniless. It wasn't that the old man didn't have any money, it was just that he hadn't left it to Consuela. Jake didn't say why Consuela was cut out of the will and I didn't ask. However, she was bequeathed the villa on the Cap, but with no money to pay for its upkeep and the running of it, she turned the stables into a bathhouse and set herself up in this blackmail racket.'

He paused, pressed his fingers to his tired eyes then returned his hand to hers. 'According to Jake she'd been doing it for about a year before Peter came along,' he continued. 'I can't remember when Jake said he found out about it, but when he did he started making it his business to get the boys out of France and either safely back to their families or over to the States, where his father uses his influence to get them set-up there. Why are you smiling?'

'No reason,' Sarah answered, thinking of how Louisa was going to love this part of the story. 'Go on.'

'Well, according to Jake, there was one thing he couldn't do and that was get his hands on the videos before they were used for blackmail.'

'But why would he want to?'

'To stop it from happening, or so he claims. So, he struck a bargain with Consuela. In return for something he's never told me about, he would take the videos to the women concerned, or their husbands, and make himself responsible for collecting the money. And as far as I know that's exactly what he does.'

'You mean he's also the one who hands the videos over just for the hell of it?' Sarah said, her admiration for Jake suddenly teetering on the edge of repugnance.

'I don't know,' Morandi sighed. 'I wish I did. All I know is that the blackmail is still going on, that money in quantities like I've never seen before is changing hands all the time and that I wish to God I'd never got involved.'

'You still haven't told me exactly how you did,' Sarah reminded him.

'Jake got me to masquerade as an Italian, someone who had connections with the Mafia because that would impress Consuela and make her more inclined to trust me, and go to her offering my services as a producer. I'm pretty sure she had me checked out, but Jake took care of that, don't ask me how because I don't know, but I can only assume he was able to do it because he does have Mafia connections. Anyway, she hired me and now I go in, set up the cameras, collect them the next day and then I edit them together.'

'But you still don't really know which of them is behind it?'

'On the face of it it's Consuela, but the truth is, Sarah, I don't know whether I've been taken for one hell of a ride here, because if Jake really is trying to frame Consuela for blackmail, which is what he claims he's doing, then he's got more than enough evidence now. I know, because I'm the one who keeps the records, who logs all the dates, all the transactions, everything, so why doesn't he just hand it and her over to the police and let us all get on with our lives?'

Since it was a rhetorical question Sarah merely squeezed his hands and settled herself more comfortably in the clutter of burnt papers, melted videos and heat-buckled film cans.

'Is it,' he asked himself aloud, 'because he's the one who set up the bathhouse? Is he the one who's profiting from this loathsome extortion? Consuela says he is. She won't tell me what he's holding over her to make her go along with it, but according to her he's behind everything. She says he was the one who set up the bathhouse, that he's the one who hires the boys, brings in the rich women and collects the money. But there are so many lies, I just can't keep track of them any more.'

'Have you ever considered going to the police and letting them sort it out?'

'All the time. But how can I when Jake knows where Peter is, where my whole family is? Not that he's ever threatened anything, but I just don't want to take the risk.'

'Does that mean, in your heart, you really do think Jake is behind it?'

'God knows,' he sighed. 'For all I know they're in it together.'

'But let's just say for a moment that it was Consuela who started it. What do you think it was that Jake used to bargain with her to get her to let him in on it?'

'What do you mean?'

'Well he can't just have sailed in out of the blue and said OK, let's go fifty-fifty, can he? Not if she had it all set up very nicely for herself already. Why would she need him? So my question is, what does he have over her that would persuade her to let him in on it?'

'I've no idea. He's never said.'

'This might be totally off the wall, but you don't suppose it might have something to do with his wife, do you?'

Morandi frowned. 'I didn't even know he was married.'

'Consuela told Danny he was.'

Morandi shook his head. 'I don't know anything about that. All I know about is the unholy mess I've managed to get myself in and I just can't see a way out of it.'

Sarah thought for a moment. 'What about Mexico?' she said. 'Where does that fit in?'

'I don't know. I don't ask because I know more than I want to know already.'

'But it could have something to do with the remote places where the boys are held prisoner after being confronted with Hobson's choice?' she suggested.

'Yes, it could, I suppose, I've never really thought about it. But to be honest, Sarah, I don't think anyone's being held prisoner. Neither do I think anyone's been shot. OK, I might be kidding myself here because I don't want to believe it, but if all those boys had gone missing, don't you think at least one of them would have been traced back to Consuela by now?'

'Yes,' Sarah said deflating slightly. 'Yes, I suppose they would.' Then realizing that meant Jake had returned to a better light she brightened again. 'I think Consuela's behind it,' she said decisively. 'I mean Jake is a massively wealthy man, so why would he need to do something like that?'

'You won't be able to ask me anything I haven't already asked myself a thousand times,' Morandi said despondently. 'But neither of us is going to come up with any answers, not unless we have the full picture.'

'So what's missing?' Sarah said, trying to piece together what she could.

'I would say that what's missing is what Jake has over Consuela or what she has over him. And that's still assuming they're not in it together.'

'Oh God, you're not much better as a detective's sidekick than Louisa,' Sarah grumbled.

Morandi's eyes flickered something very close to an admonishment, making Sarah realize that even after all she had heard, she was not taking this as seriously as she should. Or maybe it was because of what she had heard, it was hard to say, all she knew was that her sense of reality was once again as woefully impaired as her spirit of adventure was piqued.

'Jake has made Louisa promise to stay away from Consuela,' she said sobering herself. 'Now why do you think that is? Do you think he's afraid that Consuela might do something to harm her?'

'He could be. Or he could be afraid that Consuela will tell Louisa what's really going on.'

'Mm,' she grunted. 'I hadn't thought of it that way. I don't think Louisa has either. Though he did say he was going to tell Louisa himself.'

'Then we'll just have to see if he does.'

'What about Erik? He must know what's really happening between Jake and Consuela, surely?'

'I don't doubt for a minute that he does, but you'll never get him to tell you anything Jake doesn't want him to tell.'

'Then who else is there?'

'No one.'

'But hang on, didn't you tell me the other day that you thought Aphrodite knew more than you? Why don't we try asking her?'

'We could if we knew where she was. Not that I'd hold out much hope of her telling us anything, and I could be wrong, she might not know more than I do.'

'But she might,' Sarah said staring thoughtfully down at a pool of black slush in the corner. 'Funny isn't it?' she said turning her eyes back to Morandi. 'That she should have disappeared the very same day this place was wrecked. Are you sure you don't think she might have done it?'

'Why would she? Unless,' he said answering his own question, 'Consuela told her to.'

'I thought you said Jake employed her.'

'I always thought he did. But one thing I'm certain about is that Jake didn't order this place to be burnt. He postponed his trip to Mexico because of it, now why would he have done that if he already knew it was going to happen?'

'No reason I can think of,' Sarah said. 'So does that mean we might find Aphrodite at Consuela's, I wonder?'

'We might, who knows?'

An hour later, while Sarah and Morandi were still ploughing through the destruction of his office there was a knock on the empty door frame and two policemen walked into the mayhem, turning up their noses at the damp, acrid smell of the place.

Assuming that they were continuing their investigations into the burglary and arson and because Morandi was speaking to them in French Sarah didn't pay much attention at first. But then, seeing the way Morandi's face suddenly turned so horribly pale, she moved swiftly to his side and took his arm.

'What is it?' she said. 'What are they saying?'

'They've come to tell me,' he said, sounding as haggard as he looked, 'that Aphrodite . . . Aphrodite's body has just been found . . .'

18

Outside the air was soggy. Ancient American cars rumbled and clanked wearily through the streets, high-pitched sirens wailed their urgency, but inside the Los Mochis hotel room the air was crisp and cool and cut through with danger.

Jake was sitting in a low-backed armchair, elbows resting on his knees, hands linked loosely together. His face was taut, but for the moment devoid of expression. In front of him, seated on a hard chair and flanked by two solid Mexicans was Pedro, the scrawny old man who had led Jake the last time he was there to an out of the way hotel.

'You did well,' Jake remarked to Fernando who was sitting at a round table in front of the window, his legs stretched out in front of him and one arm resting on the other as he smoked a cigarette.

Fernando merely expelled two lungs full of smoke through his nose and followed Jake's eyes back to Pedro whose jutting bottom jaw was quivering as he looked back at the *gringo* with the patch over one eye and murder in the other.

Jake fixed him with his unshielded eye for some time, then lowered his gaze to the dingy pink carpet. 'Where is she?' he said, the mildness of his tone making it all the more ominous.

'I don'ta know,' Pedro answered.

'Where is she?'

'I don'ta know, they don'ta tell me.'

Jake lifted his head. 'When did you last see her?'

'Five weeks ago.'

'Where?'

'Like I say before, near Chihuahua.'

'Who was she with?'

'Two men, another woman and a child.'

Fernando's head came up and an icy fist clenched his gut when he saw Jake's expression.

'Who were these people?' Jake said.

'I don'ta know.'

'How do you know it was her?'

'I know her.'

'How?'

'I have seen pictures.'

'Who showed them to you?'

'I don'ta know.'

'Who showed them to you?'

'I don'ta know.'

Jake's eyes flicked towards the man standing on Pedro's right. Pedro squealed as the blow to his face brought blood spurting from his nose.

Jake was on his feet now, his back to Pedro. 'Who showed them to you?' he repeated.

'A man.'

'What was his name?'

'I don'ta know.'

Jake turned as Pedro's head jerked to one side under the force of the next blow. 'His name,' Jake demanded.

'I don'ta know. Please, *señor*, really I don'ta know.'

Jake nodded to the other man who picked up Pedro's hand and wrenched his forefinger back. Pedro screamed, drowning the sickening crunch of the finger breaking.

'His name,' Jake repeated.

'Juan.'

Jake nodded at the man again.

'No, no, I beg you, *señor*,' Pedro sobbed as his middle finger was bent to the point of snapping. 'His name is Juan Morales. Please no break my hand no more.'

'Was this man with her when you saw her?' Jake said.

'Yes, he was there.'

'Where are they now?'

'I don'ta know.'

Jake's eyes moved back to the man.

'No! No!' Pedro screamed. 'Really, I not know. Last week they here in Los Mochis, now I not know where they are.'

'You said just now you hadn't seen them for five weeks,' Jake reminded him.

'The woman, no. The men, they were here, but she no with them.'

'Where did they go?'

'They no tell me.'

All eyes were on Jake as he rested his forehead on his fist. 'What about the child?' he said.

'I not know about the child. I just see her.'

'How old is the child?' Jake said.

'Two, maybe three years old. It is hard to know with children.'

Jake stayed silent and Fernando moved across the room to put a hand on his shoulder.

Shrugging him off Jake looked at the other two. 'Get him out of here,' he said. 'Get him out of here and make him tell you where they've gone.'

As Pedro was hauled from the room Fernando moved back to the table and picked up a bottle of whisky.

'The question still remains the same,' Jake said waiting for the door to close. 'Is Consuela paying them to lie or is Martina really alive?'

Fernando shook his head and handing Jake a drink sat down on the chair Pedro had just vacated. 'I don't know, my friend,' he said. 'But we will find out.'

The days since Jake had gone seemed to drag endlessly for Louisa and not knowing exactly when he would be back was only making it worse. It didn't help either that Sarah was spending so much time with Morandi, not that she begrudged Morandi Sarah's support for she of all people knew how unswerving and comforting it was, but she longed to discuss all that Sarah had told her in more detail. However, she just had to make do with Sarah's rushed visits and updates on the police investigation into Aphrodite's murder. So far they hadn't come up with much that was new, except that the time of her death had been put before the burglary and arson so she was no longer a suspect.

In a snatched moment with Erik Louisa had asked him about the video of Danny's mother and whether or not they should tell Danny. Erik had been adamant that they shouldn't say a word. They needed to find out what Consuela intended to do with it, he'd said, and telling Danny was tantamount to alerting Consuela that they were waiting for her to move.

Nothing was making any sense any more, Louisa thought to herself as she climbed out of the pool, and she wished to God that she and Jake hadn't argued the way they had just before he'd gone.

Hearing a car coming up the lane she moved quickly to the sunbed to pick up a towel to cover herself. She needn't have bothered, it was only Sarah and seeing her Louisa felt her spirits take a much needed lift.

'Hi,' she called out, waving as Sarah pulled up at the side of the house, then started to laugh as Sarah, with a disgusting amount of energy in such heat, came bounding towards her with joy oozing out of her every step. 'No need to ask you how things are going?' Louisa remarked as Sarah gave her a resounding kiss on each cheek.

'They are blissful and traumatic, wonderful and problematic and I'm as excited and in love as I am laid back and phlegmatic.'

'You've been rehearsing that,' Louisa laughed.

'How did you guess? Anyway, how are you? How's the writing?'

'Don't ask. Are you staying long? Shall we at least have a drink together?'

'Absolutely. Where's Danny?'

'Where do you think?'

'With Erik,' they chorused.

'Come on,' Louisa said, linking her arm through Sarah's, 'let's crack open a bottle of that Saumur, I feel in need of something sparkly.'

While Louisa went into the kitchen Sarah sat on the edge of the terrace, hugging her knees and allowing her mind to drift back over the past week that had been one of the most eventful and one of the happiest of her life. She and Morandi were now lovers, had become so the night they had heard of Aphrodite's murder. It had, she supposed though she couldn't be sure, been the last thing on either of their minds when she had collected Morandi from the police station and driven him home. He had been so exhausted and so totally worn down by all that had happened he had been more in need of sleep than anything else. But it was probably seeing him so vulnerable and so bewildered by it all that had given her the confidence to slip into the bed beside him and hold him.

She smiled dreamily to herself as she thought about it now, of how he had apologized for becoming aroused, how he had clung to her nevertheless and tried to pretend that it would go away. It was she who had ended up making the first move, but, she guessed, it was his vulnerability and need of her that had overcome her fears for there was nothing to be ashamed of in comforting someone you cared about and at the time that's what she'd told herself she was doing. It hadn't taken her long, however, to realize how profoundly she was fooling herself, for any fears of a latent frigidity or a return of the sickening shame she'd felt since Colin had so cruelly belittled her, were quickly expelled by the burning heat of her desire and the compelling, primeval need to feel Morandi as close to her as it was possible for two people to get.

What had surprised her most about that night though, looking back on it, was the incredible way that even at the height of his passion and considering how exhausted he was after all that had happened, he had still not only managed to make her come first, something Colin had never achieved whether first, last or together, but had actually, at the peak of her frenzy, made her, an erstwhile silent and on the whole passive partner, cry out for him never to stop while meeting each pounding thrust of his hips with her own. And what was more, she had then proceeded to roll him on to his back and sat astride him so that she could take over and bring him to his climax. So if anything was going to make her ashamed the next day it was that brazen act, but far from feeling ashamed she had felt proud enough of it and the amazing effect it had had on him to do it again in the morning. Of course, he was a much more experienced lover than she was, but not once had he made her feel inadequate or awkward, to the contrary he had made her feel like the raunchiest, sexiest and most precious lover he'd ever had. And he was still making her feel like that now, several times a day.

'Oh, how easy life is when you just meet the right man,' she sighed, taking the frosted glass Louisa was handing her. 'No hang-ups, no inhibitions, no fears of making a fool of yourself, just bliss. He's a wonderful man, Louisa, truly, truly wonderful. And you really should see his paintings, they're . . . they're . . . quite simply brilliant,' she finished in a rapturous burst.

'I'm surprised you could tear yourself away,' Louisa laughed.

'He's coming here later,' Sarah said, taking a mouthful of the deliciously dry sparkling wine. 'We thought you might like to come out with us tonight.'

'Well as a matter of fact I would,' Louisa said, delighted to be asked. 'I'm getting a bit fed up sitting around here on my own with all this romance going on. But you've got to promise me you won't keep staring into each other's eyes and coming over all gooey on each other the way Danny and Erik do, because I just couldn't stand it.'

'I promise,' Sarah laughed and then was serious for a moment as she said, 'Any word from Jake yet?'

'No, nothing,' Louisa said, shaking her head. 'He's been gone for nine days now, but he didn't say when he was coming back so . . .'

'Actually,' Sarah said, pulling the corners of her mouth down in awkwardness, 'he's back. He came back the day before yesterday.'

Louisa looked away as the words wrenched at her heart. 'How do you know?' she whispered.

'Morandi told me. I thought maybe he would have called you by now.'

Again Louisa shook her head.

'Then why don't you call him?'

'No.'

'But why?'

'I just can't. Besides, if he wanted to see me he'd have called, wouldn't he?' Dear God, she was thinking as the pain dragged through her heart, I had no idea it would hurt this much.

'He's probably got a lot on his mind,' Sarah said, making an attempt to comfort her.

'Well I don't think we can be in any doubt of that, can we?' Louisa remarked with a bitterness she instantly regretted. 'Oh God, Sarah, why did we have to have that row before he went? Why did I have to make him think I don't trust him when I do? Deep down in my heart I know he's not lying to me. OK, I know what Morandi said, but even he's not sure whether it's Jake or Consuela and it's Consuela, Sarah, I'm telling you, it's she who's behind all that's going on, I just know it.'

'I'm sure you're right,' Sarah said softly, not necessarily because she believed it, but because right at that moment it was what Louisa needed to hear.

'Thank you,' Danny said, crossing one smooth, bronzed leg over the other as she helped herself to ice from the silver dish Consuela was offering. 'So let me get this straight,' she said as Consuela moved back to her own chair and sat down again. 'You're not talking to me now because my parents have asked you to, more because you think they would like you to. Have I got that right?'

'Absolutely,' Consuela laughed, 'and so much more succinctly put. But it's also because I feel a certain friendship has developed between us these past few weeks that allows me to take you into my confidence.'

Danny smiled and sipped her gin and tonic. She didn't usually drink this early in the day, but when it was so hot and so unbearably sticky a gin and tonic, with lots of ice and a thick juicy wedge of lemon, slipped down rather well, she found. Consuela, as usual, was drinking fruit punch. Danny had never known her to drink anything else, neither had she ever known her to look anything other than perfect, as she did now, with her thick, blonde hair held in a navy velvet slide at the nape of her neck and a plain, pale violet short-sleeved cotton dress with matching pumps.

Danny turned to make an idle study of the sloping gardens and the small, private beach at the end, allowing Consuela to look at her, unabashed. They were in Consuela's private sitting room where the cool, refreshing air coming in from the sea and the pastel colours were as serene and relaxing as Consuela herself.

'You really are quite exceptionally beautiful,' Consuela murmured after a while.

Danny's head came round in surprise for she was certain there had been a catch in Consuela's voice that suggested she was very near to tears.

'I'm sorry,' Consuela said, moving a hand to her hair, which she didn't quite touch, then lowering it back to her lap. 'It's just . . . No, it's nothing, please, forgive me.'

Danny watched, fascinated, as Consuela composed herself then gave her a bright, generous smile.

'We have talked before about Jake,' Consuela said, seeming to Danny's mind to be a lot more nervous than she sounded. 'And I think, my dear, that it is time we spoke of him again. No, no,' she said, lifting a hand as Danny made to interrupt, 'I am not going to try to persuade you to stop seeing him, but what I am going to do is tell you the whole truth about him and then you must make up your mind whether you wish your association with him to continue.'

'OK,' Danny said, feeling gloriously smug that she was going to have this handed to her on a plate when Sarah and Louisa were tying themselves up in knots trying to work out was what going on.

'As I'm sure you know,' Consuela said, 'Jake arrived back in this country five days ago from Mexico, so I think we should begin with why he was there.' For a moment it seemed that she was going to lose it again, but after taking a deep breath and forcing her wide mouth into a shaky smile, she said, 'He was there looking for his wife.'

'Why, has he lost her?' Danny quipped, and could have instantly bitten out her tongue on seeing the pain that crossed Consuela's face.

'Yes, you could say that,' Consuela said, then after a pause, she added, 'Jake's wife, Martina, is my daughter. I'm sorry, *was* my daughter. She is dead now, she died three years ago. Jake killed her.'

Danny's eyes were wide. 'He killed her,' she repeated on an incredulous breath.

'Yes,' Consuela said, lifting a trembling hand to her face. As she closed her eyes a single tear rolled down her cheek and she used her fingers to wipe it away. 'I'm sorry,' she said, her voice high-pitched with emotion. 'It is still very hard for me to speak of. But yes, Jake killed her. He murdered my baby. He took her out in his boat and he . . . She drowned, but he had beaten her so badly they tell me that she was dead before she went into the sea.'

'Oh my God,' Danny murmured, unable to think of anything else to say.

'But it is even worse than that,' Consuela said, and Danny could see what a very real effort she was putting into making herself go on. 'When Martina went into the sea she was carrying Jake's baby. She had only two months to go and he killed them both. His wife and his own child.'

'Oh no,' Danny breathed, even more bereft of words than before. 'But why?' she said pulling herself out of the soporific shock. 'Why would he do that to his own wife?'

Consuela's answering smile was the saddest Danny had ever seen. 'You have not lived in America,' she said. 'You will not have heard about Jake before you met him here. But always there have been rumours about him and his cruelty to women. He is a sadist of the very worst kind. I begged Martina not to marry him, but she wouldn't believe what she'd heard. He was so kind to her then, so gentle and loving and she adored him. When it started, when the real violence began, I took her away from him. It wasn't easy, because he used to keep her locked up, but we managed it, eventually, and I had her taken to Argentina where my friends looked after her. But he found her and then . . . Then he took her onto his boat and he beat her until she was . . . dead.'

By now Danny could feel tears starting in her own eyes.

'And now,' Consuela continued, 'I am punishing him. I know it is a wicked thing to do, but I have to avenge the life of my only child. So I have arranged for rumours to reach him that Martina is still alive, that she is hiding somewhere in Mexico and now he goes there to look for her. He is afraid, if she is alive, that she will tell everyone what he did to her, how he tried to kill her and then he will go to prison. So he only looks for her now to kill her, to make certain she is dead. He has heard recently of a woman with a small child. It is I who pay people to tell him these things. I want him to suffer, I want him to know what it is like to be so afraid, the way Martina was so afraid. He should be in jail for what he has done. He was arrested, but his father paid a great deal of money to hush it all up and buy his son's freedom. They all say it was an accident now, but I know it was not.' Reaching for the box of tissues beside her she pulled one free and quietly blew her nose. 'So maybe now, Danny, you understand why it is that I fear for you and for whatever relationship you have with him. He is a wicked, evil man and you are as innocent and beautiful as Martina.'

'But I don't understand why you still let him come here,' Danny said, frowning her confusion.

Consuela's slim hand was clenched at her throat, her distress showing in the way she was rubbing her thumb between her fingers. 'I have no choice,' she said. 'There are things in my life that I have done that I am not proud of, things that were the foolishness of a young woman, but are now being used to torment me. I have no idea how Jake found out about them, but that isn't really important, what is is the fact that he knows.

And now, if I do not allow him to use the bathhouse for his extortion, he threatens to expose what I have done. It is not such a great thing, but Jake, he will make certain that it ruins me. I don't care for myself, but I care for Martina. If I am not in the position I am now in then there will be nothing I can do to avenge her death.' Taking a deep breath she sipped shakily on her punch. 'You understand,' she continued, 'it is why I so rarely leave the house now. I do not wish to make any new friends only for Jake to exploit them. And with the friends that I still have from when my husband was alive I do all that I can to try to warn them of what is happening. It isn't easy, for if Jake were ever to learn of the way that I try to inform them he would expose everything that goes on here and very likely, with the cleverness of his lawyers and the influence of his father, I would be the one to finish up in jail.'

'My God,' Danny said in a hushed voice. 'It's so horrible I just don't know what to say.'

'There is nothing to say,' Consuela smiled. 'It is a burden I must carry, but I am hoping that very soon now it will all be over. I am receiving a lot of help from lawyers that Jake knows nothing about, but . . .' Her voice trembled on a sudden surge of emotion and she bit her lips as she twisted the pendant around her neck. Danny saw the way her large, gentle eyes filled with desperation. 'I need so much help,' she said, hardly able to get her voice through the choking anguish in her throat, 'and I know I have no right to ask you this,' she went on, swallowing hard, 'and please, if you wish to walk out of this house and never come here again you must feel free to do so for I, of all people, will understand . . . But I was thinking, that with your skills as an actress, that maybe there is something we could do that would see him in jail where he belongs.'

Danny's curiosity was piqued, but more importantly she was thinking of Louisa and how there was no question that she must do whatever it took to get him out of Louisa's life. This was no longer a contest between two friends as to who won the man, this was, as Consuela had just put herself through great pain to illustrate, a matter of life and death.

'Just tell me what you want me to do,' Danny said.

Consuela smiled as tears of relief and gratitude flooded her eyes. 'It is not a good thing I am asking of you,' she said, 'and if you wish to say no then please say no. I would not hold it against you, I would never do that, because what I am asking you to do is stage your own murder.'

Danny's mouth dropped open even as a tremendous thrill of excitement reverberated through her. 'Are you serious?' she said. 'You mean stage my own murder and make it look like Jake did it?'

Consuela nodded. 'That is what I mean.'

'But how on earth would we get away with it, given that I'm not really going to die?'

'I have friends who would help us,' Consuela answered. 'Friends who have known what it is to have Jake Mallory try to ruin them. Together they have a great deal of influence, especially here in Europe, and though it is doubtful we will see him in jail, if I could just make sure that he never came to Europe again then maybe I could pick up the pieces of my life and start over.'

Danny's mind was racing. 'But it's going to take one heck of a lot of setting up,' she said.

Consuela smiled. 'The technicalities of it are much simpler to organize than you might think. But so much is dependent on you and your ability to manipulate the people around you, especially him.'

She was watching Danny closely, sensing that the enormity of what she was asking her to do was going to take some time to sink in. But it would, sooner or later, and Consuela was prepared for the barrage of questions when they finally came. In the meantime, she smiled fondly. 'Sadly there is no script for you to follow,' she said, 'and it is I, mainly, who will direct you, but I'm sure that between us we can make this work.'

'I've had a great deal more experience working without a script than you might imagine,' Danny said, eyebrows raised as she smiled back at Consuela. For the moment she really couldn't see how they could possibly pull this off, but she certainly didn't want Consuela to doubt her skills as an actress.

'Good,' Consuela said getting to her feet. 'And now, before we start going into the details of how to carry this out I have something for you.'

Intrigued, Danny's eyes followed her across the room to where she stopped in front of a painting and pulled it out from the wall like a cupboard door to reveal a small safe behind it. 'This,' she said, handing a small package to Danny, 'is a video of your mother and one of the boys in the bathhouse.'

'What!' Danny gasped. 'My mother! But she said she knew nothing about the bathhouse.'

'Of course she did,' Consuela smiled. 'You're her daughter, she wouldn't want you to know that she'd ever slept with anyone other than your father.'

'No, I suppose not,' Danny muttered, taking the video and looking at it as though it were something completely alien. 'But why are you giving it to me?'

'Because I had it on good authority that Jake was about to put it to use, which was why I arranged for Morandi's office to be burgled. I knew I had to get that video out of there, but then it occurred to me that there might be more copies, which was why the person who carried out the burglary went back and set fire to the place. It is yours now to do with as you wish. Maybe you would like to keep it to remind yourself, should you ever need reminding, what kind of man Jake is, but if I were you I would destroy it.'

'Can I take a quick look?' Danny said, suddenly strangely excited by the idea of watching her mother have sex.

'By all means,' Consuela answered, obviously surprised, but waving her towards the TV nevertheless.

Danny only watched the first two minutes before feeling horribly ashamed at the way she was prying into her mother's life. 'That's enough,' she said, pushing the stop button. 'I won't need any reminding, let's burn it.'

Consuela took the video from her and carried it over to the hearth where she began screwing up a newspaper to build a fire. 'When this is done,' she said, 'perhaps it would be a good idea for us to refresh our drinks and sit down to discuss how we are going to put this plan into motion. And Danny,' she said, stopping to look up at her with eyes steeped in gratitude, 'I just don't know how to thank you for agreeing so readily to help. I have come so close to asking other friends so many times but I have never quite had the courage. Of course, they are prepared to do things that don't involve them personally, they are happy to use what influence they have to help me, but until I met you there was no one I could ask to do such a terrible thing as we are going to do. I pray that God in His mercy will forgive me for taking vengeance into my own hands, but please, if at any time you wish to stop, if you feel that things are moving beyond your control and you are afraid, then you must tell me and we will call it all to a halt. Jake is a very clever and a very suspicious man. He won't be easy to fool and you must be aware of the danger you face should he ever learn of what we are doing.'

Danny nodded soberly.

'There is just one other thing,' Consuela added. 'Jake has no idea that I am aware of who Morandi really is and probably it's better it stays that way.'

'Oh God, yes, Morandi,' Danny murmured to herself. Sarah had been seeing a lot of him lately and, if Danny had overheard correctly, he'd spun Sarah some sob story about his little brother which Sarah had swallowed. God, women could be so gullible when it came to men. Not that Danny judged herself to be an exception, because, God knows, she'd made her share of mistakes. Take her infatuation with Jake for example. She'd always known he was rotten, that he had sides to him that were as well concealed and insidious as the many sides to her own character. But never, not ever, would she kill any one, least of all her own child the way Jake had. And really she was surprised at Sarah, for anyone could see that Morandi was a fraud with that phoney Italian accent and little boy lost look he'd so cleverly cultivated. However, she didn't imagine that Sarah was in the kind of danger Louisa was in, which was why Danny had to make Louisa her priority.

'Hi,' Sarah called out from the kitchen as Danny walked onto the terrace. 'Erik's been calling you all day.'

'Did he say where he was?' Danny asked, throwing her bag on the table and going to the fridge for some wine.

'At his apartment.' Sarah turned from the salad she was preparing and treated Danny to a quick appraisal. 'Well, you're looking extremely pleased with yourself,' she commented. 'Where have you been?'

'At Consuela's,' Danny grinned, taking two glasses from the shelf and filling them with a pale rosé wine. 'Any olives?'

'In the cupboard behind you,' Sarah answered pouring a thick, yellowy oil over the lettuce.

'Where's Louisa?' Danny asked, sprawling out across two chairs at the kitchen table.

'I don't know. Her car's still there so I thought she must be out somewhere with you, but obviously not.'

'Then maybe we can take it she's somewhere with Jake,' Danny said, chirpily.

Sarah didn't turn round. 'What makes you think that?' she said guardedly.

'Oh come on, Sarah,' Danny laughed. 'I'm not stupid. I know she's seeing him. And, quite frankly, under any other circumstances I'd wish her good luck of him.'

Sarah turned slowly to face her, her blue eyes narrowed suspiciously. 'What do you mean?' she said.

'I mean that she's won. It's her he wants, so she can have him – or at least she could have him – with my blessing.'

'I don't get this,' Sarah said.

'No, I know you don't,' Danny laughed. 'But you will once I've told you all that Consuela's just told me. Where's Morandi, by the way?'

'With Aphrodite's relatives. They're taking the body home tomorrow. He felt he should spend some time with them.'

'Mmm,' Danny grunted. She'd forgotten about Aphrodite,

maybe that was something she should bring up the next time she saw Consuela. In fact, she thought with a sudden dizzying flash of inspiration, if Jake and Morandi were responsible for Aphrodite's murder, which they probably were, then it would be a simply brilliant stroke of genius if she were to die the same way – in water, with a knife sticking from her back. Oh God, this was getting better all the time. 'Anyway,' she said, reining in her excitement, 'you'd better sit down, because what I've got to tell you is going to knock you off your feet.'

Pulling out a chair Sarah sat down and fixed Danny with sceptical eyes. But her expression soon started to change as Danny told her what Jake had done to his wife and her mounting incredulity and alarm as the whole story unfolded was, Danny considered, extremely gratifying.

Danny held nothing back, not even the brief glimpse she had taken of her mother's indiscretion on video. The only thing she didn't divulge was the way she and Consuela were now planning to stage her murder. Consuela had been all for involving Sarah and Louisa if Danny felt she could trust them, but Danny had said no. It had nothing to do with trust, it was simply that she knew Sarah would never approve and she hadn't wanted to tell Consuela that Louisa was seeing Jake. If she had then Consuela would very likely have wanted to speak to Louisa herself and this was Danny's show, not Louisa's. So she had given as her excuse the fact that though they would almost certainly be willing to do something to help Consuela out of her terrible situation, they had no skills as actresses and would be highly likely to give the game away and end up putting themselves in danger. Consuela had immediately seen the sense of that and agreed that it was better to keep it between themselves and the handful of others who were going to support them. This was another little triumph of manipulation for Danny, which only went to prove how utterly brilliant she was at getting people to say and do, even think, exactly what she wanted them to – and, of course, it illustrated perfectly how right she was for this role.

However, by the time she finished telling Sarah what she

wanted her to know, her elation was starting to fade, for the look on Sarah's face was at last serving to remind her of how very serious all this was.

Sarah was on her feet, getting more wine. 'That's a pretty gruesome tale,' she said soberly as she refilled their glasses. 'And it's not that I don't believe it. In Jake's case I find it only too easy to believe, mainly because Morandi suspects him of being behind what's going on too. But I'm afraid I just can't accept that Morandi is willingly working with Jake. I've been with Morandi a lot this past fortnight, I've listened to him, I've seen the way all this is affecting him, so nothing you say is going to persuade me that he's involved the way you say he is.'

'It's not me saying it,' Danny pointed out. 'It's Consuela. And if you like, I'm sure she'll agree to speak to you herself, because I don't have any evidence to prove that Morandi is a liar. I'm just taking her word for it, but if you spoke to her, if you saw the way all this is affecting her, you might change your mind.'

Sarah was shaking her head. 'I won't,' she said, 'because he's not lying.' Her heart suddenly turned cold then as she heard herself sounding exactly like Louisa when Louisa defended Jake to her. Both of them, she realized, were only going on gut instinct and though it was hard to believe that they could both be wrong, there was, if she were being totally honest with herself, a chance they might be. But no, she only had to picture Morandi's face in her mind's eye, his fear that Aphrodite's murder had been carried out as some kind of warning to him, and she just knew that he was as helpless a victim of this as Consuela claimed to be. However, it wouldn't do any harm to talk to Consuela, she thought, feeling horribly disloyal, if nothing else she might be able to shed some light on things for Morandi.

But what about Louisa? How were they going to persuade her that Jake was all that Consuela said he was? Maybe she should speak to Consuela too?

'Yes, I'm sure Consuela would agree to that,' Danny said

when Sarah put it to her. It wasn't a case now, she realized, of whose show it was, it was a case of getting Louisa as far from Jake as they could. One woman was dead already, two including Aphrodite, and no matter how much Danny wanted to steal the limelight in all this, Louisa's life was infinitely more important than her own glory. And, should Louisa die, there would of course be no glory, there'd be only tragedy and heartbreak and an insufferable guilt that she, Danny, had stood in the way of Louisa finding out the truth for such trivial, self-seeking ends.

'Do you think she's with Jake now?' Danny said quietly.

'She could be,' Sarah answered. 'But Jean-Claude has been out all day, she might have gone somewhere with him. You know, Danny,' she went on, 'I don't think Jake does mean her any harm. He's always been honest with her about the fact that there would be no future for . . .' She stopped and stared at Danny, horrified at the way her heart was flooding with dread as the 'no future' suddenly took on a whole new meaning.

'Maybe you'd better tell me just what Jake has been saying to her,' Danny said.

'Is that Jean-Claude coming back?' Sarah said hearing a car outside.

It was, but Louisa wasn't with him.

'I think, before we go any further,' Sarah said as they walked back into the house, 'that we should contact Consuela to see if she knows how we might get hold of Jake so that we can try to get Louisa back here.'

'Good idea,' Danny said, going to get the phone. Then suddenly remembering that it was after Consuela had hidden Martina from Jake that he had beaten Martina to death, she wondered if it was such a good idea. If Jake thought they were about to take Louisa away from him then God only knew what he might do.

'Maybe I should call Erik,' she said. 'He'll know how to get in touch with Jake and maybe he'll go and get Louisa himself.'

'No, I don't think we should do that,' Sarah said. 'He could be just as likely to warn Jake of what we're doing.'

'But Erik's not involved in any of this,' Danny protested. 'OK, he and Jake are friends, but . . .'

'Oh Danny,' Sarah groaned. 'How can you say that when you know how close they are? And I'm sorry that I'm the one who has to point this out to you, but remember Aphrodite's body was found in the Port de Fontvieille, right underneath Erik's apartment.'

'What are you saying?' Danny said bristling. 'That Erik killed her? You've got to be out of your mind if you think that. Erik wouldn't hurt a fly. For God's sake, he's known all over the world, if there was anything shady about him don't you think we'd know about it?'

'Not necessarily,' Sarah answered, thinking with a disheartening degree of despondency of how Danny was now doing the same as herself and Louisa in blinding herself to the possibility that the man she had fallen for could be as guilty as the others. 'Two women are dead,' she said flatly. 'We know that Jake killed one and the chances are Erik killed the other.'

'You don't honestly think that if Erik killed Aphrodite he'd dump her body right outside his own front door, do you?' Danny cried.

No, Sarah had to agree, that put like that it didn't seem very likely. But if Erik didn't do it, then who did? Which also begged the question that was whoever really had done it trying to make Erik the scapegoat?

'My money's on Morandi,' Danny said, casting Sarah into further turmoil as she voiced the unthinkable suspicion that had just entered Sarah's head. 'He's the one who's here all the time, working with Jake,' Danny went on. 'He's the one who puts those videos together, he's the one who's hiding behind a false identity and he's the one Aphrodite accused of being a blackmailer.'

Sarah looked so crestfallen and beaten that Danny reached out for her hand to give it a comforting squeeze. 'I'm sorry,' she said softly. 'I didn't mean to sound so brutal.'

'It doesn't matter,' Sarah said bleakly. 'It's better that we thrash these things out now before any of us go in any deeper.

But even if you're right about Morandi, I still don't see that that puts Erik in the clear, because he was the one who asked Jean-Claude to look after a quarter of a million dollars worth of pesos for Jake, so he's got to know what's going on.'

It was Danny's turn to look shaken now for this was the first she'd heard about Erik asking Jean-Claude to look after money. And as Sarah saw her face blanch she tightened the grip on Danny's hand. 'The most important thing now,' she said, 'is Louisa. We've got to find out where she is and get her to come home.'

19

Louisa was sitting between Jake's legs on the blue cushioned pads of the *Valhalla's* steering station, the binnacle nestled comfortably between her knees, her hands under Jake's on the helm, her head resting back on his shoulder.

'Tell me what you see,' he said, his breath warm on her ear as he turned to whisper.

'I see,' she began, looking at the horizon, 'the most beautiful sunset ever. I see land. Corsica?' she said, turning to look up at his strong, dusk-shadowed face.

He nodded.

'And I see yachts in the bay. And I see the moon, very pale and silvery. And I see the sea turning scarlet. And I see . . . What else do I see?'

He pointed towards a rock jutting out of the side of the bay like a giant paw.

'I see a rock,' she said.

'And on the rock?'

'I see a house.'

He laughed. 'A hotel. It's where we're heading. You and I.'

'Oh,' Louisa said, a ripple of desire coasting warmly through her.

He tilted her mouth to his and kissed her softly, but with an intimacy that held no regard for the crew, and as the warmth eddied and rushed inside her she felt herself melting against him.

'Are you happy?' he murmured, gazing down into her eyes.

'Mmm,' she nodded. 'Very.'

He smiled, stroking his fingers down the side of her face

and over her neck. 'I'm sorry,' he said. 'I know I should have called you sooner, but . . .'

'It doesn't matter,' she said, putting her fingers over his lips. He kissed them, drew them into his mouth and lightly bit them. Then hearing the breath catch in her throat and seeing the way her beautiful, velvety eyes darkened, he took her fingers away and pressed his mouth hard over hers.

'We have to talk first, you know that,' he said gruffly.

'I know,' she murmured, her lips touching his as she spoke. 'But I want you so much that whatever you tell me isn't going to make a difference. So why do we have to wait?'

'Oh, Louisa,' he moaned as she pressed herself back against his hardness. 'Don't do this, please.'

'Then don't make me wait,' she whispered.

'You won't thank me if I don't.'

'I told you nothing you say is going to make a difference,' she said, keeping her voice low. 'I want you inside me, Jake. I want to feel you close, pushing all the way into me.'

'Oh Jesus,' he groaned and then his lips were crushing hers, his tongue pushing deep into her mouth as he pulled her fiercely against him.

'If you two lovebirds are gonna continue like that then you'd best let me take her in,' Bob said gruffly.

Laughing, Jake let Louisa go. 'It's OK, I'll do it,' he told Bob, grinning at Louisa's narrow-eyed scowl as she very astutely realized that he was using the docking of the *Valhalla* as an excuse to put a little distance between them for a while and therefore get himself back under control.

Wandering towards the bowsprit to sit down and watch the approach into the small, picturesque bay, which was at that moment ablaze in the sunset, Louisa curled her legs under her and listened to Jake's commands as the sails were brought down and all the many preparations for coming into shore were made. She barely understood what he was saying, for sailing jargon was totally unfamiliar to her, but in this instance it was the sound of his voice that she loved, not what he was saying.

It had been the most wonderful, memorable day so far,

which had started early that morning when Marianne had come for her. She almost laughed to herself now as she recalled the way she'd tried to put up a fight, of how she'd told Marianne to tell him that she wasn't available. It hadn't taken much persuading on Marianne's part to get her to change her mind however, and neither had it taken her very long to pack the overnight bag Marianne had told her she would need. In fact, she'd done it in such haste that she'd forgotten to leave Sarah a note. But it wasn't important, Sarah would be sure to guess where she was – if, indeed, Sarah actually went back to the villa today.

During the hour's drive over to St Tropez, where the *Valhalla* was moored, Louisa had played out in her mind all she was going to say to Jake when she arrived. It started out with a heated and serious objection to the way he always expected her to drop everything when it suited him and a demand to know why he hadn't called since he got back, and ended up with an apology for the way they had fought before he'd gone. Somewhere in between was something to do with what Morandi had told Sarah, but Louisa couldn't quite remember what now, and in any event, as it turned out she hadn't actually got around to saying any of it. Not because she'd lost courage, or melted like some tragic heroine into his arms the moment she saw him, but because when she and Marianne had arrived at the *Valhalla* he hadn't actually been there. And when he had turned up, a few minutes later, he'd been so busy giving instructions to set sail and had been surrounded at all times by the crew that the opportunity hadn't arisen until they were out at sea, by which time he'd taken the sting out of her indignation by saying, 'Stop frightening me, looking at me that way. I know I'm in the shit, but could you please just smile a moment 'cos you're scaring the crew.'

That had made not only Louisa laugh, but everyone else in earshot, and deciding that the very fact that she was there on board was evidence enough that she forgave him, she let her umbrage go. What was the point in going over what had happened the last time, or the reasons why he hadn't called, when all that really mattered was that they should enjoy every minute of what time they had together?

After that, as the *Valhalla* rose and dipped gently through the waves with a glorious sea breeze filling her vast, white sails, Jake had handed the wheel over to Bob and shown her round. It was during their brief excursion below deck to the astonishingly luxurious cabins and state-of-the-art galley, that he had given her her first kiss of the day.

'Do you have any idea how much I love kissing you?' he'd smiled, running his fingers through her soft, caramel hair and gazing ironically into the depths of her huge, brown eyes.

'I think I might be getting the drift,' she'd laughed as he'd lowered his head to kiss her again.

They hadn't stayed long below since one of the crew was still working on a fault in the air-conditioning and without it the cabins were suffocatingly hot. By contrast, however, the spacious aft-deck, where they whiled away most of the afternoon, was blissfully shaded by an awning and wonderfully aired by the steady summer breeze coming in from the east.

Louisa had watched Jake come alive during those hours in a way she'd never seen before. It wasn't really anything that he said, or anything that he did, it went much deeper than that. And that was when she realized what it was that was making him look the way he did – it was his great and consuming love of the sea. He was so attuned to it it was as though he breathed with it. He seemed to know its every nuance, its every vagary and vice, was so receptive to its inconstancy and bewitched by its sorcery, it was as though the strength and contentment within him were a part of the power and serenity of this great expanse of blue.

For a while she had almost felt jealous that the sea and all its magic had the power to move him so deeply, but as he spoke to her about it, pulling her into his arms and making her watch it with him, she had realized that for him to share this intensely personal side of himself was the greatest, most poignant gift he could give her.

At last the *Valhalla* was docked and with the sun now having disappeared altogether and night shrouding the small pockets of light that illuminated the pathway leading up to the hotel. Louisa felt Jake's hand slip into hers and hold it tightly. It had only been a few minutes since they'd left the *Valhalla*, but already she could sense the change in him, as though an ill-wind had suddenly tossed him into a storm. She glanced up at his face and saw how pinched it had become and knew that it was because he was preparing to tell her what she was now almost afraid to hear. Her fear wasn't that it would change her feelings for him, she knew nothing could do that now, it was because she just didn't want anything to spoil today. But the spectre of his past, of all that he was involved in with Morandi and Consuela and Erik, was already stalking them as though it too had sailed with them from St Tropez, lurking in the shadows, and was now creeping behind them ready to pounce.

But she wasn't going to let it take away the precious moments that lay ahead. She didn't want it there, open and sore and bleeding between them, as they made love. She wanted, when he held her, to think of him and only him. She knew it wouldn't be easy to persuade him, but she had to make him see that as soon as he let his secret go there would be no taking it back. There would no longer be what there was between them now, an unsullied, unspoken bond that had tied him to her because of her innocence of it all.

But as it turned out he didn't need any persuading, for the moment he closed the door of their room behind him and saw the way she was standing there with fear and courage and a desperate need for him burning in her eyes he pulled her into his arms.

'Hold me, Louisa,' he murmured into her hair. 'Just hold me.'

And as she clung to him, pressing herself to him and willing him with all her might not to push her away now, she felt the power of his desire spreading through him. She moved against his hardness, looking up into his face, tracing his mouth with her eyes then gazing boldly, pleadingly into his eyes.

'Oh, Jesus Christ,' he groaned as he lifted her in his arms. 'Are you sure?' he whispered as he laid her down on the bed.

'Yes, I'm sure,' she said, and then she was kissing him with a passion and a desire she had never known in herself. The smell of him, the feel of him, the taste of him was consuming her as his hands and his mouth moved over her. Taking the hem of her flimsy blouse she pulled it over her head and lay back on the bed, feeling the caress of his eyes on her breasts that were crying out for his touch. And then his mouth was on them and his hand moved to her waist, unfastening her belt and pushing inside her shorts. His lips were on hers now, his tongue probing deeply and wonderfully. She fumbled with the buttons of his shirt and pushing her hand away he undid them himself, stripping the shirt away then standing up to remove his jeans. His eyes remained on hers as she too removed her shorts.

He started to speak then stopped himself, closing his eyes as though to cover the pain.

'It's all right,' she whispered.

He laughed and looked at her again, his eyes shining with love.

And then he was naked and as Louisa's eyes drank in the sheer beauty of his uncompromising masculinity, the hard muscles of his thighs, the firm dark skin of his abdomen and the solid, straining, enormity of his erection she could feel the power of her desire as though it and only it was controlling her body. She lifted herself up and took him gently in both hands, then lowering her head she drew him deep into her mouth.

'Oh God,' he murmured as her teeth sank softly into him and her tongue and her lips pulled at him. His hands moved into her hair and his head fell back as with her small, slender fingers she lightly caressed his balls and his thighs and his buttocks. 'Louisa,' he choked, 'Louisa,' and pulling her away he pushed her back onto the bed and lay down with her.

'Tell me what you want,' he whispered, sliding his hand down over her belly and pushing his fingers gently inside her.

'Tell me how I can make you feel the way you're making me feel.'

'I already feel it,' she said, her words echoing in his mouth as removing his fingers and running them back across the moist, hard bud he rolled onto her, kissing her and pressing himself to her.

Then at last it was as though the guilt of not holding onto his promise left him as the storm of his need broke and pushing his legs between hers, he began to lower his mouth down over her body, sucking hard on her nipples, biting them, pulling them right into his mouth, then kissing them, licking them and soothing them. With one hand he pushed her legs wider while with the other he held her tightly. Then his lips were descending to her navel, into the neat, dark thatch of hair between her legs and again he was kissing her, stroking her with his tongue, drawing the silky, tender flesh between his lips and she knew ecstasy then as though her entire self were dissolving into it.

'Jake, please,' she sobbed, writhing beneath him as she felt the first stirrings of climax.

His mouth came back to hers, warm and sweet and tasting of her as he kissed her. She circled his waist with her legs, using them to pull him to her. Then raising himself up on one arm he looked long and hard into her eyes as he lowered his hand and guided himself to her. She could feel the tip of him entering her as he pulled his hand away, and with their eyes still locked she felt him slowly, very slowly, start to penetrate her.

'Oh my God,' she murmured as she felt the moist, narrow depths of her yielding to his hardness.

He pulled back, pushed into her again, deeper, yet still careful not to hurt her. 'Are you OK?' he whispered.

'Yes,' she whispered, then suddenly cried out as he thrust himself hard into her.

'Ssh, ssh, it's all right,' he said, kissing the corner of her mouth.

'I know,' she breathed, tightening her arms and legs around him. 'Oh Jake, I want you so much.'

'I'm right here, right inside you now. Do you want that I stop for a moment?'

'No! No!' she cried. 'I want you to make love to me. I want to feel you do that again and again.'

Raising his hips he began to move gently in and out of her. 'Is this OK?' he said, feeling the blood pulsing wildly through him and knowing that he wasn't going to hold out much longer.

'Harder, Jake,' she gasped. 'I want you to do it harder,' and then he was hammering into her, throwing the force of his powerful body behind it, while searching for her mouth and tightening the grip on her hands.

She lifted her legs higher, arching her back and cried out again as he suddenly changed motion so that he was rubbing himself against her clitoris as he pounded into her.

Then he was wrapping her in his arms, holding her as close as he could as he felt the soaring pulse of her climax begin.

'Jesus Holy Christ,' he seethed, pounding her and crushing her and grinding his hips savagely as it kept on coming.

'Jake,' she said, all the strength in her now clenching fervently around him. 'Jake,' she whispered again.

He sucked her lips between his, holding her spine to stop her falling against the bed. He was as far inside her as it was possible to get now and he held her there, circling his hips and feeling her climax reaching its peak, pulling at him, grasping him in long, shuddering convulsions before starting slowly to subside.

At last he let her back go and fell breathlessly over her, keeping himself buried inside her. They were hot and sticky and their sweat was mingling like the heat of their uneven breath. But gradually their hearts slowed to a normal, steady pace and the aftermath of tension slowly released their limbs.

'Mmm,' Louisa moaned contentedly and luxuriously as her legs slid from his back. She opened her eyes and turned to find him gazing into her face.

'That was amazing,' he said softly.

Her eyes started to dance.

'It was . . .'

'Oh please don't give me marks out of ten,' she groaned, making him laugh.

'You're off the scale,' he said, kissing her. 'But I knew you would be.'

'But it was you who took me there,' she smiled. 'I think somebody's got it wrong about quantity and quality, or maybe it's just that you have both,' she added making him laugh again.

'Oh, no, no, no,' she complained as he started to withdraw. 'It feels so cosy like this.'

'You're incredible,' he chuckled. 'I just want to know why you happened to me, because I sure as hell don't deserve you.'

'But you've got me anyway and I dare you to do that all over again,' she grinned.

But it was no good, she couldn't stave off the spectre any longer and as he gently withdrew himself and kissed her briefly on the mouth, she sent a silent plea to God that she was going to be able to deal with whatever he told her now.

'Are you hungry?' he said, sitting on the edge of the bed and reaching for his shorts.

'No. Are you?'

He shook his head then turned to look at her. His eyes were submerged in an emotion she didn't at first recognize, then realizing with a sharp pang in her heart that it was guilt she lifted his hand and kissed it.

'I told you, nothing's going to make a difference,' she whispered.

His face remained grim and lowering his hand to her breast she held it there. He ran his thumb back and forth over the hard nipple, but she could see his mind was elsewhere and when she took her hand away so too did he.

She watched him pull his shorts on, staring at his back, his broad, muscular shoulders, the tapering of his waist and wanted to touch him.

'Did you bring something to cover yourself?' he said, unravelling his jeans.

'Do we have to get dressed?'

'Trust me, you'll want something by the time I've finished.'

Pulling herself up Louisa walked over to the door where he had put her overnight bag and took out a knee-length cotton wrap. As she turned to put it on she could see how his eyes were avoiding her nudity and suddenly she wanted to scream. This was so unfair, why did it have to be like this? Why couldn't they just be together and make love the way everyone else did without any ghosts coming to spoil it? But she merely slipped into the wrap, belted it and returned to the bed, sitting cross-legged on the edge.

It was a small room, but carefully, almost lovingly furnished with subtle, expensive fabrics, two enclosed casement windows that looked out over the sea and french doors that opened onto a white filigree balcony. Jake walked over to the mini-bar, his thin white shirt still unbuttoned and hanging loosely down over his hips, as he helped himself to a beer.

'Would you like something?' he asked Louisa, twisting off the top of the bottle.

She shook her head and watched him as he picked up an armless easy chair and carried it over to the bed to sit in front of her.

'Oh God, I feel so nervous all of a sudden,' she laughed shakily, pushing her fingers into her hair. 'Do I really need to know?'

'Do you want to know?' he asked, sitting forward and resting his elbows on his thighs.

She nodded. 'Yes, I suppose I do. But maybe I should tell you I already know about the bathhouse. Morandi told Sarah.'

Jake chewed thoughtfully on his bottom lip for a moment, then looked down at the beer he was holding in both hands. 'I don't know what Morandi told Sarah,' he said, 'but he doesn't have the full picture. Only Erik has that. And Consuela, of course.'

'But are those women being blackmailed?'

'Sure, some of them are,' he answered. 'Those I don't manage to get to first. But there aren't so many of them these days, not since I got Consuela to cut me in on it.'

'But why did you do that?'

He stared at her for some time, but she could tell that he wasn't seeing her as in his mind he mulled over the best way to answer that. Then his eyes moved past her and he said, 'I had to know what she was doing. I had to be in a position to get something over her so's I could find out the truth of what happened to my wife.'

Louisa's heart dipped horribly, but she remained silent in the face of the anger that was now darkening his eyes and clenching his jaw. But his voice was still gentle as he spoke.

'Martina,' he said, 'my wife, is Consuela's daughter. We were married for three years before she died in a boating accident off Puerto Vallarta in Mexico.'

'Oh God, I'm sorry,' Louisa murmured.

His answering smile was grim. 'But it wasn't an accident,' he said, 'she was murdered, at least I think she was, but I still don't know for sure. The other boat came out of nowhere, they were on the *Moonshine*, our boat, before I knew what was happening and I was knocked unconscious. When I came round they were gone, and so was Martina. I stank of alcohol, which they must have poured all over me as well as down my throat and the *Moonshine* was drifting way out at sea with no other vessels in sight. So I took her in, went to report what had happened and two days later I found myself under arrest for the murder of my own wife.'

He paused for a moment as the pain and disbelief he must have felt at the time seemed to come back and steal threads from his voice.

'There was no body,' he said roughly, his breathing ragged with suppressed emotion, 'and the search that followed didn't turn one up either. So in the end, after my father had pulled a few strings, I was released from a hell-hole of a Mexican jail. I flew straight to Buenos Aires to find Consuela. I just knew she had to be behind it, and she was there, waiting for me.' A note of savagery had crept into his voice now and his hands were tight on the bottle he was still holding. 'And do you know what she told me?' he said, with a bitter, incredulous laugh. 'She told me that her people had found Martina's body and taken it to where she – Consuela – was staying and that Martina had been certified dead by a doctor right there in Buenos Aires. Death caused by severe blows to the face and head that had crushed her skull before she'd been thrown into the sea.'

For a moment Louisa thought he was going to break down, but after swallowing hard he continued. 'By then Consuela, the woman who had paid for the murder of her own daughter, had had Martina buried. She'd kept it all hushed up for my sake, she told me. She didn't want to see me go to jail for the rest of my life, or face a death penalty, or even bear the stigma of what I had done. Shit, the way she carried on she nearly had me convinced I'd done it. But I knew she had and I knew why. Carmelo, Martina's father, left everything to Martina when he died. He was worth millions and not one penny of it, with the exception of the villa on the Cap d'Antibes, went to Consuela. He'd never warned us he was going to do that, but he did, and his reasons for doing it have died with him. But piecing things together since, listening to those who knew Consuela and Carmelo when he was alive, it seems she had a pretty rough time in her marriage. He used to beat her, kept her locked up for months on end, shit, I don't know what he did to her, all I know is she never wanted Martina to know what her father was really like. It's the only decent thing I've ever known Consuela to do.

'Anyway, after Carmelo died and we found out about the will Consuela went to pieces. Martina spent as much time with her as she could, but we hadn't long been married and she didn't like to be parted from me for long. So Consuela came to the States to stay with us. Martina and I talked endlessly with lawyers to see if there was a way she could give her mother the money, but one of the conditions of the will was that nothing other than what was stipulated should go to Consuela. Martina could do whatever else she wanted with her inheritance, but she couldn't give it to her mother. So we paid a great deal of it over to various charities in Argentina, saying it came from Consuela so that no one would know that her husband had done what he had and therefore salvaging her dignity.

'It was while she was staying with us that I made what I knew even at the time was a mistake, but I never dreamt it would turn out to be the greatest mistake of my life, nor how much I was going to have to pay for it. I slept with the woman. Don't ask me why, I barely know the reasons myself, except I felt sorry for her and what started out as comfort somehow turned into something else. Afterwards I couldn't look at her without hating her, but I guess it was myself I hated for being so goddamned weak to have let things get out of hand that way. I told her she had to go, to pack her bags and be on the next flight back to Buenos Aires and that was when it all really started. She said if I pushed her out, sent her back to where she no longer even had a home, she'd tell Martina what had happened. I tried to persuade her to go to France where she did have a home, I even offered her the money to keep it running, but she wouldn't go. She wanted to stay right there in San Diego, with us, where she got the most comfort in her bereavement, she said. So I had no choice. I had to let her stay because I just couldn't stand the thought of Martina finding out that both her husband and her mother had betrayed her.

'It was a living hell,' he went on quietly. 'Every time we were left alone in the house together she was at me, pestering me to go to bed with her again. She said if I didn't she'd tell Martina we were sleeping together anyway. It got so that I was nearly at the point of telling Martina myself just to get the goddamned woman out of my life. Martina must have sensed the friction between us because in the end she was the one to tell her mother she had to leave. The two of them hadn't been getting along so well either. Consuela was disrupting our lives in every possible way even to the point of coming into our bedroom at night and sitting there, crying, saying she didn't want to be alone.

'So Martina asked her to go and I don't ever want to have to live through another scene like that again in my life. Of course Consuela told her she and I had been sleeping together and I made the mistake of denying it. So Consuela proceeded to describe me in the minutest detail, my technique, the way I kissed, everything. Obviously Martina had to believe it then, but it was her mother she turned on, not me. The only good thing to come out of it was that Consuela had blown it. She couldn't stay now and she had nowhere else to go, except France. I offered again to give her money to keep the villa running, but Martina wouldn't let me. She said her mother could sell the villa and live off that, but we weren't going to give her a penny. When Consuela had gone I explained to Martina what had happened. She said she forgave me and we never talked about it again.'

His face was grey and haggard in the glow of the room, his beer still untouched. Louisa's eyes were steadily watching him, but in some strange, inexplicable way it was like looking at a shell. He was no longer there in that room, he was back in San Diego, reliving the nightmare.

'The sickest part of it then,' he continued, 'was that I had kept it all from my father so that when we threw Consuela out it was to him she went and it was he who gave her the money that, as we found out later, went into creating the bathhouse. The money was legally documented, more fool my father, and the first we found out about the bathhouse was when Consuela contacted me threatening to reveal where her funds had come from, thereby insinuating that my father was behind the blackmail she had gotten into, unless I gave her a sum equivalent to Martina's inheritance. I went to my father, we consulted lawyers and between us we decided to ignore her. That was the gravest mistake of all, but we didn't realize just how grave until a couple of months down the line when, to punish me, or to let me know that she still had power over me, or God only knows why, she paid to have Martina, her own daughter, her own flesh and blood, killed. You might ask yourself how any sane person, how any mother, could do that to her own child just to get back at me, but we're not talking about a sane person here, because she's totally *insane* and that's what makes her so damned dangerous. She doesn't look insane, most of the time she doesn't act insane, but take it from me that woman is as close to being a psychopath . . . What am I saying here? She *is* a psychopath. That's why I told you to stay away from her. I don't want her finding out about you because if she does I don't even want to think what she might do. And that's why I say that Danny's not doing herself any favours going around telling people she's sleeping with me, particularly when she's not. My eye,' he said, touching the loose flesh of the disfiguring scar, 'Consuela did that. More accurately, she paid someone to do it about six months after Martina died. At the time of Martina's death Consuela told me, as brazenly as you like, that she'd keep the murder covered up if, after a respectable amount of time mark you, I'd marry her. That way she'd have me, the Mallory fortune and Santini's fortune too. I told her to go straight to hell and six months later someone broke into my house with instructions to cut out my eyes, both of them, so that I'd never be able to look at another woman again. Consuela got someone to call me up on the phone while I was still in the hospital to tell me that.

'We, my father and I, knew then that we had to do something to stop her doing any more damage, not only to our family, but to her so-called friends, the one's she was bleeding a fortune from. We already knew how she'd started giving the evidence of what these women were doing in the bathhouse to their husbands just to see those women end up with nothing, the way she had, *worse* than she had. We had lawyers in the States, in Argentina, Mexico and in France, working on building up a case against her. It wasn't hard, she'd hurt a lot of people by then who were more than willing to talk, but Consuela is no fool, she'd covered her tracks much better than we'd realized. Then she got wind of what we were doing and the next thing we knew my father received an anonymous call telling him that Martina was still alive and that if we didn't back off she really would be killed.

'At first we didn't believe it, but since neither of us had ever seen the body I wasn't prepared to take the chance that she might be lying. So we called the lawyers off and set our own investigation in motion. My father greased the right palms in Buenos Aires and we had the body exhumed. And that was when we found out that there was no body. Oh, there was a grave all right, and a coffin, but inside the coffin was just a pile of ash. So someone had died, but whoever it was had been cremated and there was no way of telling whether or not it was Martina.

'Then the people working for us started to come back with reports that Martina had been seen. It was a goddamned nightmare. I didn't know which way to turn, I was driven half out my mind. Then my father came up with the idea that I should go to France and tell Consuela that unless she came up with the truth about Martina we were going to put the whole thing into the hands of the FBI. It was a bluff because neither of us was prepared to contact the Bureau when there was a possibility Martina was alive. Then one of the lawyers came up with another idea, that I should try to get myself in on Consuela's operation. If I managed it and it then came to a point of law obviously I'd be as guilty as she was, but that was the point. She had to think that I was prepared to commit the crime too otherwise she'd never let me in. The only problem was why would I do it, when it was common knowledge that I didn't need the money. But that was easily overcome by getting her to think that she was coercing me into doing it to find out what I could about Martina.

'So I sailed the *Valhalla* over to France – taking the boat made my stay seem a bit more permanent than if I'd flown in – and what I found when I got there turned my stomach. There she was surrounded by young kids, all boys, getting them slaving for her, innocently screwing her friends and looking for all the world like Miss Benevolence herself. The boys didn't have a clue what they were into, though a couple of them did get to find out and as far as I know she paid them off and sent them on their way. But when I got involved she wanted me to give them the Hobson's choice I expect Morandi told Sarah about.'

Louisa nodded then cleared her throat. 'Yes,' she said.

'Well, the hell I was going to do anything like that. She had to be crazy if she thought I'd even entertain it, but I let her think I was going along with it, though my guess is she knows that I'm paying them off out of my own pocket – like all the rest of her goddamned spoils are coming out of my pocket, but I don't think she's wise to that. But she doesn't really care what I do with those kids just so long as nothing disturbs her nice, cosy, little set-up and she manages to keep me on the run. Anyway, like you must already know, Morandi's brother was one of the kids who found out what was going on and when I met up with him here in Corsica – which I do with most of them, together with a lawyer, so's to get out of them everything they know – somehow it came about that this kid had a brother who was making low-budget movies over in Britain. So the lawyer and I took the boy back ourselves so that I could try to get this brother to come work for me. I needed someone who could put those videos together and who could keep a record of everything and everyone involved. Morandi agreed, fortunately he spoke Italian and French, so we gave him a bogus identity through some dubious Sicilian contacts of the lawyer's. Being Italian helps when you're setting up business in Nice. I've never been too comfortable about keeping Morandi out of the whole picture, but I was always afraid that if he did know everything he might just go and blow it.'

'Sarah tells me that he doesn't know which one of you to believe,' Louisa said. 'Apparently he's considered going to the police, but he's afraid to in case something happens to his family.'

'Shit,' Jake muttered under his breath. 'Well, I guess it's better that he stays afraid for the moment, because we're pretty close now to finding out where Martina is.'

'You mean she is alive?'

Jake nodded. 'Yeah, I think so. It's still hard to know whether or not Consuela is paying people to give me false information, but the last time I was in Mexico . . .' He stopped, looked down at his hands, then getting up from the chair he walked over to the window. 'The last time I was in Mexico,' he said, staring blindly at the bobbing white lights of the yachts in the bay, 'I heard that the woman they're saying is Martina has got a child with her. Martina was seven months' pregnant when she disappeared.'

'Oh my God, Jake,' Louisa murmured, wanting to go to him, but knowing that right at that moment he wouldn't welcome it.

'It's a . . . It's a girl,' he said, his voice breaking up on the fear and emotion lodged in his throat. 'I'm haunted night and day about what they might be going through,' he went on gruffly, disguising his grief with anger. 'But even now I still don't know whether it's some cruel, twisted trick on Consuela's part to torment me, or whether there really is a woman and child. A woman and child who are mine, who I have to keep looking for until I know for sure.'

They were both silent for a long time then, until Louisa got quietly up from the bed, went to the bar and poured him a brandy. She handed it to him, wordlessly, taking the warm, stale beer away. She didn't have to look at his face to know that he was crying, neither did she have to be told that he needed to be left alone for a while.

Dressed in her shorts and top she pulled the door quietly closed behind her and went downstairs to order some sandwiches. They took a while to be prepared by which time she knew it would be all right to go back.

She found him standing where she had left him, a dark profile in the moonlit window, his brandy finished, the tears gone.

He turned to her and smiled as she came into the room, then watched her as she laid out the sandwiches on a small, round table.

'Come on,' she said, holding out a hand towards him. 'Try to eat something.'

He came towards her, took her hand, but instead of sitting

down he put his glass on the table and pulled her into his arms. 'I love her, Louisa,' he said, his voice once again choked with emotion. 'I love her more than I've ever loved anyone in my life. She was my whole world. Nothing, just nothing, mattered more than her. We were so happy . . .'

'It's all right,' Louisa whispered, tears of unbidden envy and loss and overwhelming pity burning her eyes. 'I understand.'

'Do you?' he said, pulling her back to look into her face.

She nodded, then biting her lip to try to stop the tears she turned away.

'I don't know why we had to meet when we did,' he said, watching her walk over to the bed. 'All I know is that being with you has been the best thing that's happened to me since all this began.'

'Then I'm glad I happened to you,' she said, sitting down.

'But you're not glad that I happened to you.'

'I don't know,' she said honestly. 'But I do know that I'm glad we made love before you told me.'

'To be truthful, Louisa,' he said, 'I wasn't intending for us to make love at all. I knew that once I told you you wouldn't want to and then I'd have gone back to spend the night on the *Valhalla*.'

'Then why did you bring me all this way?' she asked, more hurt than she wanted to think about by what he'd said.

'I brought you because I wanted to take you on the sea. I wanted to share something with you that was special to me, something that we could both hold in our memories and never forget.'

She smiled as her heart tripped on the pain and used her fingers to wipe away the tears. 'Have you thought about what you'll do if Consuela is lying?' she said.

'Yeah. I'll go back to the States and pick up again. But that doesn't mean there's a future for us, Louisa. I can't marry again now, not after all that's happened.'

'No,' she said softly, wishing that this didn't all sound so final.

'I'm sorry,' he said. 'I didn't want to hurt you.'

'I know.'

'Do you want that I leave now, come back for you in the morning?'

She shook her head. 'No, I want you to hold me and tell me you're a bloody fool who should have told me all this in the beginning.'

'I would have,' he said, pulling her into his arms, 'except for one thing. I met you at Consuela's. I didn't know who you were, what she might have told you, what you might tell her. All I know is that I looked across the room and saw the most beautiful pair of eyes looking back at me and for the first time since Martina I allowed myself to think about what it might be like to hold a woman again.'

'But you'd been with Danny the night before,' she reminded him.

'That doesn't even begin to compare,' he said. 'That was nothing more than a release. With you I knew it would be different. But I couldn't allow myself to make love to you when I knew something was happening between us and I couldn't carry it through. I didn't want to do that to you, but neither could I stop myself seeing you.'

'But we have made love now,' Louisa said shakily.

'Yeah, we sure did that,' he smiled. 'But it's not going to happen again.'

'But why?' Louisa protested. 'You're not going yet. It's not all over yet. There's still some time left for us.'

'I know that, but I don't want you falling in love with me.'

'Oh God,' she laughed through her tears, wanting to scream that it was already too late for that. But she didn't, because she knew that even though she'd thought he was falling in love with her too, that in reality whatever he did feel paled by comparison with what she'd seen in his eyes and heard in his voice when he talked about Martina.

Letting him go she walked into the bathroom and turning on the tap she splashed handful after handful of cold water on her face. When finally she looked up again he was standing at the door watching her in the mirror and as she looked back her heart seemed to twist from its roots. Would she ever get over this? she asked herself. Would she ever find anyone else who would look at her that way, who could make her feel so happy and so goddamned miserable?

'Are you OK?' he said.

She nodded. 'Yes, I'm fine, but I want to talk to you.' She turned to face him, knowing she was going to sound a good deal stronger than she felt. 'I asked you once before not to make me beg,' she said, 'and now I'm asking you again. I don't want this to be the end. I want to make love with you again, I want to take everything from this that I can so that when you're gone I'll have more than just memories, I'll have the knowledge that I really did mean something to you.'

'You've got to know that already,' he said, picking up her hand and squeezing it.

'*Please*,' she said, 'don't make me beg.' Then she laughed. 'I think I'm already doing it, aren't I?'

'Not quite,' he smiled, lifting a hand to tuck her hair behind her ear.

'If I promise not to fall in love with you, if I promise to take responsibility for myself . . .'

'Sssh,' he said, pulling her against him and kissing her forehead. 'Like I told you before, I'd never let it go so far as making you beg. If you want that we carry on, then that's what we'll do. You know what you're up against now, you know that I can't love you . . .'

'Don't say any more,' she interrupted. 'All I need to know is that when it does all end you won't just disappear without seeing me before you go.'

'No, I won't do that,' he said.

For a long time then they stood together, holding each other and letting the comfort they got from each other wash over them.

'So what do we do now?' he said, when finally he let her go.

'We go to bed and we see . . .' She shrugged. 'We see what happens, I suppose.'

'I think I know what's going to happen,' he smiled.

An impish light pushed its way through the sadness in Louisa's eyes and holding her close he turned and led her back into the bedroom.

20

'Look, why don't you just talk to Consuela and hear what she has to say?' Sarah pleaded. 'At least then you'll have both sides of the story straight from the horse's mouth.'

'I don't want to talk to Consuela,' Louisa said through her teeth. 'I don't *need* to talk to Consuela, but maybe you'd like to talk to Jake then *you* can hear both sides?'

'It's not me who needs to hear it, it's *you*,' Sarah cried, thumping a hand on the dining-room table. Then regretting her moment of temper she continued in a more placatory tone. 'OK, I understand that all he told you rang true,' she said, 'it does for me too, but I've spoken to Consuela and I have to be honest, Louisa, I don't know which of them to believe. Maybe if you spoke to her then we could come up with the answer together.'

'Sarah, it's out of the question. I am not going near that woman and that's my final word.'

'Danny, you speak to her,' Sarah said, turning away.

'Look, Louisa,' Danny began calmly, sitting forward and folding her hands on the table, thinking she might enjoy this role as mediator, would probably like to chair television debates, now she came to think of it. 'I know you and I have had our ups and downs about Jake, and it's true, I did lie about sleeping with him. OK, I fight dirty when it comes to getting what I want, but we have to put that behind us now. He's rotten, I always knew he was rotten and now you know . . .'

'Danny, you're wasting your breath,' Louisa interrupted. 'I'm not speaking to that woman, even if you bring her here, I'm not speaking to her.'

'God, you're so stubborn,' Danny seethed, though secretly

she was quite delighted with Louisa's refusal to see Consuela since it kept her, Danny, at the centre of things. On the other hand though, she didn't want Louisa spending any more time with Jake, because there was no question in her mind who was telling the truth and now she was going to tell Louisa why.

'While you were over on Corsica getting your pretty little ass screwed off by Jake Mallory,' she said, 'I was on the Cap d'Antibes at Consuela's talking to Jake's father.'

'What!' Sarah gasped as Louisa's face paled. 'You never told me.'

'I'm telling you now,' Danny smiled, superciliously. 'Maybe you'd like to meet him, Louisa,' she offered, turning back to Louisa.

'No, thank you,' Louisa said, pushing back her chair and standing up.

'Louisa, for heaven's sake!' Sarah cried. 'If Jake's father was with Consuela then . . .'

'How do you know it was Jake's father?' Louisa snapped. 'Have you ever met Jake's father before, Danny? Have you ever seen a picture of him?'

'Oh come on, she's not going to lie about something like that,' Sarah said.

'Maybe not, but Consuela would. And let me ask you this, Danny, if you're so convinced that Consuela's telling you the truth then why are you still seeing Erik? After all, he's supposed to be in on it all with Jake, isn't he?'

'That's because he believes what Jake's told him,' Danny said. 'He hasn't spoken to Consuela, he hasn't heard her side of things.'

'Then why don't you ask him to?'

'OK, I will. But my guess is I'll come up against as much stubbornness and misguided loyalty with him as I'm coming up against with you. Which only goes to prove how persuasive Jake can be and I'm perfectly prepared to accept that if he'd told me all he's told you I'd probably have believed him too. Except for one thing. I *know* he's a liar. I recognized it in him the first time I met him, which was why I didn't want you to have anything to do with him. And do you know how I knew he was a liar, because I'm a liar too. You know I'm a liar, I've lied to you a lot these past few weeks, but I'm nothing like as expert at it as Jake is and I swear to you on my own mother's life, Louisa, I'm not lying to you now. I've met his father, I've listened to him tell me virtually everything Consuela's told me and I've listened to how he cut Jake off from the family right after he'd got Jake out of that Mexican jail. So Jake has no money and that's why he's doing what he is at the bathhouse.'

'Oh, do me a favour,' Louisa cried. 'If that were true then why is Consuela letting him do it?'

'She won't tell me why, all she'll say is that she hasn't always been completely above board herself and Jake knows about whatever it is she did. And now he's using it and the threat to ruin her completely if she doesn't let him use the bathhouse, which incidently Consuela has documentary proof was paid for with Mallory funds.'

'I just told you that myself,' Louisa responded angrily.

Danny gave a sigh of exasperation. 'OK, look, we're all agreed that this is a vicious battle Jake and Consuela have got going between them, the gloves are off, no holds barred and all that, she's telling him his wife is still alive . . .'

'And for all you know she is!' Louisa interrupted. 'Now we might as well end this conversation here and now before we three end up falling out over something that's not even our fight.'

'But it will be if Jake does to you what he did to his wife,' Danny pointed out. 'And that's what we're trying to protect you from.'

'Jake didn't do anything to his wife,' Louisa seethed. 'All he did was love her and make her pregnant and then that fucking monster of a woman sitting there festering like some deadly spider on the Cap d'Antibes blew his whole life apart.'

Sarah was looking very undecided now, was feeling so torn by the two of them that she didn't know if she had the courage to tell them what she was going to do, never mind coping with the guilt of actually doing it. In the end, glancing at her watch, she decided to keep it under her hat a while longer.

'Look, Louisa,' Danny said, trying to inject into her voice all the concern she really felt, 'we both know how you've made mistakes about men in the past . . .'

'One man!' Louisa shouted. 'One man and that was a mistake anyone could have made.'

'That's precisely my point,' Danny said. 'Anyone can make a mistake, anyone can fall for the charm, and God knows Jake's got enough of that to attract himself a whole harem of women. Sound familiar? The bathhouse? Who do you think gets the women there in the first place? He does, Louisa. He brings them in, he pays Morandi to get them on camera, and then he extorts the money from them. There are records of his abuses of women all over the United States, his father told me that himself. He's managed to cover most of them up, but he's not prepared to do it any longer. And that's why he's here. Jake's his son, he doesn't want to see him go to jail for murder, but he will see him in jail for blackmail.'

At last, Danny thought, as she took time out to notice how shaken Louisa really was, I seem to be getting through to her. 'Look, kiddo,' she said, reaching out for Louisa's hand, 'Sarah and I, we're with you all the way on this. We're behind you in everything you do, but you have to admit that there are times when you can be your own worst enemy.'

Louisa was shaking her head. 'No,' she said, taking her hand away. 'He's not lying to me, I know he's not and nothing you throw at me from my past is going to convince me he is.'

'OK, but you've been warned, Louisa. This isn't just the odd burst of violence we're talking about here, though God knows that would be sickening enough, it's murder we're talking about. *Murder*. Do you hear me?'

'Yes, I hear you loud and clear. Go and shout it outside Consuela's!'

Danny's eyes moved hopelessly back to Sarah. 'Explain to her, will you,' she said, 'how men like Jake operate.'

'How the hell do I know?' Sarah cried.

Danny turned patiently back to Louisa. 'Men like Jake can't help themselves,' she said, 'they need expert counselling or, in some cases, locking away all together. I'd say Jake is one of the latter, well obviously he is if he's gone so far as to kill his own wife. Anyway, the main point of it is that a misogynist, a man who pathologically hates women . . .'

'I know what the word means,' Louisa snapped.

' . . . doesn't come with the label stamped on his forehead,' Danny continued unperturbed. 'So how are any of us supposed to recognize them? More to the point, how do we stop ourselves becoming attracted to them? On the whole, if we find out beforehand what they're like, or if we sense it the way I did, we back off, as I have done. But with someone like you, Louisa, someone who has known violence from childhood . . .'

'Oh for God's sake!' Louisa cried. 'What is it with you and my bloody childhood? It's got nothing to do with you . . .'

'But you still have nightmares about it, I know, because you've told me yourself. And what's really frightening me here, Louisa, is that there's something in you, something I don't think you're even aware of, that attracts violence to you. Almost as though you want it to happen.'

'Danny, for God's sake,' Sarah said darkly. 'You're making it sound like she's some kind of nut.'

'No, I'm not,' Danny objected. 'I'm just trying to make her face up to the fact that she's been damaged by her childhood.'

'When you've finished discussing me as though I'm not here,' Louisa said bitingly, 'then perhaps, Sarah, you'd like to tell Danny what you told me about the way people used to talk about Danny's peculiar behaviour towards me? Because from where I'm standing we're witnessing a perfect example of it right now.'

Danny was wide-eyed as Sarah seemed to shrink in her chair and Danny looked from her to Louisa and back again. 'There's nothing peculiar in my behaviour towards you, Louisa,' Danny said, tearing her eyes from Sarah. 'Unless caring about a friend's welfare, a friend's *life*, is peculiar.'

'But why do you care so much?' Louisa challenged. 'Why

do you always think that you've got to save me from something . . .'

'Because you so often do need saving. And wouldn't you do the same for me if you saw me screwing myself up?'

'Oh God,' Louisa groaned, putting a hand to her head, 'this is getting us nowhere. Why don't we all just stop the amateur analysis and the mystery solving and go and get ourselves a drink in the village?'

'Good idea,' Danny said cheerfully slapping the table. As long as Louisa was with her she knew that Louisa was all right, so wherever Louisa wanted to go was OK by her.

'I'm afraid I can't,' Sarah said, already wincing as she prepared herself to break her news.

'Why not?' Danny retorted grandly. 'You can always give Morandi a call to tell him where we'll be, or leave him a note if he's already on his way.'

'As a matter of fact he is already on his way,' Sarah said, looking at her watch. 'He should be here any minute and then . . .' She looked at Louisa, her bottom lip pulled down at the corner as she felt the unpalatable taste of disloyalty, 'and then we're driving back to England,' she finished lamely.

'You're what!' Danny hissed, as Louisa stared at her aghast. The idea of staying here on her own with Danny was about as welcome at that moment as a sojourn in a funny farm. Come to think of it, it was much the same thing.

'I'm sorry,' Sarah said. 'He wants to go. He wants to get away from all this before . . .'

'Before what?' Louisa said, the skin of her face feeling as though it was being stretched over her bones.

'Before Consuela or Jake or whoever it was who killed Aphrodite, does the same to him.'

'I don't believe this,' Louisa cried, throwing up her hands. 'Why the hell should anyone want to kill *him*?'

'I don't know,' Sarah cried defensively. 'Why the hell should anyone want to kill Aphrodite? He just thinks that he's better off away from here and he wants me to go with him.'

'So you're going, just like that? Deserting the sinking ship,' Danny trilled dramatically.

'Yes, I'm going and quite frankly I think you should come with me. Both of you. This has all got too big now. We're in over our heads and I think we should get out while the going's good.'

'Oh, honestly Sarah, you're always making mountains out of molehills,' Danny said.

'There are no molehills where murder is concerned,' Sarah answered gravely. 'And I think all of us have been treating this far too lightly for long enough. If there was a murder on our doorsteps in London we wouldn't be sitting around like fucking Charlie's Angels trying to solve the puzzle, we'd let the police get on with it. I don't know whether we've all been drunk on the sun or what, but in my opinion it's time now to sober up and let those who are paid to solve crimes solve them.'

Danny was frowning. She didn't know what to think about Sarah's departure, because though on the one hand she would have no competition for the glory of rescuing Louisa, they sorely needed Sarah's common sense to act as some kind of filter between them.

'Will you come?' Sarah said, looking at Louisa.

'No,' Louisa said shaking her head. 'I've only got this short time left with Jake . . .'

'What about me? Why aren't you asking me?' Danny objected as Louisa walked over to answer the phone.

'I already have asked you,' Sarah said. 'But if you like, I'll ask you again? Will you come?'

'No.'

Sarah rolled her eyes.

'It's Morandi for you, Sarah,' Louisa said, bringing the phone over.

'Hi,' Sarah said into the receiver. 'I thought you'd be . . .' She stopped as Morandi interrupted her, then Louisa and Danny looked at each other as Sarah's face started to turn horribly white.

'OK, OK, it's all right, just calm down. I'll be right there,' she said in the end and rang off.

'What is it?' Louisa asked.

Sarah's eyes were darting around the room. 'It was Morandi,' she said.

'Well we know that,' Danny snapped. 'What did he say?'

'He said . . . He said . . .' Her eyes came to a stop as she looked first at Danny then at Louisa. 'He's at the police station in Nice,' she said. 'He's been arrested for Aphrodite's murder.'

When Sarah returned from the police station later that evening Danny and Louisa were waiting for her. During the time she was away Louisa had tried calling the number Jake had given her, but the mobile phone, as the message repeatedly told her, was out of operation at this time. Erik couldn't be found either and Danny had wanted to drive down to the *Valhalla* to see if they were there. Louisa had talked her out of it, not only because she strongly doubted Jake and Erik were there, but because the *Valhalla*, as far as she knew, was still in St Tropez which was too far to go tonight when they both should be there when Sarah got back.

'What's happening? How is he? What did he say?' Danny fired at Sarah before she was even half out of her car.

'I only spoke to him for a couple of minutes,' Sarah answered, 'the rest of the time I was just sitting around waiting, not understanding one damned thing that was going on.'

'But did he do it?' Danny demanded.

The look Sarah gave her brought a flush of bridling offence and embarrassment to Danny's cheeks. 'Of course he didn't do it,' Sarah seethed.

'Then why have they arrested him?'

'Because obviously they *think* he did it!'

'Come on, let's get you inside,' Louisa said, seeing how very unnerved Sarah was by it all. For her part she had spent the past three hours trying extremely hard to stop herself jumping to conclusions, which hadn't been easy considering Danny's enthusiasm for the bizarre. However, she thought guiltily to herself, if one good thing had come out of this it was that Sarah would be staying – at least for the time being.

'Has he managed to contact Jake?' Louisa said as she handed Sarah a drink and sat down beside her on the sofa.

'No,' she said shaking her head.

'Well of course he hasn't,' Danny cried exultantly. 'Jake's not going to make himself available to a man he's just framed for murder, is he?'

'Danny!' Louisa snapped. 'One more comment like that and I'm going to slap your face.'

Danny shrugged and slumped into the sofa opposite.

'He wonders,' Sarah said to Louisa, 'if you could try contacting Jake. He needs a lawyer and I just don't know where to start.'

'But surely he must know someone himself,' Danny said. 'Or better still, why doesn't he ask Consuela to recommend one? I'll call her now . . .'

'He was with Consuela when Aphrodite was killed,' Sarah seethed. 'And Consuela is denying it.'

Danny's mouth formed a perfect O as she tried to think of something to say and failed.

'Wasn't anyone else around while he was there?' Louisa asked gently. 'Someone who can corroborate it?'

'Apparently not. Or no one he saw, anyway.'

'Well then, it seems to me that he wasn't there at all,' Danny remarked. Sarah and Louisa glared at her. 'Oh come on,' she cried, 'that house is swarming with boys, if Morandi was there then someone would have seen him. And if Consuela's saying he wasn't there, then I would say she's telling the truth.'

'Yes, well you would,' Louisa retorted.

'Why would she say he wasn't if he was?' Danny demanded.

'Because, you idiot,' Louisa snapped, 'she could be the one setting him up for this.'

'If she was setting him up then she wouldn't have invited him to her house at the precise time Aphrodite departed this world, would she?' Danny pointed out in a very superior manner.

'God, are you really that thick, or are you just pretending to be?' Louisa groaned. 'She had to know where he was to make sure he didn't have an alibi, so where better than at her house where she could later swear he wasn't?'

'Or,' Danny said, 'he might have done it.'

'Danny, it'll be me who swings at you in a minute if you don't shut up,' Sarah barked.

Danny nursed her drink in the crook of her arm and gazed thoughtfully up at the ceiling.

'So what happens next?' Louisa asked, turning back to Sarah.

'I don't know. I'll go back there again tomorrow, I suppose, though God knows if they'll let me see him.' She sighed heavily. 'If only I spoke the damned language, at least then I might have some clue as to what was going on.' She buried her head in her arms and started to cry softly. 'You don't think he did it, Louisa, do you?' she choked.

'No, of course I don't,' Louisa said, putting an arm around her, but as her eyes came up to Danny's she knew that even if Sarah hadn't detected the lack of conviction in her voice, Danny had.

Danny gave a rueful smile and going to sit the other side of Sarah, put an arm around her, saying, 'Come on now, it'll be all right. It'll all work for the best in the end.' Again she and Louisa's exchanged glances and Louisa suddenly realized that despite the way Danny appeared to be treating all this as some kind of game, in her heart she really did care about what was happening; in fact, in those brief few moments she seemed as bewildered and as afraid as Louisa and Sarah.

'I just don't understand it,' Consuela said, raising an agitated hand to her head as she paced her bedroom. 'Why on earth would Morandi have said he was here when he must have known that I would say he wasn't.'

'I don't know,' Marianne said, equally at a loss as she watched the tail lights of the police car disappearing down the drive.

'I mean, if he was looking for an alibi,' Consuela continued, her normally serene face pinched and pale, 'then why on earth didn't he choose someone who he'd at least set up for it? Why choose me when he knows he wasn't even here that day? And he didn't even warn me he was going to use me, not that I'd have given him his alibi, but how can he think he can get away with telling the police something that they can find out so easily isn't true? It doesn't make . . .' She stopped suddenly and turned to Marianne.

'What?' Marianne said. 'What is it?'

'Someone's going to come forward and say they saw him coming in here,' Consuela said, her eyes moving wildly about their sockets. 'Someone's going to stand by him and at the same time they're going to brand me as a liar. Oh my God!' she cried, covering her face with her hands.

Marianne moved swiftly to her side and led her gently to the bed.

'By tomorrow the police will be swarming all over the house,' Consuela cried, 'and God only knows what they'll find. Morandi's planted something here . . .'

'But what could he have planted? He hasn't been here for at least a fortnight and we'd have found whatever . . .'

'It'll be in the bathhouse,' Consuela said, jumping to her feet. 'He didn't come into the house, so whatever it is, it'll be in the bathhouse. Get the boys, we have to make a search, now!'

'What exactly do you think we'll be looking for?' Marianne asked, hurrying along the landing after her.

'I don't know. Papers, a video . . . No, papers. Some kind of record detailing all that's gone on here and laying everything at my door. Oh God, Marianne,' she cried, clinging to the banister and turning to look back at Marianne. 'If they manage to brand me as a liar, if the police get to find out about all this blackmail, then maybe . . . Maybe, they'll manage to make it look like I killed that poor girl.'

Marianne stopped breathing. 'Where were you when it happened?' she said.

'I don't know. What am I saying? Here of course. I never

go anywhere, you know that. And the boys, they were here too. Except Jake and Morandi will say I paid someone to do it.'

'But unless they find someone who will actually come forward and *say* you paid them then there isn't a problem,' Marianne pointed out.

Consuela almost collapsed with relief. 'Of course,' she said. 'You're right.'

'What about Jake's father?' Marianne said as they reached the bottom of the stairs. 'Are you going to wake him?'

Consuela froze for a moment. Then suddenly agitated again she pressed her hand to her mouth. 'Go and wake him, Marianne. Tell him to come down to my study immediately. If Jake's about to bring all this to a head then David must be told.'

21

'Danny, I've already told you, I don't want to hear another word on the subject,' Erik said firmly.

'But . . .'

'Danny!' he warned, putting the view-finder back to his right eye as he scanned the colour transparencies on the slide box in front of him.

Danny grinned, she loved it when he was masterful. 'How do they look?' she asked, coming to peer over his shoulder.

'Not bad,' he murmured.

'*Not bad*! Here, let me take a look,' she cried, snatching the view-finder from him. 'They're fantastic!' she declared, gazing rapturously down at the pictures of herself.

Erik laughed and went to sprawl out on an ivory leather and stainless steel armchair beneath the window of his Monaco apartment. 'You're fantastic,' he said, leering outrageously at her naked breasts and making her laugh.

'Do you really think so?' she said, girlishly twirling a finger around one of her nipples.

'Yes, I really think so. Now off you go and make me another coffee,' he said, stretching luxuriously. 'I've been up half the night . . .'

'Yes, where were you?' Danny said. 'I tried to call you I don't know how many times.'

'I was over at St Tropez with Jake.'

'Doing what?'

'Mind your own business. Now go and get that coffee.'

'You do know that Morandi's been arrested, don't you?' she said, staying where she was.

'Yes, we know. Jake has it all in hand and while we're on the subject I don't want you going near Consuela's again. Have you got that? Stay away from her. No, no, no,' he said, raising his hand as she made to interrupt, 'I know what she's told you and it's up to you what you believe, but here's where it stops, Danny. You're not to go there again, do you hear me?'

'Yes sir,' she said, bobbing a curtsy. 'Would you like that coffee now, sir?'

'Yes. And make one for my guests while you're at it.'

He grinned as Danny's eyes darkened with the thrill of serving his imaginary guests. She was never happier than when playing some role or other and the things he came up with seemed just about to blow her mind – his too come to that.

As Danny wiggled off to the kitchen, her tight black mini-skirt barely covering her bottom, Erik got up, wandered to the window and stared down at the Port Fontvieille where Aphrodite's body had been found. What next, he asked himself wearily rubbing a hand over his unshaven chin. He thought of Morandi sitting there in his police cell probably scared half out his wits. Would he talk? Erik wondered. Would he blow it all now? Since it didn't bear thinking about he put it from his mind and went to sit down again.

A few minutes later Danny wiggled her way back into the room carrying a tray of coffee. She'd obviously popped into the bedroom while the coffee was brewing because she was now wearing a pair of black stiletto heels and one of his bow ties as well as her mini-skirt.

He watched, feeling himself grow harder all the time, as she went through the charade of serving his 'guests', asking them if they took milk and how many sugars, before setting their cups down. Her breasts looked so firm and heavy as she bent over that it was only with supreme self-control that he managed to stop himself reaching for them. But it wasn't a part of the script, so he merely continued to watch her until she slopped coffee into a saucer and turned to him in dismay.

'Come here,' he said, beckoning her with his finger.

Danny tottered meekly towards him.

'I apologize for her clumsiness,' he said to the absent guest. Then looking up at Danny he nodded towards the floor.

Immediately Danny bent over and tugging her skirt up to her waist Erik cracked a hand hard over her bare buttocks three times.

When he had finished Danny straightened and turned shamefacedly back to the guests. 'I'm sorry,' she whispered to the empty chair.

'Wait by the door,' Erik barked, picking up his coffee.

Obediently Danny turned back to the kitchen door then stood quietly by as Erik sipped his coffee and ignored her.

She was marginally less aroused than she normally was during their games since there was so much else going on in her head. She desperately needed to speak to Consuela again because between them Sarah and Louisa had somehow managed to dent her conviction that Consuela was telling the truth. Except of course she knew Jake was a liar. She'd even spoken to his father who looked and sounded so much like Jake it was almost scary. But she had to find out what was going on where Morandi was concerned, because the last thing she wanted was to find herself starring in the wrong cast, and since Erik wouldn't discuss it there was only Consuela she could ask. She'd have gone straight to Consuela's that morning had Erik not called and told her to come here.

Now, as she looked at his handsome, though tired face she wondered what it must be like to be Swedish. He looked Swedish, she decided, not that she'd ever met a Swede before, but she imagined they probably all had blond hair and suntans, though not all of them would have such a wonderful mop as Erik, nor such a genuine tan. Theirs probably owed more to ultra-violet beds than the actual sun, because, though she wasn't absolutely certain about this and she could be thinking of somewhere else entirely, wasn't it night for half the year in Sweden? Yes, she was sure she was right, because that would account for how they found the time to learn such perfect English and got to be so utterly brilliant at sex, there was nothing else to do.

As Erik put his cup back on the table she immediately straightened her shoulders and gazed blankly at the window. A very painful amount of lust was suddenly biting into her loins as she felt his eyes sweep over her. Oh, life was going to be so wonderful married to him, she thought, for having someone else to play out her scripts with was, she realized now, what she'd always been looking for. And he was so good at it. She never gave him the lines, he seemed to know all of his own accord what was expected of him and that alone made him the perfect man for her. And, she mustn't forget, it also served yet again to prove how expert she was at getting people to fall in with her performances without even realizing that it was she who was guiding them. What a shame she couldn't get him involved with what she and Consuela were planning, but if she had any failings at all – and right at that moment she couldn't actually think of any – then it certainly wasn't that she couldn't keep a secret. Even from Erik.

'Here,' he said, lolling back in his chair and lifting one leg up over the arm of it.

As Danny walked towards him he unzipped his shorts and took out his erection. He looked up at her, then pointed wordlessly at it.

Dropping compliantly to her knees Danny took it in her hand, licked it all over then inserted it in her mouth.

Erik's hand came down on the back of her head, pushing her down harder. Jesus, did she know what she was doing when it came to this sort of thing!

After a while, assuming boredom with one of the most magnificent blow jobs he'd ever had, he pushed her away and looked contemptuously into her face. But his expression instantly changed when he saw that there were tears in her eyes and her bottom lip was trembling.

'Sweetheart, what is it?' he said, moving towards her and cupping her delicate face in his hands. 'Did I hurt you?'

'No,' she sniffed. 'No, it's just that . . . It's just . . .'

'Come on, what is it?' he encouraged, his limpid blue eyes anxiously searching hers.

'Do you really love me, Erik?' she said.

'Danny, I'm crazy about you, you know that. Why else do you think I asked you to marry me?'

'It wasn't because Jake told you to, just to get me off his back?'

'Oh, darling,' he said, folding her in his arms. 'We've been through all that before. There are a lot of things I'd do for Jake, but marrying a woman I don't love isn't one of them.'

'Are you sure?'

'Of course I'm sure. And as soon as my divorce comes through I'll prove it by marrying you and making you as happy as I possibly can.'

She smiled shakily. 'Are you proud of me?' she said.

'Of course I am,' he laughed. 'What man wouldn't be proud of a woman as beautiful and crazy as you?'

'Do you really think I'm crazy?'

'You're the craziest woman I've ever known,' he said. 'Now come on, what's really the problem?'

'Nothing,' she said, shaking her head. 'I just want to make sure I'm doing the right thing.'

'In marrying me?' he smiled. 'I hope you do think it's the right thing, because I certainly do.'

'Yes, in marrying you. But in everything else too.'

'Well now, that's a bit of a tall order, because we all make mistakes from time to time. And as wonderful as you are you're no more infallible than the rest of us.'

'I know that, but honestly Erik, I really do believe what Consuela told me about Jake. No, I know you don't want to talk about it, but we have to. You see, I'm afraid for you. I'm afraid that he's convinced you to see things his way and that he'll end up dragging you down with him. And I just couldn't bear for anything awful to happen to you.'

'It won't,' he assured her, pulling her back into his arms. A few seconds later he tensed as her hand crept along his thigh and wrapped itself around his semi-erect penis, hardening it almost instantly.

'Kiss me,' he murmured, lifting her lips to his and pressing gently against them as his tongue moved into her mouth.

'I love you, Erik,' she whispered, when he let her go. 'I mean I think I really love you.'

'I love you too,' he smiled.

She stood up, then climbing onto his lap and lowering herself carefully onto him, she said, 'Do you think our marriage will work?'

'Yes, I do,' he groaned, closing his eyes as the wet, exquisite heat of her engulfed him. Then looking up at her and taking her large breasts in his hands, he smiled. 'I don't say that I'm not going to have my hands full, in more ways than one,' he said softly, 'but yes, I think we'll work out.'

'Did you say that to your other wives?' she asked, moving slowly up and down.

'I don't remember, but even if I did, you're different, Danny. A whole lot different. All I hope is that you don't end up breaking my heart, because until I met you I never knew anyone who had the power to do that.'

He laughed then as Danny's mood instantly brightened at the prospect of having such power. 'I won't break your heart,' she promised. 'But just you make sure you don't break mine.'

'No, but I'll tell you what I am going to break,' he said, sucking first one then the other of her fat, rosy nipples into his mouth, 'is all kinds of records for how many times a day I can make love to my beautiful wife.' Just thank God, he was thinking to himself, that she never delved too deeply, for, love her and adore her as he most truly did, there were certain things happening right now that he very definitely didn't want her to know anything about.

Three days had gone by since Morandi was arrested, and while Sarah motored backwards and forwards to Nice and Danny came and went in her usual fashion, Louisa spoke only briefly on the phone to Jake. He'd found Morandi a lawyer, she knew that and he, or at least his crew, had sailed the *Valhalla* back round the coast to Golfe Juan. But not until that morning, when Marianne had come to collect her and drive her to his beautifully converted old barn in the Var, with an ancient round tower attached to one side and a lovely view down through the sparkling trees to the Lac de St Cassien, had she actually known where he was.

She stood now in front of the vast, empty hearth, whose chimney-breast rose all the way to the ribbed oak beams of the ceiling, gazing up at the old stone walls and the mezzanine that overhung the room and, as far as she could make out, housed some kind of study – certainly it was lined with leather-bound volumes and she could see a big, antique mahogany desk. Jake walked up the flagged steps from the kitchen, carrying a tray and looking somewhat baffled about what to do with the teabag in Louisa's cup.

'You seriously want milk in that?' he said, as she whisked the teabag out and put it back on the tray.

'Just a little, thank you,' she answered, her eyes dancing with laughter at his foreigner's confusion about the way the English took their tea.

Then, as abruptly as it had come, the lightness of his mood once again vanished.

She'd sensed from the moment she walked in the door and Marianne had driven away, that he was on edge. Even when he'd kissed her he'd seemed somehow distracted and she wasn't quite sure whether or not she should ask him what was wrong. It seemed such an absurd question considering all that was obviously on his mind, so hoping that eventually he would get around to telling her, she asked if she might take a look around.

'Sure,' he said, seeming suddenly to remember she was there. Then he laughed and looked up at the beams. 'This is about it,' he said, sweeping a hand to indicate the vastness of the barn, 'except the bedrooms, of course, they're in the tower.'

'Can I see them?' she shrugged.

'Go right ahead. That there,' he said pointing to a door to one side of the chimney, 'is my room. The others don't get used much. You have to go up to the gallery to get to them.'

Louisa pushed open the door he'd indicated and looked

inside. What she saw surprised her, delighted her in fact, for though it was an undoubtedly masculine room with its French boat bed and heavy armoires, the sun was pouring in through the window bouncing off the round, grey walls and filling the room with light. And, she guessed, if one were sitting up in the bed there would be a perfect view down to the lake.

'What a wonderful way to wake up in the morning,' she commented, glancing back over her shoulder.

'What?' he said. 'Oh, yeah, it's pretty amazing, mmm?'

'How long have you had the house?' she asked.

'A year, I guess. I don't use it as much as I'd like, but it's good to have somewhere to come when I need to get away from the crew.'

'But of course it still has its view of the water,' she teased.

'Not quite the same as the sea,' he smiled. 'But it'll do. How are you doing with that tea? Can I get you some more?'

'No, I'm fine thanks,' she assured him, wishing she could get beyond this odd, unapproachable air he seemed to have cloaked himself in.

'I think,' she said, closing the bedroom door and going to stand behind one of the kelim sofas, 'that I should tell you that Danny knows about us.'

'Yeah, I know,' he said, chewing his bottom lip.

'Doesn't it matter?' she asked, surprised by his lack of reaction.

He looked up. 'There's nothing to be done about it now. If she knows, she knows.'

Louisa blinked, not quite sure where to go from there. What she really, very desperately, wanted to ask him was where his father was right now, but she couldn't think of a way to approach it that wouldn't seem as though she were doubting all he'd told her while they were in Corsica. And she didn't doubt it, she truly did believe that for whatever reasons Consuela had got someone to masquerade as Jake's father, but it would just be nice to hear Jake confirm it.

'Do you think the lawyer might be able to get Morandi out of jail soon?' she ventured.

Again she was interrupting his thoughts. 'Uh, no, he won't,' he answered. 'Morandi's better off where he is right now.'

'But he didn't do it, did he?' she said.

'Not as far as I'm aware. Are you sure you don't want more tea?'

'No, thank you. This was revolting enough.'

He grinned and at last she felt she had his attention. But suddenly he was pacing the room leaving her once again at a loss, so walking around the sofa she sat down and put her cup on the low, wooden, coffee table.

As she watched him she found, to her horror, that she was evaluating how she might feel if he really was a murderer. She looked at his hands and tried to imagine them brutally attacking a woman, smashing and beating her face until she was dead then lifting her up and throwing her into the sea. But all she could see were the hands that had touched her and stroked her with infinite tenderness and care. Hands that she longed to reach out for now and hold between her own, or feel sliding into her hair, as she asked him to tell her what had happened to have disturbed him so badly. It didn't seem to be Morandi's arrest, or the fact that Danny knew about them, so, was it, she asked herself dolefully, the fact that his father was at Consuela's?

'At Consuela's!' he laughed incredulously when she at last blurted the question out. 'Is my father at Consuela's? What, are you out of your mind? My father's in San Diego where I spoke to him just before you got here, so what the hell is all this about?'

Louisa explained what Danny had told her.

'Bullshit!' he said. 'Either she's making it up or, like you said yourself, Consuela's got someone there who's making out to be him.'

'You don't seem very put out about it,' she remarked.

'Why should I be? I know where my father is so she's going to have a hard time proving someone else is him if it comes to the test, don't you think?'

'Yes,' Louisa smiled, wanting just to throw herself in his

arms with sheer relief. Instead, as he reached for the phone and punched out a number, she got up to go and look out of the window down through the hazy bands of sunlight streaming through the trees to the lake where the sun was glinting in fine, sharp blades from dazzling pools of light. That was how he made her feel, she thought idly to herself, bright and shining and filled with light, but just as ephemeral.

'Erik?' he said. 'Yeah. What time are you leaving? OK. Get hold of Danny before you go and get her to tell you what she knows about some guy she met at Consuela's . . . I'm not sure when, at the weekend, I guess. He's saying he's my old man. Yes, that's right. Louisa just told me. Yeah, she's right here. OK, find out what you can, but don't call me back. I want this line free,' and he rang off.

Feeling him come to stand behind her Louisa rested her head back on his shoulder and lifted her folded arms for him to slide his underneath. He smelt wonderful and she turned her face a little to inhale the delicate scent of pine mingled with his own maleness and, of course, that ubiquitous, though barely detectable, tang of the sea.

'I'm sorry,' he said softly. 'I guess I'm not much company today.'

'It doesn't matter. I know you've got a lot on your mind.'

'But more importantly right now, I've got you in my arms. I was afraid you might have changed your mind since the weekend.'

'No,' she said, pressing her lips softly to his neck. Then turning in his arms she continued to kiss his neck while slowly unbuttoning his shirt. She lifted her face and gazed up into his clouding eyes as she pulled his shirt open and ran her hands over his hard, pectoral muscles and up to his shoulders. Beneath the wiry hair his skin was soft and smooth and lowering her mouth she traced her tongue around his nipples. She expected him any minute to pull away and return to whatever was bothering him, but he didn't, and as he pulled her up and gazed half-laughingly, half-wonderingly down at her she could see that at last he really was with her.

'How about I do that to you?' he said darkly, starting to unfasten her buttons. She looked down, watching his hands as he pushed her blouse aside and brushed them over her breasts. Then she was holding his head, twisting her fingers through his thick, glossy black hair, as he stooped to suck her hardened nipples into his mouth. The power of the sensations shooting through her was sapping the strength from her legs and he scooped her up in his arms.

As he carried her to the bedroom he was staring hard into her eyes, until breaking the gaze Louisa buried her face in his neck and began kissing his ear.

'I'm gonna miss you,' he said, lying down beside her.

'I'll miss you too,' she smiled, not wanting to think about it now.

Again he was looking at her in that strange, almost expressionless way. Then seeing the confusion in her eyes he said in a voice so soft she barely heard him, ' "Look not in my eyes, for fear they mirror true the sight I see, And there you find your face too clear And love it and be lost like me." '

As she realized what he'd said Louisa's heart tightened with a slow warmth that seemed to spread into her whole being. 'That's beautiful,' she murmured. 'Did you write it?'

'No,' he smiled. 'It's Housman.'

They lay quietly looking at each other for a while, stroking each other's bodies and imprinting every feature of the other's face in their minds. Then rolling her onto her back he knelt over her and pulled her skirt and panties down over her long, slim legs. When finally his eyes returned to hers she saw a heartrending sadness that made the desire in them seem all the more poignant. And without either of them moving, she felt him touching her, closing around her, sinking beneath her skin and loving her as she had never been loved in her life.

'Jake,' she whispered, the emotion in her voice rippling hopelessly in her heart.

'I know,' he whispered and lowering his lips to hers he kissed her and never stopped kissing her the whole time he made love to her.

'Louisa,' he said, holding her in his arms when it was over and stroking her as he gazed out of the window, 'there are a lot of things I want to say to you, you know that, don't you?'

'Yes,' she said.

He gave her a quick squeeze. 'I'll never forget you, you know.'

'I'll never forget you either,' she whispered through the lump in her throat.

'Maybe there's a time for us in another world, another life.'

'I hope so. Jake, you're leaving, aren't you?'

'Sssh,' he said, pulling her head onto his shoulder and kissing her.

'Jake, please tell me,' she said, hardly able to push her voice through the tears and panic that were choking her.

'No, I'm not going yet,' he said.

A few minutes later he eased himself gently from their embrace and went to answer the phone. He'd left the bedroom door ajar and hating herself for doing it Louisa tiptoed over to it to see if she could hear what he was saying. But all she heard was him telling someone to keep in touch.

When he came back it was obvious that the call had upset him and she could feel him moving away from her again.

'Come on.' he said, picking up his clothes. 'I'll take you back to the villa.'

'Jake, please, will you tell me what's going on?' she implored.

'Not right now,' he answered. Then looking at her he put a hand under her chin and said, 'Do you mind? I don't want to talk right now, but I'll stop by at the villa later, OK?'

Dumbly she nodded and started to pull on her clothes.

'Do I get dinner if I come?' he asked, obviously making an effort to lighten things a little.

'Yes,' she shrugged. 'You can have dinner. I don't know who else will be there, but . . .'

'Just so long as you're there, that's all that matters,' he interrupted and tweaking her nose he walked out of the room, stopping as he reached the door to say, 'By the way, no one except Marianne and Erik knows where this house is, or even that it exists, so please, keep it to yourself.'

22

When Jake arrived later that evening Danny was still in the shower and Louisa and Sarah were having drinks on the terrace with Jean-Claude.

'Sarah's in a terrible way,' Louisa whispered to Jake when she went to greet him. 'I think it might help if you talked to her.'

'*Shit!*' he seethed under his breath, obviously either having forgotten that Sarah would be there, or just not wanting to talk to her. 'Who's that with her on the terrace?'

'Jean-Claude, our neighbour. Erik's friend.'

'OK. Get Sarah to come inside. Is there somewhere we can talk?'

'You can use my study, Sarah knows where it is. Danny's here too.'

'Is she?' he said sourly. 'Well what a cosy evening we're going to have.'

Not long after Jake and Sarah disappeared inside Danny sauntered down the steps from the small terrace outside her bedroom to join Louisa and Jean-Claude. The instant Louisa saw her her heart sank. Obviously there wasn't much left of the bottle of wine she'd taken with her to the shower.

'Hello, Jean-Claude,' Danny drawled, flopping unsteadily into a chair. 'Or should I say *bonjour*. Oh no, hang on it's *bonsoir* now, isn't it?'

'*Bonsoir*, Danny,' he said politely.

'What's that?' she demanded of Louisa, pointing at Louisa's drink.

'It's a kir,' Louisa said, not bothering to hide her exasperation.

'I think I'll have one of those.'

'Don't you think you've had enough?' Louisa retorted.

'Nope. Whose car is that over . . . Oh my,' she grinned, putting a hand to her face. 'It's Jake's car. So where is he?'

'In the study with Sarah.'

'Giving her a bit of a seeing to, is he?'

'Danny,' Louisa winced.

'Sorry,' Danny said, reaching out for an olive. 'So what brings you over here this evening, Jean-Claude?' she asked, pulling the stone from between her teeth.

'Sarah and I invited him,' Louisa answered, knowing that she and Danny were heading fast towards a particularly ugly scene if Danny kept this up. As if it wasn't enough that Jake had turned up in a foul mood.

'Do you know what?' Danny said to Jean-Claude who, Louisa thought admiringly though with embarrassment, seemed quite unperturbed by the rudeness in Danny's manner.

'What is that?' Jean-Claude asked, smiling benignly.

'Louisa is my favourite person in the whole world,' Danny announced with a grin.

'Oh, Danny, for heaven's sake, shut up,' Louisa groaned.

'She doesn't choose her men very well, but she's pretty good at choosing her friends,' Danny continued unabashed. 'Aren't you, Louisa?'

'I think we should just continue as if she weren't there,' Louisa said, turning to Jean-Claude.

'Oh no, don't do that, Louisa,' Danny pouted. Then quite suddenly she started to laugh.

Louisa glared at her and just as suddenly she stopped.

'Can I refresh your drink for you, Jean-Claude?' Danny offered, getting to her feet.

'No, no, I am fine, thank you.'

'OK. Well, I'll go and get myself one, excuse me,' and she made an airy path into the kitchen.

'I'm sorry,' Louisa said to Jean-Claude.

'Please, think nothing of it,' Jean-Claude smiled. Then

looking warmly into Louisa's eyes he said, 'Are you going to tell Jake that you 'ave told me all that is going on?'

Louisa pulled a face. 'I don't think so,' she answered. 'At least not while he's in the mood he's in tonight. So please, when he comes back, don't say anything, will you? Just pretend you don't know him.'

'That won't be difficult when I don't,' Jean-Claude twinkled merrily. 'Though I 'ave to confess I feel I do now you've told me so much about 'im.' And then his eyes were serious. 'It is going to be very 'ard for you when 'e goes, is it not?'

Louisa's lips flattened in a smile as she nodded. 'I have to admit, Jean-Claude,' she said, 'that if Consuela is lying about Martina and she really is dead, that I can't stop myself hoping that maybe, I don't know, in a year from now, two years from now, that he will reconsider and we can, well, try again.'

'You would not be 'uman if you did not think that way, he said, patting her hand in a fatherly manner. 'But let me give you a little word of advice. Don't rush 'im. If it is the case that 'is wife is dead, 'e will need to grieve for 'er all over again.'

'I know, you're right,' Louisa sighed, linking her fingers through his.

'*Oh là là*,' he chuckled, 'you are much prettier when you smile and 'e is 'ere, no? 'e comes to see you because in 'is 'eart 'e loves you. No one will ever be able to take that away from you, Louisa. No matter what 'appens in the future, whether 'is wife is still 'ere or whether 'e chooses not ever come to back, what you 'ave 'ad now will always be special for you. And for 'im. 'e 'as done all 'e can to make sure of that. And think what a very courageous man 'e is, that 'e can think of someone else's 'appiness at such a time as this in 'is life. Oh, no, no,' he said as she made to interrupt. 'I know what you are going to say, what 'e 'as no doubt said 'imself, that 'e 'as been very selfish to take from you what 'e 'as, and I agree, 'e 'as been selfish, but 'e is only 'uman too, Louisa, and remember, 'e 'as been going through a very bad time, 'e needs solace, like any other man would need it in such circumstances. And 'e 'as been honest with you from the start by never making any promises 'e knew 'e couldn't keep. So what you 'ave 'ad together, what my beautiful country, she 'as 'osted, is a little touch of summer madness that will always remain in your 'eart.'

'You're a very special man, Jean-Claude,' Louisa said softly. 'Thank you for that. And thank you for understanding and believing all that I've told you. It's not that I blame Sarah or Danny for not believing it, they're too mixed up in it all themselves, but it's so good to talk to someone who isn't.'

Leaning against the counter in the kitchen Danny was staring desperately at the bottle of wine she had taken from the fridge. She knew she shouldn't have any more, that if she did she would feel terrible in the morning, but it was so tempting, so very tempting, to drown tomorrow in the wine of tonight. She wasn't ready for tomorrow, she hadn't had enough rehearsals and she was so afraid she was going to blow it.

She turned to splash more wine into her glass, then hearing Jake's voice in the hall she smashed the glass into the sink. Did he think she was so simple, of such little account, that she was going to let him get away with deceiving her friend the way he was? Did he truly believe that he just had to tell Erik to stop her doing something and she would stop? Did he really think he could just brush her to one side as if she didn't matter, as if she hadn't recognized the evil that was in him, when they both knew she had? Well she was going to show him and she was going to make damned sure when it was all over that he knew it was *she* who had outsmarted him and it was *she* who still had Louisa and still had Erik. She just wished she'd had a few more rehearsals, because she couldn't afford to make a hash of this, not now she knew that Jake himself had killed Aphrodite – and what was more, Consuela had told her *why* he had killed her.

Hearing Sarah's nervous laughter coming from the terrace Danny's heart went out to her. Morandi was going to take the rap for what Jake had done, Jake was already seeing to that, unless she, Danny, did something to stop it. She had to get

Jake out of the country before he did any more damage to any more people and then Consuela and his father could clear up the mess after him. Poor Morandi. Jake hadn't done anything to back him up on using Consuela as his alibi and nor was he going to. Oh, he'd let Morandi think he was going to, but he'd never had any intention of doing it, that was obvious now. Even Erik had expressed surprise that Morandi was still in jail.

Still, she thought, padding off to her bedroom with a sudden return of exuberance, Morandi wouldn't be there much longer and then Sarah would be happy, so would she and Erik and Louisa would just be thankful to be alive. Roll camera!

'Oh no, don't go,' Louisa was saying, as Jean-Claude made to get up. 'Stay for dinner. There's plenty.'

'No really, I shouldn't interrupt your evening any . . .'

'You're not interrupting,' Sarah told him. 'You're more than welcome here, you know that.'

Jean-Claude looked uncertainly at Jake who, even through his continuing black humour, managed a smile. 'Stay,' he said. Then catching Louisa's eye he added, 'please. Stay.'

'So what have you got cooking?' Sarah said to Louisa, plunging into the awkwardness.

'Nothing. It's all cold and it's more or less prepared so we can eat when you're ready.'

'I just need to run upstairs and change,' Sarah said. 'I've been in these shorts all day.'

'OK,' Louisa said, smiling inwardly at Sarah's lift in spirits since she'd spoken to Jake. She'd managed, in a quick whisper, to let Louisa know that Morandi was likely to be released the following day, but the circumstances behind it she hadn't yet been able to relate.

'I'll just go and finish off the last minute things.' Louisa said. 'Are you sure you don't want anything to drink, Jake?'

'No. I'll just take wine with dinner,' he answered, taking one of his own brand of cigarettes from his pocket. Then, as Louisa and Sarah disappeared inside, he clicked down his lighter and inhaling deeply, said to Jean-Claude, 'Sorry, you must think me pretty rude, it's just been a trying day one way or another.'

'Please, don't apologize,' Jean-Claude said, 'we all 'ave them from time to time.'

Jake was on the point of saying something else when Danny appeared wearing an extremely expensive and extremely revealing white lycra swimsuit. 'Oh, Jake!' she said feigning surprise. 'What on earth are you doing here? And you, Jean-Claude, still here I see. Well, isn't this cosy?'

'The pool's that way,' Jake said, waving a hand vaguely in the direction of the pool.

'Gosh, how observant you are,' Danny remarked. 'Incidentally, did Erik tell you, I've accepted his proposal?'

'He told me,' Jake sighed.

'I'm so excited,' she said to Jean-Claude, bunching her hands together over her chest. 'I've never been married before. Oh, but you have, haven't you, Jake, you must tell me what it's like. Maybe you could give me a few hints . . .'

As Jake's face turned murderously dark Jean-Claude said quickly, 'I 'ave been married too, Danny, maybe I could give you a few 'ints.'

'Oh, no,' Danny said, wagging a finger, 'I don't want the bedroom secrets of gays, it's those of real men I'm looking for. Men who get deliciously rough with their women, not men who bugger young . . .'

'For Christ's sake, Danny!' Jake exploded

'Oh, I'm sorry,' she gasped, putting a hand over her mouth, 'did I say something to upset you?'

Jake nodded towards Jean-Claude as though to tell him to go into the kitchen and let him handle this.

Jean-Claude needed no further bidding and going inside he found Louisa humming to herself as she dressed the salad and organized the cutlery.

'Oh, Jean-Claude,' she said, starting as he came in. Then grimacing when she saw his face she added 'He's not being difficult is he?'

'No, 'e is being as charming as 'e can under the

circumstances, at least with me 'e is. Can I give you a 'and with something?'

'Yes, could you get the plates from the cupboard over there,' she said, nodding over her shoulder towards it, 'I just need to wash off these eggs. Where did you say Didier was tonight, by the way?'

'Oh, 'e is down in the village, with 'is friends. 'e will be 'ome soon, I expect. Louisa? Louisa? What is it?' he said, putting the plates down and going to her.

She said nothing, just continued to stare at the half-open window. Jean-Claude followed her eyes and then he too could see what she was seeing. The slant of the window was such that it was reflecting what was happening on the terrace, where, with one hand idly massaging Danny's exposed breast, Jake was gazing down into her eyes and listening to what she was saying. She was smiling, Jean-Claude saw, then suddenly Jake laughed and grabbing her to him he crushed his mouth passionately over hers.

Louisa turned away, dropping the eggs in the sink.

'No,' Jean-Claude said, pulling her back. 'Go out there and face it.'

'No. You go out there. Just go and break it up, please.'

'You want to pretend it 'asn't 'appened?' he challenged.

'For now, yes. I'll deal with it later, when Danny and I are alone.'

By the time Jean-Claude stepped onto the terrace the embrace was over and seeing him coming Danny wandered off to the pool. Jake watched her go, then turning to Jean-Claude and seeing the expression on Jean-Claude's face he said, quite matter-of-factly, 'She saw.'

Jean-Claude nodded.

'Where is she now?'

'Still in the kitchen, I believe.'

Pushing aside a chair Jake walked into the kitchen.

'Hi,' Louisa smiled as she saw him come in.

'Quit pretending. I know you saw.'

She shrugged. 'It's OK, it's . . .' She stopped abruptly as he suddenly grabbed her by the arm and pushed her up against the wall.

'So, I kissed her,' he raged, 'What the hell? I kiss who I want to kiss, same as I screw who I want to screw . . . I'm married, you know that, I love my wife . . .'

'Jake, you're hurting me,' she protested.

'I told you it couldn't go anywhere with us,' he growled, tightening the grip on her arm, 'I warned you . . .'

'Jake, let me go!' she cried.

But still he had hold of her and as his eyes blazed furiously into hers Louisa thought of Martina and felt suddenly sick with fear and a heartbreaking despondency that she had been so horribly, so unbearably wrong.

He let her go, so abruptly she staggered.

'I told you, it's no big deal,' she said shakily as he started to turn away.

'No, that's right!' he said, turning back. 'It's no big deal. None of this is a big deal. We had a good time together, but I told you that what we had was for the here and now. So why the hell did you have to go and fall in love with me?'

'I never said that!' she cried. 'Never once have I told you . . .'

'Oh dear, I haven't just walked into a lover's tiff have I?' Danny smirked from the doorway.

Jake's eyes stayed on Louisa as hers did on him, but she just didn't know what she was seeing. Suddenly he turned away, snatched his keys up from the table and walked out.

'Not staying for dinner?' Danny smiled as he went past her. There was no reply, then Danny and Louisa were alone in the kitchen.

'Well, at least you've had a taste of what he's really like,' Danny said, turning back to Louisa.

'Danny, if I were you, I'd just shut up,' Louisa warned, her voice trembling with fury.

'Oh, come on, you knew all along what he was like,' Danny said, helping herself to a handful of peanuts. 'You just wanted to fool yourself. I don't blame . . .'

'Danny. I'm warning you,' Louisa said, her hand tightening around the knife she hardly knew she was holding.

'Louisa, for heaven's sake, I only did it to prove to you what he was like! And look how much persuading he took. The very second your back's turned he's got my tits out. Mind you, I have to say, it was pretty nice.'

'One more word,' Louisa threatened. 'Just one more word and I'm telling you, Danny, you're going to find this knife between your fucking ribs, because I've taken just about as much as I can take of you . . .'

'Louisa!' Danny reprimanded. 'I was only trying to help. And I'd better tell you now, that the real truth is Jake and I have been sleeping together all along . . .'

'You're a liar!' Sarah yelled from the door. 'I don't know what's the matter with you, Danny, whether you're sick in the head or you just can't stand the fact that he prefers Louisa. But you say one more thing, one more lie comes out of your mouth, then it'll be me sticking that fucking knife into you.'

'OK, come on, that's enough,' Jean-Claude said, coming in from the terrace. 'Let's all just calm down, shall we?'

'Oh, Faggot Galahad to the rescue,' Danny jeered and suddenly her head swung back as Louisa slapped her hard across the face.

'You bitch!' Danny gasped, real fury blazing in her eyes, but as she made to retaliate, nails brandished like claws, Jean-Claude grabbed her, wresting her arms behind her.

'Let me go!' she yelled, twisting and kicking. 'I said, let me go!'

'She needs a fucking straitjacket, that's what she needs,' Louisa hissed.

Danny stared at her, eyes dazed with confusion. This wasn't supposed to happen, this wasn't a part of the script. What had gone wrong? They were all turning against her? 'Get out!' she suddenly screamed. 'Just get out, the whole lot of you! It's my villa, so pack your fucking bags and go!'

'With pleasure,' Sarah snapped, and taking Louisa by the arm she marched her out of the house.

*

The following morning, having spent the night at Jean-Claude's Sarah went off early to see Morandi's lawyer in Nice and Louisa, having grudgingly decided that she should try to make peace with Danny, was on the point of going over to the villa when Jake drove up the lane.

She stood at Jean-Claude's gates, wearing the now crumpled ivory silk dress she'd been wearing the night before, and waited for him to come to a stop.

'I need to talk to you,' he said, looking straight ahead.

She could see by the way he was gripping the wheel and from the hard line of his jaw that his temper hadn't improved much overnight. 'I don't know, Jake,' she said, her heart stinging with the bitter conflict of her emotions.

'Please,' he said, turning to look at her. His lips were pale, his scarred eye was covered by the patch, but the one she could see was bloodshot and heavy with tiredness.

Walking around the car she got in beside him and half an hour later, after a drive that made her thankful to still be alive at the end of it, they were in the sitting room of his house.

'I wanted to say I was sorry,' he growled, as she walked away from him towards the fireplace.

'You could have told me that back at Jean-Claude's,' she said, turning to face him.

'I know.' His voice was tight with anger, but there was something in him that seemed to be reaching out for her. He was fighting it, she could see that as clearly as she could see the struggle to control his temper. She made no move towards him, his sudden burst of violence the night before had left her more shaken than she wanted to admit, but even so she still wasn't afraid of him. 'I wanted you here,' he said.

'Why?'

'I don't know why,' he seethed. 'Does there have to be a reason?'

'Jake, for heaven's sake,' she cried. 'What is wrong with you? What's happened to make you so angry? And why are you taking it out on me?'

For several seconds he just stared at her, then wrenching the patch from his eye he threw it down on the sofa. 'Plenty has happened,' he said savagely. 'Too much.' Then lifting his eyes back to hers he said. 'But you're right, I shouldn't be taking it out on you.'

She continued to watch him as he sank down on the sofa and propping his elbows on his knees bunched his fists in front of his mouth. They were silent for a long time, until finally, his eyes closed and he let out a deep groan of anguish. 'I told you I couldn't love you,' he said, his voice cracked with anger. 'I warned you, but you didn't listen.' He got to his feet and began to thrash angrily about the room. 'Why didn't you listen?' he raged, slamming a hand on the surface of an antique chest. 'I told you I love my wife, so why didn't you listen?' He swung round, looking at her as though he meant to hit her.

Louisa stood her ground, her dark eyes flashing the challenge.

'For Christ's sake!' he suddenly cried. 'What is it with you? Why the hell are you doing this?'

'Doing what? What am I doing, Jake?'

'You're standing there looking like . . .' He let his voice go and dropped his head, bringing a hand to it and pushing his fingers through his hair. 'You're driving me crazy,' he said brokenly. 'You've got me so I can't think about anything except what I'm doing to you.'

'Jake . . .'

'No, don't say anything, I don't want to hear it.'

She stood silently, not knowing what else to do. That he should feel this way was everything she wanted, but not when it was causing him such torment.

At last he looked up and she could see from the look in his eyes that for the moment the storm had passed. 'Come here,' he said wearily, holding out his arms. 'Let me hold you.'

She went to him, tears filling her eyes, love and pain and longing flooding her heart.

Long minutes ticked by as he held her, rocking her back

and forth and gently stroking her hair as he stared absently towards the window.

'I love you, you know that, don't you?' he said.

'Yes,' she whispered.

He pulled her head back so that it was resting in his hand. 'But I've got no right to say it.'

'It's not about having the right, Jake. It's about us and what we feel, now, here today. You can't help it, any more than I can.'

His eyes moved over hers as though trying to find a way into her mind. 'I want you, Louisa,' he murmured. 'I want you very much right now.'

'I'm here,' she said.

Taking her hand he led her into the bedroom. He undressed her himself, looking at her and touching her as though seeing her for the first time. Then removing his own clothes he lay down with her. As their bodies entwined, his so big and masculine, hers so slender and feminine, she could feel their love pulling them together more surely and more commandingly than the physical movements of their limbs. When he was inside her he turned his face away and she wondered, from the way he was squeezing her hands, if he was crying. And as the tears rolled down her own cheeks she felt the anger building in him again and held him as the frenzy of his emotions vented itself in the pounding of his hips and in the brutal way he crushed his mouth to hers. He was hurting her, but there was nothing she could do to stop it, and neither did she want to. But at the last, he was gentle and tender and let his tears mingle with hers.

'They've found her,' he said quietly. 'I'll be leaving tomorrow.'

He was lying on his back now, one hand on his forehead as he stared up at the ceiling, the other holding her.

Louisa said nothing. There was too much sadness and pain in her to speak.

'That with Danny, last night,' he said. 'It meant nothing, you know that, don't you?'

Still she couldn't speak.

'I was trying to prove something to myself, I guess.' He laughed dryly. 'It didn't work.' He closed his eyes. 'God, what a fool, what a bloody fool I was to think that hurting you would make this easier.'

'Where is she?' Louisa said, in a soft, shaky voice.

'In Mexico. My father got the call yesterday from Fernando to say that Fernando had seen her.'

'Fernando?'

'An American-Mexican who's been working on finding her since all this began.'

'So Consuela's been holding her own daughter hostage all this time?' Louisa said incredulously.

'Yep,' he said shortly.

'Did Fernando say anything about your little girl?'

'Yeah, she's there.' He paused, then in a voice gruff with emotion he said. 'Her name's Antonia.'

As she felt the pain engulf him she tightened her arms around him. 'Are they with Fernando now?'

He laughed bitterly. 'If only they were. He was driven somewhere blindfold, allowed to see them, then was sent back to tell me how much it was going to cost me to get them back. I received that call this morning, just before I came for you. There are still a few loose ends to tie up here then I can go get them.'

They were quiet for a while as Louisa fought to keep lodged in her heart the choking knot of emotion and stop it making her cry out for him not to go.

'What about you?' he said, giving her a quick hug. 'What will you do now?'

She opened her mouth to answer then closed it again as the pain and denial rose up from her heart. She couldn't bear to think of what it was going to be like here without him and neither could she bear the idea of returning to London. She didn't know what she was going to do, the days and weeks and months ahead seemed so bleak. 'I suppose I'll start by trying to sort things out with Danny,' she said. 'She threw Sarah and me out of the villa last night.'

'She did?' He shook his head. 'God, that woman. I don't know how Erik can stand it.'

Her heart jolted as he raised his arm to look at the time, but he made no attempt to get up. 'You never did tell me exactly what Consuela told Danny about me,' he said.

She pursed her mouth at the corner. 'Do you really want to know?'

'Probably not. Just give me the outline.'

When Louisa had finished, having told him of his apparent abuses to women, how he was supposed to have killed Martina, and how his father had cut him off he was silent for a long time, obviously deep inside his own thoughts.

'And Danny swallowed it all,' he said finally.

Louisa nodded. 'There was a terrible scene between us after you'd gone last night, if I remember rightly I actually threatened to stick a knife in her.'

'You did?' he said surprised.

'Yes. So did Sarah.'

'She doesn't seem to have too many friends right now, does she?' he remarked. 'Unless she counts Consuela as a friend.'

'Well hopefully I can put an end to that when I tell her you've found . . .' She stopped, suddenly not wanting to say the name. 'Do you think Consuela knows you've found her? Is it she who's demanding all the money?'

'I don't know. It's hard to tell. It could be that her own people have turned on her and are out to make even more money than she's paying them. I won't know 'til I get there.'

'But you truly don't believe this is another hoax?'

'No. Fernando wouldn't lie.'

She was looking at his chest, watching the lazy movement of her fingers as she ran them through the coarse, dark hair and wondering what terrible fear and anxiety, what trepidation and nervousness must be pounding in his heart as he thought about the future, of how hard the road ahead was going to be as he tried to pick up the pieces with his wife and child from whom he had been parted for so long. And for her it was almost impossible to make herself accept that she was never going to see him again, that she was truly losing the one man in the world she felt she could really love. Would she ever, she asked herself wretchedly, get over that wonderful, astonishing, and maybe once in a lifetime *coup de foudre* that had finally brought them to this?

'So Danny's there all on her ownsome, is she?' he said, swinging his legs over the edge of the bed and sitting up.

'Until Erik comes around. Or unless I get there first.' Why did they have to be talking about Danny now, when he was preparing to go, when there was still so much she wanted to say, wanted to hear? But she knew why he was doing it, he was trying to keep away from territory that was only going to cause them both more pain.

'Erik won't be there today,' he said. 'He's been held up in Paris, won't be back until tomorrow.'

'Is he there for you?'

'No. He's there on his own business.'

'Does he know you're leaving?'

'He will when I call him.' He turned to look back at her. 'I'm going to take a shower, do you want to come with me?'

She smiled as her throat tightened. 'One last thing for us to share?'

He nodded, then swallowed hard as he reached out for her hand.

'What time are you leaving tomorrow?' she asked as they walked into the bathroom.

'Mid-afternoon to Paris, from there to Mexico City.'

'Can I come to see you off?'

He looked down at her. 'Do you think that's wise?' he said, brushing a hand through her hair.

'Probably not, but at least I'll get to see you one more time.'

'OK,' he said, and stooping to kiss her he pushed the door closed behind them.

23

Jean-Claude looked up from the *Nice-Matin* as a shadow from the open french windows fell over him.

'Hi,' Sarah said, dropping her bag on the coffee table and kicking off her shoes as she sat down. 'Where's Louisa?'

'I don't know,' Jean-Claude answered. 'I think she must 'ave gone out with Danny.'

'Oh,' Sarah said surprised. 'So they've made their peace?'

'I imagine so. Louisa went over there a couple of hours ago and just after I saw Danny's car leaving.'

'Well Danny's back now,' Sarah said. 'I just saw her car in the drive. I'll go over and see what they're up to in a minute, but first things first. Have you eaten?'

'Not yet, no. Are you hungry?'

'Ravenous. Which was why I popped into the *poissonnerie* and ordered a whopping great paella.' She glanced at her watch. 'It'll be here in about ten minutes. I've ordered enough for all of us. Is Didier around?'

Jean-Claude gave an indulgent smile. ''e 'as something of a sore 'ead after a late night,' he said. ''e is still sleeping. I will wake 'im when the food arrives.'

'OK. Do you mind if I give Danny and Louisa a quick call and tell them to get themselves over here?'

'Of course not,' Jean-Claude answered, waving her to the phone. ''ow did things go with the lawyer?'

'If I say French bureaucracy will that do it?' Sarah responded.

Chuckling, Jean-Claude returned to his paper.

'Oh God, you don't mind Danny coming, do you?' she said, giving an anxious, apologetic grimace as she dialled the number.

'No. Though 'opefully she 'as calmed down a little after last night.'

'Hopefully,' Sarah muttered. 'Hi, Danny, it's me. I've just . . .' She came to an abrupt stop and pulling the receiver from her ear she gazed at it blankly. 'She hung up on me,' she said incredulously. Then hitting the connectors she dialled again. The phone rang and rang until finally Danny picked it up. 'Danny,' Sarah said crossly. 'Is Louisa there?'

'No.'

'No? Well, have you seen her today?'

'No. Now get off the line, I'm waiting for a call,' and with that Danny slammed down the phone.

'The cow,' Sarah said angrily, putting down the receiver. She turned thoughtfully, worriedly, to Jean-Claude who was looking at her over the top of his paper. 'Well she obviously hasn't calmed down,' Sarah said. 'But I wonder where Louisa is if she's not over there?' It was the strangest thing, she was thinking to herself, but ever since she'd got up this morning she'd had the weirdest feeling inside. She couldn't say exactly what it was, but it seemed, she thought, to be coming from the air. It seemed even stiller than normal, almost eerily still. There were no birds, there was no breeze, not even the faintest rustle in the trees and she was sure that the temperature must have risen above a hundred.

''er car is there, is it not?' Jean-Claude said.

'Yes,' she answered, her eyes drawing focus. 'At least I think it was.' She went to the window and craning her neck to see over the thick clusters of oleanders she said, 'Yes, her car's there. So where can she be? Unless she's with Jake.'

'I'm sure that must be it,' he said. 'I didn't see him, but . . .'

'Oh, here they are,' Sarah said, feeling a bewildering flood of relief as the Mercedes swept into the drive. 'And by the look of their faces they haven't patched it up either. Shall we have some wine with lunch?'

'But of course,' Jean-Claude said, making it sound like a silly question.

A few minutes later Louisa came in. Even with her sunglasses on there was no mistaking the fact she'd been crying.

'Here,' Sarah said, thrusting a glass of wine at her. 'Come and sit down. What happened? Did he apologize for last night?'

'Yes,' Louisa answered.

'So why the glum face?' Sarah said, as Louisa started to bite her lips.

'They've found his wife. He's leaving tomorrow.'

'*Oh là, là*,' Jean-Claude murmured.

'They've *found* her!' Sarah said. 'You mean she's alive?'

Louisa nodded. 'Please, do you mind, I don't really want to talk about it just now. I'll tell you later.'

'Of course,' Sarah said, peering worriedly into Louisa's face.

'It's OK,' Louisa said, patting her hand. 'I'll be all right. I just need some time to get used to it.'

Sarah hugged her. Naturally, no one could be anything but glad that Martina was alive, though what the poor woman must have been through these past three years hardly bore thinking about, but it was just so awful for Louisa that it all had to end like this.

'That'll be lunch,' Jean-Claude said, hearing a car pull into the drive.

As Sarah made to get up he put a hand on her shoulder and pushed her gently back to her knees. 'I'll see to it,' he said in a low voice.

Looking up at him and smiling her thanks, Sarah turned back to Louisa. 'Will you see him again before he goes?' she asked.

'Yes,' Louisa croaked. Then clearing her throat she said, 'How's Morandi?'

'Would you believe,' Sarah said, pulling a face, 'he's sitting there in his cell writing blue movies about the police?'

Louisa chuckled. 'No, I wouldn't believe,' she said.

'Then you're right. He's not. He's a bundle of nerves and he looks terrible.'

'But I thought he wasn't under suspicion any more?'

'So did I. But some kind of bureaucratic nonsense is keeping him in jail. The lawyer didn't bother to explain what, at least not to me. I left him explaining it to Morandi.'

'They're very co-operative letting you see him so often,' Louisa commented, her mind barely on what she was saying.

'Well I only get five minutes, but it's better than nothing. I guess that's France for you, even the police have a romantic side. Still, at least now we know he'll be out soon.' Then looking immediately contrite she added. 'I just wish it could have turned out a bit more happily for you.'

'Well, never mind, that's life,' Louisa said, feeling the tightness of pain move throughout her body as everything in her cried out for him. 'When do you think they might let him go?'

'Search me,' Sarah sighed, glancing at the phone as it started to ring.

'Sarah, it's for you,' Jean-Claude called from the kitchen.

Getting up to answer it Sarah gave Louisa's hand a quick squeeze saying, 'That'll be him now. At least he's the only one I gave this number to. Unless it's Danny of course.'

But it was Morandi's lawyer and as Sarah listened to what he was saying, despite the shaft of burning hot sun on her skin, she felt herself turning to ice.

'I don't believe it,' she murmured as she put the phone down. 'I just don't believe it.'

'What? What's happened?' Louisa said.

'They're not letting him go,' Sarah answered, still dazed by the shock of it. 'Not only that,' she said huskily, 'they've just added another charge. Extortion.'

Louisa's eyes closed and as her head started to spin she thought she was going to be sick. 'But Jake said . . .' she began, but what had Jake said? 'Not that I'm aware of,' that's what he'd said when she'd asked him if Morandi had killed Aphrodite. 'Oh my God, Sarah,' she said. 'You don't suppose that he was double-crossing Jake and working with Consuela do you?'

'I don't know,' Sarah said, her face deathly pale. 'I just don't know anything any more. And I hate this silence. Where are the damned birds?'

It wouldn't be long now, Danny was thinking to herself, as she floated on the surface of the pool staring through her polaroid lenses at the sun-bleached sky. Just one more call, one more person to get into place and it would begin. The witnesses, her rescuers should it turn nasty, were all where they should be. She didn't feel as nervous now as she had last night, but it was always that way, the nerves generally disappeared when the performance began. And it had begun, for ever since she had left Consuela's, just under an hour ago, she had been summoning the flair and genius inside her. There were no lines, just a silent, spectacular performance that called for cameras all around the pool. And fate and fortune were with her, directing her, had been pulling the performance from her even before she'd known it. Last night's fiasco was the prelude, without it today couldn't have happened. That's how she knew she was receiving a near divine inner guidance, for when she had felt them all turning against her she had almost lost it. She had come so close to throwing her arms around Louisa and begging forgiveness for the way she had hurt her. But she hadn't. It was all proving so easy and she couldn't think now why she had been so frightened and nervous last night.

She was glad she'd had that long talk with Consuela this morning, recalling it now was soothing her. She had come away with everything at last in perspective. She now knew exactly why she was doing this and why it had to be done. A last minute work-through of character and motivation was invariably invaluable, but even so, Consuela had said, 'If at any moment you feel you don't want to go through with this, even if it's right at the last minute, then don't think twice, pick up the phone and it will be like nothing has ever happened.'

But there was no question now of her backing out. She was so ready for this performance. She wondered how easy it was going to be for them to get Jake here, but maybe, after she'd spoken to him on the phone this morning when he'd tried to call Louisa, he'd come anyway. That had been another unexpected twist that had gone even further to prove that this was all meant to be. She hadn't told him Louisa was at

Jean-Claude's, she'd told him that Louisa didn't want to speak to him. Then she'd invited him to come and make love to her, but she hadn't put it like that, she'd put it in a way that few men could resist. Consuela had been delighted when she'd told her. So maybe he would come anyway, but they still had their plan to get him here, just in case.

Swimming lazily to the steps she climbed out of the pool and as she walked towards the terrace she was watching her reflection in the window. She had chosen her costume with care and just to see the way she looked was igniting her lust. Her swimsuit was black, had only a bikini bottom from which two long straps hooked up over her shoulders, pulling the bottom high on her hip bones and revealing her breasts totally.

It was a strange sort of day, she thought to herself as she sat down, so silent and so unbelievably hot. She'd remarked on it to Consuela that morning and Consuela had agreed, there did seem something unnatural about today. Danny wondered if Louisa had noticed it. She didn't know why it should matter whether Louisa had or not, but for some reason it seemed important. Ah yes, she knew why, when it came to writing the script later this peculiar, breathless silence would be important for the ambience.

She blinked as for an instant her mind went blank. The telephone rang and rushing into the house she snatched it up, urgently saying hello. The adrenalin was pouring into her veins, excitement was gleaming feverishly in her eyes.

'Danny?'

'Yes.'

'Are you alone?'

'Yes, I'm alone,' she confirmed starting to shake.

'Good. Are you ready?'

'I will be by the time you get here.'

He laughed.

She laughed too.

'See you soon,' he said and rang off.

As Danny put down the phone every nerve in her body was buzzing like a live wire. Exhilaration was coursing through her.

She slid a hand over the front of her swimsuit, pushing it between her legs. She was going to screw him one more time, she was going to have a murderer's cock inside her. She reached out for the edge of the table as her knees suddenly turned weak. Oh, what a shame the real cameras weren't here, for to recreate later what she was feeling now was going to be almost impossible.

She walked onto the terrace, waving an arm towards the woods to give the signal that he was about to arrive. None of them knew that she was going to screw him, right there on the terrace, it wasn't a part of the script, but just think of what power it would add to the scene.

A few minutes later she heard his car coming into the drive and going back into the house she began stroking her breasts. Soon his hands would be doing this. A killer's hands would be moving all over her body and as she goaded him and jeered at him and forced him to beat her the telephoto lenses would be watching.

Then suddenly, from out of nowhere, a terrible fear struck like a hammer. She hadn't actually seen anyone in the woods, she'd just assumed they were there. But Consuela wouldn't let her down, Consuela had said they were there, but what if they weren't? She needed to see them. She had to be sure. She didn't want to be alone with a killer, but how could she find out now, as he was coming up the drive, if the others were there? Her heart was thudding in her ears, there was sudden terror in her throat. She couldn't think. She didn't know what to do. She needed Sarah and Louisa. Her hand flew to her mouth, trembling violently against her lips as she heard his engine die. Then turning, crashing against the table, she grabbed for the phone.

'Jake,' Louisa cried. 'Jake, I'm sorry to call you now, I know you have a hundred things . . .'

'It's OK,' he said, getting out of his car, the mobile phone resting on his shoulder. 'I already know.'

'About Morandi?'

'Sure. I'm on my way there now.'

'What happened, do you know? Why was he . . .'

'Consuela spoke to the police this morning, that's how it happened. She's trying to get her accusations in first. Tell Sarah not to worry, we'll have him out of there, it's just not going to be as soon as I thought. I've got to go now, I'll call you later.'

When Louisa rang off she turned to find Sarah's anxious, bewildered eyes looking up at her from the sofa. 'He's on his way to try and get it sorted,' Louisa told her, then smiled at the way Sarah seemed to deflate with relief.

'Was it Consuela who accused him?'

'Yes.'

'Thank God for that, for one horrible minute there I was almost suspecting Jake again.'

'I know. I feel a bit like the *Valhalla* tossing about in a storm these days, don't you?'

'Tell me about it,' Sarah remarked. 'Anyway, what are we going to do about Danny? Do you think we should go over there?'

'Mmm, yes,' Louisa sighed. 'We've got to try and thrash this out between us once and for all. The trouble is I just don't know if I'm up to her saying any more about Jake right now. If she does, we're only going to end up having another row.'

'Then why don't we leave her to stew in it for a bit longer,' Sarah said, 'and go and at least try to be cheerful guests and eat some of that paella.'

'You're right,' Louisa said, as they walked outside to join Jean-Claude on the terrace. 'It really is horribly quiet today, isn't it?' she remarked.

An hour later Didier still hadn't emerged from his hangover and Louisa was collecting up the used paella plates while Jean-Claude and Sarah sipped their coffee, when they all turned as they heard someone running up the drive.

'*Jean-Claude! Jean-Claude!*' Erik shouted, running onto the terrace and almost collapsing against a pillar. 'Get the police,' he said breathlessly.

Jean-Claude was on his feet. 'Erik, what is it?' he said, going to him. 'What 'as 'appened?'

'It's . . . It's Danny!' Erik gulped, his face stricken with horror. 'You've got to call the police.'

'Why?' Louisa cried, dropping the plates and starting towards him. 'Erik, what's happened to her?'

'Just call the police!' Erik seethed, dashing his fist through the tears streaming down his ashen cheeks.

'Where is she?' Sarah demanded.

Erik was sobbing so hard he could barely catch his breath. 'The police,' he choked. 'Please, just call the police.'

Their faces pinched with fear, Sarah and Louisa looked at each other then together started from the terrace.

'No!' Erik yelled. 'Don't go over there. Please, don't go.'

Louisa started to run, Sarah was right behind her as they raced up the drive to the villa, shouting Danny's name.

'Oh my God!' Sarah suddenly gasped, covering her face with her hands.

Louisa swung round, then she saw too.

Interminable seconds passed as they stood frozen in shock, then Louisa began moving towards the pool.

'No,' she murmured. 'No, no, no. Oh, Danny, no! *Danny*!' she cried, throwing herself down at the edge. 'Oh please God! Please, please, please God, don't let her be dead. Danny, speak to me . . .' she begged desperately reaching out her hand.

But Danny just floated silently in the bloody water, her thick black hair spreading like strands of silk, her arms and legs hanging loosely, her face submerged in the gentle undulation as the blood around the glinting knife in her back congealed in the baking sun.

The next two hours passed in a daze as the blazing sun slanted its rays of blistering heat through the open windows and the humidity outside seemed to drip from the trees. Louisa and Sarah sat huddled in Jean-Claude's sitting room, speaking to the police, and heard, but didn't see, the commotion going on over at the villa. Neither of them could collect their thoughts sufficiently from the shock to give very coherent answers, but Jean-Claude, who was acting as their interpreter, was doing his best. Erik's interrogation was going on in another room, his French was good enough for him to fend for himself, but his shock was also rendering him almost incapable.

At some point, they didn't know exactly when, Danny's body was taken away and the forensic experts were now combing the villa and its grounds. Louisa didn't know if anyone had contacted Danny's parents yet, she didn't want to ask because she just couldn't think of how terrible this was going to be for them. There was only one thought in her mind, one agonizing thought, that if she hadn't been so feeble as to not want to hear Danny insulting Jake again then she and Sarah would have gone over to the villa and somehow they might have prevented this.

Uppermost in Sarah's mind as all her other thoughts collided in her head, was the way that both she and Louisa, just the night before, had threatened Danny with a knife. Of course, they both had alibis, she had been at the police station this morning and Louisa had been with Jake. Both of them had returned to Jean-Claude's, all their movements could be accounted for, but it still didn't stop the horrible fear that someone might suspect them. But worse, so very much worse, was the memory of their parting words to Danny. How were they ever going to forgive themselves? How were they ever going to live with the guilt?

At last the police left. For the time being the villa opposite was off limits they were told, but they could, if they wished, go over now to collect what they needed. Jean-Claude went for them, knowing that at this point neither Sarah nor Louisa knew anything about the blood in the house and he didn't want them to see it. Only he had been inside the house and only he had seen Danny's body when it was dragged from the pool, so he knew how savagely her face had been battered, how her body had been slashed, in the minutes before she had been stabbed in the back and thrown into the pool.

When he had gone, Sarah and Louisa, their hands clinging to each other's, cried some more. They didn't know what to say to comfort each other, neither could they offer any solace to Erik who was sitting in a corner, staring blindly at the garden, his face so haggard with grief that neither of them could bear to look.

Didier came quietly into the room. 'Louisa,' he said softly.

Louisa looked up, her face was ravaged by the tears she had shed.

'I must tell you,' he said in pained, apologetic and broken English, 'that I 'ave just seen Madame Name-Drop and she tell the police that she see a black car leave the villa.'

Louisa's eyes dilated as she looked at him. Then as though it was coming at her, thundering towards her, from the end of a long dark tunnel, the memory of what Jake had said that morning suddenly exploded in her head. 'So Danny's there all on her ownsome, is she?' he had said.

'Oh my God,' she spluttered, thrusting a hand to her mouth.

Erik and Sarah were staring at him as though unable to take in what he had said. Didier looked back, shrugging his shoulders helplessly. 'She did not say the car is a Mercedes,' he said lamely.

'Jesus Christ!' Erik suddenly cried, seeming at last to come to his senses. 'I've got to speak to Jake! I've got to tell him what's happened,' and leaping to his feet he dashed from the room.

While he was gone Louisa tried to make herself tell Sarah what Jake had said that morning, but every time she opened her mouth the terrible fear in her heart seemed to open like a gulf and swallow the words.

Erik wasn't gone long and when he came back he looked agitated almost to the point of panic. 'Sarah,' he said, 'you've got to get Morandi to tell you where he's hidden all the evidence against Consuela.'

Sarah looked at him with dazed, uncomprehending eyes.

'Sarah! Did you hear me?' he barked.

'Yes. Yes, I heard you,' she mumbled. 'Where has Morandi hidden the evidence?'

'When are you seeing him again?'

'In the morning.'

Erik didn't seem to know if this was soon enough and putting a hand to his head he started to pace the room.

'Where's Jake now?' Louisa asked dully.

'On his way out of the country,' Erik answered. 'He was with Morandi at the police station when it happened, but he can't hang around to answer questions. He has to get to Mexico.'

'Oh God,' Louisa choked, closing her eyes as she fell back against the sofa. So many thoughts started racing through her head, but the most important one of all was that whoever's car it had been over at the villa, it hadn't been Jake's. For the moment that was all that mattered, the fact that she would never see him again was something she would deal with later.

Sarah's heart was thudding horribly as she turned to look at Louisa. Obviously in thinking only of the relief that Jake hadn't done it, Louisa had forgotten that her only alibi for this morning was at that very moment leaving the country.

'What do you mean, she's dead?' Consuela whispered, turning to Marianne.

'She's dead!' Marianne cried, verging on hysteria. 'I thought it was all a hoax, I thought we were only staging it . . .'

'Marianne!' Consuela gasped. 'What are you saying? Are you saying that I . . . Oh my God!' she sobbed, burying her face in her hands. 'Marianne, Danielle called me just before it was due to happen. She told me she didn't want to go through with it so I called the whole thing off.'

'Oh God,' Marianne breathed. 'Consuela, I'm sorry. I just didn't know what to think. When I heard . . . When they told me what had happened . . . I thought, oh God, I'm sorry.'

'Sssh, sssh,' Consuela soothed, taking her in her arms. 'I don't blame you for what you thought. It has been very hard for you all this. But Danny, poor Danny, what on earth is this going to do to her parents? Has anyone told them yet, do you know?'

Marianne shook her head. 'I don't know. I only heard it from the policeman who wouldn't let me go up to the villa. And when I saw that he wasn't one of the actors . . . I realized . . . I knew something had gone horribly wrong.'

'Why were you going to the villa?' Consuela asked, confused.

'I was going to get Louisa . . .' She stopped as she suddenly realized that she'd betrayed herself.

'For Jake,' Consuela finished for her, smiling. 'It's all right, I know all about Louisa. Danny told me this morning.

'I'm sorry I never told you,' Marianne wept. 'I thought if I didn't then maybe he would just disappear with her and leave us alone. I know it was a silly thing to think, but . . .'

'It doesn't matter,' Consuela assured her, patting her hand. 'But I don't understand why you were running this errand for Jake when as far as you were aware he was supposed to be at the villa himself.'

'I just assumed, when he called me and asked me to go there, that you had called everything off. But then, when I got there . . . Oh, Consuela, who could have killed her? Who would have done it if it wasn't Jake? And it couldn't have been Jake, he was in Nice with Morandi at the police station.'

'How do you know that?' Consuela asked curiously.

'Because he called me just now in the car. He told me Danny was dead, but I already knew. He said . . . He said that I was to tell you that burning Morandi's office wasn't going to save you, because the records weren't there. And then he said, he told me, that you had killed Aphrodite and you had killed Danny and he could prove it.'

'But how can he when I've never left this house,' Consuela cried, agitatedly. 'The boys are all here to bear me . . .' Her eyes came back to Marianne's. 'Why was Jake giving *you* messages to give to *me*? I thought he knew nothing about us.'

'So did I. But he must have found out.'

'Oh dear, this is all so terrible,' Consuela said wringing her hands as she turned away. 'I never dreamt he was so clever as to do all this to me. I must speak to my lawyers, I must warn them what's happening. Where is Jake now, do you know?'

'No. All he said was that he was going to Mexico, but earlier now than he'd planned.'

'Then you must get onto the police and warn them,' Consuela said urgently. 'He mustn't be allowed out of the country. Not now.'

'But if he didn't do it,' Marianne protested.

'It doesn't matter,' Consuela said firmly. 'The police will still want to speak to him. Oh heavens!' she gasped, throwing an unsteady hand to her head. 'His father. I must speak to his father and tell him what has happened. Oh, this will be so awful for David, such a terrible blow. He's on the yacht over in Cannes. I must call him right away and tell him to come.'

'You mean that really is Jake's father?' Marianne said shocked.

'Of course it is,' Consuela answered, seeming shocked that Marianne hadn't realized. 'I haven't been lying to you all this time, Marianne. It's Jake who's been lying, remember?'

Marianne nodded dumbly. 'But if he didn't kill Danny, Consuela, then who on earth did?'

Consuela was shaking her head mystified and once again showing signs of despair. 'I don't know, Marianne,' she answered. 'I truly don't know.' Then she looked up, a sudden thoughtful and suspicious frown creasing her brow. 'Tell me, who found the body? Did Jake say?'

'Yes. It was Erik.'

As Consuela's eyes dropped she turned to the window and looked out. 'Erik,' she repeated under her breath. 'Of course, Erik.'

24

Three days had passed since Danny's murder. The press had congregated at the end of the lane, held at bay by the police, but many of them had found their way into the trees surrounding Jean-Claude's house. The second any of them stepped outside the sound of cameras drowned the incessant croak of the cicadas and if either of them left by car it was a horrible and gruelling business trying to get through the urgent clamourings at the end of the lane. So on the whole they stayed indoors.

Jake had contacted Erik to tell him that he had managed to get out of France and was now en route to Mexico, but where he had called from, or when he would call again, Erik had no idea. It was hard for Louisa to imagine what might be happening to him now, but with so much going on around her she could hardly bear to think about it. One of the worst parts of these three days had been having to face Danny's father. Her mother was still in London, under sedation, so David Spencer had flown down with Danny's aunt Rebecca who owned the villa, to collect Danny's belongings and drive her car back to England. The body was flown back the same day.

Faced with David's despair both Sarah and Louisa had wanted only to escape. Their guilt at the way they had treated Danny these past few weeks, snapping at her, ostracizing her, that last dreadful evening was too much to bear. It was Erik who had spent the most time with David, offering what comfort he could and listening for hours as David put himself through the heartbreak of remembering his daughter.

Now David and Rebecca had gone and with their passports in police custody Sarah and Louisa could only sit waiting at

Jean-Claude's for the next interminable visit from the detectives investigating the case. The fact that Louisa had no alibi for that morning was causing them some concern and since neither she nor Erik knew how to get hold of Jake there was nothing she could say to put their minds at rest. It wasn't that they suspected her of the murder, but she wished Jake was there to corroborate where she has been that morning.

Louisa's main concern now was to help Sarah and Erik sort through Morandi's paintings, for the evidence of all the blackmail had been secreted in the backs. It hadn't been easy to persuade the concierge to let them into Morandi's flat, especially when the police had declared it out of bounds, but Erik had taken care of that with an excessively generous bribe, just as he was going to take care of handing the evidence over to the lawyer, who in turn would take it to the police.

It was during the early evening of the fourth day, after Erik had returned from the lawyer, having been there since ten o'clock that morning, that news reached them through Marianne that Consuela's passport had been seized. It wasn't quite as much as they'd hoped for, but they cracked open a bottle of champagne nevertheless. They all needed something to lift their spirits, even if it was going to be shortlived.

Knowing now of Marianne's association with Consuela none of them could be sure whether or not to trust her; on the one hand she was giving them information about Consuela, but on the other she was refusing to leave the house on the Cap d'Antibes and come and stay at Jean-Claude's. However, Erik considered that she was probably of more use to them if she remained at Consuela's, they just had to be careful about how much they told her.

The next day, to everyone's horror, the finger of suspicion was suddenly pointed at Erik. He had changed his flight from Paris to an earlier one on the morning of the murder and they had only his word as to how long it had taken him to drive from Nice airport to the villa. The time of the murder had been placed at around thirty minutes after the plane touched down. It was possible, providing there had been no hold-ups at the airport or on the autoroute to get to the villa in that time. Erik insisted that the drive had taken him closer to forty-five minutes, but he had no way of proving it. When asked if he could produce an autoroute ticket to prove that he had passed through a *péage* on that day he couldn't do that either. But since few people kept the tickets the police weren't particularly suspicious of that and, though it wasn't actually impossible, the likelihood was so remote that anyone could have done that drive *and* committed a murder – which the experts assured them would have had a timespan of no less than five minutes and probably not more than eight – Erik was ordered to surrender his passport and was then released from his interrogation and told to stay on the Côte d'Azur until further notice.

'I just don't understand,' Louisa said to Erik as the two of them, having managed to escape the press, strolled along the edge of the sea at La Napoule just before dawn one morning, 'why Consuela hasn't been charged yet. With all the evidence we handed over you'd have thought they'd have gone straight round there and arrested her.'

'I'm sure they did go round there,' Erik answered, still looking drained after his ordeal the day before and the sleepless night that had followed. 'But Consuela will have some pretty powerful lawyers working for her, make no mistake about that.'

'But there are sworn statements from the victims,' Louisa interrupted. 'No one can refute that.'

'True. But they'll have to contact everyone who made those statements to make sure they weren't coerced into making them. And now Aphrodite's and Danny's murders have been linked it'll be that the police are most interested in.'

'Of course,' Louisa sighed. Then stopping and scuffing her feet in the sand she said, 'If only they could come up with some proof that Consuela was behind the murders.'

'They will,' Erik assured her.

'Will they?' Louisa sighed. 'I'd feel more confident about that if they'd only let Morandi go. Why are they still holding him?'

'Because he still doesn't have an alibi for that afternoon. At least he does, but Consuela is still swearing he wasn't there.'

'Oh God, it's all got so complicated,' Louisa groaned, feeling vulnerable and confused and horribly low after her own sleepless night. And as the wretched tears started again she said, 'It's all gone so wrong. Nothing was meant to turn out like this and I wish Danny was here so that I could tell her I'm sorry. I wish we were all back in London. I wish we'd never come here, if we hadn't she'd still be alive. And we only came because of me. Because she thought I needed cheering up after Simon and the baby and everything. Oh, Erik, why is it we only really appreciate someone when they're not here any more?'

'Hey come on,' Erik said, pulling her into his arms as his own voice filled with tears. 'I know it's hard for you, it's hard for all of us, but please don't regret coming here. If you do that then you'll regret Danny and I meeting and you'll regret ever knowing Jake. You don't regret that, do you?' he said, tilting her face to look at her.

'No,' she said tears rolling down her cheeks. 'Or maybe yes. I don't know. It hurts so much and I want to see him again so badly.

As much as he might have liked to tell her she would Erik wasn't going to lie to her, so he pulled her head back to his shoulder and held her as she cried.

'I'm sorry, I'm being so selfish when you've just lost Danny the way you have,' she said, hugging him.

'So did you,' he reminded her. His tears were flowing freely now and they laughed at each other for the spectacle they must be making of themselves.

'You really did love her, didn't you?' Louisa said.

'Yes,' he smiled. 'I really did. 'She was . . .' He laughed and summing up all the things he wanted to say about her he said, 'She was unique.'

Louisa nodded. 'Yes, she was. I wish we could go to her funeral, but unless some miracle happens and the police give us back our passports . . .'

'Why don't we sit for a while?' Erik said, pulling her down onto the sand. 'It's so peaceful here with so few people around.'

They sat for some time, hugging their knees and watching the tide froth and lap around their feet.

'I don't think I'll ever be able to look at the sea again without thinking of Jake,' Louisa said sadly. She let several minutes tick by then said, 'Have you heard from him at all, Erik? I know I asked you not to tell me if you did, but I want to know now.'

'Yes, I've spoken to him,' Erik answered. 'He's getting his statement flown over to say you were with him the morning Danny died.'

Louisa swallowed hard. 'How is he?' she said. 'Has he found Martina yet?'

'Not yet. It takes time to do this sort of deal and the people who are holding her will want to make sure that everything is going according to their plans before they hand her over.'

'Poor Jake, it must be terrible for him, being so close and yet still not being able to see her. Do you think he's afraid to see her? I know I would be if I were him.'

'Yes, he's afraid. He's afraid of what Consuela will do if she discovers that Martina's kidnappers are negotiating her release. He's afraid of how Martina might have been treated, of what damage it might have done to her mind and to his little girl's. It'll be a long time before they'll be able to put the trauma of all this behind them.'

'Yes, it will,' Louisa whispered, feeling herself recoil from any thought of time passing when all she wanted was to go back.

'Did you ever find out who the man was at Consuela's pretending to be his father?' she said after a moment.

'No,' Erik sighed. 'I didn't speak to Danny at all after that. I tried, but she was never there.'

'Well, whoever he was he had Danny pretty convinced he was Jake's father. What's Jake's father like? Have you ever met him?'

Erik smiled. 'He's like Jake, but older.'

'What happened to his mother?'

'She died, about a year ago now.'

'Oh no,' she groaned, weighed down by sadness for him. 'What a terrible time in his life this has been.'

'I know, it's a wonder he's still sane.'

Watching her feet sink deeper and deeper into the sand Louisa felt the same burying sensation of pain in her heart. Then she raised her eyes to gaze out across the shimmering orange sea to where the rising sun was emerging from the horizon, bringing with it another day. 'I wonder what he's doing now,' she said softly.

The room was totally silent as it had been for the past hour. Tendrils of cigarette smoke languished in the faintly perfumed air. Every so often a match flared as someone lit up and once or twice one of them got up, stretched, and went to use the bathroom. Outside the ground floor suite the hustle and bustle of hotel life went on regardless, waiters wheeling trolleys through the exotic, landscaped gardens, the click of high heels on the winding concrete pathways, an incessant stream of Spanish coming from the suite next door. The light inside the room was growing dim, casting long shadows through the arches that separated the sitting area from the bedroom.

All four men were unshaven, all four had dark rings of exhaustion around their eyes. Jake was the only American, the others, Fernando, his assistant Javier, and Pedro were Mexican. The index finger of Pedro's right hand was still bandaged, there were faint marks on his decrepit, old man's face from the beating he had taken.

Pedro's bloodshot eyes moved warily towards the phones on the glass-topped table. They were like the *Americano*, silent, impenetrable, unpredictable. Throughout that long day only one had been used, the other two waited, as they were waiting.

Pedro's eyes moved on, coming to rest on the sweeping curve of the window. The shadows of night were claiming Guadalajara. His brother should be there by now. His brother should pick up the phone any second.

Javier snored and Pedro's eyes darted to his drooping figure in the corner. Using his foot Fernando flicked Javier's ankle from his knee, jerking him forward and waking him. Javier ran a hand over the stubble on his chin.

Pedro knew that the *Americano*'s eyes were watching him from beneath their lowered lids. He didn't like the *Americano*'s eyes, they seemed to bore right into his soul. Pedro wanted to be out of here. He wanted the money and then he wanted out of here. His brother should be there by now.

Another hour passed. Javier munched a pack of Doritos, Fernando ordered room service. When the food came the *Americano* didn't eat. Pedro ate, but the shrimps dried on his tongue under the *Americano*'s gaze.

Javier flicked through the TV channels, then threw the remote on the bed and tore open the door to swear in Spanish at the noisy, key-jangling maids.

Suddenly a telephone exploded into life. Everyone jarred. It was the wrong phone and everyone relaxed. The *Americano* got up from the bed.

As he spoke Jake's eyes relinquished their hold on Pedro.

'Yes, it's me,' Jake said, hearing Erik's voice.

'Any news?' Erik asked.

'No. How are things your end?'

'Hard to tell. Something's got to break soon though.'

'Are you in the clear?'

'Let's put it this way, they haven't arrested me yet.'

Jake frowned. He was in no mood for humour. 'What's the latest on Morandi?'

'The charges still stand.'

Jake paused for a moment as he thought. 'Still nothing on Consuela?'

'Not that I know of.'

'Where's Louisa?'

'At Jean-Claude's.'

'OK. You know what to do if . . .'

'I know what to do,' Erik interrupted. 'Any message for her?'

Jake stared blindly at the dry logs in the hearth. 'No,' he

said. 'Just keep her away from Consuela. I'll call you in a couple of days.'

Putting the receiver down Jake picked up a can of beer and cracked it open. His eyes had returned to Pedro and Pedro's hand twitched with the desire to cross himself as he inwardly prayed that his brother was picking up the phone right now.

The storm would be sure to break tonight, Consuela was thinking, as she wiped a handkerchief around her neck and gazed out of her bedroom window at the swirling clouds. Please God, let it break, for this humidity was unbearable. She wondered what it was like in Mexico, if the heat was getting to Jake the same way, then sighing through clenched teeth she dropped her forehead against the cool pane of glass.

The call telling her he'd made it there had come two hours ago, but still she hadn't heard from the people holding Martina. But they would call, she told herself. As soon as they got her message they'd be in touch for she was prepared to match what Jake was offering and half as much again. They wouldn't be able to resist that and they knew she'd be true to her word, she'd never let them down yet. And Jake was an unknown quantity, they wouldn't know if they could trust him, so they'd be sure to want to continue to do business with her.

That's what Martina was to them, a business. It had kept them in tequila and tortillas, smart American suits, flashy European cars and luxurious haciendas for over three years now, they wouldn't risk giving that up. Please God, they wouldn't take that risk, for whatever else happened in this unholy mess, Martina must not be returned to Jake.

Seeing Marianne's white Golf coming up the drive Consuela took a fresh handkerchief from a drawer and wandered back to the bed to lie down. She was wearing a thin, cotton nightgown, much like a hospital gown, her face was colourless, her eyes red-rimmed and sore. Poor Frederico, he was so worried about her, was fussing around her like a mother hen, keeping the other boys at bay and seeing to the running of the house. He was so loyal and so capable, thank God he was there, for these had been difficult days, the most difficult since Martina's kidnap from the boat. Consuela wished to God now that she'd never let it be known that Martina was still alive. She'd only done it to torment Jake, but no matter how passionately or convincingly she'd denied it since he still hadn't given up the search.

She looked across to the door as Marianne came in.

'How are you?' Marianne asked, moving to the bed and sitting on the edge.

'I'm fine,' Consuela said weakly, wrapping Marianne's hand in hers. 'Where have you been?'

'Just for a drive. I needed to get out for a while.'

'Did you manage to speak to Louisa?'

Marianne shook her head. 'No. Erik is with her all the time. I can't get her alone.' Her eyes lost focus for a second as she lifted them to the satin draperies of the bedhead. 'I keep asking myself what they want with her now,' she said quietly.

'Maybe they don't want anything with her,' Consuela said. She turned her head on the pillow and stared out at the milling clouds. 'If only the police would let her go back to her own country she would be safe then. Why won't they, do you know?'

'Erik says it's because she was with Jake the morning Danny was killed and now that Jake's no longer here he can't bear witness to that.'

'But why should it matter where she was that morning?' Consuela said, confused.

'I don't know,' Marianne confessed. 'But apparently there was some kind of a fight between Danny and Louisa the night before and Louisa threatened Danny with a knife.'

'*Oh là là*,' Consuela murmured. 'So now Louisa has to account for all her movements before they will let her go?'

'I imagine that's the case,' Marianne said, lowering her gaze to their entwined fingers. 'Erik says Jake's statement is on its way, but we've only got Erik's word for all this and . . .' She got up, suddenly agitated, and walked across the room.

'What is it?' Consuela said gently.

'It's just . . . It's just that I can't make myself believe that

Erik would have done that to Danny,' Marianne answered in a pained and bewildered voice. 'He could never have got from the airport in time and besides, I just can't believe he's the sort of man who would kill someone simply because Jake told him to. It doesn't make sense, not when Erik's who he is, when he has an international reputation . . .'

'You've never heard the story of how they met, have you?' Consuela said wearily. She seemed to let her mind wander for a moment, then said. 'They were young offenders both of them way back in their teens, in New York. They met in some kind of correctional facility and they've been as close, or as the English say, as thick as thieves, ever since. I don't think there's much they wouldn't do for each other, they both have souls as black as a demon's and faces and charm to sway any girl's heart.'

Marianne dropped her head, letting her hair curtain her face. This was all so confusing, she didn't know who to believe any more, who to turn to for advice and she felt so caught in the middle that it was like standing at the centre of a street where it was only a matter of time before disaster struck.

'I just wish I could speak to Louisa alone,' she mumbled. 'The trouble is, now that she knows about you and me I don't think she'd trust me. There doesn't, as far as I can make out, appear to be even a fraction of doubt in her mind about Jake. She truly believes everything he's told her about Martina, she even believes that Martina is alive.'

Consuela's eyes closed for a moment, then summoning a smile she held a hand out towards Marianne. 'Come and sit down, *chérie*,' she said, patting the bed. 'Sit down here and listen to what I am going to tell you.'

By the time Consuela had finished Marianne had curled herself into a ball and was resting her head in Consuela's lap. Had she been looking into Consuela's eyes she might have felt a moment or two of unease, but no more than that. As it was, her only thought was for Louisa and how she could get Louisa away from them all.

'Louisa! For God's sake, what's the matter?' Sarah cried, as Louisa got out of her car looking so shaken she seemed almost on the point of collapse.

'Nothing,' Louisa mumbled. 'It was nothing . . .' Then throwing her arms around Sarah she clung to her as if terrified Sarah might leave her.

'What is it?' Sarah pleaded. 'What's happened? Where have you been?'

'I went to Antibes,' Louisa said shakily. 'I bought some things in the market there . . .'

'Yes,' Sarah said, holding her by the shoulders and encouraging her to go on.

'Then I was walking back down the hill, towards my car,' Louisa said haltingly, 'and I saw . . . Oh Sarah, I thought I saw Danny.'

Sarah's eyes rounded with horror, then pulling Louisa back into her arms she said, 'This has all been such a strain. It's a bloody nightmare, it's no wonder you're seeing things . . . Oh, poor Louisa. Poor, poor Louisa. Come on, come inside, I'll make you some tea.'

'Sarah,' Louisa said, stopping her. 'She saw me too. She saw me and . . . She waved, Sarah. She waved at me.'

Sarah's face creased with concern as her heart thudded with alarm. 'We'd better speak to Jean-Claude about getting you to a doctor,' she said gently. 'You must have something to help you sleep or you're going to make yourself ill.'

Louisa allowed herself to be led into the house and a few minutes later she, Sarah, Jean-Claude and Didier were sitting on the terrace drinking coffee. Louisa was feeling a bit stronger now, the shock was wearing off and she could almost raise a smile at the way she'd dropped her shopping in the middle of the street, allowing it to scatter and roll down the hill as she'd stood there staring into the café. Then she'd run, as fast as she could through the crowds, to her car.

'I feel such a fool now,' she said self-consciously. 'I mean, obviously it wasn't Danny. But it looked so much like her. And you know, the strange thing was, at first, when I first saw her,

I almost went running over to her. Then I remembered that she was dead and I felt this horrible panic come over me.'

'It's not unusual after a bereavement to think you are seeing the person you 'ave lost,' Jean-Claude remarked solemnly. 'But I think Sarah is right, we should get the doctor to give you something to 'elp you sleep.'

'Did you see her face?' Sarah asked.

Louisa shook her head. 'Not really. Whoever she was, she was sitting with some other people inside the café. But then, when she looked up and saw me and then waved . . . Well, that was when I dropped my shopping and ran. What an idiot,' she grimaced, shaking her head. 'Obviously the woman must have been waving to someone behind me, but I didn't think of that. All I thought was that I was seeing a ghost.'

They all smiled politely, then sat staring thoughtfully into their cups until a rumble of thunder growled through the swelling, darkening clouds, bringing their heads up.

'I wish this storm would break,' Sarah sighed. 'It's been hanging around like this for two days now.'

'It'll be a bad one when it comes,' Jean-Claude warned. 'There is very much electricity in the air.'

'Where's Erik?' Louisa asked.

'He popped over to Monaco to pick up some things from his apartment,' Sarah answered. 'He'll be back later. He told me he spoke to Jake again early this morning. They still haven't got to Martina.'

Louisa pressed her lips together and returned her eyes to the dregs in her cup. 'Did Jake say anything else, do you know?' she asked, knowing it was selfish to be thinking of herself when he was going through such a terrible ordeal, but she couldn't help it.

'I don't know,' Sarah answered. 'But I'm sure Erik will tell you if there's a message for you.'

'There won't be,' Louisa stated flatly. 'It's over now, he won't send messages because he knows that if he does it'll just keep my feelings alive.' She looked up and forcing herself to smile she said. 'What news is there on Morandi?'

'The same,' Sarah sighed. 'He's still sitting there terrified out of his mind that he's never going to get out and even more terrified of what's going to happen to his kids if he doesn't.'

Jean-Claude looked around the table and seeing so many glum faces he said, 'Who's for a game of scrabble?'

Everyone was, for it was one of the few things that could make them laugh right now, since Jean-Claude and Didier played in French and Sarah and Louisa played in English – and all four of them cheated like crazy. But the best thing about it was that it helped take their minds off the way the entire world seemed to be taking a pause, holding its breath, and waiting for the storm to break.

It was just after lunch when the telephone rang and Jean-Claude passed it to Sarah. 'It's Morandi,' he told her, returning to the terrace where at last Louisa was sleeping, albeit fitfully, in a reclining armchair.

Didier was down by the pool collecting the cushions from the garden furniture before it rained and as Sarah went inside Jean-Claude sat down at the table, returning to the reports his accountant had sent him and wondering if he could put off going into Cannes. Probably not, he thought, seeing that several of the documents needed signing urgently. A few minutes later he looked up as Erik pulled into the drive at the same instant as Sarah came out of the kitchen and stared at him with a beaming, yet incredulous smile.

'They're letting him go,' she declared. 'He just told me they're letting him go.'

'But that is wonderful,' Jean-Claude exclaimed.

'What is?' Erik said, walking up the steps to the terrace and dropping his keys on the table.

'They are releasing Morandi,' Jean-Claude answered.

Erik turned to Sarah, eyebrows raised in surprise. 'When did you hear?'

'Just. He called to ask me to go and pick him up.'

'Does that mean they know who killed Aphrodite?' Erik said.

'I don't know. All he said was that he is no longer a suspect and they are letting him go.'

'So what are you waiting for?' Erik laughed. 'Go get the man.'

But Sarah didn't move. She was looking at Louisa and wondering how the hell she was going to break the rest of the news to her. Morandi was being released, she was to go and pick him up, collecting her passport at the same time then the two of them were to be out of France by the end of the day. But how was she going to leave Louisa when Louisa was in such a bad way?

'It's OK,' Erik said, putting a comforting arm around her when she explained. 'I'll take care of Louisa. You just get Morandi out of here and back to those kids of his and think yourself lucky to be out of it all.'

Sarah nodded, but the terrible guilt and fear she felt at leaving Louisa was crushing. 'Will you come with me over to the villa to pack up my things?' she said, turning to Jean-Claude. She couldn't ask Erik because she couldn't put him through the pain of having to walk into that villa again.

'It's OK, I'll take you,' Erik said, turning to gaze across at the shuttered villa.

'But I don't understand why they're not letting me go too,' Louisa cried as she and Erik sped along the autoroute back towards Antibes. They'd spent the past hour at the police station in Nice waiting for someone to come and explain why her passport wasn't being returned and now Louisa's nerves were so on edge and her frustration was at such a pitch she wanted to scream.

'They will,' Erik assured her, 'just as soon as Jake's statement gets here.'

'But why is it taking so long?'

'Nothing in this country moves fast, except the drivers,' Erik answered, but it raised not a glimmer of a smile from either of them.

'I hate this bloody country,' Louisa said angrily. 'I hate it.

If they hadn't kept us waiting so damned long at that police station we'd have been at the airport in time to see Sarah off. Why the hell didn't she wake me up before she went to get him, is what I want to know?'

'We thought it best to let you sleep on for a while.' Erik answered. 'We assumed I'd be able to get you to the airport, hopefully in time for the same flight if your passport had been released. But she'll call you as soon as she gets to England, I'm sure.'

Louisa sat quietly then, staring out of the window and wishing she didn't feel so sick and so afraid. If only Jake were there, she knew she wouldn't feel half as bad, but it did her no good to think that way so she tried to push him from her mind and think about something else.

'I started to pack up some of your things when I was over at the villa with Sarah,' Erik said, glancing across at her. 'Do you think you're up to finishing it off, or would you rather leave it for a while?'

'No, I'll do it when we get back,' she answered. 'I want to be ready to get out of here just as soon as they let me. What are we going to do about Sarah's car? We can't just leave it at the airport.'

'We'll have to until she sends the keys down for us to collect it,' Erik answered. 'I imagine she'll kick herself when she looks in her bag and realizes she forgot to leave them.'

He stopped at the *péage* in Antibes, tossed some coins into the net and drove on through the barrier, turning up towards Valanjou. When they got there it was to find a note from Jean-Claude telling them that he and Didier had gone to Cannes.

'Are you sure you feel up to this?' Erik said as he and Louisa walked in through the gates of the villa opposite.

Louisa nodded and swallowed hard. Whatever she did she mustn't look at the pool, but to her dismay she found that just the innocuous stillness of the villa's creamy walls and white, slatted shutters was unsettling her. The thought of the hidden, darkened interior was even more daunting and she expected, at any minute, to find herself turning back.

As he inserted the key in the lock Erik gave her hand a quick squeeze. 'Come on,' he smiled, 'it'll all be over with before you know it.'

Louisa stepped in through the door and as Erik flicked on the lights she felt her heart start to pound. She hadn't really known what she'd expected to find inside, but that everything was so clean and neat and exactly the way it had always been was somehow as unnerving as it seemed irreverent. She didn't know where exactly Danny had been stabbed before being thrown into the pool, but the trail of blood from the terrace had told her that something had happened inside the house. It was hard to make herself accept that having borne witness to such a terrible act the house could remain so unchanged and as her eyes swept through the arches, over the large clumpy furniture, the glass tables and ornate chests she felt a shiver of unease run down her spine. It was as though the house had somehow soaked the events into its ambience, making them invisible now, invisible, but still there, heavy, ominous, grisly in the silent, stuffy air.

'I don't know if I can go any further,' she said, turning back to Erik as he closed the door.

'OK,' he said, putting his arms around her. 'Just give yourself a minute, then if you still feel the same way we'll go back.'

She stood quietly in his arms for a moment, then slowly started to shake her head. 'I'm sorry,' she said, steeling herself bravely. 'I'm being feeble, come on, let's get it done,' and taking his hand she led him past the table that no longer bore any trace of Danny's blood, and up the small staircase to what had just a week ago been her room.

'I made a start on your study,' Erik said when they reached the door. 'Shall I go on with that?'

Louisa nodded and smiled. 'Thanks.' Then watching him disappear into the study she turned and taking a deep breath pushed open her bedroom door and turned on the light.

Everything was exactly as she'd left it.

Walking over to the bed she hauled out her suitcase from

underneath then laid it open across the lace duvet cover. Overhead the thunder continued to grumble.

Louisa stood where she was, looking at the cupboards. She was afraid to open them, she realized, afraid of what she might find inside. Then telling herself to stop being ridiculous she marched over to them and pulled them open. There were her clothes hanging just as she'd left them, swaying slightly in the draught caused by the doors opening.

Humming tunelessly to fill the silence she started to take them from the hangers, folding them and carrying them over to the bed.

'Do you want to put these in your case?' Erik said, startling her as he came into the room. He was holding up the power cables for her portable computer.

'Oh yes, yes please,' she said taking them from him.

'Why don't you open the shutters and let some air in here while you pack?' he suggested.

Louisa looked at him, not knowing how to tell him that she didn't want to see the pool.

'Here, I'll do it for you,' he said, walking to the window, pulling it open then throwing out the shutters.

'Thanks,' she said breathlessly.

Fifteen minutes later she was all packed and the few possessions she'd had in the study were piled on the landing between the two rooms.

'Here, let me take that,' Erik said as she snapped her suitcase closed, and heaving it from the bed he laughed. 'You women, I sometimes wonder how you'd manage if you didn't have us guys to do the lifting for you. Are you ready?'

'Yes,' she nodded, turning off the light as she followed him from the room.

They were halfway down the stairs when Erik suddenly remembered they'd left the shutters open. He was so laden down with her suitcase and computer and a holdall that Louisa had no choice but to say she would go back to close them.

When she got to the window she closed her eyes, reached out for the shutters and pulled them together. Then fastening the catch on the window she turned back and almost leapt from her skin when she saw Erik standing at the door.

'Sorry,' he said. 'I didn't mean to startle you. Anything else to come?'

'No,' she answered, and casting one last look around she followed him back down the stairs.

'There, that wasn't so bad was it?' he said when they got outside.

'No,' she smiled, letting her breath go slowly and not adding that never again in her life would she go into a house where someone had been murdered.

'I see,' Consuela was saying into the phone. 'And where is he now?'

As she listened to the reply her eyes flickered towards the man who was watching her. '*En route* to Posada Barrancas,' she repeated. 'What time will he get there? Yes, yes, I understand. When he arrives give him a message from me. Tell him that if he goes anywhere near my daughter he will be shot. There will be no questions asked, he will simply be shot dead.' Again she listened. 'Yes, I have made the arrangements. The money will be there for you by tomorrow. I've never let you down before. Yes, I know it's a lot of money, but this is my daughter and my granddaughter we're discussing. Call me back when he gets to Posada Barrancas. And remember to give him my message.'

As she replaced the receiver Marianne came into the room. Consuela walked over to her and putting her hands on Marianne's shoulders she said in a tone so grave that Marianne's skin prickled, 'You must go for Louisa, Marianne. You must go for her now. This has all become very serious and there isn't much time. I have just heard, ten minutes ago, that Morandi and Sarah have not arrived in England.'

Marianne's face drained.

'*Please*, go for Louisa,' Consuela said urgently.

'But how am I going to make her come?' Marianne said helplessly.

Consuela glanced back over her shoulder to the man standing

behind her. 'David will go with you,' she said as he nodded. 'He will persuade Louisa. Now please, go and get her. Don't bring her here, it will only frighten her. Take her somewhere where she will feel safe. But don't lose any time, Marianne. Jake has got very close to Martina now and if he should get to her then it won't only be Martina's life that is in jeopardy, Louisa's will be too.'

'But why?' Marianne cried. 'I don't understand. Please explain why.'

'There isn't time now,' Consuela answered. 'David will go with you, he will explain on the way.'

Marianne turned to him, then quickly snatching up her keys she said, 'No, I'll go alone.'

25

The rusty railway carriage creaked and groaned on the tracks, keeling and rocking as it made its laborious ascent into the rugged, pine-covered mountains of the Sierra Madre. The sun was blistering the dry, soulless landscape, lizards and snakes slithered between grey, slate rocks seeking shade; in the deep crevices of the valleys river beds lay exposed and parched.

Jake's eyes were closed. He wasn't sleeping, but hoped he soon would. He and Fernando had boarded the train four hours ago, there were four more to go before they reached their destination. Inside he was calm, his iron self-control had wrestled with his anger and suppressed it. That they were completely in the hands of the negotiators who were leading them blindly into God only knew what was getting to Fernando, but not to Jake. There was nothing to be gained from dwelling on the fact that had they known their destination before boarding the train they could have chartered a plane to take them into the mountains. The negotiators – the kidnappers – hadn't seen fit to provide them with that information until just over an hour ago when a steward had passed Fernando a note telling them to alight at Posada Barrancas where their next contact would be waiting for them. To the kidnappers this was a game, leading them from Guadalajara to Chihuahua and then on this interminable rail journey to Posada Barrancas, the highest and one of the remotest points of the great craggy peaks of the Copper Canyon. And since they had no choice but to play the game, Jake, whose patience had long ago learned to stand the test of the much more formidable and unpredictable opponents of wind and tide, saw no point in getting himself worked up about something over which he had no control. What he needed now was sleep.

The air-conditioning coughed and sighed, packed up, then a few minutes later groaned back to life. Fernando was watching Jake, he was also watching the Mexican further down the carriage, slumbering beneath his sombrero. A few minutes ago, at La Junta station, the Mexican had slipped out of the train to use the telephone. The Mexican's name was Alvarez – he was one of Fernando's men. Alvarez had contacted Javier to inform him of their destination and expected time of arrival. Javier, Fernando's deputy, had remained in Guadalajara keeping Pedro hostage until such time as he received word of what he was to do with the old man.

Jake shifted in his seat and stretched his long legs into the aisle. After a minute he got up and went to another torn and dusty seat the other side of the carriage. He hadn't slept in thirty-six hours. Again he closed his eyes.

For an hour or so as he drifted somewhere between sleep and consciousness he was vaguely aware of the long, deafening blasts of the train whistle and of others moving about the carriage. Then quite suddenly his eyes flew open. Louisa. He was thinking about Louisa, recalling the softness of her skin, the beauty of her eyes, the exquisite sensation of her legs circling him as he pushed deep inside her. He was aroused by the memory of her, hungry for more, needful of the soothing sound of her laughter, the uncomplicated joy of her presence.

Jesus Christ, he muttered to himself as a spark of anger erupted through his calm. She had no place here. She was in the past. He would never see her again and in his wakefulness he bitterly resented her intrusion at a time when his mind should be focused on Martina.

At last, just after four in the afternoon, Jake and Fernando stepped off the train at Posada Barrancas. A sweaty clutch of back-packing tourists bustled past them, sinking thankfully into the air-conditioned interior of the train. As the makeshift station cleared and Jake moved across the decayed wooden planks that served as a platform, he could feel himself becoming lightheaded. The air was so thin, the sun was blazing. Fernando steadied himself by putting a hand on a rail and waited for his dizziness to pass.

Two dirt roads meandered off into the hills in opposite directions and as the train lumbered on down the track the only other sign of life was a Tarahumara Indian selling her woven baskets and copper bangles which were set out on a woven cloth beside the station. Fernando approached her, but before he spoke Jake touched his arm and nodded towards a dust cloud in the distance. A vehicle was coming towards them. Then appearing from out of the bushes behind them a flat-faced Indian dressed in filthy, unbuttoned and rope-tied western clothes and baring rotten teeth in a grimace against the sunlight loped past Alvarez who was sprawled on a single bench, seemingly waiting for the next train.

The Indian came to stand beside Fernando. Jake's face was inscrutable as he pulled back into the meagre shade offered by the deteriorating overhead timbers and listened to the Indian speaking to Fernando in a dialect he didn't understand.

Fernando's mouth started to curve in a malicious smile, then dragging his eyes from the Indian he turned to Jake and interpreted. 'He has brought a message from your mother-in-law. She wants you to know that if you go anywhere near her daughter you will be shot.'

Jake pulled his eyebrows together and as he turned his eyes on the Indian the Indian took a step back, shaking his head and raising a hand as if to remind them he was only the messenger. Then with several furtive and frightened backward glances at Jake he scurried around the station wagon that had now halted beside them and disappeared into the rocks. Fernando glanced over his shoulder and Alvarez promptly started after the Indian.

The driver of the station wagon, a leathery faced Mexican with heavy eyes and wiry grey hair, stood at the side of his vehicle watching Alvarez scramble up over the rocks, then scratching his head he turned and introduced himself as the chauffeur for the lodge where rooms had been reserved for them.

When they reached the lodge, an incongruous grey stone chateau-like building with an orange tiled roof and a haphazard array of cabins that sprawled upwards through the trees towards the rim of the canyon, Fernando collected the key to the furthest cabin while Jake inspected the horses that were tethered to a rotten fence outside. In front of him the hillside sloped gently away from the lodge to the dozen or so shacks and a church at the heart of the valley. Beyond the mountains rose dramatically towards the languid blue sky. There was no one in sight, no sound of life, human or otherwise.

Their cabin, a mere speck on the rim of one of nature's most rugged and cavernous gorges, was basic and unwelcoming. It was made of stone and wood and had two windows, one overlooking the canyon, the other overlooking the wide sweep of the valley. As they walked in Fernando threw his gun on the nearest of the two beds and sat down heavily, running his hands down the back of his neck to ease the tension and tiredness. Jake walked to the window between the beds, pulled aside the bright flowered curtain and gazed out. His strong face was as implacable as it had been throughout the journey, the strain showed only in the deepening lines around his eyes. Again he was thinking of Louisa, unable to dispel the need to hold her and reflecting with fear on how the timing of what happened here, in this remote and desolate part of the world some ten thousand or more miles from where she was, was going to affect her.

'You do realize, my friend,' Fernando said, 'that the message from Consuela was an admission that your wife is alive.'

'Yes,' Jake said shortly, watching a vulture rise majestically from the depths of the canyon.

Fernando sighed. 'But we knew that anyway.'

Letting the curtain fall Jake picked a towel up from the bed and nodded towards the phone. 'See if that works,' he said. 'If it does get onto Javier in Guadalajara and tell him to contact

Erik and let him know where we are. I'm going to take a shower.'

The shower did nothing to soothe the increasing turmoil inside him. The dread of what the next few days, maybe hours, would bring was sliding as coldly through his veins as the icy water was sliding over his skin. Every time he thought of Martina now he saw Louisa. It was Louisa's voice he was hearing, Louisa's eyes that were watching him. And the resentment he felt towards her for standing between him and his wife at such a time was made all the more bitter by the knowledge that he had only himself to blame. He should never have allowed himself to become involved with her, but this was no time to be dealing with his conscience, no time for regrets. Once he saw Martina he knew all other thoughts would be erased from his mind. Getting to her was all that mattered now.

'Jake! Is that you?' Erik shouted over the crackling line an hour later. 'Where the hell are you?'

'You won't have heard of it,' Jake answered curtly. He wanted this line free. He didn't want to handle anything more than what was happening right there. 'What is it?' he snapped.

He listened, without interruption, to what Erik was telling him and as each second passed so the strain in his face deepened.

'OK,' he said finally. 'You know what to do. You know where to take her. Do it *now*, Erik,' and he slammed the phone down.

Fernando was looking at him. 'What was that?' he said.

'It doesn't matter,' Jake answered. 'Nothing that need concern us right now.'

They turned as a figure moved past the window, both snatching up their guns. The door opened. Alvarez came in and they relaxed.

'Just a local,' Alvarez told them, referring to the Indian he had followed. 'He wasn't armed. My guess is someone slung him a few more pesos than he's used to and told him to deliver the message. There's no knowing if they'll come back for an answer . . .'

'They won't,' Jake said.

They settled down to continue the wait. Fernando and Alvarez played poker by the torpid light of a brass lamp while Jake stared absently at the vast, fiery fingers of the setting sun that stretched out of the horizon across the fading sky.

At last the phone rang. Jake turned as Fernando picked it up. He listened for a moment then handed it to Jake. 'It's him,' he said, and as Jake took the receiver there was a discernible change in the air as Alvarez cleared the table of cards while Fernando picked up his gun and started to load it.

'Go outside.' The voice at the other end of the line was heavily accented with Spanish.

Jake's eyes moved to the door. Fernando and Alvarez were watching him.

'She is outside waiting for you,' the voice told him.

'How do I know this isn't a trap?' Jake said.

'You don't,' and the line went dead.

Jake replaced the receiver. He turned to Fernando then pulling a gun from his waistband started slowly towards the door. Reading the situation Fernando moved to the window. Jake waited as Fernando peered round the curtain, scanning the dusk shrouded valley. Alvarez moved in behind Jake. Fernando shook his head. No sign of life.

Keeping his gun raised Jake eased the door open. Alvarez slipped behind it, peering through the crack, while Jake flattened himself against the wall the other side. Again they waited, and still nothing happened. Jake stepped into the doorway. If they were going to shoot him he was making himself a perfect target. But he'd been that any number of times by now. The money had changed hands, there was a chance they were keeping their side of the bargain.

The temperature was falling fast. A swift breeze was moving through the Apache pines, loose rubble drifted over the barren scrubland of the hillside. He felt a hundred eyes on him and saw no one. Then in the semi-distance someone came out of the shadows into the dwindling light. It was a woman. Her black hair was lifting in the breeze. Her tall, erect figure was being pulled to one side, something was holding her right arm. Then a child, holding her hand, tottered out from behind her and Jake's pounding heart froze.

'Martina?' he whispered, realizing that until this moment he had never truly allowed himself to believe he would ever see her again.

She couldn't have heard him, but as though she had she turned in his direction. Still he couldn't see her face, but he knew beyond doubt now that he was looking at his wife. The danger surrounding them suddenly vanished. All he knew was the joy, the incredulity, the unbearable swell of love and relief and urgency coursing through him.

'Martina,' he said again, his voice choked with emotion.

Her head tilted curiously to one side as she saw him start towards her. Then fear locked her limbs, and for an instant she looked about to run.

'Martina,' he called.

'Jake?' her voice was barely audible.

He started to run.

'Jake!' she cried. 'Oh God, Jake!' and she was running to him, leaving the child behind her. Her long legs carried her towards him, her hair fanned out behind her, her arms were reaching for him. He could see the beauty of her eyes, the redness of her mouth, the brilliance of her smile. She was alive! So beautifully, so radiantly alive! Her mouth opened in a cry of pure joy. 'Jake!' she called again, laughing and crying.

'*Jake, no*!' Fernando yelled, but his words were drowned by the blast of gun fire.

Three bullets hit Martina's chest. Her arms flew out, her head jerked back, her knees buckled.

Fernando raced out the door, Alvarez was already firing.

Martina's face was frozen in shock.

Jake caught her, clasping her to him. 'Martina!' he cried, going down with her. 'Martina! No!'

'Jake, is it really you?' she whispered, touching his face.

'Yes, it's me,' he choked. He pulled her to him, burying her face in his chest, feeling her warmth, touching her hair.

'Jake. I knew . . . I knew you'd come . . .' she said breathlessly.

'Yes, my love. Yes, yes, yes,' he said, kissing her face, stroking her hair and holding her. 'Martina,' he sobbed. 'My love . . .'

Fernando ran forward, spinning and stumbling, waiting for the bullet that would bring him down. But all had gone silent now. Only the distant echo of the final shot could be heard echoing through the bowels of the canyon. Something moved further down the hill. Fernando spun round, throwing himself to his knees ready to fire. A small figure stumbled into the dim light. Fernando's heart was seized with horror as the child tottered towards Jake and Martina.

Fernando threw himself towards the child.

Terrified, she looked up.

Fernando reached her before she got to her parents and swept her into his arms. She was sobbing and straining to get to her mother. Fernando held her close, turning her face to his shoulder, unaware of the tears running down his own cheeks as he looked down at Jake and Martina.

'Jake,' he said, his voice thick with anguish. 'Jake, my friend.'

There was no response. Jake's eyes were staring sightlessly ahead, out to the great, swirling mass of the sky. In his arms Martina lay quietly, her fingers were touching his face, her blood was smeared on his chest. His thumb moved gently over her cheek.

Behind them the roar of helicopters was swooping over the rim of the canyon. Whether they had come to spirit away the killers or whether it was the police Fernando had no way of knowing. He went to kneel beside Jake, still holding the child. 'Jake,' he whispered. 'Jake, can you hear me?'

Jake lowered his eyes. The child reached out for her mother and Fernando let her go. Seeing her Jake's eyes closed tightly. Then pulling her into his embrace he held them both, burying his face in their fine, black hair. 'I'm sorry,' he whispered. 'Oh God, Martina, I'm sorry.'

Louisa spun round, unsure where the voice had come from, but recognizing it instantly as Marianne's.

'I'm over here,' Marianne called in a whisper.

Louisa glanced back over her shoulder to see if Jean-Claude was in sight. He wasn't, neither was Didier.

'Why are you hiding?' Louisa said, coming out into the lane and seeing Marianne crouched behind the bushes.

'Louisa, you have to come with me,' Marianne said urgently. 'Sarah hasn't turned up in London and no one knows where she is.'

Louisa's eyes rounded with horror. 'What do you mean, she's not in London?' she cried.

'She didn't arrive. I don't know if she's even left France. Louisa, please, you have to come with me. I swear I'm not taking you to Consuela, but I just don't think it's safe for you here either. My car's at the bottom of the lane, I'll explain what I can as we go. Come on, *please*, before Erik gets back,' and grabbing Louisa's arm she ran with her down the hill.

The moment the press caught sight of Louisa they came surging towards her in one horrifying mass. The police leapt to attention, forcing them back as Marianne pushed Louisa into her car and ran around the other side. They were gone so fast that no one had a chance to follow and as they sped out of Valanjou, heading towards the autoroute, Louisa listened as though in some kind of stupor as Marianne told her about Danny and how Consuela had persuaded her to stage her own murder and make it look as though Jake had done it. As it turned out Jake had had the perfect alibi, but Erik hadn't. So had Erik done it, or had providence just played into Consuela's hands in making the timing such that Erik could have done it? Marianne had no way of knowing, all she did know was that she couldn't bring herself to believe that Erik was a murderer.

'And neither,' she went on, 'can I make myself believe that Jake means you any harm. He's never really spoken to me about you, but it was plain enough for all of us to see the way he felt about you. It was mainly that that made me start looking at him differently. I used to hate him, when I was first working for him I despised him for what he was doing to Consuela, but then things started happening, I started to hear things that just didn't add up any more. Like if Jake gets to Martina he'll give Erik the order to kill you.'

Louisa stared at her dumbfounded, feeling her mind ebbing away from reality and still dazed by the speed at which Marianne had taken her from Jean-Claude's.

'Consuela spun me some story of how Jake and Erik made some kind of a pact when they were young to abuse and manipulate women as a means of sport, but I've never seen anything like that in either of them and believe me I've searched for it. And Erik's known all over the world, if he was doing that sort of thing he'd have been found out a long time ago. But Consuela had Danny convinced of it, I'm pretty sure of that, at least where Jake was concerned.'

'So are you saying you think Consuela might have killed Danny?' Louisa said, feeling horribly disconnected from what she was saying.

'I don't know what I'm saying,' Marianne answered. 'But obviously someone killed her and that same someone very probably killed Aphrodite too. And what's frightening me now is that you might be next.'

Louisa's face paled as a blade of fear sank deep into her heart. 'But why? Why would anyone want to kill me, I haven't done anything . . .'

'Neither did Aphrodite or Danny,' Marianne interrupted. 'Or not that I know of. But they both knew what was going on at Consuela's and so do you.'

'So do you,' Louisa pointed out.

'But I believe Consuela. At least she thinks I believe her and for now that's what's important. And I've seen the way all this has shaken her up, she looks terrified out of her mind. She's spent the last two days making frantic calls to Mexico trying to outbid Jake for Martina's life and quite frankly I just don't know who to trust any more. What I do know though, is that things are coming to a head. For all I know they already have, which is why you'll be safer where no one can get to you. I'm taking you to Jake's place for now, but you won't be able to stay long because Erik at least will be sure to know about it.'

Louisa had desperately wanted to protest Erik's innocence, but the fact that Sarah hadn't turned up in London dried the words on her lips. She felt sick with fear and with an unbearable mistrust of Erik who might just have purposefully manipulated things to make it look as if it was all just bad luck and the lack of French urgency that had stopped her seeing Sarah before she'd left.

The rain started as they arrived at Jake's house. Louisa ran inside, grabbed the phone and dialled Sarah's number in London. It rang and rang, but there was no reply. As she turned to Marianne she could feel herself starting to shake, but Marianne appeared even more distraught and kept peering from the window to check they hadn't been followed. In the end, when she was sure they hadn't she told Louisa she was going to get food.

'Keep the doors locked,' she warned. 'And find yourself some candles because if this storm gets any worse we'll be sure to lose power.'

The rain was coming down in torrents as Erik's Jaguar came speeding up the lane to Jean-Claude's and skidded to a halt.

Jean-Claude tore open the front door as Erik dashed up over the steps. One look at Jean-Claude's face was enough to turn Erik's blood to ice.

'What is it?' he demanded, looking wildly from Jean-Claude to Didier. 'Jesus Christ!' he cried reading their expressions. 'She's not here is she?

Jean-Claude shook his head.

'I don't believe it!' Erik yelled. 'I told you I was coming for her. I told you not to let her out of your sight . . .'

'She'd already disappeared when you called,' Jean-Claude answered. 'I tried to tell you, but you rang off before . . .'

'Jean-Claude, don't you realize what's going on here?' Erik

shouted irrationally, for no, they didn't know, at least not yet. 'If Consuela gets anywhere near Louisa there's no knowing what'll happen to her,' he went on, swinging round as the telephone started to ring.

Jean-Claude picked it up as Erik started to pace, grinding the heel of his hand into his head. He'd just heard what had happened in Mexico and if he'd been in any doubt before, which he hadn't, he now knew exactly what they were dealing with in Consuela. That any woman could pay for her own daughter to be shot and in such a way was beyond human understanding. And now, if she had Louisa, if she knew the way Jake felt about Louisa then . . . Jesus Christ, he didn't even want to think about it.

'It's Marianne,' Jean-Claude said holding out the receiver. 'She says Louisa's with her. She wants to speak to you.'

Erik snatched it up. 'Marianne,' he barked. 'What the hell's going on? Let me speak to Louisa.'

'She's safe,' Marianne answered. 'I've taken her somewhere where neither you nor Consuela will find her.'

Erik's relief was fleeting. 'What the hell did you do that for?' he raged. 'She was safe here, for Christ's sake . . .'

'Was she?' Marianne's voice was shredded with anguish. 'I don't know who to believe any more, Erik. All I know is that Louisa shouldn't be with either of you, not until . . .'

'Marianne, listen to me . . .'

'No, Erik. You listen to me. You tell me why Sarah and Morandi haven't turned up in London. You tell me what's happened to them. You and Morandi were the last ones to see Sarah, so where is she now?'

'What the hell are you talking about?' Erik cried. 'Sarah's in London.'

'Then why isn't she answering her phone?'

'Christ knows! Look Marianne, you've got to tell me where Louisa is . . .'

'I told you, she's safe and once I know who's telling the truth I'll bring her back.'

'Marianne! *Marianne!*,' he shouted, but the line had gone

dead. He slammed the receiver down and rounded on Jean-Claude. 'Go through Louisa's things and see if you can find a number for Sarah,' he said, starting to dial again. 'I'll try Morandi.'

As he waited for the connection he quickly related what Marianne had said, then a few minutes later, having spoken to Morandi, he turned to Jean-Claude with a terrible foreboding in his eyes.

Jean-Claude's face visibly paled. 'What is it?' he said. 'Sarah's all right, isn't she?'

Erik nodded then snatching up his keys he started for the door.

'Where are you going?' Jean-Claude cried, running out into the rain after him.

'I've got to get out of here before the police arrive,' Erik shouted back.

'What? Erik! What's happening?' Jean-Claude shouted.

'There's not time now,' Erik answered, starting up his car. 'I'll call you later, but start saying your prayers Jean-Claude, because if what Morandi just told me is true then all I can say is God help us all.'

26

Louisa was pacing the room, wringing her hands and trying desperately to keep herself calm. Almost two hours had passed since Marianne had said she was going for food and there was still no sign of her. The shadows in the room were lengthening, the woods outside were darkening and the storm had already disconnected the power and phone lines.

Her wide, luminous eyes moved about the candlelit room, to the darkness of the gallery above, inching back down the wooden staircase to the heavy, antique bureaux and chests. They were trembling under the might of the storm. She tried to comfort herself with the assurance that Marianne would be back any minute, but not for the first time her heart jolted with the fear that she had walked into some kind of trap.

She forced herself to think of Jake and of how certain she had been of his feelings, but the crashing thunder and howling wind cut through her thoughts making him seem so remote, so detached from his home and her life. What had happened between them suddenly felt as distorted and unreal as the shadows looming large and menacing in the candlelight. She stared down at the sofa where he had sat the morning before he'd left, struggling desperately with himself not to tell her how he felt. She turned and gazed into the fireplace, followed the huge funnel of the chimney-breast up to the ceiling then dropped her eyes to the door of his bedroom. She started as a giant bolt of thunder crashed overhead. She was still looking at the door. Could she bear to go in there now and look at the bed where they had shared such passion and such love? Did she really want to torment herself by gazing down at the emptiness of it now, the impervious shell that had contained them and remained unmoved, unchanged by it. The memory of the villa and how it had seemed so indifferent to what it had seen was still raw in her mind, but this wasn't the same. This wasn't tragedy this was joy, no murder had been committed here, only acts of love.

As she walked slowly, painfully, towards the door the candle shook in her hand. The tempest was reaching its peak. Daggered flashes of lightning were forking through the trees and the thunder, sharp and angry, rumbled and crashed through the heavens. But still she moved towards the door, going to it as though being pulled by some unknown force. She rested her hand on the door handle. Her breathing was ragged, her heart unsteady, but when she tried to connect with her feelings, they were strangely elusive. She felt oddly lightheaded, caught somewhere between memory and reality, unable to touch either.

The door creaked as she pushed it open. She took a step into the darkness then lifted the candle. At that instant a flash of lightning lit up the room and as she looked down at the bed her heart turned over. It was just as they'd left it, unmade, still rumpled from their lovemaking. It could have happened just an hour ago and as she felt the need for him rush through her she put a hand to her mouth and whispered his name out loud. She stood there for a long time, then putting the candle on a table she went to lie down. As she buried her face in the sheets and drew her knees up to her chest she could smell him so strongly that he might have been there with her. Her heart closed around the emotion, locking it deep inside her as she felt his breath on her face, his hands on her skin, his body joining with hers. And as the need for him grew so the might of the storm seemed to recede. She knew now that what he had felt for her had been as real and as powerful as all she'd felt for him, she knew too that she shouldn't be here, that as confused as Marianne had been she should never have allowed her to take her from Jean-Claude's.

Closing her eyes she drew the pillow tighter to her face. She knew she was afraid, that she was pushing the fear deep inside her to stop herself panicking, but as the minutes ticked by and the rain pounded the windows it was becoming harder and harder to keep her fear at bay. The suspicion that something terrible had happened to Marianne was stalking her, but she was refusing to let her imagination accept it.

After a while she got up and looked anxiously towards the window. To her relief she saw a bright, clear moon emerging over the lake. The wind had blown the clouds away, the storm would be over soon.

She went to sit on the brick dais of the fireplace and clasping her hands tightly together prayed desperately for Marianne's return. The furniture creaked and cracked the way old furniture did and each sudden noise was stiffening her nerves and making her more afraid than ever. Then suddenly her head came up as her blood turned to ice. Someone was calling her name.

'Lou-is-a!'

She shrank back into the cavity of the chimney, her heart pounding wildly, her limbs weak with terror.

'Lou-is-a!'

'Oh my God!' she murmured, pressing her knuckles to her mouth. But it was Marianne. It had to be Marianne. Probably her car had gone off the road and she was calling for help. She had to go out there, she had to make sure, but dear God, what if she was wrong? What if someone was waiting out there for her?

But that was nonsense, she tried to tell herself. If someone wanted to get her she was trapped inside the house . . .

'Lou-is-a!'

As the sound of her own name coasted a trail of terror through her Louisa pulled herself up and moved slowly, cautiously to the window. At first all she could see was her own reflection inching stealthily, shakily towards it. Then, as she looked through the shadowy ghost of herself down through the trees to the lake, her whole body stood still with paralysing terror. There was somebody on the lake. Somebody, no more than a dark profile against the rippling current of moonlight, was sitting in a boat and waving to her. Then suddenly it was as though her heart was being wrenched from its roots as she realized who it was.

'Oh no,' she muttered, backing away from the window. 'No, no, no, no. Oh, dear God, help me. She's dead, I know she is . . .'

She spun round and threw herself towards the phone. Grabbing it she started to dial, her fingers moving frantically as if her panic could inject it with life. 'Hello!' she cried, rattling the connectors. 'Hello! Hello! Please somebody. Please!'

The only reply was the dying, whining wind and the thundering beat of her heart.

'Please! Please!' she begged hysterically, banging the phone with her fingers and randomly pressing the buttons. 'Oh Erik! Erik! You must know about this house. You *must*.'

Suddenly she swung round and stared wildly at the door as she heard a car crunching the gravel outside. Erik! It had to be Erik! Or Marianne!

She sprang to her feet, started towards the door, then abruptly drew back as her mind began to whirl with crazy, irrational thoughts. What if it wasn't them? What if it was Danny? Danny who was dead. What if it was the person who had killed Danny? Horrible, deranged visions of her own murder were flashing inside her head. She couldn't think, she couldn't move, all she could see was her blood on the walls, her broken body lying battered and torn on the floor, her eyes staring sightlessly up at the roof . . .

A car door slammed and as footsteps approached the house she backed up against the sofa, grabbing it to stop herself falling. Her eyes, wide and petrified, were riveted to the door. The footsteps stopped. The handle turned, was rattled, then turned again.

'Louisa! Louisa!' Marianne called.

Relief buckled Louisa's knees and she staggered to the door. 'Marianne,' she cried, throwing back the lock and wrenching the door open. 'Oh, Marianne, thank . . .' She stopped, looking past Marianne to where Consuela was standing in front of the Golf.

'It's all right,' Marianne said softly in Louisa's ear. 'There's nothing to be afraid of.'

But Louisa was already backing away.

'Please,' Consuela smiled, coming towards them. 'I know it is difficult for you, seeing me here, but I swear, Louisa, I mean you no harm.'

'Consuela has something to tell you,' Marianne said, standing aside as Consuela walked into the house.

Louisa's eyes were darting wildly between them as she continued to move away.

'This will probably be very hard for you to hear,' Consuela said, a note of compassion shaking her voice. 'But you must believe me when I say it was even harder for me.' Her face was haggard, her eyes were heavy with pain and her entire body seemed to be drooping.

'We have just heard, an hour ago,' she continued, with effort, 'that Jake . . . that Jake found Martina earlier today and this time there is no question, he has killed her.' She staggered slightly and Marianne caught her. Then turning her eyes to Louisa Marianne said solemnly.

'I heard it myself on the news, Louisa. He tried to get away, tried to take Consuela's granddaughter with him, but they caught him. He's in custody now.'

Louisa's eyes were blazing. 'You're lying!' she yelled. 'Both of you! You're lying. Jake would never kill anyone! Never!'

'Louisa, please,' Marianne said, casting an anxious look at Consuela. 'We're telling you the truth. It's all over the news . . .'

'I don't care! I don't believe it! He wouldn't do it I'm telling you. He loved Martina . . .'

As Consuela flinched Marianne tightened her hold. 'Louisa,' she said firmly.

'No, I don't want to hear it,' Louisa cried, covering her ears. 'I don't want to hear your lies.'

'Louisa, Erik and Morandi have vanished too,' Marianne said. 'No one knows where they are . . .'

'But Sarah's back in London!' Louisa shrieked. 'Sarah's in London. Nobody's done anything to her. She's in London!'

Consuela and Marianne exchanged glances, but neither of them refuted it.

'And who's that out there?' Louisa shouted pointing to the window. 'Who is that on the lake you're trying to make me think is Danny?'

Frowning her confusion Marianne walked to the window and looked out. Louisa watched her, breathlessly. 'There's no one there, Louisa,' she said turning back.

'But there was,' Louisa raged. 'So who is she?'

Marianne went to put a comforting arm around her. 'This has been a very stressful time,' she began.

'Don't,' Louisa said, furiously slapping Marianne's arm away. 'Don't touch me. There was someone out there. I saw her with my own eyes, so don't try telling me I'm seeing things because I know what I saw and there was someone on that lake. Someone who knew my name, who shouted my name and waved to me. Someone who looked just like Danny. So who is it? Get *her* to tell you who it is!'

Marianne turned helplessly to Consuela who shook her head.

'I don't know who it could be,' Consuela said, 'but if she's right and someone is out there then it's all the more reason to get her away from here.'

'No!' Louisa cried. 'No. It's all the more reason to call the police.'

Consuela looked at Marianne. 'I'll wait in the car,' she said.

'The police have already been called,' Marianne said, turning to Louisa as the door closed behind Consuela. 'They're out there now looking for Erik and Morandi. They know about you, they want you to go into Nice where they can give you your passport and get you out of the country before anything happens to you.'

'Then why didn't they come for me themselves?' Louisa demanded.

'Because it was easier for me when I know where the house is,' Marianne answered.

Louisa's mind was in uproar. She didn't know what to think, or to say, or to do. Nothing in the world was going to persuade her that Jake had done what they'd claimed he had, but she'd just seen for herself how distraught Consuela was . . .

'Louisa, please come,' Marianne coaxed gently.

Louisa looked at her with wide, uncomprehending eyes and sensing the pain in her turmoil Marianne took her in her arms. 'Louisa, if I hadn't heard the news with my own ears I wouldn't be asking you to do this,' she said. 'But I did hear it and now I honestly believe you could be in danger if you stay here alone.'

Everything inside Louisa was recoiling from what Marianne was saying, she wanted to strike out against it, rant and rave that Marianne was lying, that Marianne had been tricked and was now tricking her, but the words just wouldn't come. She wished she could say that she wanted to stay where she was, safe and secure in Jake's house, cocooned by the memory of their love, but she knew she didn't want to stay here. The figure on the lake, the looming trees, the miles of empty countryside were as frightening and as bleak as the terrible fear that Marianne was telling the truth. She was so torn that all she wanted was to run. But run where? There was nowhere to go, nowhere to hide.

'Come on,' Marianne whispered, easing her gently towards the door. 'It'll be all right. I promise you, everything will be all right.'

Seeing them come out of the house a barely discernible smile curved Consuela's lips and with eyes as bright and glittering as the moonlit lake she turned to the night shadows and willed Jake to come for her now.

Squashed into a telephone booth at the edge of a remote Provençal village Erik pressed his coins into the slot and dialled Jean-Claude's number.

'Jean-Claude! Is that you?' he said when the ringing stopped.

'*Oui, c'est moi,*' Jean-Claude confirmed. 'Where are you?'

'Who's with you?'

'Just Didier.'

'I'm in the Var, about fifteen minutes from Jake's place. Have the police been?'

'Yes, they arrived about ten minutes after you left. They want to talk to you again about Danny's murder.'

'That's what I was afraid of.'

'I've 'eard the news, Erik, I know about Jake's arrest, so what's going on?'

'I'll tell you when you get here. Has Marianne been in touch again?'

'No.'

'Well someone's been to Jake's place, that's for sure, but they've gone now and wherever they are I think we can assume they're with Consuela. Tell Didier to stay by the phone and get yourself over here.'

After giving Jean-Claude the directions and telling him to make sure he wasn't followed, Erik sped back through the winding, leafy roads to Jake's house. Dawn was just breaking and the lanes were still wet from the storm. He was unshaven, unwashed and starving. He should have thought to tell Jean-Claude to bring food, but it was too late to turn back now, with any luck Jean-Claude would already have left and it was vital that he got his car off the road as quickly as possible. The police wouldn't only be looking for him with regard to Danny's murder now, they'd no doubt be wanting to talk to him about the way he had stormed into Consuela's house during the early hours of the morning, brandishing a gun and demanding to know where Consuela was. Either the boys weren't saying or they genuinely didn't know, but having satisfied himself that Consuela was nowhere on the premises he had left.

An hour later Jean-Claude pulled up outside the converted barn in his Renault. Erik came to the door and could have embraced him as Jean-Claude thrust a baguette and a lump of cheese at him and stalked into the house.

'Things are looking very bad for you, Erik,' Jean-Claude said sternly. 'You are my friend, but I want you to tell me that I am not making a mistake in trusting you.'

'You're not making a mistake,' Erik assured him. 'I know how it must look, but believe me, Jean-Claude, if the police decide to haul me in now then the chances of our seeing Louisa again are right out the window.'

'I don't understand,' Jean-Claude said, sitting on the brick fireplace.

Erik fixed him with haunted, bloodshot eyes. 'Jake's wife was killed the moment he got to her,' he said. 'They shot her right in front of him, right in front of the child too. I'm not sure what happened after, but obviously Consuela must have arranged things to make it look as though Jake could have done it.'

'*Mon Dieu!*' Jean-Claude murmured. 'But surely Jake 'ad people with 'im who can swear that isn't true.'

'Yes, he did. But for now it's their word against the word of Consuela's people. And what won't help is that this isn't the first time Jake's been arrested for Martina's murder. He was when she first disappeared and I don't know about you, but I don't even want to think about how he must be feeling right now. He loved his wife, Jean-Claude. He never stopped loving her and to see her die that way . . . All I can say is that I hope to God no one ever hates me the way Consuela hates Jake.'

'But why does she 'ate 'im so much?'

'It's a long story and as irrational in its madness as it is in its roots, just suffice it to say that she's made busting up Jake's marriage one of her great missions in life. Well, she's succeeded now and what we have to concern ourselves with is finding out where the hell Consuela and Marianne have taken Louisa. The trouble is, the one person who might just be able to give us the answer to that is the one person we can't contact. Jake.'

Jean-Claude was looking as alarmed as he was confused. 'But what would Consuela want with Louisa now?' he said. 'Surely she 'as 'urt Jake enough . . .'

'If Jake had managed to free Martina then Consuela would have held Louisa hostage to try and force Jake and Martina apart again,' Erik interrupted. 'But now that Martina's dead Louisa is Consuela's safety net. She knows that if Jake is released he'll come after her and believe you me it's only going to be a matter of time before Jake gets out of that jail. And once he does and Consuela finds out he's on his way I'm sure you don't have any problem imagining what sort of position that'll put Louisa in.'

Jean-Claude didn't. 'Which is why we 'ave to find 'er before Jake is released,' he said.

Erik nodded. 'And which is why I can't run the risk of the police taking me in for questioning about Danny's murder right now. Apart from having to find Louisa, I've got to stop Jake getting to Consuela, because there's no doubt that after what she did to Martina he won't even hesitate, he'll kill her and to hell with the consequences.'

Jean-Claude shook his head solemnly. 'Do you 'ave any idea who did kill Danny?' he said.

'I'll lay money it was the guy who's making out he's Jake's father, whoever he is. Consuela doesn't seem to want to soil her own hands, she pays other people for that. I've got to hand it to the woman, she sure seems to know what she's doing when it comes to stitching people up. And now I don't know whether to hope for Jake's quick release or not because the longer he's in that jail the worse it looks for me and him, but as soon as he comes out God only knows what'll happen to Louisa.'

They were quiet for some time before Jean-Claude got up to try the phone. It was still dead. 'I take it the nearest phone is in the village I came through,' he said, taking his car keys from his pockets.

Erik nodded. 'Who are you going to call?'

'Didier. We need to know what's 'appening. If the police 'ave been for you again, if Jake 'as been released, if, by any miracle, Marianne 'as been in touch.'

'Jake's release will probably be on the news when it happens,' Erik answered. 'But I don't reckon it'll be for a day or two at the very least.'

'Then that gives us some time,' Jean-Claude said.

Left alone with his tiredness and his thoughts Erik felt his grief for Danny swelling in his throat. There had been no time yet for him to deal with that and it wasn't going to help anything if he gave in to it now. What he needed to do was somehow get hold of Jake and tell him what had happened here, for if Jake knew that he was putting Louisa's life in danger by coming after Consuela then surely to God he wouldn't do it. But the only way of contacting Jake right now was through his father and when Erik had called San Diego several hours ago David Mallory had already left for Mexico. And now Erik didn't have the first idea where the hell anyone was and the very idea of trying to contact a Mexican jail from a phone booth in France was so absurd it was almost laughable.

'Sarah? It's Erik.'

'Erik! Oh, thank God,' Sarah cried. 'What's happening? What news on Louisa? Have you found her yet?'

'No,' Erik answered. Almost thirty-six hours had passed now since Louisa and Marianne had left Jean-Claude's and Erik was only calling Sarah now out of desperation. Just thank God that when she'd spoken to Jean-Claude Jean-Claude had told her what had happened to Martina, because Erik didn't think he could face explaining it again. He'd known Martina and in his way had loved her too. 'Sarah, I know it's a long shot,' he said, 'and I know if you knew where Consuela might be holding her you'd have said, but I have to ask. Can you think of anywhere. Somewhere that might just give us a lead?'

'It's all I can think about,' Sarah answered, 'but I can't come up with anything. I only wish I could. I take it you haven't managed to make contact with Jake to ask him?'

'No. You'll have heard the news so you know he's still in jail.'

'What's happening to his little girl, does anyone know?'

'His father is down there, I imagine he's taking care of her, but I don't know anything for sure except that things must be moving in Mexico because the police here are searching for Consuela.'

'Well surely that's a good thing,' Sarah said hopefully.

'Yes and no. They found Marianne's car this morning. There was no sign of Marianne. The car was abandoned in a ditch over in Villeneuve-Loubet. Apparently an eye-witness is saying that he saw a man getting out of it during the early hours of yesterday morning and from the description I'm damned sure it's the man who's been making out he's Jake's father.'

'Who is this man, Erik?' Sarah cried. 'He keeps cropping up, someone must know who he is.'

'I only wish they did. But I'm not going to lie to you, Sarah, Buenos Aires, where Consuela's from, is crawling with hired killers.'

'I don't believe this,' Sarah muttered. 'It's insane. Consuela's got to be out of her mind to be going to such lengths just to break up a marriage.'

'Insane or not, she's doing it,' Erik replied.

'But why Danny and Aphrodite? It doesn't make sense. They were nothing to do with Jake and Martina.'

'That's a question you'll have to ask Consuela,' Erik answered. 'But my guess is Aphrodite knew too much and Danny was being used to frame Jake for murder. If he'd gone down for that then Consuela would have succeeded in busting the marriage apart without having to kill her own daughter.'

Sarah's mind was spinning. This was all too much to take in, but she must think. She must be able to come up with something to help Erik find Louisa, but every suggestion she made Erik had already thought of.

'I'm sorry.' Erik said, his voice so tired and defeated he sounded almost on the point of collapse. 'Look, I have to go now,' he said. 'But if anything else comes to mind, anything at all, then call Jean-Claude straight away?'

'Of course. Same goes for you, keep in touch. And Erik.'

'Yes?'

'Take care of yourself.'

27

Louisa lay very still. The bitter taste of chloroform soured her lips and a thick, musky odour clung to the stuffy night air. All that covered her was a thin, soiled sheet bunched over her thighs and sluggish blue rays of moonlight seeping in through the grimy, barred window. Her wrists were bound to the iron bed. Her arms were numb, her heart was aching with terror.

The mewling cries that rang with an almost human despair had stopped now, but the charged silence was even more terrible. Her eyes stole warily through the darkness waiting for something to move. Nothing did. With a desperation bordering on madness she longed to bury her face in the pillow and scrunch herself into a ball, for lying as she was, naked and helpless, she had never felt more vulnerable nor more afraid in her life.

Earlier, when she'd dragged herself listlessly from the depths of a druggish sleep, she'd still had her clothes and had been free to move about the cluttered, cobwebby attic. Now all she could do was lie there, trapped in the gaze of wildly staring eyes that gleamed with demented humanity in the cracked, shadowy faces of long-neglected dolls. Even the broken chests and torn, scratched armchairs seemed to breathe a slow, watchful menace.

She longed for the anger of earlier that had kept her fear in check, when she hadn't allowed herself to lie there like some limp, tragic heroine waiting to be rescued. She'd been determined then to get out of there before they did to her what they'd done to Marianne. She hadn't seen the shooting, but she'd heard it and though a nauseating panic was swelling like a tide inside her, she had pushed it aside, using the thought of Jake to give her strength. She had no idea what had happened in Mexico, all she knew was that Consuela had lied. The fury she felt at herself for doubting him was as bitter and torturous as the guilt. But there would be time later to deal with that, what she had to concentrate on was getting out of there.

From the window she had seen tall, shuttered windows across what appeared to be a narrow alleyway. Pots of wilting geraniums were hooked over the sills, old laundry dangled in the heat. The air of normalcy was as ominous as the charged, motionless silence. Moving to one side she'd peered down the street. She saw red-tiled rooftops, more tightly shuttered windows and the stark rectangle of a church tower glinting in the sunlight. There was no sound of footsteps, no car engines, no dogs barking, birds singing or children playing. Her heart had given a sickening twist. It was impossible to say for sure, but she thought she was in the sinister village where she had once met Jake and where the only signs of life were empty cars, closed shops and a newly painted *Mairie* with firmly locked doors.

As fear pulsed adrenalin into her veins she had turned back into the slanted room. It was crammed full of things. Bureaux, chests, tattered armchairs, chipped porcelain, a broken doll's house, a rusty birdcage, faded pictures in thick, ornate frames, old, discarded knitting, tapestry-covered journals with corroded brass locks. There was hardly an inch of surface or wall that wasn't bearing a relic or a cobweb. Dust motes danced frantically in the sunlight that was streaming through the window.

To her horror she'd found the only door led into a bathroom, yellowed with age and corroded beyond use. That was when panic had devoured her anger, making her heart thump with the crazy fear that there was no other door. But there had to be, how else could they have got her in here? She searched the walls with her hands, knocking aside pictures, feeling for cracks, trying to find a hidden panel that would make something in the room move.

Dropping to her hands and knees she'd thrown aside rugs and furniture, desperate to reassure herself that she hadn't been walled up in this forgotten mausoleum. Martina's three-year kidnap was tightening her throat with panic. The floor-boards were warped and cracked. Long, thin crevices snaked between them, but there was no sign of a trapdoor. Tears of frustration burned her eyes as she cast herself from side to side, overturning chairs, knocking over boxes, hunting furiously for something she was becoming increasingly terrified wasn't there. But it had to be. There had to be a way into this place and therefore a way out. But there wasn't and as the insanity of it reached her, sliding into her senses with the same inane menace of the wide-eyed dolls and empty clock faces she began beating her fists on the floor and screaming out for help.

She knew now that the door was behind the tall, heavy dresser, but even had she been able to get up from the bed there was no way of opening the door from the inside. The dresser was part of the door, it couldn't be moved aside.

Tears trickled from the corners of her eyes as hopelessness and despair weighted her. Her swollen face throbbed with pain.

When he'd come, the man who looked so appallingly like Jake, but older, he'd stood staring at her, his chilling eyes surveying her as she'd backed into a corner. When he told her to take off her clothes she refused until he smashed an iron fist in her face. With blood pouring from her nose and mouth and sobbing with terror she had removed her clothes. He shoved her down on the bed and made her open her legs. Then taking a thin wire from his pocket he had jerked her arms over her head and tied her wrists to each side of the iron frame.

He hadn't raped her, as she'd thought he was going to, instead he'd jammed the barrel of his gun into her and warned her if she screamed again he'd blow out her brains through her cunt. Then delivering a second, dizzying blow to her face he'd left.

That had been just before five o'clock – she knew because the church clock had chimed the hour minutes after he'd gone. Now it was sometime between eleven and midnight and the terror inside her was as consuming as the helplessness. She knew there was no one in the room with her, if there were she'd have heard them come in, but someone was breathing, a thin, nasal wheeze and the old chair beneath the window kept rocking.

Suddenly the chair began to pitch wildly as though someone had left it and a strange, descending chill congealed the air. Stifling a scream Louisa jerked her knees to her chest in a vain effort to protect herself. There was someone standing beside her, someone looking down at her, she could feel them, sense them. She heard a gentle rustle, then the creak of floorboards as though someone were walking away. She lay rigid with terror, not daring to breathe. There was a thud on the floor over by the dresser that masked the door, then a faint scratching she'd thought earlier was mice, began again.

'*Au secours!*' The plaintive cry drifted like a mist, turning Louisa to ice.

The scratching became louder and faster. '*À l'aide. À l'aide.*' The voice was tortured with despair. '*S'il vous plaît. À l'aide.*' The pathetic cries became fraught with panic, the clawing and scraping took on the desperation of madness. Suddenly things were falling to the floor, furniture was moving, a doll flew across the room and smashed against the wall. Louisa cried out. Her voice was drowned by the tortured groans of hysteria. Had Consuela been there she could have told her about Marie-Thérèse, the poor, demented girl who had been kept locked up in this room until she had eventually died of hunger and despair. But Consuela wasn't there and as the tormented cries for help grew ever more frantic and the scraping and banging jarred like physical blows on Louisa's nerves she started to scream and cry out to God in terror.

Two floors below in the shabby, stone wall kitchen, Consuela's eyes darkened. The neighbours were well used to screams from this house for everyone knew the story of Marie-Thérèse. But Louisa's screams were different.

She looked across the long wooden table to the man sitting opposite her, the man who had for the past three weeks gone under the name of David Mallory. His real name was Oscar

Delacroix, or so he claimed. Consuela didn't care what his real name was, all that concerned her was his fortunate likeness to Jake Mallory. Surgery had helped of course, for the right price men like Delacroix were prepared to do anything. And for some things they didn't require paying at all.

'Go and shut her up,' Consuela snapped. 'And make sure you do it this time.'

When Delacroix had gone Consuela turned her eyes to Frederico. He was fiddling nervously with a saucer, spinning it, rolling it and catching it. Sensing Consuela's irritation he stopped. Her normal serenity was spiked through with fury. Her eyes were glacial, her beautiful lips pressed harshly together.

She wasn't fool enough to imagine Jake wouldn't get himself out of that jail, but she was afraid he was going to manage it much sooner than she'd bargained for. It didn't bother her that he would come for her, she expected it, it was why she had Louisa, but with the police searching for her here in France she couldn't move from this house. Neither could Delacroix. Someone had seen him dumping Marianne's car. It wouldn't matter that they had to stay holed up here were it not for the fact that they'd left Marianne where someone was going to find her sooner than Consuela wanted them to.

With time no longer on her side she knew how grave an error it would be to make any panic decisions. She wasn't sure if Jake knew about this house, tucked away in a dark, cobbled, back street of Chateauneuf. If he didn't she'd have to find a way to let him know. She was relying on the fact that when he came he wouldn't bring the police with him. If he really meant to kill her, he wouldn't. But of course he meant to kill her, after what she'd done to Martina she'd be a fool to doubt it.

She looked again at Frederico's young, frightened face. She should never have got him involved in this. He couldn't handle it. Getting him to masquerade as Danny in order to convince Louisa she was insane had worked so far, and with Marie-Thérèse for company upstairs it would have continued to work, but they could go no further with it. There wasn't the time.

So what did she do with Frederico? One word to Delacroix was all it would take to erase the problem.

She got abruptly to her feet and walked to the narrow staircase beside the hearth. When she reached the room above she sat in front of the mirror and looked at herself. She saw what the rest of the world saw, a beautiful, elegant woman in late middle age. The casing was perfect, but the inside was eaten away with a rage and a bitterness so profound it was as though every organ of her body had been affected by it.

She started to laugh. The mirth welled up from deep inside her, vibrating her body, issuing from her lips, pealing through the silence and causing tears to flow from her eyes. What a performance she had given all these years, what fools she had made of them all, for none of them had ever guessed that beneath her delicate, pampered skin and saintly smile beat a heart of such festering malice it was destroying them all. Except Jake, of course. He knew, but he'd never been able to tell. What joy it had given her to see his impotence, what pleasure she had gained from his torment.

She'd told him three years ago that he would never have the woman he loved and now he could be in no doubt that she'd meant it. She had vowed to destroy him and that was exactly what she was doing. He would live out his life in misery, knowing that the two women he had loved had died for that very reason. Her teeth gritted with the thrill of the power she had over him, the power he handed her just by loving. Had he left Martina alone, had he never tried to find her then Martina would still be alive. He would know that by now and no matter that she had paid the man who had shot Martina, Jake, being the man he was, would always blame himself. He was a victim of his own conscience, something she would never be. She'd kissed goodbye to her conscience a long time ago, she'd had no further use for it. What the hell did she care about anyone? Who the hell had ever cared about her?

A lifetime's resentment glittered in her eyes as she put a hand to her head and peeled away the sleek, blonde wig. She was an old woman now, old beyond her years. What hair she had was grey and wiry, her scalp was dry, the skin cracked and flaking. It was a grotesque cap around a face that had clung desperately, defiantly to its beauty. But what good had beauty ever done her? Where were her joyful memories? What had happened to the love? Who had taken her share of life's pleasures? What right had they to those pleasures when they should have been hers? She'd watched the burgeoning joy around her, she'd seen the light of love in eyes that had blinded themselves to her pain. She'd lived the lie, she'd hidden the misery and buried the resentment. She'd played her part, suffering silently and alone, watching the years pass, seeing no end to her hell and knowing that no one, not even those she had once trusted and loved, cared what was happening to her.

The betrayal had been so bitter, the hurt so deep and the pain and humiliation so severe that the only way she could bear it was to pretend. What an actress she had become, as accomplished as any Hollywood star or any whore. She had performed so convincingly, had enacted an existence of such blissful contentment and wifely adoration that in the end it was she, the helpless victim of a cruel and vindictive fate, who had crushed all the beauty and goodness from her soul. What need did she have of such things when they had been so treacherously and unforgivably abused? She had sacrificed her youth and her innocence, all her hopes and dreams, for a family who had cared more for their good name and the rebuilding of their fortune than they had for the plight of their own daughter.

That daughter no longer existed. Consuela de Santiago, whose Spanish blood was as blue as any royal's, whose nature was as wayward and flirtatious as the sun that had sparkled over her charmed and happy life, had died forty years ago the day she married Carmelo Santini. Now she was no more than a shell, a beautifully sculpted frame that like a coffin contained the long-decayed ruins of her dreams, the ashes of her hopes and veins that seethed with hatred and vengeance. After her parents had turned away, refusing to incur the wrath of the mighty and powerful Santini, she had never again told a living soul of the pain and degradation, imprisonments and penury he made her suffer. She had watched her friends feign ignorance and carried her burden alone. She had played her role, kept up appearances, maintained her dignity while all the time nurturing the hatred that would one day ruin them all.

Now the pretence was over. The curtain had fallen with Martina's death. Martina, the fruit of Santini's loins, the only truly precious gift he had ever given her. Were it not for Martina then maybe she would have tried to take back something of her life. Maybe she would have gone away somewhere and started again. Poverty would have been no hardship when compared with the violence and oppression of her marriage. Anonymity would have been a blessed release from the pretence and the fear. But that was before Santini had given her his bastard daughter, the child of a whore, the one weapon with which she could get back at him. So she stayed, for what would Martina's life be without a mother to love and protect her? What chance would she stand with a father who behind his public facade of Christian righteousness and human compassion was nothing more than a sadist and a gangster who, like so many others in their godforsaken land, had connived and cheated, corrupted and extorted his way into the corridors of power? She couldn't leave an innocent child to the mercy of a man she knew to be a monster, now could she?

She had dedicated thirty years of her life to Martina and as far as she was able had come to love the child. But no emotion flourished in her with the same might as her hatred for Carmelo Santini. Publicly they were a golden couple blessed with beauty and riches, privately he took his pleasure inflicting misery and humiliation on his high-born wife. Words of criticism or complaint were repaid by months of confinement in this very house so far from her homeland – and the breakdowns that had very nearly annihilated her sanity were treated by those whose silence could be bought. Never was a word either printed or spoken against her feared and revered husband whose concern for his wife's health was as false as his tears. He was the son of Italian peasants with no breeding and no morals. Being the head of a *frigorifico* was just a cover for his racketeering, drug-running, pimping and gambling. His rivals never survived the contest, his wife never gave him a son.

But Martina had everything, Consuela saw to that. She raised her to be the fine, spirited and noble young lady she herself had once been. Nothing of her father's atrocities ever reached her ears, neither did the truth of her birth. As soon as Consuela learned what Santini and countless others were doing to an entire generation of Argentinians, dragging them from their homes, imprisoning them and even killing them, she had begged him to send Martina to the States, wanting to preserve the love and respect Martina had for her father.

She gave a sudden, shrill laugh. Why had she done that? Why had she cared what Martina thought of her father when Santini had never given a damn about anyone but himself? Why hadn't she let his precious daughter see him for the depraved and sadistic monster he was?

Consuela's mouth was trembling. Her nostrils flared as she struggled for breath. She knew why, but in the end Santini had cheated her even of that. All their married life he had sworn that when he died his fortune would be hers. It was his Christian duty, he'd insisted in his deep, sarcastic drawl, to make amends for all the pain he had caused her and to repay her for the love she had given Martina. She would be a wealthy woman with the freedom she had always craved. She hadn't believed him until he'd shown her his will and sworn before God and a priest that he would remain true to his word. But of course he'd lied and as they'd closed the lid of his coffin she had heard his laughter rumbling through the bowels of hell. He'd left her with nothing. Nothing, unless she left Argentina and lived the rest of her life in a luxurious villa she had no means of maintaining, or a house – this house – where so many of her worst nightmares had taken place.

Then, just a few short months later Martina, ungrateful bitch that she was, had thrown her out of her life, refusing to see Jake Mallory for the adulterous, deceiving bastard that he was – that all men were.

Consuela choked and spluttered as a great heaving sensation welled from the depths of her. Hatred and fury were spewing their poison into her veins. She wanted no more of this charade, she was done with the shackles of pretence, she was rotten right through to her soul and had no more reason to hide it. Consuela de Santiago had avenged herself on all who had betrayed her. She, the greatest actress of them all, had seen the friends who had spurned her pay with their dignity and their fortunes. She, the dazzling, faithful and noble Spanish wife of an Italian *mafioso*, had taken his spoiled and haughty daughter's freedom and bestowed a punishment on her and her fornicating husband that he would never forget. Now he knew the price of turning Martina against the mother who had sacrificed her life for a daughter who wasn't even her own. Now he knew what it was to suffer as she had suffered.

As she looked in the mirror she saw the light of dementia gleaming in her eyes. She'd seen it so many times before. Her lips were cracked, her skin was sallow, her face was gaunt and old. Her beauty was being erased by the unleashing of her venom, the perfect casing was crumbling beneath the seething might of her hatred. There had been no justice for her in this life, she expected none in the next. Her faith had been eroded by the years of abuse, her belief in salvation she had buried along with her conscience. Her only joy now was to see those who'd wronged her grovel for her mercy, to see the man who had taken Martina and her fortune pay for the way he had cast her aside. She had shown him what it was to lose someone he loved, not once but twice. She had let him know the indignity of prison, the way she had known it, then she had drawn out his suffering with the uncertainty of Martina's death. She laughed, loudly. He would be in no doubt now.

Delacroix was behind her, holding her steady as the breath heaved in her chest and the malice twisted her face. Their reflections were blurred in the dwindling light, his eyes, so like Jake's, gazed down at her with indifferent confusion. She had tried once to put out Jake's eyes so he would never look at another woman, he would surely be praying now that she had succeeded. Danielle Spencer had paid with her life for their one night of passion. Did he know yet, she wondered, that she had Louisa Kramer? If he did, had he guessed where she was? She hoped so for when he came she knew there was every chance he would kill her on sight. It was what she wanted, that he didn't stop to ask questions, that he gave her no chance to beg for mercy, for once he'd done it, the very instant he'd fired the bullet, he would realize what a terrible, irreversible mistake he had made. And if he didn't kill her right away, well then he would realize what a terrible mistake that was too.

'You see, Jake,' she rasped on a laboured, choking breath, 'either way, you can't win. Dead or alive I have more power over you than God Almighty Himself.'

Marianne had been waiting a long time now. Though night had long since stolen the light from the room it was still suffocatingly hot and the stench of her own bodily waste was making her retch. Her cheeks were wet with tears, her heart ached with the pain of Consuela's betrayal and the fear she might never be found.

She'd regained consciousness early that morning, had heard Erik downstairs, ranting at the lifeless telephone, banging around in the kitchen, then finally she had heard him leave. There had been nothing she could do. Her arms and legs were bound so tightly that her circulation had all but ceased. The gag cut agonizingly across her mouth, the rag in her throat was impairing her breathing. Her head throbbed so relentlessly she could barely open her eyes.

The king-size bed on which she lay was hard up against the wall. When she'd come round she was scrunched into the furthest corner facing the wall, her hands and feet tied tightly to each other behind her back. The stiffness in her limbs and the weakness of hunger had made it hard for her to move, but gradually, inch by inch, while praying desperately for Erik's return, she had finally managed to manoeuvre herself to the edge of the bed. When he came, if he came, she would let herself fall to the floor and pray that he heard.

Thanking God for blessed mercies Erik tore open the door to Jake's house – the telephone was ringing! As he ran for it he tripped in the darkness, falling against a chest and sending the nearest lamp crashing to the floor. He swore and grabbed for the phone.

Upstairs Marianne's bound and twisted body lay on the floor, sobs silently racking her. She had lost her balance and the crash downstairs had masked the sound of her fall.

'Erik? Erik, is that you, son?'

'David!' Erik cried. 'Thank Jesus Christ. I've been trying to get you . . .'

'Erik, listen to me,' Jake's father interrupted over the crackling line. 'They released Jake late last night . . .'

'Can I talk to him? I've got to talk to him, David. Can you put him on?'

'He's not here, son.' David Mallory's tone told Erik all he needed to know. Jake had paid off lawyers and the police to keep his release from David as long as they could, then had got himself to the nearest airport and had very likely called David when he was already out of Mexico.

'I don't know what route he's taking to Europe,' David Mallory went on, 'but that sure as hell'll be where he's heading. I haven't been able to find out how he got out of Mexico yet, but I'm working on it, it might give us some clue as to where he'll make his connection before Nice. Meantime, it's over to you, Erik. You've got to stop him. Don't for God's sake let him get to that woman or he'll kill her.'

'I'll do my best,' Erik answered, at last finding a light switch. 'But as far as I know he's the only one who might know where she is.'

Marianne was inching painfully, desperately towards the door. She could hear every word Erik was saying.

'Are you coming over?' Erik asked David.

'No. I've got his little girl. I'm taking her home.'

'Of course,' Erik said. 'How is she?'

'Afraid. She wants her mommy.' David paused. 'Do your best for Jake, son. He's in a bad way. He's as mad as hell and there's no telling what he might do to get to that bitch. Personally I'd like to see her dead, but I don't want Jake spending the next twenty years in jail. He's got a child here that needs him. Remind him of that.'

'I will. And David, should he get in touch with you before I find him you've got to make him tell you where Consuela could be. Tell him she's got Louisa.'

Marianne's eyes were fixed on the sliver of light coming in through the door. It wasn't quite closed. She had to get to it, she had to knock it closed so Erik would hear. She knew where Louisa was. She could tell him. She could help him stop Jake if only she could make him hear.

'. . . you've got to find that girl, Erik,' David Mallory was saying. 'You've got to stop him getting anywhere near Consuela, because if he does . . .'

'I know, I know. You don't have to spell it out,' Erik interrupted, frowning up at the gallery. 'Take down this number.' He reeled off Jean-Claude's number and went on, 'If you find out anything call. I'm going to the police now, let's just hope they don't take it into their heads to arrest me, but we're going to need their help on this. Will they know about Jake's release yet?'

'I'll see they do by the time you get there.'

'Great. And who knows, by some miracle they might find Marianne, the girl who worked for Jake. She'll know where Consuela is. But for all we know she could be in on it all, or worse, she could be dead.'

Oh Erik! Erik! Marianne cried inwardly. *I'm here. Please God, tell him I'm here!*

Erik slammed down the phone.

Marianne was almost there. Her chest was burning with pain as she struggled to make a sound.

Erik snatched up his keys and started for the door. He paused, looked up at the gallery again, then moved on.

No! No! Don't go! Marianne silently screamed.

As Erik reached the door a car skidded to a stop beside his own and Bob, the first mate on the *Valhalla*, leapt out.

Marianne inhaled a breath of relief then pushed on.

'Is he here?' Bob shouted.

'You mean he's already in France?' Erik cried in disbelief.

'I saw him taking off in the Mercedes from the port.'

'You didn't get to speak to him?'

'Not a chance. He was gone before I could get ashore.'

'Jesus Christ!' Erik seethed. 'There's no time to go to the police, we'll have to call them. Do you have his licence number?'

'Sure.'

Marianne thrust herself frantically forward. She was so close now, so very close. She could hear Erik speaking to the police. He was shouting, making too much noise. He'd never hear the door close. She must wait. She positioned herself precariously on her side, praying she wouldn't roll before she was ready. At last she heard the phone go down. She jerked her shoulder and fell back instead of forwards.

Bob and Erik raced out of the house. Erik stopped to lock up. Marianne shoved her hips against the upstairs door, barely grazing it, but it clicked shut.

Erik turned the key in the lock downstairs, pocketed it and turned to his car.

'Where are we going?' Bob cried, jumping into the passenger seat.

'I wish the hell I knew,' Erik answered, looking briefly at one of the upstairs windows. Then flooding the drive with his headlights, he slammed the car into reverse, turned and sped off into the night.

Marianne rocked from side to side, weeping and sobbing and begging hopelessly for them to come back.

28

Consuela replaced the phone and turned to Delacroix. Her slanted eyes were glittering. She started to speak then paused as the church clock began chiming the hour.

Delacroix turned to the night-darkened window. The rare sound of footsteps could be heard passing, receding into the distance. The room was stuffy, smelt of his cologne, old cooking and cigarettes. A dull lamp in one corner cast an arc of insipid orange light over the cast-iron stove and old-fashioned china sink.

The last chime on the clock sounded.

'He's on his way,' Consuela said, her smile ruminant and catlike.

Delacroix nodded.

'So considerate of him,' she went on, her eyes unfocused in thought, 'to call at my villa to announce his arrival. But I imagine he had to check there first. Frederico told him where to come. It seems he already knew about this place, so we must assume he knows the layout too. I estimate it will take him thirty-five minutes to get here, but we'll work to twenty.' Her gaze went to Delacroix and rested there as she quietly contemplated the night. 'As you know, I don't expect to live through this,' she said, 'so when it's over take the car, drive to Milan and be on the first plane out. Your payment will be waiting when you feel it safe to return to Buenos Aires.'

Delacroix was fascinated by her. She was so calm it was scary. He slid a pack of Gitanes across the plastic tablecloth towards him. Even with twenty minutes they had time to spare He knew what he had to do.

He lit the cigarette, puffed smoke into the pungent air and remarked, 'You look better with the wig.'

Consuela raised a uninterested eyebrow. That he had seen her without it the day before didn't concern her. Her eyes glowed with a slow, purposeful fervour.

The most chilling of all insanities, Delacroix mused, was one that was as controlled as hers. It was so reasoned a court of law would probably declare her sane.

'I'm going upstairs now,' she said. 'Be sure to put out the light before you leave.'

She mounted the narrow, winding stairs, turning on lights as she went, then off again as she reached the next landing. She moved unhurriedly towards the attic door then stopped for a moment to pat her hair into place.

She pressed down on the handle and the heavy door, weighted by the dresser, swung slowly open. The light inside was on. The room was quite empty.

She gave a small sigh of satisfaction then closed the door behind her. She walked over to the bed and looked down at the blood. There wasn't as much as she'd hoped for, but it would suffice. She turned the sheet over. There was more there. She positioned it so it could be seen then went to make herself comfortable in a shabby armchair.

The minutes ticked by.

She wondered if Marie-Thérèse was watching her. Marie-Thérèse, so many years walled up here alone in this room. If all went to plan they would spend their lives everlasting together. It seemed fitting.

Some while later the clock outside chimed the half hour. Consuela's eyes moved to the corner. There was a faint scratching noise. She smiled.

'Marie-Thérèse!' she gasped, clutching her throat. 'Marie-Thérèse!' Let me go.'

She laughed. She'd scared Santini half to death with that once when he'd come to let her out. Sinner that he was, he was still a god-fearing Catholic. He believed in the possession of evil spirits. She'd spent four months in a convent after that.

She picked up the gun beside her, turned it over in her hands then laid it on her lap in the folds of her skirt. She didn't think she'd need it, she was quite certain Jake was going to kill her, but it was there, just in case.

He'd be here soon and she idly wondered whether she would get the chance to tell him about Louisa before he pulled the trigger.

There were no lights on the Mercedes as it crept slowly, almost silently into the village. It came to a halt in front of the *Mairie*. The engine stopped. Nothing, nobody, moved. The night was breathless and still.

Jake got out. His eyes moved across the roof of the car to the man getting out the other side.

They waited a moment, then began the descent down buckled, stone steps into a narrow, cobbled street.

The only witness to their presence was a fat, pampered cat sprawled drowsily on a doorstep. Ornate lamps pooled soggy light into the shadows. Minutes later they were at the door of the second to last house. No light seeped through the shutters. No sound came from within.

Jake looked at the man beside him, slid a gun from his pocket and nodded. The man gingerly twisted the doorknob. The latch clicked, the door opened and Jake sprang inside. Everything was still. Behind him the man flicked a switch and the room filled with a sickly orange glow.

Jake edged around the table, moving towards the stairs. The man stayed where he was, guarding the door.

Jake glanced back over his shoulder. His face was pale, his eyes black and empty. Again he nodded, then turning he started quietly up the stairs.

The man turned off the light and closed the door. He waited one minute then crept silently across the kitchen.

Jake took each room at a time. Everything was as motionless as a picture. The gun was steady in his hand. His heartbeat thrummed in his ears. His muscles were tensed, his eyes alert.

He reached the attic door and dropped the gun to his side. He turned the handle and the door swung open.

The first thing he saw was blood on the empty bed. His eyes zipped across the room.

Consuela smirked.

He raised the gun with both hands, aiming it straight at her head. 'Where is she?' he said.

The cellar was as black as Russian earth. A single candle flickered in one corner. Louisa was hunched beside it, still naked, her wrists and ankles bound with razor sharp wire, her face bloodied and swollen. Her cheeks were caked with dry tears, saliva dribbled from the corner of her mouth. Terror had made her pee in the dirt beneath her. Jake had arrived, they'd heard him come in. She knew the plan. She knew what was going to happen.

Delacroix was at the top of the steps by the door. She could just make out his crouched figure in the dim light. His gun was still pointing at her. He was waiting for the signal. The instant a gun fired upstairs Delacroix would kill her.

Jake was waiting. Neither of them moved. Consuela's smile was waning.

'What have you done with her?' Jake said.

'Who? Martina?' Consuela enquired.

Jake flinched and Consuela's smile returned.

'You know who.'

Consuela nodded. 'You know, I'm wondering,' she said, crossing her legs and interlacing her fingers, 'if you've yet realized that were it not for your fortunate alibi with the police at the time of Danny's murder, you would be in prison now and Martina would still be alive.'

'Then that proves you're not as clever as you think.'

She shrugged. 'Martina's death means nothing to me. I don't think you can say the same.'

Jake's face was ashen, it was the only sign of the insupportable grief he had yet to face. 'You know you're not getting out of this alive,' he said, 'so for pity's sake let her go.'

'*Pity's* sake?' she repeated.

'What difference does it make to you if she lives?' he seethed.

'To me? None. But it does to you. Oh, I don't expect you're capable of loving her now, not after the trauma of Martina's death, but being the man of honour that you are . . .'

'For Christ's sake, woman, aren't two deaths enough?'

'Three,' she corrected. 'You're forgetting Aphrodite. But she doesn't really count in the same way, does she? I had her killed because she saw Frederico breaking into Morandi's office. Not quite the same thing.'

'What will it take to let Louisa go?' he said.

Consuela looked deep into his eyes, smiling the smile of a woman who knows she can't lose. 'Make love to me one last time,' she said.

A look of unmitigated disgust twisted Jake's face. 'I'd rather die,' he hissed.

'Or you'd rather Louisa die,' she amended. 'Tell me, can you remember what it was like to make love to Martina?'

Her words seared into the heart of his pain.

'She loved you so much, you know?'

His strong, handsome face was taut and unmoving.

'Do you remember how happy you were, the two of you? It was so hard for her, being parted from you.'

Jake's eyes bored in hers.

'It wasn't so hard for you though, was it? It took a while, but you found someone else.' She laughed softly.

More seconds ticked silently by.

'She knew you had someone else. She knew about all the women you betrayed her with. She died knowing that. She died knowing that you no longer loved her.'

The scene on the Mexican hillside was replaying vividly in his mind. He held onto it, reliving the joy and the love in his wife's face as she'd run towards him. She'd known he still loved her. The pain was crippling him.

'What do you think of your daughter?' Consuela asked. 'How

old is she now? Two? Almost three.' She smiled an indulgent grandmother smile. 'They tell me she's like Martina. Is that true?'

He didn't answer.

'So I'm told she thinks one of the kidnappers is her father. She calls him Daddy. And why shouldn't she? He was there in her mommy's bed every morning.'

'I know what you trying to do, Consuela,' he said, 'but it's not going to work. I have no intention of spending my life in jail for you. Oh sure, I'm going to kill you, but before I do I'm going to tell you why I won't go to jail.'

She raised a curious eyebrow.

'You've got a gun sitting right there in your lap. If your prints aren't on that gun now they will be after I shoot you – in self-defence.'

She nodded. 'And what about Louisa?'

'I'll find her.'

Consuela laughed and shook her head. 'You think you're so smart, don't you? Well go on, go ahead and shoot me. Then go find her. She won't be . . .' Her head suddenly jerked to one side as two shots exploded into the room.

'You fool,' Consuela said as she realized he'd fired past her. 'You bloody fool.'

Louisa's wide, petrified eyes looked at Delacroix. He was at the bottom of the steps, three feet away. His face was masked in darkness. All she could see was the gun. Nauseous fear strangled her. She didn't want to die, but knew beyond doubt that she was going to. They'd heard the gun shots, Delacroix's finger was tightening on the trigger. Beyond the terror she felt a strange, unworldly sensation. She was drifting from reality, moving into a timeless void.

When it came, as the gun exploded and she fell back against the wall, for a fleeting, eternal second she was surprised to feel no pain. Just the jolt of her body hitting the wall and the echoing sound of the gunshot . . . But no pain, no pain at all.

At the sound of a muted gun shot Jake's head whipped round. He stared into the empty landing.

Consuela watched him, waiting for him to register what had happened. Downstairs a door opened then closed. The muffled sound of someone moving about reached them.

A few minutes later Jake's eyes narrowed as he saw a shadow move at the end of the hall. He turned back to Consuela.

She was holding the gun loosely in her hands and smiling.

'If you don't have the courage to shoot me, Jake,' she said, raising the gun, 'then I'll . . .' She stopped, her face draining as a stranger stepped into the room.

Her grip tightened on the gun. Her eyes were darting between them. She lifted the gun higher, turning it ready to fire. It flew out of her hands as three bullets tore into her.

With his finger still pressed tightly on the trigger Jake watched her contort. He held her eyes as she glared up at him. There was no emotion in his face.

Consuela tried to speak. The air bubbled in her lungs. Blood pumped from the wounds in her chest. Her teeth bared and her eyes gleamed like a demon's. Then Jake's voice drove into the heart of her rage as he told her what by now she had guessed – Frederico had betrayed her.

Her fingers clawed at the chair as she tried to heave herself from it. Blood spewed from her mouth.

The two men watched her impassively as she fell from the chair. Her fingers reached towards the gun. The other man kicked it out of the way.

Downstairs the house was coming alive with noise. Doors banged open. Heavy footsteps thundered on the stairs. Someone shouted. Jake turned. Two men barged past him into the room. Jake looked at the other man who was looking at him. Then throwing his gun on the bed Jake pushed his way past the police who were crowding the way and ran down the stairs.

The door to the cellar was open. More police were inside. Jake forced his way through, stepping over Delacroix's body.

Louisa was slumped in the corner, naked and pale and bleeding where the wires had cut into her.

Kneeling beside her Jake turned her towards him. Her eyes were closed, her face was bruised and cut. He lifted her carefully into his arms, stood and carried her from the cellar. As he passed he was barely aware of someone putting a blanket over her, he was back on a Mexican hillside, carrying his wife in his arms and feeling the love and pain and grief pull through him like a devastating tide.

A detective cleared the way and Jake carried Louisa out into the night. As he walked down the street, heading for the square, two policemen followed.

Erik came sprinting towards him, Bob hard on his heels. 'Jake!' Erik cried. 'Jake, is she all right?'

'She's alive,' Jake answered.

Amongst the police standing at the foot of the steps he spotted Frederico. Their eyes met. Jake nodded briefly then walked on.

A rescue vehicle was parked next to his. When he reached it he handed Louisa over. She was alive, traumatized and unconscious, but alive. He couldn't go with her. It was over now. It was all at an end.

He watched as the rescue vehicle drove out of the village. Inside he was numb. There would be time later to feel. Too much time.

As Erik's hand touched his shoulder he turned. They looked at each other in the grey light. There was no need for words. Each man knew what the other was feeling.

'I'm going to the *Valhalla*,' Jake said.

Erik nodded.

Bob walked to the Mercedes and opened the passenger door for Jake to get in.

Erik watched the tail lights disappear through the police cordon at the edge of the village then turned as Frederico came over to him.

'I've just told the police where to find Marianne,' he said. 'She's at Jake's house in the Var.'

Erik stared at him.

'They didn't kill her,' Frederico said.

Erik turned as the man who had gone into the house with Jake walked towards him. 'Fernando?' he said.

Fernando nodded.

The two men looked at each other, seemingly oblivious to the commotion going on around them. 'Who are you?' Erik said.

Fernando's eyes slanted. 'I think you know,' he said.

Erik nodded. He'd long suspected that Fernando was a Federal Agent.

'Who told the cops where to come?' Erik said.

Fernando's eyebrows flicked an admission.

'But not in time to stop Jake.'

'He killed her in self-defence.'

Erik didn't know if that was true, nor did he care. 'I think one of us should call Jake's old man,' he said.

'You go ahead,' Fernando told him. 'There's a bit of clearing up to do around here. Where can I find you when I'm through?'

'At whichever hospital they've taken Louisa to.'

'OK.' He paused. 'You've been a good friend to him, Erik.'

'He didn't deserve what happened to him.'

'No man deserves that,' Fernando said. Then added, 'It's going to be a long time.'

'Yes,' Erik said, 'I know.'

Sarah came in on the first flight in the morning. Jean-Claude was waiting for her at the airport and drove her straight to the hospital in Grasse. Louisa was waiting for them, ready to leave.

They returned to Jean-Claude's where Didier had prepared a meal. No one was particularly hungry, but they made a quiet, valiant effort. They sat, as they had just a week ago, on the wooden terrace overlooking the lawn. Everything looked as it always had. Nothing had changed, neither the sounds nor the smells, nor the clinging, claustrophobic heat of the sun.

Louisa's face, discoloured by the cuts and bruises Delacroix had given her, looked so fragile and vulnerable that Sarah longed to hug her. But she knew better than to fuss over her right now. It was a long road ahead, a very long road that would begin that afternoon when she would have to relive the terrible ordeal of the past seventy-two hours for the police. After that there was the wait until she was free to return to London, the counselling that would surely have to come and, worst of all, the press. The story had been all over the papers that morning, reporters even now were clamouring to get past the police and up the lane to the villa. And for all they knew telephoto lenses were peering at them from the trees even as they ate.

Louisa picked up her wine and catching Sarah's eye she smiled. Immediately her hand went to her mouth as a cut on her lip reopened. She laughed, shakily, and grabbed a napkin to dab it. 'Don't look so worried,' she said huskily. 'I'm fine. All in one piece. We'll be able to go home soon.'

Sarah's eyes moved to Jean-Claude. They smiled at each other, then catching sight of the infamous, interminably nosy Mrs Name-Drop striding by with Rudy while making an intent, totally unconvincing study of the sky they all burst out laughing. It relieved the tension for a while, but as they talked Sarah was still watching Jean-Claude. What would they have done without him? This kind, sensitive man who had taken them in as though they were family. He would be with Louisa this afternoon, translating for the police as she gave her statement and no doubt doing everything in his power to make it as painless for her as he could.

When they'd finished eating Louisa wandered down to the pool and stood staring into it. After a while Sarah went to join her.

They were quiet for a long time. Then a lump rose in Sarah's throat as Louisa's hand slipped into hers.

'Want to talk?' Sarah said softly.

Louisa's eyes were still gazing sightlessly into the clear, sparkling water. 'I'm not sure,' she whispered. Then looking up she smiled. 'Would you do something for me?' she said. 'Would you be there when I leave the police station?'

'Of course,' Sarah answered.

It was around six in the evening when Louisa and Jean-Claude finally came out of a back door of the main police headquarters in Cannes. Sarah was sitting in her car, illegally parked outside. She watched as Louisa spoke to Jean-Claude, kissed him on either cheek then walked towards her. Sarah knew where they were going. She had no idea if it was the right thing to do, but she wasn't going to argue, all she was going to do was drive.

As they headed out of Cannes along the coast road, Louisa said, 'Did you see Erik this afternoon?'

Sarah nodded.

'How was he?'

'He seemed OK. Tired. Exhausted. But on the whole, OK.'

'Where did he spend the night?'

'He spent most of it at the hospital with you and Marianne, the rest with the police.'

Louisa turned and looked out of the window. She didn't ask where Erik had spent the morning, she could guess.

The sun was blazing a glorious deep, red glow over the Mediterranean, the rippling waves looked syrupy and peaceful.

When at last they reached their destination Sarah parked the car and they walked together through the milling evening crowds. After a while Sarah stopped outside a café.

'I'll wait here,' she said. 'You go on ahead.'

Louisa smiled her gratitude and Sarah watched her turn and walk on.

Louisa continued to the edge of the harbour then stood gazing out to sea. In the wonderful light of the setting sun the *Valhalla* looked as magnificent and celestial as its name.

The great hull rocked gently in the waves, the vast white sails flapped proudly on their masts.

She knew he had been sailing last night, knew in the weeks and months to come that he would do a lot of sailing, seeking his solace in the great blue expanse that he loved so dearly. Her heart was filled with compassion and longing. She wished there were something she could do to ease his pain, but knew there was nothing.

She wondered if he was on board now. It didn't matter. He would be gone soon, returning to a life she could only imagine. And she . . .? She smiled. She didn't know yet what she was going to do, the only thing she was sure of was that she would never forget him. And bidding him a silent farewell in her heart she turned back to where Sarah was waiting.

29

FIFTEEN MONTHS LATER

The sprightly, jubilant sound of church bells jangled out over the Wiltshire village. Confetti snowed over the gathering as women in flowered hats with matching shoes and handbags jostled for position around the bride and groom, like the autumn leaves fluttering to the roots of the trees. Men in sober grey morning suits, paisley waistcoats and mint green cravats hovered awkwardly on the periphery waiting to be told what to do. Overhead the sun dazzled its way through the clouds, peering between them like the beaming faces of villagers peering from their curtains. Everyone loved a wedding, especially one like this that was flowing with happiness and ringing with laughter.

In fact it wasn't a wedding, it was a blessing, for Sarah and Morandi had married two days earlier at a registry office in London. They'd spent that honeymoon at Lucknam Park, a few miles away, the next they were spending in slightly more exotic climes. At least Sarah assumed they were, Morandi was in charge of that and she couldn't imagine he'd let her down. Well, she could, but she wasn't going to dwell on that.

She was as radiant as any bride could be, all decked out in creamy lace frills and oozing bubbles of joy as big as her new six-year-old stepson could blow them. Morandi's expression ranged from bewildered to forlorn to furious depending on who he was looking at the time. Right now he was at the upper end of the scale as he clapped a hand over his son's face and the bubblegum popped in a fine, pink splodge over a pair of cheery, freckled cheeks. Morandi looked at his hand in dismay.

His first wife, Dolly, passed him a handkerchief as his second wife, Tina, cuffed her son round the ear.

'It was the only way I could get him to wear a suit,' she responded through her teeth to Morandi's glare.

Laughing, Sarah scooped little Nigel up in her arms and planted a kiss on his nose. The cameras went crazy and Nigel gleefully poked out his tongue.

Sarah's sisters were arranging the bridesmaids, all eight of them, since they included all nieces and all daughters and stepdaughters, while her bemused and slightly tipsy father tried to work out exactly how many grandchildren he now had. The total was so awesome he reached into his pocket for his shiny, new flask – a gift from Sarah that morning.

Group photographs over, it was time now for the bride and groom, chief bridesmaid and best man. Morandi treated his fifteen-year-old son, the best man, to a murderous glare. In return Gregory grinned at his old man and winked. Sarah gave a splutter of laughter, smothering it quickly as Morandi turned his unamused eyes on her. The boy had dyed his hair *green*! There was nothing funny about that. On today of all days, the wretched monster had dyed his hair the colour of his grandmother's hat and then spiked it towards the heavens like he'd just plugged himself in. When he'd walked jauntily into the church earlier, swaggering up the aisle and making bows to his appreciative siblings, it had been all Morandi could do not to sock him one. And Sarah, typically, thought it was great! Still, at least his daughters hadn't let him down, that was providing he was prepared to overlook the ripping fart the youngest had trumpeted at the end of the first hymn. Sarah had almost gone to pieces and for a moment there Morandi had thought the vicar was going to lose it too. What a family!

Louisa was on the footpath leading down to the gate, standing with Sarah's relatives and watching Erik position the main players. Her sides were aching she had laughed so much. Morandi and his family were the best entertainment she'd seen in ages and Morandi's dolorous expression combined with his efforts to disguise his son's hair by resting an elbow on a low hanging branch thereby drooping the foliage over Mark's head like a wig was causing tears to run down her cheeks.

At last it was time to depart for the reception. Louisa helped Erik stow his cameras back in their cases then waited while he signed a few autographs. He gave a quick few words to the local paper who'd turned out more because of the astonishing tip off that Erik Svensson was photographing the wedding than for the wedding itself, then they climbed into his car and drove off to the local country club.

There was even more hilarity to come and as the day wore on and the champagne flowed as freely as the laughter, Sarah's excitement coupled with her wicked and lively sense of humour finally worked its magic on Morandi and he eventually, though grudgingly, relaxed. The speeches were shot through with innuendo and ribaldry and a touching amount of affection for both newly-weds. Morandi could only stare in open-mouthed amazement that his appalling, green-haired son could be so articulate, never mind witty. Actually he knew he was a wit, his hair proved that, but that he could string two sentences together that didn't contain either the word tosser or wanker was such a pleasing revelation to Morandi that he decided he might relent and let him come and live with them after all. Sarah was all for it, of course, if she had her way the entire brood would be living with them, but so far Morandi had put his foot down. He wanted her all to himself and vying for her attention amongst his boisterous flock made him feel almost as ridiculous as he did when he danced.

However, the champagne had oiled up his limbs nicely and his wife seemed so impressed by his writhings and jivings, even if his children didn't, that he threw himself into it body and soul. He wished, when he came to see the video later, that he hadn't, but at the time it had felt like sweet revenge on a family who had dished out more than their fair share of embarrassment.

Louisa, he told her, as he attempted to emulate her fantastically supple rendition of the twist, looked ravishing. So did Erik. In fact Erik looked so delicious with his recently acquired tan Morandi decided to kiss him. The two of them then proceeded to rock and bop with such astonishing vigour and expertize that they drew a hand-clapping, foot-stomping crowd around them that burst into uproarious laughter as their heads collided whilst taking a bow.

The revelries continued long after Sarah and Morandi had departed for their secret honeymoon destination. Both families knew how to have a good time and everyone agreed, even Morandi's previous two wives, that they'd never enjoyed a wedding so much. But by midnight it was time to be getting back to their various homes and hotels, the children were tired, three of them had been sick and Sarah's grandmother was about to get started on her 'When I was a girl in the war' stories.

When Louisa and Erik returned to their hotel Erik stayed in the bar for a nightcap with Danny's parents, while Louisa went on to bed. It had surprised everyone that Danny's parents had come, Sarah had thought they'd back out at the last minute. But they seemed to have enjoyed themselves, even though just to look at them it was plain to see that they were no closer now to getting over Danny's death than they had been a year ago. They had tried in a rather awkward and embarrassing way to draw Louisa into their family, but Louisa had gently resisted, knowing that she could no more fill the gap in their lives than they could in hers.

Throwing her hat and her bag on the bed she went to sit in front of the mirror and resting her chin in her hands stared back at her reflection. She'd drunk a lot more than she'd realized and now that it was beginning to wear off she could feel herself becoming maudlin. Another reason not to have stayed downstairs with Danny's parents. It had been a wonderful day, too wonderful to spoil with painful memories and tears. Which, she realized, suddenly springing up from the chair, she was about to do because her mind was so full of Jake that her heart just couldn't stand it.

Of course she'd known that she couldn't get through the day without thinking about him, that would have been too much to expect, especially when she didn't get through any day without doing that, but today had been even more difficult than she'd expected. In its way, it had frightened her, or was it just the alcohol that was making her afraid that this awful, unbearable waiting for something that just might never happen was going to go on for ever?

It wasn't that her life had stood still this past year, or that she had spent her time living in the blind, self-deluding hope that one day the phone would ring and it would be him, for that had already happened. The first time he'd called had been last October, a year ago yesterday. They'd only spoken for a few minutes, just long enough for him to tell her that he was sorry he hadn't stayed around to say goodbye and that he hoped she was recovering OK. When she'd asked him how he was his answers were vague and she'd got the impression that someone else was in the room with him. He'd rung off then saying he'd call her again in a couple of weeks, but he hadn't, not until the new year, by which time she had managed to convince herself that she would never hear from him again.

The second call had come early one morning as she was preparing to sit down and write. It would have been midnight in San Diego and though there was no slur in his voice to suggest it, she couldn't help wondering if he'd been drinking. He'd sounded much more positive than he had the last time and to her amazement he had actually talked about Martina. He knew now, through the confessions of her kidnappers, that Martina had never suffered physically during her three years of imprisonment. She had been moved from one luxurious *hacienda* to another and given everything she wanted, except of course her freedom. Jake now had in his possession the journals that had been in the attic where Louisa was held hostage, so he knew that Consuela hadn't actually been Martina's mother, but it was something he'd never made public. He'd gone on to ask how things were going with her and had sounded pleased to hear she was getting her life back together. Perversely this had upset her, mainly because she'd sensed that once she'd got her new series off the ground, the one she'd started in France, he could disappear quietly from her life and stop feeling guilty about the mayhem and madness he had dragged her into.

By the time his third call came Morandi had put her back in touch with Gaston Olivier, the Parisian film financier she had met at the Colombe d'Or, who was already a fair way down the road towards getting together a group of European producers to back her series. Jake had sounded impressed, had wanted to know all about it and had even offered a few words of advice in dealing with the Germans, something, as it turned out, he had considerable experience of.

His calls had continued to come, on and off, ever since, but instead of making her feel closer to him, they somehow seemed to make him more distant. She put it down to the time difference, to the thousands of miles that separated them, but in her heart she knew that it was because he rarely talked about himself or his daughter. That part of his life was completely closed to her and there were times when she felt she was talking to a stranger. A few months ago there had been hazy, badly focused pictures of him and Antonia in one of the Sunday supplements. Obviously the photographer hadn't been invited into the grounds of the Mallory ranch, but what he had managed to capture was enough to tell the tale. A little girl trotting around a paddock on a pony, her father holding the reins, then swinging her up in his arms and laughing and shaking her. Then the same little girl on her father's shoulders, clutching his hair as he jogged her around the garden and obviously shrieking with delight. The two of them rolling in the grass, or walking hand in hand, or gazing earnestly into each other's eyes as they talked. A sleepy Antonia with a thumb in her mouth and her head on Jake's shoulder as he carried her towards the house. And then a few weeks later, the one that had torn at Louisa's heart, the picture of Jake and Antonia Mallory sitting at the helm of a yacht, both with patches over their left eye.

She'd told him the next time he'd called that she'd seen the pictures, but he hadn't wanted to discuss it and afterwards he hadn't contacted her again for over a month. She realized it was because she had intruded further into his life than he was prepared to allow, but she hadn't known what she could do to repair it. She couldn't be blamed for what she saw in the press and Erik had tried to comfort her by telling her how hard Jake was finding it to deal with his conflicting emotions. His love for Martina had by no means died with her and his grief, his sense of failure and guilt combined with his feelings for Louisa were tearing him apart. To love another woman after what his wife had been through, to have loved that woman while Martina was still alive, was, to him, unforgivable. And now he was punishing himself by denying himself something he desperately wanted while devoting his life to his and Martina's daughter. Louisa understood all this, but there were times, like now, when the need to hold him, to comfort him and show him that it wasn't wrong for him to love her was so urgent she could hardly bear it. And of course there were other times, usually when she was tired or hadn't heard from him in a while, when the hope that they would eventually make it was eroded by the fear that he was never going to allow it.

Sarah had been to California. She and Morandi had gone to see her photographs hanging in the Mallory yacht clubs along the coast and to carry out the commissions she had received as a result. That had been three weeks of pure agony for Louisa, as she'd lived in dread of what Sarah might say if she saw Jake. And her worst nightmares had come to fruition when she'd next spoken to Jake and he'd asked if she was serious about any of the men she'd been seeing. It was true, in her less optimistic moments she had tried dating other men, but it hadn't worked. She'd even tried sleeping with one of them, and that had been a disaster. It all felt so wrong, so disloyal and out of sync with the truth. It was like looking at yourself in the mirror and seeing someone else's face. It didn't belong, just like these other men didn't belong in her life. Of course Sarah had told him in the hope of jolting him into some sort of action, but if she'd consulted Louisa first Louisa could have told her that she was wasting her time. To lose Louisa to another man now was exactly what Jake felt he deserved, but like it or not, she'd told him angrily, he wasn't going to get it. There had been a long, excruciating silence before he'd said that she had to make up her own mind what she did with her life, that it had nothing to do with him.

To her surprise and relief he had called again after that, just over three weeks ago now and probably because it was that time of the month and she was feeling tense anyway, she had told him she was fed up, miserable and whether he wanted to hear it or not she still loved him and she was sorry if it offended him, but there didn't seem to be any signs that she was going to stop. It hadn't been what he wanted to hear and his answer was something she wished to God she had never heard.

'I told you a long time ago there would never be a future for us,' he'd said, 'and now I'm telling you again. Get on with your life and stop kidding yourself there's ever going to be anything between us.'

Tears were streaming down her face and her heart was so filled with pain she could barely speak. 'Then why do you keep calling me, Jake?' she said. 'Why are you doing this to me if you don't feel the same way any more?'

'Look, things are good for you now, Louisa,' he said. 'You've got it together, Olivier will open doors for you . . .'

'Jake, please. Can't we talk about this? Can't we at least see each other and try to . . .'

'Don't make this any harder, Louisa,' he interrupted. 'Us getting together would be a mistake, you know that. It'll only hurt you more and I can't handle any more guilt right now.'

'It's all about you and how you feel, isn't it Jake?' she cried. 'Well I'm sorry about Martina, *really really* sorry, but can't you see the way you're messing up my life, letting me think that there might be some hope, that the next time you call you might just say something that will show me you're getting over all this. You're keeping me hanging on, calling me, asking me how things are going, saying you're interested in my life, when the truth is you don't really give a damn, do you? All you want is one less person to feel guilty about.'

There was a long and terrible silence before he said, 'Louisa, it's going to be easier on you if you try to come to terms with the fact that I don't love you. I'm not sure now that I ever did . . .'

'Oh Jake, please, don't say that . . .'

'I'm sorry,' he said, and the line went dead.

She hadn't heard from him since and this time she knew beyond any doubt that she wasn't going to. It didn't stop her hoping of course, but she knew she was a fool to do so. The trouble was he seemed to be filling her mind even more now than ever. She felt like a shell sitting in London or Paris while her thoughts and her heart were in San Diego – a city she didn't even know. She spent hours writing him letters that she knew before she started she'd never send. Her eyes were always straying to the clock, calculating the time difference and wondering what he might be doing now. She even rang the airlines to find out flight times to San Diego whilst knowing she would never go. Everything she did seemed such a pointless exercise and she hated the way he had stolen the purpose from her life.

Gritting her teeth in anger she kicked her shoes into the corner of the room. What was happening to her, for Christ's sake? She was so eaten up with self-pity she could hardly think beyond it. Maybe Sarah was right, she should fight for him, she should get herself over there and make him tell her to her face that it really was over. Would he have the courage for that? Perhaps more to the point, would she? Besides, did she really need telling to her face? It had been bad enough on the phone, but at least then she had been in the privacy of her own home. And what was the point in making a fool of herself, of putting them both through such horrible embarrassment when he'd made himself perfectly plain – there was no future for them, he didn't love her and maybe never had. So wasn't it about time she started making herself believe that? Wasn't it time now to put it all behind her and accept that as much as she liked to tell herself otherwise, he wasn't coming back. He still belonged to Martina and as far as she could see he always would.

The following morning Erik drove them both to the airport where he was getting a plane back to Rio to continue with the shoot he had interrupted. Louisa took his car on into London, spent twenty minutes trying to park it, then ran through the rain with her luggage back to her flat.

There were four messages on her answer phone and as usual her heart tightened with the hope that one of them might be from Jake. The thought made her want to smash the machine against the wall. If just once she could look at that damned thing without thinking of him then there probably would be a message. As it was, her ridiculous, infuriating hope felt like a jinx. Deciding to ignore it she went to unpack her wedding outfit, made a cup of coffee and opened the mail. It was only when the phone rang an hour or so later that she remembered the messages.

The first was from Sarah, ringing from the airport, with a message for Erik. Sarah was having her first major show when she returned from honeymoon and Erik was handling the publicity. The second was from Jean-Claude asking how the wedding had gone and apologizing once again for not being able to make it over. The third and fourth were from friends inviting her for dinner and to see a movie. Of course none of them had been from Jake, she knew he wasn't going to call, so why, Goddammit, did she keep doing this to herself?

'I hope that husband of yours has told you how fantastic you look tonight,' Erik said, coming up behind Sarah and whisking her glass from her mouth to kiss her.

'Erik!' she cried, throwing her arms around him. 'I was beginning to think you weren't going to make it.'

'As if,' he laughed. 'Anyway, seems like you're doing pretty well without me,' he added, casting an approving eye around the crowded gallery. 'And a few red stickers, I see. My God, what's that!' he suddenly cried, spotting one of Morandi's little *chef d'œuvres* nestling shyly between two towering framed pictures of the *Esterel*.

'Sssh,' Sarah giggled, 'he'll hear you,' and taking Erik's arm she turned him to one side to explain. 'I said he could hang a few because he looked so down in the dumps that no one was showing any interest in his work.' She started to laugh. 'You know what Michael, the thirteen-year-old said? "You're not going to let the old tosspot put his rubbish up, are you?" Erik, if you'd seen Morandi's face! I'm not sure whether it was the tosspot, old or rubbish that did it, but he looked so devastated I couldn't back out then. And besides, look, four of them have sold.'

Erik was grinning and seeing the way Sarah's eyes were sparkling he had no problem working out who Morandi's mysterious, never mind misguided, benefactors were – in fact, even as they spoke Sarah's father, under an assumed name of course, was making his bewildering purchase.

'So where's Louisa?' Erik said, scanning the crowd again and waving to a group of his trendy staff over in one corner. 'It's a great turnout,' he remarked, 'better even than I expected.'

'That's because your name was attached to it,' Sarah reminded him. 'Anyway, Louisa's not coming.'

'What! You're joking!'

'Erik!' Morandi cried, slapping him on the back. 'When did you get here? I didn't see you come in.'

'About five minutes ago,' Erik said, 'and Sarah's just told me Louisa's not coming. I was really hoping to see her tonight . . .'

'Has Sarah told you why she's not coming?' Morandi asked, gazing adoringly into his wife's eyes.

'Come on you two, the honeymoon's over,' Erik laughed as Sarah gazed back at Morandi.

'That's what you think,' Sarah murmured. 'Anyway, prepare yourself for this . . . Louisa's not coming because . . .' and pulling Erik's ear down to her mouth she began to whisper.

'I don't believe it!' Erik cried when she'd finished. 'I just don't believe it. I never thought she'd do it.'

'Well she has,' Sarah told him, glancing around and hoping that none of the press had overheard what she'd just said. They didn't seem to have and as her eyes returned to Erik's he started to laugh and shake his head as though he was still having a problem believing it.

Someone who was having even more of a problem believing it was Louisa herself, for never would she have dreamt she'd do something like this. But it was only now, as she stood there on the tarmac at Los Angeles airport waiting in line to board the small plane to San Diego that the enormity of what she was about to do seemed to be reaching her. Right up until the moment the 747 had touched down at LAX she had been convinced she was doing the right thing. She'd talked it over with Sarah for days before booking the flight and once it was done it had seemed to strengthen her resolve even further. She knew he was never going to call her, knew that nothing so romantic and sixpenny novelish as him turning up on her doorstep was going to happen, so she'd taken destiny into her own hands and flown over six thousand miles to . . . To what? What was she going to do, apart from make a complete fool of herself? She took a deep breath. She was going to call him from the hotel and tell him where she was. Then she was going to say that if he still didn't want to see her she would just turn around and go home.

'There's not a whole lot of room on board, ma'am,' one of the ground staff shouted over the noise of the engines, making her jump as he broke into her thoughts. 'Would you like to store your hand baggage in the hold?'

Louisa looked at the man in his bulky headphones and leather jacket and wanted desperately to say no, she would rather turn right around and go back into the airport. 'Thank you,' she said, handing it over. Then turning to look at the great blazing orange ball of the sun as it sank down over the Pacific she said, 'Do you have a lot of sunsets like this?'

'We sure do, ma'am,' the man answered. 'Would you like to step aboard now.'

It seemed only minutes later that the aircraft was taxiing down the runway, soaring outwards and upwards as though to shave the curved edge from the dazzling, melting crescent of the sun and carrying her relentlessly, inexorably towards a city she now never wanted to see.

This all felt so horribly wrong that she wished she could wake up and find out it was all just a nightmare. What on earth was he going to think? That she was insane was probably the best she could hope for. Whatever, he obviously wasn't going to be pleased because if he'd wanted to see her he'd have told her. In fact, what he'd told her was that he *didn't* want to see her. So what was the matter with her? Did she really have to have it spelled out this way?

The grinding nerves in her stomach intensified as she reminded herself that she had to give this a try, if only because she had to satisfy herself that she had done everything in her power to give them a chance. And if he turned her away then at least she would know that she really was wasting her time to go on hoping. And she must stop asking herself what kind of self-respecting woman went chasing after a man this way, because she knew that it was a woman who felt the man was worth fighting for. The maddening thing was that it had all seemed so easy when she was just talking about it, doing it was another thing altogether.

Her brown eyes were wide and anxious as she stared out at the darkening night sky. Each passing mile seemed to be draining her confidence, dissipating it, shredding it like the propellers breaking up the meandering drifts of cloud. She fought hard to keep it locked firmly inside her, but there were so many doubts, so much misgiving and apprehension that by the time the plane swooped down over San Diego she knew her nerve had failed her completely. She felt pathetic and angry as she pressed her way through the crowds in the arrival hall, thankful only for the fact that no one could see her shame. She collected her luggage and made her way to the exit, thankful for one other thing – that in this country that suddenly felt so foreign at least everything was in English. Catching a quick glimpse of her reflection she almost wanted to laugh. Her tawny hair fell softly over one cheek, the fine bones of her face, her slender neck, the black sweater and leggings she'd chosen for comfort, all gave out an elegance and poise that she was so very far from feeling. Then pushing hurriedly out through the big glass doors she discarded the faint hope that Sarah might have called him to tell him she was on her way. If Sarah had, he hadn't responded.

In less than half an hour a taxi delivered her to the hotel in La Jolla, a district of San Diego that appeared as resplendent in bright white Spanish style buildings, glittering lights and gently swaying palms as it did in wealth. Though she didn't know where exactly La Jolla was in relation to Rancho Santa Fe where Jake lived Sarah had told her that it wasn't far. But it didn't matter how far it was, she was quite resolved now that she was going to save them both the embarrassment of calling him.

Before getting into bed she picked up the phone and dialled Sarah's number. Maybe Sarah would say something to help pull her out of this jungle of indecision and misgiving.

'Hi, where are you?' Sarah said.

'At the hotel in La Jolla.'

'Oh, I see.'

Louisa frowned. For some reason Sarah sounded disturbed by that.

'Have you called him yet?' Sarah asked.

'No. I don't think I'm going to.'

'Oh,' Sarah said.

Louisa's heart turned over at the flatness of Sarah's tone. She'd felt sure that Sarah was going to encourage her to call, but it seemed that Sarah had undergone a change of heart too.

'When did you get there?' Sarah said.

'About an hour ago. Sarah, I really wish I hadn't done this now. It feels all wrong. But I just can't reconcile myself to coming all the way home again without calling. Tell me what I should do. For God's sake tell me what I should do!'

'Oh shit,' Sarah groaned. 'I wish I was there with you.'

'I wish you were too.'

Sarah took a breath, then very gently she said, 'Louisa, I have to tell you this . . . He knows you're there.'

Louisa's eyes closed as her heart folded around the cruel rejection Sarah's words had conjured. 'What do you mean?' she whispered. 'How does he know?'

'I called him just after you left in the hope he might come to meet you at the airport.'

'I see,' Louisa said, her eyes moving sightlessly over the heavy, brocaded curtains. *This couldn't be happening. Sarah hadn't done that. He couldn't know she was there, please God, he couldn't.* 'Well, I guess I know now what I came to find out,' she said.

'I'm sorry,' Sarah said miserably. 'I didn't know if I was doing the right thing, but Morandi thought it might go better for you if Jake had some warning that you were coming. Oh God, Louisa, I've ruined it for you now and you're such a long way away . . .'

'No, you haven't ruined it,' Louisa told her, wanting so desperately to see him now that it was consuming every part of her. *He knew she was there and he hadn't come!* 'What you've done is given him the choice of whether or not he wants to see me.'

'What are you going to do?'

'Book myself on the first flight out tomorrow.'

There was a pause before Sarah spoke again. 'Maybe you should try calling him anyway,' she said. 'He might feel differently once he hears your voice.'

'I don't think so,' Louisa answered. 'I'm going to ring off now, I'll call you again with my flight details. Can you pick me up from Heathrow?'

'Of course.'

After calling the front desk to reserve her flights Louisa lay down on the bed, hugging herself and trying to contain the crying ache inside her. It felt so much worse now that they were in the same city, so much more vital now that she knew it wasn't possible. It was so bad she could hardly bear it. She could sense his anger at what she had done as though it were there in the room, stealing through her as unrelentingly as the pain of the rejection. She felt such a fool, such an intruder in a city that was his. It was where he belonged with Antonia and his father – and his memories of Martina. What they had shared in France belonged to that one isolated summer and she had no right to trespass beyond it. He had told her so many times that there was no future for them and she'd sworn, even to herself, that she believed him. But of course, she hadn't, if she had she wouldn't be here now, putting herself through such unnecessary pain and humiliation.

The night passed in a blur of misery and fury at her own stupidity, all she wanted was to be on a plane back to London, to be as far away from him as she could get.

Her breakfast was served on the wrought-iron balcony overlooking the incredible blue Pacific. She had no appetite so leaning her elbows on the balustrade she cupped her face in her hands and stared out at the faint grey smudge of pollution on the horizon. The gentle ocean breeze carried the flowery scent of the gardens below and the distant sound of traffic. She could hardly bear any of it as the need to know what he was doing, where he was in this city she would never see, lapped over her heart like the waves lapping the shore.

An hour later she called down to reception for someone to come and collect her bags. When they'd gone she stood staring at the phone. Its silence throughout the night had told her all she needed to know, but still she was asking herself if she could really have come all this way just to turn around and go back? It seemed insane, more insane than having come here in the first place. And quite suddenly, without giving herself time to think, she took his number from her bag and dialled it. A man's voice, not Jake's, answered after the second ring.

'Hello,' she said. 'Could I speak to Jake Mallory please?'

'I'm sorry, ma'am,' the voice answered, 'he's not at home right now. Can I give him a message?'

'No, no message,' she said and with her heart pounding through her ears she hung up. She guessed that he was probably there, that he had told whoever answered the phone to say he wasn't at home. For one terrible moment she wanted to scream, to lash out at him and tell him how much she hated him for making her behave like this. Seeing his number in her diary she picked up a pen and scored thick black lines across it. If only it were so easy to blot him from her life. But she would, she'd have to now – and, feeling a bitter resistance to the comfort she tried to draw from the fact that there could no longer be any wasted hours of hope or futile dreams of reunion, she picked up her bag and turned towards the door. Now all she wanted was for the hours to melt into minutes, the distance to contract into nothing and to find herself back in London where she could perhaps pretend that she had never embarked on this fool's mission.

Pulling the door open she checked in her bag for the key. Then as she looked up her eyes dilated in shock. She tried to speak but no sound came out as she felt herself faltering in the dark intensity of his eyes. His shoulders were resting against the opposite wall, his hands were in his pockets and as he shrugged himself away from the wall for one panicked moment she almost turned and ran back into the room. But the compelling anger and pain in his expression stopped her.

As he gazed down into her frightened yet defiant eyes and saw how tired and torn apart she looked, his mouth hardened even as he raised a hand to stop her closing the door.

'Why have you done this?' he growled.

Her mouth trembled as she answered. 'Why do you think?' she answered, pain edging her voice with anger.

He turned and stared off down the corridor, his hand still resting on the door above her head. He was so close, so unbearably and overwhelmingly close, yet there was a barrier between them that was holding her away, pushing her back with the same force as his magnetism drew her.

She looked at the bandanna knotted untidily at his throat, the brilliance of his white shirt that made his hair and his skin seem so dark, the rise and fall of his chest as he breathed, the hard set of his jaw as he turned his haunted eyes back to hers. The telltale signs of grief were etched deeply at the sides of his mouth, the ageing shadows of sleepless nights ringed his eyes.

'Why didn't you call last night?' he said gruffly.

'Because I knew when I got here what a mistake it had been to come.'

He nodded. 'So?'

'So I'm going home,' she said angrily.

He dropped his head, wiping a hand over the inky black stubble on his chin. Despite the distance he was holding her at, despite the resolute hardness in his heart, he could feel her moving into him the way she so often did at night, the way she had in those hours before Martina died. The thought was like oil on the flame of his anger. She had no place in his life, so why had he come here? Why didn't he just let her go? Her vulnerability was stealing into him, filling him with the crying ache to hold her, to crush her in his arms and forget everything that had gone before. But the guilt of loving her more than he had loved Martina was so heavy within him he couldn't find a way past it.

He raised his eyes back to hers and the delicacy of her face, the fullness of her lips and the troubled depths of her luminous eyes closed around his heart like an excruciating, comforting pain. He harboured no fool's dream that they could pick up where they'd left off, it just wasn't possible. But to go on hurting her this way was no answer; to assuage his guilt by denying her his love, by shutting her out and blinding himself to what existed between them was only going to cripple him further. The words came almost of their own accord. 'We should talk,' he said.

She looked long into his eyes before slowly shaking her head. 'No. You're not ready and I . . .'

'We need to talk,' he interrupted harshly.

'How can we,' she cried, 'when you're in this kind of mood and . . .'

'You took that risk by coming here,' he snapped.

'And I was a damned fool to have done it, so I don't need you coming here and making me feel even worse than I already do.'

His jaw tightened, but as he rolled his eyes and a ghost of the irony she remembered so well stole into them she felt tears start to swim in her own.

'Jake, please,' she said, swallowing hard. 'I don't know what to say, I don't know what to do either, but I've booked my flight home now and . . .'

'Cancel it,' he said.

'I can't,' she whispered, lowering her eyes.

'Why?'

As she shook her head she could feel the emotion tightening her throat, choking off her answer. It was so hard to be sure if he really wanted her to stay or if he was only saying it because . . .

'Why?' he repeated, putting his fingers under her chin and lifting her face. The surprising gentleness of his touch, the probing tenderness in his eyes sank deeply and painfully into her heart.

'Because I don't think you really want me to.'

'I want you to,' he said, fighting against the words even as he spoke them. But they were true, he wanted her to stay. He wanted . . . His eyes dropped to her mouth, then with a humourless laugh he closed them and let his hand fall away. How could he be thinking of making love to her now, of holding her exquisite, slender body against his own, when he was so damned mixed up, so unsure of what he really wanted, it was driving him crazy.

She could sense the dilemma in him as acutely as she could sense her own fear. But he needed her, she felt so sure of it, but still she was afraid. Slowly, tentatively and hardly daring to breathe, she reached out to touch him, resting her hand lightly on his chest as she watched his eyes open and gaze into hers.

'Will you cancel it?' he said.

She nodded.

His eyes were burning into hers as covering her hand with his he drew her into the circle of his arm and brought his mouth harshly down on hers. The taste of him, the smell of him and the feel of him was like a slow burning power spreading its heat through her veins. But it wasn't right, his passion felt like a punishment. She tried to push him away, but he held her firmly, letting go of her mouth and wrapping her in his arms as he buried his face in her neck. 'Don't go,' he whispered.

'I won't,' she said, holding him tightly. 'But stop hating me. Please, stop hating me.'

'I don't hate you,' he said, pulling her back to look into her face.

'Then what is it?'

His eyes looked searchingly, almost desperately into hers. Didn't she have any idea how much he had suffered for loving her? But no, she didn't, how could she, he'd never told her. He'd shut her out and made her suffer too.

'It's a whole lot of things,' he said, holding her against him. Then a light of incredulous laughter flickered in his eyes as he added, 'You took one hell of a gamble coming here and I've got to tell you I was pretty damned mad when Sarah called to tell me you were on your way. But then, when you didn't call last night was when I realized . . . Well, I guess I realized that I couldn't let you go without seeing you.'

'And now?'

His eyes held hers. It wasn't the moment to tell her that he still didn't know if he could forgive himself for loving her while Martina was still alive, that was something they would have to deal with in the days, maybe the months, to come. What mattered now was that he took the uncertainty from her eyes by letting her know that whatever was waiting for them in the future, good or bad, he wanted to be there for her the way she was here for him now. And the only way he could start was by letting the love show in his eyes as he gazed down into hers and offered her the single most precious thing in the world to him, 'Now,' he said, 'there's a little girl not too far away from here who I think is going to be happy to meet you.'

DANCE WHILE YOU CAN

Susan Lewis

arrow books

Acknowledgements
My sincere thanks to G. V. Hardyman and Christopher Dale of Clifton College, Bristol. To Victoria Walcough of Christie's, South Kensington. Lindsay and Bob Hall. My friend Fanny, who not only introduced me to Sark but gave me unstinted support throughout the book. A very special thank you to Patrick Early of the British Council in Cairo, and John Kelsey-Fry. And, of course, Laura and Toby.

To Dad and Gary, with love

From the moment I met her, there was never any doubt in my mind that one day I would have to kill her. Perhaps it was a genuine vision of the future, though I recall no images, not even the vividness of the fire that was to consume so much. I felt only the overwhelming need to protect myself, and all that was mine.

Elizabeth Sorrill. She was blessed with the kind of beauty I had only dreamed about, bringing love and laughter to my brothers, while all the time she nursed the pain of a love she had lost – a love she would never give up.

And what right had she to that love? I am a woman, I have known love, I have known the pain of loss. Have I spent my life making others suffer for it?

But I know now that I have never experienced anything like the love that bound Elizabeth and Alexander. It was a love that not only bridged the gulf of class, but survived years of parting, the agony of rejection, and that most destructive of emotions, guilt. Do I envy her that love? No, I pity her. A love of that depth, that strength, extracts its own price. I was the one to call in the debt, and I have no regrets. Why should she have had it all? What was her suffering compared to mine? My brother gave her the world – but it was my world too, and I lied, cheated and murdered to get it back. Yet all the time my enemy – my invincible enemy – was not Elizabeth, nor Alexander, but the love they shared.

Why was their love so indestructible?

I rest my head against the wall. There is nothing to see here, only darkness, but my nostrils flare at the cloying stench of my surroundings. Among the few, almost indistinguishable sounds, I can hear myself laughing. Laughing and laughing. The bitter irony of it is, if anyone could answer me that last question, then here, at the end, they would hand me the key to life itself.

As it is, it is they who hold the key – Elizabeth and Alexander.

– Elizabeth –

– 1 –

'*A schoolboy*! You're telling me you're in love with a *schoolboy*?'

Already wishing I hadn't said anything, I met Janice's incredulous gaze. 'I didn't say I was in love with him, I only said . . .'

'Yes, I know what you said. You said you can't stop thinking about him. And the way you've been moping around here, well, I can't believe how dense I've been. But a schoolboy, Elizabeth. Do you know what you're doing? Do you realise what it means?'

'I'm not doing anything, and it means you're getting everything out of proportion, as usual.'

'You've been stuck down there at that school for too long, it's turned your mind. Christ, I could understand if it were one of the masters. But a boy!'

'If you saw him you wouldn't call him a boy.'

'Well, how old is he? Fifteen, sixteen?'

'Nearly seventeen.'

'And you're twenty-one. And this is 1964, and you're probably one of the most beautiful women I've ever seen in my life. You've got to get away from that place, Elizabeth, and fast. Junior matron at a boys' public school, I ask you! I never understood why you went there in the first place. So what's happened between the two of you? You haven't . . .'

'Of course not. We danced together at the end of term, that's all.'

'Danced! I can hardly get a word out of you because you danced with a schoolboy? There really is something wrong with you, Elizabeth Sorrill. I'm going to have to find you a man, and fast.'

Janice liked her 'and fast's, but just at that moment they irritated me. I'd come to spend the summer holidays with her, in the bedsit we used to share in Putney when, like her, I'd been a nurse at the Meadford Clinic. But I'd only been there a few months when a vacancy had come up for a junior matron at Foxton's Boys' School, down in the west country. I'd lied about my age, collected my references from Mrs Carey at the Meadford, and gone. I'm not quite sure why I did it, except it seemed like a challenge and I'd never really felt at home in London. That was six months ago.

'I take it you do want to find a *man?*' Janice said, when she realised I wasn't going to say anything.

'You don't have to say it like that, and as a matter of fact, I don't.'

'Elizabeth, think about it! This relationship can't go anywhere, and you'll land yourself in a whole heap of trouble.'

'Stop moralising. I danced with him, that's all, and I like him. He's . . .'

'Spare me. You're going to tell me he's tall, dark and handsome, and he's got a winning smile.'

'As a matter of fact he is tall, dark and handsome. And as for his smile, one of his teeth is crooked. What I *was* going to say was that he's made me feel as if I belong at the school – not easy in a place like that. I have a lot of fun there now, more than I ever did flitting round pubs in the Kings Road. I'm happy, Janice. I feel as if I belong there, as if I have a place there – and it's all down to him.'

'Down to *him?*' She looked at me and I could feel one of her 'and fast's coming. 'Don't you realise the effect you have on people, Elizabeth. No, you don't, do you, you never did. Look at yourself. You're all the things the rest of us dream about; sensuous, long-legged, voluptuous; you've only got to move and something happens to a man. Jesus, there are things about you . . .'

'Janice . . .'

'Like the way you make someone feel they're the most special person alive. What's the name of that song "From a Jack to a King". Even the bloody sun comes out when you laugh. And it's not just men, you have that effect on women too, so God only knows what you're doing to those poor little buggers down there, locked away in that school. Try looking at yourself through their eyes. One day you just appear in their lives; you don't speak like them, you don't act like them, nobody knows anything about you. You're a mystery . . .'

'Stop talking rubbish. I'm just an ordinary person, Janice, like anyone else. I don't talk about my past because it's too painful. But you know what happened, how my parents were killed, then I came to London and trained – with you – as a nurse, so why don't you drop all this nonsense about a mystery?'

She sighed. 'You really don't know what I'm talking about, do you? You say things in that funny, rich, accented voice of yours and everyone stops to listen. I'll bet he's smitten: I'll bet they all are. Well, I'm going to get you out of there, and fast. It's time you came back to the real world. What's his name, anyway?'

'Alexander. Alexander Belmayne.'

If her eyes had been any rounder they'd have burst out of her head. 'Alexander Belmayne! The one you wrote to me about? The one you couldn't stand, who made your life a misery?' She covered her face with her hands. 'Jesus, you're in bigger trouble than I thought.'

'You always dramatise everything, Janice. OK, so I didn't like him at first, but only because I hadn't got to know him. That's all.'

'*That's all!* You nearly left at Easter because of him, remember?'

'I wish I'd never told you now. And I'm going back to Foxton's at the beginning of next term, so you can forget about finding me another man, another job or another anything.'

'Then all I can say is, don't come crying to me when he gets over his schoolboy crush. Except he won't, will he? Men never get over women like you. It's just left for the likes of me to pick up the pieces.'

She flounced out, but I knew she'd be back. We'd quarrelled before and it usually ended with one or other of us storming off. It gave us time to reflect on who was right and who was wrong.

But of course, Janice was right: I was ignorant of the way I looked, the way I was. And if I'd left the school then, as she suggested, got away, who can calculate how much pain might have been avoided? But all that seemed important to me then was that Foxton's, a school of just over two hundred boys, should remain the centre of my world. I couldn't see what I might be doing to Alexander, or he to me. Naturally there were others there, like Miss Angrid the senior matron, whom I'd come to care for a great deal, but it was Alexander who'd made me feel . . .

But I'm getting ahead of myself. Things moved so fast, and so much happened that sometimes I have to think quite hard before I can remember how it all started. Then I laugh, because it is madness to think for one moment that I might really have forgotten.

– 2 –

It was just after lunch on a cold spring day when Miss Angrid, the senior matron, picked up her well-thumbed volume of Shelley and turned her chair to face the fire. 'Well, at least that's over for another six months,' she said, referring to the medicals that had been going on for the past two and a half days. 'Why don't you treat yourself to the afternoon off, go and explore the village? There's no point in hanging around here, unless you want me to read to you, that is.'

She peered up at me from under her whiskery eyebrows, knowing full well I'd do anything rather than sit through a recital of *Prometheus Unbound*. She laughed as I grabbed at my starched cap and shook out my hair. 'Beautiful,' she said. 'Too beautiful. I wonder if I've done the right thing, taking you on. Still, wouldn't be without you now, even if you do run at the mention of Shelley.'

I was on the point of making good my escape when Christopher Beadling, a spotty, skinny little thing from the second year, knocked and came in. 'Left my blazer behind, Miss,' he said, and looking at me he blushed and started to snigger – along with the boys who were huddled around the 'grub' cupboard outside.

'Next door in Miss Sorrill's surgery,' Miss Angrid answered, then looked at me. 'No idea what they're planning?' she said, after he'd closed the door behind him.

'Not a clue.' But they were up to something, that was clear. Some kind of initiation ceremony Miss Angrid had called it, when she'd warned me that the boys would be bound to take advantage of my first night duty alone. 'Insufferable beasts!' she said now, and went back to her book.

I'd been at the school almost two months by then, and was settling in quite well, although I still felt quite overawed by my surroundings sometimes, and had to pinch myself to make sure I wasn't dreaming. The whole place was much grander than I could have imagined, with its endless gilt script lists of honoured old boys and its portraits of Foxton's achievers. The corridors were dark and dank and smelt of beeswax and boiled cabbage. The boys were such a contrast to their gloomy surroundings that I was still sometimes surprised when I heard them stamping around and shouting and laughing. And the way everyone spoke made me wish I could be rid of my rounded, half west country half London accent, and become one of them. But I was working away quietly on that, along with everything else. Ever since I'd arrived I'd felt a kind of excitement bubbling away inside me. It was as if I was waiting for something to happen; like a chrysalis almost ready to burst.

When I got outside, because the sun was shining and I'd seize on any excuse not to have the embarrassment of using Tonto, I decided to walk back to the cottage.

Tonto was the nickname the boys had given the golf-cart that Miss Angrid used to ferry herself to and from the cottage where both she and I lived, she on the bottom floor, I on the top. 'Quite self-contained, quite separate,' as she had told me when she'd first shown me round. It was on the edge of the school grounds, closing the only gap in the thick hedge on the south side of the field beyond the rugby pitch, and sandwiched between Foxton's copse – five trees, some bushes and a pond – and the farmland behind. From my bedroom window I could see the statue of Arthur Foxton, the school's founder, far in the distance, standing in the courtyard in front of the school like a general in front of his army.

As I passed the sixth form common room Godfrey Barnes opened a window, gave a long wolf-whistle and asked if I'd like to go in for tea. I said I might pop back later, provided they didn't make me take part in another debate on the economic and trade whatsits of Britain joining Europe. Last time, I'd said I thought England was already in Europe, and they'd all laughed so much that I'd had to get out the atlas next day to reassure myself that I was right.

'How about telling us what you thought of *Lady Chatterley's Lover*,' Richard Lock called out. 'You have read it, I take it?'

'Bits of it,' I admitted.

'No prizes for guessing which bits. Did you know there are thirty fucks or fuckings, fourteen . . .'

Time to walk on, I thought, suppressing a giggle. I'd got as far as the front entrance when the main door opened.

'Miss!'

'Yes, what is it?' I said, trying out my haughtiest voice. I was never like that with anyone else, but for some reason with Alexander Belmayne I couldn't help myself. He was in the fifth form, one of the most popular boys at the school, and without a doubt the best looking.

'Er, it's nothing, Miss, only that, well . . .' He looked up at the sky as he sauntered towards me. 'Isn't it good to see the sun, Miss? Been jolly beastly weather lately, it's much better here in the summer. Can get outdoors more.'

I looked at him, knowing I was blushing, and unable to think of anything to say.

'I was just wondering, Miss.' He was looking straight into my eyes. 'If you're not intending to take Tonto back to the cottage, then me and a couple of the others were thinking about taking in a few holes on the golf course. Miss Angrid would never know, she'd think Tonto was with you. We'd take good care of it.'

I took a step back, shaking my head. 'I'm sorry, if it was mine it might be different, but . . .'

He held up his hands for me to stop. 'It's OK, Miss, I understand. I shouldn't even have asked.' Then, smiling to himself, he turned back inside.

I was glad he'd given in so easily as I didn't know how long I could have held out against him, and it wasn't until I started back down the drive that it suddenly dawned on me: there was nothing to stop them taking the cart anyway. And if it got damaged . . . It would be better all round if I took Tonto with me, and at the same time I'd show Alexander Belmayne I wasn't quite the idiot he took me for.

Reversing Tonto out of its space, I flicked the switch that shot out the little orange indicator arms at the side. The third form had installed them about a month ago, but unfortunately they either came out together or not at all. I shifted the gear lever to go forward. It must have been two or three seconds before I realised I was still going backwards. I pressed my foot on the brake. Nothing happened. I turned round to see if anything was in my path only just in time to avoid a collision with the Headmaster's brand new Rover. It was a narrow miss, and I was still on the move. Then suddenly the machine roared and I was hurtling round the car park.

Just missing the ha-ha, I shot round – and to my horror saw Mr Lear's red Ford Popular coming towards me. I yanked the wheel but it was too late. Tonto gouged itself right along the wing of the car. After that, things happened so fast I didn't know where I was until I shot out of the seat and skidded across the gravel, tearing my stockings and scattering the contents of my bag. Tonto, tipping on its side, groaned to a stop, I covered my face with my hands, taking deep breaths to try and steady myself.

A loud tapping brought me to my senses. Two floors up a cluster of faces was pressed against a window, every one of them laughing fit to burst. Someone waved, and suddenly I was so angry I wanted to scream.

As I ran into the school, tears streaming down my face, I bumped straight into Alexander Belmayne. 'You!' I screeched. 'It was you, wasn't it? You didn't want to borrow the cart at all, you just wanted to make a fool of me. Well, you're going to pay for this. Now get out of my way!'

'Look . . .'

'Don't touch me! It's too late for apologies.'

Miss Angrid's face turned white with anger when I told her what had happened, and how I had been tricked into using the golf-cart. 'Yes, that's Belmayne's style all right.

Come with me,' she barked and marched me straight off to the Headmaster.

Mr Lorimer's first concern was for his Rover. When he found I'd managed to avoid it, he was sympathy itself – at least, as far as I was concerned. 'Get Belmayne here,' he snapped. Miss Angrid bustled out of the study, and all of a sudden I felt hot and dizzy, and started to shake.

'Sit down, Miss Sorrill.' He waved me to the brown leather Chesterfield. 'It must have been quite a shock for you. Can I get you something?'

'No, no,' I muttered, trying to pull my skirt down over my grazed knees and cover the holes in my stockings.

He picked up the phone and buzzed through to his secretary. 'Find Mr Lear and have him come to my study as soon as he can. He should be sitting prep for the fourth form.'

We waited in silence. Mr Lorimer, in his gown and grey suit, stood with his back to me, staring out of the window. I was acutely aware that my hair was loose around my shoulders, and tried to tuck it into the collar of my coat.

At last Miss Angrid came in with Alexander Belmayne.

'Thank you, Miss Angrid,' Mr Lorimer said, walking around his desk, 'that will be all.' Miss Angrid looked disappointed, but no one argued with the Head, so she turned and closed the door behind her.

'Belmayne,' Mr Lorimer looked the boy straight in the eye, 'you know why you have been summoned here?'

Alexander's face was white. 'No, sir.'

'Were you responsible for Miss Sorrill's mishap in the golf-cart, Belmayne?'

'No, sir.'

'Miss Sorrill seems to think you were.'

Alexander's eyes were fixed on the floor.

'As a prefect of this school you don't need me to tell you that the punishment for this irresponsible display and the resulting damage could be expulsion?'

I gasped, and Alexander's head snapped up. He dashed the dark curls out of his eyes and glared back at the Head. The threat had only roused him. I could see that the Head would have no easy victory.

And so it proved. Alexander was ordered to name names, but he refused, and consistently denied he'd had anything to do with the golf-cart. It was clear the Head didn't believe him, and the interrogation started all over again when Mr Lear came in. All the time my eyes were riveted on Alexander's face. He didn't look at me once as his grey eyes flashed and the shadow on his chin seemed to get darker as he fought to control his temper.

I don't know how long we were in there, but it felt like hours. Alexander handed over his prefect's badge and Mr Lear laid a cane on the desk. In their eyes Alexander might be just a boy, but he was taller than both of them, and already filling out into the man he would soon become. My heart went out to him as I realised what this was doing to his pride.

In the end Mr Lorimer drove me back to the cottage. 'I shall speak to Lord Belmayne before I make a decision about what to do with the boy,' he said, when I asked what would happen to Alexander. 'In the meantime Mr Lear will take charge.'

The next time I saw Alexander he was on his way to bed with the rest of the fifth form. I stood on the surgery landing watching them pass. He didn't look at me, and neither did anyone else.

'Pity it had to be Belmayne,' Mrs Jenkins said, as she turned over a page of the newspaper.

I looked up from the crossword puzzle I was doing. The Latin teacher was between lessons and had come to my surgery for a cup of tea.'Why?' I asked. 'I'd say it's a pity it had to be anyone at all. I mean, it *was* dangerous.'

'True, but more of a pity it was Belmayne.' She pushed her empty cup across the table. 'Of course, it's your own fault. All this silent treatment, I mean. You let the boys think you were their friend, didn't you? Shouldn't wonder if you don't actually encourage them to misbehave sometimes – what about that snowball fight you became embroiled in three weeks ago, most undignified. I know you're young, Elizabeth, but you have a position to maintain – and buying the boys Brylcream when you go to the village so's they can look like Elvis Presley is ridiculous. Lucky Miss Angrid put a stop to it before Mr Lorimer found out. You can't pretend to be one of them and then go and report the very one they all idolise. They'll never forgive you, you know, at least, not until Alexander does. I saw him earlier, on his way out to the rugby pitch. Must have been quite a thrashing Mr Lear gave him, I could still see the marks.'

'But it was almost a week ago!' I said.

'Precisely. Mr Lear is very fond of that car of his. Unfortunately the Lord Chief Justice seems to have rather a lot on his plate right now, if this article is anything to go by,' she went on.

'What's the Lord Chief Justice got to do with it?'

She looked down her nose at me. 'Surely you know the Lord Chief Justice is Alexander's father.' She went back to the paper. 'Those damned gypsy types! Here,' she passed the newspaper as she got to her feet, 'read that. It might give you some insight into what kind of man Lord Belmayne is – and his son is going to be.'

I wasn't going to show her I was interested. I waited for her to leave before I picked up the newspaper.

> The Lord Chief Justice, Lord Belmayne, is again locked in bitter conflict with the family of gypsy murderer Alfred Ince. The family have always claimed that Ince, sentenced to death for the notorious 'farm murder' in 1954, was innocent. Lord Belmayne, who presided over the long and much-publicised trial, at which several members of the Ince family were arrested for contempt of court, has since been the victim of continuing harassment.
>
> This is not the first time the Ince family have taken up residence on the Belmayne estate. Some weeks ago there were violent scenes when Lord Belmayne had them evicted from his land. More recently, Belmayne property, in London and Suffolk has been subjected to acts of vandalism, and Lady Belmayne is said to be suffering from shock following an incident in which a brick was hurled through the window of her Belgrave Square home.
>
> According to local sources, the gypsies arrived back on the Suffolk estate in the early hours of yesterday morning. Lord Belmayne, whose outspoken comments on the trial in South Africa of African National Congress leader Nelson Mandela have recently won him considerable publicity, spoke to me shortly afterwards. 'These people are causing anguish to my family and my staff. I will do everything in my power to have them removed.' It has been suggested by his estate manager that acts of perversion involving under-age girls and boys, are being practised at the gypsy camp, but Lord Belmayne refused to comment. In a heated speech in the House of Lords on Thursday he once again . . .

There was a knock on the door. 'Sorry to bother you.'

It was Mr Ellery, the chemistry master. 'A bit of a burn to the old fingers in the lab. Should be wise to it by now, of course, but they all think they're the first. Loathsome little creatures they can be at times, third formers. They heat up a glass, you see, and leave it on my desk for me to pick up.'

I led him over to the sink and put his hand under the running cold water then went to the medicine chest to find a cotton bandage. 'It'll be a bit painful for a while,' I said, as I dried his fingers.

'No matter. I'll live.' He looked down at my desk and with his other hand pulled the newspaper round to read the article about Lord Belmayne. 'Unlucky,' he said after a couple of minutes. 'Still, the press is usually much harder on him than this.'

'Have you met him?' I asked.

'Several times. His son is here at the school.' He looked at my face. 'But, of course, you already know that. I gather he's coming down on Sunday, after chapel.'

'Oh.'

'Cheer up. Young Belmayne will get no more than he deserves. He could have caused a very nasty accident.'

'But he didn't,' I said, 'and now I just wish the whole thing would go away. I was getting off to a good start before all this happened.'

'Mmm, shame,' he said, making me feel worse. 'Just a pity it was Belmayne.'

'That's what Mrs Jenkins said,' I muttered.

'Well, boys will be boys. I'm afraid you're going to have to get used to it if you want to survive at Foxton's. Now, I'd better be getting back. Heaven only knows what havoc they've wreaked in my absence.'

Absent-mindedly I watched him go. The door was almost closed behind him, when suddenly he came back in. 'I've been meaning to ask. Do you play bridge, Miss Sorrill?'

I looked up. 'Bridge?'

'Just a thought,' he shrugged, then left.

The following Sunday was an exeat, so straight after chapel most of the boys went off to spend the day with their parents. After lunch Miss Angrid and I roamed the empty dormitories looking for sweets and comics before she went back to the cottage, leaving me alone in my surgery. I'd been trying for days to think of a way I could approach Alexander and see if we could put the Tonto incident behind us, but he looked so hostile whenever I saw him that I couldn't seem to pluck up the courage. Mr Ellery, whom I'd been to the Bistro with the night before, had reminded me that I was a member of staff, and as such could call him into my surgery any time I liked – but it wasn't as easy as that. I'd been nervous of Alexander ever since I'd arrived, even though during my first week he'd gone out of his way to make me feel welcome. After that he'd left me to my own devices, and secretly I'd been glad. There was something about him that made me feel self-conscious and awkward.

I was going over all this in my mind when suddenly the door opened and he came in. 'Alexander!' I felt myself blush to the roots of my hair.

It was plain that he was in a filthy mood. 'Mr Lorimer would like to see you in his study,' he said, and without waiting, he turned and walked out.

I knew who the grand-looking gentleman was the instant I walked in, and felt myself shrinking inside. 'Please, sit down, Miss Sorrill,' said Mr Lorimer. 'Lord Belmayne has asked to speak to you, so I shall leave you together.'

Lord Belmayne was a handsome man, older than he appeared, I guessed, but with a magnificent head of grey hair, and piercing grey eyes. I could see straight away where Alexander got his looks from – in this case, angry ones.

'I believe I owe you an apology for the childish and

irresponsible behaviour of my son,' he said, barely looking at me. 'I am only thankful that you sustained no injury.'

His presence was so overpowering, his manner so cold, that when I opened my mouth to speak, nothing came out.

When he was satisfied that I wasn't going to say anything, he went on. 'Rest assured that Alexander has been sufficiently punished, both by the school and by myself, and I trust nothing like this will happen again.' He glanced towards the door, then, clutching his hands behind his back, he walked to the window. I had been dismissed.

– 3 –

As term went on my life became more and more of a misery. Apart from tasteless practical jokes involving dead mice and spiders and the stealing of my underwear from the laundry room – later found wrapped around Arthur Foxton's head – none of the boys took any notice of me. They just filed past on their way to bed, and at meal-times they were respectful but silent. All sickness was reported to Miss Angrid, while I sat in my surgery hoping someone would come in; but apart from Mr Ellery, no one did.

It was he who told me that Alexander's punishment from his father was to miss his skiing holiday with the family at Easter. As the walls of the room Alexander shared with Henry Clive were plastered with posters of skiers, I could see how severe a punishment that was for him. Well, good, was all I could say – it was less than he deserved! That was how I felt when Mr Ellery told me, but my mood swung without warning, and instead of the outraged, injured party, I became again the junior matron who remembered how kind Alexander had been when she'd first arrived and known no one . . .

By the end of term I was so unhappy I decided I had better leave. I would go away for the Easter holiday, and simply not come back. But on the last day I knew I couldn't walk out on Miss Angrid without telling her.

She listened while I explained how my friend Janice kept writing to me about the great time she was having in London, how she was combining nursing with a bit of part-time modelling and had hundreds of boyfriends – I blushed when I admitted that I'd never even had one. 'You see,' I said, 'I keep reading in all the magazines what people my age are doing, and I'm not doing any of it. The only thing I've got that shows I'm a bit up-to-date is the poster of George Harrison on my bedroom wall, and a Mary Quant minidress I sent away for. I know I should have given you more notice, and if you like, I'll come back until you find someone else. Janice's cousin has got a shop in Carnaby Street, I might be able to work there. It's not because I don't like it here, or anything like that, everyone's been really nice to me, it's just, well, I don't think I can stay any longer. I miss London, you see.'

'But really,' Miss Angrid said, 'you're going because of the boys?'

I looked away. I should have known she'd see through all that.

She gave my hand a squeeze. 'Would you believe me if I told you all this will blow over?'

I shook my head.

'It will, you know. They're behaving childishly, of course they are, but you have to remember that's exactly what they are – children. And as for Alexander, well, he's a popular boy with a lot of pride, but he'll get over it.'

'He won't! He hates me!'

'Now you're sounding like one of the juniors! Speaking for myself, young lady, I'd miss you a great deal if you went. You've brightened this place up more than you realise, even Mr Lorimer's commented on it. Oh, you're a bit of a handful sometimes, I'll admit that – especially when you take it into your head to defend yourself from catapults with a catapult of your own! – but there's no harm done, and you've won as big a place in most of our hearts as I happen to know we have in yours. And now you're blushing again, goodness you do blush easily, don't you? Well, maybe you're right, you should be up there in London modelling or working in a fashionable shop. But unless I've got you completely wrong, I don't think that's really your scene, as they say. So come along with you now, you don't strike me as someone who gives up that easily.'

I fished around in my sleeve for a hanky, keeping my head lowered so she wouldn't see I was crying. 'Now, how about giving it until the end of the summer term?' she said, passing me a tissue. 'And I think you'll find that if you try talking to Alexander, he'll listen. He's far too decent a chap to bear a grudge for long.'

'Is he?' It was pathetic how much I wanted that to be true.

'You take my word for it. So are you going to stay?'

I nodded. I wasn't brave enough to put my arms around her, but I wanted to.

'That's my girl. And now there's something I have to tell you. Mark Devenish, the little boy in the first year who suffers with homesickness? Well, his aunt came to the school early this morning. Mark's mother died last night. He's in Mr Lorimer's apartment now, they're waiting for you.'

I don't know why Mark's aunt left him behind at the school. I didn't like to ask, but I'd never seen a child look so lost and unhappy. He ran into my arms when I walked into the room, and I kept his face buried in my shoulder so he wouldn't see that I was crying too. Poor little mite, he was only eleven and had hardly any friends. How could everyone have deserted him?

I took him back to the cottage so that he didn't have

to watch the other boys getting ready to go away for the holiday. He had a pack of cards in his pocket and taught me how to play Trumps. I gave him some lemonade and cakes, but he didn't eat anything and he didn't say much either. But every now and then I saw his eyes fill with tears, and I put my arms around him while he clung to me like the frightened little child he was.

When Mr Lorimer knocked on the door later that afternoon I was touched by the way his face softened when he looked at Mark. He ruffled his hair and listened while the boy told him how he'd beaten me at seven games of Trumps, and I winced when he added that he'd won three-and-six off me.

Luckily Mr Lorimer laughed, then he turned to me. 'I'm afraid it seems we've got another casualty on our hands, Miss Sorrill. Miss Angrid's taken a tumble down the stairs. Mr Parkhouse has taken her to the hospital, though she insists it's no more than a sprain.' He glanced at Mark, who for the moment was happily engaged in looking through my records. 'Perhaps you wouldn't mind walking down to my car with me a moment.'

He waited until we got outside before he spoke again. 'I'm glad of this chance to talk to you, Miss Sorrill, because I want you to know that I am aware things haven't been easy for you lately, and I'm sorry for it. However, Miss Angrid tells me that you wish to stay on at the school, and I want you to know how grateful I am. You have a naturalness in dealing with the boys that makes me very glad of the contact they have with you; your lack of pretension is good for them. I'm sorry if I've embarrassed you, but your contribution to the welfare of the boys has been much appreciated.'

All these compliments in one day, I'd have to offer to resign more often .... 'Thank you,' I said graciously, thinking how grown-up and dignified I seemed to have become lately.

'There is another matter, Miss Sorrill. In light of Mark's

fondness for you, and the fact that Miss Angrid will not be mobile for a week or two, I was wondering if I could impose upon you to remain at the school over the Easter break? You will, of course, receive suitable remuneration.'

'Oh, that's all right, I'll be fine in the cottage.'

He gave me a strange look, then said, 'If you would be so kind as to bring Mark to my apartment around six, after he's collected his belongings from the dormitory, I'll talk to him about going to the funeral.'

Poor little Mark. It looked as if his guardians were only too glad to pass all responsibility for him over to the school. If that was the case, it was probably better for him to be with us; I'd been lonely enough after my own parents died to know how awful it was to be with grown-ups who didn't want you.

As it turned out, I didn't see very much of him. He stayed in Mr Lorimer's apartment and the two of them only joined us for meals. Sometimes I saw them going off in the Rover or strolling about the grounds, but every night I went to say goodnight to Mark, and stayed with him until he fell asleep.

For the rest of the time there was Miss Angrid, who qualified – leaving all competition standing – as the world's worst patient. I wheeled her round the grounds and watched television with her, but apart from that, and her Shelley readings, there wasn't very much to do with all the boys away. So when Mr Ellery popped in during the week he was nearly bowled over by the welcome he got. Mark was at the cottage with us that day and his face lit up when he saw that Mr Ellery had brought his Monopoly set. I'll bet the four of us made more noise over those games of Monopoly than any of the boys did on the rugby field – mainly because Miss Angrid kept trying to cheat.

It was on Easter Sunday that Mark showed me a letter he'd been nursing for days. I'd thought it must be from his aunt, but I could hardly believe it when

I saw it was from Alexander Belmayne. He'd written to Mark to say how sorry he was to hear about his mother. Miss Angrid beamed all over with pleasure when I told her.

'Alexander is Mark's house captain, that's why he wrote. It will make the world of difference to the lad. The others won't dare to be unkind to him once they find out Alexander's written to him.' She looked at me. 'You see, he's not such a bad sort, is he?'

When all I did was look back at her she shook her head and handed me the letter. 'You've got too much pride, young lady, and you know what that comes before.'

Two days before the holiday was over, Mr Ellery and I were strolling along the sixth form corridor on our way out to the kitchen garden. I was laughing so hard at something he was saying that I didn't hear the voices coming from inside the common room.

'No sixth formers here, are there?' Mr Ellery asked, even though he already knew the answer. 'Intruders! Burglars!' He started an exaggerated tiptoe towards the door. 'Get ready to run for help.'

I covered my mouth, trying not to giggle, and waited while he pushed the door open.

'Gotcha!' he cried. I heard a scuffle, and then Mr Ellery said: 'Belmayne! What are you doing here?'

My heart turned over.

'Watching TV, sir,' came the reply.

'This is the sixth form common room,' Mr Ellery pointed out, as if Alexander didn't know.

'Yes, sir. But I thought as they weren't here, sir . . .'

Mr Ellery waved his hands. 'Never mind about that, why are *you* here? You're not due back until Wednesday.'

'My grandmother is going on holiday, sir. She'd forgotten to tell my father. Mr Lorimer knows all about it, sir.'

'Did you know anything about this?' Mr Ellery turned

to me. I shook my head. 'Well,' he said to Alexander, 'what are you going to do with yourself?'

I stepped inside the door in time to see Alexander shrug. His face reddened as he saw me, something Mr Ellery must have noticed too. 'Well, I'm sure we'll find something to keep you occupied,' he said. 'What are you watching, boy?'

'Football, sir.'

'Don't forget to turn off the set when you leave. I'll speak to you later.'

'He's a strange boy, isn't he?' I commented, as we strolled out into the garden.

'Who, Belmayne?' He sighed. 'Academically speaking, he's near brilliant. And he's a great kid, you know. Too much charm, too much wit, and too good-looking by half – but you can't help liking the boy.'

'You can't?'

He laughed. 'Come on, enough about him,' and grabbing my hand, he pulled me up over the hill.

At the top there was a swing that the boys had made in a tree. I sat in it while Mr Ellery pushed. He was flirting with me, but when I pretended not to notice he pushed me higher and higher until I was screaming out for him to stop. In the end I managed to throw myself off, fell over, rolled down the hill and knocked over the bins full of dead leaves.

He came running after me, obviously scared stiff I'd injured myself, but when he saw I was laughing, he reached out to pull me to my feet. 'You're far out, do you know that?' he puffed. 'And come to that, so are your legs.'

'You shouldn't have been looking!' I cried, as I picked the leaves from my uniform.

At that moment I happened to glance up and saw Alexander standing at the window of the music room, watching us. I don't know why, but it suddenly seemed as though the sun had gone in and I shivered.

'Cold?' said Mr Ellery. 'Come on, let's go back inside. I'll get someone to come and clear this lot up.'

We walked round to the front and went in through the main door just as Alexander was coming out of the music room. 'Go and clear up the leaves outside the walled garden, boy, will you?' Mr Ellery said.

Alexander glared at me so fiercely I nearly took a step back, then he brushed past us. Mr Ellery called after him. 'I don't care much for your attitude, Belmayne. You can come back here and apologise to Miss Sorrill. Now!'

Alexander turned round, but didn't come back. 'I apologise,' he said.

Mr Ellery and I parted company at the bottom of the stairs – where I waited until he'd disappeared into the staff room before turning to follow Alexander.

I found him refilling the bins as he'd been told. The gathering of dead leaves was normally a punishment, and one reserved for the younger boys, so I understood why he was mad at having to do it. He looked up, but when he saw it was me he went back to work.

'Can I help?' I offered.

'No thanks.'

I stood there for a while, watching him. Slowly I became aware of a kind of churning inside, and felt so jittery that I was glad he didn't look up. Eventually I said: 'I've come out here so we can have a chat. Will you listen to what I've got to say?'

He stopped what he was doing and stood up, looking straight ahead.

'Look, I don't mind saying I'm sorry, or that I'm really unhappy about all that's happened. And I thought that as we have to live under the same roof, it might be better if we tried to get along together. How about starting by looking at me when I'm speaking to you?'

To my surprise, he did – and the dreaded colour started to creep into my face.

'That's better,' I said. 'Now, I don't want to go over what's led to all this, and I don't expect you do either. All I will say is that if you had thought about what might happen before you doctored that stupid golf-cart, then you would have known that . . .'

'And what makes you so damned sure it was me who doctored the golf-cart?' he snapped. 'Did you see me do it? No. Let's face it, you've had it in for me ever since you started here. You . . .'

'Don't you shout at me, Alexander Belmayne. You tricked me and you know you did.'

'I did not trick you, you stupid woman!'

'How dare you! I'll have you know . . . No, don't you interrupt me, I'm not listening to another word from you.'

'Why? Afraid of what you might hear?'

'I'm not afraid of you!'

'*No?*' He stepped towards me – and I stepped back. 'Look at you!' he shouted. 'Not quite so stuck up now, are you? Now you can listen to me for a change. I liked you, did you know that? I thought you were all right. I bothered to welcome you into this school, and what did you do in return? Ignored me. Whenever you saw me coming you walked the other way. If I spoke to you, you put on that hoity-toity voice of yours though with everyone else you were as nice as pie. As I said, I don't know what I'm supposed to have done, but you must have got your own back by now. So why don't you leave me alone!'

'I never ignored you. After my first week it was you who ignored . . .'

'Did you know, it was me, *me* who told everyone it didn't matter if you weren't quite like the rest of us. *Me* . . .'

'I'm common! Is that what you mean?'

'Yes, common!' He glared at me. 'And now tell me this. Did it ever occur to you that the golf-cart might have had a genuine fault? No. You were adamant that someone had played you a trick. Well, they had, as it happens, but it wasn't me! You've lost me my prefect's badge, got me a caning and lost me my holiday too. So if you came out here trying to beg forgiveness, forget it, it's too late.'

'Beg forgiveness! From you! You conceited little . . .'

'So why did you follow me out here?'

'I was played a trick by someone and I'm suffering for it. And if it wasn't you, why did you say it was?'

He answered through clenched teeth. 'In case you didn't notice, I didn't say it was me.' He started to walk away.

My mind was in a spin. 'But you took the blame,' I shouted after him. 'Why did you do that if it wasn't you?'

He turned to look at me, his eyes filled with contempt. 'I should have sneaked? Is that what you're saying? Sneaked on someone else?' He was spitting the words, and his face was white. But as he turned away from me again, I saw that he had begun to smile. It was a bitter, contemptuous smile, and before I knew what I was doing I had caught hold of him and started pummelling his shoulders.

He put his arms up to protect himself, but I didn't stop. 'You nasty, small-minded, arrogant little creep! You think you're really smart, don't you? Well, here's what *I* think of you!' And I slapped him sharply round the cheek. Immediately, he grabbed my hands. Then, looking down into my face, he snarled, 'Why don't you just leave here? Go away somewhere, as far as you can get, with your own sort. You don't belong here.'

I tore my hands free, and turned quickly before he could see there were tears in my eyes. I stood with my back to him, for some reason unable to walk away. He was the first to speak.

'I'm sorry. I had no right to talk to you like that.'

I didn't answer, so he came towards me. 'Please don't cry. I'm sorry, really I am. I don't know why I said that.' He put his hand on my shoulder. 'I didn't mean it.'

I shrugged, and then I was able to walk away.

Later, when I was alone in my surgery, I tried to remember everything we'd said, but all I could really think about was how everything inside me kept going hot and then cold, and how sick I felt. I stood up and sat down, made tea and didn't drink it, opened a book and couldn't read, started to leave the room and came back.

I knew I shouldn't have hit him, but then he shouldn't have spoken to me the way he did. And he shouldn't have apologised to me like that either – I didn't know why, he just shouldn't have!

The day before term was due to begin, Henry Clive, Alexander's room-mate, arrived back at the school. His face was nut-brown after his skiing holiday, which I don't suppose cheered Alexander up much. I'd kept out of Alexander's way since I'd hit him, but it was obvious he'd told Henry about it, because when I saw them they started laughing. It seemed that every time I turned a corner they were there; I wanted to shrivel up, I was so embarrassed.

And there they were again, coming out of the pool house as I wheeled Miss Angrid past in her chair.

She was still chuckling away at something she'd said, when Henry yelled out and came sauntering over to ask how she was. She was delighted. Alexander followed and stood to one side as Henry and Miss Angrid joked with each other. I knew he was watching me, but I wasn't going to give him the satisfaction of making me blush.

'Well, Belmayne,' Miss Angrid said, turning to look at him, 'you're too old to have wet your pants, so why are you standing there like a dog with a guilty secret?'

He grinned. 'How are you, Miss Angrid?'

'Better, better. Now what's all this I've been hearing about you two putting on a play next term?'

'It was supposed to be a secret,' Henry groaned.

'Nothing is secret from me,' Miss Angrid answered, 'you should know that by now. Come on, out with it, what is it?'

'Actually, it's something Alexander's written,' Henry answered. Of course, it would be! I continued my study of the sky. 'And Mr Lear,' Alexander put in.

'Don't let him take any of the credit,' Henry objected, 'he's only helped you with the research.'

'More respect from you, Henry Clive!' Miss Angrid barked. 'So, what's it about, this play of yours?'

'You'll have to wait and see,' Alexander teased. I knew he still had his eyes on me and was laughing quietly to himself, so I smiled at Henry – who wasn't even looking at me.

'How long shall I have to wait?' Miss Angrid asked.

He shrugged and looked at Henry, who looked back at him. 'Oh, sorry, thought you'd said something,' Alexander grinned, as he shot a look at me. 'How long? Couple of weeks, I suppose.'

'Who's in it?'

'Us.'

'Surprise, surprise. Is there room for anyone else? I suppose not, with two such overgrown egos.'

Alexander and Henry laughed. 'I told you, you're just going to have to wait and find out,' Alexander said.

'Well, off you go, then,' said Miss Angrid, 'dry your hair, the two of you, before you catch cold. And reserve me a good seat for the play!'

'Things any better between you and Belmayne?' Miss Angrid asked, as the boys stalked off and I started to wheel her back to the cottage.

'I told you, he hates me.'

'And I suppose you hate him too?' she chuckled.

'Yes.'

Later that evening I was in my surgery listening to the radio and getting ready for the start of the new term, when there was a knock on the door and Henry Clive came in.

'Can I have a word, Miss?' he asked.

I reached out to switch off the radio. 'Of course. Come

and sit down.' And struggling not to show how pleased, or how surprised I was to see him, I waved him towards the chair at the other side of my desk. 'Nothing the matter with you, is there?'

'Oh no. No, fighting fit.'

I raised my eyebrows and looked him over. 'I don't suppose I can argue with that.'

He laughed. 'No, it's nothing to do with being ill. It's, well, it's something that I'm not really sure whether I'm allowed to ask.'

'I've never known that stop any of you before.'

'You won't be offended?'

'I don't know, do I?'

He shrugged. 'Fair point. It's only that, Alexander and I, we were wondering . . . You know Miss Angrid mentioned our play this afternoon? Well, afterwards when we were talking about it, we had a brilliant idea. You see, there are only three characters in it, and we need a woman for one of them. We were going to use one of the other boys and dress him up, but as, well, you're a, you know, woman . . .' The blush that had been steadily creeping up over his cheeks suddenly rushed into full blossom. He waved his hand in the air as if to say, Oh what the hell. 'Well, we thought that maybe you would play the part.' He sat back, obviously glad that was off his chest.

I looked at him in amazement, I think my mouth even fell open. 'You want *me* to be in your play?' I said. He nodded. 'I don't . . . I mean, are you sure about this? What about Alexander, won't . . .'

'Oh, don't worry about him,' Henry interrupted. 'Anyway, it was his idea. Call it an olive branch, if you like. Look, the fact is, after what happened, you know, when you hit him, and he said sorry to you, and you cried . . . Well, he feels bad about it, and we really do need someone in our play, so what do you think?'

He waited while I thought. 'And you say it was Alexander's idea?' I said, finally.

'Yes. So, will you do it?'

'I don't know. I mean, I've never acted before.'

'Well, you've only got to learn the lines and move about the stage where necessary. Alexander's directing it, he'll show you what's to be done.'

'What sort of part is it?'

'You'll be playing my wife.' He announced it with such pride that I could hardly keep myself from laughing.

'All right,' I said, 'I'll do it, on condition that my role involves nothing dangerous.'

'Now what could be dangerous about being my wife?' He grinned and got up. 'First rehearsal tomorrow morning at eleven, in the history room, before everyone gets back.'

– 4 –

With my invitation to play the part of Beth Wonderful, wife of Heeso Wonderful everything changed. It didn't surprise me one bit to discover that Alexander Belmayne, the director, was a tyrant and a bully. He propelled me round the history room like I was an Aunt Sally – but I told him that if he pushed his luck too far, I'd beat him up again. His answer, because he thought it was witty, was: 'Oh beat me, beat me!' Still, I showed him. Not only could I act, but when we needed flowers for the set I made chrysanthemums out of wood-shavings from the carpentry room, which I painted with my nail varnish; and when we needed curtains for the stage, I borrowed them from the Headmaster's drawing room. Well, he was the only master who had really big windows, and we did take care of them . . . .

There might have been quite an awkward moment when

Alexander told me I was going to have to learn to 'speak posh'. I over-reacted, I admit it, but it was a sore point with me.

'Oh, there goes the prima donna again, tossing her head and stomping out. Just like a woman,' he called after me.

'That's why we cast her,' Henry said. 'And tact is not your strongest point.'

'Don't worry, she'll be back,' I heard Alexander say, just before I slammed the door. That was it! Nothing would get me back now! That was until he came and knocked on my door . . . .

'All right, I'll beg if I must,' he said. 'Please, please will you come back?'

'No!'

'You're a stubborn, high-minded . . .'

'I suppose you'll be calling me common next!'

He burst out laughing, and so did I.

We put on our play at the end of the third week of term. It was called *The Wonderfuls*, a comedy about an old man – played by Alexander – who (to quote Alexander's uninspired programme notes) tried to show the Wonderfuls - a prosperous, self-seeking twosome – how superficial and meaningless was their way of life. The old man never quite succeeded, as the Wonderfuls were too stupid and too pompous to understand, but the outrageous dialogue - most of which even I knew owed more to Bernard Shaw and Oscar Wilde than to Alexander Belmayne – had the staff, as well as the boys, corpsed with laughter.

When the play was over the three of us stepped forward to take our bows. Then Henry and Alexander presented me with an enormous bouquet, and to great whoops and cheers from the entire school, I wept like a waterfall.

Mr Ellery seemed as pleased as Miss Angrid that the

war between Alexander and me was over. In fact the only person who wasn't obviously delighted was Mrs Jenkins; she thought us too frivolous for words – though I noticed it didn't stop her coming to my surgery for cups of tea. I didn't mind that so much, I just wished she'd stop reading to me from the newspapers. Anyone would have thought she was the only person in the world who had a husband in Fleet Street.

'I can't get over the change in you,' Mr Ellery said one evening a week or so later, when we were dining at the local bistro. 'You're so happy. The boys adore you, you know. I've never known anything like it. Everywhere I go these days I come across boys talking about you. Yesterday I found a touching ditty by one of our first year poets, describing you as a changeling.'

'A what!'

'A princess sneaked from her cradle by elves.'

I burst out laughing, but Mr Ellery said, 'Well, he might have a point. None of us knows anything about you, where you come from. Is there a mystery?'

'No. I just don't like talking about myself. Anyway, there's nothing much to tell.'

'There must be something.'

'Even if there was, I wouldn't tell you because you're teasing me.'

'Me!'

I threw my napkin at him. 'Yes, you!'

'Then I suppose I'll just have to join your fan club and theorise along with the rest of them. Do you know, every notebook I come across in the lower school these days has got Bobby Moore's name scrubbed out and yours plastered right across it?'

'Not the upper school?' I complained.

'Ah, the upper school take themselves much more seriously, so they're a little more, shall we say, subtle about it.'

'Oh yes? In what way?'

'In that they daren't let me see because they know I'll get jealous.'

I could have kicked myself for falling into that one.

'Have I embarrassed you?' he asked, without a trace of embarrassment.

'Yes.'

'Good. Then perhaps I'm getting through to you at long last. I mean I've hardly seen you these last weeks – I have to fight my way through a throng of adoring adolescents just to get to you.'

Later, we strolled back up the hill to the school. 'Cup of tea wouldn't go amiss,' he said, when we reached the door of my surgery.

Recognising the look in his eyes, I smiled. 'I'm right out of tea, I'm afraid.'

He rested his hands against the wall either side of me, and looked down into my face. 'Two minutes,' he pressed.

I heard a movement at the top of the stairs and looked up. It was Henry Clive. 'Sorry, Miss,' he stammered, 'I was looking for . . .'

'Yes?' said Mr Ellery, 'what were you looking for?'

'Nothing, sir.'

'Spying, were you?' said Mr Ellery, sounding unusually sharp for him. 'Back to bed, boy. I'll speak to you in the morning.'

'What's all the noise out here?' said Miss Angrid, coming out of her surgery. 'Be quiet, the pair of you, you'll wake the boys.'

'Sorry, Miss Angrid,' Mr Ellery said, sounding for all the world like one of his smaller pupils.

She turned to me. 'Come in here a moment, will you, Elizabeth.'

I pushed my way past Mr Ellery, throwing him what I hoped was an apologetic look. Miss Angrid closed the door behind me. 'That saw him off, eh?' She might as well have shouted it. I burst out laughing.

'Shame Henry Clive saw you, it'll be all round the school tomorrow.'

'We weren't doing anything,' I pointed out.

'Don't have to, the boys will fill in the missing spaces. Anyway, I must get back to the cottage in time for Billy Cotton. You'll be all right, will you?'

'Fine.' For someone who claimed she couldn't bear TV, her devotion to *Billy Cotton's Band Show* was amazing. And *Coronation Street*, and *Peyton Place*.

'Oh, by the way,' she said, popping her head back round the door, 'the second form are planning a midnight feast in the Hardy bathrooms. Keep an eye out, will you?'

'How on earth did you find that out?'

'I know everything there is to know around here,' she answered, then tapped her nose. 'You'd do well to remember it.' And chuckling to herself, she closed the door behind her.

Although I was still smiling as I went into my own surgery, I couldn't help but feel a bit disturbed by what she'd said. For some reason it sounded like a warning.

It took no time at all for the rumours to start. Miss Sorrill and Mr Ellery. Anonymous notes started to appear under my door, with outrageous sketches of what the boys assumed us to be up to. I had to give them credit for imagination, even though I was shocked by how much they knew about sex. Mr Ellery was getting the same treatment, but he found it funny.

'It won't be long before Mr Lorimer finds out, you know.' Mrs Jenkins eyed me with hostility as she sat sipping tea in my surgery.

'There's nothing to find out.'

'The boys are very astute, Elizabeth; they miss nothing. And I'll tell you, I've noticed myself, the way you've been throwing yourself at Richard Ellery. It won't do, you know. Anyone can see he's embarrassed by the situation. I suggest you keep yourself to yourself a little more.'

The old cow! How dare she! 'How can I keep myself to myself,' I snapped, 'when Mr Ellery keeps fawning after me like some puppy dog!'

'Miss Sorrill!' she gasped. 'You're talking about one of the masters of this school!' She pulled herself up from the chair and strode towards the door. 'Your conceit has obviously grown to preposterous proportions. Perhaps you are not such suitable material for Foxton's after all.'

'You've got no right to talk to me like that,' I cried, and jumped at the violence with which she slammed the door.

Her attack was so unexpected, not to mention unjustified, that it was several minutes before I could pull myself together. It was unusual for me to stand up to one of the staff like that – but she deserved it. I'd been edgy ever since the rumours had started; there were some boys who obviously saw them as much more than a bit of fun – Alexander and Henry, for example, had really cooled off towards me; I'd hardly seen them lately.

I went off to the dormitories to make sure the boys had cleaned under their beds and tucked in their hospital corners. My mind was only half on what I was doing, but I made an attempt to note who had not performed his duties correctly, ready to chalk them up on the board. If their number appeared, they had to report to matron.

When I got to the Lawrence fifth form room which Henry and Alexander shared, my heart sank. It was in a terrible state. I decided to tidy it myself, at least that would avoid a confrontation.

The drawers were half open, with clothes hanging out, so I took them out one by one, folded them neatly and put them away. It was as I was closing the last drawer that I noticed the blue suede winklepickers in Alexander's shoe rack. He had special permission for the shoes, but was only allowed to wear them when he was performing in the school pop group – they should not have been in his room, but downstairs in the clothes cupboard outside Miss Angrid's surgery. As I pulled the shoes out, a small red book fell on to the floor. I opened it to the first page, and found in beautifully proportioned calligraphy the name 'Beth'. I closed the book quickly, but my heart was already beating faster. No, I told myself. Just because I had played the part of Beth Wonderful in his play . . . No, it couldn't be.

'What the hell are you doing?'

I dropped the book and spun round. 'Alexander!' I gasped.

He snatched the book from the floor and turned back to me, his face white. 'I'm sorry,' I mumbled. 'It fell out of the shoe rack, I was just . . .'

'Go round snooping in everyone's diaries, do you? Or is it just mine?'

'I told you, it fell out and I opened it to see what it was. I didn't read any of it, so don't worry, your secrets are safe.' I tried to laugh.

He stared down at me, and for a minute I thought he was in pain. Then he flung his hand through his hair, sweeping it away from his face before he turned and thumped the wall. 'Just go,' he said.

'I'm sorry, Alexander, really, I'm . . .'

'I said go!'

'Alexander, please . . .'

'Please what?' He swung round.

'Look Alexander, I know I shouldn't have looked in the

book, but I told you, I didn't read any of it, only the inside cover.'

'Well, that was enough, wasn't it?' And before I could stop him, he had stormed out of the room.

– 5 –

Miss Angrid looked at the thermometer, shook it, and walked off across the room. 'Nothing wrong with you, young lady.'

'But I keep going all hot, and then I feel queasy. I've been like it for weeks. And my heart-beat keeps going up and down as well, it's really peculiar.'

She came back out from behind the screen. 'Good heavens, what on earth are you crying for? I told you, there's nothing wrong with you.'

'I don't know why I'm crying.'

She folded her arms over her chest and smiled. 'Well, I think I do. It's very likely a combination of the time of the month, and the heat. You'll be all right in a couple of days. Off you go now, or you'll be late for the film.'

'What film?'

'That James Bond film the upper sixth have all been dying to see.'

'All right, I'm going.' I blew my nose and got up from the chair.

'Elizabeth!' Miss Angrid called as I got to the door. 'Aren't you going to take your bag? Dear me, I don't know what's got into you these days. You'll forget your head next.'

It was Commem. weekend, and I was wandering across the lawns with some of the junior boys, stopping while they introduced me to their parents – and trying to ignore Mr

Ellery as he pulled faces at me through the crowd. I heard a voice I vaguely recognised, looked up and saw the Lord Chief Justice walking across the lawn towards me, with the Headmaster. I caught his eye and smiled. I might just as well have smiled at one of the cherubs over the doorway; he looked right through me and held his hand out to someone pushing past me. I watched him for a while, then realising that Mr Lorimer was scowling at me, I turned to work my way back into the crowd.

Alexander and Henry were rather overdoing their enthusiasm for the school band, and I giggled as several parents swung round at the sound of Darren Goodchild blasting his trumpet into Henry's face. Though he gave no sign of it, I knew Alexander was aware of me watching him. I wished I could just go up to him and say something – the trouble was, I didn't know what. Ever since that day in his room, he'd changed towards me.

I looked around for my faithful followers, and found that for the moment I had been deserted. Suddenly I knew I had to go inside or I would disgrace myself by crying in public. Just why I wanted to cry I didn't know, but I'd been doing a lot of crying for no reason lately.

I let myself in through the music room just in time, and groped for my handkerchief. I sat down at the piano. Then I got up and walked around the room. I didn't want to go back to my surgery because Miss Angrid would be bound to come and turf me out again. But the music room proved to be no refuge. Mr Ellery came in so quietly that I almost leapt out of my skin when he spoke.

He laughed, and asked me why I wasn't outside on this bright and beautiful summer's day. I told him I'd come inside to cool off.

'And the tears?'

I looked up, and to my horror they started again.

'Don't tell me it's the condom,' he said, referring to the

little package I had received that morning. 'I think you're losing your sense of humour, you know.'

'My sense of humour!'I cried. 'Just tell me what was funny about that filthy object, or what was inside it.'

'But it was only glue.' He grinned. 'Perhaps someone's trying to tell you they're stuck on you.

'That's not even funny.'

'No, perhaps not. And you think Belmayne had something to do with it?'

I shrugged. 'No, not really. But . . . oh, I don't know.'

We both looked out of the window to where Alexander was standing with his father. 'You two haven't fallen out again, have you?'

'No. Well, at least, I don't think so.'

He grinned. 'Tell you what, I'll have a word, put him straight about a few things, that should do it. Now, how about some coffee?' And he started to usher me towards the open French windows.

'No, I can't go out there looking like this,' I said. 'I'll go and freshen up first.'

As I got to the door he called out. 'I take it you know what Alexander's problem is, Elizabeth?' He winked, then went off to join the party.

The next day was my twenty-first birthday. Not that I could tell anyone at Foxton's that, having lied about my age to get there; as far as Miss Angrid was concerned, I was twenty-three. It was also the day of the summer ball at St Winifred's Girls' School, and Alexander's pop group had been rehearsing in the music room all day.

I busied myself in the surgery while I listened to them playing, and at some point I must have drifted into a world of my own, because I only realised the music had stopped when there was a knock on the door and Alexander came in.

He watched me from the door, moving his hand across his forehead to sweep the hair out of his eyes. 'I – ' he glanced over his shoulder, and I saw Henry outside, leaning over the banister to talk to someone below – 'that is, we, would like to invite you to the dance tonight.'

I didn't seem to be able to do anything except stand there and stare at him. Then Henry turned round. 'Haven't you asked her yet?' he said.

Alexander spread his hand over Henry's face and pushed him out of the way. He was still looking serious when he turned back, but when he saw I was laughing, he laughed too.

'You mean the dance at St Winifred's?' I said.

'Yes. Everyone's dressing up and Mr Ellery said he'd take you in his car.'

'It's either that or Tonto,' Henry chipped in.

Alexander rolled his eyes, and I said: 'Then it'll have to be Mr Ellery's car.'

Mr Ellery picked me up at seven o'clock sharp and wolf-whistled so loudly I nearly ran back inside. 'You're sure going to knock them off their feet in that,' he said, watching my hem-line wriggle further up my thighs as I settled into the car.

'You don't think it's too short?'

'Are you kidding? It looks terrific!'

But just walking in through the door of the school hall told me that I was all wrong. The girls from St Winifred's all had long dresses – real ball dresses – and in my tight-fitting Mary Quant mini-dress, I felt like a totem pole. But it was too late to turn back, so I just told myself that I was older than them, so allowed to wear what I wanted. And with Alexander singing on the stage, I clapped my hands and tapped my feet, and laughed at all the boys as they tried doing the Locomotion. The Headmaster kept glowering at me, but I was having too good a time to care. 'Up and down and round and round we go again,' Alexander sang, and everyone kicked off their shoes, let down their hair and twisted themselves silly. The boys, looking very different and almost grown up in their black polo sweaters and grey slacks, spun the girls off their feet to 'Rock Around the Clock,' and even lined up to have a go at the Madison.

Alexander sang the first line of 'Doo Wah Diddy Diddy,' and everyone cheered as Mr Ellery spun me out into the middle of the floor.

'Everything all right?' he shouted, as he twirled me round.

'Perfect. By the way, what did you say to Alexander?'

'Let's just say I put him right about a few things.'

'Like what?'

'Me and you.'

'Was that what was bothering him?'

'You know it was,' he shouted – and Henry Clive caught my hand and turned me round to dance with him while someone else took over the drums.

It seemed no time at all before the band took their bows, and after that the lights went down for the final record of the evening. The end of the summer ball, the end of the summer term. It was one of my favourites, 'Sealed With a Kiss' by Brian Hyland.

I picked up a coke and smiled as Mr Ellery invited the St Winifred's headmistress to dance; then turning round, I saw Alexander leave the stage. As he started to walk towards me my heart began to pound and suddenly I was hit by panic. I reached out for a bottle to refill my glass, but his hand closed over mine, and without looking at him I put the glass down and followed him out on to the floor.

I hardly dared to move, I was so aware of his arms round me. I could feel his breath on my cheek as he sang the words to the song:

I don't want to say goodbye for the summer,
Knowing what love we will miss,
Let's make a pledge to meet in September,
And seal it with a kiss.

His legs were moving against mine and I knew he was holding me too close, but I couldn't break away. I kept my head lowered against his shoulder and my hands rigid on his back. After a time I realised I was shaking – and that he was, too. Mr Ellery caught my eye, but I looked away. I was so full of feeling, I thought I would suffocate, and the panic I'd felt earlier sprang into life again. And then the music faded and he pulled away. I looked up and saw that his face had the same look it had worn that day in his room when I found the diary; and then his expression softened and his eyes seemed to sink into mine. I looked at his mouth, and as he started to lean towards me the lights suddenly came up.

The Headmistress clapped her hands and started to shoo her girls out of harm's way. Alexander was still watching me as I searched the room frantically for Mr Ellery. I found him waiting for me at the door and ran over to join him.

All the way back to Foxton's in the car, Mr Ellery chattered on – and all I could do was smile and nod. I couldn't speak, I couldn't think, even. I just wanted to be alone. When I got back to the cottage, I ran straight to the mirror in my bedroom. My eyes looked bigger than normal, my skin was flushed, and then I realised I was hot, too hot. And I wanted to be back on the dance floor. I wanted to hear him sing those words again, I wanted the lights to be down, I wanted him to . . .

I clapped my hands over my face. I wanted him to kiss me.

– 6 –

So that was how it started. A silly prank, a play and a dance. Janice and I didn't discuss it again, but when she drove me to Paddington on the last day of the holiday she said: 'You're heading for a fall, Elizabeth. It's all wrong and you know it.'

But it was she who was wrong. I'd had six weeks in which to get things into perspective, and I'd already made up my mind that when term started I would keep out of his way. Now that he was in the lower sixth and his room was in the stable annexe, that shouldn't be difficult . . . . And it wouldn't have been difficult if, despite my resolutions, I hadn't found myself taking the weirdest routes around the building just on the off-chance of bumping into him. And it seemed that every day there was something he had to pop into the surgery for, or a reason why I had go to to the sixth form common room. Nothing was ever said, but sometimes I would catch him looking at me and know he was remembering the night of the dance. Mostly I avoided his eyes, though, because I too couldn't forget that night.

Then I went down with a bout of flu. Miss Angrid flatly refused to let anyone near the cottage until I was out of bed and brought up the get well cards, fruit and flowers herself. After six days I ventured out as far as Foxton's copse which was little more than ten paces from the front door. Once it was known I had left the cottage, I was bombarded by boys wanting to accompany me on my walks, and one evening Alexander and Henry arrived in Tonto to take me for a drive round the grounds. After that, even when I was better, the three of us met every evening for a walk if the weather was fine, or a chat in the common room if it wasn't. Sometimes, of course, Alexander was too busy or had to go somewhere with one of the masters. Those evenings always seemed empty.

Before long I was beginning to find I couldn't sleep for thinking about him. I wanted him to kiss me so much that sometimes I had to bury my face in the pillow to stop myself screaming his name. I took to standing naked in front of the mirror, looking at myself. I'd never taken much notice of my body before, but now it seemed the most important thing in the world. I hated my breasts for being too big, but when I touched them I cried tears at the way it made me feel.

By Christmas I was looking at him, wondering about him in a way that shocked me. When I saw him playing rugby it was as if everything inside me was aching. I looked at his legs and his shoulders, and the way he moved; his hair, how it fell over his eyes; the way he'd rest his hands on his knees, getting his breath back. And then I'd wait for his smile when he looked at me, and my heart would flip over to see that silly old crooked tooth.

The day before the end of term I invited some of the boys over to the cottage for mince pies and hot punch. I did it purposely in the hope that Alexander and Henry would stay on later, and they did.

They were sitting on my battered old sofa listening to records when Henry suddenly said: 'I know! Why don't you come and stay with us for Christmas?'

At first I thought he was speaking to Alexander, but he was looking at me. I laughed. 'I don't think your parents would reckon much to that. Anyway, I'm already going somewhere.'

Alexander got up and went to stack more logs on the fire. I watched him as he squatted in front of it, resting his elbows on his knees and staring into the flames. Henry's eyes met mine and I shrugged. It wasn't at all like Alexander to be this quiet.

I turned back to finish wrapping a present for Miss Angrid, and my pen shot straight across the gift tag when Henry suddenly clapped his hand to his forehead and cried: 'Oh hell, I've got a present for you, Elizabeth, I forgot to bring it with me.' He looked at Alexander.

I knew immediately what they were up to, and even though there was nothing in the world I wanted more than to be alone with Alexander, I was suddenly afraid. 'You don't have to get it now,' I said. 'Give it to me in the morning, before you go off.' I picked up the small parcels I'd wrapped for them and handed them over. 'Not to be opened until Christmas Day.'

'Not allowed,' Henry objected. 'We've got to open them now. We can have our own Christmas, the three of us. I'll go and fetch your present.' And he was gone before I could stop him.

Alexander sat down on the chair next to the fire. 'You're quiet this evening,' I said.

He stood up, stuffing his hands in his pockets, and began to pace the room. His back was towards me as he stopped. 'What *are* you doing at Christmas?' he asked.

I was taken back by the angry tone of his voice. 'I told you, I've got plans,' I answered steadily.

He turned to face me. 'You're spending the time alone, aren't you?' he said, fixing my eyes with his.

I swallowed hard. He was right. Janice had gone to the Caribbean with her parents, so I had booked myself into a small hotel in London where I was planning to read Edna O'Brien through the holiday, until I could come back to Foxton's again. 'No, of course I'm not. Honestly, Alexander, I don't know what's got into you.'

Suddenly he was beside me. 'If you must know, I don't much like the idea of you being on your own over Christmas,' he growled. 'That's what's got into me!'

'But it's nothing to get angry about, and anyway, I told you, I'm not going to be on my own.'

'Then who are you spending it with? I know you haven't got any family, so who . . .'

'That's none of your business,' I retorted. He looked hurt, and immediately I was sorry. 'I'm going to London, I'm staying with some friends.'

'What friends? You never talk about them.'

'That's because they're not part of my life here at Foxton's. Come on,' I said, trying to sound bright, 'what are you doing over Christmas?'

'You know what I'm doing.' Suddenly he leaned towards me and my heart turned over at the look in his eyes. 'Elizabeth, let me come with you. I can tell my parents I'm staying with Henry.'

'Alexander you can't! It's ridiculous even to think of it. Your parents will want to see you, and you'll want to see them too.'

'I don't. I want to be with you.'

His cheeks were red with embarrassment and anger, and I didn't know what to say. He sat down beside me, and took my hand. I tried to pull away, but his grip was too strong. 'Alexander,' I gulped. 'Stop it, please. Look, I think you'd better go before you say something you regret.'

'I won't regret it. Damn it! Stop treating me like a child! You know how I feel about you.'

'Alexander!' I jumped up from the settee. 'Don't say any more. Boys – young men, young men still at school, you're bound to have crushes, I understand that. But, Alexander, you're taking it too far. You're making a fool of yourself.'

I could see I had hurt him deeply. 'Do you know how it feels?' he said. 'Do you know what I've been going through these past months, since that night at the dance? If you didn't care, then why?'

'Oh Alexander, I do care.' What was I saying? 'I like you. I enjoy your company and I thought you enjoyed mine. It was no more than that Alexander, honestly, no more than that.'

'You're a liar!' he yelled. 'You led me on. You made me think you felt about me the same way I feel about you – and all the time it was just a pretence. Now I can see you for what you really are. You're nothing but a lonely old spinster, pampering your ego at my expense.'

'Stop it! Stop it! I wasn't leading you on, I. . .' I started to reach out to him but wrenched myself away and went to stand behind the sofa, using it as a barrier between us.

'You've been laughing at me all the time, haven't you?' he shouted. 'I can see you now, telling Mr Ellery everything, and laughing at the way I haven't been able to do my work, the way I haven't been able to do anything for thinking about you. I was nothing more than a figure of fun, was I?'

I pushed my hands up to my face. 'You're wrong Alexander, believe me. I wanted, you were . . . oh please, please go.'

'I'm going, and don't expect either of us back. You see, you even had Henry fooled. Even he saw the way you were with me. But that's it from now on, Elizabeth, it's over for all of us.' He reached into his pocket. 'And here! Here's your Christmas present. Merry Christmas!' He flung it down in front of me.

The door slammed behind him, and suddenly I knew I couldn't let him go like that. He was at the bottom of the stairs when I tore open the door. He looked up as I called out his name. Then almost before I knew it was happening, I was in his arms. I knew it was wrong, but I couldn't let him go.

He led me back into the sitting room and pulled me on to my knees in front of the fire. 'I'm sorry,' he whispered, reaching up to wipe away my tears. 'I'm sorry for everything I said.'

'Me too.' I lowered my head, but he lifted my face and kissed me.

At first his lips were gentle, but as his hands closed around my face I clung to him, needing to feel him closer.

'Tell me you love me, Elizabeth. Please, tell me,' he murmured.

He kissed me again, and this time I felt his tongue move against mine. I twisted my fingers through his hair and was saying the words before I even realised.

'Now will you let me come with you?' he asked.

I shook my head. 'Please, look at it sensibly, Alexander. You can't come, you mustn't. Just because we've admitted to the way we feel doesn't make it right. You have to go home to your parents, and I'll go to London. Then after Christmas . . . well, who knows? I think it would be better if we don't spend any time alone together after this.'

He put his hand over my mouth. 'Don't say that. Don't ever say that again. I'll agree to go home for the holiday, but only if you agree that you'll see me afterwards, only if you promise that you'll still love me when I come back. Elizabeth. Please, promise me, Elizabeth.'

In the end I was too weak to refuse. I loved him too much already.

– 7 –

I couldn't have made a bigger mistake than to go to Mr Billings's little hotel off the Bayswater Road. He was a kind and jovial man who told me with pride that I had the only room with a bath, but the wallpaper and curtains were drab and, feeling the way I did, once the door had closed behind him it was a struggle to hold back the tears. The big armchair under the standard lamp was just right for sitting and reading in, but I never got any further than the first few lines of *Girl with Green Eyes*.

I went for walks round the shops or in Hyde Park, and

tried as hard as I could not to think about Alexander – but I thought about nothing else. At night, listening to the sounds from the street, I sat by the mirror and ran my fingers over my lips, remembering what it was like when he kissed me. And always I'd end up wrapping my arms around myself, wanting to cry out with the need to touch him.

On Christmas morning I opened the present he'd given me. I'd said once, when we'd all been talking about what we would buy if we had lots of money, that I'd buy some expensive French perfume called *Y*. He'd remembered. I wished so much that he was there then, that I was almost stifled by the longing. And because I was shaking when I opened the parcel, I dropped it, and the bottle smashed. All Christmas Day I sobbed into my pillow, and most of Boxing Day too. I couldn't bear to think of losing him, not yet.

It was two days after Christmas, late in the afternoon, when Mr Billings knocked on my door. I must have been asleep because there seemed to be a fuss going on in the corridor, and I heard someone call that she thought she'd seen me going out. I pulled myself up from the bed, my book thudding to the floor. As I opened the door and flicked on the light I could see Mr Billings at the top of the stairs.

His face lit up when he saw me and he started to speak, but I was looking past him. It couldn't be. I was dreaming. He didn't know where I was . . . .

'. . . nice to have visitors, especially at Christmas,' Mr Billings was saying. He clapped Alexander on the shoulder and pushed him towards me. Then I heard Alexander refusing the tea Mr Billings was offering, and in a daze I let him take my arm and pull me inside the room. When the door was closed he turned to look at me, lifting his hand and pulling the scarf away from his mouth.

'Merry Christmas,' he said quietly.

My voice seemed to come from somewhere far away

inside me. It shook as I said, 'How did you know . . . ? What are you doing . . . ?' He put his hand on my face and I moved into the circle of his arms, and his mouth, still cold from the wind, was against mine, and his arms were holding me tight. He let me go and my eyes flew open.

'Alexander . . .'

'Just tell me you love me, Elizabeth. Please.'

Cupping my face with his hands, he kissed my eyes and my nose and my cheeks, and then my mouth again. 'I couldn't think, I couldn't sleep, I couldn't eat. I had to come. Tell me it's been the same for you too. Tell me you love me as much as I love you.'

'I love you,' I whispered, my voice breaking as I tried not to cry.

He took off his coat and put it on the chair. I looked away, but he put his fingers under my chin and turned me back again.

I tried to smile. 'I don't want to wait any longer,' I whispered.

He kissed me slowly, and his fingers were shaking as he started to unbutton my dress. After a while he lifted my hands and nodded for me to undress myself while he took off his own clothes. Most of the time I kept my eyes on the wall opposite because I was afraid to look at him, and afraid he might be disappointed in me. And then he was standing next to me, running his hands over my arms and I buried my face in his neck.

He undid the catch at the back of my bra, then gently pushed me away from him. As he pulled the straps down over my arms and my breasts fell free, I heard the breath catch in his throat. I tried to cover myself, embarrassed by the way my nipples were standing out. He took my hands away and drew them to him. 'Look at me, Elizabeth,' he whispered. 'Look at me here.

I looked down, mesmerised by the way my hands were moving over him, and then as he took my nipples between his fingers, my hand tightened around him. I looked up as the sound came from the back of his throat, as if he were choking. And then my hand and my arm were suddenly wet.

'Oh my God!' His voice was thick with fury and disgust. He turned away, burying his face in his hands.

I stood there, not knowing what to do, and then he pushed past me and escaped into the bathroom.

He was standing in front of the washbasin when I went in, one hand on each side, staring down into the sink. 'Alexander,' I whispered.

'Don't,' he growled. 'I don't want your pity.'

I walked over and leaned my head on his shoulder. 'I love you,' I said. 'Don't be angry. Sometimes these things happen the first time.'

'How do you know?' he snapped.

I slipped my arms around him and started to kiss his shoulder. He turned round and crushed me hard in his arms. 'I just couldn't stop it,' he whispered.

'I understand,' I said.

Picking up a towel he wrapped it round his waist, then sat down on the edge of the bath. I cradled his head in my arms, running my fingers through his hair. He had tried to be so brave for both of us, and now I knew that it was my turn.

'Will you come back in now?' I said, eventually. He nodded, so I took his hand and led him to the bed, where we lay down together.

'Elizabeth,' he whispered into the silence. 'What you said just now, that these things sometimes happen the first time . . .' He lifted himself on to one elbow and looked down into my face. 'I wish I could find the words to tell you how much you mean to me.' I closed my eyes and pulled him down to kiss me. After a while I pushed my tongue into his mouth, and it wasn't long before I could feel the passion rising in him.

His voice was gruff as he spoke. 'Do you think we could try again?'

I nodded, then found I had to swallow hard as he lowered his mouth to my breasts. When he lifted his head again, he pulled me against the length of his body, and I could feel him hard against my belly. I was afraid, and closed my eyes as he slipped my pants down over my legs. And then he began to tease me with his fingers. I had never felt anything like it before. I stiffened, clamping my thighs against his hand, and then I looked up into his face and tried to say his name.

He took his hand away, and easing my legs apart, he lay down on top of me. Then very slowly I felt myself opening to him, pulling him towards me, until with one gentle push we were together. He touched his lips against mine, then pushed again. I gasped at the pain, and he stopped.

'Are you all right?' he whispered, looking down into my face.

I nodded, and my whole body swelled with love as we started to move together. He pushed his hands underneath me and lifted me closer to him. And as I wound my legs around his, he started to move faster until his breathing became laboured and heavy, and then he called out my name as with one final push he fell against me.

I wrapped my arms around him, holding him still. Our bodies were sticky and damp, and his heart was thudding against mine, but I didn't want him to pull away yet. He lifted his head to kiss me, and I felt his tears against my cheeks.

Finally he moved away. I knew immediately that something was wrong, and I was terrified that he regretted what we had done. I had given myself to him so easily, what if he despised me for it now? I wanted to speak as I watched him sitting there on the edge of the bed, his head in his hands, but my tongue was paralysed with fear.

'Tell me what I have to do,' he whispered. 'Tell me what it is you want.'

When I didn't answer, he turned to look at me. 'You're so beautiful, Elizabeth, and what you have just given me . . . But it must be the same for you.'

I closed my eyes against the surge of relief, and reached out my arms to him. 'Just be here,' I whispered, 'all you have to do is be here.'

'But I can give you more,' he insisted. 'I know I can. Tell me, show me how to do it.'

'I don't know,' I answered.

He looked into my eyes and I saw the doubt in his. 'Can I try?' he said.

I nodded, and as he started to stroke my body and then push his fingers between my legs, I suddenly knew what it was he had to do. So taking his hand, shyly, I held it where it was. 'There,' I said. 'Just there.' And as he touched me, and began to stroke me again, I experienced something so beautiful I could never even begin to describe it.

We slept for a while and when I woke up his fingers were tracing tiny circles around my nipples. He was frowning, as if he couldn't really believe what was happening to my body, then he smiled when he realised I was watching him.

'Can I make love to you again?' he whispered.

Later, after I'd been downstairs to fetch tea and sandwiches, we talked, and I tried to pretend I was angry when he told me he'd looked in my diary before leaving school, and that was how he'd known where to find me.

'It's no use you frowning at me like that, Elizabeth,' he said, sitting naked on the end of the bed and ripping apart a turkey sandwich with his teeth. 'I know you were glad to see me. You were, weren't you?' he added when I didn't answer.

I shrugged. 'Sort of.'

'Sort of?' he choked. 'Then I'd hate to think what physical state I'd be in now if you'd been really glad to see me. And stop looking at me down there, you know what it does to me.'

'I'm not looking at you anywhere,' I objected. 'Now tell me, what about your parents, where do they think you are?'

He shrugged. 'In London.'

'Doing what?'

'Well, not sleeping with the junior matron of Foxton's, that's for sure.'

I stopped smiling. 'Don't, Alexander, please don't say that.'

'I'm sorry. They think I've come down to see a show with some of the other boys.'

'Are you only staying one night?' I tried to keep the desperation from my voice, but already my heart was beating so hard that I tried to cover it with my hands.

He must have sensed how I was feeling because he came across to my chair and knelt down in front of me. 'I'm not leaving you now, Elizabeth, I can't.'

He looked so young, so brave. What was to become of us?

It was two days later when we finally ventured out to the theatre. We went to see a matinée of *Happy Days*, the Beckett play that, despite a really morbid theme, had us gripping our sides with laughter, as Winnie, buried to her waist in earth, tried to fill her days by filing her nails and rummaging around in her handbag.

All through the play Alexander held my hand, and every now and again he leaned over to kiss me, just as he did when he thought I was asleep. I kissed him when he was asleep too, because he looked so young then, and vulnerable, and I knew that despite his outward confidence he was as afraid as I was that something might destroy our happiness. There were times, too, when he couldn't hide his bewilderment at what was happening to him, and he would gaze at me for minutes at a time, then beg me to tell him how much I loved him – and I'd laugh and say silly, romantic things until he laughed too.

When the show was over we decided that as we were having such a good time, we would splash out and find a noisy restaurant somewhere in Covent Garden. And we were just heading for The Bistro, tucked behind the market, when the unthinkable happened and Alexander spotted Mrs Jenkins walking down the street on the arm of her husband. Quickly Alexander pulled me into a shop doorway, took me in his arms and buried my face in his neck.

Mrs Jenkins sailed by and didn't even look in our direction, but we stayed in the doorway for several minutes after she had gone, numbed by how close we had come to discovery. We looked at each other. This, we knew, was only the beginning. In the privacy of our little room in Bayswater, it had been easy for us to tell each other how bravely we would face the world. The reality was different.

The evening ruined, we walked back to the hotel in silence. By the time we arrived I had made up my mind what I was going to do. Seeing Mrs Jenkins had made me almost sick with shame: I, like her was supposed to be a responsible member of the school staff. Suddenly I could imagine the accusing eyes of Alexander's parents, Miss Angrid, Mr Lorimer, Mr Ellery, and the rest of the boys who had placed their trust in me. I had been crazy to allow things to go this far. Had I ever really, in the past few days, thought about what I was doing to Alexander, stopped to consider what effect all this might have on him? He was too young to know his own mind, he was headstrong, determined and spoiled. He might look and behave older than he was, but that didn't change the fact that he wasn't yet seventeen. Our relationship had to stop now, no matter what pain it might cause me, because that was nothing compared to the damage I would cause him if I let it go on.

Before he could push open the door of the hotel, I stopped him and made him turn round to face me. 'Alexander,' I said, softly, 'I want you to go inside now and collect your things. No. No. Please don't say anything, don't let's argue, I couldn't bear it. We've got to say good-bye, my darling, so let it be now, before the outside world can spoil what we have had together. I've decided that it would be for the best if I don't come back to Foxton's in the New Year . . . .'

'Elizabeth.' He put his hand over my mouth. 'I'm staying here with you. Come inside, please. We have to talk, I know we do, but don't try to push me away like this.'

My voice was constricted by the loss I was already feeling. 'It's easier this way, Alexander. If we talk it'll only make it more difficult. I'm going for a walk. Please, take your things . . .'

'You said you loved me, Elizabeth.'

Almost choking on my tears, I shook my head. 'I do, Alexander, but I can't. I can't . . . .' And tearing my hand away from his, I ran off down the street.

I expected him to follow, and when he didn't I had to bite my lips hard to stop myself from screaming out in an effort to fill the emptiness. I walked about for over an hour, hardly knowing what I was thinking or where I was going. I was terrified of going back, but knew I had to. It was the first step I had to take in facing my life without him. I steeled myself as I walked in the door of my room – and he was there, sitting on the bed, waiting for me.

I closed the door, quietly watching him through sore and swollen eyes. He stood up, reaching out for my hand, and led me across to the bed.

'Sit down,' he said, 'I want you to listen. I don't want you to interrupt, will you promise me?'

I nodded dumbly.

He went to sit in the old tapestry chair, and with his dark head on one side, he looked across the room at me, in the half-light, holding on to me with his eyes. 'I know everyone will think that I can't know my mind at my age, that I'm ruining my life – and all the other things they'll say. But it doesn't matter what other people think, Elizabeth, because none of it will change the way I feel about you. Of course it isn't going to be easy, especially when I know that even you think I'm too young for what we have between us. All I can say is that in all the books and films I care about and, in all the life I've witnessed – even though I've only seen such a little of it – love has never recognised age. I love you, and I want you to go on being the most important part of my life. I don't care about anything else. I know there will be times in the future when other things will be important to me, too – but always, no matter what, it will be you that I love. Nothing will change that, Elizabeth. I can't put into words what it is that you've done to my life; all I know is that it won't mean anything without you. And if you leave me now, you'll be hurting us both, more perhaps than either of us can understand.

'What I'm trying to say is very simple really. Not only do I love you now, I know already that I'm going to love you forever. And if you don't believe me, then maybe we'll have to wait forever for you to find out. Either way, it won't change the way I feel. So please, don't shut me out of your life.'

It was now almost completely dark, and I could hardly see him across the room. It was a long time before I stood up and walked over to him. He held out his arms, and sitting down on his lap, I held him, rocking him back and forth and wiping the tears from his cheeks.

'Like you I don't know what the future will hold, but let's hope our love is strong enough to face it.'

– 8 –

I would never have thought it possible, but as time went on I grew to love Alexander more and more. Once we were back at Foxton's the agony of being so close, yet not able to touch, was so intense that the only way to control it was to try and laugh about it. The way Alexander deliberately went around looking as if he was in the worst kind of physical torment made me laugh till I cried. 'But this is the way I really feel,' he said, when I told him he was overdoing it.

In between lessons he'd dash up to the surgery, close the door behind him and kiss me so hard and so quickly that I hardly knew he was there before he was gone. And at the end of each day we'd always manage to go for a walk, or if it was raining I'd slip down to the common room for a cup of coffee, just as I had with last year's sixth form. Even though there weren't many times when we could be on our own, we still managed to make love twice during the first weeks of term.

The first time was in a barn that was a two-mile hike from the school. But I didn't mind about my muddy shoes and wind-torn hair when I got there – still holding the note he'd left inside his pillow-case that morning, asking me to meet him at four, when the sixth form were normally in their rooms studying, or playing records in the common room. Afterwards, when our bodies were bruised and tender, I giggled at the way I'd thrown off my matron's uniform and tumbled into the hay with him – at the way we'd laughed and frolicked together like two lambs in a field.

As several of the boys regularly visited both Miss Angrid and me in the cottage, no suspicions were aroused by Henry and Alexander coming too – though it caused some heated arguments between us when I wouldn't let Alexander come more often, and alone. But there was one occasion, early in the evening, when he did come, just as I was about to get in the bath. The inevitable happened, and it was only a matter of seconds after we'd finished dressing that Miss Angrid knocked on my door and walked straight in.

She eyed us suspiciously, and afterwards I was so shaken by the narrowness of our escape that it caused the first serious rift between us. I was stunned by the fact that Alexander didn't seem to care, and yelled at him for being immature enough to think that Miss Angrid would be on our side. He hated being reminded that he was younger than me, so he hit back by saying that I was using my position to hide the fact that I was ashamed of him.

'Well, I'm not exactly proud of what we're doing,' I said.

His face turned white. 'So, you are ashamed. I'm nothing more than a randy little schoolboy who suits your . . .'

'Don't speak to me like that! I wouldn't be doing this if I didn't love you, but this kind of stupid irresponsible behaviour of yours sometimes makes me wonder how much longer we can go on. You're not to come here again, do you hear me?'

'Agreed! And don't even think about slipping notes inside my pillow-case, I'll burn them before I even read them.'

We smouldered in silence for two days, until his resolve weakened and I found a note pushed under my surgery door. He wanted me to know that he hadn't meant anything he'd said, that he didn't mean to be cavalier, it was only that he loved me so much that he wanted the whole world to know. He could see now how childish that was, so would I forgive him and meet him later in the woods? I ignored it. There was another note the following day, and two more the day after that. Still I ignored them. The last note was delivered to the cottage, and told me to go to hell.

Which is where I stayed, until he caught my eye at dinner and made me laugh. But that still didn't stop me from getting into a state. I was so worried about what we were doing, so afraid of it all and how it would end that I just didn't know what to do. That was how he found me one afternoon, alone in my surgery, sobbing my heart out.

He looked at me, his face saying nothing as he reached out his hand and pulled me up into his arms. I tried to turn away.

'No! Don't!' he said, angrily. 'For God's sake, why are you making us suffer like this?'

'I don't know what to do,' I said. 'I love you, I do, but Alexander . . .'

'Look, we both knew this wasn't going to be easy, so don't let's make it any worse. Now come on, just let me hold you.'

And I let him hold me, because just at that moment I didn't care who might walk in and find us. I loved him, and that was all that mattered.

'They're back!' Alexander cried. 'The bloody gypsies are back!'

Henry looked up from his newspaper and Alexander winked as he saw me coming towards them. It was late in the afternoon, and they were sitting next to the tennis courts, reading that morning's papers and calling out the odd rude remark to the boys who were playing tennis.

'Thank God I'm not at home,' Alexander said. 'I can see my father now, his face will be an ugly shade of purple and that snakey vein in his neck will be throbbing away. Nobody's life will be worth living.'

Grinning, Henry took the paper from Alexander and handed it to me.

'Did you read that bit about them being vermin?' Alexander said, looking up at me. 'As my mother says, we're never going to get rid of them if father doesn't cut out the vitriol. Still, it's true what he's saying. I saw them when I was there at Christmas, filthy beggars. I wonder if it's true that they're running a child prostitution ring. The local rag said it was.'

'Not only the local one,' said Henry. 'There's something about it here.'

'Henry, dear boy, what on earth are you doing reading *that*?'

I laughed. 'You're such a snob, Alexander Belmayne.'

'Couldn't agree more,' said Miss Angrid, coming up behind us.

Alexander pulled a face, then turned back to Henry. 'What does it say?' he asked.

'Headline stuff. As you say, all about the child prostitution thing. Your father is quoted as saying something about calling in Rentokil to deal with it.'

Alexander gave a yell of laughter. 'Renta who?' I said.

'Rentokil. The pest control people,' Miss Angrid enlightened me.

'Sounds like my father,' said Alexander. 'No doubt he's pissing himself with excitement at the forthcoming battle.'

'Alexander!'

'Sorry, Matron, momentarily forgot myself.' And as he threw her a kiss, I had to turn away before she saw me laughing.

'Anyway,' I continued, as Miss Angrid strolled off, 'what are you two doing here? I thought you were going to the theatre this afternoon.'

'Mr Lear's gone sick,' Henry answered, draining a can of shandy. 'Titus Andronicus leftus in the lurchus.'

Alexander held his can out for me to drink. 'All I can say is, I'm glad I'm not at home now. Just having those people in the vicinity makes a chap itch in his bed at night.' He stood up and came to put his arms around me, kissing the back of my neck.

'Alexander!' I cried, jumping away from him. 'For God's sake, someone might see!' He laughed and I glared at him, but at the same time heard myself telling him to come to my surgery after supper.

Henry stretched and yawned. 'You know, I've been thinking,' he said. 'We ought to try and find a way to take you up to Oxford with us, Elizabeth.'

A smile stretched painfully across my face as I watched Alexander sit down again and pick up a paper. It was something I didn't allow myself to think about – the time when they would have to leave.

'Hope the females at Oxford are a bit more desirable than the ones at St Winifred's,' Henry mused. 'I can just see it now. Orgies and more orgies. Maybe I ought to be getting in a bit of practice. Can't have you running off with every available female in the place, Alexander.'

As I started to walk away I heard Alexander say, 'Henry, old chap, what's happened to your brain?'

There was a pause, then Henry said, 'I didn't mean anything. Just wasn't thinking. Tell her I'm sorry, will you?'

A few minutes later, hearing my surgery door close, I walked out from behind the screen. 'You don't have to say anything,' I said, before he could speak. 'But we're going to have to face it, you know. When you leave here, well . . .'

'It's a long time away yet, Elizabeth. Besides, me being at Oxford won't change anything. We'll still see each other, all the time.'

He kissed me, and not for the first time I felt myself beginning to fall apart. I would lose him, I knew I would.

He was grinning as he let me go. 'And what's so funny?' I said.

'You.'

'Me! Why?'

He shrugged. 'I don't know, you just are. I love your

hair,' he said, taking off my cap and pulling out the hairpins. 'Ebony hair and ebony eyes. Lift up your skirt, I want to look at your legs.'

'Can you come to the cottage later tonight, after ten?' I said, as he ran his fingers under my suspenders. 'I want you to make love to me.'

His face was suddenly serious. 'I'll be there,' he said.

I'd bought us some wine, and put out some crisps and peanuts, but when he arrived all that was forgotten. Later, when we were sitting in front of the fire with our clothes all over the room, he started to talk about what we had done. It had been the first time we'd had oral sex. I don't know why – probably because I'd been feeling insecure all day – but suddenly I burst into tears.

He stopped what he was saying straightaway, and moved round to sit next to me. 'What is it?' he said. 'I thought you'd like it. I'm sorry, we won't do it again.'

I laughed then. 'Of course I liked it,' I said. 'That's why I'm crying.'

He gave me one of his lop-sided looks. 'And I suppose I've got to work that one out for myself.'

I sighed and leaned my head back on his shoulder. He picked up his wine and held it to my mouth, then, taking a sip himself, he pulled the chair round so he could rest against it.

'What are you thinking?' he asked.

'I'm thinking that one day I hope you'll look back on all this and remember it the way it was. You know, how much we loved each other, how much we taught each other . . . .'

'I don't like the sound of what you're saying. We'll be looking back together, won't we?'

'All I'm trying to say is that, if for some reason that doesn't happen, I hope we'll always be a very special memory for each other.'

'Stop it, Elizabeth. Stop saying things like that. It's what

Henry said this afternoon, isn't it? Well, I might as well tell you now, I won't be going up to Oxford. I've decided it will be easier for us if I don't.'

I smiled at that. 'You will go to Oxford. If you don't, then I really will leave you. Anyway, I'm just being morbid, Alexander – ignore me. Where's the wine?'

He got up to get the bottle, and when he came back I watched him as he poured. 'Smile, Alexander. I want to see your crooked tooth.'

He laughed and then sat forward, bringing his mouth to mine. And all my insecurities went away, because every time we were together we became more a part of one another.

A few mornings later I was sitting with Miss Angrid, packing up first-aid boxes for the Easter Outward Bound course, and idly chatting about the current experiment of introducing St Winifred's girls into the sixth form lectures at Foxton's. Deciding that the girls were, without a doubt, an unnecessary distraction for boys who were trying to achieve a decent grade in A levels, she went off to make a cup of tea – but when she came back and settled herself in her chair, instead of picking up her cup she took a long, hard look at me.

I felt uncomfortable, and tried to laugh. 'It's me, Elizabeth,' I said. 'You look as though you're seeing me for the first time.'

She shook her head. 'Oh no,' she said, 'not the first time. I've seen you plenty of times, my dear.'

'What a strange thing to say.'

She sighed heavily, and reached out for her tea. I waited for her to go on, trying to ignore the alarm bells that were already ringing inside my head.

It was a while before she spoke again. 'All that chit-chat just now about the girls . . .' she began. 'Well, I suppose there's no point in beating about the bush. You know what I was leading up to.' She stared at me, waiting for me to answer. 'Do you know what you're doing?' she asked, bluntly.

'Packing the first-aid boxes,' I quipped.

'Elizabeth.'

I felt myself colour, and looked away.

'I saw him leaving the cottage the other night,' she said.

When I looked into her face I understood the silent request for no lies, and though I wanted to deny it, tell her she was imagining things, I found I couldn't. I got up from my chair and went to stand by the window. 'I don't know what to say.'

'There's nothing to say. It's what you have to do that matters.'

I swallowed hard. I wanted to shout at her, call her a nosy, interfering old woman who should mind her own business. But in my heart I knew she was right.

'His work is falling behind,' Miss Angrid went on. 'He's failed his end of term Latin. Did you know that? No, I thought not. He's taking English today, yes?' I nodded. 'Mr Lear thinks he's going to flunk that too.'

'Does Mr Lear know?' I gasped.

'No. But questions are being asked. He's always been ahead of the others, way ahead. He's been called in by Mr Lorimer, did you know? The boy is besotted with you, Elizabeth. He can't see straight or think straight. If he fails his A levels next year, well, you don't need me to spell out what that will mean.'

I shook my head. She was telling me, in as kind a way as she knew how, something I already knew. I was ruining his life.

'Do you think I should leave?' I said, after a while.

'No.' She was emphatic: if I left he would be even more distracted than he was now. What I had to do was to speak to him myself, try and make him see sense.

'Are you going to tell anyone what you know?' I asked her.

She smiled, and it was the first time I had seen that strange, whiskery old face, close to tears. 'No,' she said. 'I think I know the way you feel about him, Elizabeth. Others will think you have led him on, that you're playing with him. But I know. I've seen it from the very beginning.'

My heart turned over. 'I tried not to,' I said.

'I daresay you did. But it's too late now, it's done. Just get him through his A levels, that's all I ask. Once he's at Oxford then the whole thing will fizzle out. He's too young for all this, and the same goes for you. You should be out with people your own age.'

'They say the truth always hurts,' I smiled.

She took my hand. 'I'm very fond of you, Elizabeth. The last thing I want is to see you hurt. But I think you know in your heart what it is you have to do.'

That night I asked Henry if he would come for a walk with us. We'd stay in sight of the school, then no one need have any cause for suspicion.

Alexander shouted and raved when I told him what Miss Angrid had said. At first he was intent on storming back to the school and telling her just what he thought of her, but between us Henry and I managed to stop him. Finally, after he had calmed down and we'd talked it over between the three of us, Alexander and I struck a bargain. If I would agree to go away with him, just the two of us, at Easter, then he would knuckle down to some serious studying the following term.

As Alexander's parents were travelling to France to see his sister and her husband, they weren't too put out when he told them he was going to help supervise one of the junior Outward Bound courses. We took separate trains to Penzance station, where I hired a car, and then we went off to a cottage we'd rented just outside Zennor.

During that two and a half weeks I tried a thousand times to tell him it was over but I couldn't do it. It was as if everything he did had the sole purpose of making me happy, and he was so happy himself that the idea of spoiling things was too painful even to contemplate. I knew he was pretending we were married from the way he tried to help in the kitchen, or fought with the carpet sweeper, or walked up to the bar in the local pub to order my drink without asking what I wanted. It was the first time we had been free just to be ourselves, the first time we hadn't had to look over our shoulders and worry that someone might see us. He was a different person, even more confident, so grown up, so protective – though of course we had our share of rows. It was a wonderful taste of what our life together could be like – and that made it all the harder for me to tell him that at the end of the holiday I didn't want to see him again . . . . For I'd decided that was the only way to do it. If he thought I was ending it because someone else had told me it was the right thing to do, he wouldn't accept it; but if I could somehow persuade him I didn't love him any more, then he would have to let me go.

I waited until our last day. We'd run out of milk so I walked down to the village to get some while he stayed at the cottage. I was surprised when he said he wasn't coming with me, because we'd hardly been apart for a moment the whole holiday. At least it gave me time to prepare what I was going to say. I was gone a long time, walking round the churchyard, staring out over the bleak moors, telling myself that I was doing this because I loved him, because it was the best thing for him – and trying not to think about how much I was going to hurt him.

He was looking out of the window when I opened the garden gate, and I could see he'd been worried by my long absence. My heart went out to him, and I had to fight to stop myself from smiling and waving.

I took a deep breath as I went in through the door. He was still standing by the window, watching me come in, and I could tell straightaway that he was up to something. Then I saw what it was. Hanging from one of the oak beams was a banner, and on it was written: *Please will you be my wife*?

He was obviously nervous – and yet I'd never seen so much love in his eyes. 'I didn't know whether to put, "Please will you marry me", or whether you would like the word wife,' he explained. 'I can do another saying whatever you like, only the . . .'

I broke down and cried then, and immediately he was holding me, and I was clinging to him, begging him always to love me, never to leave me . . . . In the end he managed to calm me down and went to make some tea. I started to laugh when he brought it back, and then I couldn't stop laughing. It was as if I had lost him, and now he'd come back to me. He laughed too, but I knew he was confused.

'I'm laughing because you're an idiot, and because I love the word wife, and because I love you so much I think I'm going to burst with it,' I said.

'Does that mean you will marry me, then?' he asked, searching my face.

'It means I'd marry you now, this minute, if we could . . . .'

'Please don't give me a list of reasons why we can't. I only want to hear you say yes, then we'll talk about when.'

'Ask me again.'

'Will you marry me?'

'Yes.'

It wasn't until later in the day that we were able to discuss it sensibly. By then, even though I couldn't let him go, I had made him agree that we wouldn't talk about marriage again until he came down from Oxford.

'I'll still want to, you know,' he whispered.
'I'll pray to God every night that you will.'

– 9 –

Because we realised now what would happen if anyone found out about us, we both behaved more responsibly when we got back to Foxton's for the summer term. All the same, Alexander obviously found it very hard to be discreet, so on my free evenings I went to the pub so that he wouldn't be tempted to come to me at the cottage or the surgery. The rest of the time wasn't so bad, except that there were always other people around; but at least we did see each other, and we left notes for one another inside his pillow-case every day.

Then – predictably, perhaps – Alexander found a way round our difficulties: he discovered an abandoned railwaymen's hut a mile or so from the school . . . . We met there at least once a week, and were so careful that we didn't even tell Henry about it. Alexander approached it from the railway tunnel, a hundred yards along the track, while I, after a quick lunch-time drink, wandered behind the pub, climbed a stile, made a mad dash across a field full of cows, then picked a path through the remains of the station, to find him waiting – once with a railwayman's hat on, a flag, a whistle, and a toy train on the track.

I never told him, perhaps because I thought he might be unhappy about it, that I'd made a friend at the pub. Her name was Ruth. Her family lived in the village, she told me. She talked a lot about herself and made me laugh when she told me about all the boyfriends she had and the way she kept them dangling.

'You'll have to meet Peter,' she said one day, after she'd

told me in detail what the two of them had been up to the night before. And the next time I went to the pub, Peter was there too.

One day, very casually, I mentioned Ruth and Peter to Alexander. He was jealous, just as I'd thought he might be, so I didn't refer to them again.

Towards the end of term Alexander's parents came to the school to find out from Mr Lorimer how he was doing. The report they received wasn't brilliant, but it was better than either of us had expected. Of course, Alexander's father wasn't too happy about it, and he let Alexander know it. He grilled him all day, then took him and Henry down to the village for dinner.

I had arranged to meet Ruth in the pub at seven-thirty. Peter had been in London on business for the past couple of weeks, so I was rather surprised to find him there too. We settled down in the corner of the bar with our drinks, and while Ruth and Peter talked about London I wondered what Alexander was doing at that moment.

'You seem a bit quiet this evening, Elizabeth,' Ruth said. 'Nothing the matter, is there?'

I looked up. 'Sorry, I was miles away.'

'Miles? Or a few hundred yards up the hill at Foxton's?'

'If you ask me, she's hiding a secret lover up there somewhere,' Peter chipped in. 'Come on now, who is it? The Latin master? The English master? I know, it's the Head!'

'That's typical of you,' Ruth said. 'Everything's got to come down to the same thing in the end, sex.' She turned back to me. 'Ignore him.'

I liked them so much. I wished I could introduce them to Alexander.

'Tell me,' Ruth said, 'don't you ever miss London? That was where you were before you came here, wasn't it?'

We chatted about where I used to work in London, and the places I used to go. Lord Belmayne's visit to the school had unsettled me, and my mind was only half on what I was saying, but neither Ruth nor Peter seemed to notice.

When I got back to the cottage at about half past ten, Alexander was waiting for me. I knew straightaway he'd been drinking; he was hiding in the bushes of the copse, and was making very heavy weather of getting out of them.

'Where've you been?' he said, as I tried to pull him up.

'You shouldn't be here. Where's Henry?'

'Gone to sign us in,' he slurred. 'Always good to see the old parents, you know, but they do go on. Any chance of some coffee?'

When we got inside the cottage he insisted on making the coffee himself, then crashed over the arm of the sofa on his way to the kitchen. 'Just how much wine did you have?' I asked.

'Not much. Must have been the brandy that did it.'

I eased him onto a kitchen chair, and he sat patiently watching me until I went to the fridge for the milk, when he came and put his arms around me.

'I wish we were married,' he said, lifting my hair and kissing the back of my neck. 'We will be, won't we? One day, you will marry me?'

'Yes,' I said. 'Yes, I will.'

'I nearly told them about you today.'

I tensed. 'You didn't though, did you?'

'No. But I'm going to. During the summer break. I'll go home for a few days, tell them then . . . .'

I was shaking my head. 'No, no, you mustn't. Not yet.'

'. . . then we'll go away somewhere, just the two of us. Where do you want to go?'

I started to protest. 'Just answer the question,' he said. 'Where shall we go?'

I could see there was no point in trying to reason with him now. 'You suggest somewhere,' I said.

'Sark. It's a little island just off Guernsey. Very romantic.'

'Are we taking Henry with us?'

'Are we hell!'

I pushed him away and he followed me back into the sitting room. 'I don't suppose I could persuade you into making it a honeymoon, could I?' he said, weaving his way round the sofa.

'You could not.'

'Thought you might say that. Still, we can always pretend. I'll book it in the name of Mr and Mrs Belmayne, how does that sound?'

I smiled as my heart turned over just to hear the words.

'Ah, I almost forgot. Damn! I must have left it in the bushes. Now stay right there, and don't move.'

When he came back again he went to the record player, and put on the record he'd brought in with him. As the music began to play he pulled me to my feet and wrapped me in his arms. 'Remember?'

How could I forget? It was 'Sealed With a Kiss.'

'Happy birthday, and happy anniversary, darling,' he said, as we started to dance.

'Anniversary?'

'It was a year ago tonight that I held you for the first time, and we danced to this record.'

I looked up into his face, and wondered what I had done to deserve someone so hopelessly romantic.

'Now close your eyes, I've got another surprise for you.'

I did, and as his lips pressed against mine I felt him fumbling with my left hand. It was an eternity ring.

'With my love, my heart, and my life,' he whispered.

When I went up to London for a couple of days, just before the end of term, I gave Alexander the excuse that I had to help Janice out of some trouble. He wasn't very keen on my staying away overnight, but I pointed out that as he was due to play cricket at a school in Dorset, then he wouldn't actually miss me too much.

Miss Angrid was waiting for me when I got back, she was holding open the door to her surgery. 'Elizabeth, come in will you?' The moment I saw her face I knew something was wrong; despite the heat my hands turned to ice. All I could think was that something had happened to Alexander.

She closed the door behind me and walked over to her desk. 'What is it?' I asked, and was shocked by the deadened sound of my voice. I tried again. 'Paul Raven, wasn't it measles?'

'No, Elizabeth,' she said, gravely, 'it's not Paul Raven.' She looked down at the newspaper on her desk, then turned it to face me.

I looked down at the page and at that moment I knew what it was like to feel the whole world fall out from under me. 'EXCLUSIVE: LORD CHIEF JUSTICE'S SON IN LOVE NEST WITH GYPSY.' For an instant I thought I was going to faint as the walls of the surgery seemed to close in around me.

I had never dreamt, not even in my worst nightmares, of anything like this. Front page, glaring out for all the world to see. Huge black letters, and a picture of Foxton's. A smaller picture in the bottom right hand corner showed the gypsy camp on Lord Belmayne's estate. I read the first few lines of the article. 'Following the allegations of gypsy child prostitution on the Suffolk estate of Lord Belmayne, the Lord Chief Justice, our reporters can now reveal that Lord Belmayne's son, the Hon. Alexander Belmayne, has been pursuing a life of debauchery at the elite Foxton's Boys' School with a gypsy love of his own . . . .' The words became a blur and I had to grip the edge of the desk to steady myself. Miss Angrid pulled up a chair for me, then handed me a glass of brandy.

'Alexander,' I said, trying to get up. 'Where is he? Has he seen it?'

Miss Angrid reached out to stop me. 'He's in the Headmaster's study. With his father.'

I closed my eyes and felt my hands begin to shake again. My stomach was churning, and I thought I was going to be sick. Miss Angrid pulled up a chair and sat next to me. She took my hands and started to rub them. 'Elizabeth,' she said, 'look at me.'

I dragged my eyes to her face.

'I know you grew up on the fair, child, Mrs Carey told me when she gave me your references. There's nothing to be ashamed of in that. But you've got to tell me, dear, are you anything to do with the Ince family?'

I shook my head. 'No.'

'Then why does the newspaper say you are?'

I swallowed hard, trying to control my voice, but it was coming in short gasps. 'I don't know,' I said. 'The fairground, they must think . . .' I looked at her. 'I'm not a gypsy, not the way they mean it.'

Miss Angrid squeezed my hand, then in her gruff, deep voice, she said, 'Does Alexander know where you grew up?'

'No. It never seemed important.' I looked up at her again. 'I knew that one day our relationship would have to end, and I've tried, honestly I have. But oh, don't let it be like this. Please, Miss Angrid . . .'

I jumped as the buzzer sounded on her phone. She patted my hand and went to answer it. 'Yes,' she said. 'Yes. I will.' Her face was grim as she put the receiver down. 'It was the Head. Lord Belmayne wants to see you.'

I couldn't face him. My eyes, my face, my whole body ached. 'They're wrong! Please, Miss Angrid, you've got to tell them, they've made a mistake.'

Miss Angrid placed her hands on my shoulders. 'It's too late, child. I tried to help you before, but now there's nothing I can do.'

Suddenly I was in her arms, and she was rocking me

back and forth like a baby. When she let me go I saw tears wending their way through the strange pattern of lines on her face. 'I'm going to miss you, Elizabeth,' she said. 'Probably more than you'll ever know.'

I held my breath, trying to take it in.

'I'll walk down with you,' she said, and led me to the Headmaster's study.

Lord Belmayne waited for the door to close behind the Head, then, keeping his hands clutched behind his back, he turned away from the window to face me. 'So,' he said, 'you have succeeded in making fools of us all. I hope you are satisfied.' He glared at me, but when I tried to speak my voice had disappeared.

He leaned forward and put his hands on the desk. 'You do realise you could have ruined my son's life? But that's what they put you here for, isn't it? To make a laughing stock out of me – and out of my son, a seventeen-year-old boy. You failed the first time, didn't you? Over that golf-cart business? He might have been expelled then, but for the fact that I happened to believe in his innocence. But he still took what punishment was going, because *you* insisted. And now it's you again – *you* who have managed to get his name spread across this filthy rag. Except that your dirty little trick has misfired again, because he won't be expelled this time either. Oh no! No, it's you who are going, Miss Sorrill. But before you walk out of that door I want to know exactly who you are. Ince's granddaughter, are you, or his niece? Or are you just an obliging friend?'

'I'm nothing to do with the Ince family,' I cried. 'I'm not a gypsy. I didn't . . .'

'Listen to me, young lady. I did everything in my power last night to stop this going to press. In the end I failed, and do you know why? Because they'd done their research. They had the facts, and the facts speak for themselves. So I'll ask you again, who are you?'

'My dad was a showman. I grew up on the fairground, but . . .'

'Fairgrounds! Gypsies! It's all the same thing!'

'No! It's not! Please listen to me. I love your son, and he loves . . .'

He slammed his fist down on the table. 'Don't waste your lies on me! You are nothing to my son, do you hear me, nothing! If you ever go near him again . . .'

'I'd never do anything to hurt him, I swear it. Never!'

'Names! I want the names of the people who put you up to this.'

My hands were over my face. 'It's all a mistake. Ask Miss Angrid, she'll tell you!'

But he wouldn't listen. He was determined to find a connection between me and Alfred Ince. And if there was no connection, as I insisted, then he wanted to know why I hadn't told the truth about my past when I'd first come to the school. Why, of all the schools in England, I had chosen Foxton's? And of all the boys in the sixth form, why I had chosen his son? The questions were coming at me so fast that my mind was spinning and anything I tried to say came out wrong. Why had I gone to London the day before? he wanted to know. How much were the journalists paying me for my story? What further filth were they going to print? How much longer was this vendetta going to carry on? Was there no human decency in people like me?

'I want you out of this school within the hour,' he finished, 'do you hear me? Out! And I am personally going to see to it that you never set foot inside a decent school again.'

Miss Angrid drove me back to the cottage in Tonto. I knew the boys were watching us from the windows, but I couldn't bring myself to look up. As we got out of the cart Miss Angrid stopped me. 'I think you should know who is responsible for this, Elizabeth. It was Mrs Jenkins.

I gather she saw you in London at Christmas? Well, she's been keeping an eye on you ever since. And with her contacts in Fleet Street . . . You made some friends at the local pub?' I nodded. 'Reporters.'

It was a nightmare.

Miss Angrid walked me up the cottage stairs to my sitting room. Alexander was there. Miss Angrid looked from one to the other of us, and left.

I could see the strain on his face and guessed that his interview with his father had been no easier than my own. He had a copy of the newspaper in his hand. 'You shouldn't be here,' I whispered.

His voice was cold and sarcastic. 'I've come to say good-bye.'

'Oh.'

'How could you, Elizabeth?' he yelled suddenly. 'You've made a fool of me, and of my family. Why did you do it?'

'I didn't,' I said. 'You've got it wrong, you all have. Please listen to . . .'

'Stop lying!' he shouted. 'Why else did you go to London yesterday if it wasn't to do some deal with this filthy rag. I want to kill you, do you know that?'

'Please, Alexander . . .'

'It's too much of a coincidence, Elizabeth. There they are on my father's land, and you're here at the school. My father's right, isn't he? It's a set-up. Well, here's what you've achieved. Go on, pick the filthy rag up. Keep it with you. Then whenever you're feeling down you can gloat over what a fool you, Elizabeth Sorrill, made of the Belmayne family.' He looked at me with loathing. 'And to think I believed you when you said you loved me.'

Miss Angrid came in. 'Alexander,' she said quietly, 'I think that's enough.'

He snatched up the box that he'd stuffed with the books and records he'd lent me and walked to the door. As his hand hit the handle he turned to look at me, and the hatred and pain I saw in his eyes I knew I would never forget.

Miss Angrid came to stand beside me at the window, and together we watched him walk across the field to the school. I looked down at the ring he'd given me, only two days before. Now I would never have the chance to tell him why I went to London. I was carrying his baby.

– Alexander –

– 10 –

It has taken me a long time to come to terms with my behaviour in the years that followed Elizabeth's departure from Foxton's – and from my life. Now, with the benefit of age and experience, I know why I did what I did. But still it is with shame that I recount these years, and the considerable pain I caused not only myself, but others too. At a time when every student's mission in life was to make the world a better place, I went up to Oxford, consumed by anger – an anger that burned more fiercely with every passing year as my struggle to deny the void Elizabeth had left in my life grew ever more desperate.

For though she had lied to me and made a fool of my family, I couldn't forget her. Because of her my first year at Oxford is mostly lost now, dispersed, along with the sweet-smelling smoke of the marijuana that provided my only respite from the confusion and resentment that burned in my heart. And yet, on the surface, I behaved much like any other student. Now and again, if it took our fancy, Henry and I might make our way to the occasional lecture, but mostly we spent our time indulging in intellectual debate on how we, as students, should assume responsibility for world peace. Peace was the watchword of the times – though, ironically, despite our long hair and our fashionable socialism, there was very little that was peaceful, or indeed socialist, about our behaviour. We roared around Oxford in the new Mercedes 230 SL my grandmother had equipped me with on my eighteenth birthday, we threw outrageous, extemporised parties, raged against the establishment, and took aggressive advantage of the trend for making love not war. Sex was made easy for me by the succession of girls flocking to my door as though I were the reincarnation of Giacomo Casanova himself: the scandal of the 'gypsy love affair' lived on. All I had to do was crook a finger and they would all but fall at my feet. I relished the way I could use them, then just walk away.

It was sometime during my second year that the boredom of easy conquest was alleviated by a new turn in events. Students in Paris struck out at the Gaullist Government, creating an unprecedented furore among students worldwide. My participation in sit-ins, boycotts and rallies was both vigorous and vociferous. We felt the time had finally come to make ourselves heard, to condemn the forsaking of revolutionary vocation for capitalist comfort, and to make known our disgust at the atrocities that were being committed all over the world. Along with thousands of others Henry and I marched on London to demonstrate against the war in Vietnam, against the Russian invasion of Czechoslovakia, and against UDI and the oppression of blacks in Rhodesia. Demonstrations and protests became as much a part of the times, as Janice Joplin, hippies and pop concerts .... And pop concerts offered yet another opportunity for rolling up a joint, taking off your clothes and making love in the grass. After a concert everything was peace and harmony and everyone loved the world.

It was after a concert – The Festival of the Flower Children – that I first met Jessica. A crowd of us had gone back to Henry's and my rooms at Brackenbury Buildings to listen to more music, but I was bored, only half-stoned, and in need of a new woman. The superior-looking chick who sauntered into the room late in the evening – so strikingly out of place among the spaced-out-flower children with her silent, condescending scrutiny of her surroundings and her obvious awareness of her own sexuality – fitted my bill perfectly.

At first I only watched her, as she stood alone, taking in

the scattered bodies through a blue haze of pot and incense. She didn't seem to be looking for anyone in particular, nor did she seem to care that she was the only woman in the room who wasn't in kaftan and plaits. In fact looking at her, petite as she was, was like watching the pages of *Vogue* flutter into animation.

'Far out,' Henry muttered in my ear.

'Who is she?'

He shrugged. 'Never seen her before. Ask your friend.' And with a grin he nodded to someone behind me.

I turned to find a girl whose name I had forgotten glaring up at me in doped paranoia. I recognised the look immediately: I had screwed her three times – which, in her book, gave her some sort of territorial rights on me. Clutching my arm, she dragged me outside, and since there were several people on the landing freaking out to Cream, she pulled me down the stairs. 'Her name's Jessica Poynter,' she hissed.

'Really?' I drawled, stuffing my hands into my pockets and leaning back against the wall. 'Wouldn't care to introduce me, would you?'

She slapped my face, harder than they usually did, and stormed off. I looked after her, rubbing my jaw and grinning, then turned back up the stairs and pressed my way back into the party.

When I found Jessica Poynter she was studying the obscene faces of Ensor's *Intrigue*, something I had stuck on the wall to brighten the place up.

'I find it beats looking in the mirror,' I said.

She gave me an unhurried once-over, then turned back to the painting.

I watched her, amused by her deliberate indifference, and let my eyes wander slowly from the thick pencilled lines that sloped from the inside corners of her eyes towards her temples, to the knee-high white socks that finished at least nine inches below her hemline. Her dress was crocheted, and as far as I could tell she wore nothing underneath.

‘So, it’s the famous, or should I say infamous, Alexander Belmayne.’

I smirked, and lifted my eyes from her barely concealed breasts to rest on her whitened lips.

‘Is it true what they say about you?’ she said, without looking at me.

‘Depends what you’ve heard.’

She took a step back and put her head on one side, still studying the grotesque faces on the wall. At last she lifted her eyes to mine, using her lack of height to perfection. ‘They say you despise women.’

I wasn’t unaware of this popular myth, spread mainly by the rabid feminists who were sprouting up all over Oxford, most of whom had availed themselves of my services on more than one occasion. But this was the first time someone had actually come right out with it – or at least come out with it before I laid them rather than afterwards.

I laughed. ‘And how would you like me to answer that?’ I said.

‘Whichever way you choose.’

‘I choose to get you a drink,’ I said, taking her empty glass.

I was gone for some time, and half expected her to have disappeared by the time I returned, but she was still waiting. Why were they all so predictable?

‘Thank you.’ She smiled up at me as she took the drink, and I couldn’t fail to notice the challenge in her eyes. ‘You didn’t answer my question. Do you despise women?’

I sighed, feeling suddenly bored. ‘I despise women,’ I said, and turned to go.

She caught my arm. ‘I won’t do anything to change that.’

‘You couldn’t.’

‘I couldn’t?’ She laughed softly, and I was arrested by her condescension, or maybe it was aggression.

'I haven't seen you before,' I said.

'Somerville. I study hard.' She shrugged when I didn't answer. 'Isn't that why we're here?'

'It could be.'

She smiled slowly. 'Just as long as we come out with what we want at the end of it.'

'And what do you want?'

She cast her cool gaze over me again. It was answer enough.

I held the silence between us, keeping my eyes on hers. Then I said: 'Sleep with me tonight.'

'Is that what you want?'

'Yes.'

'Do you always get what you want?'

'Usually.'

'But not always?'

I shook my head. 'Can I see you again?'

'I shall be around.'

I laughed, and for a fleeting second she looked unsure of herself. 'I'll take you for a drive tomorrow,' I said.

'In the famous Mercedes? Not tomorrow. Make it the day after. My parents are coming tomorrow.'

'Can't I meet them?'

She seemed surprised, and this time her eyes were mocking me. 'OK. Come for tea. Four-thirty.' She looked across the room, then smiled. 'If you're desperate for some company in your bed tonight, it looks as if your friend Henry has finished with Rosalind Purbright. I'm sure she'll be more than willing, she usually is.'

I raised an eyebrow at that. 'And if I did take Rosalind Purbright to bed tonight, would you mind?'

'Why should I?'

'Maybe because I want you to.'

'OK, then, I'll mind. Should I also slap her face tomorrow, or would you prefer me to slap yours?'

'I've already had mine slapped twice this week.'

'It's a very slappable face.'

'Thank you,' I said. 'So is yours.'

She laughed and raised her face in invitation. I caught it in my hand, and eased her back against the wall, feeling her skin through the holes in her dress. She looked up at me, her lips slightly parted, and suddenly I wanted to enter her, there, in the middle of the party. From the way she was looking at me, I knew she wanted it too.

As I bent my head to kiss her she slipped her hand between us, and began to caress me through my jeans. I groaned into her open mouth, and caught her hair in my hands. In response she pressed her hand harder against me, and for one horrifying moment I thought I was going to come.

Then, abruptly, she pushed me away. 'Ciao,' she said, and dropping her empty glass into my hand, she left.

I didn't meet Jessica's parents the following day, as for some reason they couldn't make it – which was just as well as I had a rugger match I'd forgotten about. I invited Jessica to come along and watch, but she wasn't interested.

I saw her a few times over the next month or so, but almost always in the company of the arty types she mixed with, and if we did spend any time alone and I raised the subject of sex, she simply sighed, 'Is that all you ever think about? There's so much more to life, you know.' And when she wasn't dabbling around with the History of Art, she'd take off for Hull or somewhere, to organise the fishermen's wives or Dagenham to join the sewing-machinists in their strike for equal pay. She was teasing me, I knew, and for the time being it amused me to let her. But before much longer I'd put a stop to it and give her a session she'd never forget – before moving on to someone else . . . . Meanwhile, I concentrated rather more than I was used to on things like lectures and tutorials and put Jessica and her art and feminism, out of my mind. She'd find out soon enough that Alexander Belmayne never went crawling after a woman.

Then Henry told me she was screwing Guy Hibbert, one of our group. I fell straight into the trap, and my fury knew no bounds when she coolly responded to my dinner invitation with a note informing me that she would be otherwise engaged. However, she went on to say that her parents were arriving the next day, and as I had expressed a desire to meet them once before, if I was still of a similar mind they would be arriving around four thirty.

I screwed up the note and hurled it against the wall. And to demonstrate just what I thought of her, I set out in search of Rosalind Purbright and promptly humped seven bells out of her.

Four-thirty the following day found me at Somerville College. I had taken the trouble to root out a pair of my least torn jeans, and I'd got a nurse from the Radcliffe Infirmary, whom I'd been seeing on and off, to iron me up a decent shirt. I was annoyed with myself for making an effort, and even more annoyed by Henry's amusement.

Jessica and her family were waiting when I arrived. Her mother had planned a picnic, so we piled into her father's Bentley and set off for the countryside. We stopped somewhere on the road to Stratford and found a 'nice, shady little spot', as Mrs Poynter became faint in direct sunlight.

We looked ridiculous, the four of us sitting there on the side of the road, but I was the only one who seemed to feel it. Mr Poynter soon fell into a heated argument with Jessica on whether or not women should be allowed to join the Stock Exchange.

'Never heard anything so ridiculous in all my life,' he grunted. 'Women! On the Floor! What nonsense will you come out with next?' He stuffed another chicken leg in his mouth. Mrs Poynter took out a little battery-operated fan which hummed a monotonous circle about her face. Jessica looked at her with contempt, but to my relief she dropped the argument with her father and poured me some more wine. I tried not to look at my watch. It could be a reasonably pleasant afternoon, I thought, if only the old man would shut up; and even better if Jessica and I could be alone.

'So,' said Mr Poynter, delving into his teeth to remove a piece of chicken, 'what are you reading, my boy?'

'Law,' I answered.

'Yes, of course, law. Met your father once. Can't remember where now, probably at the House. How is he?'

'Very well the last time I spoke to him, thank you, sir.'

'Oh, it's so hot,' Mrs Poynter complained. 'Fetch my parasol from the car, darling, will you?' She blinked at Jessica. 'She's such a good girl,' she said, when Jessica had gone. 'Have you known each other long?'

'Not really,' I answered. She nodded, and batting away the flies that seemed dementedly attracted to her, she appeared to lose interest in me.

Jessica came back with the parasol, then lay down on the grass beside me. Her bra-less nipples were very evident beneath the thin cotton of her T-shirt, and my jeans became uncomfortably tight as she trailed her fingertips over her breasts before letting her hands fall to the grass.

'Ever get rid of those blasted gypsies, did he?' Mr Poynter asked.

I tensed, but before I had to answer Jessica said, 'Have either of you heard from Lizzie recently? I haven't had a letter for ages.'

'She's somewhere in Turkey,' her mother answered. 'Heaven alone knows why she should want to go there. I just hope she doesn't bring back anything nasty.'

'Lizzie's my sister,' Jessica explained. 'She dropped out

of university and went off round the world to find herself. Two years ago, haven't seen her since.'

'Very enterprising of her,' I remarked.

'Enterprising, you say,' Mr Poynter jumped in. 'Downright irresponsible, I call it.'

'Yes, that too,' I said, and heard Jessica giggle.

'Have you known each other long?' Mrs Poynter said. She leaned against a tree and closed her eyes, blissfully unaware that she'd already asked once.

'Not very,' Jessica answered, stretching and yawning. 'Alexander wants me to sleep with him. What do you think I should do, Mummy?'

I choked.

'Oh heavens, I don't know, dear. Is it necessary?' Her mother was smiling pleasantly, eyes still closed. Mr Poynter was ripping apart another chicken leg, and looking bored.

Jessica flung herself back in the grass and laughed. 'I'm not sure really,' she said. Then abruptly she jumped to her feet and held her hand out to me. 'Let's go for a walk.'

I got up, and mumbling something to her parents, followed her across the field. 'Did you have to say that?' I said, when we were out of earshot.

'No, I don't suppose I did. But it was worth it to see your face.'

'Don't they mind? I mean, you sleeping with men?'

'They've never seemed to.'

'Unusual parents. Especially with a daughter.'

'But it's all right for a son?'

'I didn't make the rules,' I said, holding up my hands in defence.

She pulled me to a halt and turned me to face her. 'And I'm changing the rules, Alexander.'

She looked beautiful. Her blonde hair, piled carelessly on top of her head, was curling in wisps around her neck, and her intelligent eyes studied me, waiting for my response. When I didn't answer she shrugged and started to gaze around her. After a while she lifted her arms to the sky and let her head fall back. When she spoke it was as if she were reciting poetry, and slowly she brought her eyes back to mine. 'Tell me Alexander, because I need to know. Who do you really think I am? What is my purpose in this world?'

It wasn't the first time I'd heard her ask these questions, and I knew just how serious she was. I looked at her. She was a mystery to me. Her search for meaning and value to her life took her further from me than any earthly distance could. In a way it made her more desirable – I wanted to possess her and make myself her only purpose.

'Is purpose just another word for fate?' I asked. 'Or are you using it to evaluate your movement through life?'

She stared back at me, surprised and intrigued – surprised because I had never taken her seriously before, and intrigued because I had managed to say something that she considered worthy of thought. 'I can see your intention is to penetrate my psyche,' she said, eventually, and then started to walk slowly on across the field.

Relieved that the pondering of life's little complexities seemed to be over and not a little pleased with my own stimulating but unanswerable contribution, I started after her. It was a sleepy summer's day, and these lovely Oxfordshire cornfields were wasted as a setting for a discussion on the meaning of life.

When we reached the stile to the next field Jessica climbed over. As I made to follow she stopped me, putting the stile between us. 'Would there be a purpose to us consummating our relationship?' she said.

Only just managing not to groan, I looked around, trying desperately to dredge up another piece of mind-boggling profundity. When I looked back at her she was still watching me. The moisture on her lips caught the sunlight, and she had unclipped her hair.

'I think there would be,' she said, and smiled. 'I want to be naked. I want you to be naked.'

I felt my penis swell at her words, and reached out to touch her. Her mouth was already open, and as I pushed my tongue deep inside, she took my hand and placed it on the small mound of her breast. 'Harder,' she groaned, as I began to rotate her nipple between my finger and thumb. 'Harder.'

Quickly I leapt over the stile. Her hands slipped down to my waist and she was unzipping my fly. I was solid by now, and could feel the blood pulsating through me. She pushed at my trousers, dragging them down over my thighs, then reached up to slip off her T-shirt. I fumbled with the zip on her jeans, but she pushed me away. 'I'll do it,' she said. 'Undress with me.'

Naked, we walked into the field beyond. The corn came to our waist, but there was no one around to see us. After a while she stopped, and sank to her knees. Her face was on a level with my penis, and lifting it away from my belly, she covered it with her mouth. I held her head and moved with her, feeling her teeth rub against me. After a while she let me go and looked up into my face. I pushed her back and lay down beside her, manoeuvring myself to kiss her behind the clutch of blonde pubic hair.

I waited until I felt her muscles start to contract, then sat up quickly, holding her legs apart ready to enter her. She licked my lips, sinking her teeth gently into them, and clawed her nails across my buttocks. I positioned myself above her, then making her look into my eyes, I thrust into her with all my might. She screamed out. I thrust again, paused, then again. I knew I was hurting her, but she cried out for more. I was going to come soon, but she wasn't there yet, and I wanted to make her scream out again – scream and scream. She looked up at me and I saw she was laughing. 'Think of your life, Alexander. Think of everything in it and use it, push it into me. I want it all.'

I lowered my head and kissed her savagely on the mouth, then grabbed her legs and pushed them up, so high her knees were almost on her shoulders. 'That's it, oh yes,' she groaned. 'I can feel you coming to me. All of you. Use it, Alexander! Use it to fuck me!' I was looking down into her face, it was contorted with lust. 'Was she as good as this?'she snarled. 'Your gypsy?'

I stopped dead.

She laughed. 'Is that who you're thinking of now?' she said, writhing beneath me and twisting her fingers through my hair. 'The gypsy slut?'

My hands slipped round her throat, almost strangling her, then with all the strength I had left I hammered into her, so hard that she cried out for me to stop. But I kept on going, thrust after thrust, driving her into the ground, crushing her beneath me, and not looking at her once. Let her scream, let her struggle, she was going to pay for that mistake. And then my climax was upon me, crushing me, blinding me, choking me, and it was my voice that cried out – a single name – as my body exploded into hers.

She was trapped beneath me. When she tried to move, I felt sickened and rolled over on to my back. I could hear her breathing, and after a while she started to move again. Finally she pulled my face round to hers. She was masturbating.

'Watch me,' she whispered.

I felt only disgust. She saw it, and laughed. Then her back arched from the ground, and she moaned as waves of orgasm surged through her body. I watched her, hating her.

'So her name's Elizabeth, is it?' she said, as we stood at the stile putting our clothes on. She was pulling on her jeans, and seeing her slight body writhe its way into them, I had to fight the urge to crush her with my hands.

'You're still angry,' she said, when I didn't answer. 'Just think for a moment, Alexander, and you will see that your anger was the purpose to our love-making. You needed to face up to your pain.'

'What pain? You don't know what the hell you're talking about, so just shut up!'

'You're angry inside, Alexander, it's why you're the way you are. You need to face it, and I want to help you. I told the Federation I could, and I think I have, though maybe you don't realise it yet.'

'Federation! Do you mean to say you've been discussing me at your lesbian orgies! You're sick, do you know that?'

'No, Alexander, it's you who are sick. In the way you abuse women, you're sick. And by abusing us you're abusing yourself. I was right, it's because you still yearn for the gypsy. Does it hurt terribly?'

I turned away. 'Poor Alexander,' she cooed.

'Shall we change the subject,' I snapped.

'Sure. But if I can face it, and handle it, why can't you? After all, if we're going to get married I'm going to have to live with her too, aren't I?'

I spun round. 'If we're what!'

She was laughing, and I'd never hated anyone so much since the day I found out the truth about Elizabeth.

She started to climb the stile and I grabbed her arm. 'You'd better get this into your head now, Jessica. I've no intention of marrying you, or anyone else for that matter. So –'

'OK,' she said, and dropping a kiss on my cheek, she skipped over the stile and began running back across the field.

– 11 –

I hated her, yet I was obsessed by her. The harder I tried to stay away the more I found myself going to her. It was as if she had spun a web and trapped me; when she felt like it she crept out of her lair, sated her lust on me, and then discarded me. Weeks turned into months and still I was seeing her. Her independence and elusiveness almost drove me out of my mind. Her quest to find a purpose in life continued and she made it clear that this was something more than I could supply. Her need for identity, recognition, a status, was the source of endless fights between us, but she could no more stay away from me than I could from her.

Henry despised her, but that only served to make her more acceptable to me. When she and I decided to move from our respective colleges and find ourselves a small house on the outskirts of Oxford I thought it was going to be the end of my friendship with him.

'You're insane,' he yelled at me, standing in the doorway of my room as I packed.

'Maybe,' I said, taking the Ensor from the wall and grimacing as I remembered the first night I had met Jessica.

'She's no good, Alexander. She's sleeping with other men, you know that, don't you?'

I nodded. 'Yep, I know that.'

He punched his fist against the wall. 'How can you just shrug it off? Jesus, I don't think I know you any more.'

I laughed at that. 'This is beginning to sound like a lover's tiff, Henry.'

He didn't even smile. His eyes were brilliant and I could see that he was struggling with himself. I turned away and began stuffing my shaving equipment into a bag.

'It's Elizabeth, isn't it?' he suddenly burst out.

I turned back to him, my razor still in my hand. This was a forbidden subject between us, and had been since before we left Foxton's.

'It's Elizabeth. Jessica's told me all about it. She lets you think of Elizabeth when you're screwing her, doesn't she?'

I felt the blood draining from my face. 'You're out of your mind – '

'No! It's you who's out of your mind. Listen, do you know why she does it? Why she lets you carry on this insane delusion? It's so that you will never completely own her. So that she can walk out on you whenever she feels like it. She's using you, Alexander. You're her cause, her challenge. If she can conquer you, break you even, she'll have scored *the* great victory for womankind.'

'You don't know what you're talking about.'

'I bloody do. I'm Not Fodder for the Male Chauvinist Pig! Christ, it's emblazoned all over her T-shirt! She's made you a laughing stock, Alexander, the way you go running around after her. And you don't really think you're going to get Elizabeth out of your system by – '

'Out of my system! What in hell's name are you talking about? So I made a mistake when I was a kid – why can't you do as I did years ago, and forget it? And as for all that crap about – '

'It's not crap. Jessica told me herself, she's told everybody. What is it she does for you, Alexander? Put on a nurse's uniform?'

'For Christ's sake!' I yelled.

Henry's face was white. His eyes fell to the razor I was still holding. 'Why don't you use it now?' he said. 'Slit your wrists and be done with it, before Jessica does it for you. Because take it from me, Alexander, she'll destroy you.'

Before I could answer he had stalked out of the room, slamming the door behind him.

I didn't see him for several weeks after that, but I was so busy with Jessica I had no time to think about him. Intellectually my life took a new turn as I entered her bohemian world of artists and writers, and languished away the days posing nude while she stood at her easel creating unrecognisable portraits of me. This was her surrealist period.

The novelty of living together soon wore off though, as Jessica started to introduce her feminist friends – the lesbian brigade, as I irreverently called them – into our house, and returned to her old habit of attending women's rallies in far flung corners of the country. At that time the Women's Liberal Federation, the organisation she belonged to, was trying to bring about government legislation for equal pay. They had plenty of other causes too such as free contraception, maternity rights for working mothers, laws against sexual harassment in the workplace, Jessica's old favourite about allowing women to join the Stock Exchange – in fact so many that I often lost track of what Jessica was doing, and got fed up with the endless political wrangling that I seemed to get caught up in whenever she was at home. It wasn't that I didn't believe in what she was trying to do, it was just that I was growing a little weary of helping her cope with the basic contradictions in her behaviour. On the one hand she believed passionately in every one of the Federation's feminist ideals, but on the other, she was not only living with one of the common enemy, she was actually falling in love with him. She could not come to terms with this – and nor could I. It wasn't as if I expected her to cook for me, wash up after me, iron for me, they were all tasks I could and did perform for myself; but sometimes, when she was feeling particularly warm towards me, Jessica insisted on doing these things. She did them because she loved me, because she wanted to do them, that was what she said at the time – but afterwards she would fly into a terrible rage and nothing I could do or say would convince her that she hadn't drastically diminished her status as a modern, liberated woman. All men wanted women for was to slave for them, she'd yell at me; they wanted to parade them as status symbols, and then drive them home and father children on them in their own image. There was nothing to compare with the arrogance and stupidity of the male ego! And all this because she had darned a hole in one of my socks, so small that I hadn't even noticed it was there.

After an altercation that very nearly came to blows just

because I asked her to post a letter for me, I walked out of the house. I was sorely in need of male company. I sought out Henry and in no time at all we were slapping each other on the back as if our quarrel had never taken place. Robert Lyttleton, a chap who had come up from Eton a year after us, and knew Henry's family was now occupying my old room. The three of us began to spend a lot of time together, mostly at Brown's or the King's Arms. And Parson's Pleasure was a convenient male-only retreat that I frequented because I knew it annoyed Jessica.

This isn't to say that I stopped living with Jessica, of course. Our erratic and eccentric relationship continued along its rocky path, painfully cemented by a compelling mix of hatred and lust. I thrived on the way I could torment her because she loved me; she tried desperately not to mind about the other women I had – and hit back by taking lovers herself. I, at least, was happy with the way we were, and didn't intend to change it.

So when, after Finals, I had the idea of inviting Miss Angrid up to Oxford for the weekend, no one was more surprised by the suggestion than me. From the look on his face, Henry was pretty flabbergasted too.

'Just think of the old dragon,' I said, before he could say anything, 'waddling her way round college telling everyone to stop biting their nails and tuck their shirts in. It'll be a kill.'

'Where will she stay?'

I shrugged. 'Why not with me and Jessica?'

Henry's eyes widened, and I realised that perhaps that wasn't such a good idea. This was confirmed later when Jessica rounded on me and demanded to know how she was expected to cope with a morbid old bag of a matron hanging round her all day. Why on earth had I invited her in the first place – or was I just kinky about matrons?

In fact I had been having second thoughts about the invitation, but after that jibe I went ahead and composed a letter to Miss Angrid the same night. The following week I received a reply saying she'd love to come, and could I book her into that nice Eastgate hotel – the Ruskin suite if I could manage it – where she had stayed the last time she had been up.

On our four-hundred-and-twenty-pounds-a-year grant, plus the six hundred pounds allowance we each received from our fathers, Henry and I managed to stretch to the Ruskin suite, and I was at the station to meet Miss Angrid on the designated Saturday. I was annoyed to find how nervous I was at the prospect of seeing her again, and silently berated Jessica for forcing me into it. And the fact that my heart gave an Olympic-style somersault as Miss Angrid stepped off the train annoyed me even further. However, the situation was saved by the Mercedes. She made no comment, except to purse her lips and glance at me over the top of her new spectacles, but it was a look I remembered so well that I very nearly threw my arms around her and danced her round the car park.

Henry was waiting at the hotel and leapt from his seat when he saw us come in. He then proceeded very nearly to buckle his back by trying to sweep her off her feet. Her face was beaming so hard it looked painful.

When lunch was over, she produced a well-thumbed guide of the city and took us on a tour, dragging us from monument to museum, college to library, impressing us like mad with her vast knowledge of the place, until at last we arrived at Balliol where she insisted Henry show her his room.

I almost choked when I saw Henry's face; it was as if we had stepped back in time. Miss Angrid was duly horrified at the state of Henry's room and demanded to know who was responsible for letting him get away with it. Henry whispered to me that his scout was away, and we both heaved a sigh of relief at the narrow avoidance of past and present worlds colliding . . . .

We dined with her that evening. I stayed longer than I'd intended, mainly because with Miss Angrid there, Jessica suddenly seemed an intrusion in my life, an irrelevance. But I had to face her wrath sooner or later, so leaving Miss Angrid and Henry to their brandies and reminiscences, I went home. Jessica wasn't there. Her wardrobe was empty and there was a note on the bed. I didn't even bother to read it. I knew she'd be back.

The following day Henry was taking part in the Eights Week races, so I took Miss Angrid for a stroll over to Magdalen to see the deer park.

'So you'll be going down at the end of the month,' she remarked, as we wandered past the tower and on to the bridge.

'Mmm,' I waved to a couple of friends emerging from beneath the bridge in a punt.

'What do you intend to do with yourself then?'

'Bar School.'

'And Henry?'

'Same.'

'And are you still determined to practise criminal law?' she asked, leaning against the side of the bridge.

'Yes.'

'Is your father any happier about it? I thought after all that business – '

'Not really, but we don't row about it any more.'

'How is he? I read in the paper he'd not been well. Heart, wasn't it?'

'He's better, I think. Apparently the doctor's told him he's got to take things a bit easier, but you know what he's like.'

'And your mother?'

'Oh, she's fine. Gave her a bit of a fright, naturally, but now Lucinda's had the baby she's got something else to occupy her mind.'

'Of course. I was forgetting you had a sister. She married a Frenchman, didn't she?'

'Etienne. And now they've got a son. And before you ask, I'm sure they'll be putting him down for Foxton's – unless Etienne insists he has a French education!'

She laughed. 'Now, what about you? Who's this Jessica Henry was telling me about last night?'

'Henry told you about Jessica?'

'He did. But I had already guessed there must be someone, otherwise you and Henry would be sharing digs together. So, what's she like? Why haven't I been introduced?'

'She's gone to keep her grandmother company for the weekend.'

She eyed me suspiciously. 'Mmm. Serious, is it, between you two?'

I answered with a shrug, then deftly manoeuvred her round to telling me the news of Foxton's. Mr Lear was now the Deputy Head, I was surprised to hear, and Mr Ellery had married a new English mistress who had joined the school just after I left. Foxton's had been slaughtered at rugby by Monkforth Abbey for three years running, she added with disgust. 'Seems they forgot how to play the wretched game after you'd gone. You got a blue, I hear?'

'You hear a great deal down there at Foxton's,' I laughed, and pushed myself away from the wall to walk on. She followed, a pace or two behind. 'And the other matron?' I asked, after a short silence. 'I've forgotten her name now. Is she still there?'

'Miss Austen. Yes, she's still with us.'

When we came to the other side of the bridge, we wandered down the steps to the river bank. It was several minutes before I realised Miss Angrid was no longer walking beside me. When I turned round I found her watching me, her hands bulging the pockets of her cardigan and her blue rinse tilted to one side.

'Is something the matter?' I asked. And when she didn't answer I looked at my watch. 'I know! It's time for tea.

There's a great tea shop not far from here. No hot buttered toast, I'm afraid, but they do a terrific scone with homemade jam and fresh . . .'

'Why don't you ask, Alexander?' She waited, her eyes steadfastly holding mine. 'It's why you invited me here, isn't it?'

I stared out across the river. I hadn't been conscious of any motive, but maybe that was because I hadn't allowed myself to be. It was all so long ago now – I couldn't even picture her face any more. So why was my heart beating faster? Why did the palms of my hands feel damp?

I looked back to Miss Angrid. She was still watching me. 'I can return to Foxton's without mentioning her name if that's what you want,' she said. 'It's up to you.'

I sat down on the grass and rested my elbows on my knees. After a while she came and sat beside me. I couldn't meet her eyes as I spoke. 'Have you heard from her?'

'A postcard.' She fumbled in her handbag. 'Here, I brought it in case you wanted to see it.'

I looked at it for a long time, but didn't take it from her. 'When did she send it?' I asked finally.

'Just over a year ago.'

'Do you know where she is?'

'No.'

'She doesn't say on the card?'

'No.'

I laughed, and knew it sounded bitter. 'Well, that's it then, isn't it,' I said, getting to my feet. 'She could be dead by now for all we know.'

Miss Angrid said nothing. 'Well, what am I supposed to say?' I shouted angrily. 'She went out of our lives four years ago. She knows where we are, if she wanted to get in touch she would. I gave up losing sleep over her a long time ago.' It wasn't what I'd meant to say, but somehow the right words wouldn't come.

Miss Angrid sighed, and held out her hand for me to

help her to her feet. 'It's no good, Alexander,' she said, 'I can see it in your eyes, even after all this time. I thought maybe you'd have got over it by now, but common sense tells me I wouldn't be here if you had.' I turned away so she couldn't see my face, and she sighed again as she looked out over the river. 'She was very special, wasn't she? I don't suppose any of us really knew how much you two meant to each other. You were both so young. All I can say to you now is, stop punishing yourself and – from what Henry tells me – everyone around you too. It's been a long time, Alexander, time enough for you to come to terms with what happened. That's the only way you're going to stop hurting, you know – and when you stop hurting, then it really will be over.'

I swung round to face her. 'It is over! For God's sake, what do I have to do to prove it? Yes, she did mean something to me, but you said it yourself, it was a long time ago. I was a schoolboy. Things are different now. Things, *I*, have changed.'

She sighed and hitched her bag across her elbow. When she looked at me again her eyes were sad, and she shook her head slowly.

I glared at her, and in that instant I felt such rage well up in me that I wanted to strike out at her. Why wouldn't they all stop tormenting me? Why wouldn't they believe me when I told them it didn't matter to me any more? There was another woman in my life – there had been for more than a year. Damn it, surely that must mean something!

I was glad when Henry joined us for tea at the Eastgate and sensing the tension between Miss Angrid and me, immediately set about breaking it. He almost succeeded, but I refused to be drawn completely; knowing that he thought the same as Miss Angrid angered me.

Later I drove Miss Angrid to the station and waited with her until her train was ready to leave. As I was closing the door of her carriage she turned quickly and pushed a note into my hand. The sudden lurch of my heart must have shown on my face, because she shook her head.

I waited until I got back to the car before I unfolded the note, then smiled as I saw it was a verse from Shelley. I read it slowly.

> Life may change, but it may fly not,
> Hope may vanish, but can die not,
> Truth be veiled, but still it burneth;
> Love repulsed – but it returneth.

I banged my hand hard against the steering wheel. Damn! Damn her! What did it take to convince her that not only was I no longer in love with Elizabeth, I was in love with someone else? Jessica was a bitch, but I couldn't live without her; we were made for each other, Jessica and I, and the rest of the world could go to hell. And what was more, I now knew exactly what I would do to show the rest of the world that Elizabeth meant nothing to me any more – absolutely nothing.

•

'What do you mean, no?' I stormed. 'You mean you're refusing?'

'That's precisely what I mean.' Henry walked slowly across the room to refill his glass, then sauntered back to his chair and sat down. 'Then I'll have to ask Robert Lyttleton, I suppose,' I said.

'You can always ask.'

I swung round to face him. 'Look here, Henry, I'm getting married. It's supposed to be one of the most important days in a man's life. I'm asking you to be there, with me.'

'And I'm saying that I don't want to be. In fact I don't want to be there at all. I refuse to sit and watch my best friend make a fool of himself. The whole thing's a sham, Alexander, as you well know.'

'A sham! Good God, man – '

But Henry interrupted me. 'Look, it's been ever since Old Anger came to visit. She got under your skin, didn't she, about Elizabeth? OK, OK, it's all over, I've heard you say it a thousand times. I believe you, all right? You don't have to marry Jessica to prove it.'

That took the wind clean out of my sails.

'You see, I'm right,' he went on. 'Practically everything you've done in the last four years has been because of Elizabeth. Your reputation as a stud and a heart-breaker was such a legend that the biggest feminist in Oxford came gunning for you. The only trouble was, she fell for you too. They all do, Alexander, because you're a bastard. Because you don't give a shit about any of them, except to make them pay for the fact that you feel you've been "betrayed" by one of their sex – a girl you *claim* you don't even love any more. Well, if you don't love her any more then why not stop behaving like this? Stop now, before you make one of the biggest mistakes of your life.'

'Impossible,' I said.

'It's not!'

'I mean, it's impossible for it to be the biggest mistake of my life. I've already made the biggest.'

'When you were no more than a kid. And you're still behaving like one.'

'I've already asked her,' I said.

'Tell her you've changed your mind.'

'Why should I do that? I haven't.'

He gave an exasperated sigh. 'Oh, to hell with it. If you want to ruin your life, then go ahead and do it. I can see that nothing I've got to say is going to stop you.'

We sat through a long silence before either of us

spoke again. Finally I caught his eye and grinned. Reluctantly, he grinned too. 'Have you fixed the date?' he asked.

'June 19th.'

'Why does it have to be so soon?'

'Why not?'

He shrugged. 'And if Elizabeth were to walk through that door now, what then?'

I jumped up from my chair. 'For God's sake, Henry!' Then I gave a half-hearted grin. 'If she did, I could invite her to the wedding.'

He laughed. 'You really are a bastard.'

'It's why Jessica's marrying me, or so you would have me believe.'

'I can think of no other reason. Apart from the title, I suppose.'

It was my turn to laugh. 'Let her have her title, what the hell? We understand each other, Jessica and I. She's just the sort of wife I need. If you didn't hate her so much, you'd see it too. She's a perfect barrister's wife. For one thing she's great at dinner parties. She's witty, intelligent, and she's got her art which gives her something to do besides making my life a misery with the lesbian brigade.'

Henry looked at me aghast. 'I take it you've never said that to her.'

'Would I be alive to tell the tale? Anyway, shall I go on? She's got an independent, though I admit, sometimes warped mind. She's beautiful. Good child-bearing hips with which to produce the Belmayne heirs. What more could a man ask?'

Henry's look was sardonic as he said: 'I thought you of all people would know the answer to that.'

– 12 –

'I just can't think where they've got to.' Jessica stood back from the mirror, eyeing herself critically. Around her our bedroom was in its almost permanent state of chaos. Damp towels lay where they'd been dropped, shoes spilled from the wardrobe, the contents of Jessica's handbag were strewn across the bed that only an hour before had been rumpled by our love-making, and the clothes we'd been wearing that day were draped in an untidy heap over the chaise-longue. I kicked a towel out of the way before she tripped on it, then stood behind her, watching her in the mirror. Her fingers hovered around the pearls at her throat, then adjusted the thin halter strap of the dress that had cost me eighty-three guineas the week before because I had turned up over an hour late for an exhibition where two of her paintings were being shown. She was beautiful. Her fine blonde hair was swept up from her neck in a cluster of curls and held in place by a sapphire and diamond hairpin, the family heirloom my mother had given her almost a year ago on our wedding day. It matched her dress perfectly.

'Probably just delayed in traffic,' I said, still watching her.

She leaned towards the mirror and peered at herself through narrowed eyes. 'What do you think of this eyeshadow? Do you think it's too heavy? I've got a lighter one.'

I shrugged, and carried on tying my tie. 'Personally speaking, I think you look ravishing in anything.' I looked at my watch.

'Now you're trying to rush me,' she complained. 'Well, I shan't be moved until you express a preference.'

'I like the one you're wearing,' I said, and she laughed. 'Come here.' And taking me by the arm, she turned me round for inspection. 'Mmm, yes, you'll do,' she decided, flicking invisible specks from my DJ. 'Have you got the tickets?'

I patted my pocket to make sure they were there, then caught her by the hand before she sailed back to the mirror again. She turned in my arms and I brushed my lips against her bare shoulders. She smelt good.

'One kiss?' I said, my mouth very nearly on hers.

'No, you'll smudge my lip . . . Oh Alexander, now look what you've done,' she grumbled as I let her go, but her eyes were bright and I kissed her again.

'I wish someone had warned me what a trial it would be to have a husband around when one is trying to get ready for a ball,' she laughed, picking up her lipstick. 'Oh God, where can they have got to? Why aren't they here yet?'

'Maybe Lizzie's flight was delayed,' I suggested. 'Shall I ring the airport?'

'Yes, yes. Good idea.'

But British Airways confirmed that the flight from Melbourne, due in at six-thirty, had arrived on schedule.

'Well, what do we do now?' I noticed the warning blotches of colour rising on her cheeks, as they always did when things weren't going according to plan.

'We go without them,' I said. 'Henry's got their tickets. Anyway, it's a long flight, Jess, maybe she's tired.'

'You don't know Lizzie.'

'Then maybe they've gone straight there.'

'Oh, don't be ridiculous, Lizzie has to get ready first. No, they must be on their way. Let's wait another five minutes. Did you pour me a gin and tonic?'

We went downstairs to the drawing-room where we waited for five minutes, and then a further five, while

Jessica paced up and down the room, her heavy skirts swishing around her ankles. My earlier surge of affection had by now diminished, and I was watching her with increasing irritation. Sometimes her behaviour so resembled that of a spoilt brat that I was tempted to put her over my knee and spank her, hard. In fact I had done it once, but predictably, Jessica had become so aroused by my aggression that we ended up writhing madly on the kitchen floor. Ever since I wondered if she misbehaved purposely in order to get me to do it again. But, watching her face become almost ugly with ill humour, I doubted if sex was on her mind just at this moment.

Marriage to Jessica was everything I might have expected, had I only stopped to think. We never stopped competing with each other. Jessica feigned disinterest in almost everything I did, and declaring she wasn't some bovine creature content to sit at home and chew the cud of her husband's success, forced her artistic triumphs down my throat – along with her resentments, her jealousies and her feminism. I was repeatedly unfaithful, but the strange thing was that even though my feelings for her were so ambivalent, I was always sorry for what I'd done when I saw how hurt she was.

But as time went on, and despite all my efforts, our incompatibility out of bed became more and more destructive. I couldn't help imagining how my life could have been, should have been, if only . . . Elizabeth . . . In the end everything came back to her. I couldn't understand it. It was more than five years ago.

Jessica tutted, and I looked up as she began to pace the room again. I sighed. How different it would all be if I were married to Elizabeth. There would have been none of the rage that had almost crippled me at Oxford. None of the resentment that made me want to hurt any and every woman, even now, who crossed my path. Dear God, I'd been only a boy then, why hadn't she understood? I hadn't meant to be cruel, to turn my back on her the way I did.

I knew she'd loved me – what was it that had made her stay away?

Damn! I jerked myself to my feet. Why was I still suffering like this? And even if she did come back into my life, what the hell could I do? I was married now. Just think about that, Alexander Belmayne. Married – when you swore to her that you would always love her. Married to Jessica, and why? To prove that you didn't love her any more, when all the time, if you'd been man enough to face the truth . . .

'Damn! Damn, damn and damn!' Jessica slammed her glass down on the table and went to look out of the window. I swallowed my irritation and went to pour myself another drink – I knew better than to get into a fight with Jessica before we went out – but I was finding it increasingly difficult to hold my tongue. I hadn't wanted to go to the Berkeley Square Ball in the first place, but Jessica had found a possible new patron for her paintings in George Mannering, who owned a small gallery in Knightsbridge, and as he was going to the ball Jessica saw it as another opportunity to court him.

It had been my idea to invite Henry, saying he could escort Jessica's sister Lizzie, who was returning to London 'for several months, but possibly for ever, who knows?' Henry had leapt at the idea, and the stirrings of conscience I had felt on behalf of Caroline, whom he'd been seeing a little more regularly than his other girlfriends, were eased. Henry was without a doubt the current Deb's Delight, and had even been listed in *Harpers & Queen* as one of the country's most eligible bachelors – something that had made us both yell with laughter.

We now had four more dinners to go at the Inns of Court, one last batch of exams, and then, hopefully, we would be called to the bar. My determination to practise criminal law had wavered not at all, and my father no longer raised any objections – with hanging now firmly abolished, any anxieties he had about my being involved in a repeat of the Ince affair were laid to rest. So, providing I gained the results required, I would enter chambers at the Inner Temple where Lord Green was one of the benchers. It would be said that my father had put in a word for me, but I could shrug that off. Since my father had become Lord Chancellor, no matter where I went people would accuse me of being 'the protégé of the woolsack.'

The clock on the mantelshelf began to strike nine. 'Right, that's it! We've waited long enough,' Jessica announced. 'They'll just have to get themselves there.'

Obediently I put my drink down and walked across the room to fetch her cloak. Suddenly I felt sorry for her. I knew she had been looking forward to seeing her sister, and the Berkeley Square Ball was the perfect opportunity for welcoming her home in style. 'Cheer up, darling,' I said, putting her cloak around her shoulders and fastening it at her neck, 'after all, you've still got me to keep you company.'

Immediately her face softened – but I found myself turning away.

Everyone from our set was at the ball, half of them already three sheets to the wind, and the other half struggling to catch up. As Jessica and I walked into the marquee I heard her swear under her breath as her heel sank in the mud, and took her by the elbow to help her along. It proved to be a rocky journey over to the champagne, as her high heels were sucked and plucked from the ground.

'If you dare to say you told me so,' she hissed under her breath, 'I swear I'll kick you.'

Robert Lyttleton was in the middle of the crowd, wearing an extremely attractive middle-aged woman on his arm. Robert was second only to Henry in the playboy stakes these days, and, if my information was correct, he was poised for a takeover: his rise at the Foreign Office had been meteoric, and he was undoubtedly bound for foreign climes in the very near future – but word had it he needed to acquire a wife first.

He introduced his companion as Rachel, then immediately turned his attention to Jessica. Jessica rose to his flattery as she always did, and I felt a stab of jealousy as I wondered, not for the first time, if they had ever been to bed together at Oxford.

'So you're Alexander Belmayne,' Rachel was saying. 'I've met your mother once or twice. How is she?'

I tore my eyes away from Jessica as she threw back her head and laughed at something Robert had whispered in her ear – and found myself looking into Rachel's rather bewitching green eyes. They held mine in an openly seductive gaze while her lips, full and smiling, parted to reveal a set of perfect white teeth. Probably because of my sudden surge of jealousy, I was almost overwhelmed by the impulse to lean forward and kiss her, brutally, but I was saved by someone knocking against her and spilling champagne over her hands. She laughed softly, but didn't take her eyes from mine as she ran her tongue over the tips of her fingers.

'How is she?' she repeated, when I didn't answer.

'Who? Oh, my mother. She's very well, thank you.' I glanced quickly at Jessica, but she had joined a group of friends and looked as though she had all but forgotten me.

I danced with Rachel, remembering to look up occasionally to see if Henry had arrived, but there was no sign of him. So I concentrated on Rachel. I had known, since the moment I'd taken her in my arms to dance, where things were leading. Normally I was bored by women who threw themselves at me, but with Rachel's soft, mature, slightly overweight body moving seductively against mine, I felt myself responding handsomely to the promise of something new.

She held her glass out for more champagne and I went off to oblige. On my way I looked around for Jessica, but she seemed to have disappeared, and for a fleeting moment I felt wildly free – but the feeling was quickly followed by the fear that Robert Lyttleton might have taken her off somewhere. I'd never felt jealous of any other man, but for some reason it was different with Robert Lyttleton. He was so damned smooth, so damned good at everything. As far as I was concerned Jessica could screw whoever she liked just as long as it wasn't him – although these days Jessica never seemed to screw anyone except me.

I had several more dances with Rachel; I took her to supper; and after supper I danced with her again. By this time it was almost one in the morning. Still there was no sign of Jessica. And I knew from the way Rachel was looking at me that she was ready to do something about the erection that had been pushing its way between us for the best part of the evening. Taking her somewhat roughly by the arm, I started to steer her towards the nearest exit.

'Oh darling, there you are!'

I froze. Beside me I heard Rachel mutter an expletive, and several seconds must have elapsed before I was sufficiently in control of myself to turn round. Jessica's hair had slipped anchor and was cascading about her face. Her lipstick was smudged and there was a bow tie round her neck, its ends dangling between her breasts.

'I've been looking for you everywhere, Alexander. Isn't it the most perfectly wonderful ball? Aren't you glad you came now? I told you you'd love it.'

With that she blinked several times, before fixing Rachel with one of her cold stares. Then, taking me by the arm, she said to her: 'Sorry, I didn't catch your name, but I'm sure you won't mind if I take my *husband* away for a dance, will you?'

I glanced apologetically at Rachel, but she only smiled, and inclining her head vaguely in Jessica's direction, she disappeared into the crowd.

'There was no need to be so rude,' I said, attempting

to hold Jessica upright as we bumped our way through a fox-trot.

'So sorry, darling,' she hiccoughed. 'Oh, look at you, you're angry with me. Maybe you would have liked my blessing on your little liaison instead. You were about to go and fuck her, weren't you?'

'You have a vivid imagination,' I said, 'and you're drunk.'

'Ah, but not too drunk to catch my husband in the act. Or at least, very nearly in the act. Tell me, out of interest, where were you planning to do it?'

I looked at her for a moment, trying to gauge her mood before I answered. 'In our bed,' I said, finally.

'Oh, very naughty.' She threw back her head and laughed uproariously. 'You always get ratty when you're found out. I suppose she looks like Elizabeth, they usually do, don't they?' She screeched with laughter again. 'It's about time you learned that I know everything about you, Alexander, everything.'

'Then you'll know that I'm tired of this conversation, and I think it's time I took you home. Get your cloak.'

'Get it for me.'

'I said get your cloak.'

She usually knew when she'd gone too far, and more often than not it was a reference to Elizabeth that did it. She walked off, leaving me in the middle of the dance floor as she weaved her way through the crowd. I wasn't sure whether or not she was intending to come back again, but nevertheless I looked round for Rachel. She was in the midst of a group of people I'd never met, and caught my eye before I reached her. It was clear she didn't want to provoke a scene with Jessica, so she quickly gave me her address and told me to meet her there the following afternoon at five.

Jessica did come back, together with her cloak and naughty-little-girl look. She giggled most of the way home in the taxi, and kept trying to open my trousers, but I wasn't in the mood. In the end she gave up and started to suck her thumb, knowing it annoyed me.

When we pulled up in front of the house, the lights were on in the drawing-room. 'It'll be Lizzie!' Jessica cried, and I felt a wave of relief. My first thought had been that it was burglars.

We let ourselves in quietly and Jessica crept along the hall to the sitting room. When she got outside the door, she stopped and turned round. 'Do you hear anything?' she whispered.

'She might be asleep,' I said.

Jessica looked undecided for a moment, then turning the handle, she pushed the door open and burst into the room. 'Lizzie!' she cried.

I walked in behind her, and as Lizzie and Henry looked up from the sofa I felt a grin spread across my face. The timing of our interruption was immaculate – though, catching a glimpse of Henry's expression, I guessed he might want to contest that. Jessica appeared quite unperturbed, though she couldn't have missed Henry's surreptitious attempt at doing up his fly. He threw me a look, then got to his feet and stood back as Jessica and Lizzie embraced each other. 'You might have given us a bit more warning,' he muttered.

'From the look of you, old chap, it was too late for that. By the way, those yours?' I nodded towards a pair of white silk panties that were lying on the floor beside the sofa.

'Alexander, come and meet Lizzie. Isn't she simply divine?' I gave Henry one last grin, then turned to greet Lizzie. Until that moment I hadn't really been able to get a good look at her, so lifting my eyes from her discarded panties and preparing to embrace her in a brotherly way, I was caught completely unaware. She wasn't quite as small as Jessica, nor quite so beautiful, but she had something, something that defied words and oozed sex appeal in quantities I'd never have thought possible.

'Well, come along,' Jessica urged, 'give her a kiss.'

I don't know if I imagined the brief press of her body against mine when I put my arms about Lizzie, but just her touch was enough to make me pull back as if an electric current had shot through me. She laughed, and her eyes swept over my face. 'Well, Jess, he's every bit as handsome as you said he was. I'm sorry I missed the wedding now, Alexander. I might have been able to persuade you to change the bride.'

Jessica laughed, and putting her arm around her sister, ushered her out of the room and upstairs, eager to show her the bedroom that had been prepared for her.

I turned to Henry. 'Jesus Christ!' I exploded, as soon as I gauged them safely out of earshot.

Henry burst out laughing. 'Too much for you to handle, my friend. She'll have you for breakfast. And if Jessica gets to find out about it, she'll carve you up for dinner.'

I shuddered. 'Well, you sure as hell didn't waste any time,' I remarked.

He held up his hands in defence. 'Don't look at me, old chap. It was her. From the minute I picked her up at the airport she was all over me like a rash.'

Laughing, I walked over to the bar and poured us both a brandy. Upstairs I could hear Lizzie shrieking with delight as Jessica showed her around. Henry sat in an armchair looking like the cat that got the cream, as he described, in minutest detail, the incomparable body he had been taking advantage of all night and fully intended to take advantage of again. One look at Lizzie was enough to tell anyone that she would have been the one taking advantage, but I refrained from saying so.

Eventually Jessica called out that it was getting late, and Henry got up to go. At the door he clapped his arm round my shoulders. 'See you in the morning, old chap. Try not to overdo it tonight, more exams tomorrow don't forget. Oh, and tell Jess I won't be staying for dinner tomorrow night, I'm taking your ravishing sister-in-law out instead.'

'Tell you what, give her one from me next time, eh?' I grinned.

'Oh but, Alexander, surely you can do that for yourself.'

Henry and I swung round together – to find Lizzie standing on the stairs. She was wearing a transparent pink lacy affair, and was starkers underneath. My eyes were transfixed as she sauntered down the last few stairs and came to stand between us. Her lips were wet and her nipples stood out firmly against the gossamer-thin fabric.

'Good night, Henry,' she purred, sliding her arms around his neck. And opening her mouth I saw their tongues meet. Her eyes never wavered from mine.

I was surprised, a couple of weeks later, when I arrived home one afternoon to find Caroline Truman, Henry's ex, waiting outside the house for me. With an admirable effort at holding back the tears, she asked me what she had done wrong. Why didn't Henry call her any more? Couldn't I talk to him, please, get him to say he'd meet her, if only for an hour? Though I'd always liked Caroline, I was annoyed that she had managed to corner me. Even if I was partly responsible for the split between her and Henry, it wasn't as though I'd forced him into Lizzie's arms. Rejected women were all the same, crying and sniffling, and all but begging a man to go back to them, even when it was quite clear he didn't want to. And what the hell could I do about it? I suggested a good shopping session and a few more cocktail parties, and if she still felt lonely after that, well there was always me. She walked off in disgust.

And as the invitations continued to stream through the letter-box – opening nights, concerts, exhibitions – I like Henry, soon forgot about her. Almost every night there were parties or clubs to be attended, places to be seen at, bottles of champagne to be drunk and new games to be played. Our own wild parties became the talk of the town as windows and doors were thrown open to the world, and the dignified quiet of Belgrave Square was rocked to its foundations. Somehow, during this orgy of frivolity, Henry and I managed to accomplish the dining of four more dinners, and having mysteriously achieved our finals, were called to the Bar.

I couldn't help noticing during this time that it wasn't only Caroline's company Henry was denying himself; every female who threw herself his way – and plenty did – was rejected, so that he could concentrate his inimitable charms on Lizzie. And the more Henry saw of Lizzie, the more I saw of Rachel. I knew that all too often when I made love to Rachel I was fantasizing about Lizzie, but it was the safest way of trying to work my sister-in-law through my system. I had told Jessica time after time to speak to Lizzie about walking round the house naked, but Jessica was too busy with her own life to worry much about what Lizzie's magnificent breasts were doing to mine. As far as Rachel was concerned, I eased my conscience by assuring myself that, attractive though she was, she was still rather lucky to have someone of my age interested in her. Besides, she was my companion in another kind of fun that I had been growing rather attached to of late – gambling.

Jessica I saw little of. Since Lizzie's arrival she had redoubled her efforts on behalf of the Women's Movement, showing off to her sister and trying her damndest to enlist her in their war against men. Lizzie was as bored by it all as I was, though she managed to hide it a little better. But dedicated as Jessica was to her cause, she wasn't one to let it get in the way of her own personal glory. When she wasn't holding meetings in the parlour at Belgrave Square, which she had commandeered for the use of the lesbian brigade, she was either in her studio at the top of the house or at George Mannering's gallery in Knightsbridge.

And things were coming along 'frightfully well' with her art, she assured me whenever I remembered to ask. George thought it showed 'unusual potential,' and was sure she would be ready for an exhibition of her own within the year. I couldn't stop my eyes from flicking to the paintings that adorned the walls in Belgrave Square when she told me that, and wondered what my mother would say. There had been an uneasy truce between my mother and Jessica ever since my mother had descended upon the house, having heard that Jessica was hanging her paintings alongside the masterpieces my mother, and my grandmother before her, had worked so hard to acquire. Secretly I thought my mother very restrained when she merely remarked that she felt Jessica's *chefs d'oeuvre* looked somewhat incongruous beside the buhl, the ormolu and the passementerie. Jessica sulked for three days after my mother's visit, and claimed I'd given her no support whatever in what was a matter of fundamental importance to her. Rather flummoxed, I objected that I was being thoroughly supportive, in that I was prepared to suffer the paintings without complaint. Not a wise choice of words, and the price I paid was a new dinner service.

But there was no getting away from it, Jessica's paintings were, to put it mildly, extreme. The only thing I had ever recognised in any one of them – and they were coming off the easel by the dozen – was a rabbit, which had been tucked away – 'rather cleverly,' I remarked – in the corner of a painting she called 'The Warren.' Of course the title had given it away, but I had been rather pleased with myself all the same – until Jessica's wrath descended upon me with all the subtlety of the erupting volcano the painting was supposed to depict . . . . I never did manage to find out the reason for the rabbit. Nor did I venture to guess her subjects again after that, but meekly accepted my role as one of the uninitiated and waited until she was ready to explain precisely the feeling she had tried to capture in the painting, and then assured her that indeed she was getting it across. She never believed me, of course, but it was a little charade that satisfied us both.

In fact, it was through her art that I first began to notice a change in Jessica. We'd been talking on and off for some time about starting a family. Jessica's first reaction, when she realised I was serious, was one of horror.

'*You* want a baby! Don't make me laugh, Alexander. What would your friends say? I mean, it's hardly the macho image you try so hard to cultivate, is it? With your ridiculous male pride, I'm astonished you even have the guts to say it.'

'Jess, I said it because you're my wife. If I can't tell you, then who the hell can I tell? And as for the macho image, *you*, astonish *me*! I'd have thought you'd be more likely to accuse me of vanity in wanting to reproduce myself.'

She laughed. 'Yes, there is that, too. Anyway, it's out of the question. I'm sorry if you're feeling broody, darling, but I'm not.'

I wasn't going to give up that easily, and she knew it. Nevertheless I was surprised when she listened, without ridicule, to my case. Afterwards I listened to her explanations of why it was a bad idea. They started with the fact that she was too young and ended with the totally predictable statement that she was *not* my brood mare.

But eventually, and without a detailed feminist analysis of what this might do to her as a person – which I had expected and indeed prepared myself for – she agreed to stop taking the pill. I should have been warned then, for Jessica never gave in easily on anything, particularly where the 'exploitation of her womanhood' was concerned. But my reaction was so positive that it surprised even me; I hadn't realised until then how very much I really did want a child. I was even slightly embarrassed by it. Jessica couldn't resist teasing me, but it was an affectionate teasing, and for a while we were closer than we had been for a long time.

Even Lizzie got caught up in the spirit of it all, and was

already treating her sister as though she were pregnant. Jessica lapped up the attention, and our love-making took on a tenderness that had been alien to us until then. Oddly enough, though, contented as I felt at the way things were going, I was still finding it impossible to stay faithful. If I didn't see Rachel, or someone else, for three or four days, then I became jumpy and irritable. I never stopped to question why, I guess I just assumed that this was a natural state of affairs for someone like me. The only thing that mattered was that Jessica should not find out, so I took her on trips to Paris, bombarded her with flowers and did everything I could to make her happy. That lasted for about three months, and then things began to change.

Up to this time, Jessica's paintings had always been bright and over-filled with colour; garish even, some might say – not me, of course. But now a kind of morbidity was creeping into them. There were only two or three of them at first, that had found their way on to the walls of our bedroom. As this was an essentially feminine room, full of chintz and lace, the paintings created an almost ghoulish contrast, and their greys and blacks, smudged over with violent streaks of reddish brown, made me uncomfortable. But when I ventured to suggest to Jessica that perhaps they might be a little more at home in the garden shed, instead of flying at me in a rage she merely looked at me with what I can only describe as sightless eyes, and smiled into the distance.

I mentioned it to Lizzie one evening, but she only shrugged. 'Oh, you know what artists are,' she said, 'they're all a little insane, couldn't do it if they weren't. And Jess is a genius, you know.' I thought that was taking sisterly devotion a little too far, and decided to drop the subject.

'Where's Henry tonight?' I asked. We were having dinner, just the two of us; Jessica had gone off to an exhibition in Fulham with George Mannering. That was another thing.

Before she always used to invite me to go with her to art exhibitions, but now, despite the fact we were getting along so well, she was almost secretive about where she was going.

'Henry? Henry's sulking because I told him we were seeing far too much of each other.'

'I thought you were becoming rather attached to him,' I said.

She shrugged. 'Maybe.'

Sensing she didn't want to talk about it, I sat back to finish my wine. I noticed that another of Jessica's morbid paintings had appeared on the dining-room wall, this one directly opposite the chair I always occupied. I stared at it for some time, not liking it any more than I had any of the others. Then I realised that she must have hung it there on purpose, and for no accountable reason I felt the hair prickle at the back of my neck.

'Something the matter?' Lizzie asked. Her voice startled me, and it must have showed. 'You seem very edgy tonight,' she said.

I laughed. 'Deep in thought. Devilling for a particularly unpleasant murder trial at the moment, it's probably getting to me a bit.'

Mrs Dixon had stayed on that night to fix the meal, so when we had finished I helped her clear the table before going to find Lizzie in the drawing-room. She was sitting on the floor, reading a magazine, and barely looked up as I walked in.

I sat down on the sofa and stretched my legs out in front of me. It was a warm night and the windows were open. There were no sounds coming from outside and I lay back to enjoy the peace, for once free of the restlessness that normally plagued me. I watched Lizzie's hair as it fluttered in the breeze, and her small hands as she flicked over the pages of the magazine. My mind wandered back to the hour or so I had spent with Rachel that afternoon, when I knew that once again, in my mind, I had been making love to Lizzie. But I would make it up to Rachel when I saw her later at the Clermont. . . . My eyes snapped shut, and I was immediately aware of feeling restive again: I'd lost a lot of money last time I was there, more than my quarterly allowance, and I was only going again tonight in an attempt to win it back. I glanced over at the clock. I'd have to be leaving in half an hour.

'It's so hot in here, don't you think?' Lizzie stretched, and I noticed that the top two buttons of her blouse were undone. She leaned forward and at the same time threw her hair back over her shoulder. Her right breast was almost completely exposed. Then tossing her magazine to one side, she uncurled her legs and lay down on the floor. Her short skirt wriggled up around her hips and I caught a glimpse of white panties as she lifted one knee.

Slowly her eyes came round to meet mine, and I watched as she dampened her lips with her tongue. She was smiling and I didn't dare to move, the suddenness of sexual tension was shooting through the air like currents of electricity. She's your wife's sister, I kept telling myself. Anyone, you can have anyone, but leave her alone. My eyes were still on hers. She's Henry's, you can't do it, it's not worth losing a friend for. I clenched my teeth, and my fingers were biting into the arms of the sofa, but I was all too aware of the ache in my groin that was making a mockery of my resistance.

'I do love these warm nights, don't you, Alexander?' she purred, running her hands down over her breasts and letting them fall to the floor on either side of her. 'They always make me feel, mmm, so . . . good.'

'Lizzie, do you think Jessica's having an affair with George Mannering?' I blurted out. Suddenly the air was clear. Lizzie's knee went back to the floor and she sat up.

Her eyes flashed at me for a second before she spoke. 'Are you serious?' she said. 'George Mannering?'

Of course I wasn't serious. Jessica's devotion to me these days was more than evident, and George was a pretty poor specimen of manhood by anyone's standards, let alone Jessica's. I shrugged, 'Well, haven't you noticed how strangely she's been behaving lately?'

'You said that earlier,' she very nearly snapped. 'Strange? In what way?'

'Her God-awful paintings for one thing.'

That seemed to annoy her. Apparently she was prepared to bed her sister's husband, but was not prepared to have the said husband speak detrimentally of her sister's art. I watched her face, sensing the inward struggle. The question she was asking herself, I knew, was, how desperately did she want me in the sack? If we argued over Jessica she'd never regain the earlier mood. In the end she shrugged, and I was aware of Jessica's art sliding neatly into second place as she said: 'She seems perfectly normal to me.'

I couldn't ignore the brief feeling of victory, but had myself fully under control by now. 'Henry said he saw her in Harley Street yesterday.'

'Is there something strange about Harley Street?'

'Of course not. It's only strange that Jessica was there when she told me she was going to Bristol for some meeting or other.'

Lizzie yawned loudly, making it clear she was becoming bored by the subject of her sister. 'All I can say is, a girl's got to have some secrets, even from her husband.' She stopped as if something had suddenly occurred to her, then turned to look at me. 'You're not jealous, are you?'

'Jealous! What of?'

'I don't know. Her art?'

I looked through to the dining-room, at the painting that was hanging there. 'Not jealous, no,' I said.

She got to her feet and ambled over to look in the mirror. The silence hung heavily in the air, and I knew she hadn't given up on me yet. 'I think I'll go and take a shower,' she said, looking at my reflection. 'Care to join me?'

I laughed. 'Thanks, but I have to go out.'

She gave a long and enigmatic smile before she turned round. 'Rachel waiting, is she?'

'Rachel?' I said, surprising myself at the innocence in my voice.

'Rachel Armstrong. The woman you go to see most afternoons, in Lennox Gardens.'

I closed my eyes, feeling suddenly very tired. When I opened them again she was still watching me. 'How do you know about Rachel?'

She tapped the side of her nose. 'Now that would be telling, wouldn't it?' she said.

'Does Jessica know? Is that what all this is about?' I waved my hand towards the painting.

'Jessica? Oh no, I don't think Jessica knows. And I won't tell her if you won't.'

My breath escaped in a long drawn-out sigh. 'Why do I get the feeling that there are going to be conditions attached to that?'

She gave a low, throaty laugh. 'Because there are. Shall we begin by taking that shower?'

I closed my eyes and tried to pray that Mrs Dixon had already gone home. I tried to pray that Jessica wouldn't walk through the door, and last of all I tried to pray for resistance. But all I could hear was the sound of Lizzie taking off her clothes, until there was no sound any more.

When I opened my eyes she was standing naked in front of me, holding out her hand.

What could I do? I had no choice.

– 13 –

It was past midnight when I walked upstairs to the gaming room of the Clermont. The cashier greeted me in a friendly manner and I wondered what he would say if I pushed over the bank statement that had fallen through my door that morning.

A low murmur erupted from the roulette table as I reached it, and I saw three towers of black chips being added to Rachel's substantial collection. Her slanting eyes flickered in my direction, but she gave no other sign of having registered my presence. I guessed she was angry with me, and in turn I was angry with her. OK, I was late, but her reaction to it stifled me. Deciding I had no desire to witness her further success, I went to watch Robert Lyttleton trying his hand at chemmy, before taking my place at a blackjack table.

From the start I played recklessly, doubling and splitting wherever I could, and I raised the table to a thousand in the first hour. The inspector recorded my drop as I won almost every hand, and I had nearly twenty thousand pounds worth of chips at my elbow by the time Rachel joined the crowd that had grouped around me.

She ran her hands over my shoulders and stooped to whisper something in my ear, but I wasn't listening. This time I had pushed ten thousand pounds to the centre of the table and the dealer had just peeled a second three from the shoe. Her eyes moved across the short distance between us.

'Split,' I murmured, and placed my cards side by side to make two hands. The entire twenty thousand was at stake.

The six of spades landed beside the three of diamonds. 'Nine.' The dealer's voice was the only sound in the room. 'Seven,' she said, as the four of hearts joined the three of hearts on my second hand.

With the next card my first hand totalled sixteen. The king of diamonds slipped and spun as it came to rest on my second hand. 'Seventeen.'

I didn't have to look at the old woman who was playing beside me to know that she was holding her breath. Surely I would stop now, no one in their right mind would carry on. My heart was thudding so hard against my ribs, I thought I could hear it through the hush that had engulfed us. I knew everyone was watching me, fascinated and horrified to see whether I would go on.

'What!' It was Robert Lyttleton's voice that hissed through his teeth as I nodded. Several people shuffled and strained to come closer.

I waited as the next card was turned over. The voice of the dealer was matter-of-fact. 'Twenty-one,' she pronounced. The woman beside me totalled nineteen. And then I turned to the dealer.

'Stand-off.' And the dealer calmly pushed ten thousand pounds in my direction, followed by another ten.

I sensed that the old lady wanted to leave, that the presence of the crowd had unnerved her. But my crazy bravado had captured the entire casino and she too stayed to watch.

'Ten.' I felt Rachel's thighs pressing against my arm.

'Double,' I said immediately. Once again my stake was twenty thousand. The dealer wasted no time in revealing the next card.

'Blackjack,' she pronounced the word quietly, as if she

herself couldn't believe it. The tension must have filtered through to her because her hand trembled as she turned over her final card. The hum that threaded through the crowd was one of incredulity and excitement.

I had won fifty thousand pounds.

I stared up at the faces that bobbed over me. Everyone was smiling, reaching out hands to congratulate me. Fifty thousand pounds wasn't a large amount to most of them; what had impressed them was my nerve – the nerve that had not stuck at seventeen, and the devil's own luck that had delivered blackjack on a stand-off.

'Champagne,' Robert said, clapping me on the back. 'Your treat.'

I felt Rachel's hand slide into my trouser pocket and at the same time was aware of someone tugging on my arm. Removing Rachel's hand, I turned stiffly to see who was trying to attract my attention. It was the woman who had been playing beside me all evening.

My lofty expression dissolved as she smiled. She reminded me of my grandmother. She too had that paradoxical air of reckless safety about her, leaving you in no doubt that an hour in her company would be worth three with most other people. 'Won't you join us downstairs?' I offered.

She shook her head. 'Thank you, but no. Time I was in my bed.' She had a deep, commanding voice that was surprising, coming from such a frail body. 'I just wanted to offer my congratulations. There aren't many who would have taken a card again on seventeen.' She was looking searchingly into my eyes, as if seeking something that only she might be able to find. Then her face broke into a smile again. 'You know, if the old adage is true – lucky at cards, unlucky in love – then I fear for your heart, young man.' And laughing at her little joke, she bade us all good-night.

Robert grinned. 'And yet another conquest with which

to swell the Belmayne harem,' he quipped. 'Now, are we going downstairs or aren't we?'

'Why don't you be a darling and go find us a table?' Rachel jumped in before I could answer.

Robert saluted her. 'At your service, ma'am. What'll it be?'

'The best they have, of course,' Rachel answered, and chucking him under the chin, she turned him round and gave him a gentle push in the direction of the stairs.

The second she turned back I knew we would not be joining Robert. Her expression was one of naked desire – and it was only then that I realised I had an erection. How long I had had it I didn't know, but I knew that winning had acted like an aphrodisiac on us both. We needed to fuck, and couldn't wait.

Outside in the car my fly was open before I could get the engine started. I dropped the keys, and as I stooped to retrieve them I felt her fingers circle my penis. I cried out as the juice began to surge from my body, and tearing her hand away I pushed her back in her seat. 'Wait!' I snapped, and starting the car I drove out of the square, only narrowly missing a police car.

When we reached Lennox Gardens I reversed up against the railings and turned the engine off. Rachel started to get out, but I pulled the door shut again. The power I felt swelled in my chest, almost choking me. 'You want to fuck,' I said, 'then you do it my way.'

Her mouth trembled, and leaning over I crushed it with my own. 'Get into the back seat.' She started to protest, but I ripped open the front of her dress and scooped her breasts free. 'Do you want it?'

'Yes. Oh God, yes,' she groaned, her head rolling back against the seat.

'Then get in the back.'

For a moment she looked at me, then as her eyes dropped

to the erection she had lifted free of my trousers, she turned to do as I told her. I waited until I heard the back door close, then, almost exploding with the need to humiliate her, I got out of the car. When I made no move to join her in the back seat she pushed open the door, watching my face as I gave her my brief instructions.

Obediently she turned away and lifted her legs on to the seat. And forcing her on to her hands and knees, I ripped her underwear and penetrated her from behind.

That night was the first time I had truly fucked Rachel. I couldn't say we made love, because there was nothing tender about the act that took place in the back of the car; but now, having possessed Lizzie, I could concentrate on Rachel and all that I wanted to do to her. I was drunk with the power of my success. From now on this was how it would be with me and Rachel; I would make her a slave to my lust, just as I was a slave to Lizzie's.

When I finally returned home the sun was threatening to break the horizon. I looked up at the bleached façade of the house in Belgrave Square and thought of my wife lying in bed, obediently waiting for me to come home. And my sister-in-law in the next room, who only hours before had panted beneath me, begging for more as I thrust into her. And then I thought of the fifty thousand pounds I carried in my pocket.

My blood began to move faster, charging me with the same surge of sexual arousal I had felt when I'd won at the Clermont. I was ready for more. I wanted to win again. I'd go to Lizzie. I'd show her who called the shots around here. And I'd do it while Jessica was under the same roof.

I crept up the stairs, and passed the door to Jessica's and my bedroom without even stopping to look in. At the end of the landing I stopped at Lizzie's door and pushed it open.

In the dim light that filtered through the curtains I could see that another head lay on the pillow beside hers. The sheets were in a tangle around the two bodies and for a moment I felt an insane jealousy, wanting to kill him, whoever he was. Then realising that it must be Henry, I closed the door.

My own bed was empty.

Almost bursting with rage, I went downstairs to see if Jessica had waited up for me, but there wasn't even a note. I made myself some coffee and slumped into an armchair to wait. If Jessica had walked in at that moment I might have tried to kill her: everyone did as I said, everyone wanted me and I controlled everyone – with the exception of my own wife.

I must have dozed, because I noticed by the clock that it was ten minutes past seven when I heard a noise at the bottom of the stairs. Heaving myself up from the chair, I swore as my half-drunk cup of coffee tumbled to the ground, spreading a dark stain across the carpet. I stared down at it, wondering what to do. Then I heard the front door close and footsteps outside.

Quickly I ran to the front door, wanting to tell Henry about my win. But as I looked out into the grey London dawn it wasn't Henry I saw, getting into his BMW, but Robert Lyttleton starting up the engine of the E-type Jaguar he'd brought round to show off the week before.

As he drove away, I stood trying to sort out the thoughts that were spreading through my head.

I didn't hear anything, it was more an awareness of the presence of someone else that made me turn and look back through the open door.

Lizzie stood halfway down the stairs. Her hair was tousled, her mouth a deep, savagely-kissed red. Her eyes were watching me, taunting me into speech, but I wasn't looking at her. I was looking at the woman standing beside her, one arm draped over the banister, her bare foot beating a tattoo on the floor. Their smiles reached me in waves of triumph, leaving me in no doubt as to what it was that had been happening in the room at the end of the landing.

'Hello, darling,' Jessica murmured. And as I moved towards the bottom of the stairs, she threw back her head and let out a screech of laughter.

I have no clear recollection of what happened after that. All I knew was a blur of colours, crashing around me, blinding my sight, blinding my reason. Sounds of manic laughter, and then screams, deafening me, piercing my brain. And blood. Blood on my hands, blood on the walls. And all around me pain and chaos and destruction.

I looked around at the paintings on the wall. I'd never noticed them before. They were very like the paintings that adorned the walls of Belmayne House in Suffolk. I shifted my eyes restlessly from one to another, until yet again I was confronted by Monet's 'Roche-Blond at Sunset'. Normally I enjoyed looking at Impressionist paintings, but now, different though they were from Jessica's doom-laden canvases, they somehow reminded me of her, and heightened my guilt.

I stirred in my chair and turned back to the newspaper. A report on page two outlined the background of the forthcoming Haley Weinberg fraud case, and again I felt guilt. Jeremy Corbyn had been handed the brief two months ago, and I'd been devilling for him. I should ring chambers and at least let him know where I was. But I didn't.

I'd been with Rachel for four days – four days during which I had alternately slaked my fury on her body and gambled like a lunatic at the Clermont, where I was now in debt to the tune of eighty-five thousand pounds. I blamed Jessica. Thinking about her, I could feel my fingers digging into the palms of my hands, the unholy images crowding into my mind as I remembered the early hours of that morning. If only she hadn't laughed.

The door opened and Rachel came in. She was wearing

the sable coat she had purchased with her roulette winnings the week before, and just the sight of it made me want to lash out at her.

'You still here?' she said, dropping her bag on to a chair.

'As you can see.'

She went to hang up her coat. Coming back into the room, she said, 'That's a Morant,' and nodded towards the table that was propping up my feet. I removed them. 'And now you can do the same with those cartons,' she said, indicating the remains of the Chinese take-away I had had sent round earlier. I scooped them up and stuffed them into the waste-paper basket next to my chair. Rachel sighed and went to get herself a drink.

'Scotch for me,' I said, and went back to the newspaper.

'Get it yourself.'

'For Christ's sake, I'm only asking you to get me a drink.'

She spun round to face me. 'Alexander, I'm getting a little tired of you lately. Isn't it about time – '

'Forget it! Just forget it!' I yelled. 'I'll get my own.'

We smouldered through the silence that followed; turning pages, and ice clinking against glasses, made the only sound.

It was Rachel who spoke first. 'You didn't tell me you destroyed her paintings.'

I shot a glance at her, but she was still flicking through the magazine. When she realised I was going to say nothing, she looked up. 'Why did you do it?'

'Why did I do it? You can sit there and ask me why I did it?'

'She went to bed with another man. She was unfaithful. Is the whole of your life built on double standards, Alexander?'

'We were supposed to be trying for a baby, for God's sake! What if I hadn't come in when I did and then found out in two months' time she was pregnant? The child might not have been mine – and I wouldn't even have known! And let's not forget, she wasn't the only one in the bed with Robert Lyttleton that night. Her sister was there too, her own fucking sister! And in *my* house! She's – '

'Oh shut up, Alexander. I'm tired of your tantrums. And I still say no matter what happened you shouldn't have destroyed her paintings.'

'Have you seen them? They gave me the spooks. I couldn't stand them any longer. Anyway, she was asking for it.'

'It's you who are asking for it, Alexander. You think you can do whatever takes your fancy, don't you, and be damned to how anyone else feels about it. Well, it's time you woke up to the fact that the world wasn't created for the sole purpose of satisfying the bottomless appetite of Alexander Belmayne's ego. Your life is a mess, and you've only yourself to blame. Look at you! What you've done to yourself God only knows, but what you've done to your wife is unforgivable. And who are you, anyway, to sit in judgement on her art? Just who the hell do you think you are?'

I opened my mouth to speak, but she stopped me. 'You're nobody, that's who you are. You're not fit to sit in the same room as decent people. You think those good looks of yours give you the right to behave just as you please. You don't care who you hurt or what you might be doing to those who love you, like your wife. Do you know why she did what she did? Because she knew you were coming round here. She knew that all the time you were telling her you loved her, you were lying to her, cheating on her – and what she's done is to show you that two people can play at that game, and you don't like it. They're none of my business the dangerous games the two of you play with each other, but I'm telling you, Alexander, your pretty face means nothing. It's what's underneath that's important, and you've got nothing underneath. You're shallow and empty, and a waste of space.'

She got up to refill her glass. Her voice was calmer as she turned round, but her eyes were still cool and hard. 'I want you to leave, Alexander. Now. Go back to your wife, if she'll have you. Go anywhere. I don't want you here any more.'

I leapt up from my chair then, and bunching my fist, I thrust it between her legs. 'How about here, Rachel? Don't you want me here any more either?'

She glared at me and I laughed. 'You can't live without it, Rachel. You'll be begging me for it within a week. Well, here's one last one to be going on with.' I started to fumble with my fly.

'You touch me, and so help me, Alexander, I'll kill you.'

I laughed again. 'You want me to rape you, is that it? You want me to rough you up again. What'll it be this time, Rachel? Shall I tie you up? Or shall I just beat you?' My hand was still between her legs and she made no move to back away.

Suddenly she slumped forward, pushing her glass on to the table. 'Alexander, stop it,' she pleaded. 'Just stop. This anger, this violence, it's destroying you. Look at yourself – what's happening to you?'

Slowly she removed my hand. She held it between her own two hands, and uncurled my fingers, looking down at them as she did so. 'Oh, Alexander,' she sighed, 'I'm so sorry for you, though God knows why. Her paintings, Alexander, how could you have done it?'

I turned away, feeling small and loathsome in the suffocating well of my guilt. 'How did you find out?' I asked.

'Robert told me.'

I felt myself beginning to tense. 'Robert Lyttleton? That must mean Jessica's seen him again.'

'No. It means Henry is looking for you.'

'Does Robert know I'm here?'

She nodded. 'He does now. I saw him this afternoon.'

'In his bed?'

She smiled. 'No, Alexander, not in his bed. Incest never did hold any appeal for me.'

My head snapped up. 'Incest?'

'Robert's my son. Don't tell me you didn't know.'

I wrenched my hand away from hers. Her face was soft and smiling, but all I could see were the lines that fanned at the corners of her eyes, the broken smoothness of her neck – and for a brief moment my eyes glazed and I thought I was looking into the face of my own mother. My stomach churned. Rachel was Robert Lyttleton's mother. And while I fucked his mother, he fucked my wife. He fucked my wife's sister. And my wife and her sister . . .

'Jesus Christ,' I choked. 'Jesus Christ.'

She turned away and went to pick up her drink. I watched her, hating her, and as she looked back at me my hatred turned to disgust, all-consuming disgust that sucked at my insides, making me want to rip out my guts, tear at my skin, anything to exorcise myself of this obscenity. For it was I who had dragged them all into this sordid gutter. Jessica, Rachel, Lizzie, and countless others I had abused along the way – they had all been nothing more than pawns in my own sick game of mysoginistic power. All I'd ever wanted to do was hurt them, humiliate them, and then walk away, leaving my contempt entrenched in their souls.

My head dropped as my shoulders began to heave. Dear God in heaven, when would it all end? How much longer could I go on living with this pain? Where was she? Dear God, where was she?

– Elizabeth –

– 14 –

Everyone was laughing. Bright lights flashed, children screamed; 'Sugar, Sugar' blared out of the speakers, and somewhere in the distance a siren brought the dodgems to a standstill. People wandered about with their goldfish and coloured balloons, hugging themselves into scarves and hats to keep out the bitter wind that cut across the common. I tucked the scrap of newspaper back in my pocket and waited while a little boy rummaged in my basket for a ticket. His cheeks flushed with excitement as he pulled one out and tore it open. No prize. The child's face fell and his father, who had earlier returned my smile, now gave me a look I knew only too well.

I turned away, withdrawing into myself, needing to escape, if only for a moment, this prison of festivity.

My uncle was watching me as he handed out darts, shouting to the crowds to come and try their skill. He didn't trust me, I knew that, but he had taken me back because they had been short-handed that summer, and I'd had nowhere else to go. That was five years ago now. I leaned against the side of my stall and closed my eyes. Oh, when would it stop hurting?

Someone called my name. It was Edwina, the old hag whose husband ran the big wheel. I could never look at the big wheel without thinking about my parents. It had been theirs, before the storms blew it over, killing them both. If things had been different, and they'd lived, then maybe I'd never have left in the first place.

'You're right to be getting on with things, girl,' my uncle had said the day I told him I was going to leave the fair.

Violet May, the fortune teller, had been looking after me until then, but I was a constant reminder to my uncle that he was shirking his duty by not taking me in himself. 'You've got your education, your mother saw to that, so off you go.' As he opened the door of the London train for me, I wanted to tell him I'd changed my mind, but by the time I'd turned round he was already walking away.

I'd been fourteen then but sometimes it seemed like yesterday . . . .

Edwina yelled at me again, indicating the little queue of children waiting to buy tickets from me. I gritted my teeth and looked away from her. Edwina had always hated my mother, and after she'd died, had turned her resentment on me. And as soon as I'd walked back into the fair, only hours after I'd watched Alexander walk out of my life, Edwina had been there screaming at me, telling me she knew what I'd done, she'd read the newspapers – I was a trollop, and they didn't want my sort here. My uncle, along with the others, had stood by and watched. In the end I'd picked up my bag and started to walk away, but Violet May came after me. She would hear none of my going to Janice; the fair was my home, she said, it was where I belonged, never mind Edwina. And I'd stayed because I couldn't face Janice trying to find me another man, another job, or anything that might end the way things had ended at Foxton's . . . .

'I've won! Miss! Miss! I've won!'

I looked down into a pale excited little face and smiled as the girl beamed up at me . . . . That was all a long time ago now. Everything was a long time ago now.

I took one of the cheap biros down from the shelf, and checking that no one was watching, I slipped it into the little girl's pocket. Then I handed her a teddy. I put my finger over my lips to show her that the two prizes were our secret.

'Edward's here, Mummy!'

I looked up as Charlotte ran over to the stall. She gave the girl with the teddy a shy smile, and watched her walk away. 'Edward's in the caravan,' she said, turning back to me and trying to sweep the thick black curls from her eyes.

'Is he?' I said, smiling as I lifted her up over the counter. 'And don't tell me – he bought you a candy floss.'

Her grey eyes rounded with amazement. 'It's all over your face,' I laughed, and as she hugged me I felt my heart swell.

'Ouch, you're hurting me,' she complained, struggling to get away, and putting her down again, I watched her skip off through the fair. 'Come on,' she called, peeping back round the lucky dip, 'he's waiting.'

My hand tightened around the scrap of newspaper in my pocket, and taking it out, I read it one last time. A year. He'd been married for a whole year and I hadn't even known.

There was no point in fooling myself any longer. I'd waited, I'd never stopped loving him, but now, just like when my parents had died, I knew that it was time for me to move on.

It was Violet May who had introduced me to Edward Walters, the tycoon art dealer. They'd first met more than twenty years before, when Edward's wife started to visit the fair to have her fortune told. And after Edward's wife died, Violet May had carried on visiting him.

That was until Charlotte was born. Since then it was Edward who came to visit us, travelling the country as often as his business would allow – all because he was besotted with a baby girl. I knew he was lonely, it was what had drawn us together, even though he had a brother and sister who lived with him at their country estate in Kent. He tried to persuade me to take Charlotte down there, but I wouldn't go. His elegant city suits and expensive tweeds, his easy composure and the distinction of his greying hair and wise blue eyes, all reminded me that I had already proved I didn't belong to his world.

But I was always pleased when he came to the fair – though no one could be quite as pleased as Charlotte. It was odd, watching this distinguished-looking man take such time and trouble with my daughter. He radiated warmth and kindness. It was rare that I spoke about Alexander, but Edward sensed that I still loved him, and even though he knew it might mean that he would have to say good-bye to Charlotte and me, he had offered to find him for me. I suppose it was because I was afraid that I wouldn't let him. Alexander had been little more than a boy when we'd been in love; by now he would have changed, probably forgotten all about me. No, I didn't want to find him, I told Edward, I just wanted to stop loving him.

As time passed and my confidence started to come back, I grew more and more attached to Edward. I looked forward to seeing his tall figure stride through the crowds, to hearing his jocular voice when he crept up behind me and asked if he could buy a ticket. I laughed when he was sad, because he was only sad when he remembered his age. He was old, he kept telling me, too old for me. What could I possibly want with someone who was fifty, past his prime, and ready to fall apart at the seams?

'Then I'll just have to stitch you back together, won't I?' I said. That was after the first time we made love.

Though I had been determined not to make comparisons, it was impossible not to. But Edward was here, and Edward loved me. Alexander was no more than a dream now. So why did I keep on believing that if only I waited just a little bit longer, he would come?

'But he won't, child,' Violet May said, on the night Edward asked me to marry him. I'd told him no, as gently as I could, but the hurt I saw in his eyes almost tore me apart. He held me in his arms, and I despised myself for what I was doing to him, but he only wiped away my tears and told me he understood. In the end, not knowing what else to do, I had run to

Violet May and asked her to look into the crystal ball for me.

I sat before her in the warm dimness of her caravan and searched her fleshy face, trying to get her to meet my eyes as she spoke, but she wouldn't, and I knew she was lying.

'You've got to tell me,' I whispered. 'Please, I want to know.'

'I told you child, he won't come.'

'Look, I know you want me to marry Edward, but if there is any chance, any chance at all . . . Please, Violet May, tell me the truth.'

She peered into her crystal ball again, then with a gesture of impatience, pushed it to one side. 'Give me your hand,' she wheezed.

She studied it for a long time, until finally she looked up and I saw that her eyes were swimming with tears. She shook her head, slowly.

'Violet May!' I cried. 'Tell me!'

Then she smiled, and the icy hand that had been pushing my heart into my throat seemed to draw back. 'Did you see him, Violet May? In the future, was he there?'

She nodded. 'Yes child, he was there.'

'Does that mean . . . ?' I swallowed. 'Does that mean I will see him again?' I stammered.

'Yes, you will see him again.'

'When? Violet May, tell me when? Is it soon?'

She shook her head. 'It is a mysterious thing, this love you share with him. It has a power beyond my understanding, but the seeds of fate have already been sown. There are still long roads to be travelled before you see him again. When you do, Elizabeth . . . Don't do it, child. It will only bring pain. There is death and hatred, such hatred. And foreign lands . . .' But I wasn't listening. All that mattered was that one day, it didn't matter when, we would be together again . . . .

Leaning against the side of my stall remembering the

confidence I'd felt then, how happy I'd been as I left Violet May's caravan, I could hardly hold back the tears. Like a fool I had waited, believing in my heart that he had meant it when he'd said he would always love me. But he was married now, and I was nothing more than a memory.

'We got tired of waiting.'

I jumped – and Edward laughed as he held his hand out for mine. Charlotte was bouncing up and down beside him, wearing his deerstalker and pleading with him to play her new game. As I looked at them I knew in my heart it was time now to get on with my life. I put my basket down and let myself out of the stall.

Edward's eyes were searching my face, and as the wind swept up my hair he brushed it back. 'Why do I get the feeling you want to tell me something?' he said.

'Because I do,' I whispered. 'I'd like us to get married, Edward, if you still want me, that is.' And seeing the way his mouth trembled, I wondered how I could have been so blind as not to have realised a long time ago how very much I loved him.

– 15 –

Slipping the ring on to my third finger I turned my hand to the chandelier and nearly gasped as tiny splinters of light shot between my diamond and the crystal above me. Edward was standing beside me, watching my face, waiting for me to speak. I put my arms around him and hugged him. 'Darling, it's beautiful,' I said. I looked at the diamond again, then laughing, I threw out my hands. 'I just don't know what to say.'

'Then don't say anything,' he said. 'Just as long as I know you like it, that's all that matters.'

Like it? I could hardly believe what was happening to

me. After all, less than two years ago I had been just the girl from the fair. I'd always read about people who were wealthy then, though I'd seen them often enough, at the fair, and at Foxton's too, but it was as if they belonged to another world. And now here was I living in that world, Edward's world. He did everything he could to make me a part of it, but still at times I couldn't help feeling like an intruder, as if I had borrowed someone else's life and at any time it might be snatched back again. Violet May would tolerate none of that talk, though, and told me to grow up and mind when I was well off. It did me good to go and visit her from time to time, it brought me back to earth. I had no regrets at leaving the fair; once again my uncle had been glad to see the back of me. As for the others, I had always been 'too hoity-toity' for them anyway.

David clapped his hands. 'Champagne!' he called, and on cue the double doors that opened out into the West Hall were thrown wide and Christine, outrageously overdressed in her new Zandra Rhodes and a tiara, wheeled in a trolley laden with two bottles of Dom Perignon and four glasses.

Edward rolled his eyes, and Christine stuck out her tongue. 'Mmm, very ladylike,' he grunted, then laughed as she blew him a kiss.

'Well, come along, David.' She thrust a bottle of champagne at him. 'What are you waiting for?'

Edward slipped his arm around my shoulders and waited until everyone was holding a glass. 'It's not often a man gets engaged two years after his wedding,' he said, 'but it was a good idea for an anniversary present, even if I say so myself.' He gave me a gentle squeeze and as I looked up into his face I could see that his sister and his brother were for the moment, part of another world. 'To you,' he whispered.

'To Elizabeth,' Christine and David echoed, and the moment was broken.

After we had drunk the toast, and another to Edward, we sat down. Wanting to remain close to him, I curled up on the floor at his feet. He always sat in the same chair, the one on the left-hand side of the hearth. David's was the chair on the right, and many was the night I had sat just like this, at Edward's feet, studying the intricacies of the eighteenth-century fireplace, while the two of them discussed Edward's next trip to Paris or Rome, a forthcoming auction or the needs of one of their many collector clients. I felt comfortable and safe, and smiled as I hugged my knees to my chest. I was almost happy.

The last thought slipped into my mind before I could stop it, and I tossed my head back, as if trying to shake off the introspection. It had come, not as a spontaneous, pleasurable thought, but as if it were struggling to establish its presence while at the same time denying me its sentiment. Feeling guilty, I rested my head against Edward's knee and reached up for his hand.

Christine and David were arguing gently. 'Oh do be quiet,' Christine said, as she flicked David on the shoulder.

'Your problem, young lady,' he retorted, 'is that you go looking for trouble.' He was referring to the fracas Christine had become involved in at the village store that morning, and since Edward had been in London, it was David, the younger of the two brothers, who had had to go and smooth Mr Russell's feathers. They were always dragging Christine out of one scrape or another. She had been only a child when their parents died, so the brothers had brought her up. She was devoted to them both, but we all knew Edward had a special place in her heart.

'More champagne anyone?' she said, holding up the bottle.

I held out my glass. 'What time is Rupert arriving?' I asked. Rupert was yet another in the long line of Christine's escorts.

'I didn't invite him in the end, thought it might be nicer if it was just family.' At the slight emphasis on the word family, I looked round, but no one else seemed to have noticed.

'Quite right too,' Edward said. 'Not, of course, that I have anything against Rupert,' he added quickly.

Christine laughed and dropped a kiss on his head. '*You* don't have anything against anyone,' she said.

'What time are you setting off tomorrow?' David asked, turning to me.

I looked at Christine. 'We thought about nine-thirty, didn't we?'

'About that.' She went to sit down again, and as she crossed one leg over the other I saw her looking at mine. 'We all know you've got wonderful legs, Elizabeth, but please stop showing them off. Envy-green clashes with my dress.'

'There's nothing wrong with your legs, Christine,' David remarked, 'which is more than I can say for your navigation, incidentally. Are you sure you're leaving yourselves enough time tomorrow?'

'My legs are fat, I'm fat,' said Christine – and David rolled his eyes in a here-we-go-again pantomime as Christine launched into another bout of destructive self-criticism. According to her she looked like a roundhead, with her mousey club-cut hair and circular face, but in fact she was rather beautiful, and her short fringe and round blue eyes made her look much younger than thirty. That was a compliment she had no time for, however. What really obsessed her were her freckles, and she spent hours soaking her face in lemon juice in the hope of getting rid of them. And if anyone dared to tell her that what she lacked in height she made up for in personality, they were sorry for it, especially David, since he was the one she resembled. Why couldn't I have been tall and slim like Edward? she would ask pathetically.

'You know,' Edward said suddenly, 'I think I might come along to the auction tomorrow after all.'

'Oh no!' Christine protested. 'You said you were going to leave it all to us. Besides, it'll be Elizabeth's first auction without you – how's she ever going to learn if you're always there?' She looked at me. 'You're mad, you know. Why you should want to get involved in all this wheeler-dealering when you can have a nice easy life at home here, I don't know. Anyway,' she said to Edward, 'I shall be there if she comes unstuck – which she won't.'

'Then don't forget, if you feel you don't want to go through with it all you have to do is place your bid with the auctioneer before the sale begins, he'll do the rest.'

I smiled at the way he was trying to protect me, but Christine snorted. 'As if she's going to do that.'

'We all know you wouldn't,' David said, 'but you've had a lot more experience at this than Elizabeth has.'

The argument continued as Edward told us yet again how much he was prepared to go up to in order to secure the neo-classical Bullock sofa, one of the items being auctioned at a country house sale over in Sussex the following day.

I was becoming a little more used to this new world of mine now, but it had taken time. I had had no idea of just how wealthy Edward was, and at first I was overwhelmed by the lavishness of his generosity. My wardrobes were brimming with clothes flown in from the best couturiers in the world – and with alarming frequency they were packed into a fifteen-piece set of Hermès luggage as we flew off to distant, exotic places where Edward conducted his business and I explored and socialised. We both attended every royal function that Edward was invited to – and there were many – and were constantly entertaining clients, either in West End restaurants or our London home – businessmen, film stars, celebrities of all kinds. There were charity balls at least twice a month, some in London but most of them in New York, Dallas or Hong Kong. At these functions, Edward hardly ever left my side. He advised me, because I insisted, on how I should dress, how I should speak and how I should eat.

He loved me, almost to the point of idolising me, and was never happy unless I was with him. He still couldn't believe that I really did love him, when he was so 'old and decrepit', as he put it, and I was so young. His devoted attendance on me was his way of trying to hide this insecurity, and it was because of his insecurity that I loved him.

The pomposities and eccentricities of the people who belonged to Edward's world of art and antiques also took me some time to get used to. But with time, and again a great deal of patience on Edward's part, my knowledge of the business increased, and even in that most difficult of worlds I began to feel more at ease. Walters & Sons was one of the largest art dealers in the country. Nevertheless I was relieved that we rarely invited people down to our house in Kent. It was the family home, and David's particular refuge. Since the accident had killed Edward's first wife and left David's face badly scarred he'd given up his post as a university professor and now lived in virtual seclusion.

Soon after Edward and I were married I had taken over the running of the household while Christine concentrated on carving herself a niche in the family business and joined the board of directors. She was almost as passionate about antique furniture and old masters as David was. Not that Edward wasn't too, but anyone who really knew him knew that his heart had been captured long ago by the mysterious works of ancient Egypt. There was a room on the second floor of Westmoor – the Kent house – filled with limestone reliefs, faience bowls, broken grey granite faces and schist and marble statues. It was known simply as the Egyptian Room.

I often teased Edward about his passion for all things Egyptian, knowing that he was, in a way, made vulnerable by his obsession. Whenever he had spent some time in the Egyptian Room he would emerge looking dishevelled and child-like, almost as though he had been playing with a forbidden toy. I was reminded of my days at Foxton's, when I caught one of the younger boys up to no good – and Edward was so like a boy, especially in the way he tried so hard to please me. It was impossible not to love him. His great passion was King Tutankhamun and his excavated tomb. On that he could wax lyrical for hours.

I couldn't help wondering what Alexander would make of my new life – wondering, too, if he ever thought about me. To be thinking of him so frequently after all this time, and when my life was now so complete, was madness, I knew. But how could I help it, with Charlotte there, looking more like him every day? What would I do if he were to walk into my life now?

'Elizabeth! Elizabeth! Where are you?'

I blinked, wondering how long they had been calling my name. 'Sorry,' I laughed. 'I was miles away.'

'We could see that,' said Christine. 'We want to know where?' Sometimes her manner of asking questions was hard, accusatory even, and I felt Edward's hand move through my hair as if to take away the edge of her sharpness.

At that moment the double doors were thrown open and Jeffrey, the butler-cum-chauffeur-cum-part-time chef, walked stiffly into the room. 'Mesdames et messieurs, dinner is now being served in the Baroque Room,' he announced.

Everyone burst out laughing, and as if someone had removed his backbone, Jeffrey fell against the door and laughed too. 'Honestly,' he complained, as we filed out of the room, 'no one ever takes me seriously. By the way, love the rock, Mrs Walters.'

'Thank you, Jeffrey,' I said, and offered up my hand for him to have a better look. As he gushed his delight and Edward looked on with pride, I couldn't help remembering the ring Alexander had given me, the one that had cost a fraction of this, and sat untouched now in a little box upstairs. I swallowed hard against the unexpected nostalgia. Why, tonight of all nights, was I thinking about Alexander?

Over dinner I noticed that Christine seemed agitated, but when I asked if there was anything on her mind she smiled brightly and said no. David and Edward smiled indulgently; they were used to her erratic moods and had learned to ignore them. I listened as she talked about the furniture she had taken to the restorers that day, then abruptly changed the subject to discuss a board meeting called for the following week. I tried to fight back the niggardly envy. It was ironic; she envied me my looks and figure, and I envied her the respect she had earned through her knowledge of antiques. It seemed to me that Christine always had something of value to say, while I could only engage in the kind of affected small talk favoured by art dealers' wives. I hated myself for minding. I was luckier than any woman deserved to be, and would be grateful to Edward for the rest of my life. But still, I couldn't stop myself from being envious of Christine, not only for her intelligence but also for the freedom she had to be herself. She didn't have to hide what she was really thinking, or bear the guilt of not loving her brother enough . . . .

I caught her grinning in my direction, and smiled back. She really was much more striking than she realised. I'd asked her once why she had never married. 'What, and give up all this?' she'd cried. 'Why should I do that? And now I've got you and little Charlotte too, what more could I want?'

I was to find out.

Charlotte dipped her head and stared at the floor. Her hands were clasped in a knot behind her back and I could see her little shoulders heaving up and down as she struggled valiantly to accept her undeserved fate. 'I do understand, Mother,' she said, her eyes still riveted to the carpet. She shifted her weight on to one leg and a little knee poked out from under the rags of her skirt. 'Will there be some mending for me to do while you are gone?'

I caught David's eye across the room, and had to turn away so that she wouldn't see I was laughing. Ever since David had taken her to see Cinderella, the entire household had been both wittingly and unwittingly playing the roles she cast them in. Needless to say, she was Cinderella; I was the wicked step-mother, and Christine and Jeffrey the ugly sisters. I suspected that Canary, her nanny – called after her bright yellow uniform – was expected to appear at any moment as the fairy godmother, and deliver her to Prince Charming – Edward. David was a less than enthusiastic Buttons.

She was waiting for an answer, so putting on my best haughty face I glared down at her. 'You mean you haven't already scrubbed the grates today, you lazy child? What do you think you're about? Off to the kitchens with you.'

'Yes, Mother,' she murmured, and keeping her head lowered she sidled past me and let herself out through the door.

'Charlotte!' I called, just before the door closed. Her face peeped back in. 'Did you call, Mother?' she said. 'Have I done something wrong? Oh, please don't beat me, Mother.'

That was too much, and I burst out laughing. 'Come and give me a kiss before I go,' I said.

'Oh, Mummy! You've spoilt it all now.' Then seeing I was laughing, her face turned pink and she ran into my arms. 'Can't I come too?' she said.

'Not today, darling. I have to do something for Edward. I thought you were doing something for him too. Weren't you making him a cushion to put your glass slipper on?'

Her face brightened immediately. 'Oh yes,' she said.

Then hugging me tightly, she pressed her mouth to my ear. 'Canary's making it really, but don't tell.'

'No, of course I won't,' I whispered. 'Now, how about that kiss?'

It was wet and slobbery, and very long. She had walked in on Edward and me a few nights ago and caught us kissing – not that she hadn't seen us kissing before, but this time she had wanted to know why we took so long over it. Edward had done the explaining, and it was now her mission in life to perfect the art of long kissing. She practised on anyone who would allow her close enough, which was all of us – but not on Edward; he was Prince Charming, and destined to be the recipient of the final, perfect version.

'Hey, how about one of those for me?' David said.

She slid out of my arms and ran across the room. David, stooping to catch her, was knocked off his feet as she bowled into his arms.

'I think I'll leave you two to it,' I said, laughing as they rolled across the carpet.

I found Christine organising Jeffrey into the van, listing the errands he needed to run before he drove over to Rowe House to collect the sofa. It made me both pleased and nervous to think that Edward was so sure I would succeed in obtaining it. It had been quite a battle to get him to let me go to this auction, but I had explained as gently as I could that, like so many other women these days, I needed to prove that I could be more than just a wife.

'But darling,' he had said when I'd first suggested I might take a more active role in the business, 'I love you being "just a wife", as you put it. I want you and Charlotte to be happy and not to have to worry about anything. You are happy, aren't you?'

'Of course I am,' I answered. 'It's just that I want to share more with you.'

By the time I had persuaded him to see it my way, he actually seemed to like the idea of his wife being a working woman. 'Who knows, you might have a seat on the board before long, and then there'll be no stopping us, will there?'

And provided I pulled it off at this auction, then who could tell, he might well be right.

'All set?' Christine said as we got into her Volkswagen Beetle.

'I think so.'

'Good God, Elizabeth, you sound like a lamb going to the slaughter. It's only an auction, you know.'

At eleven-thirty we hurtled up the drive of Rowe House and lurched to a stop at the front door. I say lurched because Christine had very little regard for a clutch. I was so relieved that we had survived the ordeal of her driving and arrived in one piece – albeit late – that the auction seemed as nothing in comparison.

The house was sombre, even menacing inside, but I refused to be daunted. Christie's had set up an office in the library, so I went off to register, and Christine, spotting someone she knew, wandered off in the direction of the stables. I wasn't unduly worried by her disappearance for it was some time before Lot 137 was to be auctioned, so I sat and watched the other dealers as they made their bids for the various items of Queen Anne and Regency furniture. There were several paintings too, one of which fetched the staggering sum of one hundred and eighty-five thousand pounds. I was beginning to feel a little sorry that Edward had set a limit on what he was prepared to pay for the Bullock sofa – the idea of bidding and winning whatever the cost, held a certain appeal. But there would be time enough for that sort of thing in the future; what was important now was to show Edward that I had the confidence to carry out his instructions. I knew the American collector who wanted the sofa was important to him, and I sent up a silent prayer that no one would outbid me. I looked at my catalogue for the hundredth time and the neat figures written beside Lot 137: fifteen thousand pounds. I felt comforted as I looked at the picture beside it. Surely no one would want to pay so much for such an ugly piece. I might even get it for less.

In what seemed no time at all Lot 135 went under the hammer, and I looked round for Christine. A Minton porcelain and brass lamp was Lot 136 and I heaved a sigh of relief as she appeared in the doorway.

'Ready?'she said, sitting down in the chair next to me.

'Of course,' I answered, despising my stomach for calling me a liar.

The auctioneer was speaking. 'I offer you Lot 137. Who will start the bidding: Ten thousand pounds. I have ten thousand pounds. Ten thousand five hundred. You sir, you at the back, eleven thousand? Yes, eleven thousand.'

Within seconds I was overwhelmed by the certain knowledge that I was invisible. I looked at Christine in panic. She must have sensed my fear because instead of turning to look at me, she fixed her eyes on the auctioneer and nodded her head.

'Eleven thousand five hundred,' he said. 'Twelve thousand. A new bidder in the middle there. Twelve thousand five hundred.' Had it really been me who had pushed it up another five hundred?

'Twelve thousand five hundred. Your bid at the moment, madam. Twelve thousand five hundred. Thirteen thousand.'

I nodded. 'Thirteen thousand five hundred.'

I felt a movement beside me but was too tense to look round. 'Are you bidding, madam? Yes. Fourteen thousand.' The woman beside me had entered the bidding, and calmly folded one leg over the other as I raised my card.

'Fourteen thousand five hundred. Fifteen thousand.' Suddenly it occurred to me that the woman next to me must have seen my catalogue and would know what I was prepared to go to.

'Fifteen thousand five hundred.' I hadn't moved, and the woman beside me would not be bidding against herself, so there must be someone else in the arena. I leaned to one side, peering between the backs of heads to see if I could spot who it was.

'Sixteen thousand.' I caught my breath. Had the auctioneer thought I made a bid?

'Sixteen thousand five hundred.' It was the woman again. I looked at her, hating her and wanting to shout that she had cheated. How had everything got beyond my reach so quickly?

'Seventeen thousand.'

My head swung round and I felt as though I were caught in a nightmare. All around me people were bidding, and I had lost. Didn't they know my husband wanted that piece of furniture? Didn't they understand that I couldn't let him down? Why didn't they stop?

'Eighteen thousand.'

My hand shot to my head.

'Eighteen thousand five hundred.'

Christine turned to look at me, her smile triumphant, and I knew that had she been in my shoes, she too would have carried on.

'Nineteen thousand. Nineteen thousand five hundred.' I wouldn't allow myself to look at the figure on my catalogue. What would Edward have done? He would go on, I knew he would. The woman beside me was slumped in her chair, now intent on watching me, and whoever it was at the front of the room who was bidding against me.

'Twenty thousand pounds.'

Would no one make the auctioneer stop? I couldn't go any higher.

'Twenty-one thousand pounds. Twenty-two thousand pounds.' People were stirring in their seats and turning round to see who was bidding against the man at the front.

'Twenty-six thousand pounds.'

To hell with everyone. I was going to win that sofa. No matter what it cost, that sofa was going back to Westmoor.

'Twenty-seven. Twenty-eight. Twenty-nine. Thirty thousand pounds.'

Suddenly I stopped. Thirty thousand pounds. Twice the figure Edward had set down. There had been no let-up in the bidding, no hesitancy from the man in the front row. He wanted that sofa too. He was going to have it.

'Thirty-one. Thirty-two. Thirty-three. Any advance on thirty- three? Are you going on, madam?' The auctioneer's gaze was fixed on me. The room was silent. Everyone was waiting for me. Christine's eyes were gleaming and I noticed the moisture on her forehead. Had I done wrong? She had said she wouldn't interfere, that she was only there to lend me moral support. But surely if I had gone too far she would have stopped me. Gone too far? Was I mad? I had more than doubled what Edward had said he was prepared to pay. I couldn't go on. Feeling slightly sick, I slumped back in my chair.

'The George Bullock sofa, sold for thirty-three thousand pounds.' The hammer went down, tearing through my nerves like a sweeping scythe.

'Damn!' Christine muttered.

My eyes stung as I looked at her. 'Oh my God, should I have gone on?' I gasped.

She shook her head irritably. 'No. No, it's just that he didn't say who bought it.' She craned her neck to get a better view of the front row. 'Who is it?' she hissed.

I could only see the back of his head. I was feeling nauseous, all I wanted to do was to get out. I stood up and began to clamber my way along the row, to the door.

I stumbled as I got to the end, and a doorman caught me and supported me by the elbow into the hall.

A few seconds later Christine followed. 'Take me home,' I breathed. She put her arm around my shoulder. 'Come on, don't take it so hard. Someone has to lose and let's face it, you put up a hell of a fight. I would have lost my nerve long before that. Just wait 'til I tell Edward, he'll be so proud of you he'll probably . . .'

'No!' I cried. 'You mustn't tell him. Please, Christine. He was so clear about the fifteen thousand pounds. He mustn't know, he'll never trust me again.'

'Stop being so dramatic, he'll have a good laugh about it, you'll see.'

I caught both her hands in mine and begged her not to tell him. To her it might seem unimportant, but she didn't understand.

'Honestly, Elizabeth,' Christine said later, as we were driving back to Westmoor. 'I don't know why you're so afraid to tell Edward, you must know he'll forgive you anything.'

Which was precisely the reason I didn't want him to know. I didn't want him to forgive me. Just for once, I wanted him to be angry. I wanted him to rant and rave at my obstinacy, shout that I'd almost cost him eighteen thousand pounds. I wanted to have to beg his forgiveness, suffer his silent anger – anything that would instil a passionate emotion in us both. But I could see already in my mind's eye his kind and patient face, the look of sorrow in his eyes as he blamed himself for putting me in a situation that had caused me so much distress. Already I could feel his suffocating arms around me.

Christine dropped me at Westmoor, then went on to meet Rupert. Edward was still in London, Charlotte was in the nursery playing with a schoolfriend, and David had gone to the village. The house was quiet; it smelt of polish, and the silver gleamed in the sunlight that streamed in through the windows. I couldn't think of anything to do. I toyed with the idea of taking one of the horses out across the common, but it didn't really appeal. The latest editions of *Vogue* and *Harper's* were on the coffee table, I might find some new menus, we were giving three dinners in London the following week. But who cared about menus? The past week I had had the auction to look forward to. Now it was over, and those brief minutes of excitement had only intensified my restlessness.

I flopped down on the sofa and stared, unseeing, at the porcelain and the paintings that adorned the room. I must have dozed off because it was past five when Edward touched my cheek, and taking my hands, pulled me to my feet.

'Congratulations, darling,' he whispered. 'And thank you.'

I blinked, trying to pull myself from sleep. 'Thank you? What for?'

He laughed. 'For the sofa, of course. Well done.'

'But . . .'

'Edward!' I looked up as Christine came into the room. 'Ah, there you are,' she said. She turned to me, her face incredulous. 'Elizabeth! What happened? How did it get here?'

'Jeffrey brought it, of course,' Edward answered.

We both turned to stare at him. 'Jeffrey?' I repeated.

'Yes. Why are you both so surprised? He'll be taking it on to the warehouse later. It's in the library now.'

'The sofa?' I said. 'But how?'

Edward laughed. 'What on earth has got into you two? Did you or did you not go to the auction this morning and acquire one sofa?'

'We did – it seems,' said Christine.

'Well then, shall we go and take a look at it?'

As soon as I clapped eyes on it my heart began to thump.

What on earth had happened? The man in the front row had made the final bid, so how had it arrived here? And in God's name, how much had we paid for it?

Edward voiced the question. I looked at Christine, but her voice seemed as far from her throat as my own. 'Well?' Edward prompted.

'Uh, I think we'd better take a look inside the envelope,' Christine suggested, picking it up from the seat.

My worst fears were confirmed as she read out the total. 'Thirty-three thousand pounds?' Edward echoed. He turned to me. 'I thought . . .'

'Why don't we all go and sit down,' Christine interrupted. 'I've no idea how this has happened but I'm sure we can get to the bottom of it.'

Edward listened patiently as Christine explained. By the time she had reached the end of the story Edward was laughing. 'My poor darling,' he said. 'And all for me. Well, there's obviously been some confusion at Christie's end, I'll get on to them and find out who the rightful owner is.' He dropped a kiss on the top of my head before he left the room.

When he returned a few minutes later, with David, he was no longer smiling. 'I'm still not sure how it happened, Christie's are looking into it. But the sofa is ours.' He paused as David handed him a drink. 'For thirty-three thousand pounds.'

I closed my eyes and groaned. 'I'm sorry, Edward, what can I say? I don't know . . .'

He came and put his arms around me. 'Sssh. It wasn't your fault. It seems that someone contacted one of Christie's staff, asking him to act on my behalf.' He turned to Christine. 'Do you know anything about it? Who it might have been?'

Christine shook her head. 'Shall I check with the office, see if anyone there placed it?'

'They'll have gone home now. We'll try in the morning.'

His arms tightened around my shoulders. 'Don't blame yourself, darling. It was just some stupid muddle.' But his voice held no conviction.

I pushed him away, 'Edward, how can you sit there and take it so calmly? OK, you'll get some of the money back, but whichever way you look at it this has cost you personally something in the region of eighteen thousand pounds. And I am responsible. Me! *I* have messed it up.'

'Elizabeth.'

I looked at him, and for one blinding instant I wanted to slap him. I realised then that in a perverse way I was almost glad at what had happened. It had shaken him. He hadn't got angry, nothing ever made him angry, but he had not been completely unmoved. Someone's head would roll for this – not mine, of course – but Edward would fire whoever had placed the bid. I wanted to be there when he did it. I wanted to watch him be unkind to someone.

I stared at him, shocked by my thoughts. 'I'm going upstairs,' I said.

'I'll come with you.' He was already on his feet.

'No, Edward! Don't you understand? It was my fault! If I'd stopped at fifteen, as you told me to, this would never have happened. At least let me feel guilty about it.' I swept out of the room, aware that I had hurt him deeply and feeling more wretched than ever.

An hour later there was a knock on the door and Edward let himself into the bedroom. One look at his face was enough to send me running into his arms. He forgave me my outburst, and in his calm, gentle voice he explained that this was what he had been afraid of all along – afraid that if he did allow me to become part of the business we would end up fighting with each other. Didn't I understand that, as his wife, I was far more important to him than any old sofa or painting could ever be?

Yes, I understood that. I understood too that it wasn't my failure at the auction that had really upset me, but the way

I had hurt Edward by suggesting that just being his wife wasn't enough to make me happy. Edward wanted above all things to make me happy. He loved me, and I owed him so much – all the fun, the laughter and the loving of a proper family life. I had to get a grip on myself, and put a stop to whatever it was that was driving me to try and ruin it all.

Edward never did get to the bottom of what happened at Rowe House. I often wondered how hard he tried. Though he fought to hide it, I was never in any doubt that my decision to take no further part in the business was a great relief to him. I had made the decision – but it didn't stop me feeling unnerved by the way all the doors to his professional life seemed closed to me after that. It was only many years later that the truth of what happened at the auction came to light – years during which Alexander returned to my life more than once, and was, in the end, to take control of events that very nearly destroyed my life.

A week or so after the auction we were all once again in the drawing-room at Westmoor. I was beginning to hate that room. Like Edward's adoration, its portraits and its statues seemed to stifle me – no matter how often I tried to tell myself how fortunate I was. I stood at the window, watching the rain outside. Edward looked up from *The Times* and asked me if I was feeling all right.

My reply must have sounded irritable because he put aside his paper and came to stand beside me. I turned away. How could I tell him that I didn't want to fly to Paris that night? That I was bored by Paris, bored by Rome, bored by New York? I longed to do something different, something unplanned, impulsive. I felt as if my whole body were on the point of exploding, with frustration.

'Isn't he simply divine!' Christine exclaimed, giving me the diversion I needed.

David caught my eye and winked. 'And just who are we gushing about this time?' he asked.

'Alexander Belmayne, of course, who else?'

I froze in Edward's arms. Had Christine found out somehow, and was this her way of tormenting me? No. I was being paranoid. How could she possibly know? I didn't dare look at Edward – but he couldn't know either; I'd told him about Alexander, but I'd never once mentioned his surname, and everyone thought Charlotte looked like me.

Edward shook his head and went back to his chair. 'He's not in the papers again, is he?' he said. 'What's he done this time?'

'It says here that his father has bailed him out.'

'Bailed him out of what?' David was only half listening.

'The debt he got himself into through gambling. There's a picture of him here coming out of Annabel's with some woman. God, he's beautiful. It says here that 'the Belmayne marriage is on the rocks and according to close friends his wife has moved out.' Mmm, sounds hopeful. I don't suppose we could invite him for drinks when we're next in London, could we, Edward? Elizabeth, are you all right, you look positively pale today.'

Edward dropped his newspaper immediately. 'Christine's right, you know, darling. Come and sit down. Call Mary, David, get her to bring in some tea.'

I allowed Edward to lead me to a chair. He was talking to me, rubbing my hands. It wasn't the first time Christine had read aloud articles about Alexander, but this time her words rang in my ears with terrifying clarity. Now I knew why I had been behaving so badly, and what it was that was forcing me to reject Edward. Did I really still love Alexander as much as my reaction said I did? Wasn't it all buried somewhere in the past? Why had it come back now to haunt me? I looked into Edward's face. What was I doing here with this man? Everything around me was alien – and somewhere out there Alexander was alone, alone as I was here, in this room. Then, for one wild moment, I was back in Bayswater, sitting on the bed, looking at him and listening as he swore that he loved me, that I would never be able to shut him out of my life, because no matter what happened in the future, it would always be me he loved.

I clutched at Edward's hand. I loved Edward. I would never do anything to hurt him. He had to save me from this . . . .

I turned abruptly as the door opened. Canary came in, brandishing a long stick with a star glued to one end. Jeffrey followed her, miming the blowing of a royal trumpet, then bowed and swept his arm to usher someone in through the door. And there was Charlotte, her black hair curled round her face, her satin dress sprinkled with stardust and a glass slipper balanced on the cushion she held out to Edward. Her face was beaming as she looked round the room and her eyes – his eyes – pleaded with mine for approval.

Too late I stifled a sob, and before anyone could stop me I ran from the room.

– Alexander –

– 16 –

Jessica and I were reunited the day Henry married Lizzie. She'd been living with her parents at their house in Holland Park and we'd neither seen nor spoken to each other for over six weeks. I hadn't really cared much when she went – at least it meant no more of those macabre paintings would find their way on to the walls. Lizzie had remained at the house with me, a situation that, amazingly, seemed to cause no speculation. In fact, Henry all but lived with us, so it was only when he was out that Lizzie turned her insatiable appetite on me. I didn't like myself too well for my weakness in giving in to her, but she blackmailed me by threatening to tell Henry. I didn't know whether or not she would actually have carried out the threat, though I rather suspected she wouldn't – which only went to show what an altogether contemptible character I was.

Henry and Lizzie tied the knot at Chelsea Register Office, with a reception afterwards at the Ritz. Jessica was there. I was surprised at my feelings when I saw her. She'd lost weight and her eyes seemed larger in her pale face. Watching her, as she mingled with the other guests, brought back all the shame I felt at the things I had done to her. One way or another she had suffered at my hands ever since we'd met.

At first we were uncomfortable with each other, but the readiness with which she turned her back on the rest of the party told me she was as keen as I was that we should at least make an effort. She put up a good show of enjoying her freedom, laughing and chattering as if she hadn't a care in the world. But I knew her too well. Every time a waiter passed she helped herself to a drink, and as the day wore on I could see how close she was to breaking-point. In the end I took her home and put her to bed. The following day we drove round to her parents' house and collected her things.

In the weeks that followed our reconciliation we did something we should have done years before – we talked about our relationship, and our feelings for each other. I was shocked to discover that for the past year, up until the time she left me, she had been taking drugs. It was the only way, she said, she could cope with the fact that I didn't love her. And the morbid paintings on the walls of our home had been intended to represent her womb as time passed and it shrivelled and discoloured in infecundity.

'But it was all my fault really,' she said. 'I was so confused about you, and because I was suffering, I wanted to make you suffer too. I was afraid that if I couldn't give you children, you would use it as a weapon against me, and because I was afraid of you, afraid to talk to you, the only way I had of expressing myself was through my paintings . . . I've always thought that you still loved Elizabeth, you see, and I suppose that's what it's all been about really. I wonder if you know how it feels to live with someone, and love them, knowing all the time that they love someone else.'

I was appalled to think that I could have lived with Jessica for so long, and not known anything of the pain she was suffering. In fact, I probably *had* known, the trouble was I hadn't really cared. Now I was simply grateful for the opportunity to try, in whatever way I could, to make it up to her.

I saw to it that we spent every possible minute together. One of my favourite ways of relaxing was to sit in the corner of her muddled studio, now once again filled with bright and vivid colours, and watch as, naked – and it had to be naked, she assured me – she tied a paint brush to each hand and rotated so that the tips of the brushes swept over the canvas. I was no more *au fait* with her peculiar form of art than I had been before, but it reminded me of our days at Oxford, and that touch of nostalgia drew us even closer together.

I noticed quite early on how much she was drinking, but if I ever mentioned it she became defensive. 'I'm just having a bit of fun,' she hiccoughed, when I came home early one afternoon and found her sprawled on the sofa, the best part of the way through a bottle of gin.

'But Jess, darling, that bottle was full last night.'

'Are you having a go at me, oh Godalmighty Alexander? Why are you home early, anyway?'

'I live here, remember? Now come along, let's get some coffee inside you.'

'Not one of your little babies?' She giggled as she saw me flinch. 'Still haven't got me pregnant, have you, Alexander?'

'Jess, stop before you say something you regret.'

Suddenly she burst into tears. 'I'm sorry. I didn't mean it. I don't know what I'm saying. I don't know what I'm doing any more. You confuse me. You've never loved me before, and now that you do, I don't know how to handle it. What shall we do? Shall we go and see someone? I know you want to have a baby. *Well I'm not damned well giving you one!*'

I walked out of the room, knowing it was pointless to stay. When she sobered up we'd talk again. And maybe she was right, we should go and see a specialist – after all, we'd been trying long enough with no results. But how could we even think about having a baby with Jess in this state?

So we muddled on from row to row, each more acrimonious than the last. But I was certain that once she was pregnant, everything would change; then at last she would allow herself to believe how much I cared for her. To have something in our lives that we could share and love together was what we both needed.

It was on the day Jessica and I finally plucked up the courage to go for our fertility tests that I received instructions in the Pinto case. No one – with the possible exception of Raddish, the clerk at chambers – was more surprised that I was. It was a case that had been in and out of the press for some time and I came across it when I had to attend a Section I at the magistrates'court. The committal proceedings were brief, and I barely met Ruth Pinto. However, I succeeded in getting her bail, and it was because of this, her solicitor told me, that she later insisted I should be the one to continue with her case. He was determined to make it abundantly clear that the decision had nothing to do with him.

The British Government, or more precisely, the Ministry of Defence, had accused Ruth Pinto of stealing top-secret defence documents and selling them to one of the hundred and five Russian diplomats who were subsequently expelled from Britain. These documents, I was told – I never got to see them – outlined certain key details of Royal Naval manoeuvres in the Baltic.

The case, with much press coverage, lasted four days, and the interaction between myself and prosecuting counsel was bitter, amusing and, for me, increasingly exhilarating as my certain, and public, victory drew closer.

The night before the final day of the trial Jessica and I dined at home. I was edgy because of an unexpected turn in court that day, when Pinto's boyfriend took the stand and all but handed the prosecution their case on a plate. I'd have my work cut out preparing my summing up before I went into court the following morning, so I was even more depressed than usual when I realised that Jessica was drunk.

I watched her across the table as she helped herself to minestrone. She slapped the ladle back into the bowl and I stared pointedly at the mess she had made. She glared back at me, then picking up the ladle, she emptied it over the salt and pepper.

Swallowing hard on my anger, I held out my hand for the ladle. 'I'd like some of that soup, please.' For a moment I thought she was going to throw it at me. Instead she burst out laughing, and soon I found that I was laughing too.

She stopped. 'Why are you laughing?'

'I was laughing because you were.'

'But you don't know why I was laughing, do you? I was laughing at you, Alexander, so you were laughing at yourself. The great Alexander Belmayne, he who knows everything. I suppose you think you know what's wrong with me tonight, don't you? Yes, of course you do, because you know everything. But even if you did know, which you don't, what would you care? What do you care about anything, except yourself?'

'For Christ's sake, don't you think I've got enough on my mind tonight of all nights, without having you and your childish tantrums to contend with. Either tell me what's on your mind, or shut up. Frankly I don't care which.'

We glared at each other, the air between us simmering. In the end I put my napkin on the table and stood up. 'I'm going to do some work. Why don't you do yourself a favour and go upstairs and fiddle around with your paintbrushes. It might improve your temper.'

I saw a dangerous gleam leap into her eyes and her fingers tightened on the knife beside her. I turned away, and as I walked into the hall the telephone began to ring, drowning the string of obscenities she was screaming after me. Suddenly I felt all the old antipathy surging back into my veins. I'd tried, I kept on trying, but there was no point; I didn't know what she wanted, or what I had to do to make her happy. She couldn't accept my love, and now she had me so confused I didn't know which way to turn.

'*Answer that bloody phone!*' she screamed.

I picked up the receiver. 'Someone sounds out of sorts.'

'Father.'

'Haven't rung at a bad time, have I?'

'No, as a matter of fact, you've rung just *in* time. How are you?'

We chatted for a while until I realised that he was actually saying nothing at all. It wasn't in my father's nature to indulge in idle chat – here was someone else who wouldn't come right out and say what they were thinking. Trying to keep the irritation out of my voice, I asked him if there was something on his mind.

'No, nothing really. Just wanted to know how you were feeling about the Pinto case. The jury goes out tomorrow, doesn't it?'

'That's right.'

'Mind if I offer a word of advice?'

I did, but nevertheless told him to go ahead.

'Go easy on the summing up,' he said.

I looked at the receiver, uncertain whether I had heard him right. 'I beg your pardon.'

'You heard me. In your own and your client's interest, go easy on the defence. That's all. Goodnight, son. Love to Jessica.' And he'd gone.

I slammed the receiver down and spun round to find Jessica standing in the doorway. 'What did he want?' she asked.

'Good question. He's someone else who's talking in riddles tonight. Now, if you don't mind I'm going to my study and I don't want to be disturbed. By anyone!'

'In that case, I'll go and fiddle with some paintbrushes,' she spat, and flounced off up the stairs.

My summing up speech would have been difficult enough to prepare without my father's words ringing in my ears. 'In your own interest,' he had said. But just how could it be in my interest deliberately to lose the case which is what I supposed him to mean and see the girl go to prison? With the sort of press coverage the case was receiving I'd be on the map if I won, and there weren't many barristers who could say that at the age of twenty-four.

Then it dawned on me: I was being subjected to government pressure . . . . Outraged, I picked up the phone, ready to demand that my father – more accurately described, under the circumstances, as the Lord Chancellor – should explain exactly what he was after. I didn't even finish dialling; it wouldn't be any use, he wouldn't tell me anything. I must simply ignore him. The girl was clearly innocent, and it was my job to see that justice was done.

But the doubt had been planted, and the question that until then I had refused to ask myself – why had the government decided to proceed with the prosecution at all when the defence case was so strong? – danced about in my mind until I couldn't see the papers in front of me. I dropped my pen and rubbed my fingers over my eyes. Something was wrong with this case, something fundamental that I must have overlooked. And I was convinced that whatever it was, was staring me full in the face – which only added to my frustration.

'In a better mood, are we?'

I turned to see Jessica leaning against the door. 'I told you I didn't want to be interrupted,' I said.

'I was bored upstairs alone, and you know how you

getting angry always turns me on. I thought you might like to play.' She ran a hand over the thin white silk of her blouse, pulling it tightly against her skin. The pink nipple stood out enticingly.

I looked at it for a moment, then sighed as I turned away. 'Jessica, I'm not in the mood.'

The ice clinked against the glass as she finished her gin and tonic. For a second or two there was silence, and then the glass smashed against the wall in front of me. The ice cubes melted across the pages on my desk, turning the ink to an illegible blur.

'Actually, darling, it wouldn't make a lot of difference to me if you were in the mood. What I need right now is a *real* man.'

I made no answer. I could neither trust myself to speak nor move.

'Got any suggestions? How about one of the husbands of the hundred wives you've fucked?'

'Jessica, just get out of here.'

'At least there's one thing you can be sure of, there won't be any little Belmayne bastards running around anywhere, will there?' And she swept out of the room.

I was behind her like a shot. 'What the hell was that supposed to mean?'

She stopped, and staggered against the wall as I turned her round. 'What do you think it means, Alexander darling?'

Blood was pounding through my ears and my hands were sweating, but I forced myself to remain calm. 'You've had the results?' I said.

'To the little testie-westies we had? Yes.' She started to laugh.

I caught her by the wrists and pinned her against the wall. 'Well?' She gave a nervous giggle and looked away. I shook her, and twisted her arms painfully behind her back. 'Well?'

She giggled again, but couldn't meet my eyes as she spoke. 'Well', she sighed, 'it would seem that your little testie-westies simply don't work, Alexander. It had to be one of us, didn't it? And it's you! Defunct, I think the word is. But don't worry, I'll stick by you, darling.'

'Are you trying to tell me. . . ?' I looked at her, and felt myself physically recoil.

'That you're infertile? Yes, that's exactly what I'm telling you. You can't have babies, Alexander. You can't have heirs, because what's coming out of you is nothing.'

I let go of her. She was lying. She had to be lying.

'What's the matter? Not going to cry, are you? Not Alexander, the big man. It's not the end of the world, you know, and as I said, your loving wife is prepared to take on your deficient manhood. Now how's that for devotion?'

I walked slowly down to the sitting-room and sank into a chair. Several minutes later she followed me in, another drink in her hand. She stood in front of me, smiling, waiting for me to speak.

'Why Jessica? Why did you have to tell me like that?'

'You mean, with the contempt you always treat me to? Hurts, doesn't it, Alexander? And after all you've put me through, all you've done to me, at last you've got what you deserve.' She gave a sickening laugh. 'Just look at you, all white and shaking. I wonder what your darling Elizabeth would say if she could see you now. Well, I'll tell you something, she wouldn't stay with you, no woman would, because you're a sexual cripple. You're pathetic, do you know that? Pathetic!'

Looking at her then, her bright blue eyes bloodshot and puffy, her skin mottled, I felt myself drowning in the sorrow of our lives. 'Shall I tell you something, Jessica?' I said quietly. 'Shall I tell you the truth about me? The truth is, you were right. I've only ever loved one woman, and that was Elizabeth. She was everything to me. I begged her to marry me, but she said I was too young. I asked her again and again, because I thought if she left me I'd die – and that's just what I have been doing, all these years, dying. But it's my fault, because I turned my back on her at a time when she needed me. I'll never forgive myself for that, never. But I'm paying for it. And you, Jessica, are the price.'

– 17 –

After that night I could no longer be in any doubt about our marriage. The way I had used the one weapon I knew would wound Jessica more than any other was unforgivable, but the shock of hearing I was sterile, and the way she'd told me, had pushed me over the edge. 'Defunct', she had called me, 'a sexual cripple', and I would never forget the look on her face when she'd said it. It haunted me, persecuted me, and I started to see that same look on the face of every woman I met. Triumph and contempt. I understood it – they saw it as their just revenge – and I felt everything they meant me to feel; inadequate, futile and sick.

Somehow I dragged myself through the days that followed. Ruth Pinto was acquitted – despite the judge's summing up, which I have to say was shamelessly biased. However, she was free to go, and as she shook me by the hand she said something that was only to make sense to me later:

'I don't know what will happen to my life now, Mr Belmayne. I was convinced my stupidity, coupled with your inexperience, would put me in prison.'

That evening the papers led on the case. Triumph was mine, and Henry held a party to celebrate at his flat in Eaton Square.

'Oh come on now, no false modesty,' he protested when I tried to tell him that it had been an open-and-shut case from the beginning. 'You wait 'til the morning, you won't be able to see old Raddish for the pile of briefs he'll be carrying into your office.'

I laughed, and promised to pass my overload in his direction. Robert Lyttleton was the next to congratulate me. We saw very little of him these days, as he slogged it out at the Foreign Office, working his way towards that elusive overseas posting. Whenever we did meet, we neither of us referred to his affair with my wife, nor mine with his mother. I was glad that these near-incestuous involvements, and my jealousy, had not affected our friendship – even though I had no idea at that time just how valuable a friend Robert would turn out to be.

Now he nudged my arm and nodded towards Lizzie as she slid past us with a tray of hors d'oeuvres. 'She's not wearing any knickers, you know.'

'And how would you know that?' I enquired.

'She showed me.'

I shook my head, not in the least surprised. 'I take it Henry was nowhere in sight?'

'Then you take it wrong, old chap. Henry was right there with me. In fact, he told her to do it. No, Scout's honour,' he said as I started to protest. 'Henry, old chap.' He grabbed Henry's arm as he sailed past with Caroline. 'Did you or did you not instruct your wife to display her private parts to me?'

'Guilty.' He looked at me. 'Don't tell me you want to see them too? I'm sure she'll oblige if you ask. Or would you like me to make the request on your behalf?'

It wasn't until much later that I was able to get Henry alone and ask him just what was going on between him and Lizzie. 'Apart from a series of orgies, you mean? Very little,' he said.

'I assumed you were happy together.'

'I fuck her, that's all she wants. She's happy.' He was smiling as he spoke, but I knew him too well.

'Are you seeing Caroline again?' I asked.

'As often as possible.' The smile faded. 'I should never have given her up.'

'Then why don't you leave Lizzie?'

'Why don't you leave Jessica?'

We looked at each other for several minutes before he spoke again. 'Well, we sure made one hell of a mistake when we got into bed with those two, didn't we? The question is, which of us is going to be the first to do something about it?'

The following morning when I arrived at chambers I found a stack of newspapers on my desk. Perhaps Henry was right, I would see a few more briefs coming my way now, and God knew I needed something to take my mind off the situation at home.

I sorted through the mail first, then picked up the papers to read them again. There was still something that unsettled me about the Pinto case, not that I seriously expected to find the answer in the press.

'Telegram for you, sir.' I waited for the junior clerk to go before I tore it open. You didn't have to have lived through the war to experience a certain trepidation at the delivery of a telegram.

There were only two words to the message – two words so unexpected that my legs gave way beneath me. I was stunned, transfixed, feeling my heart slow and somersault. I tore my eyes away and turned to the window, as if expecting to find an explanation there. The distant noise of the city faded even further as I heard her voice speaking those two words. All these years had passed, and now, suddenly, today . . . I gazed down at the telegram again, my eyes hungry, wanting there to be more. Still there were just the two words: *Congratulations, Elizabeth.*

I must have sat there at my desk for almost an hour, staring into space, as slowly I unlocked the doors of my memory. I could see Foxton's so clearly that I might have been there yesterday. I heard the stampede of feet and the babel of young male voices as boys descended from dormitories. I saw the old building slumbering amid its lawns, the clearly-marked sports fields. I saw the classrooms, the dining-room, the Head's study. Then the cottage, the surgery and the railwayman's hut. And almost, just fleetingly . . . I jerked my head up, half expecting to see her eyes laughing back at me. But there were only the blank walls of my office in front of me, and I dropped my head in my hands. I had shut it all out for so long now, so much had happened since, and with the pain of the last few days . . .

I met Henry that evening at El Vino's. As the day wore on and the telegram worked its way into my subconscious as well as my conscious mind, I had ground myself into a near catatonic state of frustration and resentment.

'Two words! Two lousy words! Why doesn't she say where she is, for Christ's sake?'

Henry handed the telegram back. 'So I take it you want to know where she is?'

'Of course I do! I'm surprised you even need to ask.'

He shrugged, and let a long silence elapse before he spoke again. 'You don't need me to tell you how much you hurt her, Alexander. Maybe she's afraid you'll do it again.'

'Then why the telegram?'

'I think you can answer that for yourself.' He held up his hand as I started to speak. 'As far apart as your worlds were, you two were right for each other, you knew it, she knew it, we all knew it. Even Old Anger tried to make you face it, didn't she, when she came up to Oxford? I suppose this is Elizabeth's way of letting you know she still thinks about you, perhaps even that she wants to see you again. And if you want my advice, then go and find her. With everything that's happening to you at the moment, well . . . find her before you hurt anyone else, because I think quite enough people have suffered as a consequence of your bleeding heart.'

My immediate impulse was to get up from the table and tell him just what I thought of his agony aunt routine, but he caught hold of my arm and pulled me back down again.

'I'll tell you this for nothing, Alexander. You weren't the only one who missed her after she'd gone. I think about her too. And I've never understood why you refused to talk about her, especially to me. I'm supposed to be your best friend, for God's sake! So, you can talk now, and you can start by telling me – because I've always wanted to know – why the hell you let her go so easily.'

I felt my anger diminish, only to be replaced by the onset of that burning misery I had thought never to feel again. 'I wish I could answer that. All I know is that my father sounded so convincing. I think he even told me he had proof to connect her with those damned gypsies. I believed him when he said she'd made a fool of me; somehow at the time it all added up. But I tried to find her afterwards. You must remember that.'

Henry nodded. 'I also remember the pride that made you give up. The same pride that has hurt so many people since. So what are you going to do now?'

'What the hell can I do? It's as if she's some sort of a ghost come back to haunt me. She's there, but I can't touch her. Why now, after all these years, and like this?'

We neither of us had the answer to that, and the next two weeks dragged painfully by. I couldn't concentrate on anything as visions of the past flooded my mind to drown the present. My eyes strained across busy streets, trying to pick her out amongst the crowd. Every time the phone rang, the door opened, the postman knocked . . . The agony of waiting seemed endless. My relationship with Jessica deteriorated even further. Ever since the night she had told me I was incapable of fathering children, I had taken to sleeping in another room. Jessica, I soon discovered, was seeking solace in the arms of her new mentor, Thomas Street. I didn't care. If anything, I was glad. Jessica embodied all that was wrong with my life, and all I wanted was to get as far away from her as I could.

Then one morning I received a telephone call from my father. He wanted me to meet him at his club; there was a matter of great importance he needed to discuss with me.

My heart leapt into my throat. Had he found Elizabeth? Was he going to tell me that he had made a mistake all those years ago? My obsession was such that it didn't occur to me that my father might want to see me on an entirely different matter.

True to form, he wasted no time in coming to the point. The Pinto case. As I listened to what he was saying, I remembered all too vividly the hollow feeling I had had when I won. Now here it was again, this time stripped of its pretence, and revealed in all its horror. Ruth Pinto had been a British agent, not a Soviet one. The information she had been 'acquiring' for the Eastern Bloc had in fact been given her by the Minstry of Defence – and her communist masters were beginning to suspect her. The court case had been staged to allay their suspicions and to save Ruth, for once justice had been seen to be done, after a reasonable lapse of time she would have been quietly released from prison, whisked away somewhere and given a new identity. The bottom line, my father told me, was that the pseudo-trial had been engineered to save her life. As it was, due to my 'brilliant defence', she had been acquitted. Her body had been found the night before in an East Berlin street.

The whole thing seemed incredible. If my father hadn't been the Lord Chancellor I would have accused him of reading too many spy thrillers. What I wanted to know most of all was why I had not been told the truth from the beginning.

'That's simple,' my father answered. 'There were agents from the KGB in court. If you had known what was going on, it would have been bound to show in your defence. These people aren't stupid, Alexander. The whole thing had to be conducted as a bona fide case.'

'Then why the hell didn't the prosecution make a better job of things? They practically handed it to me on a plate.'

'You do yourself an injustice. What no one was prepared for was just how cleverly you would conduct the defence. Now don't flare up. You're still an inexperienced barrister. The brief could have gone to anyone, it just so happened that you were the one who attended the Section I at Clerkenwell. You became the obvious choice.'

'So I was set up?'

'No need to dramatise, Alexander.'

'I said, I was set up.'

'In a manner of speaking, yes.'

I drew breath to deliver my outrage, but he held up his hand to stop me. 'The case is closed now. But there is one other thing I wanted to tell you before you read it in the press. I shall be retiring at the end of this session.'

'Retiring!' I echoed. 'But you're only sixty-four.' Alarm bells began ringing in my head.

'And your mother is not far past fifty.' I was touched by his loyalty in not revealing her actual age. 'She's still young, Alexander, and I want to spend some time with her before it's too late. Nothing wrong in that, is there? You should try it some time, good for the old heart.'

'Heart? Have you had more warnings?'

'There's plenty of life left in this old dog yet. But yes – ' and I saw the veil drop from his eyes – 'the doctors are insisting. And what with your mother nagging away at me too, she'll probably do for me long before the old heart goes! I've given in. She's won – but then women always do.' He smiled as he spoke of my mother; they were still very much in love, even after all these years.

I swallowed hard. Though we had had our differences over the years, I loved my father.

'Come along, old chap,' he laughed, reaching out and clasping my arm, 'enough of the long face, can't have you weeping into your soup, now can we? Besides, I shan't be going anywhere yet awhile, that I can promise you. And as for you, well, you'd better brace yourself for the public humiliation that is very likely on its way.'

Never one to pull punches was my father.

The only good thing about finding myself back in the newspapers was that it might prompt Elizabeth to get in touch with me. But the days passed, and I heard nothing.

From time to time I took the telegram out of my pocket and looked at it, vainly searching for the telephone number that wasn't there. Henry and I met in El Vino's every evening, ostensibly to mull over the day's events in court, but in reality to commiserate with one another over our unfortunate marriages. Steeped in self-pity, I wasn't backward in pointing out to him that at least he saw Caroline.

'Not the same,' he slurred. 'I want her there all the time. Do you know, for the first time in my life someone else's happiness is more important than my own. Isn't that amazing?'

'Isn't that love?'

'Don't let's get shlushy, old chap.' And he got up to get more drinks.

'Do you think Elizabeth's happy?' I asked him when he returned.

'Can't be. Wouldn't have sent the telegram if she was.'

I knew I hadn't wanted him to reply in the affirmative, but thinking of her, maybe alone somewhere, and unhappy, was unbearable. 'I'm going to find her, Henry. If it kills me, I'm going to find her.'

– 18 –

Jessica was preparing the house for the big send-off we were giving Robert Lyttleton. At last he had attained his overseas posting, and would be flying to Baghdad at the beginning of the following week. It had been Jessica's idea that we hold the party – as much, I guessed, to avail herself of another opportunity of flaunting a 'real man' in my face, as to say good-bye to Robert.

At various intervals during the morning she bumped open the door of my study to regale me with yet another problem that had cropped up, and enquire whether I didn't think I should do something about it. My refusal was unvarying, and she would slam out again, hissing obscenities – under her breath so the hired help wouldn't hear. After lunch, which was a sandwich behind the now locked door of my study, Lizzie and the florist arrived. Unable to think why it hadn't occurred to me before, I snatched up my coat and went off to play a round of golf with Henry.

Later, when we returned to Belgrave Square with Henry boasting his victory, Jessica and Lizzie were nowhere to be found. 'Gone shopping,' Mrs Dixon informed us. So Henry and I decided to make a start on the champagne. By five o'clock they still weren't back, and Henry sauntered off to Eaton Square to get his head down for an hour.

I was in my study when I heard Jessica and Lizzie come in, but didn't bother to get up. I was going over a file that a private investigator had delivered to my chambers the day before. Not that there was anything much to read – all I'd been able to give him to go on was the telegram, and that, he discovered, had been sent from a post office in Chelsea. It heightened my frustration no end to think that she could be so close. I picked up the telegram and read it again. Then angrily I crumpled it into a tiny ball. Damn her! Why was she doing this to me?'

A snigger from the doorway brought me round sharp. Jessica was holding two glasses while Lizzie filled them with champagne. 'Poor Alexander,' she sighed. 'Is he dreaming about his long lost lover again, do you think?'

Lizzie tutted and giggled. 'Would you like some champagne, Alexander darling?' She held the bottle towards me, but I ignored it and glared at Jessica.

'I don't think Alexander wants any champagne, Jess.'

'No, I guess not.' Jessica clinked her glass against Lizzie's. 'Let's drink to my darling husband. Should we tell him our little secret, Lizzie? What do you think?'

'I don't know. Shall we?'

Jessica looked at me. 'No, I don't think so. He'll only get cross.' And, giggling, they started to walk out of the room.

'Tell me what?' I demanded.

'Nothing,' Jessica threw over her shoulder. 'Come along, Lizzie, let's go and see how Mrs Dixon is getting on in the kitchen.'

'Have you been holding something back from me, you bitch! What is it? A letter? Where have you hidden it?'

'Oh, he thinks he's had a letter,' Jessica said. She turned back to me. 'No darling, not a letter.'

'Then what?'

'I'll tell him, Jess, shall I?' said Lizzie.

'Yes, you tell him.'

'Alexander. What's my name?' She smiled and nodded her head. 'I think he's beginning to get it already, Jess. That's right, Alexander, my name's Lizzie. And what is Lizzie a derivative of? That's right, Elizabeth. Congratulations, Alexander.' And shrieking with laughter, they walked out of the room.

After they'd left my study I sat staring into space, not daring to move, afraid of what I might do if I did. Eventually I picked up the phone and rang Henry. Briefly I told him what had happened. He swore he would beat Lizzie to within an inch of her life, but by that time my temper had abated, and a feeling of defeat had set in. I told him not to mention it, saying that it would be better if from now on we just forgot it had ever happened.

The evening didn't go with the swing we had hoped it would. Jessica and I could barely be civil to each other, and matters weren't helped by the presence of Robert's mother. Naturally, neither Jessica nor Lizzie could resist the odd oblique, barbed reference to our affair. I was past caring, but there were twelve others present, mostly old friends of Robert's; they, and Rachel, were clearly embarrassed. Robert got roaring drunk, so did Lizzie. Jessica disappeared for half an hour at one stage, and then I noticed Robert was missing too. I felt sick. My only hope was that she would get pregnant. It would be good enough grounds for a quick and uncomplicated divorce.

Around eleven several people drifted off, and I walked Rachel to the door.

'I couldn't help but notice how bad things are between you and Jessica,' she remarked, as I held out her coat for her.

'An understatement, Rachel.'

'You look tired, and you've lost weight.'

'That's what a bad marriage does for you.'

'Then get out of it. You're young, you don't have any children to consider. Get out now, while you still can.'

'I'm seriously thinking about it.'

'Do it. I know things didn't work out well for us in the

end, but I cared about you, Alexander. I still do. And despite everything I said that day, I know that behind that handsome façade of yours there's a good and decent man. The trouble is, between you, you and Jessica are suffocating him.'

I gave a sad smile, and drew her into my arms. 'Did I really treat you so badly, Rachel?'

'One way or another you've treated everyone badly. Time to stop, eh?' She opened the door.

'Excuse me, sir. I'm looking for Lizzie Roseman.'

Rachel and I turned to find a tall blond man standing on the pavement outside, shuffling uncomfortably from one foot to the other as if he were more than ready to move on. The collar of a purplish check shirt appeared above the neck of his fur-lined leather jacket, and his jeans, which had seen better days, were stuffed inside the legs of what looked like size fourteen cowboy boots. All he needed to complete his appearance was a cork-dangled hat and a can of lager.

'Er, maybe you know her better as Lizzie Poynter,' he said, when neither Rachel nor I answered him. 'I'm told her sister, Jessica, lives here.'

'I think I'll be on my way,' Rachel said. She leaned over and kissed me on the cheek. 'Think about what I said.' And she ran off down the steps. The man smiled pleasantly as she passed him, and doffed the invisible hat. I followed her down the steps and asked what he might want with Lizzie. He hooked his thumbs through his jean loops, as if trying to give himself a confidence he was clearly far from feeling, and leaned against the pillar of the porch. I listened in stupefied silence as this stranger, who had appeared out of the darkness on a cold and windy March night, told me who he was, and why he was looking for my sister-in-law. In the end I asked him to wait, and went inside to fetch Henry.

I let him take a good look at the man standing at the door before I made the introduction. 'Henry Clive, meet

John Roseman. Or should I put it another way. Henry, meet Lizzie's husband.'

After the shock had worn off, a rather cosy little party developed. Lizzie had been horrified when John followed Henry and me in through the drawing-room door, but her horror soon changed to delight as the Australian turned on all the charm that had probably made her marry him in the first place. Henry, I noticed, sat back and watched the proceedings with detached interest.

We learned that Lizzie had married John some four years ago, while she had been travelling round Australia. By all accounts it had been something of a whirlwind romance; they'd known each other a total of three months before she walked out and left him. Quite why she walked out we were never told, but I suppose that was their business. She seemed wholly unconcerned that she had committed bigamy, and so too did Henry and John. Jessica, I noticed, said nothing, and I soon realised that she had known about John all along. It was decided that as Henry was a lawyer he should sort the whole thing out – John would do anything he had to do to help – and with that, Lizzie and her new-found husband left. To go where? Heaven only knew, and Henry didn't care.

I was dumbfounded. Between the time of John's arrival and his departure, I don't think I'd uttered more than a dozen words.

'Always did like the Aussies,' Henry said, putting on his overcoat to go. 'Get in touch with their embassy, old chap. See if they can't rustle up a little something for you too.'

'I might just do that,' I laughed. 'Something's got to be done. Robert Lyttleton had her tonight. D'you think he could be persuaded to take her with him?'

'Not a chance.'

As I turned back inside I saw Jessica standing at the drawing-room door. From the look on her face there was no doubt she had heard every word. I walked towards her, heading for my study, and as I brushed past, her voice snaked over me.

'I'll never let you go, Alexander, so don't even think it.'

In the early hours of the morning she crept into my bed and cried as though her heart might break. Understanding her pain, I held her in my arms and wondered what the hell was to become of us.

When Henry and Caroline announced the date of their wedding it was impossible not to share in their long-delayed happiness, though I had to admit to more than an occasional stab of envy. After that one night of tenderness Jessica and I had, yet again, talked long and hard about our relationship, but this time there was no point in fooling myself: I would never be able to trust her again, and whatever love I'd had for her had been killed the day I found out about the telegram. I was as faithful to her now as she could have wished but my fidelity was born of my impotency, not of love, and she knew it. She tormented and ridiculed me for what she called my 'defective organ', but if I threatened to leave her, she threatened in return to tell the world how 'the great Alexander Belmayne couldn't get it up'. She even went so far as to hang a plaque over my bed quoting William Congreve's words: *Heav'n has no rage, like love to hatred turn'd, Nor Hell a fury, like a woman scorn'd.* These two lines epitomised our relationship so perfectly it would have been laughable had it not been so tragic.

No longer able to prove myself in the bedroom, I threw myself into work. My professional reputation was growing, and I took on more than it was humanly possible to cope with. In the end Henry took me to task and tried to persuade me to seek psychiatric help before I killed myself with overwork. I told him to mind his own business, and that I was perfectly capable of sorting out my own life. But the dilemma grew. I wanted children, now more than ever. I wanted them so badly, I would find myself smiling at them in shops, or walking the parks in order to watch them play. I felt sick at myself for such a display of weakness, but my yearning was too strong to be denied.

It was on one such day, while I was walking in Hyde Park, that I felt something knock against my legs. I looked down to see a girl's small face gazing up at me – she was laughing despite her fall. She had been running away from a hot air balloon that had rolled towards her while someone was trying to inflate it. I bent down to put her back on her feet, expecting her to run away, but she lingered, looking me over in the curious way children have, until a woman appeared beside us.

'There you are, I thought I'd lost you under the balloon.'

I could see the woman was nervous at finding the child with a stranger, so I stood up and smiled, wanting to reassure her. 'No harm done,' I said, and ruffled the girl's hair. 'Definitely all in one piece.'

The girl's face broke into a smile that turned my heart over, then allowing the woman to take her by the hand, she walked off. I watched them go, the thin legs of the girl skipping along beside the elegant, though stiff figure in canary yellow.

That night was one of the rare occasions on which Jessica and I sat down for dinner together. I was relieved to see that she was moderately sober and in a better mood than usual – the following week she was to have an exhibition of her own in a Bayswater gallery. She chattered gaily on in her excitement, not really interested in what I might have to say, but obviously glad to have someone to talk to. After a time I found myself telling her about the little girl, and how I often walked alone in the park. To my surprise she seemed genuinely touched. Despite the turbulence of our relationship, there were still rare moments of tenderness between us, and when she came to sit beside me I slipped an arm around her and sighed wearily.

'What are we going to do about us, Jess? We can't go on hurting each other the way we do.'

She turned to face me, and brushed the hair away from my face. 'Do you want a divorce, is that what you're saying?'

Was that what I was saying? The truth was, I didn't think I did want a divorce. If Jessica so despised me for my infertility, how could I be sure that that wasn't the way all women felt about men like me? And despite all she said, Jessica still stayed with me. Perhaps that counted for something. In the end I said: 'I don't know, Jess. I just don't know. But you've got to admit we do seem to bring out the worst in each other.'

'Not all of the time. Sometimes we're good together. And I've been thinking.'

'What have you been thinking?' I asked, when she didn't go on. 'Come on, you're cooking something.'

'Let's just say it's something that's going to surprise you, and make you very happy.'

'And what might that be?'

'I'm not telling. Not yet anyway. But what I will tell you, is that despite the way we hurt each other, despite everything I say, I do still lo – '

I put my fingers over her lips. 'No, don't say it.'

The light went from her eyes and I heard her swallow. 'If I can't say it, Alexander, then maybe . . . Well, I know it's been a long time, but maybe you'll let me show you?'

'Oh, Jess, it won't change anything. You know that.'

But it did. It changed everything.

It was May 4th. I will always remember the date because it was Jessica's birthday. Fortunately her mother rang me the day before to remind me, thus avoiding what would inevitably have been yet another showdown between us.

Her mother was also good enough to suggest what I could buy her.

I was at the Old Bailey all day, engaged in legal arguments for a fraud case. I had thought we might finish in plenty of time for me to get to Christie's, where I was going to bid for a plique-à-jour pendant, but the judge wanted to know far more than a judge normally did in these cases, and it was past four-thirty when we came out. The auction wasn't until six, but I had to call in at chambers on the way to see if there were any returns for the following week. There were, so it was another three quarters of an hour before I got away. I dashed out to Fleet Street and flagged down a passing taxi. The traffic was especially bad, as it always was when it had been raining, and I was already racking my brains for an alternative plan if I didn't get to Christie's on time. However, after a few neat back-doubles and even more near-misses, the driver got me there.

'Hope it's worth it,' he said, as I jumped out.

'So do I,' I laughed, as I delved into my pocket for the fare. I was on the point of handing it over when my eyes were drawn to someone standing further along the pavement, outside Spinks.

The cab driver leaned over and took the money. 'Something the matter, guv?' he called.

When I didn't answer he must have driven off, because I was standing alone, people pushing past me, hurrying to get out of the rain. My briefcase fell against my legs, and still I stood there.

And then I started to run. I wasn't thinking, I wasn't aware of what I was doing or what I intended, I just ran. As I turned into St James's Square I saw her disappear into Duke of York Street. I think I called out her name, but she couldn't have heard because she didn't turn round. I ran faster, until there was no more than ten yards between us. Then she stopped, took down her umbrella and ran up the steps to Jules' Bar in Jermyn Street.

The bar was crowded, and when I looked round I couldn't see her. Someone behind me vacated a chair, so I sat down. The waitress came and I ordered a Scotch. Five minutes passed, then ten. I looked down at my glass and told myself I had been a fool. I'd been so sure it was her, but even if it had been, what then? Damn it! What kind of idiot was I, running down the street after strange women? My hand curled tightly around the glass, my eyes searching every face that passed.

I finished my drink and got to my feet. My mind, shamed by my foolish behaviour, was already turning to Jessica, trying to concoct some excuse for having missed the auction. If I hadn't stood back to let a group of people through from the bar, I might never have seen her.

I could say that at that moment the room seemed to go quiet, but of course it didn't. I could say that my heartbeat changed, but I don't know if that would be true. All I knew was that Elizabeth was there, at the bar, talking to another woman and laughing as she stirred her drink.

I tried to move and found that my feet were like lead weights. Ever since that telegram I'd thought of little else but what I'd do if I saw her again. Now that the moment had come, all I could do was slump back into my chair and order another Scotch.

After a while she picked up her bag and started to walk towards me. She would have walked straight past, but I was on my feet. Feeling my hand on her arm she turned round, and the moment she saw me the blood drained from her face.

'Alexander?'

I tried to smile. 'Hello, Elizabeth.'

We looked at each other for some time as if unsure whether there might be some mistake, until, suddenly agitated, she turned to see if the woman at the bar was watching us.

'How are you?' I asked.

'Oh, I'm fine. Fine. How are you?'

She wasn't looking at me, and I felt my control beginning to slip away. 'Can we talk?' She seemed uncertain and glanced round again, nervously. 'Elizabeth.'

She must have seen the anguish on my face, because for an instant her eyes softened. 'Not now. Christine will recognise you.'

'When?'

I could see the indecision reeling through her mind. 'Can you wait here? I can come back in half an hour. Christine has to meet someone then.'

My heart soared. It was more than I could have hoped for. 'I'll wait.'

Almost an hour passed before she returned, and in that time I experienced such dread as I have never known before or since. The crowd had thinned out a bit by then, and I had managed to get a table in the corner. I stood up and waved as I saw her come in.

'A white wine, please.' She smiled at the waitress as she took the order.

My eyes scanned her face, and it was some time before either of us said anything. In the end she was the first to speak.

'I hardly recognised you.' Her hand trembled on the glass as she lifted it to her mouth. 'You're um . . . well, you're . . . older.'

'Twenty-four.'

'Of course. Four years younger than me.'

'Almost five,' I corrected her with a grin.

She laughed, and I can barely describe the joy I felt. Seven years had passed, seven years in which she had become more beautiful, more contained, somehow more aloof. Her hair was pulled back from her face, showing small amber studs in her ears. Her skin looked smooth and olive, and her dark eyes slanted as she smiled. Everything about her was stylish, from the way she moved her hands and folded one leg neatly over the other, down to the tan suede purse that matched the suede insets of the leather jodhpur-suit she wore. She had a sophistication that was almost too perfect, yet when she laughed I saw the Elizabeth I'd known – the Elizabeth I'd loved.

'I've often wondered what happened to you, after . . .' I looked up and saw that she was watching me. 'I tried to find you.'

'I went back to my family.' She was still watching me, the challenge clear in her eyes.

'I was wrong . . . my father, we were wrong about you, weren't we?'

She nodded. 'It doesn't matter now, though. It's all in the past.'

'Nevertheless . . .'

'How about another glass of wine? My treat.'

I laughed. 'The answer is, OK, we'll change the subject.'

After the waitress had brought the wine we talked for a time about Miss Angrid, united in our guilt that we never wrote to her now. We talked about the weather, about my father becoming Lord Chancellor, and about the queues for the Tutankhamun Exhibition that had just opened at the British Museum.

She leaned forward, resting her hands on the table, and our knees touched. She jerked hers away so quickly that for a moment there was an embarrassed silence between us. Then we laughed. I picked up her hand from the table, half expecting her to pull it away, but she didn't. Twisting the wedding band round her finger I asked her how long she'd been married, trying to keep the pain from my voice.

'Almost three years.'

'Tell me about him.'

She did. As she talked I began to feel as though it had been weeks since we'd last seen each other, rather than years. She sounded bright – too bright – as she told me about Edward and David, and I knew there was something she was hiding. I didn't ask her about it, but a sixth sense told me that whatever it was was causing her pain. Then she made me laugh by telling me about Christine's crush on me.

'Christine? The woman you were with at the bar?'

She nodded. 'Quite besotted with you. A good job she didn't see you.'

I shrugged. 'Not my type. Too round. Besides, women with severe faces frighten the life out of me.'

She threw me a look, then went on to tell me about Violet May, who had gazed into a crystal ball and told her that we would meet again. When I raised my eyebrows, she kicked me. And as I gazed into the eyes that I had tried so hard to forget, I could see so clearly how empty my life had been.

She looked away, trying to hide the colour that had crept into her cheeks.

'Why did you never get in touch with me again?' I asked.

'For lots of reasons. You were so young, Alexander. You had your whole life ahead of . . .'

'A life I wanted to spend with you. You knew that.'

'You could have changed your mind.'

I looked down at our hands entwined on the table. 'There are a host of platitudes that either one of us might come out with now,' I said, 'but let's take them as read. Don't let's lie to each other. Yes, perhaps we are different people now, but that doesn't change the past. What I'm trying to say, Elizabeth, is that I want to see you again, that we can't just walk out of here as if nothing has happened.'

'No, I don't want that either. But – '

'If we could turn back the clocks, which moment would you choose?' I was half teasing her, and she laughed, but it sounded sad.

'We were on our way to Sark. And I was going to tell you . . .' She shrugged.

Putting my finger under her chin, I tilted her face up to look at me. 'What were you going to tell me?'

She smiled and shook her head. 'Nothing.'

'Will you come there with me now?'

She stared at me.

'Will you?'

She pulled her hands away then, and tucked them into her pockets. Her eyes scanned the room then fell to her wine. I knew she was going to look anywhere but at me, and I could feel her slipping away.

'Elizabeth. Please, Elizabeth, just listen to me. I probably have no right to say this, but I'm going to say it anyway. I still love you, at least I think I do, but I've got to find out for certain. And if the past seven years have been as much hell for you as they have for me, then for God's sake don't you think we owe it to ourselves to try again?'

She didn't speak for a long time, and when she did she covered her face with her hands. 'You don't know how I've dreamed that one day I would hear you say that. How many times I – ' She looked up, and through her tears she was laughing. 'Seeing you now, touching you, hearing you, I don't need to find out, Alexander, I already know.'

I reached up to wipe the tears from her face, and she turned to kiss my hand. 'The answer is yes,' she whispered. 'Yes, I'll come with you.'

– 19 –

The initial awkwardness of meeting again, this time in the cold light of morning, was augmented by Elizabeth's guilt at leaving her daughter. Throughout the short flight to Guernsey she tried hard not to let me see how she was fretting, but by the time we stepped off the plane I could tell she was near to tears. Unable to bear her anguish, I took her in my arms and told her I would book us seats on the next flight back to London.

'I want to be with you, Alexander,' she said.

'You will be. We can always see each other in London, as often as you like. I just don't want you to be unhappy.'

'I'm not. I won't be. I know in my heart that Charlotte will be all right. She's with people who love her, she probably won't even miss me.' She tried to laugh and I watched her face as she fought with her emotions. 'I can't seem to think. I've wanted this for so long, but now . . .'

'These yours, squire?'

We looked round to see a baggage-handler hauling our suitcases off the conveyor belt. It wasn't a particularly educated guess he'd made as everyone else had long since departed. I thanked him, took our cases, and turned back to Elizabeth.

'I'm afraid, Alexander. I'm afraid of the way I feel. And afraid to go back again in case I lose you.'

'You won't lose me, darling. I promise, you'll never lose me again. If you want to go home then all you have to do is say.'

For a long time she stared down at our luggage, her hands now firmly stuffed inside her coat pockets, her hair falling around her face. When at last she looked up her eyes were swimming with tears. 'I think we'd better hurry if we don't want to miss the boat, don't you?'

I felt such a rush of relief that I dropped the bags and gathered her into my arms.

'Do you suppose we're being dreadfully selfish?' she asked, when we were aboard the ferry.

'Dreadfully,' I replied, without a moment's hesitation. 'Not to mention irresponsible, self-indulgent . . .'

'You're begining to remind me of that awful schoolboy I used to know.'

'And if you remember, I was always at my very worst when I was with you.' She laughed and looked away, but not before I saw the colour that had come to her cheeks. 'Almost,' I added, 'as bad as you.'

By the time we docked at Creux Harbour the barrier that had risen between us that morning had disappeared. A horse and carriage carried us up over the steep hill towards our hotel, and Elizabeth was almost childlike in her enthusiasm for the rugged beauty that greeted us. Wild spring flowers spread between the trees and hedgerows, creating a carpet of violet blue that swayed in the breeze, and the winding pathways that eased into the long grass promised even more celebrations of undisturbed nature. On either side of the crumbling road, primroses peeped out of the banks, smiling into the face of the sun. I watched Elizabeth as she looked all about her, absorbing her surroundings, her eyes sparkling with joy.

'Oh, Alexander!' she cried, 'it's so beautiful!' And I pulled her into my arms . . . . As I kissed her it was as if all the knots inside me were unravelling. As if some secret place inside me that had always belonged to her and had lain cold and deserted for seven years, was opening up to her. I felt so alive. When finally I let her go, her cheeks were flushed, and I was embarrassed to see that several of the locals were standing at the side of the road, watching us, each one of them sporting a grin that practically hooked onto their ears.

The seventeenth-century hotel was at the top of the wooded hill that led down to Dixcart Bay. The porch was bright with hanging flower-baskets, and an old Bassett hound lay across the front step, slumbering peacefully in the afternoon sun.

After checking in we followed someone who turned out to be the chef, up the rickety stairs to our room. I hadn't missed Elizabeth's quick look as she heard me announce us as Mr and Mrs Belmayne.

When the chef finally departed, after proudly pointing out every eccentric nook and cranny of our room, which was made even more bewildering by the oddness of decor, Elizabeth went to the windows and pulled back the curtains. I went to stand beside her, and it was as I slipped my arms around her waist that I realised how very nervous she was now that we were alone. I let her go, but kept her hand in mine as we stood looking together over the gardens that sloped down to the bluebell woods beyond.

I sensed her relief when I suggested we take a walk, and once outside in the crisp May sunshine, her light-hearted mood returned. We wandered down the steep, tree-lined path to the bay where we stood for a long time, watching the tide as it roared against the cliffs. Five or six yachts bobbed on the horizon but otherwise there was no sign of human life; we could have been the only people in the world.

Feeling her hand slip into mine I looked down at her and smiled.

'Are you really here?' she whispered.

I brushed the hair from her face and touched my lips against her nose. 'Yes, my love, I'm really here.'

By the time we returned to the hotel, night was drawing in. I carried our drinks outside and we sat in the darkening courtyard huddled into our coats, watching the shifting shadows, listening to the stirrings of invisible night sounds.

We talked long into the evening, telling each other about our lives. I told her how Lizzie had sent the telegram that I had thought was from her; 'I wish it had been,' she said, and I saw tears fill her eyes.

'You haven't said up until now, and maybe it's none of my business, but where did you tell Jessica you were going?' she asked, after a while.

'Just, away.'

'But wasn't she curious to know where?'

I shrugged. 'If she was, she didn't ask.' I didn't add that

we had had a blazing row when I had arrived home late, without her birthday pendant. In fact, it was because of the fight that I hadn't had to elaborate on where I was going. I merely packed a bag and told her I'd be back in a week. Her parting words, screamed from the top of her lungs, had been: 'Don't bother!'

'And you?' I asked. 'What did you tell your husband?'

'I didn't have to. He's in New York at the moment.' At the mention of her husband, she seemed to close herself off. I said nothing, understanding that this was a part of her life that was hers alone. Then, as the moment passed, she was smiling again, and asking me about Henry.

She laughed when I told her the incredible story of his bigamous marriage. 'But now it's all worked out perfectly,' she sighed wistfully, when I'd finished. 'And when will he be marrying Caroline?'

'Sooner than they intended. She's pregnant, or so he told me when I called him last night.'

'You spoke to him last night? Did you tell him about . . .'

'Yes.'

She sighed again. 'So Henry Clive is going to become a father. It hardly seems credible. I still think of him as the boy I used to know. I'm glad he's happy.' She turned in her seat. 'And you, Alexander, are you happy?'

I picked her hand up from the table. 'Now I am. Yes.'

'Me too.'

I lifted her hand to my lips. 'What are you thinking?' I asked, when she had remained silent for several minutes.

She shook her head. 'I'm sorry, but I can't help it. I was thinking about Charlotte, wishing she was here, wondering if she's all right. I suppose it's thinking about Henry, and oh . . . I don't know . . .'

I squeezed her hand. 'Don't be sorry. Tell me about her. How old is she?'

Slowly she entwined her hands round mine and stared down at them for a long time. 'She's beautiful, she's naughty, she's everything in the world to me, just like . . .' She looked up with a quick smile. 'Was that your stomach telling us it's time for dinner?'

I laughed and tweaked her nose, and at the same time was ashamed of my relief that she had gone no further. I didn't want to confront my feelings about Charlotte. It seemed ludicrous to be jealous of a child, but I knew I was. Even worse were the feelings I experienced whenever I thought of Charlotte's father. Unbidden images of the three of them, and their togetherness, were already eating away at me like a cancer. And the fact that he had been able to give Elizabeth something I could never give her razored my mind.

When we got upstairs Elizabeth threw her coat on the bed and went to close the curtains. When she turned round she stopped as she saw me standing against the door, watching her in the semi-darkness; she started to speak, then stopped, and I held her gaze with my own. All I wanted just then was to look at her, and in the silence neither of us moved.

'Standing there like that, you remind me of the Alexander I knew when he was seventeen.' There was a slight catch in her voice.

When I didn't answer she gave an uncertain laugh, then covered her face with her hands. 'Oh God, I can't believe this is happening. Tell me I'm not dreaming, Alexander. Hold me, please hold me.'

At the note of desperation in her voice my heart twisted, and taking her in my arms I held her close. 'My darling, oh my darling. God, how I've needed you. How I've wanted you.'

I drew back to look at her. 'Don't let me go,' she whispered. 'Don't ever let me go.' She lifted her mouth and as I covered her lips with my own I felt her begin to tremble.

Wave after wave of longing swept through my body, and when, minutes later, she stepped naked into my arms, my fear of impotency was over. I ran my hands over her back, and through her heavy hair, piling it on to her head; I pulled her face to mine, moulding my lips and my tongue into her mouth. She stood against me, pressing the length of her body against mine, until gently I lifted her into my arms and laid her on the bed.

Slowly our bodies began to move together. She whispered as she kissed me and I whispered too, making up for all the years I had been unable to tell her how much I loved her. Her skin was so soft and I held her close, as if afraid she might slip away. I had forgotten what it was truly to make love with a woman, when passion was born of love, not lust; when the mouth you were kissing was the only mouth you would ever want to kiss, and the body that moulded into yours was the one without which yours would never be complete. 'Elizabeth, Elizabeth.' I said her name, over and over, never moving my lips from hers.

The hazy light of dawn was beginning to penetrate the windows when finally, exhausted by the depth of our love, we fell asleep.

Running away, expecting everything to be the same after so long, was madness of course. But madness or not, it was not the present that seemed unreal to us, but the years we had been apart. To have the chance to tell each other at last, how we'd felt when we parted, and how we'd thought of each other in the years that followed, was like a gift from heaven. Elizabeth had changed, so had I, and the changes sometimes delighted us, sometimes saddened us. But there was no awkwardness between us, everything we did felt as natural and as easy as if we had always been together. It wasn't that either of us had forgotten what we had left behind, it was simply that it didn't seem to matter. This time belonged to us. I watched her, the slant of her eyes, the slow curl of her smile and the gentle rise and fall of her breasts. The sense of recognition I had as she flicked her hair from her face, as she used her elegant fingers to emphasise what she was saying, as I watched the easy movements of her long legs when we walked about the island – was mesmerising. Just listening to her as she laughed and talked, or watching her eyes darken with love, rushed warmth through my veins.

The sea spread like wings on either side of us as we cycled north to Greve de la Ville, La Banquette and Eperquerie Landing. The road – which was no more than a cart track – was rough, and Elizabeth, not one of the world's greatest cyclists, swore as she ploughed into one pot-hole after another. I yelled with laughter when she threw her bike into a hedge, declaring she would be more comfortable on a three-legged camel. I managed to catch her as she started to stomp off up the road, and spun her round. Then making sure no one was in sight, I rubbed my hands soothingly over her buttocks and thighs, asking if that felt any better. Her eyes were bright as she answered.

The only sounds were those of the birds and the sea. As we rode on, a sweet fragrance of coconut wafted gently by on the breeze and the occasional cow favoured us with a lazy glance. Now and again we stopped, on the pretext of looking at something unusual or resting our legs, but really all we wanted to do was touch each other, and kiss.

We climbed down to the Boutiques Caves, where we sat for a while watching the waves. Elizabeth got up and strolled to the mouth of a cave to look inside. All around us there was an air of mystical romance. If you close your eyes long enough, I told her, you can hear the ghosts of smugglers hauling their booty into the bay. She stood quietly for several minutes, straining her ears for the sounds. With one eye partially open I watched her and tried not to laugh.

'Aar Haar! And what sort of contraband 'ave we 'ere?' It was my best smuggler's voice, and scooping her up in my arms I ran with her into the cave.

'Oh help! Put me down, put me down, you beast.'

I did, and she threw herself against the wall of the cave. 'Oh no, please don't ravish me, I beg you!'

'All right.' I doffed an invisible cap. 'If you don't wish to be ravished, my lady, then far be it from me to press my attentions.'

'Alexander!'

'You called, my lady?' I sighed wearily and turned back. 'Do I take it you want to be ravished, my lady?'

She nodded, and fell into my arms, almost speechless with laughter.

We roamed beaches I have now forgotten the names of, carrying our shoes and gasping as the icy sea washed over our toes. So often I felt her eyes on me, and when I turned to her she would laugh and throw her arms round my neck. And then I would watch her – laughing, frowning, running away from me, gasping for breath as she looked back to find that I was nowhere in sight. And when she came looking I would spring out from behind my rock and topple her to the ground, drowning her shrieks with kisses.

Later we rode horses out on to the cliffs that overlooked Dixcart Bay. Far beneath us the sun sparkled across the sea, and behind, keeping a lonely vigil, was Jespillière House. We walked round it, peering in through the windows. It looked as if it had been deserted for many years. We decided we would buy it, and began a game of what we would do when it was ours. We would buy two rocking-chairs for the veranda, where we could sit on balmy nights watching the sun go down over the sea. And facing the middle window upstairs we would set our bed, so that each morning we could look out and watch the day stirring into life. Elizabeth wanted chintz curtains, I wanted plain. She wanted oak panels, I wanted walnut. She wanted grey carpet, I wanted green. She wanted four children, I wanted . . .

I smiled, then taking the reins of my horse, I led it to the edge of the meadow. There was a gap in the gorse, so letting my horse go to graze freely, I dropped down on to a ledge in the cliff. To one side I found an old stone seat that had been carved into the rocks, and sat down.

Our little game of plans for the future, which had started so innocently, had ended by serving as a bitter reminder to me. I asked myself what I was doing here. Hadn't I hurt Elizabeth enough before, without needing to do it all over again? Perhaps I should tell her now, before her dreams became so real that she believed them. But how could I? What we had together, here, so far from the harsh realities of our everyday lives, was too perfect to shatter. And, just like her, I wanted to imagine our children playing on the veranda, riding their ponies in the meadow, calling to us to watch them. I needed my dreams too. What did it matter if they could never be? For now they were all we had, and I couldn't take them away from her. And though I hated myself for the lies, I would deal with them later, when we were far away from here.

I ran my tongue over my lips, tasting the bitter salt that had carried on the wind from the sea. I could hear her picking her way through the undergrowth towards me, and I dashed my hand across my eyes. I hated this weakness – this curse of infertility that made a grown man cry tears of self-pity.

She came to sit beside me and linked her fingers through mine. Somewhere in the distance a dog began to bark, discordant against the background sough of the waves. Seagulls cawed, and somewhere the engine of a speed-boat roared into life. Then all was still again.

'Alexander? Is everything all right?'

'All right? Of course it is.' Down in the bay two people were rowing out to their trimaran and I leaned forward to watch them boarding.

'You're very quiet suddenly.'

'Just soaking up the atmosphere.'

She waited. 'Alexander, you're not being honest with me.'

I sat back. How could I have thought that I would be able to fob her off with inanities? I lifted a lock of her hair and wound it round my finger, looking into her face and seeing bewilderment and fear where earlier there had been only love. I smiled.

'I know there's something,' she said, her eyes searching mine. 'Darling, please tell me.'

I slipped an arm around her. 'There's nothing. Only the fact that I love you so much it frightens me.'

For a long time she looked into my eyes. I met her gaze, willing myself not to look away. Then slowly she lifted her hands, and placing them on either side of my face, she kissed me, slowly, and with the greatest tenderness I had ever known.

On the second day I took her to Little Sark. It was a steep and difficult climb down the cliffs, but when we finally reached the bottom, I knew I had been right to come. This would be our special place, this tiny pool – Venus Pool – that was scooped deep into the rocks, hiding away beneath a hanging boulder. The water was clear and blue so that we could see the pebbles at the bottom. And behind us the sea roared on to the surrounding cliffs, growling as if to protect its young. The sun was hot and we lay down beside the pool, holding hands and feeling the breeze sweep gently over our faces. Every sense was touched by nature.

After a while I opened my eyes. I could tell from her steady breathing that Elizabeth was sleeping. I turned on to my side to look at her, and as my eyes roamed slowly over her face I felt my heart swell. Her olive skin was smooth beneath my fingers as I lightly touched her cheeks. She was the most beautiful woman I had ever known. But it wasn't only her physical beauty, there was another kind of beauty too; it was what made her the woman she was. I thought of Jessica then. She would never understand why I loved Elizabeth so much. I wondered if she would be looking for me now. Would she care at all where I was? My marriage had been a lie from the start, and I knew now what a fool I had been to think I could use it to forget Elizabeth. What a mess I had made of all our lives!

'Alexander, come down from there.' I had climbed the rocks while she slept, and was lying on the boulder that overhung the pool, looking up at the sky.

'No.' I smiled to myself as I heard her laugh.

'Please come down.'

'I can't. The tide's practically in, there's no way through. I'm afraid you're stranded.'

'What!'

'I tried to wake you but you were snoring so loudly it drowned out my voice.'

Her voice was bubbling with laughter as she answered, 'I don't snore! And I'm not stranded either.'

'How do you know?'

'Because if the tide really was coming in, which it's not, you wouldn't have left me here.'

'I wouldn't?' I raised myself on one elbow. 'And what makes you so sure of that?'

'You love me too much, that's what.'

'Do I?'

She nodded. 'Yep. In fact, I bet if I asked you to prove it by jumping into the pool right now, fully clothed, you'd do it.'

'Ask me.'

She asked.

'No,' I said, and she burst out laughing. I got to my feet and descended by the dry route.

'I missed you,' she said, as I put my arms around her.

I lifted my hand to her chin and stroked my thumb over her face. 'Shall I tell you ten reasons why Miss Sorrill is the best?' I whispered. 'One, because she looks lovely when she smiles. Two, because she says outrageous things. Three . . .'

I laughed as I saw the look on her face. 'You – you know about that?'

I nodded. 'I should, I wrote it.'

'*You* wrote it! But I always thought it was Mark Devenish! Why didn't you ever . . .'

'Sssh,' I whispered. 'Just kiss me.'

When I let her go she began to unbutton her dress, her eyes holding mine. I watched her until, naked, she walked to the edge of the pool. All around her shapeless formations of rock pushed against the horizon, and set against that harsh and uncompromising background the silhouette of her body appeared infinitely vulnerable. She glanced over her shoulder and smiled at me, but I was holding my breath at the vision of incomparable beauty. Then she was gone. The water parted and I waited for her to resurface. When she did, her hair floated round her and she smiled and waved. Then she drifted on to her back, presenting her body to me, the full breasts caressed by ripples, the thatch of black pubic hair silky at the join of her long legs. She was watching me watching her. Then taking off my clothes, I slipped into the pool and we swam together.

Looking back now, I think we both knew how selfish we were being, but at the time we were so much in love that nothing else seemed to matter. I listened for hours while she told me about the fairground and Violet May. Then I basked in her admiration as I told her about the cases I had been involved in, shamelessly exaggerating my successes. I'm sure she knew what I was doing, but nevertheless allowed me to wander on in my own fantasy world – until, with an ear-shattering snore, she brought me back to earth again.

Every day we strolled along the narrow high street, watching the women as they shopped and chatted. Elizabeth often stopped to talk to them, and the way she could make them flush with pleasure, or laugh, made me want to burst with pride. She was interested in them all; it was plain to see that people were a joy to her.

'She told me it's her anniversary so she's going to try out a new recipe tonight,' she said, as she waved a dumpy, smiling woman off on her bicycle.

'I heard,' I remarked dryly.

'Oh, you weren't bored, were you?' she teased.

'Stiff.'

She laughed, and ran on ahead. When I caught up with her she was sitting on a wall, waiting, so I sat down beside her. 'Were you really bored?' she said.

'No. But I was wondering. Is it enough, do you think?'

'Enough?'

'For these women. Do you think they're happy, you know, living here on this island. Or do you think they want more out of life? More than just looking after a man?'

She turned to face me. 'Alexander, don't tell me that on top of everything else, you're a feminist too?'

I laughed. 'If I am, then I'm definitely still in the closet! But tell me, you're a wife and mother. Is it enough for you?'

'What you really want to know is, am I one of the lesbian brigade, as you so chauvinistically call it, that Jessica belongs to?'

'Yes.'

'No, I'm not one of them. But that doesn't mean I don't agree with a lot of what they say. I just think they go about things in the wrong way, that's all.'

'So how would you go about it?'

'Me! My darling, I have neither the education nor the rhetoric to be a leader of women, but I can tell you this: they're missing the point. OK, what they're achieving materially and socially is right, admirable. But the aggression they use only makes people hostile to their cause – women included. It's a bit like the old fable about the wind and sun, isn't it? It was the sun and the warmth that made the man take his coat off.'

'And who says she doesn't have the education or the rhetoric?'

She pinched me. 'But there's another reason why I wouldn't do for them. You see, I'm hopelessly and incurably in love with a man, and that's simply not allowed.'

Though I knew I had never been so happy, dark thoughts were never far from my mind. I knew I should tell her, I even tried to persuade myself that she would understand, but I was a coward. I kept remembering Jessica's face when she told me, and I knew I wouldn't be able to bear it if my infertility was the reason Elizabeth and I said good-bye. I hated myself for the plans I allowed us to make, our undying promises that we would never be parted again, when I knew that as soon as we left the island it would all be over. Sometimes when I made love to her I was violent, but I couldn't help myself – my frustration at the futility of our love-making overwhelmed me. I knew there were times when she sensed that things weren't as they should be between us, but whenever she tried to talk about it, I would laugh and tell her she was imagining it. But as the days passed I felt my love for her turning to a pain so excruciating that I thought it would choke me.

And then there was only one more day, one more night, before fantasy must give way to reality. Elizabeth didn't want to go to Venus Pool again, she said the pain of leaving it would be too great to bear.

Dixcart Bay was deserted, and we sat down on the pebbles to watch the yachts sail in over the skyline. Later other people wandered on to the beach, an old couple walking their dog, teenagers strolling hand in hand, boys in a boat, rowing out of the bay and disappearing from sight. Neither of us spoke, we were both too aware of our looming departure. A man about my own age walked to the edge of the sea. His jeans were rolled up to the knees, and he tested the temperature with a bare foot, then turning, he waved to somebody behind us. A boy and a girl, neither of them older than six, sped towards him, and their mother followed, laughing as her husband gathered the children into his arms and swung them round. Tentatively, they ventured into the waves, the children shrieking at first, then gaining enough courage to plunge their bodies into the surf, and finally trying to splash their parents. For a long time the four of them played, oblivious to the rest of the world, and Elizabeth and I watched. Then the little boy fell. I felt my body stiffen and jerked myself up. But his father was there, ready to pick him up and comfort him. I relaxed and lay back again. It was several minutes before I realised that Elizabeth had turned her attention to me.

'Alexander, what is it that's making you so unhappy?'

'You have to ask?'

'No, there's more. I've sensed it ever since we arrived here.'

I started to get to my feet, but she pulled me back. 'Alexander, please. Don't shut me out. If there's to be any future for us, you must tell me what's troubling you.'

I already knew the truth of what she was saying. Tears were gathering in her eyes and I felt my own stinging too. Then I looked round me again and knew that if we were to say good-bye anywhere, then it must be here. Here, where we had known love again.

'Darling,' I faltered. She said nothing, only took my hand and waited. For a time I was afraid to speak, afraid to tell her how I had cheated her by making promises I could never keep. And I was afraid to lose her – which I would in the end, no matter what she said, because my inability to have children, together with my jealousy of the child she already had by another man, would tear us apart. 'Elizabeth.' The family were moving away from the sea, chasing one another to the smugglers' arch. Gently she turned my face back to hers, and waited for me to go on. 'I should have told you the truth from the beginning, Elizabeth, but I was a coward. I wanted you so badly that

I told myself it would be all right in the end. But it can't be. We can't be together, it's just not possible.'

I felt her fingers tense as I spoke, but couldn't bring myself to look at her.

'Is it because of Jessica?' she said, after a while.

I shook my head.

'Because I'm married?'

'No. Though God knows, that should be enough.'

'Then what is it, Alexander? Tell me.' There was desperation in her voice.

I took her face between my hands and for an instant I saw Jessica's mouth laughing back at me, ridiculing me. I let her go and leaned forward. 'I'm infertile, Elizabeth. It's why Jessica has never conceived. I am sterile, empty, useless, call it what you like, but I can't give you any children. I know you'll say it doesn't matter, but it will. Living with you day after day, watching you and knowing that I . . .'

'Alexander! Stop! Stop! How can you think that would ever make a difference? How little you must think of me to believe that I would be capable of turning away from you over something like that. Something that's not even . . .'

'Please, Elizabeth, don't make this any harder. I know what you're going to say next, that I will come to love your daughter as my own. Well, I can't live with your daughter, Elizabeth, knowing she is the child of another man. I know I'm a coward, but I can't do it.'

'Alexander, look at me.'

When I didn't, she pulled me round to face her. 'No, stop,' she said, as I tried to speak. 'Stop and listen to me. You're not infertile, Alexander, do you hear me? You can't be.'

'There's no point in denying it. Jessica . . . there were tests . . .' I didn't want to go on.

She started to speak, then stopped. She tried again, then threw herself away from me and ran off across the beach.

I let her go, as again I saw Jessica, heard her laughing

even, but this time Elizabeth was there too. She had turned away from me, as I'd known she would. But God, how I had prayed she wouldn't.

She was sitting beside a rock not far away, her head buried in her hands. She looked up as my shadow fell over her. I was surprised to see that she wasn't crying, though her face looked ravaged. I sat down beside her and held out my hand for hers. She took it.

Staring straight ahead I started to speak. I told her then about Jessica, about the bitter fights we had, and the cruel way I had tormented her during the first years of our marriage. And I told her how, when Jessica found I was infertile, she had taken her revenge in the scorn and contempt she threw at me, knowing that I wanted a child more than anything else.

When I had finished I raised her hand to my mouth and kissed it softly. 'So, my darling, you can see now what my infertility has done to me and Jessica. I couldn't bear that to happen to us.'

I turned to look at her and saw that tears were streaming silently down her face. 'Oh my God, what have I done?' she whispered. 'What have I done to you?' She put her hand over my mouth as I started to speak. 'There's something you must know, Alexander. Something I should have told you a long time ago. I could have saved you all this pain. But I didn't know what to do, please believe me, I was so young then, and so were you, and I didn't know what to do for the best. I'm sorry, my darling . . .'

'Elizabeth . . . ?'

'It's Charlotte, Alexander, she's . . . Charlotte is six years old.'

At first I didn't move. The sounds of everyday life continued, but all I could hear was the echo of Elizabeth's words. I was too stunned to speak or to think, and feeling myself go weak, I leaned back against the rock and closed my eyes.

How hurt she must have been to shield herself from me like that. And Jessica, how I must have hurt her too, for her to lie to me the way she had. I looked at Elizabeth and for a moment I didn't understand her. All the times she could have told me in the past week, and hadn't. I had a daughter. I closed my eyes again as tears slid unchecked over my face. I felt her arms go round me, cradling me like a child. But I couldn't respond, my heart was numb. 'I'm sorry,' she said, over and over. 'I should have told you before. I'm sorry, my darling.'

It was a long time later, when the tears had dried on my cheeks and the sun was sinking towards the horizon, that I was finally able to speak. 'Tell me about her, Elizabeth. Tell me everything about her.'

The following morning dawned dull and grey. It was the first miserable weather there had been, and Elizabeth sat at the window looking out at the rain.

The night before we had been closer than I had ever dreamed possible. This morning we were quiet. In less than an hour Jack Serle would come with his horse and carriage to take us to the ferry. Already Elizabeth was wrapped up against the weather.

The clock ticked monotonously in the corner. Elizabeth got up and said she was going for a walk. She wanted to go alone.

I waited for her in the lounge, thinking about her and wondering what the future would bring. When it was almost time to leave I went to the window and looked out, but there was no sign of her. The door opened and Jack Serle came in. He was early, and went off to the kitchen for a cup of tea.

I started to pace the room, looking at my watch. Where was she? Had something happened to her? The wind was vicious this morning, and the sea. Had she slipped and . . . ?

I went outside. The rain was heavier now, and the sound of the wind, raging through the trees that cloistered the hotel, seemed sinister. I listened, straining my ears, as if expecting to hear her.

And then suddenly I knew where she was, and I knew that I must go to her. Circling the hotel, I strode quickly through the garden behind, oblivious of the driving rain, only knowing that I had to get to her. Then I was running, through the orchard, over the stile, past Jespillière House and across the meadow. There was the barely hidden gap in the yellow gorse. I pushed through and out on to the cliff edge.

She was a small figure huddled into the stone seat, her hair plastered to her face; alone in her grief. I held her close.

'We will come back, Alexander, won't we? Promise me that one day we will come back.'

'I promise you, my darling. With all my heart, I promise you.'

How could either of us have known then what was to come?

– Elizabeth –

– 20 –

I was trying very hard not to look at my watch. Every muscle in my body was tensed to the point of breaking, and my heart thumped more rapidly as each minute passed. One o'clock on Friday at Jules' Bar, he had said.

I looked around at the lunch-time drinkers. A party in the corner that had sung 'Happy Birthday' a moment ago; a group of men standing at the bar, talking too loudly; office girls, businessmen. I turned back to my drink. He's not going to come, I know he's not going to come. The words beat a tattoo on my brain.

A shadow fell over me, and the moment I saw Henry's face I felt the blood drain from my own.

'Elizabeth.'

I tried to smile, but my heart was in my throat and I dug my fingers deep into the palms of my hands in an effort to keep calm.

He sat down. 'How are you?'

'Oh, I'm fine. How are you?'

'Yes, I'm fine.'

I rushed on. 'Alexander told me all about Caroline. I'm very happy for you, Henry. When's it to be?' I gave him a big smile, as if by doing so I could stop him from delivering the news that was written in every line of his face.

'Next week, actually.'

Neither of us said anything after that, as the waitress took our order then came back with the drinks.

'He's not coming, is he?' I whispered.

He looked down at his hands, bunched together on the table in front of him. Slowly, he shook his head.

The denial rushed at me with such force that it snatched my breath. It couldn't be true. This wasn't happening. Any minute now I would wake up and Alexander would be walking through the door. All I had to do was open my eyes.

When I did, Henry was still sitting beside me and I wanted to die. 'Is it Jessica? Is he going back to her?'

'He has to, Elizabeth.'

I didn't want to hear the compassion in his voice, I only wanted this to stop.

'There was an accident. While you were away. Lady Bel, Alexander's mother, was killed.' I closed my eyes. 'Jessica was driving. She's in hospital. The doctors say she'll be all right, but it'll be some time.' He waited a moment, then went on. 'There's something else, Elizabeth.' I looked up. 'After the accident, Jessica had a miscarriage.'

Again I closed my eyes. The bitter irony, after all the lies she had told him, was too much to bear.

'Did you know Alexander thought he was . . . ?'

I nodded. 'Why did she lie to him like that?'

He didn't answer and I could feel the pain dragging me down, swirling through me in relentless waves.

'He told me about Charlotte.'

'Where is he now?'

'With his father.'

'She's very like him, you know, Henry. She's got his curly black hair, it even falls over her face the way his does. And her eyes. They're grey, but she has tiny specks of blue in them. She knows how to use them, of course, just like he does. You know, she even laughs like . . . Henry, I don't know if I can bear this.'

He reached out for my hand. 'Come along, let's get you out of here.'

He took me back to his flat in Eaton Square where we talked until it was dark outside. I had stopped crying by then, but I knew that in the months that stretched emptily and endlessly ahead there would be many more tears. I had lost him once, and survived, but I didn't know if I could do it again. I didn't know if I even wanted to.

Henry handed me my coat and tried again to persuade me to let him drive me home. I shook my head. I needed some time alone before I could face Charlotte.

'He wants to see you, when all this is over. He's asked me to find out where you live.'

I looked into Henry's face, and felt the years slip away. It was as if we were all back at Foxton's and Henry had come to tell me that Alexander wanted me to be in their play. I shook my head. 'No, Henry. It'll only mean more pain for those who love us.' For the first time I was thinking about Edward.

'What about Charlotte?'

'One day I will tell her about him. She'll come to find him, I know she will. Just ask him to be patient.'

He walked with me to the door. 'Henry, please tell him . . .' I stopped and looked into his face. His eyes were clouded and I guessed, in his own way, he was suffering too. 'Nothing, it doesn't matter, he'll know anyway.'

I can't describe the way I felt in the weeks that followed, I only knew that the pain was more intense, more agonising than I had known anything could be. I thought about him day and night, reliving every moment we'd spent together, and asked myself a thousand times why God was punishing us like this. But even as I asked the question, I still refused to believe that this was the end.

It was this denial of the truth that proved my downfall. As I carried out the daily tasks that were expected of me, the certainty that Alexander and I would be reunited grew in my mind until everything I did was in preparation for his coming. I stocked the library with law books and had the Renaissance paintings in the long gallery replaced with Impressionists – Christine scoured the auction rooms, armed with lists of what to look out for. Westmoor was suddenly buzzing with builders, decorators, gardeners. I bullied them along, they must be finished by the time Alexander came . . . .

'But it's got to be done,' I said, when Edward told me I was going to wear myself out if I didn't slow down.

He smiled. 'I'm going to Florence at the weekend. How about taking a break and coming with me?'

I looked at him, aghast. Couldn't he see I was far too busy to go to Florence, why didn't he take Charlotte instead?

But Charlotte didn't want to go, either. At least, she did want to go, it was just that she didn't want to leave me behind.

'Leave me behind?' I laughed. 'If nothing else, it'll be good to have you out from under my feet. Why aren't you playing with your friends?'

She looked up at me with her big eyes and I felt a surge of impatience. 'Honestly, Charlotte, I just don't know what . . .'

'Why are you always getting at me? What have I done?'

'Done? You haven't done anything. Oh Charlotte, you're impossible. Why don't you take the horses out over the downs, they could do with the exercise, and so could you.'

'We took them this morning.'

'Did you?' I laughed. 'I don't know, there seems to be so much on my mind lately . . . .'

'Can we do something together, Mum? Just me and you? You know, like we used to.'

'Can't you see I'm busy, Charlotte? He'll be here soon and I . . .'

'Who'll be here soon? You keep saying that.'

I stared at her.

'Who, Mum? Who's coming?'

'Why don't you run along and find Edward if you're going to Florence?'

I found her later, sitting on her bed combing her doll's hair. She looked as if she'd been crying and turned away when she saw it was me. I had to swallow my irritation. 'How would you like to come up to London with me at the weekend? We'll go to the theatre.' Alexander lived in Belgrave Square. I'd go there, tell him everything would be ready soon.

'But what about Edward? He wants us to go to Florence.'

'We won't tell him. We'll wait until he's gone, then sneak off to London without telling anyone. Well, I suppose we'd better tell Canary. In fact, why don't we take her with us? Run along and ask her, darling, I've got a lot to finish off here, and the designer will be coming back again this evening.'

We saw an unmemorable matinée at the Savoy, drove out to Hampton Court, tore round the zoo and went to hamburger bars and cinemas. I didn't go to Belgrave Square, it wasn't time yet. But I'd go soon.

When we got back to Westmoor Edward was still away, and the delivery men were waiting to install the apparatus in the gym. I supervised them as they unpacked, making sure everything I had ordered for Alexander was there. At four o'clock I dragged Charlotte along to visit Miss Barsby who lived in a cottage just outside the estate. Charlotte loathed the old woman and did very little to hide it. I watched with mounting annoyance as she delivered her monosyllabic replies to Miss Barsby's questions. I stood it for half an hour then, making my apologies to Miss Barsby, I took Charlotte by the hand and led her out to the car.

'You're a nasty, spoiled little girl,' I said, once Miss Barsby had gone back inside. 'She's a lonely old lady who looks forward to your visits, and all you can do is sulk. Next week you'll spend the whole afternoon with her, and talk to her properly. Do you hear me?'

Charlotte sustained a mutinous silence until we pulled

up outside the house. I leaned across and threw open her door. 'Go to your room. I'll deal with you later.'

'You're always picking on me these days. I wish I'd gone to Florence with Edward, he's much nicer than you. You're horrible.'

She'd run into the house before I could catch her, and as the decorator was bearing down on me with yet more curtain samples for the new bathroom, I had to let it go for the moment. But it wasn't forgotten, and the next day, although I had promised her she could go with Jeffrey to collect Edward from the airport, I made her stay in her room.

The new tennis courts were ready, so I challenged David to a game before lunch.

'You mean you've got the time?' he teased.

'Don't say it like that. It's hard work getting this house together.'

As we strolled down to the courts Charlotte was watching us from her window. David waved out, but when I turned round she shrank back. The sun was already beating down, it was no day for a child to be cooped up in a bedroom, but when David started to plead on her behalf I shoved a racket into his hand and told him to play.

I wasn't sure whether it was the heat, or the fact that I hadn't had any breakfast that morning, but after four games I started to feel dizzy. And when I missed a fourth service David asked if anything was the matter.

After that I didn't remember anything until I woke up in my bed with the doctor gazing down at me. I tried to struggle up, but he pushed me back. Then I heard Charlotte, sobbing outside the door. The doctor let her in and she ran into my arms.

'Are you going to be all right, Mum?' she said.

'Of course I am, darling. I fainted, that's all. And it serves me right, I shouldn't have been so awful to you. Will you forgive me?'

She nodded and I started to get out of bed, reminding her that we had the summer fête to organise. At that moment the doctor came back, and when he saw me hunting round for my dressing-gown he started to shake his head. 'Back to bed for you, young lady,' he said. 'Your brother-in-law has been filling me in on all you've been doing lately and – '

'Oh doctor, honestly. It's an extremely hot day, and you know what they say, a little hard work never killed anyone. So I'd like to get up now, if you don't mind.'

The doctor put his hand on Charlotte's head. 'How about going downstairs and asking Mary to bring us up a nice cup of tea?'

Once she'd gone the doctor pulled back the bedclothes and pointed to the bed. 'In you go,' he said, 'it's about time you and I had a bit of a talk.'

I didn't get up again until early September. During those weeks I couldn't bear anyone near me except Charlotte, but even when she was there all I could do was stare at her and stroke her hair. I knew I was frightening her, but I couldn't bring myself to tell her what the doctor had told me. I couldn't even think of it myself. I had sworn him to secrecy, telling him I wanted to deal with this in my own time and in my own way.

Despite my breakdown, during this time I noticed that Edward was changing towards me. It was as if he had put a barrier between us. He was still as kind and solicitous as ever, but there was a ring to his voice I didn't recognise. How much he understood about the reason for my breakdown, I didn't know, but he was away more often than he was at home, and as far as I could tell Christine had all but taken over the daily running of his life. He talked only about her when he came to my room, and wouldn't allow me to speak at all. It was breaking my heart to see how much he was suffering, but there was nothing I could do.

Then, for no accountable reason, I woke up one September morning feeling I couldn't wait to face the world again.

Everyone looked up as I walked into the breakfast room, and the sunny smile I beamed at them so took them by surprise that Jeffrey, who was pouring the tea, allowed it to overflow into Christine's saucer.

Edward stood up and put his arms round me. His kind face looked down into mine, and I saw the lines deepen around his eyes as he smiled. They were more pronounced now than they had been and I knew I was to blame. I reached up to touch his face, then pulling him closer, lifted my mouth for him to kiss me.

'We must all go out for dinner,' I announced, pulling up a chair. 'Tonight. It will be a belated celebration of Edward's birthday. What do you say?'

Still looking somewhat bemused, they nodded. 'Yes,' Charlotte echoed, giving her egg a bashing. 'Can I come too?'

'You've to be up for school in the morning, darling.'

'Oh, Mum!' she groaned.

'Let her come,' Edward said, tousling her hair. 'We can always make it an early dinner.'

'Yippee! Will you let me choose the wine, David?'

I looked at her aghast. 'The wine?'

'I'm afraid it's her latest hobby,' David admitted. 'She heard Edward discussing it with someone on the phone, and insisted he teach her. The happy task befell me. No, no, don't worry, we haven't got around to the tasting bit yet.'

I shook my head and laughed. What would Alexander make of her? But I mustn't allow myself to think of that.

We arrived home just before ten that night, after going to the French restaurant in the village. Charlotte fell asleep in the car on the way back, and drowsily insisted that Edward take her up to bed. David poured the brandy while we waited for Edward to join us. He was a long time in coming.

'I had to tell her the story of Osiris and Isis again,' he explained, as he came to sit beside me.

'Who?'

'The great Egyptian love story of an ancient god and his goddess.'

'You must tell it to me sometime,' I said.

'Don't, or he will,' Christine warned. 'But if he does, get him to tell you all the bits I'll bet he misses out with Charlotte, like how Osiris's body was cut into fourteen pieces, and the only bit missing when they put him together again was the phallus.'

'I don't miss those bits out at all,' Edward objected.

'Don't you?' I laughed. 'Didn't she want to know what a phallus was?'

'She most certainly did, so I told her. Then she asked me if I had one, and then she wanted to know if she could see it. So I explained that it was a part of the body people didn't show each other until they got married.'

'Oh God, Edward, you're the limit,' Christine said.

'You haven't heard the best part yet. After complaining bitterly at how long she'd have to wait for that, she went off to inspect her dolls. Canary caught her. I tell you the whole thing was worth it just to see Canary's face when Charlotte said "phallus".'

I waited for the laughter to subside, then clutching my glass nervously and trying hard to sound casual, I said: 'If Charlotte was to have a little brother, she wouldn't have to wait quite so long, would she?'

I should have sensed the mood change then, but I didn't. I looked from Edward to Christine to David, not seeing the emptiness of their smiles. 'That's why I wanted us all to go out to dinner,' I went on, 'but I didn't want to say anything with Charlotte there – I thought I would tell her on our own.'

'Tell her what, darling?' There was an edge to Edward's voice that in my excitement I chose to ignore.

'That I'm going to have a baby.'

I heard Christine gasp, but she was looking at Edward. So was David. Their faces were white.

'It's due in February,' I added lamely.

There was a long silence. I turned to Edward and saw he was staring into his drink. Then David got up and said he was going to bed. Christine followed.

I went to pour Edward some more brandy. When I handed it to him he ignored me, so I put it on the table beside him.

'Come and sit down, Elizabeth,' he said eventually.

He took my hands between his and as he looked up I saw how sad his face was. That night had been the first time in months he had relaxed with me, but now, despite the love that shone in his eyes, I sensed him pushing me away. 'Darling, I should have told you this a long time ago, but you always swore that Charlotte was enough and you never wanted any more children. You see, my first wife gave birth to a stillborn child. It was a girl, and I sometimes wonder if that's why I love Charlotte so much.' He smiled. 'But who could help loving Charlotte? Anyway, the birth was difficult and my wife almost died. Afterwards she was advised not to try again, so I had a vasectomy to save her from any more pain.'

Until that moment I don't think I'd realised the insanity of what I had tried to do. I stared at him, struck dumb by the sheer horror of it.

It was some time before he spoke again. 'You don't have to tell me anything, darling, but it might help if you did.'

I buried my face in my hands. My self-loathing was so complete I couldn't speak.

'Is it Charlotte's father?'

I nodded.

'You were with him when you went away?'

I looked up into his face. I thought he had aged since I'd been ill, but now he looked almost haggard. 'Edward,' I sobbed, 'I don't know what made me say it. I don't . . .'

'Hush, hush. People often say or do things they don't mean when they are hurting badly. I know how much you love him, Elizabeth, I've always known.'

Hearing him say that, I wanted to get up and run and never stop. I wished he would hit me or shout at me, his kindness and understanding were tearing me apart.

'Does he know about the baby?'

'No.'

'Will you tell him?'

I shook my head. 'I can't. There's nothing he can . . . I'm sorry, Edward. Please forgive me. No, don't forgive me. I'll go. I'll go as far away from your life as I can. You can divorce me, I won't make any claim on you. I'm sorry, Edward, I'm . . .'

'Hush now, you're not going anywhere. I know you don't love me in the way you love him, Elizabeth, but I love you, and I love Charlotte too. I don't want to lose you.'

'But what about the baby?' I looked at him, suddenly stricken with panic. 'I couldn't have an abortion.'

He put his hand over my mouth. 'Of course not. The baby will be mine – if you allow it to be. No one need know, only the family.'

'No, Edward, I can't let you do it.'

'I want to do it, Elizabeth. But I have one condition, and I suppose even that's not a condition, I would want you to stay anyway. But if you can, I want you to promise me you will never see him again.'

For an instant I thought I heard Alexander's voice telling me to deny him, warning me not to listen. But I had to ignore it. Alexander was again a part of my past, and this man here, my husband, who loved me more than any woman ever deserved to be loved, was waiting for my answer. I made him the promise.

In the early hours of the morning I woke to find the bed empty beside me. When I went to find Edward I saw lights in the Egyptian Room and tried the door, but it was locked. I listened, and after a while I could hear him sobbing.

– 21 –

Edward didn't come back to bed at all that night. The following morning he joined Christine on an early flight to Cairo, leaving me a note to say he would ring when he got there. After what had happened it was a relief not to have to face them, and when David left a message with Jeffrey to say he'd gone up to London for a few days, I guessed he too was anxious to avoid seeing me.

When Charlotte arrived home from school, she came up to my room and we sat on the window-seat for a long time, drawing patterns on the steamy windows. As she chattered, I tried so many times to tell her about the baby, but every time I opened my mouth the words wouldn't come.

Life was so cruel, and yet in other ways so kind. While it allowed me to have Alexander's children, it would not allow me to be with him. I put my arms round Charlotte and hugged her tight. At least I would always have a part of him, but what did Alexander have? I couldn't bear to think of how unhappy he might be. I never once doubted his love, nor how much he must want to be with Charlotte and me.

But what about Edward? Last night had served to remind me just how much he loved me. Often I sensed the struggle he had to keep his feelings under control and always knew when he was losing the battle because he would go away. His love was so overpowering, at times I could almost see the way it threatened to engulf him. It was as if I wasn't real but an object to be treasured, revered almost. But it was the complexity of his sophistication and almost childlike adoration that made me want to protect him.

When he came back from Cairo three days later, I could see how relieved he was that I was still there, that I hadn't run away, and my heart twisted with pity and guilt. He talked excitedly about the deal he had in hand, but wouldn't go into detail because he wanted it to be a surprise. He asked about Charlotte, wanting to know everything we'd done while he was away. Then he laid his hand on my stomach and told me he loved me. I turned away before I could stop myself, but he didn't notice. His eyes were almost glazed as he seemed to drift into a world of his own. It was at moments like that, when he appeared so remote, that I wondered how well I really knew him.

Christine stayed in Cairo much longer than was originally planned. She rang Edward daily, but he took the calls in his study and she never asked to speak to me. After the calls he always seemed distracted, irritable almost, but when I asked him why he just said that the man they were dealing with in Cairo had an absurd passion for riddles. After one such phone call he got his secretary to book him on a flight to Istanbul and was gone for five days, during which he didn't ring home once.

Christine returned four weeks later. Edward and I were at an art dealer's party in London. He hadn't told me Christine was flying back that night, so I was surprised when she walked in around eleven. She greeted the host and his wife, throwing her arms around them in the ostentatious manner they all affected. Everyone wanted to know how she had got on in Cairo. She exchanged a quick glance with Edward – then declared loudly that they were all a very poor bunch, bombarding her with questions the minute she walked through the door and not even offering her a drink. Then she went off into a corner with Edward, and they talked quietly but heatedly for several minutes, before separating and mingling with the other guests again.

I waited, watching her from the corner of my eye as she worked her way round the room. Eventually she was standing behind me, talking to Edward's secretary. I'd been dreading seeing her, and now she was so pointedly ignoring me I didn't know what to do. Suddenly I felt a thump in my back.

'Oh Elizabeth, I'm so sorry.' Her voice was thick with sarcasm.

I smiled. 'No harm done. How are you?'

'Very well.' She looked me up and down. 'No need to ask how you are.'

I tried again. 'You've been gone ages, I missed you.'

'Did you, sister-in-law darling? And what about when you were off wherever it was with your lover? Did you miss me then? Or were you too busy to think about anyone else? You know, like the people who were left looking after your daughter?'

I stared at her.

'Oh, so you didn't miss me then. How about Edward? Did you miss him while you were away screwing another man? You know, the man whose child you tried to push on to my brother? She was shouting now, and I looked round wildly to see if anyone had heard her.

'What's the matter, Elizabeth, afraid everyone will find out what a sly, conniving little bitch you are?'

'Christine, please . . .'

'"Christine please!" I could kill you for what you've done to Edward. He's never hurt anyone in his whole life – but you've hurt him all right, haven't you, you slut! You're not fit to bear his name, you never were. Why don't you do us all a favour and take your bastards back to the gutter where you belong!'

I felt myself being dragged backwards and there was a loud crack as Edward's hand flew across Christine's face. 'Go home, now!' he hissed, then without uttering another word he took my arm and marched me out of the room.

When we arrived home Edward told me to go upstairs. He

caught Christine's arm as she made to follow me, and pulled her into his study. Once the door had closed I went back to the landing. Even though their voices were raised it was difficult to make out what they were saying, but I did hear Christine telling Edward to pull himself together and 'see the little slut for what she really is.'

The door opened then, and as Edward came out I drew back into the shadows.

'You're doing this because of her!' Christine yelled. 'She's not worth it!'

Edward turned back. His voice was too low for me to hear, but when Christine answered I knew they were no longer talking about me.

'You've got to be insane even to think of it! How the hell are they going to get in? Have you thought about that?'

'Yes, I've thought about it. All we have to do is talk to the . . .' I couldn't make out what Edward said after that because the door closed again.

It was the early hours of the morning when I finally heard Christine come upstairs. When Edward didn't follow I tiptoed down to his study. He wasn't there, but I was shocked when I saw the chaos on his desk; catalogues and leaflets were strewn all over it, and on top of the pile was a blown-up colour photograph of the Tutankhamun death mask. I closed the door quickly, feeling, for no earthly reason, that I had intruded upon something I hadn't been meant to see.

At the bottom of the west stairs I hesitated and looked up at the silent landing. There was only one light at the end of the gallery, casting long shadows across the walls. A sixth sense warned me not to go to the Egyptian Room. I remembered the way Christine had looked at Edward when she'd arrived at the party, and the oddness of Edward's manner after the phone calls from Cairo. I thought of the curious exchange I had heard only a few hours ago in Edward's study. I stood there in the half-darkness, and as my skin prickled with sentience I was suddenly engulfed by a premonition that something very sinister was going on at Westmoor.

Jonathan was born the following February, only three days after Alexander's birthday. It was a difficult birth and Edward was there throughout. Afterwards I couldn't bring myself to hold the baby, and the more Edward fussed and cuddled him, the worse I became. I was in hospital for four days, then Edward, David and Charlotte came to take us home. Christine wasn't there, nor had she come to visit.

Since the night of the party there had been an uneasy truce between Christine and me, though I knew the only reason she made any effort at all was to keep Edward happy. She was unkind to Charlotte, which caused bitter scenes between her and David. Edward sent her off more and more frequently to far-flung places in search of paintings or antique furniture; she always came back with something, and always, no matter where she was, managed to make a stop in Cairo.

One night David teased her that she was hiding a lover there. Her denial was so vehement that the two brothers raised their eyebrows, and Edward wondered if David hadn't hit on something.

Charlotte was all ears. 'Oh do tell us about him, Christine,' she begged. 'What's he like? Do you kiss him?'

'For God's sake, Charlotte, I've already told you . . .'

'What's his name?' Charlotte persisted.

Christine glared at me. I took hold of Charlotte's hand and pulled her on to my lap. 'That's enough, darling,' I said.

'"That's enough, darling",' Christine mimicked. 'God, it makes me sick the way everyone round here hangs on that kid's every word. I suppose it's going to be the same with Jonathan. No darling, yes darling, that's enough darling . . .'

'And that *is* enough.' Edward got to his feet. 'We've got guests arriving in less than two hours and there are some things I want to discuss with you before you go to New York tomorrow, Christine. Now Charlotte, how about a nice big kiss before you go up to bed?'

An hour later Edward came upstairs to our room. I was sitting on the bed, holding the baby. I turned sharply as I heard the door close, and my arms tightened around Jonathan. He was three months old now and I couldn't forgive myself for the way I had rejected him when he was born. He started to bounce around as Edward came to sit beside us, and to stop him holding out his arms for Edward, I stood up.

'It's all right, darling, I'm not going to take him away from you.'

I nuzzled my face into Jonathan's and didn't answer.

Gently Edward took hold of my elbows and sat me back on the bed. 'You've got to stop blaming yourself. A lot of mothers react the way you did after a difficult birth. As long as you love him . . .'

'It's not that,' I interrupted.

'Then what is it?'

'It's Christine. She hates me being here. I can't stand all this pretence.'

Immediately, Jonathan started to cry, and Edward took him from me. I made to snatch him back, but stopped myself just in time. Then, afraid of what I was feeling, I jerked myself from the bed and went to close the curtains, while Edward put Jonathan in his cradle. Jonathan had slept in our room since we'd come home from hospital. He'll have to go to the nursery soon, I thought, and was ashamed at how pleased I was at creating just that little distance between him and Edward.

Edward put his arms around me and I leaned my head against his shoulder. 'I've had an idea that I think just might sort everything out once and for all,' he said. 'Meanwhile, just try and be patient with Christine, darling. Despite everything, I know she loves you very much.'

I wrenched myself away and went to stand over Jonathan. I could feel Edward beside me, smiling down into the cradle, and I was suddenly possessed by the conviction that I had to get Alexander's son away from him.

A month or so later I was busy with the organisation of the charity bazaar in the village hall. Edward had been in London for days, but on the morning of the bazaar he returned, proudly announcing that he was sending Jeffrey back up to London to collect a lorry-load of saleable bits and pieces he'd managed to wheedle out of friends in the art world.

Christine went into action to help with the last minute arrangements. By now we were all convinced she was conducting a secret love affair, for she flew off to Cairo as regularly as the rest of us went up to London. At the same time I had noticed that David was becoming very friendly with a neighbour, Jenifer Illingworth, whose husband had run off a year ago with another woman.

'Why don't we invite Jenifer up to the house for dinner tonight?' Christine whispered in my ear. I was so startled that she had actually spoken to me by choice that, for a moment, I could only stare at her.

It was settled. Jenifer said she would love to come, and I laughed as I saw the pained expression on David's face. He knew two matchmaking women when he saw them.

The bazaar was an unprecedented success, for which Edward accepted the credit with outrageous immodesty. 'And things seem to be better between you and Christine,' he said, as we were dressing for dinner later.

'I think you could be right,' I admitted. I was still cautious, though.

'Good. I hoped it would work out once . . .' He didn't finish, and when I looked up he seemed intent on trying to cover the bald spot at the back of his head. I took the brush from him, and he leaned back in the chair and watched his reflection as I pampered him. 'Aaah, Elizabeth,' he sighed, after a while, 'what kind of life is it for you, cooped up here with two crusty old men, trying to hide their bald spots and matching them up with abandoned women?'

Despite the lightness of his tone I could tell he was troubled about something. Putting my arms round his neck I met his eyes in the mirror. 'It's a wonderful life,' I said. 'And you're two wonderful, crusty old men. Now what is it, Edward? What's on your mind?'

He turned round in his chair, and taking the hairbrush from me he put it on the dressing table. I knelt down in front of him and slipped my hands in his.

'You always could read me so well,' he said.

I felt a flash of irritation at the pride in his voice that we knew each other so well.

'I wasn't going to tell you now,' he began, 'but I suppose it's as good a time as any. It'll give you a chance to think it over, anyway.' He seemed reluctant to go on.

'Is it something to do with Christine?' I prompted.

'Not really. Well, in a way I suppose it is. It's got something to do with all of us, but mainly the children.'

My heart gave a sickening lurch.

'No, don't worry,' he patted my hand, 'it's nothing awful. I've talked it over with Christine and David, and they agree it would be for the best, too. Well, Christine was against it at first, but once I'd assured her it wouldn't change anything as far as she was concerned – in my will, that is – she saw the sense of it. And now, just as I'd hoped, things are getting better between the two of you because of it. So you see, it could be a good thing.'

'What could be a good thing, Edward?'

He looked at me blankly, then laughed as he realised he'd told me nothing. 'I'm sorry. And I hope you won't mind that I talked to David and Christine first, but I suppose

I needed to know if I was doing the right thing. Well, I always thought it was the right thing, but I didn't know how you would take it.'

I smiled. 'And you still won't, if you don't tell me what it is.'

'It's Charlotte and Jonathan. I want to adopt them, Elizabeth.'

I stared at him, feeling myself go suddenly cold.

He rushed on. 'I think it would be best all round. You know, if legally they were mine. I have no heirs, and when the time comes I'd like to provide for them properly. I want to be their father, Elizabeth. Their real father.'

I still couldn't speak. I looked down at my hands and saw that they were still entwined in his. I pulled them away and suddenly I wanted to scream at him. How could he be so stupid! How could he even think I would let him have Alexander's children?

'I waited 'til now to see if you would change your mind and decide to go back to their father. God, Elizabeth, if you only knew what I've . . .' He swallowed hard. 'It doesn't matter. All that matters is that you're still here, and that you seem happier. I think you want to stay. And if you do, then I want us to be a real family. Can we be that, darling? Can I be their father?'

I stood up slowly, not trusting myself to speak – and Edward talked on and on, his words hitting me like stones.

I didn't go down to dinner that night. I sat in my room, holding myself, sure that if I let go I would fall apart. I needed Alexander then as I had never needed him before. I wanted him to tell me that I didn't have to do it, that they were his children, and that nothing and no one should ever divide us. But he wasn't there, and Edward was asking, and how could I deny him when he had done so much for me? How would I find the words to say no, he couldn't have Alexander's children? And then, with a tremendous sense of relief, it occurred to me that I wouldn't have to. As they were Alexander's children, surely Alexander would have to give his permission for the adoption to go ahead, and I knew that was something he would never do.

It was then that I started upon a mindless exercise of self-torture. I told Edward I needed some time to think, and went to stay at our London house, alone.

It was a bitterly cold March night. The taxi dropped me at the corner of Belgrave Square, and through the drizzling rain I searched the imposing houses for the right number. When I found it my courage failed. Crossing the road quickly, I tucked myself in tightly against the railings and pulled my fur hat down over my eyes. The lights were on in Alexander's house, but there was no sign of life. It looked warm and comfortable, and I wondered what he would do if he knew I was standing outside. The hours slipped by until, chilled to the bone, I hailed a taxi and returned home.

The following night I did the same. And again, night after night. I never saw him, though I guessed the Mercedes parked outside the house was his. At first I got a grim comfort from the pain of being so near him, but as the nights wore on I began to despise myself for my weakness.

Then one night, when I was sickened by the knowledge that again I was going to walk away, and when my feet were so numb with cold I could hardly move, the door opened and an elegant woman, wrapped, as I was, against the wind, ran down the steps, got into the car and drove off. My heart was thumping unnaturally. Though I'd never met her, I knew it was Jessica.

Now I had only to cross the street and knock on the door. And then . . . Dear God, what would happen then? Would I really beg him to help me? Would I really tell him about Jonathan? I must. I knew that no matter what happened afterwards, no matter who got hurt, Alexander must know what Edward was planning.

But as I started to cross the road the Mercedes came back round the square and Jessica, leaving the engine running and the door open, ran up the steps to the front door. As she reached the top Alexander came out. He was laughing, and reached out to grab her. She shrieked and cried out that she had only been teasing. He wrapped his arms round her and squeezed her until she cried out again. Then he ran to the car, closed the door and drove off. Jessica stood on the pavement watching the car disappear around the corner. I could hear her laughing as she turned towards the other end of the square, waiting for him to drive round. Instead, he reversed the car back and drew up beside her. As they drove away together I could see he was still laughing, and I shrank back into the shadows as they passed.

David came to sit beside me on the sofa. 'Jeffrey told me you were back,' he said. I was in the Blue Sitting-Room, a room we rarely used, that adjoined the dining-room.

I smiled. 'I got bored, entertaining myself,' I said. 'Where's Edward?'

'He's taken the children to see Violet May. The fair's only a couple of miles away, did you know?'

Mary came in with a tray of tea which David poured and we sat quietly watching the flames shoot up into the chimney.

'Have you decided what your answer's going to be?' he asked, gently.

I shook my head. 'I just don't know what to do.' He slipped an arm round me, pulling me on to his shoulder. 'I've seen him, David, it's why I went to London.'

'I guessed as much. What did he say?'

'Nothing. I didn't speak to him.'

'Why?'

'It doesn't matter.'

'If he knew about the children, would he want them?'

I sobbed. 'Yes, he would want them. He would want them very much.'

'Then maybe you should let Edward adopt them. That way, if their father ever found out about them he would never be able to take them away.'

'No. I don't know. If Al . . . if he knew that I was even thinking about it, then . . .'

'He won't know.'

'But I'd have to get his permission.'

'You wouldn't. He's what's called the putative father. As such he doesn't have to know about the adoption.'

A dreadful buzzing began in my ears. That couldn't be true. It was the only hope I had left. 'Doesn't he?' I whispered.

David shook his head. 'Edward's already consulted a lawyer. He wants this very much, Elizabeth.'

I sat up and turned to look at his poor, scarred face. He loved his brother and knew how terribly I had hurt Edward when I had tried to tell him he was Jonathan's father. I owed Edward the adoption – that was what David was really saying.

So the adoption went ahead, and Charlotte and Jonathan were no longer Alexander's.

– 22 –

None of us would ever forget Charlotte's first day at St Paul's Girls' School. The honour of driving her fell to Edward, and as she was ten now, he allowed her to sit in the front seat; Jonathan, who didn't start kindergarten until the following week, insisted on accompanying them. Christine and I stood at the door, with Canary, Jeffrey and Mary, and all four of us had to wipe away a tear or two as we waved her off, her big grey eyes peering up over the top of the door frame of the Rolls Royce, bright with anticipation. That afternoon, as a very special treat to mark the occasion, David was going to come up to London with Jenifer Illingworth. The first Charlotte would know of it was when she came out of school to find David waiting.

The telephone call came at just after half-past three. No one was to blame. Who could have foreseen that an over-excited ten-year-old would go dashing out into the road to greet her uncle just as a motor-cyclist came round the corner?

When we got to the hospital David was waiting on a bench outside the operating theatre. Sitting beside him was a young boy wearing leathers and holding a crash-helmet. I stared at him. Christine led me away, while Edward and David stayed to talk to him.

Much later the doctor came to find us and showed us into a side ward. I think I must have cried out as I saw her little body lying on the bed, because the doctor turned abruptly and Christine put her arms round me. I pushed her away and ran over to the bed. There were tubes fixed into Charlotte's wrists, mouth and nose. Her eyes were closed and her face was as white as the pillow beneath it.

I turned back to the doctor. 'Will she . . . ? Is she . . .'

He stared at me for a moment, then with a grim face turned back to Charlotte. He didn't know.

Edward went outside with him where he learned the full extent of her injuries. I wasn't ready to hear yet. All I knew was that she might die and that, whatever happened, I mustn't leave her. I prayed then, as I had never prayed before. David prayed too. He was in a state of shock, and the doctor had tried to make him lie down in a room along the corridor. He blamed himself. If he'd been a few minutes earlier, he would have been on the right side of the road, and there would have been no need for her to run out . . . . If that taxi-driver hadn't blocked the one-way street, he wouldn't have been late . . . . Christine tried to soothe him. Edward held my hand, but didn't speak. The only sound was the bleep of the machine beside us, monitoring the unsteady rhythm of Charlotte's life . . . .

It was dark in the room. Edward was still sitting beside me. His eyes were closed, but I knew instinctively that he wasn't sleeping. Christine was there too. Her head had fallen to one side and her mouth was open. David was nowhere to be seen, and then I dimly recollected him giving in to the doctor and going to lie down.

I felt utterly exhausted. Someone had once told me that if you concentrated hard enough, you could penetrate another person's mind; lives had been saved that way, they told me. And for the past seven hours that was what I had been trying to do with Charlotte. Every ounce of energy I possessed I had poured into trying to reach her. Somewhere, deep down in the dark recesses between life and death, I had tried to grasp her and bring her back to me. Her breathing was so shallow now that her tiny ribcage barely moved. I lifted my eyes to her face. She seemed so lonely. If only it could have been me lying there. I picked up a stray curl that was stretched across the pillow and wound it gently round my finger.

'Charlotte, please,' I whispered, 'please, my darling, don't go away.

She didn't move. I looked at the black curl, and for the first time since I'd learned of the accident I thought of Alexander.

Edward opened his eyes. 'What is it?' And when he saw I was on my feet, he got up too. 'Where are you going?'

'I'm sorry, Edward,' I croaked, 'please try and understand. He's her father.'

Christine caught me at the door. 'No, Elizabeth!' she hissed. 'No! Edward's her father now. You can't do this to him.'

'My daughter is dying and you tell me what I can and can't do? I'm telling you, he's got to see her. Christine, get out of the way.' We struggled in the doorway. Christine was stronger than me and managed to grip me by the shoulders and turn me round.

'Look! Just look!'

Edward was slumped forward, his elbows resting on his knees, his face buried in his hands. 'Don't do it to him, Elizabeth. Please, don't do it to him.'

'I'm sorry, Christine. Edward, I'm sorry.' I tore open the door and started to run down the corridor. I was getting into the lift as I heard Christine scream my name. 'Elizabeth! It's Charlotte! Come quick!'

With my heart in my mouth I flew back along the corridor. As I burst into the room I saw that my daughter's eyes were wide open, dark pools in her pale face.

'Charlotte,' I breathed. Edward stood aside as I ran to the bed. 'Charlotte, my darling. It's Mummy. I'm here, angel. I'm here.'

The nurse came in and turned on the overhead light. She tried to push past me and I all but threw her out of the way. Now I was closer I could see that Charlotte's eyes were dilated and wondered whether she could see me.

'Mummy?' she croaked.

'Yes, darling. Mummy's here.'

'Mummy?'

I looked at Edward in panic. She couldn't hear me.

Two huge tears rolled from the corners of her eyes. 'It's dark. Where's my Mummy? I want my Mummy.'

– Alexander –

– 23 –

Henry gave a low whistle as his ball sailed into the sky and came to land only a few feet from the eighteenth green. 'Damn good shot, if I say so myself.' He stood back to make room for me. 'So, how much did you win?'

'Ten quid.'

'Ten! Is that all?'

'It was twenty,' I said, selecting a number one wood, 'but Froggo refused to cough up the other ten. He claimed I hadn't said the exact words.'

'So let's hear how you managed to slip in this little nugget of blasphemy.'

I placed my ball on the tee, then leaning on my club, recounted my summing up of the day before, when Froggo, the barrister originally briefed to prosecute in the Saxony case, had bet me twenty pounds that I couldn't slip the phrase 'Take up thy bed and walk' somewhere into my speech. As the case had concerned an armed wages snatch at a bedding warehouse in the East End, when I delivered the line, 'And so, members of the jury, I ask you to consider the evidence put before you very carefully, because to allow any of the accused to take up their beds and walk from this courtroom, free men, would be tantamount to inviting them to put more lives in jeopardy . . .' I'd had the gratification of a rare wince from the normally impassive Judge Burr.

Henry grunted. 'You're not normally as corny as that, old chap. Losing your flair.'

I shrugged and took up my stance to hit the ball. We both watched in disgust as it sliced off the end of my wood and rocketed towards a clump of trees, to land God only knew where, probably in the lake behind.

'Jesus, Alexander, that's the third time you've done that today. What the hell's got into you?'

'Fellow can have an off-day, can't he?'

We picked up our clubs and started off down the fairway.

'Everything all right at home, is it? Jessica's OK?'

'Henry, you're not going to start an amateur analysis on me because I've hit three bad ones, are you?'

'Just asking. Tell me, how did you fare with fair Rosalind what's-her-name?'

'Rosalind who?'

'Don't play dumb with me, old chap, this is Henry you're talking to. You know, the solicitor in the Godwin case.'

'Rosalind Blake.'

'Well, anything doing?'

'Henry, ever since you've become a respectable married man you seem to think every other man in the world is leaping in and out of bed with any woman he can lay his hands on. The fact is that I've given up that sort of behaviour for good. It's all in the past for me now, I've told you. Why won't you believe me?'

'Because it's against your nature.'

'Not when I've got a crippled wife who might not be crippled if I hadn't . . .'

'I wouldn't say the loss of three fingers on her right hand makes her a cripple, Alexander. And you hardly notice the limp these days.'

'When you live with her, I can tell you you're required to notice her limp, and every other blemish, and do penance for them several times a day.'

We parted company then as I went off to find my ball.

Life with Jessica was, indeed, even worse than it had been before the accident. Her self-confidence had been destroyed, and even though I never stopped trying, nothing I said or did seemed capable of restoring it. I couldn't blame her for not trusting me, but during her bad weeks things were so unbearable that all I wanted to do was walk away and never come back. I couldn't do it, of course, my conscience would never permit it. And should I ever be in danger of forgetting my conscience, Jessica would be at hand to remind me of the way I had disappeared with my 'slut', leaving her to tear round the countryside trying to find me.

'*I* was the one driving that car when the lorry hit us! The lorry that killed *your* mother! And my baby! You might just as well have been the driver of that lorry!'

I knew now why she had lied to me about my infertility. As it so often was, her reasoning had been convoluted and perverse: she'd wanted there to be something in my life I couldn't have; she'd wanted to see me suffer in the way I'd made her suffer all the years of our marriage. My desire to have children had been like a gift to her, she told me, because nothing hurts a man more than to have doubt cast on his manhood. When I explained that the kind of lie she'd told me could come close to destroying a man, she answered, quite calmly, that I deserved to be destroyed . . . . But once she had sensed she was losing me, getting pregnant had been the only thing she could think of that might make me stay. I made the insensitive mistake of asking if the child had been mine and she flew at me, hissing and spitting like a wild cat.

All this was while she was in the clinic recovering from the breakdown that had followed her accident. The doctor insisted that her mental condition was caused as much by the fear that she might never paint again as by the trauma of the accident – and my infidelity. The fear that she might not paint again had vanished now. She painted every day, and the centrepiece of her first exhibition after leaving the clinic had been a macabre impression of the accident. It was gruesome, and made even more so, I felt, by its dedication to me.

The affection that had grown between her and my father since he had withdrawn his resignation from the Cabinet and moved into Belgrave Square, both surprised and annoyed me. They talked endlessly about my mother and how special she had been to them both. In fact Jessica and my mother had never hit it off, and though I knew this was her way of trying to cope with what had happened, I despised her hypocrisy.

Her moods were so erratic that I took to working late into the night at chambers – anything to avoid going home. Only the week before she had presented me with a portrait of myself. She was touchingly shy about it, but the following evening I arrived home to find ugly scars daubed across it and a dagger plunged into the throat. A thin trickle of blood ran from the wound down over the frame. As I stood transfixed by the sheer horror of it, Jessica walked into the room, smiling pleasantly and waving a large brown envelope at me. 'I've been waiting for you,' she said. 'Can you give me the address of your girlfriend, I thought she might like the painting. As a memento.'

It was three years since I had gone to Sark, and still she was making me pay. At least I had never told her about Charlotte. But, hardly a minute of the day passed when I didn't think about my daughter – and the longing that swept over me for Elizabeth, for the uncomplicated way she had loved me, was at times almost unbearable . . . .

'Hey!' Henry shouted. 'Are we playing a round of golf or aren't we? You're miles away, old chap. Come on, let's get it over with. I'm freezing, and in sore need of a drink.'

We finished the round in double quick time, and sauntered back in the direction of the clubhouse. 'Henry,' I said, as we walked down the hill past the seventeenth hole, 'I want to tell you something, but I don't want you to make a big deal out of it.'

'Fire away.'

'It's about Elizabeth.'

He stopped. 'What about her?'

'You're going to think I've lost my marbles, but I think she needs me.'

When he didn't answer I went on, 'I don't know what it is, it's not something I can put into words, but I have this feeling that she . . .'I shrugged. 'Probably just my imagination.'

He turned slowly and walked on down the hill. 'Are you going to do anything about it?' he asked eventually.

'What can I do? I tried to find her once before, remember? I don't even know her married name.'

We were at the clubhouse now and Henry was bending down to take off his shoes. 'I suppose you could always try mental telepathy,' he said.

'What kind of an answer's that, for God's sake?'

'Just a suggestion, old chap.' And slapping me on the back, he went inside to order the drinks.

I saw a lot of Rosalind Blake during the build-up to the Godwin trial. She was an unusual woman with chaotic red hair and bright blue eyes that sat oddly with her somewhat aloof and efficient manner. I enjoyed her company and was rather proud that I had managed to establish a friendship with a woman in which neither of us was trying to get the other into bed.

The niggling feeling that Elizabeth needed me had disappeared, and if I thought about it at all, I put it down to a lack of sleep and tricks of the subconscious. After all, reason told me, if she had needed me, she would have found a way to contact me.

After the first day in court, with opening speeches completed and the first witnesses called, Rosalind and I went for a drink. I wasn't happy with the way things were going, and was angry at Godwin's apparent failure to appreciate the seriousness of the case. Euthanasia might be his word for what he had done, but murder or manslaughter was the way the law termed it. Rosalind tried to calm me down, saying things would be better the next day, and I snapped at her for patronising me.

We wound up at her flat. By that time, although I had drunk enough to sink a battleship, I still felt sober – though extremely morose. We'd talked all evening about Godwin and what he and his wife must have been through before he helped her out of her misery. Enough to make anyone depressed.

Rosalind's flat was a surprise. With her pre-Raphaelite looks I had expected to find her home furnished with antiques. However, hi-tech modernity seemed to suit her quite well, too. Her heels clicked across white tiles as she walked down the hall, kicking a rug into place, as she went, and I followed her into a kitchen that seemed to have every gadget imaginable.

'I know what you're thinking,' she said. 'How does anyone on my salary afford such luxuries.'

'Well, I must admit . . .'

'My husband. Ex-husband. It's all his, or would be if he came back to claim it.'

'Where is he now?'

She shrugged. 'Haven't a clue. He went off to work one morning three years ago, and I haven't seen him since.'

'But didn't he tell you . . . ?'

'Oh yes. I had a phone call a week later, telling me he didn't want to be married any longer and he was going off to do his own thing. I was devastated at the time, but more for my son than myself.'

'I didn't know you had a son.'

'He's at boarding school. Charterhouse, down in Surrey. He'll be thirteen next week. I'll go down to see him, but the best present he could have would be his father turning up. At least the bastard left enough money for me to educate his son. Be thankful for small mercies, eh?'

I sighed. 'Do any marriages work out these days, I wonder?'

'Some must.' She turned to look at me, her eyebrows raised. 'Don't tell me yours . . . ?'

'Don't let's even speak about mine.'

We took our coffee and moved into the sitting room. 'She's a feminist, your wife, isn't she?' Rosalind said, curling her feet under her at the other end of the white leather sofa. 'She did a lot of good work back in the late sixties, early seventies. I remember her name was always in the papers. How did you cope with all that? Did it annoy you?'

'Like hell. Don't get me wrong, I've got nothing against equality of the sexes. What I objected to were Jessica's motives – not that I think she knew what they were herself. But she used the cause as some sort of weapon against me.'

'Weapon? Or shield?'

I looked into her blue eyes. 'Do I look like the kind of man you need to shield yourself from?'

'You are exactly that kind of man. And I can just imagine what you were like at university. If you ask me, Jessica was a brave woman to take you on.'

'Especially when she knew I was in love with someone else.'

'You were?'

'Still am.'

'Poor Jessica. It must have been very difficult for her.' She paused. 'And the other woman? Does Jessica know you're still in love with her?'

'Oh yes. She knows.'

'I'd like to meet her. Jessica, I mean.'

'Then you'll have to get someone else to introduce you.' I looked at my watch. 'I suppose I ought to be getting along.'

'Do you have to? You could always stay here tonight.'

I was surprised but assumed she was offering me the

spare room. Only when I looked at her face did I realise she wasn't.

'Are you shocked?' she said.

'I suppose I am, a bit. I mean, I didn't come here expecting . . .'

'I know you didn't.' She put her coffee cup back on the table. I moved along the sofa, took her in my arms and kissed her, waiting for the stirrings of desire to begin. After a while she led me through the dark hallway to the bedroom at the end. As she started to undress I watched, still waiting for my own response, but not until she was lying naked between the sheets did I realise that I couldn't go through with it.

I begged her to forgive me. It wasn't because I didn't find her attractive, I told her, it was just . . . I couldn't meet her eyes, and like a petulant schoolboy I hammered my fist against the doorframe in frustration. Then, to my horror, I was sobbing in her arms.

I pulled myself together quickly, fumbling out some lame excuse about too much to drink, a lot on my mind – and bolted before I could disgrace myself further.

It was past one in the morning when I finally arrived home, to find that Jessica had packed her bags and left. It was, I knew, another empty gesture. I went upstairs, threw a few things into a suitcase and made an early start for Suffolk, where I was going to have to spend the weekend sorting out the aftermath of the heaviest snowfall for years. I left a note for Jessica, knowing she would follow – she always did.

The following Monday, when I saw Rosalind again, she made no reference to what had happened. Embarrassed as I was, I still felt great warmth for her. I was so accustomed to Jessica's sneering if I made any show of weakness that Rosalind's kindness touched me in a way that reminded me of Elizabeth.

Godwin was found guilty and received a two-year suspended sentence. Rosalind and I took him and his daughter for a quiet drink later.

When they'd gone, on impulse I invited Rosalind to come to the gallery where Jessica's latest exhibition was opening that evening. I called Henry and arranged for Rosalind to go with him and Caroline – if she turned up with me, Jessica would throw a fit.

Jessica was in good spirits when I arrived, and busy sorting out last minute details. My father was already there, giving the benefit of his advice as usual, so I helped myself to a glass of wine and stood back to watch.

Jessica's exhibitions were always well attended, and little red stickers found their way quickly on to frames. The theme for this latest one was rather sober for her, in view of her past excursions into surrealism and the abstract. We had spent a month in Tuscany that spring, and she had made the Italian hills and valleys the background for a series of paintings entitled 'Child Lost in Tuscany'. The child, which had to be searched for in every painting, bore a striking resemblance to Jessica herself, though in one or two pictures it appeared only as a foetus. She'd taken me through the paintings some weeks before, in the belief that I would otherwise never understand their hidden message. The use of the foetus was pointed enough, I thought, without her having to add: 'I like to think our child is somewhere beautiful, don't you, darling?'

As I watched her now, excited, moving with ease among the guests, I was suddenly gripped by an overpowering desire to walk out. I didn't belong in this world of hers, I never had. I hated the farce we staged every time she had an opening. People talked about us, even wrote about us, as a loving couple, when nothing could be further from the truth. It was only guilt that bound me to her now; all I really wanted was to get as far away from her as I could . . . . But she was coming towards me now, smiling and holding out her hand for mine. She whispered something in my ear that I didn't catch, then planted a kiss on my cheek.

'I've been neglecting you,' she said. 'But you must blame your father. He's invited so many people and wants me to meet them all. Did you have a good day?'

I nodded absently, then looked down into her eyes. Successful Jessica might be, but I knew how fragile she was, too. There was still a long way to go before her shattered confidence could be completely restored. She needed me now in a way she never had before. It was as if she were afraid to do anything without me, even though she couldn't stop herself hurting and resenting me.

'Jess! There you are!' My father clapped his hand on her shoulder. 'The chap from *The Times* has arrived, come and say hello. Henry's looking for you,' he added to me, as he led her away.

I found Henry and Caroline – Caroline was more than halfway through her third pregnancy – standing next to the table that had been set up as a bar. I looked around for Rosalind. 'Gone to the ladies,' Henry whispered. 'She tells me she's dying to meet Jessica. Do you think that's wise, old chap?'

'I've got nothing to hide. Besides, I don't think Rosalind is going to let on we already know one another.'

'Got you. So who is she?'

'A friend of yours, of course . . . .'

Half an hour later I noticed Rosalind standing in a corner with Jessica. They were looking at one of the paintings, and I could almost hear Jessica as she explained to Rosalind what she was trying to convey. I watched them for a while, touched by the similarity of their lives. One way or another both had suffered at the hands of the men they loved. I hoped they would become friends, they would be good for each other.

After the exhibition the six of us – Henry, Caroline, Rosalind, Jessica, my father and I – went to Langan's.

Jessica and Rosalind paid scant attention to the conversation going on round the table, they were too engrossed in one another.

Rosalind became a frequent visitor to Belgrave Square after that. She and Jessica hit it off so well that they sometimes made me feel like an outsider. Occasionally Rosalind and I would lunch together but she rarely talked about Jessica, except to say that she thought she was regaining her confidence. I had to agree. To start with, Rosalind had rekindled Jessica's interest in the Women's Movement. I was never sure which rally they were attending when, but each time Jessica returned from a march or a meeting, she was a different person. There was no bitterness in her fight for equality now; there was a new gentleness about her, which found its way into her paintings too.

Jessica's part-independence, and part-dependence on someone else, had a strange effect on me. On the one hand I felt free and able to breathe again, on the other hand I missed her. I missed the arguments and the acrimony. I missed her being there when I got home at the end of a day. I missed the way she coped with my father. Most of all, perhaps, I missed the shock of her sudden, sadistic gestures – the cruel tricks, the drunken malice, the bizarre practical jokes. So often when I arrived home now, I would find a scribbled note saying, 'Back in a few days,' or she'd ring from Rosalind's and say she was staying over. As she began to stand on her own feet, so I began to feel unimportant, unnecessary; in fact I must have been feeling something of what Jessica had felt during the years of our marriage. Of course, she had not left me. We still slept in the same bed, dined together occasionally, even went away for weekends together. But it was as if she had somehow outgrown our marriage, was learning to stand free of it.

'I think things between us are better than they've ever been, don't you?' she said one day. 'I mean, we don't fight any more. I don't hate you any more, and I don't mind so much that you don't love me.'

'Don't you?'

'OK, I'm lying. I mind a lot, but I can handle it better these days. Rosalind's been a marvellous influence on me, don't you think? She's helped me to come to terms with things. To think of myself as an individual; you know, as Jessica, rather than as Jessica-and-Alexander.'

'Do I figure anywhere in the picture?'

'Oh, don't start getting sentimental on me, not now. I've fallen for that too often in the past. You'll only end up hurting me again.'

'I never meant to hurt you.'

'I know.'

'Do you love me, Jess?'

'You know I do. And what about you? Do you think you might be able to start loving me now?'

'I always did love you. Just not in the way . . .'

'No. Don't say any more.'

'I miss you. When you're not here, I miss you, you know.'

'I miss you too. But it's best this way.'

It was after that conversation, when she had flown off to Rome for the weekend with Rosalind that I realised I had been kidding myself. I didn't miss her at all. It was Elizabeth I missed. I had deluded myself into thinking it was Jessica because for the past three years I had rarely allowed myself to think of Elizabeth – the memory and the longing were too painful. Now there was nothing to fill the hours of loneliness, no one demanding my attention, no one constantly reminding me how I had ruined her life. At last I was free to think, and all I could think about was Elizabeth.

My father picked up Jessica and Rosalind from the airport when they got back from Rome, and took them to Henry's where we were all dining that night. But by the time I arrived Rosalind had left; she'd had a phone message to say that her son had been rushed into hospital with appendicitis. Jessica had offered to go with her, Henry told me, 'but then she changed her mind. Wait 'til you see her, she looks gorgeous. If you ask me she's fancying a bit of jig-a-jig later.'

'You've got sex on the brain,' I told him.

'Me!'

'Three children in three years, I rest my case.'

'Two,' Caroline corrected, as she waddled in through the door. 'The third can't make up its mind when to arrive. I wish it bloody well would, it's no fun being this shape. Have you been up to say goodnight to your godson, Alexander?'

Two Rupert Bear stories later, I came down to find the table laid for dinner. After Sarah, Henry's second child was born, Caroline and Henry had moved out of Eaton Square to a house in Chelsea, and my father, Jessica and I spent a lot of time there.

Henry was right, Jessica did look gorgeous. She'd had her hair cut in Rome, and it looked blonder, too. It was the first time I'd seen her with short hair; it made her eyes look bigger and her mouth fuller. She was wearing her normal jeans and sweater, but somehow tonight even they looked different.

When I kissed her she put her arms around me. 'You look tired,' she said. 'Not been having too many late nights while I've been in Rome, I hope?'

I pushed her away. 'Let's eat.'

Her face darkened, but my father was already asking her to go on with what she'd been saying before I arrived. It seemed she and Rosalind were going to join a march the next day to Aldermaston, the headquarters of the Atomic Weapons Research Establishment. 'A lot of women from our group are going, and we've arranged a meeting for Thursday to report back. In fact, Rosalind and I are thinking of joining CND on a permanent basis. Well, a girl's got to protect the next generation and all that.' She looked at me, but I didn't react.

When dinner was over Henry asked me to go to his study with him, there was a brief he wanted my thoughts on. I saw him exchange looks with Caroline before we left the room.

Once in his study he took a bottle of brandy from his filing cabinet. He seemed in no hurry, and chatted for some time about Nicholas and what he was doing at kindergarten. 'Well,' I said eventually, 'where's this brief?'

'There isn't one,' he answered shortly. 'It's something else, Alexander. I don't know whether I should tell you this or not, but I'm going to. It's about Elizabeth.'

I froze. 'What about her?'

'I've got her address. It's written there, inside that envelope.' When I made no move to pick it up, he handed it to me.

The skin felt so tight over my face it was difficult to speak. 'How did you find it? Did she telephone you?'

'No. I was picking Nicholas up from kindergarten a couple of days ago, I saw her then. She didn't see me. She got into the car in front of mine and drove off. Nicholas and I followed.'

I stared down at the envelope.

'There's something else you should know, Alexander. The child she collected from kindergarten. It was a little boy, same age as Nicholas. His name's Jonathan. I've seen him, Alexander . . . .'

'Go on.' My voice was hoarse.

'There's no doubt in my mind, and well, with his age as well . . .'

There was no need for him to elaborate. We looked at each other for a long time without speaking. In the end it was Henry who broke the silence.

'It's up to you now, Alexander.'

'Why up to me? She's always known where she could find me.'

'For Christ's sake, Alexander, you were the one who broke it off. You were the one who told her you couldn't leave Jessica after the accident . . . .'

'She could have told me. If he's my son . . .'

'And since then you've done nothing, have you? You could have gone to her once everything had calmed down, but you didn't. You've done nothing . . .'

'But things never did calm down, did they? Jessica's still a mess. Am I supposed to walk out on her now, on top of everything else I've done to her?'

'You've got two children out there. Don't you think you owe them something too? Your marriage is a bigger farce now than it ever was. You make me laugh, you two, the way you go about pretending you're over your difficulties. . . . If you ask me, it's about time you stopped wallowing in guilt and got on with your life.'

I was out of my chair like a shot – but the door burst open before I could speak. It was Jessica. 'Henry! It's Caroline. The pains have started.'

Henry glared at me. 'Just think about it, Alexander,' he growled, then raced out of the door.

'Don't tell me you two were having a lovers' tiff?' Jessica scoffed. She stepped back as my eyes blazed into her.

'I'm sick of you, Jessica! I'm sick of the damned sight of you. I thought you'd changed, but even tonight you couldn't resist twisting a knife in my guilt, could you? Well, you've done it long enough, so do us both a favour and get out of my life before I do something we might both regret!'

'Oh it's too late for that, Alexander. You did it three years ago.'

– Elizabeth –

– 24 –

I watched Edward stalk off through the crowds. 'It will be a most wonderful book Mr Walters is writing.' Kamel was standing at my elbow – he seemed to have been standing beside me all the time we'd been in Egypt. Next to him was one of the museum's curators, his round brown eyes dilated with something akin to worship as they followed Edward.

The Cairo Museum was seething with tourists. I'd known nothing about a book until we returned from Aswan to Cairo – Kamel had told me. Kamel was with us to protect us, though Edward had never told me from what. His presence unsettled me, as did the crowded streets and anonymous, staring eyes that seemed to follow me everywhere. From the moment we'd arrived the city had appalled me with its frightening pandemonium of noise and disorder; Cairo was a jungle of pungent, decaying streets and crowded alleys where modern hotels and ancient crumbling houses stood cheek by jowl. It was a bizarre, amorphous place that vibrated with an almost sinister extremism. As I got to know it better, the poverty and ignorance horrified me. I talked to Edward about it but he just patted my hand and told me there was nothing to be done. I know he didn't mean to but he made me feel as if Cairo were his particular territory, and he was sorry he'd brought me.

Every day he went to the Museum to study the people and their reaction to the Tutankhamun collection. His fascination with it bordered on obsession. We'd come here for a holiday for Charlotte to recuperate, but ever since we'd arrived Edward had spent his time here. As well as doing his research, he was advising the museum authorities on the installation of an intricate alarm system. He was treated like a royal visitor, and behaved like one too. He wore his galibaya as if he had been born to it, ate nothing but Egyptian food, read Egyptian newspapers, and unless speaking to the children or me, always spoke Egyptian. He even had the heavy, musky smell of an Egyptian.

The curator fiddled with his collar. His brown, Western suit didn't fit him well. His bad teeth were exposed in a grin, and turning, I found Kamel had hoisted Jonathan up on to his shoulder. The curator looked at Jonathan just as he looked at Edward – with admiration verging on reverence. It was a look I was getting used to, but I didn't like it. Almost everyone we'd met, especially on our cruise down the Nile when we had stopped in remote villages, looked at Edward and Jonathan like that. I wondered if it had anything to do with the vast amounts of money Edward dished out to the poverty-stricken villagers, who rushed out of their mountainside homes to greet him, their galibayas billowing behind them. What Edward talked about with these men, closeted away in dark, sunbaked houses while they sucked on hookahs and drew diagrams in the sand, I didn't know. Whatever it was, though, it seemed to have a profound effect on him.

Wherever we went, Kamel went too. Sometimes he entered the huts with Edward, but usually he stayed outside with the children and me. I knew he carried a gun even though Edward denied it. And the way Kamel watched the slow movements of the villagers while listening to the distant, guttural sounds of Nubian drums, I knew he was waiting for something. Always in the distance was the Nile, a shimmery blue ribbon parting the desert. The conferences continued through the heat of the day while, forgotten by Edward, Charlotte, Jonathan and I sought refuge from the sun. The only break in the proceedings came when the cry of the Muezzin beckoned the Egyptians to prayer. Then Edward would emerge, his galibaya and turban coated in dust, and wait while a woman, her face shrouded in a tarha, wiped the sand from his face. He seemed then like a man I didn't know. Until we went to Egypt I'd all but forgotten the sinister premonition I'd had that night at Westmoor when I'd heard Christine and Edward arguing. But while I was in Egypt my fears increased like a swelling black cloud. A sixth sense told me the storm was almost ready to break – and all I wanted was to go home.

Jeffrey was at Heathrow to meet us when we flew in from Cairo. Edward was returning with Christine the next day. We drove straight to the London house in Priory Walk, where Canary was so overjoyed to see the children that I thought she was going to break down and cry. In the Scots lilt we had all missed she clucked her delight at the gifts Charlotte and Jonathan had brought for her, and listened with wide eyes while they talked of pyramids and camels and the trips they had made in a felucca.

The following day I was in the kitchen with Mary when Canary came in. 'Would you mind coming to the nursery, Mrs Walters? There's a wee matter I'd like to discuss with you.' And without waiting for an answer she left.

She was sitting in her wicker chair when I walked into the nursery, her hands folded in her lap, her papery eyelids blinking rapidly.

She got up and closed the door behind me. As she passed I could smell jasmine. 'I think it would be better if no one overheard this conversation,' she said. I perched on the edge of the wicker sofa beneath the window and waited. I could see she was uncomfortable so I smiled to try and help her relax.

'Somebody came to call while you were in Egypt,' she began. Her face remained sombre, and though she had told me nothing yet, I felt my smile begin to freeze. 'He asked to see you but I told him you had gone on holiday.'

Her words hung in the air while I tried to control the

thoughts that were suddenly careering about inside my head. 'Did he leave his name?' I asked finally.

'No.' Her face softened. 'He didn't have to.'

I knew instinctively that there would be no point in trying to deceive Canary. Alexander wouldn't have told her anything, but I could tell from those few short words that she had read the situation perfectly. 'Did he say anything at all?' I asked.

'Not then, no. But he came back again the next day.' She pulled a letter out of her pocket and handed it to me. 'He asked me to give you this.'

I stared down at the envelope, recognising his untidy scrawl. All the time Charlotte had been recovering in hospital, I'd thought about him. When I was in Egypt, watching the sun set over the Nile, I'd wished he could be there. All the times I'd felt afraid and alone – and had almost cried out for him. And now he had come. My heart was beating so hard I thought Canary must be able to hear it.

I got up. My body felt stiff and it was an effort to put one foot in front of the other. When I got to the door, I stopped. 'Canary . . . ?' She was still watching me. 'Thank you for not telling anyone about this.'

In the privacy of my own room I peeled back the flap of the envelope. My hands were shaking so badly I could hardly pull the letter free.

After I'd read it I lay back on my bed. He'd given me a phone number where I could reach him. He wanted to see me, he wanted to see his children. *His* children. Oh God, what was I going to do?

He said if he didn't hear from me by the tenth he would call again. Today was the eighth.

I lived through the next twenty-four hours in a daze. I had to stop him from coming here – but I knew that as soon as I heard his voice on the phone my courage would fail me. In the end I felt I had no choice. Edward was back from

Cairo so I asked Canary if I could use the telephone in the nursery. She folded her sewing away and left the room.

A man answered, and when I asked if I could speak to Alexander Belmayne, he said, 'I'm afraid he's in court at the moment. If you call again about five he should be here then.'

At five o'clock the children were in the nursery and Edward had gone out, so I used the phone in my bedroom. This time I was put through. As I heard Alexander's voice come over the line, my fingers gripped the phone and my mouth was suddenly so dry I couldn't speak.

'Hello? Hello? Is anyone there?'

'Alexander.'

There was a brief silence at the end of the line. 'Elizabeth.' His voice was soft and I felt tears rush to my eyes. 'I was afraid you wouldn't ring.'

I didn't answer. 'Are you still there?' he said.

'Yes.'

'You read my letter.' He stopped, and I could feel his presence so strongly it was as if he were in the room with me. 'Can I see you?'

The tears spilled from my eyes and my whole body began to shake.

'Elizabeth! Are you all right? I'm sorry, I shouldn't have done this to you. But I have to see you, I'll go out of my mind if I don't. Please, for God's sake, say you'll meet me.'

'No, Alexander,' I sobbed. 'No, I can't. Please don't ask me to explain.'

'Elizabeth! Don't hang up! Elizab . . .'

I pressed the phone back on the hook and sank to my knees, whispering under my breath for him to forgive me.

At that moment the door swung open and Charlotte came skipping in. 'Look at this, Mum, what do you . . . ?' She stopped as she saw me kneeling on the floor, then ran into my arms, frightened tears starting from her eyes. 'Why are you crying, Mummy? What is it? What's happened?'

'Hush, hush, darling. It's nothing. Nothing for you to worry about.' I smoothed my hand over her hair and felt myself being crushed from within. 'Oh Charlotte, Charlotte, what have I done? What am I going to do?'

'I don't know, Mum, but it'll be all right, I promise you. We'll make it all right. Please stop crying, Mummy.'

Jonathan let up a loud wail as he came in and saw us sitting on the floor wiping tears from each other's eyes. I held out my arms to him.

'I'm sorry,' he sobbed. 'I didn't mean to do it. Honest, Mum, I didn't mean it.'

'Didn't mean to do what, darling?'

'Whatever it was that made you cry. I didn't mean it, Mum. I'm sorry.'

I met Charlotte's eyes and through our tears we started to laugh. 'Oh Jonathan,' I hugged him fiercely, 'I love you so very much.' I reached out for Charlotte. 'I love you both so much.'

We were still sitting on the floor an hour later when the smell of Canary's jasmine perfume made me look up. She stood there for a moment, looking at me, then turned and walked away. When I reached the landing she was waiting in the hall below, holding the door to the sitting-room. Her face was grim as she watched me descend the stairs.

'It's all right,' I said as I passed her.

'I'll be getting back to the children,' she answered.

I didn't look up until she had closed the door behind me, and when I did it was as if I was being carried away on the current of my own longing. Alexander was standing there, in my drawing-room, his dark overcoat unbuttoned to reveal the sombre grey suit beneath. He could have been anyone – except for the power that drew my eyes to his face, unleashing the blood that, for a moment, had seemed to stop in my veins. He was thinner, and his handsome face looked drawn and tired. I knew I should be angry with him for coming, but when he smiled and I saw the crooked tooth my heart turned over. It was as if a magnet had suddenly drawn together the fragmented pieces of my life.

'I had to come, you know that, don't you?'

I nodded, then suddenly I was in his arms. 'Oh, Alexander, I've needed you so much.'

He held me close, crushing me, telling me he was sorry, that he should never have left me. I looked up into his eyes and touched his lips with my fingers. 'Why do our lives have to be like this?'

He cupped my face in his hands. Suddenly a door slammed upstairs and someone ran down the stairs.

'What are we going to do? You can't stay, Edward will be back soon.'

'Tell me about Jonathan, Elizabeth. Is he my son?'

Unable to meet his eyes, I turned away and went to sit beside the fire. 'What do you intend to do?' I asked, after a while.

He came to stand beside me and reaching out for my hand turned me round to face him. 'I think that rather depends on you.'

I pulled my hand away, but still his grey eyes held me. 'Please, Alexander, please go now, before anyone gets hurt.'

'Elizabeth, you've given birth to two children, my children, whom I've never even met. Now isn't it about time it all got sorted out?'

'It's too late, Alexander, there's nothing to be sorted out any more.'

His face paled. 'What do you mean? Either I am their father or I'm not. Which is it, Elizabeth?'

'I think I'm in the best position to answer that.' The door closed, and we spun round to find Edward standing there watching us. He walked towards us. 'Are you going to make the introductions, Elizabeth?' he said, never taking his eyes from Alexander.

I mumbled their names and turned away as they shook hands.

'I think what Elizabeth is trying to tell you is that Charlotte and Jonathan – those are their names, by the way, in case you didn't know – that Charlotte and Jonathan are no longer . . .'

'*No*!' I screamed. 'No, Edward. Please!'

Edward turned to me. 'But he has to know, my dear, otherwise he'll think he can come here whenever he pleases.'

I saw Alexander bristle and stepped in quickly. 'Please, Edward, let me deal with it.'

'Shut up!' I had never known Edward shout at me before. I must have recoiled – and Alexander took a step forward as if to defend me. Edward visibly shrank away from him, but his resolve remained firm. 'What I'm trying to tell you, young man, is that the children you so arrogantly assume to be yours are, in fact, mine. Three years ago I adopted both Charlotte and Jonathan.'

'Edward, stop!' I ran to Alexander's side. 'You've gone too far, Edward!'

Alexander snatched his arm from me. 'Tell me this isn't true, Elizabeth. Tell me he is lying.'

I hung my head but he caught me by the shoulders and wrenched me round to face him. 'You let this man adopt *my* children!'he spat. 'After all we meant to each other, you let *him* . . .'

'Alexander, it wasn't like that. You don't understand. I had no choice . . . .'

Edward pulled me away and shoved me behind him. His eyes bored into Alexander's. 'You have no right to come here, upsetting my wife . . . .'

'Your *wife*? And just what kind of wife is it who runs off and gets herself pregnant by another man? And what kind of man are you who steals another man's children?'

'Get out of here!' Edward snarled.

I tore myself away from Edward and ran to Alexander. 'Please, listen to me. Please . . .' But Alexander wrenched himself free. His eyes were like ice as he looked back at me. 'I'll never understand how you could have done this, Elizabeth. You, above anyone else, knew . . .'

'Enough!' Edward's voice cut between us.

'Alexander! No! Don't go!' I cried, as he started to turn away. 'Edward, let me go after him. He mustn't leave like this.'

'Stay where you are, Elizabeth. He's out of your life now.'

'How can he be? For God's sake, he's their father!'

The blow to my cheek stunned me to silence. And then, before I knew what was happening, Alexander had knocked Edward to the floor. I threw myself down beside him, but he flung me away and dragged himself to his feet. He was breathing heavily and reached out for the back of a chair to steady himself. 'Get out!' he growled. His face was grey and menacing and I felt a sudden stab of fear.

Alexander reached out for my hand and pulled me to my feet. 'Take me with you,' I begged. 'Please, take me with you.'

'Go with him now and you'll never see your children again,' Edward gasped.

'She's not coming with me.'

I spun round and my blood turned cold as Alexander's pitiless eyes swept over my face.

'No, Elizabeth. You made your decision the day you let him adopt our children.' He shook his head slowly, and at last his eyes began to thaw. 'Jesus Christ, why did you do it?' His voice was quiet now. 'They were my children, Elizabeth. My children.' Then he turned and walked out the door.

I went slowly over to Edward. He was wiping the blood from his nose, his hands shaking badly. For several minutes neither of us moved. He was still holding on to the chair, his body sagging against it. Then suddenly he slumped awkwardly to his knees and his voice slurred from the back of his throat as he tried to say my name. I looked at him in horror as he slowly rolled to the floor.

When we reached the hospital Edward was wheeled away and I was left alone. I paced the corridor, going over and over all that had happened. I detested myself, knowing that I was to blame. If I hadn't married Edward, I could have saved him all this and he wouldn't be lying here in hospital, maybe dying.

But even then I was thinking about Alexander and the pain I had caused him too. Everything was my fault. If I hadn't seen Alexander and Jessica looking so happy together that night as I stood in the dark at the edge of Belgrave Square, I would never have agreed to let Edward adopt the children. And now he was the one who was paying the price for that unforgivable act of revenge.

David and Christine arrived. Christine's face was white with anxiety and I couldn't bring myself to meet her eyes. If she knew what had brought this on she would never forgive me. I was saved from any immediate explanations by the doctor.

'Mrs Walters?' He smiled. 'Don't look so worried, your husband's going to be fine.'

My knees buckled with relief. David caught me before I fell and led me to a chair. 'But . . . what was . . . ? Is he . . . ?'

'Your husband's suffered what we call a transient ischaemic attack,' the doctor explained. 'In plain language, he's had a very mild stroke. Ah, no,' he said, as I tried to speak, 'it's nothing to worry about, he'll be ready to leave in the morning.'

'In the morning?' I echoed, hardly daring to believe it.

'Indeed. I suggest he takes it easy for a while, but there's no reason whatever why he shouldn't continue a completely normal life.'

'But what brought it on?' Christine asked.

I felt myself tense, but the doctor was still smiling. 'It can be brought on by a number of things – in this case, it appears to have been the spasm of a blood vessel in the brain.'

When we reached Westmoor late the following afternoon, Edward and I went straight upstairs. It was cold in our room, so neither of us took off our coats. Out of habit Edward went to sit on the sofa beside the empty fireplace, and motioned for me to sit beside him. We sat quietly for a long time, both of us understanding that he must be the first to speak.

Finally, long after it had grown dark and I had turned on the lamps on either side of the bed, Edward spoke. His face was still grey, though a tiny spot of colour highlighted his left cheek where he had been resting it on his hand. His hair, normally immaculate, was ruffled, and automatically I ran my fingers through it, smoothing it into place.

'I was afraid,' he said, simply. 'It is the only excuse I have for the way I behaved. No, please, hear me out. The moment I saw him I knew who he was, and I was afraid. I could see I was losing you, that I had probably already lost you. I was thinking only of myself and what my life would be like without you and the children, and the loneliness and emptiness I saw stretching before me robbed me of reason. He was so young and handsome, and there was I . . . I realised then what I had done to your life by marrying you.' He lifted his hand and wiped the tears from my face, then he sighed and smiled, looking out through the window into the black night. 'I can't keep you here any longer, my darling. I know now that I have to let you go to him. I've decided to fly to Cairo with Christine on Sunday, so that it will be easier for you when you go. But I want you to know how sorry I am, Elizabeth. Sorry for the years I've held you to me, and sorry for everything that happened yesterday.'

I was crying so hard my voice jerked from my body. 'Oh, Edward, Edward. What have I done to you?' He rocked me gently in his arms, stroked my hair and my face as if I were a child. 'I'm not going to leave you, Edward.'

He squeezed me. 'But I shall still go to Cairo. If you change your mind while I'm there, or even before . . .' The breath caught in his throat and he buried his face in my hair.

Edward flew off as planned on Sunday, but Christine didn't go with him. Instead she came up to London to spend the night with me and the children before catching a flight to Hong Kong the next day. She would be joining Edward in Cairo the following Friday.

Canary was waiting when we arrived at Priory Walk, and ushered the children upstairs to prepare their things for school the next day. Jeffrey carried the luggage up after them, and Christine and I followed Mary into the drawing-room.

'Now,' said Christine, as the door closed behind Mary, 'perhaps you'd like to tell me what's been happening.' I looked up from the tea tray. 'I'm talking about the mild stroke, the pregnant silences, your red eyes, and most of all what Edward said to you in the drive at Westmoor before he left. "If you do want to leave . . ." Isn't that what he said? So what the hell's going on?' The skin was drawn tight across her cheekbones, and her lips were white.

I put the teapot down slowly, then drew myself up to face her. 'I don't wish to be rude, Christine,' I said, trying to keep the edge out of my voice, 'and I know how much you care for Edward, but what goes on between us doesn't concern you.'

The colour flooded up from her neck into her face, turning it an ugly puce. 'It damned well concerns me when my brother is rushed to hospital with a stroke!'

'I don't think we should continue this conversation. As I said before . . .'

'Don't patronise me, you bitch! You nearly broke his heart once before, and this time you almost killed him.' She was advancing across the room towards me, her fists clenching and unclenching at her sides. 'You and your two bastards have caused him more pain than any man deserves, but let me tell you this, Elizabeth, you hurt him once more, just once more, and so help me God, I'll kill you.'I thought she was going to strike me – but suddenly, as if she couldn't bear to look at me a moment longer, she turned on her heel and walked out of the room.

I didn't see her again that day, and she had already left for the airport by the time I came down the following morning.

I resolved not to tell Edward anything about it. I knew it would upset him, and cause more arguments between him and Christine. When they returned from Cairo two weeks later Christine greeted me with a sisterly kiss as if nothing had happened, and I decided to follow her lead and keep up appearances. But from then on I was wary of her. If only I'd known how wary I needed to be.

Life resumed its normal pattern after that. Edward and I still entertained a great deal, and Westmoor became an art dealer's Mecca. On the rare occasions when we had no guests, Edward spent his time going over the plans he was still drawing up for a security system in the Cairo museum. His constant complaint was that with such a lack of security there, the Tutankhamun mask was in real danger. I did wonder why it was taking him so long to finalise the museum's security plans, but it was obviously a complex job, and Edward was nothing if not a perfectionist.

In June David returned from Gstaad with Jenifer Illingworth and gave us all the good news we'd been waiting for; they were to be married.

But as the months passed and the dreadful shock of that

day in spring wore off, I found myself thinking more and more about Alexander. I even got as far as picking up the phone, though I never rang him. Much as I wanted him, I couldn't risk causing Edward a moment's more pain. In the end it was neither Alexander nor I who made the move towards a reconciliation, but Henry.

He made no mention of why he had chosen to ring when he did, but I gathered that it was something he had been thinking of doing for some time. He spoke briefly and to the point. He didn't know why I had let Edward adopt the children, but he was sure I had had my reasons, and what he asked of me now was simply that I should explain those reasons to Alexander. He felt – and he was sure I would agree with him – that I owed Alexander at least that.

So, with a complete disregard for all the promises I had made Edward, I waited only as long as it took for Henry to ring off before I called Alexander at chambers and arranged to meet him the following day.

After that we met at least once a month, sometimes more often, on the bridge over the Serpentine. We would walk for hours, talking and laughing, as I told him about his children. He was hungry for every detail, all the little anecdotes I had stored away in my memory over the years, in the hope that one day I could tell them to him. Sometimes he came with me to collect them from school, watching from a distance, until we drove away. I can't imagine what it must have been like for him, but he never asked for more.

I had dreadful feelings of guilt about what I was doing, but although I was terrified of Edward finding out, I couldn't stop. Edward, though, seemed more preoccupied than ever lately. I sensed a distance creeping between us, and though I couldn't explain it, I knew it was of his making. On the rare evenings when we were at home together, I felt his mind was elsewhere. But if I asked him what he was thinking he'd only smile and hug me, all the time staring abstractedly into some other world.

Then, through the developing friendship between Jonathan and Henry's son, Nicholas, it became possible for Alexander to get to know Jonathan. We spent many hours at Henry's house in Chelsea, and Caroline became a good friend to me. Occasionally Caroline would bring her children round to Priory Walk; it was her idea to do that – she thought it would appear less suspicious if she were to let Edward meet her children.

Alexander and I, no matter what the weather, continued to meet in Hyde Park. Neither of us ever suggested meeting anywhere else, I think we were afraid of what might happen if we did. In all that time we had been careful never to touch one another, though sometimes his smile was so like a caress that it was all I could do not to throw myself into his arms and beg him to hold me. I can't explain how it felt to know that each time I left my car and walked towards the bridge over the Serpentine, he would be waiting there for me. And he only had to turn and look at me – the relief in his eyes at seeing me, then the slow, teasing smile of appreciation as he took in my appearance – for the laughter to well up inside me, making me feel like the happiest and most beautiful woman alive.

Then one day, when we were sitting in the little cafeteria on the edge of the Serpentine, sheltering from the rain, he started to talk about his father. 'He was very upset when I told him about you, so we now have another person riddled with guilt on our hands. He blames himself, as you and I do; he thinks he should have tried to understand us more when we were young. He'd like to make up for it, Elizabeth. What do you say? Will you come to meet him?'

'What about Jessica?'

'When she's not on a march she's at the studio she and Rosalind have rented in Windsor. She's designing publicity material for CND, and Rosalind gives free legal advice if anyone falls foul of the police. I imagine they're quite a force to be reckoned with. Anyway, she hasn't been home in weeks.'

'How was she, the last time you saw her?'

'The same old Jessica. Charming and sweet when she arrived, at my throat by the time she left. But at least she starts off with good intentions. I don't suppose I help much.'

'Why?'

'Well, for one thing I've moved all my things into another room.'

The following week I met Lord Belmayne at their home in Belgrave Square. It went off better than either Alexander or I could have hoped. Alexander teased his father because it was clear he had been expecting to see the gauche twenty-one-year-old he'd last confronted at Foxton's. I showed him photographs of his grandchildren while Alexander boasted about how closely they resembled him. I was having such a good time I didn't want the afternoon to end.

At the Lord Chancellor's invitation I went again the following week. He was waiting for me at the door; he had his coat on, and there was a car outside with its engine running. He had to rush off to a meeting, some crisis had erupted.

'Alexander's inside feeling extremely sorry for himself,' he said. 'He lost a case on Friday after locking horns with someone who's better than he is – but don't tell him I said so.'

Alexander was standing in front of the fire beneath the portrait of his mother when I walked in. His hands were clasped behind his back, and with his long legs set slightly apart he looked every bit the viscount he would one day be.

'How are you?' he smiled.

'Cold.' And I went to stand beside him at the fire. 'Your father tells me you lost a case on Friday.'

'After locking horns with someone better than I am. I heard!' He walked over to the record player in the corner. 'He was getting his own back because I told him he had a meeting to attend.'

I turned to look at him. 'You told him . . .'

'I can't take any more of this, Elizabeth.

I stood very still, feeling the colour seep into my face. 'Remember this?' he said, as 'Sealed with a Kiss' began to play.

His eyes held mine, and I was dimly aware of my heart-beat beginning to race. The fire crackled in the grate. And then he was reaching out for me, pulling me into his arms. We danced slowly, until the music had finished. His mouth was so close to mine I could feel his breath on my face. He waited, then as I closed my eyes he gathered me into his arms and carried me up the stairs.

– 25 –

The scream shrilled through the house, waking me with a jolt. Groping frantically in the dark for my dressing-gown, I ran to the door. David was on the landing in his pyjamas and Canary was running down the hall, tucking her curlers into a hairnet.

'What's happened? What is it?'

'It sounded like Christine.' David crossed the landing and threw open her door. The room was in darkness, the bed hadn't been slept in.

'Where's Edward?' David asked.

'I'm here,' Edward answered. We all turned to see him coming up the stairs and I noted, with surprise – for we had gone to bed at the same time that night – that he was fully dressed. 'Everything's all right, you can all go back to bed now.'

'But the scream,' I protested. 'What was it?'

'It was Christine. She had a bit of a shock. Nothing to worry about.' His face was haggard and as his eyes moved from mine, I saw him exchange a meaningful look with David.

Canary offered to go downstairs and make a hot drink for everyone, but David put his arm round her and ushered her back to the nursery, leaving Edward and me on the landing.

'Where's Christine now?' I asked. 'Is there anything I can do?'

'I think not.' He looked over the banister into the hall. 'David will go down to her in a moment.'

We were all at Westmoor for the summer holidays, except for Charlotte, who was now fourteen and had gone to spend a week in the south of France with a schoolfriend and her family.

At breakfast the following morning no mention was made of the night's incident, and when Christine emerged from her room, much later in the day, there were no visible signs of damage. So I shrugged the whole thing off and started devising an excuse for going up to London the following week.

In fact excuses were hardly necessary these days. Edward spent so much time in his study, or flying backwards and forwards between Cairo and London that he barely noticed whether I was there or not. I knew he was about to pull off some big deal he had been working on for years, but he never discussed such things with me and I had to confess to being guilty of complete indifference now that Alexander was back in my life.

I was in the Blue Sitting-Room that afternoon when I heard voices in the dining-room. As far as I knew Edward and Christine had gone to the warehouse for a stock check, so I was surprised when I identified the voices as theirs, and was on the verge of opening the adjoining doors when something Christine said stopped me in my tracks.

'. . . but for Christ's sake, Edward, they killed him.'

'Well, what was he doing there in the first place?'

'They said he'd fallen asleep.'

'And what about the . . . ?' I couldn't make out what Edward said after that, but Christine's answer chilled me.

'Is that all you can think about? A man's lying dead, and all you care about . . .'

Edward interrupted. 'I've been waiting too long for this to let anything get in the way now. Now, what else did they say? When are they getting it out?'

They left the dining-room then. And when I went to look for Edward later, Jeffrey told me he'd gone out and didn't know when he would be back.

I waited for the rest of the day, but there was no sign of him and neither did he ring. Christine had disappeared too, though she hadn't gone with Edward, Jeffrey said. Once or twice a foreign-sounding man telephoned, asking for her, but he wouldn't leave a message or give his name.

I drove up to London and found Alexander waiting in the flat we now rented in Chelsea. We'd been living our double lives for over three years now; it was easier for him as Jessica had all but moved in with Rosalind. Our own flat was small, cluttered with things we had bought together in antique markets and junk shops. The children's school drawings were pasted all over the kitchen walls, and photographs of them were scattered about the sitting-room and bedroom. When I arrived Alexander was in the kitchen, an apron round his waist, starting the evening meal. I was too distracted by all that was going on at Westmoor to eat much, and as Alexander talked about his day in court the feeling of depression that had been lingering about me for so long seemed to reach him too. We snapped at one another, then yelled over the washing-up, broke a few plates and drenched one another in dishwater. We made up later, in bed, but the following morning I drove back to Westmoor early.

Edward was in such a good mood I ventured to ask him about the conversation I had overheard. He didn't even flinch.

'Oh that!' he laughed. 'It was all a misunderstanding. You know what the Egyptians are like, they make a drama out of everything.'

'But I thought I heard Christine say someone had been killed,' I insisted. 'How can that be a misunderstanding?'

'Easily. As far as I can make out there was a fight and one of them fell and hit his head against something. The other one assumed he had killed him, panicked and ran. So apart from one Arab with a large bump on the head, no one's any the worse for wear.'

'But what were they fighting about in the first place?'

'Money.'

'That you were paying them?'

'Yes. But as I said, there's nothing to worry about now, everything has been sorted out, and within a few days the deal will be finalised and your husband will have pulled off one of the greatest coups the art world has ever known.'

And that was as far as I got – until Charlotte told me something she had overheard the day after she arrived home from France.

She came in from the garden to find me in her room, sorting out clothes for jumble. She sat down on the edge of her bed. 'Mum, I've just heard the strangest thing.'

'What was that, darling?'

She giggled. 'Well, it was like something out of a movie, except it happened right here, in our garden.'

It seemed she had been sitting against the wall under the parterre when Christine and David had walked out of the French windows. She hadn't taken much notice of what they were saying until Edward joined them and David said: 'I don't want to know any more than I already do, I'm going in.' Edward had laughed, and said to Christine: 'So you've spoken to your husband, and I take it you're satisfied it wasn't him?'

I interrupted Charlotte. 'Husband?'

'That's what he said.'

'But Christine's not married.'

'I know.'

'You must have misheard, darling. Is that all?'

'No. Then Edward asked Christine where the plane was coming in, and Christine said it was landing at Greg Dunne's airfield, the same as before, and that she'd given him the money.'

I put my arm round Charlotte's shoulders and tried not to laugh. 'Edward's always having things flown in from all over the world, you know that.'

'I know, it's just that, I don't know, somehow this sounded different.'

'In what way?'

'Well, David wouldn't listen, for one thing.'

I thought about this for a moment. 'Tell you what,' I said, 'why don't we ask Edward what he's expecting? I'm sure he'll be only too glad to tell you.'

And sure enough, he was. He was expecting a cargo from Hong Kong the following week, and Greg Dunne was going to call him when it had been cleared by Customs. No mention was made of the 'husband', as it was absurd to think Christine would want to hide something like that, so we just assumed Charlotte had misheard.

Over the next few days I noticed a distinct change in Edward. He almost skipped around the house, his eyes brimming with excitement; he looked younger – in the last week he seemed to have lost ten or fifteen years. There was a great deal of activity in the Egyptian Room, painters going in and out, the old treasures being removed and carefully transported by lorry to the warehouse. At night Edward tossed and turned, keeping me awake, even though we now had separate beds. In direct contrast to Edward's ebullience, Christine seemed annoyed all the time, and kept telling him to pull himself together. Then David announced abruptly that he and Jenifer were going to the house in Gstaad, and wouldn't be back for at least a month.

After David's departure Edward's behaviour changed again. Now he veered from melancholy to downright bad temper and seemed constantly on edge. On one occasion, when Jonathan answered the phone, Edward actually pushed him out of the way. It was his secretary, obviously asking him when he next intended coming to London as work was piling up. Edward barked that he would inform her of his movements when he knew what they were and slammed the receiver down. Then Charlotte came into the room, and the next thing I knew, Edward was shouting at her too.

All this was quite untypical of our normal family life, and I found it so upsetting that I decided to go to London. Jonathan was all for going, but Charlotte wasn't keen. I guessed this had something to do with Colin Newman who was playing Romeo to her Juliet in the village play, so I said she could stay behind, but Edward declared he was too busy to look after a lovesick teenager and she had to come. And so, with an eager son and a sulking daughter, I arrived in Priory Walk late one hot Wednesday night in August.

It was these small details I had to remember later, when I was giving evidence at my own trial.

Alexander called me from chambers the following afternoon. By the time we rang off, arranging to meet in the flat at seven-thirty, he'd got me so aroused I could have torn off my clothes and raped the milkman. I was still feeling flushed when the phone rang again twenty minutes later. It was Edward.

'Elizabeth, I want you to get back here as soon as you

can. Leave the children in London, Jeffrey can pick them up tomorrow.'

'Edward, I can't . . .'

'For Christ's sake, Elizabeth, this is an emergency!'

'What do you mean, an emergency?' But he had already rung off. I dialled the Westmoor number immediately, but the line was busy, and it remained busy. Suddenly all the warmth had gone out of the day and that cold feeling of dread was creeping over me again.

Alexander was in a conference, so I drove round to the flat and left him a note.

I arrived at Westmoor just after seven. Edward was waiting in the drive. As I pulled up beside the Rolls Royce, he tore open the door of my car. 'Thank God you're here.' He gulped, as if he was trying to catch his breath. 'Christine's hurt her foot, I need you to drive the car. We haven't much time.'

He ushered me behind the wheel of the Rolls. 'Where are we going?' I said.

'Just head for Dover, I'll tell you when to turn off.'

By the time we reached the A2 he had calmed down a little. I glanced at him, trying to gauge his mood, then asked again where we were going. He smiled. His eyes were too bright. 'Just wait and see, my darling. Just wait and see.'

There was a gnawing sensation in the pit of my stomach. I wanted to stop the car, demand that he tell me what was going on – but there was something about him that stopped me.

Just after we passed the Aylesham turning we turned right, down a one-track road. The sun was sinking into the trees by this time, though it was still light enough to see without headlights. After several very rough miles, Edward told me to pull in beside a gate. As we came to a halt he looked at his watch. 'We're too early. We'll have to wait.'

'Too early for what?'

'Don't ask any more questions, Elizabeth, you'll know everything soon enough.'

His eyes were fixed rigidly ahead. This was so unlike any situation I had ever been in before that I couldn't begin to imagine what was happening. What were we doing here, parked miles from anywhere, waiting for a rendezvous with God-only-knew-who? I started to tell him I was afraid, but the words dried on my lips as I realised it was Edward I was afraid of . . . .

The sound of a light aircraft droned overhead. It came into view. Edward never took his eyes off it, but he didn't say a word, and even when the plane landed about a mile away, the malignant silence continued. From time to time he looked at his watch, then at the horizon. Finally, when night was a black, solid mass around us, he told me to start the car.

It was a hazardous journey, he made me drive in the all but useless beam of sidelights. I was amazed at how well he knew the road, every twist and turn. At last he told me to pull in through an opening in a hedge, and the road became smooth and straight – it was some time before I realised that I was driving along a runway.

I was so shocked by what happened next that I could only sit in appalled silence and watch.

A man stole out of the darkness and Edward, yanking the keys from the ignition, got out of the car. They spoke for a few minutes, pointing towards the aircraft that I could now make out in the dim moonlight, then back at the car. I watched them walk away until their figures dissolved into the shadows. I was alone.

My ears strained into the silence, half expecting to hear a scream, a gun shot, feet running . . . . I looked about me, trying to fight down the nausea of fear. The bushes were great black clumps in the semi-distance and as I looked I thought I saw something move in the darkness. My nerve ends pricked, I could hear my heart thumping. Was there someone there, waiting to leap out of the shadows? Suddenly something moved in the back of the car. I spun round, my mouth open to scream.

It was Edward. He took a small package from the back seat, then got out again. The man was still there; he took the package, then waited while Edward opened the boot. I heard something being lifted and placed inside, then the boot closed. The man walked away, and Edward got back into the car. He handed me the keys and, still mute, I started the engine.

'Take it slowly,' he said. 'No lights until we reach the main road'.

All the way back in the car I kept my eyes fixed on the road. I didn't ask what we were carrying, I didn't want to know.

It was almost midnight when we pulled into the drive at Westmoor. Christine was waiting at the front door. Edward jumped out, again snatching the keys from the ignition. I followed him, standing back as he opened the boot and he and Christine eased the packing-case out. I looked down at Christine's foot.

'Put the car away, Elizabeth,' Edward snapped.

As I walked back from the garage I looked up at the house, knowing already that the lights would be on in the Egyptian Room. And suddenly I understood that whatever it was I had been afraid of for so long was here.

I was in the front hall when Edward came down the stairs. His face was flushed, and he was trembling. 'Elizabeth,' he sighed, as if one of us had just returned from a long journey. Then walking towards me, he opened his arms and pulled me into them. 'Oh, Elizabeth, today is the greatest day of my life.' He took me by the shoulders, but when I looked up he was staring past me. 'Today I have achieved what no other man will ever achieve.' And then the insane, glazed look retreated and his kind blue eyes were shimmering, threatening any moment to spill tears on to his cheeks.

He turned round as he heard Christine on the stairs. She nodded to him, then walked past us into the drawing room.

I pulled back as he took my hand, but he only smiled, and like a father coaxing a child into doing something it was afraid of, he led me up the stairs.

The lights were off in the Egyptian Room, but he didn't turn them on. I could hear him panting as he positioned me at the door, and only then did he flick the switch, flooding the room with light.

My breath caught in my throat. Gone were the ancient stone and alabaster treasures of Egypt, gone were the mummies, the reliefs, the hideous carved faces. In their place, its slanted ebony eyes staring straight into mine, while the headdress fenced blades of pure gold and turquoise which reflected like lasers from the same coloured walls and ceiling, was Egypt's – the world's – most priceless treasure: the Tutankhamun death mask.

– 26 –

My skin began to prickle and I shivered. It was as if evil were a real presence in the room's chill air. I tore my eyes away from the mask and looked at Edward. His face was beatific; I half expected him to fall to his knees in worship.

'My God,' I breathed, 'what have you done?'

'Hush, hush,' he soothed.

'But for God's sake . . .'

He gripped my hand and pulled me outside on to the landing. 'Wait, we'll speak downstairs.' Then turning away, he switched off the lights and locked the door.

He was right, no one would ever know that the Tutankhamun death mask was here, because in its place in the Cairo museum was another death mask, a brilliant forgery. And no one would suspect, because who in their wildest dreams could ever have imagined that for the past five years a small team of expert forgers had been taking advantage of the deplorable security at the museum to enter the building by day as tourists, hide in the store-room until the museum closed, then come out of hiding at night and begin their work. It seemed the only problem they had faced was the one of getting the mask out of the museum. But in the end, even that hadn't proved too difficult. The forgers had simply added the case containing the mask to a lorry-load of packing-cases being transported to Luxor, then hi-jacked the lorry on the outskirts of Cairo; later in the day the lorry was found with its cargo intact – except for the one crucial packing-case that no one had known was there in the first place.

When Edward had finished his recital I got up to pour myself another brandy. I didn't normally drink a lot, but that night I needed it. It was incredible, the two of us sitting in our own drawing-room like any other married couple, talking and drinking brandy, while my husband told me calmly and quietly how he had masterminded a crime of theft and forgery unparalleled in the art world's history.

I slept in Charlotte's room that night. Edward frightened me. All these years I'd thought I knew him, and now he was a stranger.

When Jeffrey and Canary brought the children back the next day I was terrified that Edward was going to invite them into the Egyptian Room. He didn't, nor did he go there himself. Instead he drove Charlotte to the village hall where she was needed for a *Romeo and Juliet* rehearsal, and took Jonathan on to see one of his clients in Tunbridge Wells. Business was continuing as normal.

I found Christine in her office and asked her the reason for the lie about her foot.

'Edward didn't want to wait to unpack the mask when he got back, so everything that still remained in the Egyptian Room had to be moved out to make way for it. Jeffrey and I took it all to the warehouse; you were the only one left who could drive.'

'But why couldn't he drive himself?'

'You saw him,' she answered. 'He wasn't in any state to drive.'

How I wished David was there! – I so badly needed to talk to someone. I thought of ringing him in Gstaad, but realised that the reason he had gone there in the first place was so that he shouldn't have to have anything to do with this business . . . .

Knowing Alexander would be worried about me, I rang him at chambers and for once found him there. I told him some story about Edward being ill. The night before, as I'd tossed and turned in bed, my one thought had been to ask him for help, but in the cold light of day I realised I couldn't involve him. He was a lawyer. If it should ever come out that he had known what was going on at Westmoor, his career would be finished.

At the weekend an absurd normality prevailed. Though Edward was ludicrously happy, and showered us all with gifts, no one seemed to sense that things weren't as they should be. The strangest thing of all was that Edward never went near the Egyptian Room.

The day Edward died began like any other – the children shouting to each other across the landing, breakfast in the dining-room, Christine on the telephone to the London office, and Edward lounging with the newspaper in the Blue Sitting-Room. I went to find him. I knew I didn't stand any hope of persuading him to return the mask, but I had to try before I decided what I should do next.

I suggested we went into the garden where we couldn't be overheard. As we walked he pulled my arm through his, smiling the half-crazy smile he had worn ever since the night the mask arrived. Again I was struck by the insane unreality of it all: here were a husband and wife apparently taking an innocent stroll round their garden, while all the time they were discussing the presence in their home of the world's greatest treasure.

'Superstitious nonsense,' he laughed, when I told him how I had sensed something evil the moment I'd set eyes on it. 'Now put all that sort of thing out of your mind. All we need think about is that I've finally got the very thing I've wanted all my life. And look at it in this way, it's safe here – infinitely safer than it was at the Cairo museum with that appalling security system. They don't deserve . . .' He stopped, and I could see he was trying to get himself under control. 'I'm sorry,' he said, 'it's just that it makes my blood boil to think that anyone, at any time, can break in there and take anything they want. They've no security cameras, no alarms, no . . .'

'But Edward, don't you see, you're one of the people you're talking about. You, or someone you've paid, has breached that security system and taken the most valuable piece in the museum's entire collection. Isn't there some way you can get it back there, darling? That's where it belongs, you know it is.'

'You're wrong, Elizabeth. It belongs here, with me.'

'But how can it? I mean, you're not even Egyptian.'

'Who knows who or what I was in a past life?' he smiled. 'Perhaps I should tell you about the affinity I've always . . .'

'No, Edward, I won't listen. It's madness. What's happened to you? You've always been an honest man. Why have you done this? What's going to happen to you if anyone finds out?'

'But I've already told you, my darling, no one will find

out. There's no reason for anyone to examine the mask that is in the museum now, and only an expert would be able to tell the difference.'

'Then now you've got it, why don't you ever go and look at it? You've never been near it since the night it arrived. Oh please, Edward, get it out of the house. Even if you have to keep it, please, just take it somewhere else. I can't bear it being under the same roof as Charlotte and Jonathan.'

'We could ask them what they think about it,' said Edward. 'Here's Charlotte coming now. Shall we ask her?'

'*No*!'

'I was only teasing,' he whispered, and kissed my forehead. Turning to Charlotte who was walking across the lawn with Christine, he cried, 'And to what do we owe this pleasure? I thought you were dashing off to a rehearsal?'

'I am,' she answered, 'but there's something I want to ask you first.' She seemed reluctant, and I guessed immediately it was something to do with her new boyfriend. 'It's just that Colin and some of the others are going to Devon camping next weekend,' she said, 'and they've invited me.'

'I'm sorry, darling,' I said, 'it's out of the question. All those boys and girls are at least sixteen, aren't they, and you're only fourteen and a half. It's too young to be going away for a weekend like that. And besides, Colin's not exactly the type of boy you should be mixing with, is he now?'

'You mean, because he's not the same class as us. Because his father's only a baker. Well, you're a fine one to talk!'

'I didn't mean that at all. I was referring to . . .'

'You did! You're a snob, Mother. Well, his father may be a baker, but what about yours? You grew up on a fairground! You were little more than a gypsy before . . .'

'Charlotte!' Edward's voice cut across hers. 'That's enough! I don't ever want to hear you talk to your mother like that again. Now, you heard the answer, you can't go, and that's final.'

'Who asked you?'

'Charlotte!' I cried.

'No one asked me,' Edward snapped, 'but I'm telling you. I've had just about enough of you these past few weeks. You're rude and insolent, and it's about time someone taught you a lesson. Now go to your room, I'll speak to you later.'

'You can't tell me what to do, you're not even my real father.'

Edward's face turned ashen. 'What did you say?' he breathed.

'I said you're not my real father.'

'Charlotte, come back here,' I cried, grabbing hold of her arm.

'Let go of me!'she yelled.

Suddenly Christine caught her by the shoulder and dealt her a stinging blow across the face. 'You little bitch!' she snarled. 'How dare you speak to your father like that?'

'He's not my father!' Charlotte cried. 'He's not! He's not! I hate him!'

'Take her inside, Christine,' Edward said.

Charlotte tried to fight her off, but Christine was too strong. Edward and I watched them cross the lawn until they disappeared inside the house.

'I suppose we always knew that one day this would happen,' Edward said. 'I never thought it would be quite like this, though.' He turned to face me. 'Does she know him?'

I shook my head.

'But you've been seeing him? No, don't lie to me, Elizabeth, I saw your face just now. How long has it been going on?'

'Four years, maybe longer.'

He seemed to crumple then. 'All that time,' he whispered. 'I told you you could have your freedom, but you said you wanted to stay. And all the time . . .'

When I didn't say anything, he covered his face with his

hands. 'I've tried so hard to understand you. I've done everything I could do to make things easier for you, but in the end you always go back to him. What is it about him, Elizabeth? Why is it that you can't let go?'

To have tried to explain my love for Alexander would only have added to his pain. I stayed silent.

'You've held your love back from me all these years. Charlotte's sensed it. It's what's turned her against me.'

'I didn't turn her against you, Edward. I don't know why she behaved as she did, but I swear to you, she knows nothing about her father.'

He tried to smile through his tears. 'Her father.' He turned away and started to walk slowly towards the house. His shoulders were hunched, as if trying to shield himself against any more hurt.

I followed him inside. I thought at first he was going to Charlotte's room, but as he reached the landing he turned in the opposite direction towards the Egyptian Room, and I stayed close behind him – for some reason I felt he wanted me to.

When he opened the Egyptian Room door, I gasped. The walls and ceiling of the room had been painted in turquoise and gold stripes, and with the sun streaming in through the slats in the blind, it was as if the entire room was filled by the mask.

Edward turned to me. 'Beautiful, isn't it?' And it was. We stood at the door, letting the light fall over us, absorbing us into the unholy pattern of gold and blue. Again I was aware of the ebony eyes watching me from the centre of the room.

Edward went to stand beside it. The serene face, supported by the plaited beard and resting on the magnificent collar of lapis lazuli, quartz and amazonite, gazed up at him with youth and innocence.

Suddenly my blood turned cold. Edward was touching the mask, his fingers trembling so hard they were banging against the side of the golden head.

I caught him as he collapsed, falling to my knees with him.

'The years!' The words gurgled at the back of his throat. 'Years,' he said again.

'Years?' I said. 'What about them? What is it? Oh Edward, please.' I screamed for help, but it was already too late.

Over the next few days my most difficult task was trying to console Charlotte. Nothing would persuade her that Edward had died of a stroke, she was convinced she had brought about his death herself. I didn't ask her why she had chosen to mention her real father when she did – she was suffering enough already.

Christine confined herself to her room.

It wasn't until after the funeral that I told David what had happened when Edward died. He was as baffled as I was about why, in his last moments, Edward should have been trying to say something about 'years'. None of us talked about what was to happen to the mask now, though we were all acutely aware of its presence.

The day after the funeral, Alexander rang. He had heard about Edward. I knew from the sound of his voice that he was genuinely sorry. It was so good to hear him, to speak to someone who was not connected in any way with the whole dreadful business of the mask, that I broke down and cried. They were the first tears I'd shed since that terrible morning in the Egyptian Room.

Alexander listened as I explained that I would never be able to forgive myself for the way in which Edward had found out about us. I told him that we had both lied and cheated for long enough, that it was time to say goodbye before we brought more pain into other people's lives – including the lives of our children.

His parting words echoed my own thoughts and descended over me like a dark cloak. 'God only knows why things have to be like this for us, Elizabeth. Our only crime has been to love one another. But this time I know there is something you're not telling me. So I want you to know, when you feel you can trust me, that I'll be here. Until then, please remember that I love you with all my heart.'

I was dumbfounded when I learned that Edward had left everything to me. There was, of course, a sizeable sum for Christine, but for reasons known only to Edward, it was tied up in trusts. There was a codicil to the will, to the effect that, should I die before Christine, she was to hold the money in trust for Charlotte and Jonathan. From the tight expression on Christine's face as we left the lawyer's office, it was obvious that this was not the will she had been expecting, and I knew that life from here on was going to be difficult . . . .

It started when she came to me a week later and asked for money. I was shocked – not because I would have refused her anything she wanted, but because of the amount she asked for, and the reason she gave for wanting it.

'You're asking me to pay for the forging of that mask? I'm sorry, Christine, but I want nothing to do with it. You'll have to sort it out yourself.'

'For God's sake, grow up! Don't you realise you're as deeply implicated in this as I am? You've known all along the mask was here, and haven't told anyone. You even drove Edward down to pick it up that night. You went to Egypt with him, you even went to the museum with him. In fact, if it weren't for you the bloody thing might not be here at all.'

'Me! It's got nothing to do with me!'

'It's got everything to do with you. Before you came along, the mask was just an object to him, a beautiful object that he admired. It was because of the way you treated him that the obsession started. He was crazy about you, Elizabeth, so crazy that when you abused his love, kicked him in the face time after time, the only way he could survive was to clutch at something that wouldn't turn on him, wouldn't keep reminding him that he wasn't good enough. It was all a substitute for you. So, like it or not, you're involved right up to your neck.' She paused. 'Now, fifty thousand pounds is what the forgers want. It's the first instalment of what Edward promised them. And it would be better for both of us if you paid because, as I'm sure you realise, they have it in their power to send us to prison for a very long time.'

'But I didn't know anything about what Edward was doing! Oh God, this is all too ridiculous for words. Why didn't he ever talk to me about it? I *did* love him, he must have known that. You must have known what was happening all along – why didn't you stop him?'

'Stop him! I could no more have stopped him than I could have forged the damned thing myself. He had to have it. As far as he was concerned, he was the only person in the world who could protect it. But he wouldn't have needed to protect it if he hadn't been afraid he couldn't hold on to you. He had to have something he could cherish – Edward was like that.' There was a cruel smile on her mouth as she continued. 'And you ask why he didn't talk to you about it. He didn't tell you about it because you didn't want to know. You were only interested in your lover. All you ever wanted from Edward was his money and his status. Well, you've got them – and now you're going to have to pay for them.'

'But I'm not going to pay, Christine. Do you hear me, I'm not! I'll give the mask back!'

She threw her hands in the air, then slapped them against her thighs. 'This is the Tutankhamun death mask we're talking about, not some bloody hamper from Harrods! Don't be naive! They want money, Elizabeth. Money! They've given us five days in which to pay, or they'll start leaking what they know – and that includes the murder of a museum security guard, whose body is even now hidden in one of the sarcophagi.'

'What!' It was all too much for me to take in.

'You heard me.' Her voice was quiet, but the bitterness that coated her words sent shivers down my spine. 'He was murdered, Elizabeth, because he found the forgers at work. You heard me scream that night, didn't you? That's what it was all about. I thought it was someone else who'd been killed at the time, but that doesn't matter now. Are you getting the picture? These people aren't to be messed around with. Pay – or I'm telling you, you'll live to regret it. And so will those bastards of yours, too.'

I had been sitting at Edward's desk when she'd come into the study, but now I was beside the sofa, gripping the back of it. 'I'll need time to think,' I said. 'I have to go up to London tomorrow, the children are starting back at school.'

'You can think all you like, Elizabeth, but there's only one answer, and the sooner you come to terms with it, the better. I'll telephone you tomorrow night. What time are you seeing your lover? I'll make sure I call before you leave. Or perhaps you'd like to give me the number of your flat in Chelsea?'

I walked out of the room, telling her to call me by seven. I refused to give her the satisfaction of asking her how she knew about our flat.

Long before she rang the next day I had made up my mind what I was going to do. She was mad to think I would allow myself to be blackmailed by the forgers. I would go to Edward's solicitor and tell him the whole story. Then at least the mask would be taken away, even if there were dire consequences to be faced.

Christine was furious when I told her what I'd decided. 'Don't you care about your bloody children, for Christ's sake!' she screamed down the phone. 'These people have no scruples, Elizabeth, they'll stop at nothing.'

I told myself she was only trying to frighten me. The

truth of the matter was that she had far more reason to be frightened than I did – there was evidence of her involvement in the crime scattered all over the world. So I remained firm, and ended up by putting the phone down on her.

Stupidly, I thought that would be the end of the matter – that I had only to piece together the facts before I went to Edward's lawyer and got everything straightened out. I had no idea what would happen to Christine then, but I would warn her before I made my move so that she could decide what she wanted to do.

David called me later that evening to say that he and Jenifer were returning to Gstaad. He hated to admit it, he said, but neither of them liked being in the same house as the mask. I wished I had the courage to ask *him* to sort the whole thing out, after all he was Edward's brother, but I knew the problem was mine – David had washed his hands of it before it had even entered our lives.

The resolve that had carried me through so far was shaken when I called Edward's lawyer, Oscar Renfrew, and found he would be out of town until the following week. I had assumed he would take control of everything; now I wasn't sure what to do next. I left a message for him to ring me the moment he got back.

That weekend I took the children down to Westmoor. I would have avoided it if I could, but it was the weekend that Charlotte was opening in *Romeo and Juliet*.

Christine had already gone out by the time we got there on Saturday morning, but she had left me a note attached to the previous day's newspaper. The headline on the page she had directed me to read: 'Tutankhamun Death Mask Under Scrutiny'. My heart skipped a beat, and I turned to her note before I read on. 'Dear Elizabeth, perhaps now you will believe me when I tell you that these people mean business. It won't be long before the experts discover the mask's a fake, but that is the least of our problems. Britain has no extradition treaty with Egypt, but *we* will still have to face charges of illegal import and God only knows what else this end. This leak of information to the Egyptian authorities is just a warning from the people Edward and I have been dealing with. As I told you, they couldn't care less about the mask, what they want is money. I suggest you start saying your prayers, and keep an eye out for those children of yours. Be a good girl and destroy this note when you've read it.'.

At long last it got through to me that I was in danger. Christine was right, these people would stop at nothing to get the money that was owed to them.

My first concern was the children. Charlotte was at the village hall with the rest of the theatre group, where she would be staying until after their first performance tonight. Jeffrey was with Jonathan in the garden. For the moment they were safe.

Next I called Oscar Renfrew's home. His wife answered, but said Oscar wouldn't be there until Tuesday.

'Can I contact him wherever he is?'

'I'm afraid not. He's walking somewhere in the Pennines.'

Almost sick with fear, I paced the room, not knowing what to do next. Every now and again I glanced at the newspaper article. It was an innocuous enough piece, but in my agitation I read all manner of threats into it.

At two o'clock the phone rang. It was Christine. 'Oh, thank God,' I gasped, 'where are you?'

'I'm at the warehouse. Now, listen to me carefully. Things have moved faster than I expected. Someone is on their way to see you.'

'Who?' I almost screamed.

'Customs and Excise, the Foreign Office, I don't know. What I do know is that someone here has had a tip-off from the Egyptians that Edward is in some way involved in the investigation going on in Cairo. The security guard's body has been found and the Egyptians want an investigation this end.'

'How do you know all this?'

'I just do. Now listen. The mask is still in the house and somehow or another we're going to have to get rid of it. But that's not our only problem. It'll only be a matter of time now before it's discovered that Edward's entire Egyptian collection was acquired as illegally as the mask – and that's enough to create an incident on its own. There's more. It's about time you knew everything, then perhaps you'll realise just how serious this is. You remember all those visits we made to the villages along the Nile? The purpose of those little trips was to grease the palms of the villagers – who, my dear sister-in-law, are sitting on wealth such as you've never dreamed of. All those houses are built on ancient tombs you see, full of priceless antiquities – and while the Egyptian authorities try to buy the householders off, people like Edward give them money to keep them there. In return the householders do a little excavation . . . . The bulk of the money goes to Cairo. It's used to buy arms for the PLO, or the Libyans – the Israelis even, it doesn't matter; all that matters is who's paying the right price that day. It was there, Elizabeth, going on right under your nose, and you were too stupid to see it.' She paused, and I thought I could hear her laughing softly. 'Now, just get yourself out of the house and meet me here. Make it look as though you've gone shopping, and don't for God's sake tell anyone where you're going.'

When I didn't answer she spoke again. 'Elizabeth,' she breathed, and the coldness of her voice curled my insides into a knot of terror. 'You were his wife, you have inherited everything. And I mean everything.'

I tried not to rush as I gathered my things together, to make it look as though I was going into Tunbridge Wells. As I drove into the village I saw Miss Barsby giving directions to someone, and then I suddenly remembered

I'd left Christine's note lying on Edward's desk. Quickly I reversed the car back round the bend, praying I would get to it before anyone else did.

When I finally arrived at the warehouse Dan, the warehouse-keeper was waiting at the door. I rushed past him and up to the second floor. I looked round for Christine. There was no sign of her. Because it was Saturday the place was eerily silent. I flinched at the sound of my own footsteps as I walked to the storeroom at the other end of the building.

When I pushed open the door, I cried out in horror. The entire contents of the storeroom had been smashed to fragments; all Edward's lovingly cherished artefacts were now no more than piles of dust and rubble. His desk had been overturned and the contents strewn over the floor. On top of everything lay torn canvases, all that remained of Edward's collection of old masters, and broken pieces of antique furniture.

I spun round as I heard a noise behind me, then recoiled in terror as I found myself looking into a pair of manic, staring eyes.

– Alexander –

– 27 –

It was the first time I'd been to Westmoor. On any other occasion I might have been impressed by its grandeur; as it was I was driving too fast to notice the beauty of the gardens or the breathtaking views over the countryside. I skidded to a stop outside and rapped hard on the front door.

Canary answered, but I pushed past her and was on the point of calling out when suddenly Elizabeth appeared at the top of the stairs. I looked at her, my heart somewhere near my throat. She was dressed in black. Her face was stark, and her hair, her beautiful raven hair, had gone.

She stared back at me, and then I saw the terrible fear in her eyes. Slowly I lifted my arms and held them out towards her.

She clung to me. I could feel her bones jutting through her skin. 'I didn't do it,' she whispered. 'I didn't kill them.'

'I know, it's why I'm here.'

Behind Elizabeth I could see Charlotte standing at the top of the stairs, as beautiful and tragic as her mother. Canary went to her and led her back along the landing.

It was all too bizarre to be real. In an attempt to cover up what looked as if it might turn out to be one of the biggest and most complex art crimes in history, someone had set fire to a warehouse on the outskirts of London. Daniel Davison, the warehouse-keeper, had died in the fire. Two days later Elizabeth had been arrested for murder, then released on bail. Police were still searching the warehouse debris for Christine's remains.

I spent the next three days with Elizabeth, going over all that had happened. She was still in a state of shock, and so distressed that I felt callous in the way I coaxed and cross-examined her. But I had to find out the truth. Of course she was innocent, I never doubted that, but how was I to defend her if I didn't know exactly what had happened?

I knew the Bar Council would never condone my taking the case, so when Henry told my father that this was precisely what I intended to do, I wasn't surprised that he summoned me to his office.

I leapt up from my chair. 'For God's sake, father, she's been charged with murder.'

'And arson.'

I glared at Henry.

'Whatever she's been charged with, Alexander, you cannot defend her. It's simply not ethical.'

I rounded on him. 'Ethical! Who the hell gives a fuck about ethics! This is Elizabeth we're talking about. She wants me to defend her, and I'm damned well going to.'

'Freddie Rees has offered to take her on,' Henry said. 'He's about the best.'

'She doesn't want Freddie Rees. What the hell are you doing here anyway?'

'I asked him to come,' my father answered. I hoped he might be able to talk some sense into you. Does Elizabeth know what it could do to your career if you take her case?'

'Of course she doesn't know. And no one's going to tell her. She's frightened half out of her mind as it is.'

'Do *you* realise what it could do, Alexander?'

'Do you think I care a damn about that? I've told you, I'm going to defend her.' I couldn't tell them how, when I had suggested someone else should defend her, Elizabeth had begged me not to hand the case over. She didn't understand, didn't even know, how the bar would view it, and it would have been selfish and insensitive of me to have told her. I couldn't explain that I loved her too much to let her down, and that, as far as I was concerned, what she wanted and how she felt came before my career – before anything else.

'You don't have the experience to take on something like this,' Henry said.

'Especially,' my father interrupted, 'if they find the remains of her sister-in-law.'

'They won't. She's out there somewhere, alive and well, all we have to do is find her.'

'But you don't know that for sure. Look, son, can't you see you could be jeopardising her chances by taking this case. I know how you feel, we both do, but . . .'

'Where in the rule book does it say I can't take this case? Eh? Show me!'

'It doesn't, you know that. But there is a code of practice we all follow, Alexander. It would be wiser all round if you stuck to it.'

'How d'you think you're going to keep yourself under control when the going gets rough?' my father said. 'Just look at the way you're behaving now.'

'Of course I'm emotional now, what else would you expect? By the time it comes to the trial I'll be as detached as you like.'

'And if you lose,' my father said, 'how are you going to live with that?'

'I won't lose.'

Finally my father stood up. 'I am not giving this my blessing. You have said nothing to convince me that you're pursuing the right course. You will take the case as a junior. Freddie Rees, if he agrees, will lead. It is up to him whether or not he lets you conduct the defence. If you do, then on your head be it.'

It was four months before the case came to trial. During that time I all but moved into Priory Walk with Elizabeth and the children, and we tried to carry on our lives as normally as possible. Jessica came to see me from time to time, but our meetings always ended in bitterness. Though she professed to be leading a perfectly happy and fulfilling life on her own, she still behaved like the jealous wife as far as Elizabeth was concerned. It was no surprise when she said she thought Elizabeth was guilty.

'The trouble with you, Alexander, is that your precious Elizabeth can do no wrong. She's guilty, all right, you wait and see. I hope she gets what she deserves – and the irony of it is, it'll be you that gets it for her. You can't win this case, never in a million years.'

Rosalind wasn't with her on that occasion and I was sorry for it. At least when Rosalind was around our meetings were a little more civilised.

But as time went on and Freddie Rees agreed to take the case – Freddie who, unlike my father, thought there might be something to be gained from my presenting it – Jessica mellowed, and even took to telephoning me from time to time to see how we were getting on. Freddie monitored my research every step of the way and gave endless advice and encouragement. But our real problem was Christine's disappearance. I even flew to Gstaad to speak to David about her but he had no idea where she might be. He and Elizabeth were both convinced she wouldn't have gone to Cairo as she didn't have the money to pay whoever was blackmailing her. When David refused to come to court and testify on Elizabeth's behalf, I was shaken. Elizabeth had been so certain he would. Nevertheless I took a signed statement from him, detailing everything he knew about the theft of the death mask.

And that was something else that had delivered its own staggering surprise. The mask was a fake.

'You can tell,' one of the experts from the British Museum told me, when I went down to Westmoor to see how they were getting on. 'You can tell by the holes in the ears.'

'What holes?' I asked.

'Precisely. There are no holes. The real mask has pierced ears. And what's more, the holes are quite large. Whoever made this copy deliberately set out to have his work recognised as a fake.'

'Why would he do that?'

The specialist shrugged. 'Search me. It's such an obvious mistake, and one Walters couldn't have failed to notice. Apart from that, the workmanship is incomparable.'

So that was what Edward had been saying in his dying moments – 'ears'.

I was speechless. Knowing that both Elizabeth and Charlotte blamed themselves for Edward's death, when all the time it had been this fake that had caused it, sent me into a blinding rage. The only good thing to come out of it was that Customs and Excise were suitably baffled by the expert's findings and decided that, providing the relevant import taxes were paid on the precious metals, the charge of illegal import would be dropped.

Elizabeth could hardly believe it when I told her. 'You know, Christine told me that Edward developed this obsession when he realised I would never love him the way he wanted me to. Now it seems he was cheated even over the mask. Poor Edward. All those years, Alexander. All those years I lived with him and hardly knew him. What is it that makes someone do the things he did? It can't just be love.'

'The important thing is that you don't blame yourself. There was nothing you could have done. As you said, he was cheated. And by the time he found out he had already lost his mind.' I paused. 'The person we have to worry about now, Elizabeth, is Christine, not Edward. Christine tried to kill you, and she's likely to try again.'

Her face turned white. 'You've got to face it, Elizabeth. Under the terms of Edward's will, if anything happens to you Christine gets everything. At least, until Charlotte and Jonathan are old enough to take over their inheritance.'

'By which time she will have made sure there is no inheritance to take over,' Caroline said.

I had called into Henry's on my way home. Elizabeth was staying there now, until the trial was over; with Christine's whereabouts still not known I didn't like her staying at Priory Walk alone. Henry's house was bursting at the seams with children, for he and Caroline now had four, and Charlotte and Jonathan were staying there too.

Henry walked to the door with me. 'Why haven't you told her yet?' he said.

'I will. I'll come back later and take her to the flat. I think she'll need to be alone with me when she finds out.'

The trial was set for the following Monday at the Old Bailey. What I hadn't told Elizabeth was that Michael Samuelson was prosecuting. I had seen Samuelson cross swords with barristers far more experienced than I was, but I'd never seen anyone beat him yet. Not even Freddie Rees.

– 28 –

The clerk of the court stood. Only his bespectacled eyes and the dome of his balding head were visible above the sheet of paper that bore the indictment. Behind him was Justice McKee, dwarfed by his wig and red robes, though still managing to look his usual irritated self. He cast a glance at the full public gallery. It had come as a blow to us to find ourselves in Number One Court; the oppressive dark wood and claustrophobic air were menacing. I looked up at Elizabeth. Her face was drawn, evidence of the sleepless night she had passed. The royal blue of her dress seemed to cast a bluish tinge over her skin too, and with the weight she had lost during the past months she looked almost skeletal. Behind her in the dock was a prison officer. I looked away quickly, before emotion got the better of me. For a fleeting moment I saw the court as Elizabeth must see it: strange and familiar faces, black gowns and white curled wigs. A macabre theatre.

'Prisoner at the bar, you are charged upon an indictment containing five counts. Count one. Murder. In that, you, on the fifth day of September, 1981, did murder Daniel Raymond Davison. How say you? Guilty or not guilty?'

'Not guilty.' Her voice was small but firm, and she looked at the judge as she spoke. He didn't return the compliment, and though she didn't move she seemed to shrink back into the dock.

'Count two. Arson. In that on the fifth day of September, 1981, contrary to the Criminal Damage Act 1971, section one, paragraph two, subsection . . .' The clerk's voice droned on as he related each and every word of the subsection, until he asked, 'How say you? Guilty or not guilty?'

'Not guilty.'

Three more times we went through the same performance as the counts for theft, forgery, and receiving stolen goods were read out. Then there was a hush over the room as the jury was sworn in. Eventually Michael Samuelson got to his feet. The trial had begun.

For two days prosecution witnesses filed into the court. The main focus of attention was on the murder and the fire, but since no one had actually witnessed the start of the fire there was very little evidence to be heard on that score. Finally, on the third morning, Elizabeth took the stand. For the moment, as so much of the evidence so far had been based on hearsay and conjecture, I wasn't unduly worried and felt confident that things were going our way. Nevertheless, as she took the oath Elizabeth's voice shook. Every member of the jury had his eyes fixed on her. This was their first and only opportunity of hearing first-hand what had happened that day at the warehouse.

We began by going over the details of Edward's will, something I would have preferred to avoid, but I knew that if I didn't bring it out first Samuelson would be sure to do so later.

When I was satisfied that the jury understood that the will gave Christine a motive for killing Elizabeth, I moved on to the day of the fire.

I smiled encouragingly and asked Elizabeth to begin by telling us at what time she had arrived at Westmoor on the morning of the fire, and what had happened after she found the note from Christine. She spoke quietly, but coherently, going over the details of the telephone conversation with Christine. She confirmed Canary's testimony that she had said she was going shopping, then told how she had driven her car into the village before returning to Westmoor to make sure Christine's note was not left around for anyone else to find.

'Is this note available to the court?' Justice McKee interrupted.

'I'm afraid it isn't, my lord,' I answered. We had searched everywhere for it but in the end had come to the conclusion that it must have been destroyed in the fire.

'Oh,' was all McKee said, but it was enough to throw the existence of the note into question, and add credibility to Miss Barsby's testimony that she had been directing Customs officers to Westmoor when she saw Elizabeth reverse out of the village; her implication – that Elizabeth had been trying to hide from the Customs officers – was clear.

I turned back to Elizabeth. 'After you collected the note, what did you do next?'

'I drove straight to the warehouse. When I got there, Dan, the warehouse-keeper, was at the door. I ran past him up to the second floor where my husband had a large storage area. I looked for Christine, but there was no sign of her. I had only been to the warehouse once before, but I remembered that there was a smaller storeroom at the end of the corridor, which Edward used as an office. As I walked towards it I checked all the units to see if Christine was in any of them. Then, as I pushed open the door at the end, I remember screaming out for Dan.'

'Can you tell the court why you screamed out for Dan?'

'Because everything in the room had been smashed to pieces. I couldn't believe my eyes. Even the wreckage must have been worth a fortune.'

Out of the corner of my eye I saw Samuelson scribbling. 'And what happened next?' I asked.

'I heard a noise behind me. I turned round, but before I knew what was happening I was being pushed into the room.'

'Can you identify the person who pushed you into the room?'

'No. I only know it was a man.'

'A man. But it was your sister-in-law who had asked you to go to the warehouse?'

'Yes.'

'Did you, at any time on that Saturday afternoon, see your sister-in-law?'

'No.'

I nodded. 'And what happened after you were pushed into the room?'

'I fell into the debris. It reeked of petrol. Then a lighted newspaper was thrown into the room and the door was closed.'

'What happened after that?'

'The whole room went up in flames. I managed to get to the door, but it was locked. I tried to find something to break it down with, but then I slipped and fell and my clothes caught fire. I tried to scream but nothing came out. The room was filled with smoke and I could hardly breathe.

'I threw myself at the door. Then it was as if I was being pushed back into the fire. I didn't realise at first that someone was trying to open the door from outside, so I tried to resist. Then I heard shouting above the roar of the flames and I was dragged out on to the landing.

'It was Dan. He was beating me with his overall to smother the flames and asking me what had happened, but all I could say was Christine's name.

'He must have assumed she was in the fire because he covered his face and hands with the overall and ran into the room. It must have been only seconds after that that a dresser fell and crashed on top of him. He screamed, and I tried to drag myself towards him. He was still screaming when something else fell, and then . . . he didn't scream any more.'

She was sobbing, and the judge nodded to the usher to bring her a chair. I waited, letting the silence hang over the court. Eventually she indicated that she was ready to go on.

'Did you assume Dan was dead at that point, Mrs Walters?'

She raised her hand to her eyes, rubbing away the tiredness. 'I don't know what I thought. Yes, I suppose I must have thought he was dead.'

'What did you do?'

'I was still lying on the floor. The fire was spreading fast and I knew I had to get help. I managed to drag myself to my feet, then I started to choke again. I realised I had to get outside.'

'Did you not consider using the telephone in Dan's office at the warehouse entrance?'

'I only thought of it when I got downstairs, but by then I could hear sirens in the distance and I knew help was on the way.'

'And can you tell the jury why you were no longer at the warehouse when the police and fire brigade arrived?'

She started to shake her head, and wiped the back of her hand across her eyes again. 'I panicked. I was a coward, and I panicked.'

'Why did you panic?'

'My thoughts were so confused . . . I didn't know who had started the fire, but I kept thinking about the people Christine had been dealing with, and how she had said they were capable of anything. And then all I could think of was my children, and that I had to get to them.'

'When you got home, what happened then?'

'Canary – our nanny – was coming down the stairs as I let myself in. I told her to get me upstairs before the children saw me. When we got to the bedroom she tried to call the doctor but I wouldn't let her. I knew my burns were severe, but both Canary and I are trained nurses. I think I passed out then, because it was half an hour or so later . . .'

'What time would that be?'

'Four-thirty. Canary helped me to the mirror. I told her to cut away the burnt hair. Then I sent her to the hairdressers to get some hairpieces. While she was gone I changed my clothes and put on some trousers and a long-sleeved shirt. I was trying to hide my burns because I didn't want to frighten the children.'

'Why, at that point, did you not call the police?'

She lifted her face, as if to sink the tears back into her eyes. 'I don't know,' she sobbed. 'But I wish to God I had.'

'You say here in your statement that you didn't call the police because you were trying to protect your children.'

'I was, but I was afraid, too, that if I went to the police, whoever had pushed me into the fire would try to kill me again. I wasn't thinking straight, I did everything wrong, but I knew that eventually the police would come to me.'

I turned to the jury for emphasis. 'And we have already heard from the police how helpful you were when they did. And your sister-in-law, Mrs Walters, did she contact you again?'

'No.'

'Did you have any other visitors?'

'Only the police. They came to interview me several times, then two days after the fire, they came to arrest me.'

She looked drained, and I asked the judge if we might break for lunch. He agreed immediately, knowing she would need her strength to face the cross-examination.

Samuelson started by taking her back over the terms of Edward's will.

I saw immediately what he was implying – that over a period of years Elizabeth had managed to cajole her husband into leaving her everything, and had then been determined to remove the only obstacle – Christine – that stood in the way of her children inheriting. He didn't labour the point, but he made sure the jury appreciated it.

He moved quickly to her arrival at the warehouse. 'You tell us that on arrival at the warehouse you were accosted by a man. In your statement you say you looked fully into this man's face before he grabbed you and pushed you into the fire – and yet you would have us believe that you are unable to identify him, or give any description of him.'

'That's right.'

'You are left with absolutely no impression of what this man looked like?'

'No.'

Samuelson looked at the jury, his eyebrows raised. 'Who are you trying to shield, Mrs Walters?'

She looked at me. 'No one. I'm not shielding anyone. It was as I said . . . .' She stopped as I looked away – 'Just answer the questions,' I had told her.

'Please correct me if I am wrong, Mrs Walters, but it is your intention, is it not, that the court should believe your sister-in-law wasn't at the warehouse?'

'I didn't see her.'

'So she might have been there?'

'I don't know.'

'I put it to you, Mrs Walters, that she was there. Why

else should Daniel Davison have thought she was in the fire? After all, it was a Saturday afternoon, a quiet day. Davison would have seen her enter the warehouse.'

'No. She wasn't there.'

'You claim your sister-in-law had threatened your children. Is that why you fought with her and pushed her into the fire, Mrs Walters?'

Elizabeth was staring at him in horror, as if she couldn't register the fact that he, or anyone, might really believe she was capable of doing what he suggested.

'Was that why you asked her to meet you at the warehouse? So you could kill two birds with one stone? By setting light to what was stored in the warehouse, and pushing your sister-in-law into the fire, perhaps you thought you would put your children and yourself out of danger?'

'No! No, it wasn't like that. I didn't . . .'

'You didn't what, Mrs Walters?'

'I didn't see her.'

'The jury may think you did, Mrs Walters. The jury may also think she's in hiding now because she's afraid of you. It is clear she escaped the fire, but perhaps she was a witness to Daniel Davison's murder? The murder you committed with the man you are trying to shield. Is your sister-in-law still alive, Mrs Walters?'

'No. Yes. No.'

'Yes or no, Mrs. Walters?'

'Yes.'

'She's still alive? But you say she hasn't contacted you since the fire, so how can you know?'

'I don't . . .'

'If she's alive, as you claim, Mrs Walters, then where is she?'

I could see Elizabeth was close to breaking point. Samuelson was just waiting for the moment of her greatest confusion and vulnerability to trick her into confessing. I stood up. 'My lord, I think it has been fully established that Mrs Walters has no knowledge of the whereabouts of her sister-in-law. Perhaps we could proceed . . .'

'Please sit down, Mr Belmayne.'

Samuelson smiled and left a long pause before continuing. 'We have heard Mrs Daniel Davison testify that her husband knew the goods stored on the second floor of the warehouse – the goods that belonged to the deceased Edward Walters, and now belong to you – were either illegally obtained or stolen, and that Davison had been wondering for some time whether he should report this. Is that why he had to die, Mrs Walters? To shut him up?'

'He didn't have to . . . I didn't . . .'

'And the man you met at the warehouse, was he your accomplice? After all, Davison was a big man; you would need help.'

'You're wrong! I hardly knew Dan. I didn't even know myself that the goods were stolen until I read my sister-in-law's note.'

'Note? But there is no note, Mrs Walters.'

Elizabeth looked at me, but all I could do was shake my head.

'The petrol can, found half a mile from the warehouse in some bushes. We have already heard your chauffeur testify that it is the can normally found in your car. How did it get into the bushes?'

'I don't know.'

'How did you get your burns, Mrs Walters? Why did you try to hide them? Why didn't you go to the police after the fire? What were you afraid of?'

'I don't know. I didn't kill him!'

'You are a liar, madam!' His voice boomed through the court and Elizabeth shrank back in terror.

I leapt to my feet. 'My lord! My learned friend has gone . . .'

'Yes, quite, Mr Belmayne.' He turned to Samuelson. 'I do not approve of theatrics in my court, Mr Samuelson, as well you know. Please return to a direct line of questioning and refrain from harassing the defendant.'

'I have no further questions, my lord.' Samuelson was still smiling pleasantly as he sat down.

I did a short re-examination. I would have spared her the distress of answering any more questions, but for the fact that it was important to establish fully in the jury's minds that Elizabeth had been the intended victim of a premeditated murder, arranged by Christine, to be carried out by a person or persons unknown, probably the people who were blackmailing her. Again I got her to demonstrate the obvious grief she felt at Davison's losing his life just after saving hers.

When we left court that day I was unnerved by the way things were going. Although he tried to hide it, I knew Freddie was too.

In the robing room Samuelson congratulated me on the way I had handled the case so far, subtly reminding me of how inexperienced I was. But we both knew our guns were empty of any real ammunition. The lack of facts meant the outcome now rested on our skill as barristers – whichever one of us succeeded in getting the jury on our side would win. And Samuelson had had years of practice.

At ten o'clock the following morning Samuelson rose to his feet to begin his summing up. His notes were spread out in front of him – but over the next hour he hardly needed to refer to them at all. His speech was every bit as powerful as I'd expected and I listened carefully as, step by step, he took the jury through the evidence. He did it succinctly, and in an easy language that no one could fail to follow.

'We now have no choice, members of the jury, but to conclude that the accused is an arsonist.' His voice was trembling with indignation. 'Why did she try to hide the fact that she had been in a fire, if not because she herself had started that fire? It was only when the police came to question her, and she could no longer conceal the burns, that she admitted to having been there. And where is her sister-in-law now? Afraid to come out of hiding, or . . . Well, I wonder where she is, members of the jury. It is convenient, is it not, that there are no witnesses to this crime? The only certain survivor of the fire is the woman before you, the woman who stood to benefit more than anyone from the destruction of the Bridlington warehouse. Daniel Davison had known for some time that the antiques and antiquities on the second floor were either fraudulently obtained or stolen, and it was because he was on the point of doing his duty as a law-abiding citizen that he died the worst kind of death there is – death by fire.'

He stopped suddenly, leaving the courtroom empty of sound. In the electric silence, the full horror of Davison's death came home to everyone.

Samuelson hitched his gown over his shoulders and after a few seconds looked up. 'And for what? To disguise a lifetime of cheating, stealing and lying. Remember the accused's own words when she claimed to have found the destruction in the warehouse? "Even the wreckage must have been worth a fortune." Her first observation, and one that has come with her into the courtroom. It gives us some indication, perhaps, of the way this woman thinks. Members of the jury, I'm sure you will agree that the few facts we have in this case speak for themselves. There is only one verdict, is there not? Guilty.'

Despite his pleasant smile, Samuelson couldn't have looked more like an executioner as he retook his seat.

As I got to my feet there was a shuffling in the public gallery. The Old Bailey regulars were there, the modern equivalent of the hags who knitted their way through the French Revolution, beside the guillotine. Like leeches, they sated their gruesome appetites on other people's misfortune.

After Samuelson's speech, the jury now presented to me

two rows of uniformly hostile faces. Freddie and I had been right to assume, when we put the finishing touches to my speech the night before, that they would not want another detailed review of the events of the case.

'May it please your lordship, members of the jury. It is never an easy task to present the case for the defence, and it is especially difficult for me today, when my learned friend has put such a convincing argument before you. But there is one fundamental flaw in his argument. That is, that he has no proof whatsoever to substantiate his claims.

'As he himself has pointed out, there are no witnesses to the events at the warehouse, and therefore all the evidence on that score is either hearsay or conjecture. In legal terminology, it is circumstantial evidence only. It is on circumstantial evidence only, members of the jury, that you must decide the defendant's fate. And remember too that she is innocent until proved, beyond all reasonable doubt, to be guilty.

'Miss Barsby claims she saw Mrs Walters drive into the village at two-thirty on the afternoon of the fire. Miss Roberts, the Walters' nanny, has testified that Mrs Walters returned to Westmoor just after four o'clock. According to Mr Samuelson, in that one and a half hours Mrs Walters accomplished the following: a thirty-minute journey to the warehouse, where she started the fire, argued and perhaps fought with her sister-in-law, then – after suffering extensive burns – called Daniel Davison from his post and, together with a man so far unidentified, thrust Davison into the flames; she then ran half a mile down the road to dispense with the petrol can, ran the half mile back again, and then returned to Westmoor after another thirty-minute drive. Is this likely, members of the jury? Is it even possible?

'Miss Roberts has also testified that she had overheard Christine Walters threatening the defendant. And the evidence presented by British Airways, Pan Am and Singapore Airlines makes it clear that Christine Walters was likely involved over many years in what have turned out to be extremely dubious international transactions. It was the threatened exposure of those transactions, and the defendant's refusal to bow to blackmail, that drove Christine Walters to hire someone to – in the words of my learned friend – "kill two birds with one stone" by setting fire to the warehouse and depriving Mrs Walters of her life. That, members of the jury, is why Christine Walters has gone into hiding and is not present in this courtroom.

'During this trial my client has never denied her presence at the fire, nor has she sought to deny the evidence of the prosecution witnesses. I ask you to take a look at her, members of the jury. Does she really look like the gorgon of Mr Samuelson's conjectures? Of course not. She is a decent, law-abiding citizen who has become embroiled in a series of events almost too fantastic to credit.

'There are a great many more things I could say about my client's sister-in-law, but we are not here to try Christine Walters, we are here to see that justice is done in the case of Elizabeth Walters. Justice – British justice – dictates that she is innocent until proved, beyond all reasonable doubt, to be guilty.' I smiled and looked up at Elizabeth. Her eyes were lowered, and when I turned back to the jury every one of them was watching her. 'There is so much doubt in this case that I am sure you are as surprised as I am that we are here at all. It is physically impossible for Mrs Walters to have committed these crimes; on the contrary, she was the intended victim. I leave it to you, then, members of the jury, to see that justice is done by returning a verdict of Not Guilty.'

As I sat down I felt a tap on my shoulder, and Oscar Renfrew, Elizabeth's solicitor, passed me a note. 'Holy Shit! You've done it!' I read, and I allowed myself a smile. Freddie's face was expressionless, but when I caught his eye he winked. Every face in the jury box showed a confusion of doubt and sympathy. Oscar Renfrew was right, I felt it in my bones.

The judge decided to adjourn until ten-thirty the next morning, when he would deliver his summing up before sending the jury to consider their verdict.

That night Jessica left a message at chambers asking me to see her. On my way home I called in on Henry and Caroline to speak to Elizabeth and tease her for not having faith in me from the beginning. She looked better than she had over the past few days, but the strain was still evident. I didn't feel the time was right to tell her that the next step was to find Christine – before Christine came to find her.

Jessica and I went out for dinner. We talked mainly about the trial, and I was surprised at how sympathetically she listened. I must confess it was good to have someone I could confide in after keeping my feelings under such tight control, and when Jessica told me that my father had grudgingly praised my performance, I couldn't help being pleased. Yet I had to admit to myself that his reservations about the case hadn't been entirely unjustified; defending Elizabeth wasn't the easiest thing I'd ever done, and I still wasn't sure it would turn out to have been the wisest, either.

Jessica smiled at that. 'You were so confident a moment ago.'

'I still am. Well, I suppose there's always a chance the jury could have some sort of mass aberration . . . No, what I meant was that maybe I behaved immaturely over the whole thing. Because it was Elizabeth, I wouldn't hear of anyone else taking the case. I didn't even know if it would be the best thing for her, I just felt I had to do it.' I shrugged. 'Too late for all this now, eh? Just thank God it worked out.'

After that we talked about Jessica, and what she and Rosalind were doing – but all the same, by the time dinner was over we were on the point of snapping at each other. It was probably as much to do with my intolerance as with Jessica's incurable jealousy of Elizabeth. When we got home we went to our separate rooms, and she was still in bed when I left for court in the morning.

Justice McKee's summing up wasn't exactly biased, but with his reiteration of all I had said about doubt and the lack of hard evidence to tie up the loose ends of the prosecution case, I could see that Samuelson knew he had lost.

The jury returned at two. As they filed in Henry, who was sitting behind me, directed my attention to the public gallery. Charlotte was there, and my heart gave a flutter as she waved to me. Later that day we were going to tell her and Jonathan that I was their father.

The clerk of the court was speaking. 'Members of the jury, have you reached your verdict?'

The foreman stood up. 'We have, sir.' He looked at me – and in that instant I knew.

'Members of the jury, on the first count of murder, do you find the defendant guilty or not guilty?'

'Guilty.'

'Members of the jury, on the second count of arson, do you find the defendant guilty or not guilty?'

'Guilty.'

The blood pounded in my ears as I sat rooted in shock. I had been so certain. Henry grabbed my arm, and I swung round to see that Elizabeth had collapsed.

The clerk's voice droned on as verdicts were given on the three other counts. All I could do was stand and watch as the court ushers picked Elizabeth up and held her on her feet.

'Members of the jury, on all counts you find the defendant guilty?'

'Yes.'

'And that is the verdict of you all?'

'Yes.'

'Thank you. You may sit down.'

The judge called for order. 'I know you will wish to mitigate on your client's behalf, Mr Belmayne, so perhaps we should continue.'

Freddie stood up. I barely heard his mitigation, but when I looked up I could see that the judge was sympathetic, and indeed before he passed sentence he expressed his surprise at the verdict.

Life imprisonment. Seven years, and three terms of five years, to run concurrently.

I caught up with her as she was led from court, pushing the prison officer to one side and holding on to her, trying to keep her upright.

'The children,' she mumbled, 'what will happen to the children? Oh Alexander, you will take care of them, won't you?'

'Yes, of course, I – '

Before I could say any more, she was snatched from me and taken away to prison. It was the worst moment of my life.

When I got to the robing room Henry was waiting with Caroline and Charlotte. Until that moment I had forgotten Charlotte had been in court. Seeing her face, white with terror, I took her in my arms and swore that I would do whatever I had to do, to see that her mother was freed from a prison sentence she should not be serving.

– 29 –

The following morning I went into chambers. I knew that for the children's sake, as much as my own, I must carry on as normal. Jessica had been in court for the verdict. She had called Rosalind and the two of them had sat up with me through half the night. There was a certain irony about her support, since she herself had predicted that Elizabeth would be found guilty. Before she left that morning I hugged her, and even had to swallow a few tears as she told me how sorry she was things had turned out so badly. Whether she meant between us or for Elizabeth, I didn't know, but either way I sensed her sincerity and sadness.

Raddish was coming out of my room as I walked in. 'We're going to appeal, Raddish,' I said. 'Get on to Oscar Renfrew and fix a meeting.'

'Will do, sir. There's a gentleman to see you, sir. Says he's been to your home first, and your father sent him here.'

'To my home? Did he give his name?'

'Yes, sir, Mr Walters.'

My immediate thought was of Edward, but that was absurd. David stood up as I walked in, and extended his hand. Reluctantly, I took it; I couldn't forgive him for refusing to testify on Elizabeth's behalf.

'Mr Walters,' I said, 'I'm afraid you're too late. Didn't you hear?'

'Yes, I heard. It's why I'm here.'

'Oh?' I took off my coat and hooked it on to the coat stand behind the door.

'I've heard from Christine.'

The name hung like poison in the air between us, and the hatred I felt toward this woman – whom I'd never even met – began to churn in my stomach. 'When? Where is she?'

'She rang me yesterday, after she'd heard the verdict. She's in Cairo.'

I picked up the telephone. 'What are you doing?' David asked.

'Informing Interpol.'

He shook his head. There wouldn't be any point in doing that, he told me. 'The people she's with are at least three steps ahead of anyone in Interpol.'

'How did she hear the verdict?'

'Simple. She rang someone in Fleet Street.' He paused, and looked down at his shoes. 'She was at the warehouse, Mr Belmayne.'

'I was never in any doubt of it.'

'I think you should go to Cairo and find her.'

I looked at him levelly, noticing that the scar on his face seemed to have deepened since the last time I'd seen him, in Gstaad. His thin hair looked as if he'd just come in out of a high wind, and I realised he'd been running his fingers through it nervously ever since I'd come into the room.

'She's your sister, why should you want her found?'

His face was sad as he smiled. 'Because, contrary to what you might think, I care very much for Elizabeth. I knew she wasn't capable of setting fire to that warehouse, and I knew too that my sister was. But you see, Mr Belmayne, Christine *is* my sister, and despite everything I love her very much. When she disappeared – and I swear to you I had no idea where she was – I assumed Cairo was the last place she'd go, given that she didn't have the money to pay the Pasha . . . .'

'The Pasha?'

'It means "lord". He's the one Edward and Christine have been dealing with all these years. A nasty piece of work. Anyway, after she disappeared and Elizabeth was arrested, well, I suppose my faith in British justice was misplaced, because I never dreamed Elizabeth would go to prison. I just assumed there wouldn't be enough evidence.'

'Your sister is cleverer than you think, Mr Walters. Go on.'

'That's it, really. All I know is that this Pasha character has some sort of hold over Christine. I want her out of it, and if it means facing up to what she has done, then so be it, she must stand trial.'

I was surprised by that. 'Not just a signed confession?'

He shook his head. 'But that's probably all you'll get – and you'll only get that if you can find her.'

'Oh, I'll find her, Mr Walters, that I can promise you.'

To my relief, the first class area of the British Airways flight to Cairo was almost empty, so I settled back to watch the outlying suburbs of London recede into the distance, and wondered how I was going to endure the five-hour journey.

I willed myself not to think of Elizabeth, but it was impossible. I had seen her the night before, and her face, bloodless and bewildered, was etched on my memory. It was obvious she was still in a state of shock. That worried me more than anything else: how would she cope when she came out of it and fully understood what had happened to her, and worse, what was to come? My heart sank when I thought of the abuse, even violence, she might have to suffer from her fellow-prisoners. How would she find the strength to cope, after the ordeal of the last four months and the trial itself? As it was, after just two days she looked ill and couldn't meet my eyes when she spoke. If a door clanged somewhere in the distance, she flinched, and once, as footsteps approached the room we were in, she tensed so hard her nails left deep red weals across her palms.

When I told her I was going to Cairo, she mumbled that she didn't want me to go, that it wouldn't help anything. I knew she wasn't in any state to discuss it, so I tried to change the subject, but she kept muttering over and over again that I didn't know what kind of people I would meet there, that they were evil and I mustn't get mixed up with them or my life would be in danger. I tried to make her understand that this was the only real chance we stood of getting her out, but her only answer was to say she didn't want me to find Christine.

When the time came for me to leave, a prison officer was waiting to escort her back to her cell. Elizabeth followed her down the corridor, her head bowed and her hands clenched at her sides. I waited, but she didn't look back . . . .

My head began to throb until it forced me from my seat. Maybe I was in some sort of shock too, for all I seemed able to feel was blinding rage at what so-called British justice had done to her. And I knew already that, once this was over, I wouldn't have to be asked to leave the bar, I would go anyway.

Ten minutes later I was back in my seat and signalled for the stewardess to bring me a drink. She'd been openly flirtatious when I boarded the plane, but after she realised I didn't want company she'd treated me with thinly disguised contempt.

'Alexander.'

I turned in my seat and at first I couldn't believe my eyes, 'Charlotte!'

She tried to force her smile wider. 'I knew you'd never agree to me coming,' she said, 'so, well . . .' She shrugged.

Fighting to pull myself together, I got to my feet. 'How did you get here?'

'I thought I might be able to help. There might be something or someone I remember when we get there. I know Cairo.'

I knew she had been to Cairo only once, when she was eleven. Now here she was at sixteen, her hair scooped under her beret and her eyes red and swollen, wanting desperately to do something to help her mother. I smiled and swallowed hard, then I kissed her on the head and sat her down in the seat beside me.

'You're not angry, are you?' she whispered.

'No. I'm not angry, but once we land I'm going to have to put you on the first plane back to London.'

Tears welled in her eyes. 'Don't send me back. Please! I'll go mad if I can't do something. I'll stay in the hotel, I won't even move from my room if you insist, but please, let me stay with you.'

My heart contracted as I watched her face. With her slanted dark eyes and fresh young skin she looked so like Elizabeth. I considered her a child, but she was the same age I had been when I fell in love with her mother.

'Alexander?' Her eyes were imploring as she waited for my answer. I ran my fingers over her cheek and tucked a stray curl behind her ear. 'Alexander,' her voice was soft, and shaking. 'I know you're my father.'

To hear her say those words was almost too poignant to bear.

'It is true, isn't it? You are my father. And Jonathan's too?'

'Yes,' I whispered, 'and Jonathan's too.'

She rested her head on my shoulder, her hand tightly gripping mine.

'How did you know?' I said, after a while.

She giggled. 'Because Mum was always nuts about my smile. And then when I saw her looking at you, well, I've got a crooked tooth too, see?'

I burst out laughing and hugged her before she could see the tears in my eyes.

'When all this is over,' she said, 'when we're back in London and Mother is free, can I change my name to yours?'

'It'll be the first thing we do, as a family,' I promised, and felt both bitter and sad that Elizabeth wasn't with us to share the moment.

It was past ten o'clock when we got off the plane. Robert Lyttleton was there to meet us. His career with the Foreign Office had flourished, and he was now the Military Attaché at the British Embassy in Cairo, something that until two days ago I had been unaware of. Henry had rung him to fill him in on everything that had happened, and straightaway Robert had offered his help.

I watched his face as he shook hands with Charlotte, and

was somewhat bewildered by his lack of surprise at seeing her. 'There's a car waiting outside,' he said. 'I've made your reservations at the Marriott.' He smiled at Charlotte, who was busily wrapping herself in a voluminous coat. 'I've booked a two-room suite, so you'll be sharing with your . . .'

'You mean you were expecting her?'

'I certainly was. Henry rang to warn me she was on her way, and, I might add, to give me her instructions.'

I turned to Charlotte, who was now pulling a woollen hat down over her ears. 'Henry knew you were coming?'

She nodded. I shook my head and laughed. I'd have a few words to say to him when I got back.

On the way into town Robert filled me in on what he had managed to find out so far. It seemed that Kamel – I wracked my brains for any previous mention of the name but couldn't recollect one – had been arrested. Robert was uncertain what for, though he was pretty sure it had something to do with the running of an import-export racket somewhere in the Valley of the Kings.

'But what I do know,' he went on, 'is that the police are trying to find some way of linking all this – the forgery, the alleged drugs and arms offences, and of course the murder of the security guard – to the Pasha.'

'The Pasha? David Walters mentioned him. He thinks Christine is with him.'

'He could well be right, but that doesn't help us much. The Pasha practically owns Cairo, she could be anywhere.' He waved his hand for me to look out of the window.

Little as I could see in the dark, I understood at once what he meant. Cairo looked as if it were the sort of place you could hide in forever without being found. By the light of madly winking neon signs I could see that behind the modern buildings that lined the main thoroughfare the city became immediately a maze of little streets and alleys, a warren of decaying houses and tenements, all of it seething with human life and activity. To my foreign eyes, it looked like a vision of chaos. Even the main road wasn't much better. Death-defying drivers honked their horns and jammed their accelerators with a recklessness bordering on lunacy. We ground to a halt at the base of the Sixth of October bridge, where ahead of us a policeman was yelling at a man whose body was half out of his car window. Somewhere in the distance loud yet haunting music wailed its contribution to the city concert.

As we crossed the bridge, heading for Zamalik, Robert laughed. 'Cheer up! It's not as bad as it looks.'

The Marriott Hotel was the most welcoming sight so far: white marble fountains and a golden web of cast-iron arches, it was like an island of civilisation quietly resisting the encroaching chaos. As it was nearing midnight I insisted Charlotte went to bed. Robert and I ordered drinks from room service and sat up talking late into the night.

The following morning at eight o'clock, breakfast arrived, and Charlotte and I sat on our balcony chewing rubbery toast. We overlooked the palm trees, fountains and waterfalls that surrounded the hotel pool. The air was still cold, but the sun was struggling up through a grey, low-lying mist. From the corner of my eye I watched Charlotte as she stretched out her long legs and reached for her tea. She flicked her hair out of her eyes, in just the same manner as Elizabeth always did. I felt a stabbing sense of loss. I had missed so much of her childhood. I had never allowed myself to think too long or too hard about the way I felt about her before, but seeing her now, I could hardly believe the ridiculous surge of pride I felt that she was mine.

She didn't turn her head as she spoke, but continued to look out over the gardens. 'I know you're pretending not to, but you're watching me,' she said. 'What are you thinking?'

I found I had to swallow before I could answer, and then I laughed. 'I was wondering how I came to be lucky enough to have a daughter as beautiful as you.'

She thought about that for a moment, then turned to look at me with a mischievous gleam in her eyes. 'Do you think Mum might have had something to do with it?'

'I think she had everything to do with it. After all, apart from you, she's just about the most beautiful woman alive.'

'And you're not biased, of course?'

I laughed. 'If I remember rightly, she once accused me of the same thing herself.' I sighed. 'God, that all seems such a long time ago now, probably about the time you ceased being just a twinkle in my eye.'

'Tell me about it. Tell me how you first met, and why it was you didn't marry her when I was born. I'd really like to know.'

The phone rang then and I got up to answer it. It was Robert saying he wouldn't be able to get away from the Embassy until two. I didn't relish the idea of waiting so long, but I knew that without his help there was very little I could do. On the other hand I was glad to be able to spend some time with Charlotte. She was right, it was time for her to know the truth about Elizabeth and me.

We were sitting by the pool when Robert arrived, an hour earlier than he'd said. With him was a short, scruffy-looking Egyptian dressed in what had once been a rather smart Western suit. The man grinned, showing more gaps than teeth. His name was Mohammed Abu el-Shami. We were to call him Shami, he said.

Robert explained that Shami had returned to Cairo that morning, and seemed to think that his arrival heralded an end to our problems. I regarded the weaselish little man sceptically – but I had only to listen to his broken English for half an hour to realise that he knew everyone and everything to do with the city's covert world. Favours was the currency used, and I was soon persuaded that half of Cairo owed Shami a favour – I didn't ask about the other halt. Robert had already explained to him why I was there, and he would go away now, he said, and 'begin the ball turning.'

His round face beamed with pleasure as he added, 'You have no cause to worry, Meester Belmayne. There is nothing Shami cannot do.' And he dragged a tobacco-stained hand from his pocket which he held under my nose, rubbing thumb against fingers and leaving me in no doubt as to the magic ingredient required for the performance of Shami-miracles.

That evening Charlotte and I attended a cocktail party at the British Embassy. The Ambassador, David told me, had taken a particular interest in our case, and had expressed a desire to meet us. I guessed immediately that my father had been on the phone to him.

It was a strange feeling, turning up at an official function with my daughter on my arm and I had to hide a smile as she took a compact from the beaded purse Robert's wife Susie had lent her, and checked her lipstick before we went in. She looked beautiful. Her dark hair curled loosely round her shoulders, and the long white jacket and pleated grey-and-white linen skirt – 'by Calvin Klein,' she'd informed me – highlighted perfectly the slight tan she'd already acquired. I felt ridiculously proud when heads turned as she walked in, and almost choked when she winked at me and asked if I'd feel happier introducing her as my girlfriend.

When we got back to the hotel there was a message from Shami. It told me that if I wanted to find out where Christine was, I should go straightaway to the supine statue of Ramesses II at Memphis.

Robert was still at the Embassy, so – since I didn't know how long I would be – Susie offered to take Charlotte home with her. The minute the Embassy car turned the corner, heading for Aguza, I asked the doorman to call me a taxi.

'You go to Memphis?' the driver said, as he pulled away

from the hotel. I caught his eye in the mirror. I hadn't told the doorman where I wanted to go.

It was a long drive, and once out of the glare of the city lights we were driving into a dark unknown, with a cluster of black bushes to our right and an expanse of dry, barren land to the left. Neither of us spoke. Finally, after about half an hour, we pulled off the road and the driver switched off his headlights. In the dim glow of the moon I saw no more than a sandy wasteland.

'Ramesses.' The driver was pointing. 'You wait.'

I got out of the car and started to walk in the direction he had indicated. I heard the car turn round. Then, to my alarm, it drove off.

About ten yards in front of me I could make out a building. Then the moon slid behind a cloud. I had never known such darkness. The wind whined over the desert and strange night creatures twittered and squalled. My skin prickled.

I trod carefully through the sand. Coming up against the building, I ran my hands along the smooth concrete until I found an opening. I called out, but the only answer was my own voice, echoing eerily around an open chamber. I decided to wait at the door – there was no point in going inside when it was too dark to see.

Time ticked by. Once I saw a car approaching in the distance, but it turned off before it reached me. The wind picked up. Something ran across my foot. I stepped back and it scuttled off into the night. Then I heard a noise and spun around. There was only the looming shadow of a tree, bending and creaking in the wind.

As quickly as the wind had risen, it dropped. The silence it left was eerie, and I was beginning to wonder how the hell I would get back when suddenly the chamber was flooded with light. I waited a moment, expecting someone to come out. When no one did, I made my way tentatively inside. The only sound was the flutter of a bird, disturbed by the sudden blaze of light. That, and my footsteps.

I looked round. In front of me, lying on its back in the centre of the room, was a colossal statue. I froze. The slanting, stone eyes were as sinister as the insane serenity of the limestone smile. Pugnacious arms with clenched fists pressed against the skirted torso, and below the powerful thighs and knees the right shin bore the jagged edge of amputation.

'Mr Belmayne?'

I spun round as the owner of the voice stepped out of the shadows. He was as tall as me, but slighter. His black hair was combed neatly back from his face, and greased into place. His suit was dark, his shirt a dazzling white against his brown skin. He held out his hand to me. I looked at it, but didn't take it.

'Are you the Pasha?' I asked, knowing instinctively that he wasn't.

He smiled, and the gold in his mouth glinted. 'You are very formal, Mr Belmayne,' he said, eyeing my dinner suit. 'I saw you earlier, leaving the Embassy with your daughter. A very beautiful girl.'

He shrugged when I didn't answer, and took out a cigarette. 'Shami tells us you are looking for someone.'

'Do you know where that someone is?'

He laughed. 'Maybe she does not want to be found.'

'Then why are you here?'

'I am here to show you it would be wise to return to your own country.'

'I'll leave when I've found her.'

'It is unlikely, Mr Belmayne, that you will have the chance to find her. She has asked me to deliver a message to you. It is a very short one.' He took a long draw on his cigarette then ground it into the dust.

I waited. Our eyes locked. He was smiling, mockingly. Not for one second did I doubt that he meant to use the gun he was now taking out of his pocket.

His finger tightened on the trigger and there was a dull

click. He laughed, and I felt myself breaking into a cold sweat. Again his finger moved. I didn't have time to pray for a distraction before it was upon us. I looked up at the bird, and so did he. The gun flew from his grasp as my foot connected with his wrist and my fist smashed into his face. I swung round, searching frantically for the gun. As I made a dive for it, his foot exploded into my groin and I dropped to the ground in agony. Within seconds he was holding the gun to my head. I heard footsteps, then, as something crashed into my skull, I lost consciousness.

– 30 –

I was woken by a party of Japanese tourists peering down at me. Dazed and disoriented, I blinked hard as I tried to focus on the ceiling of bewildered faces. Seeing my eyes open, one of them helped me to my feet while another, somewhat robustly, dusted me down.

Fortunately the Japanese tour guide spoke English, so I was able to ask for the nearest phone. He laughed loudly, and translated my request to his party who, slapping me fondly on the back, joined in the joke. However, after much to-ing and fro-ing I managed to hitch a lift on a horse and cart. The driver, an elderly, toothless peasant who spoke not a word of English, dropped me off at a run-down hotel somewhere on the road to Sakkara.

Once he had established where I was Robert came to collect me.

'Do you know who it was?' he asked. We were nearing the outskirts of Cairo, and I saw his hands tighten on the wheel as he prepared to do battle with the city drivers.

'No. He didn't leave his calling card. All he said was that he had a message from Christine.'

'And the message was your hasty despatch?'

'You know, what beats me,' I said, as we bumped our way through uncordoned roadworks, 'is why he didn't kill me.'

'Well, don't sound so put out. My guess is they were just putting the frighteners on. If they'd wanted to kill you they'd have done it, be in no doubt of that.'

When we got back to the hotel Robert came in and waited while I showered and changed. The hotel manager called to check that everything was all right, as the security guard he'd posted outside my door, at the Ambassador's request, had told him my room hadn't been slept in all night.

It was probably because of the manager's call that I noticed, when we left half an hour later to go and collect Charlotte, that there was no guard outside. I asked Robert if he remembered there being one when we'd come in. He frowned. He thought there had been, but he wouldn't swear to it.

I went back into the room to call the manager, leaving Robert outside, searching the corridor for the guard. But before I could pick up the phone it rang.

'Mr Belmayne?'

'Speaking.'

'You don't know me, Mr Belmayne, but I am ringing for the Pasha.' The voice was Oxford-smooth. 'It was *inshallah*, was it not, Mr Belmayne, that you came to no harm last night in Memphis. Allah smiles upon you. However, the gun was merely a means of communicating to you Miss Walters' reluctance to be found. The Pasha feels certain that you will now be willing to do as he asks so that we can avoid any further unpleasantness. All you have to do is go to the Suez Canal Bank, where the Shari el-Giza meets the Shari el-Nil. Somebody will be waiting for you there. You will be given an account number. Please place into this account one hundred and fifty thousand Egyptian pounds – roughly fifty thousand pounds sterling. When you have done this, you are to take the next flight back to London. Your seat is booked, courtesy of the Pasha. I thought you would prefer to fly British Airways. You will find your ticket waiting for you at the . . .'

'And Christine Walters?'

'I think you misunderstood me, Mr Belmayne. The money is not for the deliverance of Miss Walters. The money is merely the first instalment of what Mrs Walters owes the Pasha. And in return, because the Pasha is a generous man, he will endeavour to . . .'

'I will pay the amount you ask, not as an instalment of any deal *Mr Walters* set up with the Pasha, but for Christine Walters.'

'Mr Belmayne, you *will* pay the money. But, I am sorry to say, on the Pasha's terms, not your own.'

'I am in this country to locate Christine Walters. Until I do, then please tell the Pasha I shall not be leaving.'

'Perhaps, Mr Belmayne, you will reconsider when I tell you that your daughter, even as we speak . . .'

My mouth went dry. 'Charlotte! Where is she? What the hell . . .'

'She is safe, Mr Belmayne. Please, just do as I ask and she will remain so.' And the line went dead.

'*Jesus Christ*!' I spun round as Robert came running in. 'Charlotte! Where is she? I thought she was with your wife.'

'She is. What's going on?'

'That phone call . . .' I snatched up the receiver and started to dial. The phone rang at the other end, and almost straightaway Susie answered.

'Alexander. At last. What happened? Where . . . ?'

'Where's Charlotte?' I barked.

'Isn't she with you?'

I felt the bottom drop out of the world. 'No, she's not with me. When did you last see her?'

'About an hour ago. I dropped her off at the hotel.'

'Then where is she now?' The question was futile, of course.

I slammed the phone down and caught Robert by the throat. 'They've got her. Do you hear me?'

Robert wrenched himself free and snatched up the phone. 'I'm going to ring the Ambassador. What did the man say exactly?'

I told him. 'Have you got the money?' he asked.

'Of course I've got the fucking money. The money's nothing.'

'Then I suggest you do as they say.'

'Robert, you'd better get this into your head now. I am not leaving this country until I've got my daughter, so don't let's even discuss it.'

'Robert Lyttleton here,' he said into the phone, 'put me on to the Ambassador. I don't care if he's in a meeting, put me on now!'

He waited as the operator put him through, and I paced the room, berating myself over and over for not sending Charlotte straight back to England.

'What did he say?' I asked, as Robert replaced the receiver.

'He's getting on to London.'

'London! What fucking good will that do?'

'We'll see,' he answered. 'Meanwhile I suggest we get ourselves over to the Suez Canal Bank.'

We stopped off at the hotel manager's office. Thank God he wasn't like his fellow countrymen. Instead of the million apologies I had been expecting, he merely picked up the telephone. I had no idea what he was saying, but when he'd finished he told me to go to the National Arab Bank by the lobby where one hundred and fifty thousand Egyptian pounds would be waiting for me.

When we got to the Suez Canal Bank we didn't have to wait long before I was approached by an old woman, huddled darkly behind her gilbab and khimara.

'Eengleesh?' she hissed.

I nodded, and she handed me a scrap of paper, then

turned and disappeared into the crowd. I made to go after her, but Robert pulled me back. 'She'll have been paid to deliver the note. It'll have passed through too many hands before hers for us to be able to find out where it came from.' He took the piece of paper from me and unfolded it. The only thing written on it was a bank account number.

The transaction went smoothly and I was outside the bank again in less than ten minutes. Robert was waiting in a taxi. 'I think we'd better go to the Embassy,' he said.

'Drop me at the hotel. If anyone wants to contact me, that's where they'll try.'

But for the rest of that day we heard nothing.

The first call came the next morning. It was the Ambassador to say the tracing of the bank account had led nowhere. However, his instructions had come through from Whitehall. He was to inform President Mubarak that Her Majesty's Government would be greatly obliged if every effort would be made by the People's Assembly to ensure the safe return of the Lord Chancellor's granddaughter, forthwith.

I looked at Robert, dumbfounded.

'I don't think you realise, Alexander,just what . . .'

'*You don't think I realise*? This is my daughter we're talking about. She's been kidnapped. *Kidnapped*! Given the lunatics we're dealing with, she could be lying out there dead for all I know – and all you lot can come up with is a polite request that she should be returned! What bloody good do you think *that's* going to do?'

'You'll see,' he answered calmly. And within the hour I did.

The Cairo Chief of Police came to my room at the Marriott. With him was the British Ambassador and two henchmen. The Chief questioned me for over an hour, during which time an emergency police headquarters was set up in the Verdi Salon downstairs.

'The Pasha is being questioned,' the Chief said, as

he pulled back the curtains and looked down into the garden.

My heart thumped adrenalin into my veins. 'You know where he is?'

'We have him at headquarters. I'm afraid so far this is all we have to go on.' He took a scrap of paper from his pocket and laid it on the table. 'It is all the Pasha will say.'

We all looked at it, but it was written in Arabic. I didn't bother to disguise my irritation. 'So, what does it say?'

'It says, Mr Belmayne, the French earl curses into double figures.'

'And what the hell is that supposed to mean?'

'As it stands, nothing. We have to work it out. It is the way the Pasha works.'

The Ambassador looked bemused. 'You mean it's a riddle?'

'I suppose, yes. But it is more than that, I'm sure. I believe it will give us the clue to where your daughter is being held, Mr Belmayne.' I glared at him, certain he had taken leave of his senses. He turned to the Ambassador. 'Your intelligence agents, sir, I think they should join forces with the police in order to break this code. We have very little time.'

I snatched up the piece of paper. 'For God's sake, it's a riddle. The way you're behaving, anyone would think it held the answer to the Middle East crisis. A French earl is a count! Curses. Oaths, spells, scourges, plagues . . . Double figures. Anything from ten.'

'The ten plagues,' Robert said.

'Incidentally,' the Ambassador said, 'I have just learned . . . What is it, Mr Belmayne? Has something . . . ?'

'The tenth plague,' I whispered, and when I realised they were all staring at me, I almost yelled, 'If you knew your bible . . . The tenth plague was the death of the first-born.'

The Ambassador looked at me, appalled, and I stared

back at him. *She's dead! She's dead!* The words thumped with my heartbeat. Her face swam before my eyes, and I felt the knife of terror rip through my body.

The Chief was speaking. 'Please, don't be alarmed,' he was saying, 'it is early days yet. And now you, Mr Belmayne, you have given us a beginning.' Despite his words he looked defeated.

I exploded. 'Didn't you hear what I said? Isn't the message loud and clear? Isn't that what the tenth plague means? It's your damned country, your damned history!'

'Oh yes, that is without a doubt what it means. But that is only the surface meaning. The Pasha, he will never make anything so simple as that. You see, you break the code in minutes, or so you think. But what we do now is solve the riddle of the tenth plague.'

Observing my reaction, the Chief obviously felt it best he withdraw at that point. I had been living on my nerves ever since Charlotte's abduction, and now, with this new, implausible turn of events it was highly probable I might go over the edge at any moment.

After a sleepless night the police were still no closer to finding her. The Verdi Salon was in chaos; just about every cryptographer in the Middle East had been sectioned off to help decipher the 'conundrum', as they were now calling it. The only people keeping a reasonably cool head seemed to be the Chief of Police and the hotel manager.

Another day went by, and still we heard nothing. My father telephoned but I cut him short, wanting to keep the line free. Henry rang later, but again I terminated the call before he could get started.

On the third day, just before lunch, Robert arrived with a handful of telegrams. He passed them to me just as the telephone, which had been silent all morning, burst into life.

'Mr Belmayne? Claude de Rousse here, from *Le Monde*.'

'*Le Monde*?'

Robert pressed his fingers on the connectors and ended the call. 'I should read the telegrams if I were you. Somehow the story has leaked out. What you have there are messages from the great British public, expressing their support.'

'What!'

'Some clever hack has pieced together your story, Alexander, old chum. It's all over the press back home, so I'm told. Front page stuff. The great love story of the century, I think one of them called it. You and Elizabeth.'

'Me and Elizabeth? But what . . .?'

'You'll find it goes right back to Foxton's, I'm afraid. The gypsy and the aristocrat. It's caught everyone's imagination. How you've loved each other secretly all these years, even that you're the father of her two children. Everything's there. Haven't read it myself, of course, Henry told me. He called me last night. Said he called you first, but got cut off.'

I was listening to him in stupefied silence, while all the time a volcanic rage was rumbling through my gut. When he finished I exploded. 'This isn't a bloody soap opera!' I yelled. 'Don't they realise . . .'

The phone cut me short. Robert picked it up. 'I'm afraid Mr Belmayne isn't available for comment at the moment,' he said, and hung up. He rang through to the manager then, and asked him to instruct the operators to divert all calls from the press to the Verdi Salon.

'Now calm down,' he said, turning back to me. 'Don't you see, with the British public and the press on your side, it puts all the more pressure on the Egyptians to find her. And they will.'

'I wish I had your confidence. And where the hell is Shami?'

Robert looked at his watch. 'He should be arriving any minute. He says he knows where Christine is.'

'What! Why didn't you tell me this before?'

He shrugged. 'Thought I ought to warn you about the

paparazzi. They all flew in this morning, so we're going to have to sneak out the back way.'

'And the police? Have you told them you might know where Christine is?'

'The Chief is on his way up. Incidentally, the telegram on the top is from your wife.'

He grinned at my look of dismay. 'I'd read it, if I were you. I don't think you'll be disappointed.'

It was very short. 'Good luck, darling,' I read, 'try and stay in one piece for our divorce. Love Jess.'

I looked at Robert and saw he was laughing. For the first time in days I laughed too. 'She certainly knows how to pick her moment,' I said. 'Cable her back for me, will you?'

'The message?'

'"It's a promise."'

The moment Shami walked in and saw the Chief of Police, his eyes sank back in their sockets. He mumbled his apologies for bursting into the wrong room and started to close the door. The Chief was too quick for him and hauled him back inside.

He looked more shifty than ever as he admitted that it wasn't he who had seen Christine, but his brother. He shrugged. 'But is the same thing, no?'

The Chief shook his head, and Shami looked crestfallen. 'But I explain, my brother, he know wife of second cousin of Pasha, she take my brother to a place where they see your Christine. It is in Khan-el-Khalili, where the men they make the gold. The gold they use for King Tutankhamun mask, no?'

The Chief was eyeing Shami. 'What Tutankhamun mask, Shami?'

Shami looked round the room helplessly. 'I donno, sir. Shami, he know very little.' He turned his eyes to me. 'But my brother, he say to be at Fishawi today. Someone will lead us to the men, and maybe they tell you where is your Christine. We hurry there now, yes?'

'Yes,' said the Chief.

Shami's face was gloomy as he said his brother would not be pleased if he arrived with the police. 'Not that he no like the police,' he hastily assured us.

The Chief tossed us a wry smile and picked up the telephone. He spoke hurriedly in Egyptian, then asked us to wait a few minutes while his men arranged a decoy out of the hotel, to mislead the press.

A fleet of cars was waiting, none of them marked with police insignia. As we sped away from the hotel I noticed several of them break away from the convoy and fall anonymously into the traffic.

When we reached the bazaar the Chief disappeared inside the Sayyidna el-Hussein Mosque. Two of his men followed, and when they emerged several minutes later, they were all three dressed in traditional Egyptian garb. A police officer I recognised from the Verdi Salon approached us. He spoke to the Chief, waving his arms in the direction of the bazaar. The Chief listened gravely, nodded his head, then turned to us.

'My men are in position. They are covering the Khan el-Khalili at every strategic point. I must instruct you, Mr Belmayne, that should we encounter any danger you are to leave everything to them. Please, no heroics. You do not understand the kind of people we are dealing with here. To them everything is *inshallah* – God's will. If a man stands in their way and they have to kill him to get what they want, it is *inshallah*, they do not think twice.' He turned to Shami. 'Go ahead to the Fishawi, and no tricks, Shami, you will be being watched.'

When Shami had blended into the crowd the Chief turned again to Robert and me. 'Now, please, follow me. I will lead you to the Fishawi – it is a coffee bar a few streets from here. When you see me sit down, please go no further than a nearby stall where you should inspect the merchandise. Do not, under any circumstances, move from there unless I say so. We will be in Shami's hands. And again I stress, please, no heroics.'

A few minutes later we plunged into the pandemonium of the Khan el-Khalili. The Fishawi wasn't far, but I knew that if I tried to find my way there again I would undoubtedly fail. The Chief, in his striped galibaya and turban, blended perfectly into the coffee bar crowd. Robert and I stood innocuously by, hustled and jostled as we inspected a display of brass and copper pots. Within seconds the owner of the stall was asking us to name a price, and so as not to call unnecessary attention to ourselves, Robert entered into a long-drawn-out haggle. I made a pretence of watching them, but all the time my eyes were fixed on Shami who was seated a few tables from the Chief of Police.

Through the hanging haze of smoke and steam I could see blank faces sucking peacefully on their hookahs, while excited traders bellowed for turbid mint tea and Turkish coffee. The Fishawi was a strange place. Though decaying and filthy, it had a unique sepia-like charm; battered tables spiled out into the covered alleyway, and waiters scuttled back and forth hoisting hookahs and trays from kitchen to table.

Robert bought a copper tray.

To my dismay I watched Shami remove his shoes and hand them to a shiner. The Chief called for a hookah, and Robert bought an urn. Time dragged on.

Eventually the Chief set aside his hookah and wandered over to us. He made a pretence of admiring the brass pots while saying he could only assume that either Shami had been lying, or he himself had been recognised.

My heart sank. I moved to one side to let a woman and her baby pass, thrusting my hands in my pockets before I hammered my fists against the nearest object.

I felt a sharp kick on the leg and Robert – now so laden

with purchases he could barely move – nodded towards Shami. The woman who had just passed us was standing over him, speaking to him hurriedly. Shami listened, stroking the baby's head. When the woman had finished, she tucked the baby back into its blanket and started to move away. Shami got to his feet.

I started towards him but the Chief pulled me back. 'Wait,' he hissed.

The woman and Shami disappeared round a corner and we moved across the Fishawi. As we rounded the curve of the building I spotted the woman, pressing determinedly through the crowd. Shami was behind her. Following him, we pushed steadily on through the maze of passageways, past stalls selling carpets, jellabas, jewellery . . . . Traders dived into my path, thrusting their wares in my face, and motor-cycles roared through the crowds, but I never took my eyes from the woman ahead. Suddenly somebody screamed, there was the crash of a stall falling, and a motor-cycle skidded into a shop front. I looked up, and the woman had disappeared.

I started to run, tearing through the people, thrusting them ruthlessly aside. My eyes darted from left to right, searching the alleys. A man grabbed me by the arm, spinning me round to show me the damage I'd done to his stall, but I shook him off and charged on. A sea of startled faces loomed towards me as I pressed through the crowds. And there was the woman with the baby again, but no Shami. She was standing on a corner, looking to her right. I forced my way towards her, but as she saw me she ran on. I let her go and turned into the dark alley. It was thronging with sheep, but at the other end I saw Shami's scrawny figure disappear into a doorway.

The animals huddled round my knees in a knot of bleating, lice-ridden bodies. I grabbed at them, throwing them one on top of another as I forced my way through. There was no sign now of either Robert or the Chief.

The doorway opened into a blackened passage. I almost drew back as the acrid stench kicked at my gut. The walls were slimed with mildew and the dingy linoleum floor was coated with filth. I strained my eyes to see into the shadows. Several feet to the right was a staircase. I took it, two steps at a time. When I reached the top, I could see daylight at the end of a corridor. I rushed towards it, and as I pushed out into the fresh air I found myself faced with a maze of roofless gangways and stairwells. Turning into the nearest, I felt my foot hit something heavy and soft. I looked down into a face covered in blood. Shami groaned. I bent down to help him, and as I did so a foot crashed into the side of my head.

Then there was mayhem. I fell on to Shami, blood cascading from my mouth and nose, as my attackers trampled over me and ran back the way I had come. I dragged myself to my feet and down the stairs after them. A gun was fired and I dodged back into the shadows. Then there was the sound of running feet and voices yelling. More gunfire – and I dashed out into the street. The police were swarming in as my attackers – four of them – fled in all directions. I saw one of them dive into a twisting alley and made after him. We broke out at the other end into the very heart of the bazaar. I paused and looked round. Someone screamed, and a black Peugeot sprang out of the crowd.

Quick as a flash, I heaved a driver out of his taxi. As I started the engine the passenger door flew open and Shami, his face battered and still bleeding, leapt in beside me. 'Let's go, Meester Belmayne!' he cried.

I roared out into the traffic. Shami hung out of the window, screaming at everyone to get out of the way. Minarets and domes sped by in a blur. Behind me I could hear the wail of police sirens, while in front the black Peugeot tore through the streets until eventually it screeched into the Pyramids Road. I turned in after it, then slammed my foot on the brake as I skidded round a pack of meandering camels. The Peugeot was surrounded. I leapt out of my car. Then suddenly the camels parted and the Peugeot was speeding off into the distance. Back behind the wheel, I pressed my hand on the horn, yelling at the camel drivers to clear the way. The police came round the corner, managed to skirt the mêlée, and roared off towards the Pyramids, after the Peugeot.

By the time I was clear there was no sign of the chase. About two miles further on, where the road stretched endlessly out in front of me, I knew it was pointless to carry on. I turned round and drove slowly back. Then a police car came speeding up behind me and screeched to a halt as I waved. The Chief clambered out of the back seat.

'We've got him! Turn your car round and follow us. If you get lost Shami knows where the Alexandria Road is. And you, Shami . . .'He said something in Egyptian and went back to his car.

A few minutes later we pulled up outside a palatial villa. The gates were locked but a police officer got out of the Chief's car and spoke for some time on the intercom. Eventually the Chief joined him, listened for a while, then went back to his car and opened the back door. Robert got out and the two of them came over to me.

'The Pasha is inside,' the Chief said. 'He wants to speak to you. I have agreed to wait outside, but Mr Lyttleton will go in with you. I think you know by now that the Pasha is a dangerous man. Please, just listen and don't do anything foolish.'

I nodded and waited while the Chief went back to the intercom. A few seconds later the villa gates slid slowly open. As I drove in I saw the Chief and two police officers creep in behind me and disappear into the bushes of the garden.

Robert followed me over to the door. Tentatively I tried the handle, and to my surprise the door opened. The entrance hall, carpeted in tiger skins and ornamented with elaborate gilt mirrors, was empty. I turned back to Robert and suddenly the double doors at the end of the hall swung open.

'Mr Belmayne.'

The first thing I noticed about the Pasha was the almost overpowering beauty of his smile. The second was his height. His forehead was masked by the doorframe, but his eyes gazed down into mine as he lifted a gold-laden hand. With a long, claw-like finger he stroked his lips. His movements were almost feminine and yet his every gesture exuded menace – a sinister combination that made me shudder with revulsion.

'We will not waste words, Mr Belmayne,' he drawled. 'If you want your daughter returned, then you will ask the police to leave my premises immediately.'

Suddenly my control shattered and I lunged at him, grabbing him by the throat. 'Tell me where she is now, or so help me, I'll kill you.'

He squealed like a rabbit, his limbs thrashing about in all directions.

'Let him go!'

I wheeled round to see a woman standing at the bottom of the stairs. She was pointing a gun at Robert. Her hair and part of her face were covered by a spangled scarf, and her eyes were heavily ringed with kohl. She was looking at me and I sensed rather than saw the triumphant smile.

I let the Pasha go. He held his hand out for the gun, then casually looked Robert and me over. 'It would seem, Christine,' he said, 'that they have not yet solved my little riddle. So what we have in the child is our passport out of the country.'

Christine looked up at him, and I saw a strange, almost hypnotic adoration shine from her face. The Pasha nodded for us to go into the room behind him. Robert and I exchanged glances, but there was very little we could do with a gun at our heads.

I was already inside the room when I heard the shout. The front door crashed open and suddenly the place was filled with police. Two shots were fired, almost simultaneously. I swung round – and the Pasha's eyes seemed to bore into mine. Before he fell I saw more evil in that one look than I had ever seen before in my life. Christine screamed and ran towards him, then before any of us had time to move, she had seized his gun and was pointing it at me.

'You!' she spat. 'You! Everything that's happened is because of you and your slut! You killed my brother, and now you've killed my husband.' And before anyone could stop her she had pulled the trigger.

The bullet tore through my shoulder. Within seconds the police had seized her. Robert was hanging on to me, keeping me from falling. It must have been only minutes later that I lost consciousness.

I passed the night at the Embassy, drugged with painkillers, and my left arm supported by a sling. Robert came to see how I was next morning, and after taking my temperature and checking my wound, the nurse told him I was fit enough to leave the room. On the way to the Ambassador's office he filled me in on what had been happening throughout the night.

The Pasha wasn't dead. While Robert brought me back to the Embassy doctor, where I would be safe from the press, the Pasha had been rushed to hospital under police escort.

'And Christine?'

'She's being held at El Knater – the women's prison.' He stopped to let someone pass, but made no move to walk on again. 'I don't suppose you knew she'd married the Pasha, did you?' he asked.

I shook my head. 'No, but I suppose that's what her brother meant by the Pasha having some kind of hold over her. She's going to live to regret that marriage.'

We started to walk on. 'Why do you say that?'

'Under the laws of Islam isn't a woman her husband's property? I take it the Pasha is a Moslem?' Robert nodded. 'Then she'll have to face the rigours of Egyptian law. With the murder of the security guard, the forging of the mask, illegal import and export, kidnapping and God only knows what else they've been up to, she could be facing a death sentence.' I steeled myself before asking the next question, even though I already knew the answer. 'Has either of them told you where Charlotte is?'

Robert shook his head. 'She wasn't in the villa, the police searched it from top to bottom. But there is some good news. They've called in some egghead from the Cairo Museum who thinks he s cracked the conundrum.'

We were at the Ambassador's office now. Inside were the Ambassador, the Chief of Police and the professor. The professor was seated at a table by the window, surrounded by bibles and history books.

'It was necessary to channel thoughts in a new direction,' the Chief said, once the introductions were over. 'My friend here has done that, and now, after a long process of elimination, we have the answer.' The professor sat by, smiling benignly, as the Chief explained how the professor had come up with the solution. It was, like almost everything else I had encountered since I'd arrived in Egypt, bizarre in the extreme.

'We merely used hieroglyphs,' the professor explained, as if one might use hieroglyphs to solve any old problem. 'First, we took the rod. Do you remember? Moses' rod changed to a snake. It was God's way of showing Moses he had the power of God within him. Here,' he held up a piece of paper, 'the hieroglyph snake. Do you see?'

Robert, the Ambassador and I looked blankly at a squiggle that vaguely resembled a snake. The professor merely shrugged at our lack of appreciation. 'Then we considered the plague and how the children died. They were visited by the angel of death, yes? Flying like a bird by night over Egypt, yes? And the bird that flies by night? An owl. And the hieratic script for owl, see here?'

Again he showed us a piece of paper. On it was scribbled what looked to be the figure three.

'This is the sign for the owl. And now see, if you put them together, the sign of the snake and the sign of the owl, this is what you have.'

He waited while we passed round the results of his efforts, then taking it back from Robert, and, hardly able to contain his excitement, he said. 'This is the sign which is inscribed over a door in El Khalifa – the City of the Dead. It is the door of the Pasha's mother's house. I have no doubt in my mind that your daughter is there, so if you are ready, Mr Belmayne, we will go.'

I was too stunned by the tortured logic to do more than smile stupidly.

It was a long journey to the south-eastern outskirts of the city, and one I can barely remember now, for I spent the time praying that the Chief's confidence was not ill-placed. As we drove into the City of the Dead Robert wound up the windows to block out the stench. We remained in the Chief's car with the Ambassador while, surrounded by his men, the Chief made his way into the macabre town.

I could hardly believe what I was seeing as they stepped through the dust among emaciated animals, mud-fronted tombs and wretched, tired-looking old men. But it wasn't that that shocked me, it was the brand new Mercedes, Jaguars and most incredible of all, Rolls Royces. Robert explained that even if they became rich, some people preferred to stay with their neighbours among the ancient tombs, where they had become used to living side by side with the dead. If I hadn't already, then it was at that point that I gave up any hope of ever understanding this nation.

We had been waiting for ten minutes, maybe less, when the haunting cry of the muezzin drifted from distant minarets. Hunched and shrouded figures shuffled past on their way to prayer, and round brown eyes glanced furtively in our direction. A few minutes later the Chief came striding towards the car. Behind him an old lady, wailing loudly, was being escorted by two police officers. They bundled her into a car, and the Chief got back into his. There was no sign of Charlotte.

'She is gone,' the Chief said. 'They took her away this morning.'

'They? Who are you talking about?' I demanded, failing to keep the desperation from my voice.

The Chief nodded to his driver, then turned to face us. 'I'm sorry, Mr Belmayne, I cannot say. All I know is that she was alive when they took her. My men are taking the Pasha's mother away to be questioned, but I think she was speaking the truth when she said she didn't know the people who came for your daughter.'

I slumped back in my seat, unsure if I could take any more. None of us spoke as we were driven back to the Embassy. None of us wanted to admit that we could be right back at square one.

'Ah, Meester Ambassador, Meester Belmayne,' Shami said as we walked into the Ambassador's office. He was grinning like a pumpkin. 'The secretary she say I can wait here for you. You find your daughter, no?'

'No!'

The smile fell from his face. 'You no find her? But was my . . .' He threw up his hands in exasperation. 'He drink again,' he said, mysteriously. 'You come with me, Meester Belmayne, I take you to your daughter. Very fine, very beautiful girl, your daughter. I take you there now. She wait for you.'

'You mean you know where she is?'

'Sure. She with my brother. I take her from El Khalifa

in this morning. She no like it there. Come, she wait for you.'

I was aware of my whole body turning rigid as grim suspicion flowered into certainty. 'Have you known all the time where she is, Shami?'

Shami nodded brightly. 'For sure I know, Meester Belmayne. Shami know everything.'

I lunged at him but Robert and the Ambassador pulled me back. 'If you knew, then why have you let us go through all this?' I yelled.

Shami shrugged. 'To say mean no money, Meester Belmayne. Like everyone in the world, Shami need money.' He grinned. 'And the chase, aaah, the chase, he was good, no?'

For the moment, robbed of the power of speech, all I could do was stare at him. While my daughter had suffered in God only knew what kind of hell, with God only knew what kind of people, this man had thought no further than the money he could make and the sport to be had in making it. He shuffled his feet and grinned sheepishly from me to Robert. Then the Chief of Police ushered him out of the room before I could regain control of my faculties . . . .

– Elizabeth –

– 31 –

I had been in Holloway Prison for exactly sixteen days when Alexander brought Charlotte back to England; already it felt like a lifetime. Henry came to see me that day to tell me Alexander had taken Charlotte straight to hospital. I can't explain what it was like living with the frustration of such helplessness.

The day after he flew in Alexander, together with Oscar Renfrew, came to see me. As I was led up to the visiting hall my heart was in my throat and I felt sick with the humiliation of him seeing me like this. The first time he had come, the day before he went to Cairo, I was still too dazed to think straight. But now, as I walked soundlessly along the corridors, avoiding the eyes of the officers we passed, I was all too aware of the living hell my life had become. When I'd been told he was coming I'd brushed my hair and left it loose, but I knew it wouldn't hide the dark rings round my eyes or the dullness of my skin. Of the three outfits I'd been allowed to take into prison I'd chosen a black Chanel suit as the one I would wear for visiting days. I no longer had it. The other women, resenting the open display of wealth had ripped it to pieces and were using it as dusters to clean their cells. Very few of them spoke to me except to sneer and hiss and cat-call across the landings. I was terrified of them. I stood at mealtimes – unable to sit down because no one would let me. I ate very little, as they spat in my food or knocked it from my tray. Most of the time I was dirty because I was too afraid to go to the washrooms. It wasn't until Isabelle, my cell mate, decided to befriend me that I managed to utter more than a few words to anyone.

Without Isabelle I don't know how I'd have got through. After days of silently watching the way I was treated, she took it upon herself to protect me from the constant threats of violence and sexual abuse, and pulled strings to get me a job in the library with her. It was my only respite from the nightmare.

Just past the visiting hall, the prison officer stopped and opened the door to an interview room. There was brown carpet on the floor and the walls were bare. In the middle was a table. I went in and she closed the door behind me. A few minutes later I heard footsteps, then the door opened and Alexander was there. I had promised myself I would be strong, that I wouldn't let him know how awful things really were, but when I saw the look in his eyes my control fell apart. I had never seen a man's face so filled with love and anguish.

With one arm he held me, burying his face in my hair and whispering for me to be calm. Oscar nodded to the prison officer and she left us alone. It was some time before I could pull myself together. Throughout the time Alexander and Charlotte had been in Cairo, Henry had kept me informed of what was happening, and now, knowing they were both home and safe, all the torment and terror I had somehow managed to bottle up came pouring out. Alexander waited while I reminded him that I'd told him not to go, that I had warned him about the kind of people he was dealing with; I called him irresponsible, selfish and stupid, I even lashed out at his wounded arm. In the end he caught hold of me and turned me to face him.

'It's good to see you too,' he said.

He sat me down then and, perched on the edge of the table, he laughed as he told me how Jonathan was green with envy that he hadn't been kidnapped too, and couldn't wait for Charlotte to come home from the hospital so he could hear all the gory details.

'Don't worry,' he smiled as he saw my look of alarm, 'my

father's taking Jonathan off to the country this afternoon, so Charlotte will be spared. Canary and Caroline will be looking after her. And me, of course.'

I looked away, my heart aching. They would be together now – Alexander, Charlotte and Jonathan, and here was I . . .

He must have sensed how I was feeling because he slipped his arm out of its sling and hugged me. 'We'll have you out of here, darling,' he promised. 'I know it's difficult, but please, try and be patient.'

But I knew from the way his eyes met Oscar's that something was troubling him, and when I challenged him, he admitted it. It was the way the Egyptians had gone about interrogating Christine. Although he had no actual details of what they had done to extract the confession from her, he knew that when it came to appeal the prosecution would make a great deal of their methods and perhaps succeed in invalidating the confession altogether.

'Our only hope is for her to be present at the appeal,' Oscar said. 'Even then, there's no way of knowing if she will admit to the crime.'

But she did. Exerting every ounce of influence they had, between them the British Ambassador in Cairo and Alexander's father managed to get Christine, under heavy guard, flown to London for the appeal. It was only later I found out, that, had she not been there, there would have been no appeal.

It was almost nine months since I had last seen her, and four of those she had spent in an Egyptian prison. She was forty-three now, but looked closer to sixty. Her hair, what was left of it, clung to her skull, and as she looked up from her bony hands and shifted her weight stiffly from one leg to the other, I saw the strange pallor in her eyes. Her small, heavy-lipped mouth was drawn into sharp, parallel lines of rancour. She held herself erect, but I could see that beneath the brown serge that almost engulfed her, her emaciated body was beginning to sag with the effort.

Mesmerised, horrified, I watched her as she took the oath, almost choking on the pity and sadness I felt at seeing her like that. Then, as she looked out across the courtroom, a triumphant gleam lighting her yellowed eyes, I knew the time for reckoning between us had come.

'I am in no doubt,' she said. 'I know that by the end of this year I shall be dead. The crimes my husband and I have committed in Egypt are sufficient to earn us not one but two death sentences. I welcome them. There is nothing left to live for. My husband and my brother were my life. I am under no illusions about the way they manipulated me, the way I became a pawn in their dangerous games, the way I was used as an exchange of favours between them, but it doesn't matter. I got what I wanted. I got Salah – the Pasha. He married me because my brother requested it. He never did and never will love me, I know that, but I can accept it. For me it was enough to be his wife. He was a man who wielded immense power; he could be ruthless and tyrannical, he was malevolent, corrupt and cruel – yet he only ever treated me with kindness.

'I am telling you all this because I want you to understand why I did what I did for my brother. You see, I knew what it was to love someone who was in love with another man. My brother lived with that hell for more than twelve years. Every day was torture to him – to be with her, yet not to be loved by her. It drove him out of his mind, in fact it killed him. Salah too loved a man, but I shall be the one who is with him at the end, in a way my sister-in-law was never with my brother.'

As she continued to speak, trying to explain her blinding passion for the Pasha, it was as if she were reliving it all again, oblivious of the courtroom and everyone in it. Until Alexander told me I'd had no knowledge of her marriage, and now, together with everyone else in the court, I sat spellbound as she spoke of the obsessional and unrequited love she had for Salah – a love that, time after time, she likened to Edward's love for me.

Finally she lowered her eyes. 'Maybe now you will understand why I set fire to the Bridlington warehouse with the intention of killing my sister-in-law.' I felt my body go rigid and everything around me started to swim. 'I hated her. She brought her bastard daughter into our home, that man's bastard – ' her hand was trembling as she pointed towards Alexander, though she had not raised her voice – 'and my brother treated the child as his own. He gave them both everything they could want. And how did she repay him? She ran off with her lover again, returned to us when he had finished with her, and tried to palm her second bastard off as my brother's child. And even after lying to him and cheating him in the way she had, he forgave her, because he loved her. He even adopted her children as his own. He changed his will for them. And all the time *I* was the one helping him to realise an ambition that would save him from the final ignominy of her faithlessness. The need for the mask burned in him with all the might of his love. If he couldn't have it, there was nothing left for him. And while I helped him, *she* was back in her lover's bed. This time when my brother found out, it killed him. My sister-in-law deserved to die, and she would have died if Daniel Davison had not saved her life.' Her eyes rested fleetingly on me before she looked away again. 'If it were left to me she would not go to prison, she would rot in hell.' She paused again, and a gruesome smile dawned on her face. 'But my brother loved her. He would have forgiven her anything, and it is because of him that I am prepared to absolve her from her sentence. She is innocent.'

My hands bit into the rail in front of me as she turned and fixed her yellow eyes on mine. Her smile had widened now, and there was something so sinister about it that my mind went numb with terror. Why was she doing this? Why, when she hated me so much, was she setting me free? My whole body trembled with horror as she hissed the answer:

'Now live with the guilt.'

Her eyes were still boring into mine as a barely audible chuckle escaped her lips. She had won.

After my release, as the weeks passed I saw less and less of Alexander. I couldn't look at him and love him without seeing Christine's face and the way she had looked that last day. He tried everything he could to persuade me to pull myself together, but the more he yelled or cajoled, the more I withdrew.

Then, on the day Christine was sentenced to die – September 14th – a messenger arrived with a special delivery. Even now I find it difficult to put into words the way I felt when I opened the envelope. There was nothing to say who had torn the page from Christine's diary and sent it to me, I even wondered if she had done it herself. The entry was for September 12th and as I read, my heart was filled with the terrible loneliness and confusion she must have suffered, not only during her final hours, but ever since I had come into her life.

'From the moment I met her there was never any doubt in my mind that one day I would have to kill her. Perhaps it was a genuine vision of the future, though I recall no images, not even the vividness of the fire that was to consume so much. I felt only the overwhelming need to protect myself, and all that was mine.

Elizabeth Sorrill. She was blessed with the kind of beauty I had only ever dreamed about, bringing love and laughter to my brothers, while all the time she nursed the pain of a love she had lost – a love she would never give up.

And what right had she to that love? I am a woman, I have known love, I have known the pain of loss. Have I spent my life making others suffer for it?

But I know now that I have never experienced anything like the love that bound Elizabeth and Alexander. It was a love that not only bridged the gulf of class, but survived years of parting, the agony of rejection, and that most destructive of emotions, guilt. Do I envy her that love? No, I pity her. A love of that depth, that strength, exacts its own price. I was the one to call in the debt, and I have no regrets. Why should she have had it all? What was her suffering compared to mine? My brother gave her the world – but it was my world too, and I lied, cheated and murdered to get it back. Yet all the time my enemy – my invincible enemy – was not Elizabeth, not Alexander, but the love they shared.

Why was their love so indestructible?

I rest my head against the wall now. There is nothing to see here, only darkness, but my nostrils flare at the cloying stench of my surroundings. Among the few, almost indistinguishable sounds, I can hear myself laughing. Laughing and laughing. The bitter irony of it is, if anyone could answer me that last question, then here, at the end, they would hand me the key to life itself.

As it is, it is they who hold the key – Elizabeth and Alexander.'

As I finished reading there was no longer any doubt in my mind that it was Christine who had sent it. I could almost see her smile, the smile she had aimed at me across the courtroom. By giving me my freedom she had sentenced me to a prison from which there could be no escape – a prison of guilt. She had known what she was doing then, and this was a final reminder. Her way of letting me know that, with her death, the door was locked on me and the key taken away for ever.

As I continued to grieve for us both I withdrew further into myself, unable to speak to anyone about it and unable to pick up my life and start again.

Sometimes, from an upstairs window, I would watch Alexander as he left the house with Charlotte or Jonathan. He had left the bar and would be taking up a consultancy in the city at the beginning of the following year. He'd wanted it to be a new start for us both, but every time I saw him I was reminded of the people who had suffered because of us. If he saw me looking, I let the curtain fall back into place, unable to meet his eyes. I longed for him so much that sometimes I thought I might go mad. And the more I tried to stop loving him, the stronger my love became, so that I wanted to die rather than carry on without him. But my guilt was always there, ready to deny me even the luxury of a final release.

It was one Saturday afternoon towards the end of September when Jessica telephoned. I stared at Canary as she held out the receiver; just the mention of Jessica's name was enough to make my conscience flare. Another victim, another accuser. She was asking if she could come to see me. I refused, but she was insistent.

She arrived around four o'clock in her silver Volkswagen. My heart lurched painfully as I saw the car pull up outside. It was the same car as Christine had driven, the same colour, even. I heard her talking to Canary in the hall, then the door opened and, bracing myself, I turned to face her.

Her blonde hair, silky and smooth, glinted in the afternoon sunlight. Her face was bronzed, and though I had seen her once before, she was much more beautiful than I remembered. Her eyes widened as she took in my neglected appearance. 'Well,' she said, 'I don't suppose you always look such a mess, but I have to admit you're not at all what I expected.'

I stared at her, but her eyes had begun an assessment of the room. 'Would you like some tea?' I offered.

'I think Canary – that is her name, isn't it? – is getting some.'

I gestured for her to sit down, and slipping her jacket from her shoulders she sat in Edward's chair, folding one leg over the other, looking small and elegant and relaxed. She seemed in no hurry to start a conversation, and the frank way in which she studied my face unsettled me. Then she laughed. 'You look like him,' she said. 'My God, you actually look like him.'

I stood up as Canary came into the room. She put the tea on the table between us, then left.

'I don't imagine you've come just to look at me,' I said, as I handed Jessica a cup. 'So why are you here?' I hadn't meant to sound so abrupt but I'd been on edge ever since she'd phoned.

'I'm here to find out just what you are playing at.'

'Playing at?' I put my cup down, spilling tea in the saucer. 'I don't think you've got any right . . .'

Her voice was smooth as she interrupted. 'Elizabeth, I have lived with your ghost for more years than I care to remember. That alone gives me the right.'

I looked at her, aware of the animosity between us growing. 'OK, if you've got the right, then say what you've come to say. I'm listening.'

She fumbled in her bag and brought out a packet of cigarettes. 'I hate the gutter press, do you know that? Week after week these hacks ridicule what Rosalind and I are doing at Greenham Common, just for the fun of it – they've no conscience, no morals, and no compassion. But it's not the first time I've been one of their victims, is it? Because along with you and Alexander, Edward and Christine, I've been reaping the rewards of their mucky little exposé ever since they chose to blow your and Alexander's life to smithereens at Foxton's. They had nothing to gain by doing it, except momentarily to discredit Lord Belmayne. A few paragraphs of sensationalism with never a thought for the people whose lives they're destroying, and before you can even say "repercussion" they've moved on to their next victim. The gutter press, that's where it all began. So are you really going to sit up there in that bedroom of yours for the rest of your life, taking all the blame for everything that happened? It must be quite something to think you've got the same sort of power as God Almighty.'

She laughed. 'I mean, three people are dead and no one else shares the blame. That is what you think, isn't it? Tell you what, why not give me a bit of it? I mean, if I hadn't married Alexander then you would never have married Edward, would you?'

I felt the blood drain from my face. For a fleeting moment I thought I saw Christine, smiling back at me.

Her voice was filled with derision. 'You're pathetic. You're hurting Alexander, you're hurting yourself, and you're hurting your children – all because you can't come to terms with the fact that a lying, cheating, murdering bitch was sentenced to death in a foreign country for crimes she alone committed. Do you hear what I'm saying? *She alone*! She didn't need any help from you. You couldn't have stopped her doing it, you didn't even know what she was up to. So why are you making everyone suffer now?'

'How can you sit there and say that? Did Alexander tell you what Christine said in court? Did he tell you how I had cheated on Edward and lied to him all those years, while Alexander was cheating on you? How we took what we wanted, not caring what we might do to other people? Did he tell . . . ?'

'Alexander's told me everything. And yes, I knew he was cheating on me. He was cheating on me from the day we got married – before, even. He loved you then, and he loves you now. That's why I'm here, though God only knows why I'm bothering. Look, for heaven's sake, Elizabeth, you can't have gone through all you have to throw it away now. Pull yourself together. You're behaving . . .'

'Edward and Christine are dead, Jessica! Nothing you say . . .'

'Edward died because he was a thief and a forger who played his hand too far and was double-crossed. That bloody mask was what brought on his stroke. You know it and Christine knew it too. So how the hell can you sit there letting Alexander, Charlotte and Jonathan pay for it?

What's past is past, Elizabeth. You've got to put it behind you, and carry on.'

I looked down as the button I had been twisting broke from my cardigan and rolled on to the floor. Jessica looked too, and laughed as she got up to help herself to more tea. 'Well, now we've dispensed with Edward and Christine, let's get back to you. I'm sure you won't mind me saying so – and too bad if you do – but you're spineless, Elizabeth. An out-and-out coward. Alexander's out of his mind, letting you get away with what you're doing to him.'

'If you knew the truth, the real truth . . .'

'Elizabeth, believe it or not I do understand how you feel. No one could have come through the ordeal you have suffered and not be scarred by it. But think about Alexander. He gave up on his marriage, he threw away his career and then risked his life – all for you. What more do you want from him? I'll be honest, I don't much care about you, but don't hurt him any longer, please.'

It was several minutes before I could speak. I was too crushed by her sudden compassion even to look at her. 'Does he know you're here?' I asked.

'No.' She downed her tea then picked up her jacket. 'I came because I think you should know; Alexander and I were divorced yesterday.'

I watched her walk to the door. As she reached it she turned back, stared at me for a few seconds, then said, 'I'm glad I came. I never knew Edward but I feel . . . Well, we had a lot in common, didn't we? He with his obsession, me with my search for a meaning to life. The cross we shared was loving you two. We've all paid the price, Elizabeth, every one of us. Don't let it be for nothing.'

Long after she'd gone I sat in the chair going over everything Jessica had said. The fact was, she had been more accurate than she could possibly have known when she called me a coward. I was a lot worse even than that. But now I knew that I had to do something I should have done from the start. I had to tell Alexander the truth, so he would know why there could never be any future for us. I had to tell him how, on that Saturday afternoon in September, I had set light to the Bridlington warehouse and killed Daniel Davison . . . .

I hadn't intended to kill him, I had intended to kill Christine. From the moment I turned from the chaos and destruction in the store room and looked into Kamel's eyes, all I knew was unadulterated terror. He laughed when he saw how frightened I was, and turned to Christine who was standing behind him.

It was her idea to set fire to all the evidence against us, hers and Dan's. Kamel sent me to get the petrol can from my car. He was the one to pour the contents over the wreckage, but it was I who set light to it. Within seconds the whole room was ablaze. Kamel started to run and yelled to us to get back. But Christine stood at the door, staring into the flames. And suddenly I felt myself blind to reason, so that all I could see was that here was a way out of the blackmail, an end to the threats to my children. I lifted my hands and slammed them against Christine's back. As she staggered forward, I pushed her again. She fell into the fire, but as I turned to run she wrenched herself from the flames and caught my foot, so that I crashed to the ground. We fought, trying to force each other into the blaze. My hair was burning and her dress was alight. She was on top of me and pain seared through my hands as I grabbed her. Then with all my strength I threw her off, and she screamed out as she landed on her back in the heart of the fire. Then I watched, unmoving, as she struggled to get up. She was screaming and I could see the terror in her eyes. But still I didn't move.

Then I was knocked out of the way and Dan rushed in to drag her out. He called out for me to help, yelling that I was a murdering bitch, but all I could do was watch, paralysed by what I had done, unable to take my eyes from Christine. Before the dresser fell on Dan I saw him pull her free, but once it had fallen I could no longer see either of them. It was then that I ran away.

So I was a coward. I was a murderer and an arsonist too. And all the time he was defending me, while Michael Samuelson so nearly put together the pieces of what had really happened, Alexander's belief in my innocence never wavered. He had put his life at risk, and Charlotte's too, all to get me out of prison when I was guilty of the crime that had put me there. I had lied to him, and had gone on lying to him. And I knew it was that he would never be able to forgive.

– 32 –

By eleven the next morning my bag was packed and standing in the hall. I told Jeffrey he could take it out to the car, then turned back to the stairs.

I used the telephone in my bedroom. My heart-beat was steady now, but still my fingers shook as I dialled the number. After the seventh ring I started to replace the receiver, but as I did so I heard a voice answer.

Now the moment had arrived, my voice died in my throat.

I could hear him breathing. And then very quietly he said, 'Elizabeth? Is that you?'

I swallowed hard, willing myself to go through with it. 'Alexander, we have to talk,' I said finally.

'I'll come over.'

'No!' I took a deep breath. 'I want to tell you now. I don't want to see you, and when you've heard what I've got to say you'll understand that it's for the best that we don't meet.'

He listened in silence as I told him. Sometimes I paused, thinking that now he would speak, but he didn't. So I went on, telling him everything, exactly the way it had happened, until I got to the end.

I waited, but still he didn't speak.

'Alexander, I'm sorry,' I whispered. 'I know it's too late now, and it won't change anything, but I want you to know I love you with all my heart. There are no excuses, nothing I say can change what happened, but I just . . .'

'Why didn't you trust me, Elizabeth?'

The silence drew out until, unable to stand it any longer, I replaced the receiver and left the room.

I stayed in Sark for three days. It was cold and wintry, and not at all as it had been the last time I was there, with Alexander.

I visited all the places we had been together – the smugglers' caves, Dixcart Bay, Venus Pool. I even stayed at the same hotel. I tried and tried to recapture what we had had, to remember how much in love we had been before I lied to him, before Christine had died, before I deceived Edward . . . but my memories were drowned by the sound of his voice asking me why I hadn't trusted him.

It was late in the afternoon, the clouds were thickening overhead and the rain drizzled miserably from the sky, as I walked along the path to Jespillière House.

I had been afraid to come. Afraid because, of all the places on the island, it was Jespillière, the meadow and the cliffs around it, that held the most precious of my memories. The house was still there, dignified in its neglect, and I remembered how we had dreamed that one day it would be ours. I turned and walked on, out across the tiny meadow and down through the gorse, on to the cliff edge. My breath caught in my throat and threatened to choke me as the memories came flooding back. It was here, at the end of that week, when I thought the pain of leaving him would crush me, that he had come to find me. It was here, on this island, that Jonathan had been conceived, and where I first told Alexander he had a daughter. And now, looking back, I couldn't help wondering what would have happened if we had come here the first time he'd asked me, when he was still only seventeen and I was twenty-two. Things might have turned out very differently. Would our love, given time, have burned itself out? Had it been the separation and the desperate need for something we couldn't have that had bound us to each other all these years? But no, it was more than that, it was something I couldn't put into words.

The wind howled round the cliffs, biting my face and penetrating my clothes with its cold breath, and suddenly I knew I had been right to come. At last I was remembering him as he had been the first time we were here, when he held me in his arms and promised me that one day we would return. He would never keep that promise now, but I would always remember how in love we had been.

I looked up to the sky, letting the rain wash away my tears. It was all over now. I would always love him, nothing would ever change that.

Pulling my coat tightly round me, I took one last look across the sunless seascape. My eyes followed the tide, moving ever and steadily inwards to the shoreline below. I stood for a long time, looking down into the bay, until the darkness gathered shadows – as if trying to draw together the fractured pieces of my heart. I buried my face in my hands, drowning in the bottomless gulf of grief.

And then, even before he spoke my name, I knew. Lifting my head, my eyes blinded by tears, I turned and walked slowly into his arms.